CANDY QUINN'S DIRTY FANTASIES

CANDY QUINN

BAD SEED

Book Themes:
    One night stand, fertile tryst, risky sex with a stranger

Word Count:
4,635

~

I KNOW I look like the part of the perfect good girl. Pencil skirt, neat blouse, stockings, heels, glasses, hair tied back in a ponytail. And I have the grades to prove it. I came to college on a full scholarship and I've held onto it no problem, so far. But… that doesn't mean I don't have bad urges.

Like how I could be sitting in class, and that dreamy English professor just gets my panties so wet they're ruined for the day. I could offer myself to him, and I fantasize about it. About him bending me over his desk, slapping my ass and lifting my skirt.

Heck, sometimes I even imagine him doing it in front of the whole class. Just claiming me as they watch, forcing

1

me to look at them as his dick is rammed into me from behind.

God, that gets me so worked up.

But that's just a fantasy. I can't have that. No professor is gonna do that, and get himself fired.

And of course, I'd get kicked out of school.

So instead I just sit and squirm. And wait for class to be out.

No way the English professor's the bad boy I want him to be. But that doesn't mean I give up. I walk out of the campus, down the busy streets, books in one hand. It doesn't take long to get to the part of town where a girl like me looks *real* out of place.

Me, prim and proper, long legs carrying me over dirty sidewalk, and down a dark alleyway. There's guys here, but they're not like the ones on campus. They're hanging around outside a dingy old bar that's hidden away, and all of them look like the type that either spent time in jail or are working a rough job.

Right away one of them catches my eyes. How could he not? He's big. Tall I mean, and muscular. He's only wearing jeans, shoes and a tanktop, so I can really get an appreciation for how cut he is. Broad in the shoulders, with bulging biceps, thick forearms, and washboard abs that you could grate veggies on. And those tattoos all down his arms? Oh god, icing on the cake.

Makes me weak in the knees just looking at him.

"Hey girl, you lost or somethin'?" says a guy to my right, stepping up to me, leering. God, I love the way men's eyes can just devour a girl.

"No, she ain't lost," said the man I had my eyes on first. "Are you, girl?" he flicked his toothpick onto the alleyway and stepped out from the wall, a wall of muscle himself.

"Oh, what if I was? What if I was just some dumb girl

who found herself on the wrong side of the tracks?" I can't help but fight my smirk, my amusement. I wanted them riled up, and I enjoyed teasing them, even if it just has to be by using my words. At least for now.

The big guy is intuitive, though. He doesn't sound cocky or like he's taking a wild guess. He can see that I have no fear in me, despite how prim and proper I look.

"Sounds lost to me," said the man at my right as he stepped closer, very close to grinding up on me as he sized me up from head to toe. He even reached out to touch my blouse, feeling it between his fingers.

"No," said the bigger man, his voice so deep and gravelly as he seemed to see right through me, giving me the shivers. "She knows exactly where she is and why she's come here," he remarked, casually making his way towards me, until he was looming over me from his towering height. Even the muscly man at my right backed off, but I stood my ground.

"You're lookin' for trouble, ain't you doll?" he said to me, his face ruggedly handsome, short dark hair swept back.

I smiled up at him, and it was genuine. Truly, unforgettably genuine.

I mean, how often do you find a man who can read you like a book, just at a glance?

"Is that what they call you around here? I'm tired of finding men where trouble is their *middle* name."

His stony, hardened but handsome face cracked a hint of an uneven smile for me. It made him even more appealing. It made him look scary, even. Well, I guess scarier. He is already the kind of guy most girls would be walking away from as fast as they could.

"That and worse things," he said to me, and without delay, his big, strong hand was on my hip. "You're awful young to be seekin' out trouble here, but… that ain't no impediment," he said to me with a hint of a grin as he began to guide me down that alleyway, around a corner to an even darker corner of the city.

Even the dark alleyways have dark alleyways, I muse while my brain can still think of anything but his hard body and his harder dick.

It was a losing battle, and my knees were already trembling. Not with fear, but excitement. It felt so… wrong. Anyone who knew me would be outraged, disgusted. Especially since I wasn't on the pill, and I knew damn well that this wasn't the type of man you demand wear a condom before he fucks you in the dirty alleyway.

I was also at peak fertility. I knew it instinctively, because I always got even hornier this time of month. To the point that it just starts driving me mental, and I can't think about anything else.

It was hugely irresponsible for so many reasons, and that just made it hotter.

He didn't waste time with words, we were around that corner and he swung me about, pushing my back up against the brick wall as he pressed in upon me. He was like a wild predator, and I'd stumbled into his domain like a doe eyed fawn.

He tilted my head to the side, and his lips went right for my neck as his big, powerful hands felt my sides, slid up over my figure to fondle my breasts through that thin blouse. God, if only my parents and all the prim church and school people could see me now.

I didn't hold back my moan, didn't bite down on my lower lip like I'd have to if I were in that dorm room. That was the best thing. Not having to hold *anything* back. I guess that's what this stranger liked in me, too. He could just finally be himself.

"You take girls back here often?" I asked as I writhed against him, pushing my blonde ponytail away from my porcelain neck, letting him mark me like the slut I was.

He didn't answer me, not right away. He kissed and nipped at my neck, felt my body as he pulled my blouse open. And for a moment I hoped none of those buttons had popped off in the brute act. But then I realized if he had, I'd have an even more shameful walk back. Wouldn't be able to hide what I was up to after this.

God that got me even hornier.

"Yes," he finally said to me as his hands dove into my opened top, those rough, strong fingers sinking into my breast flesh, fondling with a greedy, powerful grip.

I was still wearing my bra since I'd come right from class, a little lacy balconette that left my nipples exposed while pushing my tits up. I liked the way my blouse felt on my nipples all day as I squirmed, but I like his hands on them even better.

"You don't get tired of having to stick it to misbehaving schoolgirls that wander into your neck of the woods?"

His light scruff scraped my skin as his lips made his way to my jaw, then closer to my lips. It made me shiver, everything he did was so rough. Even a kiss was like a jolt to the senses.

"You're not just any schoolgirl, are ya?" he said to me, staring me in the eyes. It was only a split second, but it felt like an eternity. That dark gaze of his holding me entranced before he shoved his mouth to mine, his tongue piercing my lips as one of his hands dipped low again, grasping my skirt and lifting it up.

It was almost embarrassing how wet I was. My panties were soaked, after spending all day in class with my dirty thoughts. And then, meeting him?

Yea, I was filthy, and every moment made me wetter.

5

My mouth met his back eagerly, letting go of all civility and manners as I lost myself to his body. Everything outside of us drifted away, and all that remained was him and the anticipation of him breeding me like the slut I was.

My parents would disown me if they knew what I was doing. And if I got pregnant with some random hoodlum's baby? Probably the same thing.

But all I could think about was how hot it was when he grasped my panties in his two hands and just shredded them with one tug. There was nothing between my pussy and him now, and he helped himself. Letting his hand touch my slit, feel that fiery heat, that overwhelming slickness.

"Damn. Maybe you are just another little schoolgirl slut in need of some real dick," he said to me as he toyed with my clit, making me moan and writhe. And he took a moment to pull back, to look over my exposed tits, my wet slit, before bringing those fingers up and putting them in front of my mouth.

"Suck," he commanded me.

My baby blue eyes were on him as my mouth obediently opened, and my tongue did all the things to his fingers that I wished I was doing to his cock. Of course, my tongue would have a *lot* less room with his cock, but still. I liked showing him just how right about me he was.

I was nothing but a slut in need of a dick. His dick.

Real dick.

"You like that, huh? But you'll like the real thing even better, won't you," he said to me more than asked, watching me intently as his free hand went down and unbuckled his jeans. My eyes finally dipped once he was taking out that cock and...

It was everything a girl dreams of.

To match the man himself, it was big and long. A thick

girth that was ribbed with jutting veins, the tip of it was a dark purple crown that glistened with precum.

"Now get down and show me how bad a girl you are, before I help myself to that hole I really want," he said, as his hand went from my lips to grasp my shoulder, forcibly pushing me down before him.

The alleyway was dirty, my white stockings definitely getting dirty around the knee as I was bent before him. Knowing I didn't have any say just was the cherry on the top. He would take what he wanted, and knowing that just made my clit throb with need.

My mouth opened, my lips eagerly finding the head of his shaft, my tongue teasing him for just a second as I gathered his delicious precum up. I wanted to taste him so bad, to remember this moment forever.

And from the moment I tasted that salty tang on my tongue, I knew I would.

But as much as I wanted to savour my time with his thick, manly cock, he put his fingers through my hair and forced me to lick and blow him at his pace and discretion. That guiding hand taking over as I slid my tongue in around the ridge of his tip, then went down and up his length before wrapping my lips around his shaft.

It was a strain to take him into my mouth, it wasn't used to opening that wide. But I made him fit as he force fed me that thick, meaty dick, and I felt his big, heavy balls nestle at my chin as he rocked my head back and forth.

"That's it. That's my dirty lil' slut. Ain't even worthy of bein' a whore, you're too weak in the knees for dick to risk chargin'," he growled out in his lust laden voice.

He was right, and that only made my honey leak more down my inner thighs, and I had to squirm to try to give my pussy a little pressure. It just needed to be filled so dang bad! Even being choked on his dick couldn't do anything to distract from how much I needed him to fuck my cunny.

I didn't even know where his friend was, if he'd followed. Anyone could be watching me as I kneel on the ground in my prissy pencil skirt curled up around my waist, my blouse torn open, my nipples harder than diamonds. I was so humiliated and degraded and *turned on*.

He shoved his cock down into my throat, that thick beefy length stretching it wide and sealing it shut. I was without air for a while, my nails digging into his thighs, before he finally pulled back and let me gasp for air.

"Get up here," he said, grasping me by my ponytail as he hauled me back up to my feet, which was easier said than done as I gasped. But in the flash of the moment I saw that yes, his friend was there too. Leaned back against the opposing wall, watching me with a glint in his eyes as the bigger male twisted me around and bent me over against the brick again.

The brick pricked my arms, and it made me feel so *alive*. Knowing that I was being watched, that I was going to get knocked up by some bad boy I didn't even know the name of and would likely never see again. My pussy was swollen and red, and I'd made sure to be completely waxed today so that I could feel everything And he, no doubt, could see just what a mess he'd made of me already.

He grasped my ass in one hand, prying my cheeks apart as he admired that sticky mess of my pussy, and the other took hold of his thick, long cock as it glistened with my saliva. He brought it in, and just as I predicted, he made no move to put on a condom. He just rubbed that raw tip along my slit, teased my clit so mercilessly.

"You need this, don't ya, slut?" he asked me in his dark, rumbling voice.

"Please," I begged, no longer even able to tease him and

act like I have this all under my control. That was most of the fun. Knowing it's out of my control, knowing that I'm subject to whatever this big, brute of a stranger's whims are. "I need it so bad!"

"I know you do. Just be aware, I'm goin' in raw, and I ain't pullin' out. Whatever happens is on you," he said, though he didn't give me a chance to object. He just split me open on the biggest dick I'd ever seen. I screamed out, filling the alleyway with the sounds of my cry as he shoved so much of that thick, meaty dick up into me, stretching my pussy to its limits, making me dizzy with the sensation of it all.

My arms pushed further into the brick, that painful sensation absolutely nothing compared to the explosion of pleasure erupting within me. I'd gotten exactly what I wanted, but it was even better than I could have dared hope. I had to go up on tip toe, even in my high heels, and my long legs screamed with the effort, but it was worth it.

My pussy clung to him, even though I was wetter than I'd ever been, and my tight little ass pushed up against his pubic mound. I could feel him against my innermost center, and the ache was utter perfection. I'd finally found my Holy Grail.

With both hands free now, he grasped my hips and began to pound into me. No building up to it, no easing in, he used his raw strength to just force his dick through my tight, clenching pussy again and again, at his own pace. My tits were bouncing and swaying beneath me, and he had full control as he made me squeal and moan, his own grunts and pleasured sounds lower, but no less real and sincere.

"That's it... fuck, that's the tightest lil' pussy I've had," he growled at me.

I squeezed him harder at the compliment, feeling his

pulsing veins as I ground my pussy against him. I felt like I might pass out, but at the same time, I was more alert and aware than ever before. I screamed as he pounded me, each thrust making my voice warble.

"You gonna make me yours?"

He slapped my ass hard at that, made me squeal again as my cheek stung. He reached up, grasping a hold of my ponytail and twisting my head back and to the side, so I could see him out of the corner of my view.

"You think you're worthy of bein' my girl and not just some one-time cum dump?" he growled, punctuating his question with another rough slap.

It was so cruel, and yet it was the thing that absolutely obliterated me. I felt my pussy tensing up, betraying me to the stranger. There was no holding back, that was for sure. There was no hiding the fact that his words, his sharp smack, his yanking me around was what toppled me over the brink and gave me the most intense orgasm I've ever had in my life.

He let go of my hair sharply as he continued to hammer into my pussy, even as that narrow little hole grasped his dick oh so tight amid my orgasm. He wasn't impeded by anything, he just helped himself to me at his own pace and time, reaching a hand in underneath me, grasping a breast, squeezing and fondling it, feeling my stiff nipple prod his palm as he grunted and shot off some pre into me.

"Not much to say for yourself,," he growled. "You look like some bookworm, but you fuck like a bimbo slut," he said roughly.

I was still shuddering as a powerful aftershock went through me, and a moan was all I could manage. I wanted so badly for him to claim me, for him to sneak into my bedroom at night and wake me with his cock. But I couldn't even beg him to make me his. It was all too perfect.

He was hammering me towards my second orgasm in no time, everything was so exquisite about the moment. His balls slapped against my clit up until they tightened, getting ready to unload all his seed. And he moaned, gripped me tighter as my nipple was pinched between his fingers.

"You're gonna take it all, slut," he growled, right before he pounded into me a few final times, groaning as his dick swelled and then…

I could feel it. Every pulse of his dick was another thick jet of sticky, rich cum. He blew so many strands of his virile seed into my fertile depths, and true to his word he never pulled out. He just jammed that thick crown up against the entrance to my womb and unleashed it all.

I'm not an idiot. I knew the risks, and I knew that when a girl cums the same time as a guy, those risks shoot way up. Maybe that was the knowledge that sent me toppling over the edge, left me screaming my head off in the dark alleyway as I pushed my ass against him, taking every last drop of his seed.

We both pressed into each other, our bodies melded, his seed trapped deep within me as our bodies slowly uncoiled down from their intense highs. It was the greatest rush of my life, fucked by some rough stranger in a back alley, blasted with his raw cum, watched by some rough thug.

He grasped my ponytail again, wrenching my head back.

"You still wanna be my girl, slut?" He asked me with a growl.

"More than anything," I gasped, forcing my blue eyes on him. I didn't want to mess it up. I didn't want this to be a one time deal. Sure, that's hot in its own way, but I knew that no other dick would satisfy me like his. I was going to be forever trying to find someone who could stand in his shadow.

He studied me, and again I felt like he saw right through me to my core. There was no lying or games with him possible, because he'd ferret out the truth without a word.

"Get down on your knees," he demanded as he let go of my hair then yanked his dick out of my pussy. It made me squeal from the sudden roughness, then whimper from the sad emptiness as his cum drooled out of me and down my inner thighs. "Clean me up, slut. Show me you want to be my girl," he demanded as his cock jutted out, still hard.

My legs were quivering so hard that it was easy to fall to my knees. It forced more cum from my pussy, though, and I brought a hand to my slit, cupping it as my other hand wrapped around his cock, aiming it at my face. I looked at his delicious masculinity for only a second before my mouth was taking him in again, tasting our combined juices upon every single inch of his dick.

He watched me, evaluated me. I felt so scrutinized, tested. But... didn't I say I was a good student? I always aced my tests. And this one was no different, I cleaned and teased his dick masterfully, made him give a few grunts of approval. Until at last I was done, according to him.

"That's enough," he said as I lapped around his balls, cleaning what honey had leaked down around them. And more than saying it, he yanked my ponytail off his shaft. "If you're gonna be my girl, you gotta be more than just some slut," he told me. "You gotta be a whore."

He whistled sharply before I could respond.

"Dino," he called out to the man behind him, who came immediately.

"Yes boss?"

"A hundred bucks'll buy you sloppy seconds," he shot the man an intense look, but already he was fishing out a wad of bills and slapping them into his boss' hand.

It was all happening so fast, but as I watched that money change hands, I could feel my heart begin to pound, my pussy throbbing once more. I looked up at the stranger, the one I still didn't know the name of.

Then I looked at Dino, my smile growing.

The Boss peeled off some of the bills and slipped them into the waist of my skirt as he tugged me back up to a standing position.

"Graduate from being a bad girl to being a good whore," he told me before letting go and backing off.

Dino was already unbuckling his belt excitedly. He'd been aching for this moment since he first saw me, and the fact his boss had got to me first and left me a mess, wasn't gonna be a deterrent for him at all I could tell. He needed a taste of me too.

And even though I knew that what I really wanted was the Boss... If this pleased him, then that was everything I needed. I knew then and there that I'd do anything to get his cock again, and being paid for the privilege of getting what I wanted anyways?

Icing on the cake.

I turned around again, my arms pressing against the brick as I spread my legs, bracing myself.

"My boy Dino here doesn't mind sharing his boss' pets. And I'll even let him raw you too. Though not those other guys, y'hear me?" the boss said to me firmly, as Dino got in behind me, and began to push his hard dick into my wet, cum filled pussy with a squelch of juices and seed.

I nodded my head, even as I let out a wanton moan, my back arching as I took another man into my used cunt. He was smaller, and I was so wet, but that didn't matter. This wasn't about Dino. This was about finding my true calling in life, and I was planning on acing this exam.

Dino wasn't as big as his boss, nor as strong. But still, he hammered that raw cock into me hard and fast, he made me body quake and caused me to moan all over again. And that's what I needed. I needed to feel like a woman. And they did that.

Dino pounded me, made my ass cheeks ripple and quake with each thrust, and got my tits to swaying again. And like his boss, he helped himself to groping my flesh all over, taking handfuls of my tits, pinching my nipples, ravishing me too.

But even as spent and sore as his boss had left me, I loved it all, and it was coming to an end all too soon as Dino's dick began to throb wildly.

I slammed back against him as hard as I could, my body begging for him to finish in me. The idea that he would pull out, deprive me of that sensation of his pleasure bursting into me was awful. I couldn't allow that.

My pussy tightened around him, begging for his seed, milking him with such wanton desire.

Dino didn't let me down, as I was afraid he might. He just hilted himself inside me and let his load burst out, adding to the sticky mess of virile seed that his boss had dumped in me already. I squealed and moaned with excitement, knowing that now not only had one random stranger risked knocking me up, but two had.

It was the filthiest, happiest day of my life.

THIS TIME when I walk down that alleyway, it's not looking

like a sweet schoolgirl. Butch--that's his name, I finally learned, after weeks of being his--has transformed me.

When I walk down here now, it's with fishnet stockings and leather, my tits practically bursting out of my top as I make my way over to his side.

He catches sight of me before I reach him, and that dark gaze lights up a little. He lifts his arm and puts it around me.

"'Bout time," he says to me in his gruff way, Dino giving me a nod from across the alley.

I nuzzle in against Butch, wrapping my arms around him.

"I'm late," I say, taking hold of his massive hand.

"I know that, ho," he says to me.

"No, I mean... I'm late. Like, real late... in fact, two months late," I clarify as I guide his hand over to my bare stomach, to let him feel there. I knew that meeting him was fate, and in his eyes, I saw a little sparkle. A faint grin forming on his lips.

"I said, I know," he growls at me before his lips find mine, our bodies melt into one another's once more.

BOUGHT BY THE BAD BOY

Book Themes:
    Breeding, Barely Legal, mild blackmail, Bimbofication

Word Count:
5,579

HIGH SCHOOL IS SOMETHING most people put behind them as life beckons them forward, but for me? The carefree life of summer teen days was something I never wanted to say goodbye to. And I didn't.

College? Nah.

Job? Don't think so!

Laying by the pool in my parent's luscious backyard in my string bikini, I was too busy enjoying life at a leisurely pace to waste my time on those bores. Instead I'd soak up some sun, then head inside, eat, clean up, and head out for a night on the town. Clubbing and bars, have a blast with my girlfriends, most of whom were like me; they skipped the whole bore of college and work life.

Though that one day, I was in for a rude surprise.

When I walked into the house I found my mother and father arguing, which was odd. They never fought like the parents of poorer kids. They had everything!

But when I saw them brandishing around a letter and arguing, it seemed like reality hit home.

I tried to put it behind me after they explained what was happening. They'd said horrible things like that I'd need to get a job! That they couldn't afford to cater to my lavish lifestyle — as if! — and I'd have to make my own way.

I was in tears, frankly. And even that didn't change their minds! So I knew it was serious.

I wasn't the most fun that night, not in on the laughs my friends were having, but trying not to let them realize I was about to become one of those depressing tales of woe. What a bummer that'd be!

But out of the neon lights of the club appeared a tall, dark and handsome man, dressed better than all the other guys I'd seen that night. He stood out, but not in a bad way. I guess maybe it was the way he walked with that kinda swagger like he owned the world.

It was like the calling card of the rich and famous. Warded off those that'd be too intimidated to talk to someone that was just, like, brimming with confidence.

But for me?

It made me get off my ass and start towards him. That was just what I needed. Some rich jackass to treat me like a million bucks, buy my drinks, and make everything go back to normal.

Sure, I was only thinking of one night for the second, but

every step I took towards him and my expectations grew. One stilettoed heel in front of the other, my slinky, black dress creeping up over my long legs with every step. By the time I got to him, I wanted him to be putty in my hand.

Though I was more than a little put off when he kept his cool, and managed to stand there, one hand in his pocket, looking so in control. His intense gaze turned towards me and I sensed I felt something familiar about him, though I couldn't place it. He was no older than me, but he looked far more mature.

"Surprised to see you here," he said, his deep, gravelly voice carrying over the beat of the music to my ears. He was broad in the shoulders, but fit and trim, judging by the looks of his tailored suit. "But then not," he added on, as if he knew me.

My nose crinkled and I giggled, as if I was totally in on his joke. The worst thing in the world would be to tell the stud I didn't remember him.

"It's been awhile," I said, taking a stab in the dark. I mean, it wasn't like it was a complete stab, because if I'd seen him recently, I totally would've remembered him.

"You look good," I added on.

He sized me up in return, as if truly scrutinizing me. Though even that stony, confidently handsome face of his couldn't keep him from the truth.

"So do you. Better than ever in fact," he stated, turning towards me and looking so intense. "Easy to see you've been taking good care of yourself. You're hotter than even my memories could do justice," he said so openly, looking utterly unperturbed by the confession.

As if the words didn't affect him at all, but I knew the difference. I jut my hip out, my hand on it like I was going to another photo shoot, and gave him my best smile. "So are you going to buy me a drink, then?" I asked, trying to be cocky.

"I remember a time when you would barely let me do that much," he said, cracking the slightest of little smirks as he flagged down the bartender, able to command her attention so easily, when most of us struggled. "I trust you like the same," he said, before ordering me a Cosmo, same as I'd always loved, since I was a girl.

He'd bought me drinks before — or at least offered — and I still couldn't even remember him. Maybe he was, like, ugly or something before. Lost some weight or something?

I just couldn't place him, and trust me, I'd have remembered someone like him.

"So when'd you get back?" I asked, guessing once more.

"Just last week, in fact. Rolled into town to buy a few businesses up," he said as our drinks arrived, him with a vodka tonic, sipping it as he looked me over. "I was going to look you up, but honestly, I didn't expect to stumble upon you this quickly," he leaned against the bar, his own fit form silhouetted in the dark light so well as he studied me, soaked me in like I was the main course of a meal.

"I know what you've been up to though," he said with a cocky grin.

I giggled as I took the straw into my mouth, wrapping my tongue around it before taking a sip of the drink.

"Ohh, a stalker?" I purred out.

"Not quite," he replied, taking another mouthful of his stiff drink. "I just figure there's no chance in hell that with that body of yours, you've changed since we last met. And you're still doing the exact same thing since last I touched bases with you. Am I wrong?" he asked, cocking an eyebrow in challenge to me.

I shrugged. The fact that I couldn't remember him was

CANDY QUINN'S DIRTY FANTASIES

starting to grow old, and I was getting frustrated, so I took another sip of my Cosmo and gave him a dazzling smile, flipping my long hair from my shoulder.

"I know what I want in life, is that a crime?"

"No. And I hope that means you won't blame me for pursuing what I want so damn hard either," he said with a wolfish grin, as if I was his prey. He knocked back the rest of his drink, then laid the empty tumbler on the bar top as he leaned in just a bit closer. "I know you don't remember, but when last we met I wanted something more than just a fling. You left me in the dirt." He reached out to touch his strong hand upon my hip, "I never forgot you. And like all things, I have trouble letting go of my desires."

Oh.

Oh right. It was slowly coming back to me, but I sipped my drink, making him wait for my response. As if I weren't inwardly, like, freaking out, even though I was.

"You can't blame a girl for not wanting to settle down," I purred, and I caught the barest hint of his aftershave. It was delicious. "And that was a long, long time ago."

"High School still," he responded, his firm grasp upon my hip so commanding, so strong. His presence was so masculine, so authoritative, and it was easy to see how someone like him had gone so far. "I had big plans for us, for me, but you wanted to stay here and party. Seems we both accomplished our goals, Trisha," he said with that predatory grin of his.

"Well, to high school dreams, then," I said, raising my glass in a toast before finishing it off. I'd had such a bad day, and now he was harshing my buzz. Making me feel bad for doing something I couldn't even remember.

How many men — no, boys — had wanted something more from me? Had big dreams for our future?

But that wasn't who I was. Though with my parent's impending financial crisis...

I put on a brighter smile, "But we all have to grow up sometime, right?"

He lifted his hand from the bar to lightly trail his fingers along my chin and jawline, cupping my face ever so lightly with his hard hands.

"No. Not necessarily," he said in a low, husky growl. "I've come to appreciate you for who and what you are. I don't want to change you, make you aspire to be anything but you. Though still," he said with that wolfish grin widening, "I've just got to have you all to myself. Whatever it takes."

My head tilted to the side as I looked up at him. It was a way more intense conversation than I could really have. My life was falling apart and I didn't need some guy I knew in high school coming in and trying to...

To what? Have me all to himself?

Hah. Unless he was ready for a trophy wife or something, that wasn't going to happen.

"Is that so?" I asked, raising a brow to him.

His thumb trailed along my cheek, its hard, smooth surface so calming in its own way.

"Every beautiful party girl needs someone to keep them, no? And I can just feel that you need a man right now to take you on and keep you in the manner to which you're accustomed, huh?" he said, leaning in closer, his tall form looming over me as his dark eyes bored into mine.

And I so totally did.

I guess that's what people talk about when they talk about fate.

My smile broadened, and I shrugged my shoulders a little, playing coy. "Maybe," I said with a little sing-song-ness to it.

"No maybe about it, is there?" he said, so confident in his knowledge of me, that grin never fading. "Back in high school I couldn't offer you much. Just a lot of promises. Now? Things have changed, Trish-the-Dish." He leaned in, his shaved-cheek brushing against my smooth one as he murmured gruffly into my ear. "I'm going to buy you. Make you mine. Whatever the cost. It's already decided. From the moment you turned me down and stayed here, I knew I'd come back for you."

His deep, husky words so dark, so certain, so authoritative. He had to have me, and never let me go from his thoughts in the years since high school.

And I couldn't lie... the idea of this guy pining over me for so long, that I had made such an impression on him? That turned me on like I couldn't believe. Thinking about him spending his nights at home, jerking off, moaning my name...

I let out a sigh of arousal, my smile so genuine. It was like all my silly little dreams were coming through. The world does give you what you need!

"Buy me?" I repeated, licking along my lower lip. "What makes you think you could afford me?"

There it was, that devilish glimmer in his eyes. I'd brought it out, and he looked so damn devious, so smug.

"Because I made it so, my sweet Trisha," he said in a smooth husk. "It took a while. Study, hard work, the building of a fortune. Then the buying up of your parent's company. Firing them. Buying up their debt to foreclose on their mortgage," he licked his lips as if his hunger was rising just talking about it. "All so you'd have no choice. Nowhere better to turn. Than me."

I stared at him in shock.

It wasn't even that I believed him, not really... but how could he possibly know all that if he was lying?

It made my knees quiver, and I had to hold onto the bar just to stay upright in my stiletto heels. I was gonna be sick, I just knew it, and I tried to say something but I couldn't.

And there it was again. The thought of him going through all this obsession, just for me, and I was angry and scared and it was all rollin' around within me. But the worst was how much the idea of him being so obsessed with me made me horny.

He'd obsessively planned it all, set me up so that my options were security with him, or take my chances. Live like everybody else.

It was sadistic.

And he looked to be loving it.

His two strong hands steadied me, holding me up, just like he was offering to do; he'd tear down my life, but keep me up. As long as I did what he wanted.

"I'm not asking much, Trisha," he growled, leaning in so close to me. "Not that you give up being a party girl to settle down. Just that you be *my* party girl," and the emphasis on his possession was so strong, so fierce. "Travel around the world with me on business trips. Live the high life in every major trade city on the planet. The finest booze and drugs. And have your brains fucked out by me every goddamn night."

I wanted to be so pissed. I wanted to scream, to hit him, to call him every name in the book.

But he'd found some way to tap into something that I'd hid so deep even I didn't know it was there, and I couldn't hide how my body was growing warm. That between my thighs, I was getting unbearably hot.

"Fuck you," I hissed, but there was no fight to the words.

"Oh you will," he replied without missing a beat, then

pressed in. His lips met mine and he held nothing back. He kissed me deeply, passionately, grasping a hold of my body and face, his fingers running back through my hair as he ravenously hungered for me.

I could feel his fingers squeezing at my shapely flesh, his tongue lashing at mine as the music still thrummed around us.

I admit that I was even then questioning what I was doing, and I wasn't used to that. Usually I did what felt good, and this... him?

He felt really good. His body was hard, his hands and mouth filled with passion, and he tasted like power.

But I knew he shouldn't feel good, and that kept bringing me out of the kiss, even as my tongue warred with his.

For all he'd done to shake up my life, he shook me up physically too. His hands were all over me and he was ravenous for me. Years of repressed desire bubbling out before he even got his answer from me. He even got so daring as to grab and knead my ass as we stood there at the bar, until finally we broke apart and I stared into this intense, dark eyes of his.

"I have a penthouse suite while I stay here," he said in a breathy, deep voice. "Come spend the night with me. And every night after. You're mine now, princess. And I'll keep you better than your parents ever could anyhow," he pledged to me so vehemently.

That's the point that I should've turned around and walked out and taken him to court or something. But that wasn't who I am.

I'm the girl that nodded her head because she was too horny to think straight. I'm the girl that found his sadistic obsession with me arousing. I'm the girl who needed him, bad.

The smugness was gone from his face, just sheer triumph took its place. He'd won, after all those years, and got the prize: me. He'd broke me down and claimed me, as he'd always wanted, and he was too excited to be anything else in his victory.

He led me out of the club, where a black, chauffeured sedan awaited us. The driver opened our door and Ash — I remembered his name at last — helped me on in, before climbing into the back and pouncing atop me again before the chauffer could even begin to drive.

It might've been one of the dumbest things I'd done, but it didn't feel like it. Not as his hand ran up over my ribs, then down to my naked thigh. His palm pressed against my skin, grabbing me hard as he kissed my lips, making out with me so lewdly.

Lust took me over and I was squirming against him, wanting so bad to feel his hand on my hot, wet pussy.

We were like teenagers again in the back of his car, pawing, kissing, humping. He let his hand wander up my thigh and gave me just what I wanted too; he touched his finger to my hot, wet cunny, free of panties, and he gave a low growl of desire at finding it so bare.

It wasn't a long drive, but in that time he stoked my fires higher. He teased my clit, circled it with his thumb and squeezed at my breast through my dress. All the while, his mouth worked against mine, quieting my nearly constant moans.

I couldn't remember ever being more turned on in my life.

He was just as ravenous and as the car came to a stop outside the swankiest hotel in the whole city, we could barely tear ourselves away from each other.

My hips bucked towards him, our bodies all tangled up as I reached out, touching against his hard-on through his pants, stroking him so wantonly. I pulled away for just long enough to look at him from beneath my thick lashes, and I knew I couldn't hold myself back from him.

He had to pull me from the car, lift me up out of it in fact. Though as I struggled to pull my dress down to a semi-decent level, we were walking up the stairs into the posh hotel front, making our way to the elevator.

He inserted his key for his private suite floor, and then before the doors were even shut, we were at it again. He lifted my one leg up to his hip, stroked along to my ass as our lips smacked, and he was grinding against me, pinning me to the mirrored wall of the elevator.

Though once the elevator came to a halt at his fabulously opulent penthouse, we only barely managed to get through the door before it shut again. He held me up in his arms, fondling and kissing me as we made our way towards the plush, round sofa.

He was such a colossal jerk, and really, it'd be easy to say I was only doing it because he was blackmailing me.

But because he was blackmailing me, oh man... I totally wanted it. Him. He'd built his entire world around getting me, and maybe it'd be smart to play coy, but my body was having none of that. No games, to teasing.

I broke from his kiss and immediately he went down my throat, sucking on my neck, claiming me like an animal with his love bites.

Those big hands of his pawed at me, he nipped and kissed at my neck, and all the while I could feel the pulse of his desire through his impressively sized cock. Feel the way it ground against my supple flesh, the way he so desperately needed me.

He released me only long enough to shed his blazer, growling as he suckled at my neck.

"You're mine at last," he said between suckling kisses.

I wanted to protest except the way he said *mine* made me hungry for him. I moaned, my dark hair flicked off my shoulder as he licked and kissed and nipped at my sensitive flesh. My hand went to his bicep, gripping it as my body ground beneath him.

I was horny as hell, and no matter how I tried to hide it, I couldn't.

It became especially impossible when he slid his two hands up my thighs, and lifted my dress over my hips. With my pussy bare, there was no way to hide how glistening wet it was from his hungry gaze. No way I wanted to stop him as he kissed his way down between my legs, placing pecks and suckling kisses upon the soft inner flesh of my thighs, before finally coming to taste my pussy.

One lick of it and he was moaning with such vulgarity.

"Fuck, I forgot how good your cunt tastes," he growled, lashing his tongue around my clit again immediately after, not wanting to take his mouth away from me for long.

I gasped, my hand gripping the sofa cushion as I lifted my hips towards him, not shy about wanting him to bury his face in me. I ground against him as his tongue swirled around me with expertise, and I only vaguely recalled that night we were together, and I taught him everything there was to know about eating me out.

And he remembered every last trick I'd taught him.

He devoured me not only with a great hunger and need, but such practiced attention to detail. Like my pussy had been enshrined in his memory ever since. He licked my cunny, suckled my clit and worked me so masterfully, not that I had a lot of choices about it. Though it'd be hard to argue I wanted him to stop.

I'd never had a lover who was so into it, so insatiably needy for my body, to taste my honey. He wanted it all, all of me, every part, and not just for his own physical gratification.

His need for me was more than just that. He needed to possess me, fully. Totally. As a woman and not just a plaything.

One of my legs was sprawled over the back of the sofa, the other wrapped around his head as he brought me to ecstasy faster than anyone else I'd ever been with. I couldn't believe it was even happening, but my tummy tensed up and then it was just an explosion of bliss, and I knew I was making a mess all over his face and the expensive sofa but I didn't care. I didn't care about anything except how good he made me feel, and I screamed his name so loud I figured I'd wake the people in the basement dozens of floors below.

As I was still quaking in the wake of my mind-blowing orgasm, he was lapping it up. All of my juices were his to devour, bought with his blackmail and cunning. He kissed and teased my flesh before he finally pulled away.

"That's *my* pussy, *my* dinner from now on, you hear me, Trisha?" he growled so commandingly as he stripped off his white shirt, revealing a sculpted chest, with pronounced pecs and chiseled abs. Such a gorgeous specimen of masculinity, and I hadn't a doubt that it too was for me. All part of the obsessive snare laid to catch me, and I watched as his hand trailed down, undoing his pants.

I was transfixed, my body betraying me as I stared at him with such need. Need to feel what his cock was like. I couldn't remember if we'd fucked before — probably not. I was a wicked cock tease in high school, and I wouldn't be surprised if I'd left him aching.

I bit in on my lower lip, squirming to get closer to him. I'd never needed something, or someone, so bad in my life.

He unbuckled his belt, unzipped his pants, and I could

see the cotton bulge of his manhood, that thick snake of a cock protruding. He tugged down both garments, and that meaty girth of his sprang out, so big, so perfectly shaped. It was a gorgeous specimen of manhood, and it throbbed in the air for me. Its desire so obvious.

Ash took hold of my hips and legs, positioned me just as he wanted as he got over me.

"And one more thing," he said in a low, dark growl, his eyes staring into mine as he wiped away the last remaining juices from his face to lap them up too. "No condoms. No protection of any kind. Not with me, party girl," and then he took hold of his dick, and lewdly slapped it to my pussy before teasing my entrance with his bare, purple crown.

I wish that cock didn't do such horrible things to my mind, absolutely numbing my ability to protest. That was always my one rule. Always use a condom. To make sure I did? I didn't go on the pill or anything like that. I didn't want to tempt myself to ever break my rule.

And yet there he was, ordering me to.

I'd already cum, so I should've just said 'fuck it'. Walked out that door.

But then his cock teased along my clit and I sucked in a deep breath, quivering against him.

"I'm not on the pill," I said, shaking my head and looking for where the hell I left my purse. "Always condoms."

The purse was long gone, left with my girlfriends back at the club. Forgotten when I left with the man who was blackmailing me in such a lust filled hurry.

"No," he growled to me simply, and paid me no heed as he teased my clit one final time, took one last tempting slide down along the length of my wet slit... then sank down into me. His bare cock filling me up like no other man had, our raw flesh touching, producing such a sensation that made every other care-free romp feel like a pale imitation. And he moaned deeply, his pleasure a low rumble as he shut his eyes for a moment and savoured his first penetration of his new captive.

"Ohhh fuck... no... never a condom. Not with me," he stated so certainly.

I cried out, wanted to protest, and yet my body betrayed me again. He felt... amazing. So hot, and hard, throbbing with such intensity that I could barely believe. He was so big, and it just stole every last thought from me.

The idea of pushing him off of me was like a silly, weird thought that I could never go through with.

Instead, my body clenched him, begging him further into my hot little pussy.

He tugged back his hips against the tight grip of my cunny, my folds clinging to him as his powerful hips retracted. Though the first pleasing thrust after we were both moaning again, then again with the next. And again.

It was beautiful, our bodies working together more masterfully than any of the random hookups I'd had. He was magnificent, and all those years of waiting, planning, had paid off — not just for him — as he took me his way.

I was at his mercy, and his throbbing cock slammed into me harder with each thrust. His heavy, cum-filled balls slapping against my ass as he pounded and pounded, the two of us rutting carelessly like the teenagers we once were together.

He grabbed my legs, my high heels still on, and held them over his shoulders, making it so that I couldn't squirm away from his powerful thrusts. He was fucking me so deep that it almost hurt, and I was pinned against him, my knees bent over his shoulders as he stared down on me.

He had me right where he wanted me, in every way, not

just physically. And he knew it. The look on his self-satisfied face, the utter bliss as he fucked me for the first time, really fucked me. And my very first raw fucking.

I'd never barebacked with *anyone* before, and it was like being a virgin again. The sensations... there was no comparison! It was like all those years were wasted doing pretend sex when I had his big, throbbing dick plunging into me again and again.

"Ohh fuck, you're pussy's so damn tight," he grunted out. "Dammit, you stayed so perfect all these years... more perfect than ever."

My hair was getting messed up against the pillow, my sexy dress was hauled up to my waist, and I felt trashy in all the right ways.

"You're so big," I gasped, half in protest, half in appreciation. It was a good thing I was soaking wet, because it would've been too much otherwise. But he felt so fucking amazing, so... right.

He brought one of his hands to my chest, tore my dress open as he yanked it away from my breasts. I'd have been pissed about that just a couple hours before, since I knew I couldn't afford another now, but instead I knew he'd take care of it. Take care of me.

He sank his fingers into my thick mound of breast flesh, squeezed and kneaded it as he pounded into me. I could feel his dick twitch and pulse inside me, knew what was on its way.

"Fuck Trisha, I'm gonna cum," he growled out, and I knew that each of those throbs of his steel-hard shaft was another spurt of precum into my fertile depths.

I should've stopped him, I really, really should've, but oh...

There was no chance of that. My back was arched, my stiff nipples being tugged between his fingers, pinched as he looked down at me. He was going to cum, but it wasn't going to be him weakening, not at all. He was going to claim me like an animal, and he was going to make me beg for it.

His fingers tugged my nipple, the pain jolting through me before going to my clit and almost vibrating with electricity.

"Tell me you want it, Trisha," he growled, and even though his motions didn't stop, he held back. Going a bit slower, a bit gentler, and I wanted nothing more for him to fucking pound me. To grab me and take me, manhandle me.

Claim me.

But I didn't want to be so easy! I was still fucking pissed, deep down, and so I kept my mouth shut.

But then he grabbed at my other breast, that nipple pinched between his thumb and forefinger too, and it was just enough pressure to make me quiver. I was near the brink again. I just needed him to thrust in, to let me grind against him, and then it'd all be over.

I bit down on my lower lip as I tried to bring my pussy further down his cock, to take what I wanted without giving him what he was after, but it was no use. He had me pinned.

"Fuck!" I cried out in frustration as I tried once more to flee, and he pinched my nipples harder. The words came out, uncontrollable. "Just fucking cum!"

He had that victory too.

And he seized it.

Ash's big, throbbing dick buried itself into me, that bulging tip thrust right to my deepest regions as he let loose a loud, bellowing moan. He gave all he had to hold on that long, and then the flood came.

He let loose such copious spurts of his virile seed. Jet

after jet of that cum filling me up as I ground against him, used his body for my own satisfaction until I was wailing along with him and writhing beneath him. Our two bodies coated in a thin sheen of perspiration as we felt our mind-blowing orgasms together. The two of us undulating, grinding, rocking, as he filled me up with that rich cream of his.

And I wanted every last drop. Before the night was over, I was begging in earnest like the slut I was.

❧

I WAS HOOKED.

Fucking with a condom on was unthinkable to me after that. Lord knows I tried though! But I kept crawlin' back to Ash, for more of his raw, hard cock.

Not that I had to crawl. He was true to his word, in every manner. He took me with him around the world, wherever he went. In all the poshest, most expensive hotels, keeping me full of his cock every night after a day of me enjoying the spoils of his fortune while he went to meetings.

It was heaven. Better than I ever had with my parents, he could afford anything for me, and denied me nothing.

Except the pill.

It wasn't all bliss after all, but swelling up with his baby inside me didn't put him off. And I still got to live the life of a queen, catered to at all times as I toted his baby boy around inside my belly. So maybe it wasn't love, or what I'd expected out of my life.

But I was damned happy with it.

BOUGHT BY THE BILLIONAIRE

Book Themes:
Virgin, Barely Legal, Breeding, Mild blackmail
Word Count:
5,579

~

Life on the farm was generally quiet and peaceful. Sure, there was lots of hard work, but it was uneventful generally speakin', especially since my ma and pa passed away, leavin' the property to me. But that was all fixed to change the moment that fancy black sedan rolled up to my door. I just didn't know right then I'd be ass up in the back of her before the day was through.

~

He was a slick lookin' man, with long dark hair, backswept and shiny in the midday sun, and a pair of sunglasses that must've cost more'n my car. He stepped out of his vehicle in a fitted suit, and looked better'n a catalogue model, I gotta say.

Though all of that looked completely out of place on my lil' farm. The farmhouse itself was about two centuries old, even if it did have about a dozen renovations since then, and the whole plot of land had that rustic look that city slickers liked to stop and gawk at.

Though this guy was no usual city slicker, I could tell that. I wiped my hands as I strode up the gravel drive towards him, tuckin' the hand towel into the back of my tight daisy dukes as I got close to him. Though as I studied him, his dark, piercin' eyes turned to peer right back into me in turn.

"Are you the owner of this place, ma'am?" He asked, his voice so deep and gravelly, despite his glossy, well-kept appearance.

He kinda had me on edge a little. You know, like when you meet someone that seems better off and more educated and you're just waitin' to be made the fool of? Yea, that was me, 'cause he had everythin' that the books told me was bad news. He was all calm and cool, and chose his words all careful like, and he was sexy to boot. So I knew I was in trouble.

But I smiled at him all the same, like a polite girl does, and nodded my head. "Yea, sure do. All the land from here to there," I said, pointin' out the boundaries.

He listened real closely and all that, but I could tell he had somethin' important on his mind from the get go.

"Got some bad news for you then, little lady," he said, and truly I was lil' compared to him! He was well over six feet tall, and I was well over a foot shorter'n him. "I recently acquired the local creditors to consolidate into a branch of my business," he said, reaching into his car and pulling out a thick stack of papers. "And it turns out your place is well in arrears on payments. As in, about forty years," he said, holding out the document to me. "I don't know why the debt has been put aside for this long, but it showed up after my acquisition."

"What?!"

I mean, I half understood most of what he said, but I did understand that we were in debt for forty years? I mean, that was even before my parents took over probably... I didn't have time to think on the math just then.

I pushed my fingers through my hair, fixing my ponytail before I grabbed the papers, lookin' at them like I might be able to figure out what'd happened.

He undid the front of his blazer, the only sign he wasn't fully comfortable in the hot midday sun, and stepped in a lil' closer to me. He set his sunglasses atop his head, and those dark eyes studied me somethin' fierce.

"It's all there. And the bank is set to foreclose on your place within the week. But that's why I came out. I wouldn't want to set a woman out of house and home without at least first meeting her," he said so calmly, so smoothly, as if nothin' ever fazed him.

"Foreclosed?" I asked, my jaw dropped open. "But my ma and pa owned this place outright, and they gave it to me in their will," I protested. I couldn't lose my house! My farm! I didn't have anythin' else, not in this world.

He looked me over with that hard gaze of his, and I knew then and there he had all the world in his pocket. Rich as they come, he could buy and sell people like me clear and easy. He took his time, took out a cigarette and lit it up, the grey smoke carryin' on the air before me, fillin' my nostrils with its acrid tang.

"Maybe you and I can come to some sort of accommodation, however," he remarked in his low, growling voice.

"Accommodation?" I said with a bit of a growl. I

couldn't believe what I was hearin'! This was my home, and had been since I was born!

My hands were tremblin' like I couldn't believe, and I was breathing hard and fast, and I couldn't make heads or tails of what he was talkin' about.

He offered up his silver cigarette case, a lone smoke pokin' out towards me in offerin'. "Go ahead, it'll help you relax as we sort this lil' mess out between you and I."

I had anger boilin' in me, but there was somethin' about that man, and I had no idea what it was, but it made me feel a lil' calmer. As cold and impersonal as he looked, so tall and well-dressed, with his finely groomed appearance, I got the feelin' from him that he was a safe man to have as a friend. Or whatever you could get close to bein' a friend.

So I took the smoke, and I held it to my lips as he lit it with his fancy lighter.

I was still in shock, but he was right. It made it a little easier. And it weren't like it was his fault, what was happenin'. He couldn't have known any better than I did.

"I just don't understand. My family's had this farm since long 'fore I was born..."

"I guess one of your grandparents must've mortgaged the place out way back, and it got lost in the mix," he said, taking a slow drag upon his cigarette, one hand tucked into his pocket as he looked around. "I don't want to take your farm from you though. But I have a rule that's served me well in business: never give something away for free that you could cash in on." He looked me over again, nice an' slow.

I crinkled my nose.

"I only make enough to just keep afloat," I admitted in a soft voice between the puffs of the cigarette. Everythin' was racin' through my head, that fear and anxiety windin' me up tight, but that calm way he was lookin' at me made me feel it mightn't be all bad news. At least, I hoped...

"You're a very beautiful woman," he said so calmly, reaching his hand out of his pocket and up to lightly brush his fingers over my ponytail. "You live out here by yourself? No man in your life?" he asked, smoking so casually as he leaned back against his shiny black car.

I could see clear as day that beneath his white pressed shirt, he was a man who take care of himself. His fitted clothing didn't do much to hide the bulk of muscle beneath the surface.

It surprised me, what with him bein' a businessman or accountant or somethin'. Most of them were scrawny as anythin'. At least around where I grew up.

And really, that little touch, his softer words, they relaxed me. Did a world of wonder, really, and I nodded my head. "Just me, Mister," I said. My green eyes found his, takin' him in a new, calmer light.

His full lips spread ever so slightly into a soft smile, and he reached up, cuppin' my chin in his large hand. He had a way about him, some sorta commandin' authority that made him seem so in charge, and it was comfortin' as well as unsettlin'.

"I bet you always were the kind of gal that wanted to be a mother though, weren't you?" he asked in his low voice, strokin' his thumb along my smooth cheek so tenderly.

"Well, sure, Mister. Every little girl grows up wantin' to be a mom," I said with a little roll of my eyes and a twitch of my lips. "I just ain't found anyone wantin' the same. Most the menfolk are movin' into the city for work and such."

He brushed the backs of his long fingers over my jawline, back to my ear as he smiled at me all admiringly.

"I promised my mom before she passed away I'd find a

nice, respectable woman, and make some lovely kids with her. Down to earth little brats," he remarked before taking a tug on his cigarette then exhaling a grey cloud. "Tell me, Annie — if I may call you Annie — are you on the pill?"

My nose crinkled again. I didn't figure that was a question I'd ever be asked, 'specially not by someone I just met.

But I shook my head no, my brows knit above my narrowed eyes. Sounded more like a business proposal than... than what? A regular proposal?

He took his time, casually takin' a drag on his cigarette before tossin' it in the dirt and grindin' it out with the toe of his shoe.

"Tell you what, Annie. How about you and me make our dreams come true, huh? And then this place is yours forevermore, and I make sure you're set up to last another ten generations out here." He reached to the side, pulled open the door to the back seat of his car, the luxurious interior on display, "What do you say, beautiful?"

My stomach was tied into knots as I looked at him, and there was a little tremor as I dropped my cigarette.

"I don't understand, Mister. You... you just wanna knock me up and then keep me here?"

He gave a shrug of his broad shoulders and reached up, undoing his tie, then taking off his blazer. He undid the first few buttons of his shirt and I could see a glimpse of the hard body beneath, peppered with some of his dark hairs.

"You're a beautiful girl, Annie," he said in a deep, gravelly husk that was edged with somethin' more than business. "If you've got the guts for it, I might do more than just that. Maybe I'll take you with me. Fly you around the world with me, and fuck you in every continent on earth. That is," he said, leaning down in towards me closely, licking his full lips. "If you've got the stomach for adventure."

I'm sure my eyes were wider than anything as I watched him, my breathing gettin' fast even though I didn't want it to. My body growin' warm, my knees startin' to tremble.

I stared, my mouth still open a little as I shook my head, "Mister, I ain't never been with a man before," I said, my eyes trailing over his exposed chest.

That made his grin widen, and he looked me over once more, from head to toe, soakin' me in as if I was the most beautiful creature on God's green earth. He was a very intense sorta man, who could convey all sorts of emotions with just a look, and that was somethin' I learned about him real fast.

He stroked his hand back over my hair, until his fingers was a tightenin' around my ponytail, and he was leanin' in so close barely a hairs breadth separated our lips.

"Perfect," he growled out. "Now Annie, I want you very bad right now... very, *very* bad," he stressed in his low, bestial tone. "So what's it gonna be, huh?"

His lips hung so close to mine, all it'd take was the slightest waver in my stance to make 'em brush together and have my first real kiss. So little...

I whimpered, my breath brushing against his lips, and it was like I went from zero to sixty in a half second, because suddenly I was ready to throw caution to the wind. That bit of brute force, the intensity that was in his body, in his gaze...

It was unreal, and I parted my lips softly, but didn't know what to say. It was so brazen and wrong, yet...

He sealed our lips together, my head locked in place by the strong grasp of his hand around my ponytail. His tongue snaked into my mouth, and we were makin' out somethin' fierce right away. A passion bubblin' out from him immediately as he wrapped his other arm around my bare waist, beneath my tied-up plaid shirt.

I felt nearly crushed against his hard body as he swept me literally up off my feet for a moment, that free hand of his slidin' on down my lower back, until those strong fingers was a diggin' into my rear and squeezin' my ass cheeks so tight.

God, he felt good. Strong and warm, his mouth hard and soft all at once. I was pressed into him, consumed by him, and even though I just barely met him, I was lost to his passions. The paperwork and cigarette both slipped from my hands as I wrapped my arms around his neck, lettin' him lead me, 'cause I didn't know what I was doin', not really.

I was just goin' with the flow, and what a strong current it was.

He picked me up off the ground, holdin' me with that one strong arm graspin' my rear, and I was swoonin'. Our tongues lashed one another, and though I had no experience with makin' out, it was easy to just respond to him in kind.

The low, guttural growls a comin' out of his chest were such a delight, they excited me to hear, made me feel how genuine his desire was. He kneaded the flesh of my rear until at last he turned us around, pressed me up against the car. His hand slid along my leg, liftin' up my thigh so that I hooked my legs over his hips. And then… oh boy, I could feel the throb of his manhood pressed up against me.

Sure, we had the fabric of our pants separatin' us, but it didn't feel any less primal. I mean, I was burnin' hot against him, and he was hard as steel against me. Without even wantin' to or tryin', my body was respondin' to him, grinding against him like you wouldn't believe. I mean, I definitely wouldn't have believed I'd act so wantonly after just meetin' a man.

If you'd have told me just an hour before he arrived what I'd be a doin', I'd laugh right in your face!

But there I was, in the middle of the sunny day, pressed up against a stranger's car, humpin' and grindin' with him like we was animals in the field. It was shameless, it was lewd, and by golly it was just raw need at work. I couldn't have stopped myself from grindin' up on his dick if there was a small fortune awaitin' me.

One of his big strong hands reached up, undid the front of my shirt and let my breasts spill out, bare. The tops of 'em sunkissed, but the rest a bit milky. And it was there, on that delicate porcelain skin, he grasped and squeezed at me.

I didn't have nobody or nothin' to compare him to, but the way he touched my breasts was somethin' amazin'. His hands were smooth but his grip was hard, his finger and thumb playing with my nipple, squeezing it and teasin' it until it was rock hard before he lowered his face to me and kissed me, right there on my sensitive skin.

The Spring sun was shinin' down upon my bare skin as that man hungrily devoured my flesh. His mouth workin' at my teat, tastin' me like nobody ever had before. He was ravenous, and he worked his hand down to the front of my daisy duke shorts, unbuttonin' 'em, tuggin' 'em open as he suckled at my stiff nipple, givin' a final flick of his tongue over its surface.

I had to admit... he was good. I mean, I'd never been so foolish, so blindly in lust, not ever. Not even close. But all I wanted was to go all the way with him, to feel somethin' real, that I'd never felt before. And with his calmness over top of a broilin' desire, the way he was touchin' me, I knew he had to be a pro.

And then he touched my wetness through my white, cotton panties, and it was like my world just went black but for the pleasure.

All that I could feel was the touch of his hand to my lady parts, the gentle rub of my most private of privates... it was intense. I couldn't hardly contain myself! I moaned into the warm midday air, and he nipped at my breasts with his mouth.

And then he did somethin' more daring still, he slipped his fingers in beneath the pale cotton and touched his hand to my slick folds, bare and uncovered. He circled his fingertips around and teased a part of me I never fully explored myself even.

"Oh, oh!" I cried to the wind, my back arching, my body crying out for release as I ground into that touch and then tried to shy away as it became too much. He wouldn't let me, though, and I started to quiver and quake, my nerves on fire, my tummy flutterin' like moths were let loose in it.

He did things to my body I never could've imagined before then, and he just never let up. He kept me pinned to his fancy car, kissin' from my breasts up my neck, nibblin' at my tender skin as he continued to work his fingers inside my panties. The lil' swirls of his long fingers stokin' my fires so hot I swear I could hear the crackle of the flames.

I screamed out, and I knew no one was around to hear but I still felt self-conscious and bit down on my lip real hard, tryin' to calm myself down, but that was useless. I just couldn't stop wrigglin' like a worm, letting out these little gasps that sounded like I was in pain but I wasn't feelin' no pain, not a lick.

He bit my neck and oh... I never thought much 'bout the term love bite, but I knew what it was then because it felt so good I could barely believe it.

My panties were soaked, and there he kept goin', touchin' at my most private of privates, makin' me wriggle and squirm and moan all out of control like. He kept me pressed between his rock hard body and that warm metal of his car, nippin' at my skin, and slidin' his free hand up along my figure.

He took his time, like he was appreciatin' my flesh for all it was worth. He let his hand glide on up to my breast, his fingers sinkin' into its flesh, squeezin' and kneadin' at it as he continued to tease and provoke my lil' clit.

There came a point, though I don't know exactly when, that I just completely lost it. Was like my mind went blank, and all there was was this... tension. A tightness just beggin' to be released, and when his tongue flicked over my throat once more, and his finger swirled just so, I came undone.

I would've lost my footing if not for him pinnin' me up, my knees were shakin' just that bad, and I was screaming so loud my throat hurt, but it all felt so good, it was unreal.

It was like the fourth of July, everythin' went suddenly dark and then lights went off. My body felt like it was bein' torn apart by pleasure from the inside out, but the truth of the matter was he was just bringin' me to the most pleasant point of my life to that point.

He didn't let me down easy neither, he slowly eased off, makin' me squirm and buck in his grasp as he teased my naughty bits on down from their high. He licked his way to my ear, nibbled and tugged at it with his teeth, then pulled back enough to meet my eyes.

And even then, as I was only slowly comin' off of my explosive high, he slid his fingers from my quiverin' mound, trailed a lil' glossy wetness over my belly, then licked at his fingers. Right there in front of my eyes! I watched as he tasted my own girlish honey on his digits, lickin' and sucklin' 'em clean of my flavour and soundin' like it was a delicious Christmas treat.

I stared at him through my heavy eyelids and could barely believe what I was seeing, but I was too exhausted and still tremblin' with excitement that it didn't feel so wrong. I mean, I felt like I should think it was wrong, but I didn't. Instead I found it... enticin'.

There I was, top undone, tits out in the sun, my panties soaked, watchin' a man lick his fingers clean of my juices. And it just felt so damn right! I can't help it! It did!

"You've got the tastiest cunt," he growled his words at me like an animal. He squeezed at my breast once more, then leaned in, kissin' me right on the lips! With my own flavour still lingerin' on his tongue!

Though it didn't last so long that time before he was lowerin' me down back to my shaky feet. He set me there, restin' my back to the car as he began to strip off his shirt completely, showin' off his broad shoulders, his sculpted pecs and abs. Oh lordy... what a sight he was!

I admit, I greedily looked him over, and then my hands joined in like I was nothin' more than a wanton slut. I touched his muscles, feelin' him over, and the hairs along his chest teased my palms. He was strong, so much stronger than I imagined some rich jerk from the city bein'.

And then, before I knew it, he was unbucklin' his pants, and down they came. Tugged away from his hips, I got to see the outline of a truly tremendous manhood silhouetted in black cotton. His boxer-briefs tightly wrapped around his junk, such a thick long shaft, with a big bulge of his balls beneath.

Though before I could finish appreciatin' the sight of it, he yanked down my own shorts and panties, leavin' me exposed with him.

"I need to fuck your pretty little pink pussy now, Annie," he said to me so crassly.

He was so commanding, and I wanted nothin' more than to obey. To follow through, and so I bobbed my head, even though my eyes were still glued to his package. I stepped out of my shorts, and it was brazen how little I cared that I was naked in the noonday sun.

My smooth, pale skin that was always hidden, that tan-line never quite touchin' far enough to be scandalous. Never had anyone seen me like it before, but his hands went to my rounded ass and squeezed my bare flesh.

He bent his head down and kissed me on the lips again as his two powerful hands worked at my body. We made out like that for ages, my fingers tracin' along the lines of his strong muscles, feelin' the indents and grooves between the hard bulges, until finally they found themselves down to the cotton of his drawers. It was there I found myself stroking along the shape of his tool, feelin' how big it was, the curious veins that bulged along its girth.

A low, husky groan rumbled out of his throat and then he pushed us apart, his dark eyes staring into mine from above.

He hooked his thumbs into his briefs and yanked 'em down, so that he stood fully naked with me. That thick shaft throbbing lewdly in the sun, bare and exposed between us.

"Get down on your knees and kiss it," he commanded me.

I couldn't believe what he was askin' me to do.

More than that, I couldn't believe how much I wanted to. How much I needed to just feel it, raw against me. Even if it was just my mouth.

Besides, he was so commandin', I didn't ever wanna say no to him. So I knelt down before him, a bit more cautious

47

and uncertain as I looked up along his body. Over his hard chest, his pulsin' shaft. I was so close to it that I could smell him, and see all the thick veins that bulged out of it.

I was scared, but I took it in my hand anyway, holdin' it in place as I leaned up, plantin' a kiss right along the bottom of it.

He gave a deep, lewd groan as he stared down at me, watchin' me kneel before him and kiss at his manhood. He licked his lips, ran a hand back through his thick, glossy black hair.

"Kiss it again, right on the tip. Kiss it like you mean it. Make out with my cock," he instructed me so forcefully, as if I had no choice but to obey. And truthfully, that's exactly how it felt! He was such a powerful, gorgeous man, who held all the power, and I had to obey.

So I pushed myself up higher, my knees diggin' into the gravel as I brought my mouth to the tip of his cock. I kissed it, closed lipped and cautious, but it wasn't so bad. In fact... It was nice. Felt warm and hard against me.

So then I kissed it again, lettin' my lips open a little, and then I could taste a bit of him on my tongue, and he moaned approvingly, so I did it again.

His hands went to my hair, coiled my ponytail about his knuckles as he urged me on to lick and taste his cock. Though it wasn't long before his deep, rumbling moans signalled he had enough. He tugged me back up to my feet by my hair as his dick glistened with my saliva in the midday sun.

"Get in the backseat. Hands and knees," he commanded me so roughly, guiding my head down with his grasp on my hair.

I couldn't believe what I was doin'. That I was standing up, dusting off my knees before crawlin' into the back of his expensive car.

The leather felt warm against my hands, and there wasn't a lot of room, but it was enough for me to get kinda comfortable. Well, except that kneelin' in front of a man when I was bare naked was not comfortable at all.

He got in behind me, his palms graspin' my ass cheeks, spreadin' 'em wide as he let the tip of his manhood prod at my slick lil' slit. He teased me purposefully, slidin' that bulgin', purple crown up and down my wantin' cunny, but even he had his limits.

"I'm gonna breed you like a bitch in heat, you hear me Annie?" he said roughly, right before he sank his big, bulging cock right down into my pussy, endin' all my years of virginity in one fell swoop. "Ohhh yeah," he exclaimed noisily.

I cried out, my head thrown back. It hurt! Though when he finally hilted in me, and it was just him stayin' still, throbbin'...

That part didn't hurt. Not at all. I was so wet, and I guess it made that easier, because he pulled out and I let out a little moan of annoyance because I wanted him in me. I wanted him to... to breed me!

He didn't disappoint though, 'cause he pulled back for only a moment before he was thrustin' in again. His powerful body hammerin' his dick into me again and again, his pace and strength growin' as he pummeled my ass cheeks, the loud slap of his hard body to mine resonatin' in the car. Those thick, cum-filled balls of his swingin' up, smackin' against my clit wetly as he grunted and groaned.

"Fuck you are so tight," he growled, his dick swelling inside me, makin' me squirm. "Ohh you are such a sweet lil' piece of ass Annie... never fucked a girl like you before."

I didn't wanna think about the types of girls he'd usually fucked. I didn't wanna just be a number, not really, but I did want him to keep going. What he'd did before, how he'd touched me, that was just the tip of the iceberg because when his body slammed up against mine I was in heaven.

I gripped on tighter to the leather upholstery, pushing my ass in against him, begging for more with my body as I panted and gasped for air.

It felt so good to be full of him, and the more he fucked me, the greater it got. He got rougher as time went, but my body only started to crave it more and more as he kept it up, the lil' twinge of pain with each rough thrust just enough for me to adapt to until the next.

He raised his hand and cracked a slap across my ass cheek, makin' me gasp out. Then he did it again, gruntin' himself as his dick swelled.

"Fuck fuck fuck," he crooned in pleasure. "I am gonna fill your tight lil' pussy with so much cum you burst," he boasted, and I believed him then! He felt unstoppable.

Like no man I'd ever met before, that much was for real, because he had so much power and control I felt like a doll to him. But that was nice in its own right, and he was givin' me such a pounding that I'd never complain, for even for a second.

"Ohhh," I groaned out, my body responding to him in ways I never knew it could, "You feel so good!"

We'd been doin' such naughty things in the sun for so long, our bodies were perspirin', gleamin', and his thrusts grew sharper, harder. He moaned, and I felt the slap of his heavy balls end as they tightened, gettin' ready to breed me.

"I'm gonna cum," he said, brushing his dark hair back out of his face again before slapping my ass cheek again. "I'm gonna knock your pretty lil' ass up, Annie. Beg for it," he commanded.

It was strange and felt wrong and oh so right, but I opened my mouth, and the words tumbled out. "Ohh, do it," I pleaded. "Knock me up, Sir." I didn't even know his name!

My pussy was so wet, he was makin' such a loud noise in between the cracks of his hand over my ass, makin' me smart in such a good way.

Then he let loose such a loud roar, I swear he must've upset the cows in the barn!

He plowed into me so hard and fast, lettin' loose all his desire as he took me upon that back seat. He fucked me raw and hard, his dick swellin' so stiffly, his one hand reachin' around beneath me, rubbin' at my clit, teasin' and provokin' it once more as he let loose his torrent of cum.

Those thick gouts of creamy seed shot into me, fillin' up my fertile depths beyond their capacity, just as he promised. Again and again he thrust, until finally he stilled, his balls emptyin' their load in me with those pulsatin' swells.

I trembled with excitement.

My first real, masculine load.

I was almost proud of myself, becomin' a woman, and it was with that pleasant thought that he sent me over the edge again and my pussy gripped his tool, my entire body pushing onto his more desperately.

That was my first time. But it weren't the last.

He might've been some fancy pants big shot from the city, but when we was a layin' in his backseat, pantin' and sweaty, he pulled me up against him and held me there as I dribbled his cum. In fact, that was a position I got real used to since.

Y'see, he did more than keep his promise. He knocked me up, oh heck yeah! My belly's out to here now, and gettin' about is becomin' tougher. But he's not left since, not for more than a few hours anyhow.

I invited him on in for a bite after our first time, then the night, and one day led to the next, and he just couldn't resist me, my cookin', nor anythin' else about life on the farm with me. Though I gotta confess, we had to hire help on the farm for more reasons than just the oncomin' baby. He's got a sexual appetite that don't quit! And with the hours a day I spend on my back, or my knees, boy howdy... how'd I ever get all that work done?

CAUGHT CHEATING

ook Themes:
> Cheating, BDSM, and Cuckolding.
Word Count:
4,744

~

WEDNESDAY.

That was her day. The day that Aiden couldn't tell her what to do. They day that she was just allowed to be Sarah.

It was her chance to unwind, and every week she used it to her advantage. The rest of the week, she was his, absolutely and utterly. Every command. Every wish. Every thought.

And she served him, happily. But the reason she was able to was that every Wednesday was hers.

She smiled as she stepped into the shower and felt the warm water wash away the grime. The scent of him. Tomorrow she would long for that scent, for the feeling of his strong hands guiding her, his commanding voice taking charge of her.

Today she wanted to smell like coconuts.

Her loofah soaped her body and she even caught herself singing as she explored herself. It was the same thing, the same routine every Wednesday morning. No matter how she chose to spend the rest of the day, she always started by reclaiming her body.

Her song dipped lower as the soapy material brushed against her smooth slit. He'd paid for her hair removal and it was a present she always cherished, even on this most holy of days. Her skin felt alight with sensation and she drew her hand up, rubbing along the heavy mounds of her chest. She wasn't a big woman, but she was still curvy, and the way they felt against her palm was delicious.

She tweaked her nipple and tugged it hard, feeling a wave of electricity run through her. She let herself moan as she reached for the waterproof toy that made these mornings so much brighter. It was a hot pink, and she instantly turned it on high.

Sarah wasn't fucking around today.

She had plans.

Aiden let her do whatever—or whomever—she wanted on these glorious breaks, and though she didn't often take him up on his offer of non-exclusivity, today she was going to. The only difference was that this time, she wouldn't have his permission or consent.

He'd never give it.

Tobias was his best friend in the world, and he'd never risk that. But at the party Aiden had hosted on the Saturday prior, Tobias had cornered her in the bathroom and whispered such dirty things in her ear.

The vibrator tickled her, first, and excited her clit, but it did nothing to curl her toes. Not until she remembered what he'd promised.

"Aiden told me," he'd confessed in that dark and sensuous voice. She remembered how full his lips had looked, and how they were glossy from the beer he was drinking.

"Told you what?" she'd asked, pretending to be naive.

"Of your arrangement. Your… contract. The things you do for him. The way you plead and beg to please him. The way you do everything he says, and if you don't, you get punished."

Sarah had blushed and tried to move away from him, but his firm hand had tugged at her hip, and when he'd drawn her thigh to his groin she'd felt him throb. "I want you. Just like this."

She moaned louder and her hips started to circle, the vibration warming her canal and making her insides begin to clench.

"I have to go back to Aiden." She cursed herself for being so curt, because Tobias was hot. He and Aiden could pass as brothers. They both had short hair and full lips that drove her crazy. They were both powerful and tall, and both made her feel like a woman.

"Look, you go back to him. But this week, here's what you're going to do…"

She reached out for the wall of the shower to balance herself as she fell over the precipice. Her body trembled as her scream echoed around her.

How was she possibly going to make it through to the evening?

SHE COULD SMELL the scent of cooking from outside the

front door, the open window taking its pleasant aroma out into the evening air where she stood. It was intoxicating in a way, though when he opened that door and stood before her, something more intoxicating still presented itself.

The evening was pleasantly hot, and so was the large, buff man that stood before her in the doorway. Black pants and a tight white shirt that clung to his muscular form accentuated his body, showing off the well-built muscle as his mouth broke into a wide grin.

"Sarah," Tobias said simply, stepping aside enough for her to pass as he reached out and took her hand gently in his large, strong grasp. The front of his shirt was undone low, and showed off the peppering of dark hair on his pecs.

Her stomach tightened and she almost walked away. She knew she shouldn't be doing this. Keeping secrets from the man she called Master the other six days of the week felt wrong, but he looked so right.

Her skirt was black and tight and scandalously short, her red top dangerously low, and the smell of coconuts still clung to her flesh. Her entire body felt so hot, just seeing him, just knowing what a chance she was taking.

He was the one person off-limits to her, and that just made her need him more.

"It smells delicious," she offered, immediately kicking herself for sounding so shy. She was quiet at times, sure. Respectful. Not shy.

Though as soon as the door was shut, Tobias was up against her, and she was put to the wall. "Damn, girl, you look amazing," he said in his low husk, the rumble of approval able to be felt through his chest and into her as he squeezed her hand and gazed into her eyes. "I'm so glad you came."

Fuck, he felt good. She inhaled and it felt like he was all around her. How many times had she fantasized about him? Yet she'd never acted on it, not until now. The air was almost electric between them and the pressure of his body felt so right. So powerful.

She felt so small next to him and her head had to tilt back to see him. Her brown eyes were framed with dark lashes, and her long hair tendriled down over her shoulders. He looked so damn good. It had been torture having him around, trying to be respectful of Aiden while lusting for his best friend.

"Me too," she finally whispered back, and she felt her thighs begin to dampen already.

It didn't help that his free hand came up beside her, and the tips of those strong digits touched upon her outer thigh, lightly curling up towards her black skirt. "You've got no idea how much you've been on my mind, Sarah," he said to her in a deep, confessional tone, gaze still glued to her.

The large, built man let his eyes shut for just a moment as he inhaled her coconut-laced scent, and it looked for a moment like his lips would seek out hers. Though some last moment of discipline kept him from doing so as he had her nearly pinned to the wall.

Sarah liked dominant men. She and Aiden had been together for a year, and even though he gave her freedom, she knew he was in control. Just like Tobias. They were so similar, but so different at the same time. Aiden wouldn't have paused, and Sarah found that made her knees quiver and her pussy throb with need. Just knowing how close he was but how he resisted her.

It was sweet torture, but she didn't press her lips to his. She simply let her warm, cinnamon-scented breath heat them.

Tobias was only temporarily restrained though, for his fingers curled up in under her skirt just so as he tilted his head and pressed against her. She could feel his hard body hot against her, and more still, the hot throb of his manhood.

"Why'd he have to get to you first, huh?" he lamented in his dark tone, the food forgotten as he was lost in his obsession with her. Touching her. Smelling her. Craving her.

It was like a drug and she was grateful that he was pinning her to the door, because otherwise she might have crumbled to the ground. She felt molten between her thighs and begged for him to touch nearer, to feel how much she longed for him.

Her throat felt closed off, but she managed out a small, pleading sound of longing.

Those strong, daring fingers of his probed higher, to where he should've found the cloth of her panties, but where instead there was nothing. Nothing but her flesh.

It sent a visible shiver through his broad frame, and he delighted in the feel of her bare skin at the crease where her thigh met her hips. "Damn it, girl," he cursed, his lips nearly brushing against hers as he bent down to her level, eyes staring down her top. "If only I had laid claim to you for myself first"—and his other hand went from hers up her arm to her shoulder, thumbing her shirt so that it rolled further down—"there'd be no keeping me off you each and every day. Night. Morning."

She couldn't remember feeling so stupid from lust. What was he doing to her? He was off-limits, but damn it, that was only making this sweeter. Keeping a secret from her lover, her "Master," her partner. It was torturous, but she couldn't stop herself. It was like watching a car roll out of control. Time stood still and she wasn't able to put on the brakes.

Her ruby lips parted and she whimpered his name, her

dark lashes falling over her eyes. She shouldn't do this. She shouldn't be here. Aiden... She shook the thought away. It was too late now. Too late to turn back.

She inhaled and her breasts rose towards his hand, the black lace just barely visible as it made her cleavage more pronounced.

Tobias closed the gap, his tongue dove into her mouth, and he moved a hand into her hair and grasped it tightly as he pushed her against the wall. The passion of that moment was nearly violent as he took hold of her, tongued her deep, and lifted her thigh as her skirt rolled up to her waist, nearly forming a belt.

It was the boiling over of passion, and she felt it: the throb of need in his loins as he took hold of her, claimed her for himself in that moment of lust.

Her moan was muffled against his tongue as she met him with equalled desire. She'd spent so long thinking about him, fantasizing about what he'd feel like. What he'd taste like.

Now that it was happening it was even better than she could have dreamed. Her stomach coiled and flipped as he so expertly took control of her body, and her arms flung around his neck. It had always seemed such a shame to her that Aiden didn't share with his best friend, but now he would.

Whether he knew about it or not.

There was no doubt in her mind where this was headed, and fast, and she couldn't believe how excited she was. She couldn't recall being this wet in months, despite all of the dirty things Aiden did to her. With her.

Tobias was an animal unleashed though. The fire in his own loins drove him after her so hard as he lifted her up by his one palm on her ass, fingers still locked in her hair above as they made out.

No sooner than she was elevated up like that, did he press himself between her legs, forcing them to accommodate his size as she wrapped them about him. He ground his shaft to her, only breaking the seal of their lips to longingly murmur her name on the moan that rumbled from his throat. "I'm gonna take you into my bedroom," he told her, didn't ask, just pulling her from the wall and beginning to make his way there.

She clutched him and felt like her world was spinning. It was amazing. She needed this more than anything else, and for that moment, Aiden left her mind. Everything did.

All that remained was the sensation of his heated body, his rough clothes, and hard cock probing her delicate flesh. She felt so exposed, but it wasn't like anything she'd experienced before. This was a man who she was denied. She could sleep with anyone in the world, but not Aiden's best friend.

But she was going to.

When he took her into his spacious bedroom, it became so real. He didn't lay her out on the king-size bed, he fell upon it with her, refusing to part from her for even a moment. There was a primal need between the pair that had to be fulfilled, and he tugged at the buttons of his shirt, letting it come open to reveal the hard-lined shape of his abs before going to hers, desperate to get her top and bra off as they hungrily made out.

She squirmed out of the top, revealing her smooth skin and that bra that made her breasts look so delightful. Instantly her hands were pawing at that too, struggling out of it and revealing those large, heavy orbs. Her skirt was already hiked up around her waist, and she felt so lewd and exposed. It didn't matter.

Her hands gripped his ass, pulling him in closer to her, begging for their bodies to unite.

Yet Tobias still had to finish freeing himself, and his strong body resisted her urgent tugs as he unleashed his manhood. It fell against her with a heavy slap of flesh, so thick and full it swelled with ridged veins and pulsed with a need she'd not seen in Aiden for some time. This was fresh lust, unrequited, needful, and so generously proportioned.

Maybe that was what made her accept. The boredom. The routine. She hadn't been taking full advantage of the freedom offered to her every Wednesday, though she appreciated it. But even that day off, that day to herself, had become just another part of the cycle.

This was her breaking free, and it felt glorious.

He kissed at her, a low growl in his chest as he gave in and let that insistent tug bring his groin to hers, that thick crown, only partially covered by his foreskin, nudging to her honeyed slit before quickly pressing itself in against its tight ring.

She was so wet he was able to impale her in one go, and her sensitive body tingled in response. "Ahh!" He was so needy, so hard, and her legs wrapped around his ass.

All else was forgotten as that thick, trunk-like member embedded itself into her to his root, pulsing fully inside her, straining her limits even before he began to pump. Though that too was not far off; he was a beast with a need, and he grasped a breast in one hand, squeezed it tight as he pulled back his hips then crashed into her with a loud slap of his balls striking her ass.

There was no slow, steady buildup, little care or concern, just a wild, bestial rutting as he pounded her atop his bed at an increasing speed. "Sarah," he grunted out her name. "Need you so damn bad!"

She wasn't even sure if she was saying it, but she was

certainly thinking it. Over and over the words "take me!" repeated.

They were only silenced when she screamed his name, her body arching and pressing against his. Her bare breasts flattened against his chest, her nipples prodding his bare skin between his unbuttoned shirt.

He was just like Aiden in some ways, back when they first got together, and she longed for this feeling again. Need. Desire. Passion.

How had she lived without it for so long?

They were so wrapped up in their own world, Tobias pounding into her, calling out her name in return as he quaked and trembled with his own release. It was so powerful, he battered into her as he emptied his loins with powerful thrusts. The whole of his bed groaned beneath them as they found such heights of pleasure together in one another's bodies.

It was dizzying, and even in the aftermath of their explosive rutting the smell of the burnt food and smoke that had brought Aiden in went unnoticed.

It was hard to ignore it when that other man's voice piped in from the doorway. "Sarah?"

He stood there, a look of dull-witted surprise on his face to see his woman sweaty and near nude beneath his best friend, cock still buried inside her.

It was a shock to hear him, and Tobias looked back with a start. "Jesus, Aiden!"

"Fuck!" Sarah's face went red and she tried to squirm away from Tobias, but they were too entangled. "Fuck, Aiden."

She felt shame, sure, but anger too. Anger that he was interrupting her. Anger that they were caught.

"It's not what it looks like," she said, her voice quivering even as she kicked herself. Not what it looks like? What else could it be?

He stood there, very nearly the mirror image of Tobias, but looking pissed. His fists were clenched as finally the man inside her disentangled himself, leaving her puffy labia to drool the pearly-white essence of his release.

"Damn it, man, I didn't want yo—" but Aiden cut him off, holding up a hand.

"Save it," he said, though the anger edged out of his voice. "I can't blame you," he said, stepping into the room as his gaze moved back to Sarah. "Damn it, woman, I gave you one restriction... just one." He shook his head. "I know you couldn't help yourself from her, Toby," he said. "I couldn't."

Her heart pounded and she moved to cover her body, but she didn't know why.

She thought she knew what it felt like to be exposed, but she had no idea. Not until then.

She moved onto her knees, crawled across the bed towards him, and looked up with those dark eyes. Instantly she was back to being his kittenish slave, even though her body trembled. Even though she leaked another man's cum.

"I'm sorry," Sarah mewled weakly. "I..."

She didn't get to go on further, as he put his hand about her throat and silenced her with a tight squeeze. "Toby," he said back to his friend as he gave her a harsh stare. "I'm sorry I barged in and interrupted your fun. I smelled the smoke and burning from outside, so I got worried," he explained, as if nothing were out of the ordinary but him overstepping his bounds on his friend's privacy a bit.

"Don't worry, man," responded Tobias, who stood, shirt and pants still undone as he stared with surprise.

"No reason to ruin your plans for the night though," he

said with a smile back to his friend. "I know you've wanted my pet for a long time, and you got her fair and square." He turned his hard gaze back to Sarah, "You won't mind sharing a bit, though, will you?" he asked.

She felt her cunny pulse. Her gaze was uncertain, a bit fearful, but that dark look in Aiden's gaze ignited something in her. Something deep.

She'd been his for a long time, but this was the first time in months that she felt this overwhelming need to serve him. It certainly didn't hurt that his idea made her entire body tremble with need.

She shook her head and felt her entire body flush with heat as she felt the webbing of his hand threaten her throat.

Tobias was a bit stunned with surprise, but as Aiden undid his shirt, revealing his own bare, muscular chest, the man muttered, "That's real generous of you."

Aiden simply peeled his shirt off, letting it hit the floor before he went to work on his belt. His hand only left her throat after he gave her a hard look, that one she knew so well. It meant so much without needing a word. It meant don't move, shut up, and be obedient. He saved his actual words for his friend, as he unleashed his own cock, and she was surprised to see it thicker, harder than she could remember in so very long.

"She's the finest piece of ass there is, Toby," he said, climbing upon the bed behind her, taking hold of her hips and ass as she was pushed to the edge of the bed. "But you can park your dick at her mouth for now."

He did.

It was all happening so fast, but she couldn't help but moan softly. He tasted of her. Of him.

It was exquisite. For that moment, that blissful moment, the sensation and taste enwrapped her and she was at peace until she felt her lover's hands tighten on her hips.

No, this wasn't peace. This was her most secret dream come true. Two men. Two men that she was wildly attracted to, their hands and cocks touching her and her body. Lusting for her.

Her body pushed back towards Aiden, her knees spreading and revealing that cum-slickened pussy. She was so hairless and it made her cunny even more responsive to touch.

The first thing she felt wasn't the sweet entry of her Master, but the hard crack of his hand upon her ass cheek. So hard and fast, he kept her pinned in place as he doled out that piece of punishment. "Don't let her half-ass it," he growled to Tobias before taking hold of her hair, yanking back her head before forcing it further onto his friend's cock. "Take it all," he commanded.

She was used to such rough treatment, but when paired with the hard stab of his own thick, needful cock into her cum-stained cunt, it was near overwhelming.

She'd thought Tobias so raw and passionate that very evening, showing a bestial desire that she'd not seen in Aiden in so very long. Yet to feel that molten metal dick pierce her already-fucked cunt? She knew her Master's desire was unequaled again. He kept his hand in her hair as he began to buck into her, undeterred by the gooey slickness of his best friend's cum aiding his rutting.

Fuck near overwhelming. She felt like she'd died and gone to paradise. Aiden was taking control of her with more interest and zest than he'd shown in way too long, and Tobias was reaping the benefits. She licked every bit of their combined juices from his cock, suckling him to fullness with such eager desire.

Her eyes watered from the rough smacks, from how

CANDY QUINN

deeply that thick cock prodded her throat, but it didn't matter. Nothing mattered but for this moment in time when she finally got just what she needed.

Grunting with his harsh hammering thrusts, Aiden tugged her hair roughly then pushed her head back down Tobias's dick. For his part, the beefy friend took hold of her face, moaning and panting as she kept his recently drained cock so stiff and satisfied with each slap of his balls against her chin.

Though all the while Aiden saw to her attention to his friend, he exacted his price from her. He pounded brutally, making her quake and waver beneath his blows. Only the tight hold on her waist and hips kept her up as he moaned and hammered.

It was hard to keep up, to be able to handle so much happening at once, but she reveled in it at the same time. Her throat ached, her pussy throbbed, but still as he hammered in, her toes curled in warning.

She couldn't believe it. Her body quivered and her clit throbbed as it was slapped by Aiden's hefty sac. Each thrust made her breasts bounce and pull, and the tension all toppled her over her peak. Her cry was a rumbled moan along Tobias's cock and her brown eyes looked up through her dark lashes at him as she came.

She could see in the wake of her orgasm the look of desire and longing still smoldering in that man's gaze. He'd had her, a taste of her, and he needed more. That made her climax all the sweeter, sweeter still knowing that as she satisfied him a flood of her honey graced Aiden's cock as he hammered in wildly with his own release, pumping his virile seed into her to add to Tobias's.

To be stuck between two such strong, stunning men, each so powerful as they had their hands upon her flesh, their cocks within her body.

Aiden took control of her again. He yanked back her head off that thick dick in her mouth, and without a word Tobias wrapped his hand about its girth and began to beat it hard and fast. The fire of passion was still written in his gaze as he stared at her with his huffs and grunts.

The world was ripe with sensation, and she watched as he pounded his meat with his fist until that dark purple crown exploded. White strands of cum lancing out across her face, over her lips and tongue, snaked across her cheeks and nose. It was amazing he had so much in him after only just recently cumming inside her.

Her only regret was the instinct to close her eyes, but to feel that warm, wet jism strike her was degrading and liberating all at once. It was what she hadn't even known she'd been looking for.

Aiden had given her the option to sleep with other men, but she hadn't. Not until Tobias. She knew it would never be something that could live up to her fantasies, but this...

Her pussy tightened around Aiden's cock in thanks.

He gave her a slap of her ass and a tug of her hair in response, biting her neck and growling her name with desire to show he was far from done with her. She moaned loudly in response, and her body tingled with anticipation.

DANCING FOR THE MOB BOSS

ook Themes:
   Creampie, Breeding, Bad Boy Alpha Male,
Stripping, and Mobster
   Word Count:
   11,074

~

"You ARE the hottest girl in this club tonight," I told myself in the mirror, looking over my bright blue eyes beneath three layers of fake lashes and more mascara than anyone needed. With my ruby lips, dark hair, and porcelain skin, I knew I had to be someone's type.

But I'd been on my shift for three hours, gotten twenty seven rejections, and had another five hours to go.

That was how it went as a stripper. Sometimes the guys wanted you, sometimes they didn't.

It was my job to turn their no's into yes's, but that was easier said than done when my boyfriend of three years just dumped me and I felt like a pile of shit.

"You are the hottest girl in the club," I said again, more sternly. I had to believe it. If I couldn't even convince myself of that, how was I going to convince anyone else?

Mark came up behind me, his voice hard and distracted.

"You're up after Sparkle."

"Yea, one more song, right?"

"Yea. Same set?"

I nodded my head, pushing a bang back with a rhine-stone clip as I looked over myself. I'd chosen black leather with rhinestones, and it gave me a bit of a badass edge which I appreciated. My hands ran over the flat of my stomach before I turned, looking over my ass. I was a thin girl, but toned. I stayed in shape though the gym and pole dancing. With skin as fair as mine I had to do something to stand out.

I looked up at Mark who was growing increasingly bored. It was always strange to me how desensitized the DJ could become to the sight of naked women's bodies and tried to tell myself it wasn't just because I looked hideous.

Self-confidence could be a real bitch.

"Same set," I agreed, getting excited for the break in the rap and the hip-hop. Typically I was a dance and techno girl, but tonight I needed something harder and angstier.

He went back to his booth, settling in before announc-ing, "And that's the hot little Sparkle! Remember, guys, you can take her for a private dance or get really intimate in the champagne room." He tried to sound enthusiastic, but after repeating that every ten minutes or so for the last few hours, it lacked oomph.

But the moment I heard the opening chords to my first song — the rhythm pumping my heart up and making me feel so alive — I couldn't wait to get on stage. I felt like a diva, and all the lights were on me.

I strut out to the stage, my black Maryjane stilettos carrying me steadily, fishnet tights clinging to my thighs. With each step, my leather and rhinestone skirt fluttered above the cusp of my ass, and my smile grew.

Walking up those few steps, onto the stage, I was a Goddess among men unworthy of my attention.

No longer was I sweet little Alice. No, I had fully become Ruby, and my clear eyes met each of those in the crowd.

Long legs carried me towards the pole, the thing I was most confident about. I wanted to start out slow, though, like the beat of the music before the crescendo. My spine pressed against the pole as I looked out to the crowd, my legs parted as I let my body roll down the pole's length before I was on my knees. Crawling forward, I pushed my ass back.

Guys loved that. It looked like I was taking them doggy style, and I could make my face contort into such a wanton expression of pleasure.

I practically moaned against the music as I rolled onto my back, arching it and letting them look me over as I writhed against the ground. My hands ran over my bare stomach, up to cup my breasts, squeezing them a little as my face tilted towards the crowd.

Most of them were still rather ambivalent and I had a moment of despair before I caught the eyes of the night manager, Tom, talking to someone I'd not seen before. And it wasn't the usual conversation. It was friendly, cordial, and the other man looked good.

High class.

I licked my lips and pushed down my fear of rejection, standing before instantly going up on the pole.

I had a target now. Someone to perform for.

Crawling up that large pole got the attention of some of

the crowd, my toned thighs gripping the pole between them as I wriggled. My smile broadened with the growing attention, and the beat got louder, faster. It was all working together to build to something amazing, and I let my body drop so I was upside down, clasped onto the pole with only my legs.

My hands went to my back, fingers working at the bra clasp before I got it open. I gathered the bra before it could reveal my breasts, though, because I wanted to tease. For them to know how close they were to seeing my perky tits and the hard, pink nipples beneath.

More than that, I wanted to get the attention of my target.

It didn't take long. One of the men in the crowd was getting impatient and cried out for me to, "Take it off!"

The target looked at me, watched as I smiled at him and let that bra drop away from my chest.

I hoisted myself back up, spinning around the pole, and performing such a beautiful little act for him. I was powerful on the pole, that was where I felt most at home, and once I had him in my snare, I knew he would be captivated.

He clasped his hand on Tom's shoulder, motioning to me, and there was a soft conversation before Tom gave him a nod and moved towards the side of the stage.

I spun my way down the pole, my hips circling and back arching as I showed off my ass, bare breasts cupped around the pole and reflected in the mirror ahead of me.

Next, my fingers worked into the skirt, feeling over my soft skin and tugging down the leather and rhinestone material to show off the slutty little thong beneath. My eyes went back to Tom's friend, and saw he'd moved onto one of the couches, alone and getting comfortable.

It only took a few moments before another dancer

approached him, trying to sit in his lap, but he gently rebuked her advances, his eyes on me all the while.

I had a good feeling about it. About him.

My fingers went down to my covered pussy, rubbing over it for a moment as I tilted my head to the side, licking over my lips. He gave me such a smile, and even from the stage I could see he was handsome. If I was working the floor, I might have passed him up with how much of a wreck I felt. You might think it was harder getting turned down by the ugly, old men, but no, it was way worse getting turned down by the hot guys.

The hot guys that really knew how to fill out a suit.

I'd almost lost track of the rhythm of my songs as I watched him, dancing only for him, but then I heard the DJ.

"That's the ravenous Ruby! Remember, guys, you can take her for a private dance or get really intimate in the champagne room."

I grabbed for my bra and skirt, along with the few tips I'd managed, before I went right over to my beckoning manager.

"Hey, Ruby," he said in his baritone voice. "Luc over there," he motioned towards the man he'd been talking to, "is in from out of town. He owns the chain, and requested you. Don't fuck this up, don't do anything illegal, don't..."

He kept talking, but I wasn't listening. My eyes were on Luc, and that mischievous smile he had upon his gorgeous face.

I nodded to Tom absently. "Don't worry about it."

I moved towards my target, breasts still bared and the nipples so stiff at the prospect of making some real money.

"Hi," I said as I knelt next to him, not being so presumptuous as the other dancer I'd seen him shoo away. Not that I didn't believe he wanted me in his lap. My eyes

CANDY QUINN

ran over his body, over his strong brow, his powerful jaw, his full lips.

He reached out, brushing his finger along my arm, over the raven tattoo I had there.

"What's it mean?" he asked, and his voice was accented. I'd guess Russian, perhaps, but I wasn't sure over the loud music that had turned from my metal into some watered down rap.

"Protection," I said with a small smile. "It's supposed to bring power and protection."

Those fingers of his slid up my arm, along to my shoulder. He was masculine, strong, but his fingertips weren't rough so much as just hardened. He lightly stroked my hair and seemed to take some time to appreciate me up close, as if checking to make sure I was real and not the product of some stage effects.

The smile that grew upon his face said he got the answer he was hoping for, and I was still as flesh and blood and real as ever.

"A beautiful woman like you deserves all the protection she can get," he said approvingly, letting his arm slide in behind me, holding me. "I didn't expect to find such a magnificent women here. You're more than a cut above the rest of the dancers, Ruby," his compliments delivered in that rich, masculine husk of his, making them sound all the sweeter.

I really liked his voice. I don't know why, but I had always found voice really important in a man.

But it was business, not pleasure, I reminded myself, though there was no harm in enjoying it a little. Dancing for handsome men was always a secret high for me, knowing they thought I was so hot they'd pay for me to be naked when I would have done it for free...

I smiled brightly as my hand rest against his shoulder gently.

"Thank you, Luc," I purred sincerely, my clear blue eyes finding his, fluttering over them. "Do you have any tattoos?"

"A few," he said to me smoothly, letting his fingers trace along my collarbone, enjoying the soft feel of my skin. "But seeing as I am not the dancer in this scenario of ours, mine are not so easily shared," he said with a light humour to his voice, his eyes soaking me up.

In a space devoted to watching the bodies of beautiful women, he had a way of making me feel like I was the only one in the entire place. His intense gaze was unwavering as he sized me up.

"How about I take you up for a private dance, hmm?" he said in that husky, accented voice of his. "You are working after all, it would be inconsiderate of me to monopolize your time with no reward."

I nodded as I leaned in, bringing my lips to his ear, "We could go to a room if you like," I offered. "There's bottle service there."

I pulled away, fluttering my many layers of fake lashes at him, smiling so sweetly.

"Yes," he said, looking me over, watching the motions of my lashes, how I sat there topless beside him. "Something nice and private. The club is too noisy and crowded to enjoy time with so beautiful a lady," he remarked in that accent which was growing more alluring every moment he talked to me.

He stood up, and in such an old-fashioned, gentlemanly manner, he extended his hand to take mine and helped me up off the seat.

My bra and skirt were still draped over my wrist, and I couldn't help but feel some excitement in my chest. Not just for the money, though that was clearly there as well. No, he had an aura to him that was drawing me in, making me forget all my cares and concerns as I took his hand.

He was so warm, and strong, and I found myself standing a bit nearer to him than needed. Even normally I gave my clients some space, but I simply wanted to feel him against me.

He obliged so nicely, keeping that strong hand of his upon my hip as he guided me over to the stairs. I worked that club most days each week, yet still I let him show me the way. I didn't even need to do the usual fuss, since he owned the damn club franchise. He was let on through, but dispelling any concerns of mine that it might leave him entitled and cheap, he pulled a roll from his own jacket of hundreds, and handed it to me.

"In case I get so caught up in your beauty later I forget to pay you," he said smoothly, that broad, masculine face marked by such a handsome smile.

It surprised me, but I tried not to let it register on my face as I took the offered cash and tucked it into my purse. I was smitten, and I bit down on my lips as we went past the open booths and towards the highest point of the club. It was just above the DJ booth, away from the heavy bass of the speakers, and overlooked the stages. It was huge and well decorated with soft pillows and lighting, with couches along the back and side. A table was in the centre, glowing slightly, and a bottle of champagne awaited us.

I wondered if it was the real stuff, but tried not to look greedy as he pulled the curtain across and left us in relative comfort and privacy. The glass was mirrored on the outside, so none could see us, and I knew the only way anyone was coming in was if he invited them.

The bouncers checked on us all the time with clients to

make sure we got up to no dirty business, but this wasn't just any old client, after all.

He escorted me to the couch, helping me take a seat before he went to the champagne, took a look at the label then went about serving it all by himself. Most men left that sort of task to me, but not him. He was all class.

Pouring up some into that fluted glass, he handed it to me first before returning to serve his own up. It also gave me the opportunity to see part of a tattoo that ran from his arm up to his hand. I couldn't quite make out what it was, or what significance it had by that little glimpse of its edge, however.

"How has working one of my clubs been for you?" he asked me, sounding warm despite the deep, dark tone of his masculine voice. More importantly, he seemed genuinely interested.

I leaned back, not bothered at all by my own topless-ness or the fact that I was clearly sizing him up. I crossed my legs, the fishnets making them look more toned and shapely.

He joined me and I curled in towards him, wanting his warmth pressed against me. I couldn't help it. He was probably ten or more years older than I was, with a lot more culture and class, and as I rested my hand on his chest, I could tell he was cut.

"It's the best club I've worked at," I said truthfully. The staff looked out for me, the money was good, what more did I need?

His thickly muscled arm went back around me as he got comfortable upon that sofa with me. He leaned in, slowly inhaling the scent of my hair as he let the ebon locks stroke his cheek.

"That is good," he said in his accented voice, the words

hard but said so warmly. He sipped the champagne with me, and I knew it was the real deal.

"Have you been working here long? Special women such as yourself are so hard to find, and worth holding onto," he said.

I curled into him, sipping the champagne in one hand, the other stroking along his chest. He smelled so good and masculine, some scent I hadn't words for. Spicy and seductive, kind of dark, if I were to try.

"Just the last few months."

I looked at him, over his skin, caressing him with my gaze as I relaxed and pressed my almost nude body against him.

I normally felt so calm with my nudity, but he was making me squirm, my body growing heated against his.

We could hear the music of course, and see the shows going on below through the glass, but Luc's attention was purely upon me. That's what made things so complicated for me. Having such a masculine and clearly wealthy man so focussed upon me, taking such a keen interest.

"I hope you choose to stay, Ruby," he said so genuinely. "It will give me such a great reason to come back again. Seeing you dance once more will make the trip out here very worth it."

I was used to compliments from strangers. I was a stripper, damn it. Sometimes they hoped complimenting me would get them extras like a blowjob or a discount on dances, but it never did. Sometimes they were genuine, they truly meant it, and I'm ashamed to admit that almost never did those compliments affect me. There was a part of me that just didn't accept it.

But something about the way Luc said it, the way his eyes stayed locked on mine, did more than make me believe it. It took my breath away.

I bit in my lower lip to try to hide how deeply his words affected me, but it was impossible to fully disguise it.

My hand dipped down along his side to his hip as I watched him. My gaze was the first to flinch away, though, but his hand was on my jaw, guiding it back to him in a gentle but firm manner.

That hard, powerful hand of his was rough against my smooth, soft skin, but it felt so masculine, so reassuring. He held my gaze, kept me in check. All as the music played and we sat, entwined, overlooking the club.

"I've never met such a rare beauty in any of my clubs," he said approvingly, and he was so in control, I felt like whatever he did to me I'd be powerless to stop it. Yet he was gentle, despite his raw strength, and hard body. "Nor anywhere else either," he added, guiding my head back to his broad shoulders, to rest next to his neck.

He cradled me against his chest as his hands stroked my side, my cheek.

"What do you want from life, Ruby?" he asked in that deliciously dark, husky voice of his.

That was a question I got a lot — what did I really want to do, wasn't I smarter than this? — but I didn't feel as if his words were said with malice. Just curiosity.

It made my lips twist into a grin, and I wanted to be honest. Maybe just a little.

I tilted my head, glancing towards the stage, the club, and then back to him.

"I don't wanna take orders," I grinned as I licked over my lips. "Make enough that no one can tell me what I want to do."

My answer brought a smile to his face, or at least a broader one. He seemed to enjoy holding me, just sitting there, feeling my skin, never too direct, never too crass. He touched my breasts, but never more than grazed the sensitive nipples. His was a careful, calculated touch, and he enjoyed the contact, the closeness.

Immensely, judging by the feel of what lay beneath my bottom as I sat there in his lap.

"That's an excellent goal," he commended me. "That was mine at one time too, when I was a younger man. Now, of course, I'm already there."

I couldn't help but smile as I nodded, head tilting to the side as I found my body responding to his touch.

It was highly unprofessional of me, not because I should've been able to control my arousal, but that I was losing track of where we were. I was forgetting that his touch was the touch of a customer.

I longed for more of it, and it had nothing to do with the money.

My hips ground against him instinctually, and my breath paused in my chest as I felt my almost nude body tingle with anticipation and need.

A man like him, so strong, so wealthy, so powerful, could've easily abused it. Took liberties. And with me in his lap like a purring kitten, there was no doubt between us that he had that freedom, that he could do most anything he liked and I'd have run with it. Yet a man like Luc, so hard and in control, didn't need to take what was already clearly his.

Instead, he pet my hair, my side, enjoyed my presence, my company. We sat in quiet for a while, enjoyed the closeness, the music. We sipped champagne and took it easy.

"How many nights do you tend to work, Ruby darling?"

His words broke me from my stare and I couldn't help but flush just a little at the intrusions upon my scandalous thoughts. Wondering if he'd bend me over. It I could rub him just the right way, if it'd become too much and he'd simply take me.

I licked my lips, my throat suddenly dry as I looked back at him, my hips still rocking.

"Only a couple, before my boyfriend broke up with me. Now I'm here five days."

The smile on his face told me something: that he'd gotten the information he'd truly wanted, even if it was in a very roundabout way.

A man like Luc didn't blurt out dumbly, "You got a boyfriend?" That would've been too obvious, to classless and inappropriate. No, a man like Luc got what he wanted, but never the way you expected.

"Ahh, beautiful woman like you should not know heart-break. Only how to break hearts," he said so affectionately, leaning in and nuzzling against my cheek and forehead, the scent of his faint musk so enticing.

My arms wrapped around him, tugging myself closer to him as my legs wrapped about his hips, my small body fitting so snuggly in his larger form. He made me feel protected, my thighs pressed into him, though as I pulled myself closer, I had to pause.

He throbbed against me, and that slowed by thoughts further, but I felt another hardness, closer to his side. Something with a distinctive feel.

He was packing heat.

My heart went up in my throat, and for a moment, I panicked. I didn't know what to do, what to say, and I was glad he couldn't see my expression as he rubbed his cheek against mine, because I knew I was making the deer-in-headlights look.

What do I do?

Yet Luc was never fazed. Even as my thigh touched cold steel at his hip, he just felt me up, enjoyed the feel of my waist, my hips. My breasts. Smiling all the while, so confi-dent, so in control. I would never have guessed that he was carrying around a gun on him. Yet it all made such sense, this big man, with an Eastern (maybe Russian?) accent, owned a whole chain of clubs, dressed so damn well. Lived so lavishly.

I'd never known your typical businessman to be loose with his money. They were always so stingy.

"You make me want to linger with you here all night, and into tomorrow, Ruby," he said so approvingly.

But I was fluttering against him like a butterfly.

It was one thing to know he had a gun on him. The implications...

Was he a mob boss? Oh god, was my club owned by the mob?!

Worse than that, though, was that even through my fear and anxiety, I never stopped rolling my hips, rubbing myself against his throbbing package. All that separated us were our clothes, and I was cursing that. I wanted him, bad.

And the gun...

Why'd that only make me want him more?

I was silent long enough to be suspicious, and his hand went to my jaw again, capturing my face and bringing my gaze to his.

Staring into his eyes as I so purposefully ground against his large, throbbing manhood had to be one of the most intense moments of my life. Knowing what he must be, what he held. I even managed to break that stoic, self-assured look of his enough to make him give a low moan.

"You should not break the rules," he said in a gravelly voice. "Not even for me."

Yet he never tried to stop me, and kept our gazes locked, one hand at my face, the other at my hips, grasping me firmly.

My lashes fluttered as my eyes rolled back, pain and

frustration contorting my expression as I gasped, my nipples so stiff and just yearning for touch.

I wanted him in a way that was more primal than anything I'd ever felt before, and I knew that without those words, I would've taken him, then and there. The idea of snaking my hand between us, undoing his fly, unleashing him...

Fuck, even the fact that I didn't have protection didn't stop me. The fact that I'd gotten off the pill when my ex dumped me, and the fact that I heard you're way more fertile just after stopping, even that couldn't have been enough to convince me that I didn't want Luc, right now.

But his words, they made me pause, heart racing in my chest as I still ground against him, feeling his hand on my creamy flesh.

"I won't," I promised, though I didn't know how much longer I could maintain myself. I leaned in against him just to feel the fabric of his shirt rub against my stiff nipples, and with every grind of my hips I grew wetter.

He emitted such an aura of calm, yet I could feel how his body reacted. How his heart thudded so heavily in his chest from excitement, how his cock throbbed thick and lewdly beneath me with desire that matched my own at least.

"You would, if I let you," he said to me, so certain of himself as he looked me over, and as if reading my mind he slid his hand up, cupped my breast and lightly teased my nipple, bringing such sensations to that sensitive, pink teat.

"And I have already decided I won't rest until you come back to my hotel room this night," he added on in a dark voice. His eyes so hard as he looked me over then.

I trembled against his touch, my body pulling away from him just enough so that he could play with my nipple, twist and pinch it. I was already so turned on, my mind abuzz with need, and I looked at him seriously as my breathing increased.

Then, as I sat prone in his lap, my hips still rocking against his, my pussy juices soaking through my black thong, with my nipple in his fingers, I asked the stupidest thing.

It was the type of thing you omit from retellings, because it seemed so out of character, so risky.

I asked anyways.

"Are you in the mob?"

I cursed myself. Did I even want to know? But the question already was floating between us, and I couldn't take it back.

Yet Luc wasn't even fazed by that dumb, girlish question of mine. His lips crooked back into a wry, amused smile and he stroked my cheek fondly as he toyed with my breast.

"You do not need to worry about such things," was all he said to me as he leaned in, hovering his lips so near to mine. Nearly kissing me, but stopping that fraction of an inch from making it so. Just as our loins lay pressed together, only some thin fabric separating us.

"You are safe with me," he said, his eyelids descending, leaving his gaze narrowed with desire.

Oh God.

There couldn't have been a more clear 'yes' if he'd actually have said the word.

So then why did my back arch? Why did I keep my mouth so near to his, and why did I want him to close the distance so damned bad I thought my body was going to shatter into a million pieces if he didn't touch me right then and there?

Why was he being such a stickler for the rules in the first place?

What would he taste like? He smelled of champagne, of something sweeter beneath it, a bit like cinnamon hearts. Harsh yet sugary.

I wanted to feel what his tongue would be like against mine. I licked my lips, swallowing at the thought as my pussy rubbed against his clothed cock once more, the gun still pressing into my thigh.

His hand left my breast as we stared into each other's eyes, and he reached down, cupping my ass cheek, and I swore I could feel him egg me on just the slightest bit with that grasp. His eyes shut, but only for a moment as he gave a low, rumbling moan of approval at my motions.

"You will come back to my hotel room tonight," he said, dictating what would happen to me so firmly, authoritatively. "You will spend the whole night, and eat breakfast with me come morning. But between then, I will discipline you for your tempting of the rules tonight. I like you, and I would be remiss if I did not correct your deviant behaviour, Ruby."

Discipline me?

My lips dropped open, and I swear, I tried to stop grinding my hips against him. I tried to stop searching for my orgasm against his clothed cock, but if I were to be honest, I was so damned close, and those dark words...

They were my tipping point.

I couldn't have come at a worse time, because he was looking right at me, and it was so obvious. My nipples stiffened and I pushed my toes down in my heels as my skin went goose bumpy, and I couldn't stifle the moan, even though I bit down on my lower lip.

But even if I could've hid all that, I couldn't hide the way I was trembling like a maniac, grinding against him more urgently as I toppled over that precipice.

There was no going back from that.

I'd just cum all over a mob boss — my mob boss! — in a strip club.

That was definitely against the rules.

He never scolded me, never said a word in reprimand. Instead he pulled me in close against his hard body, held me tight, and stroked my skin. His hands on my back, my side, his thumb reaching on in to tease and prod my nipple, drawing out that orgasm, making the sweet climax last longer.

He was heaven in that moment, doing the right things to make my pleasure so sweet, to draw it out longer.

When I was done, left a shivering mass upon his lap, he murmured in my ear with that deep, gravelly voice of his.

"It's okay. I know you do not do this for other clients. You'll make it up," he said so certainly, as if he had total control of everything, the club, me, the outcomes of all.

And I should've dreaded it, but oh no.

All I could think of was that I wanted more. So much more.

I pulled back enough to look at him, my eyes tracing over his handsome face as I flushed, my pale skin turning such a shade of pink.

"I've never," I promised, confirming what he already seemed to know. "I'd never..."

"I know," he said to me with such understanding. "But you are still fired," and there was no joke or humour to him as he said that. I'd broken a rule and that was that, he was a man of his word, and his word was law.

Yet there was no time to be upset about it, because with that there were no more rules between us. He pressed his lips to mine and kissed me deeply, his tongue working betwixt my lips as his strong hands held and fondled me. I rested atop him as he held me more tenderly, more lovingly than any man before him ever had.

I trembled against him, both from my lingering orgasm and the shock of his words, or the fact that I'd just thrown away a job I loved and was so good at, just for that sweet pleasure.

Worse still was that I wrapped my arms more firmly about his neck, holding myself to him as he kissed me, his tongue glancing against mine. A moan reverberated through us and I was barely certain if it was mine or his, but I was still shaking, my entire body worked up to a state I'd never felt before.

We made out for so long like that, his manhood straining beneath me until even that giant mobster couldn't contain himself. He stood up, me in his arms as if I were but a feather pillow.

He held me like that for a time before he finally set me back to my feet. His hand rested upon my cheek again, drawing my gaze to his for a shared moment.

He broke away only to pull away the curtain and gesture to a man — one of his henchmen? — that I'd not seen before. He certainly wasn't a bouncer with how well dressed he was.

"Bring something warm for the lady to wear out, and get the car ready," he instructed before turning back to me and pressing our lips together once more without delay.

My knees were so weak I had to rest against him, desperate for his warmth.

I had never gone home with anyone from the club. I'd never even been tempted.

But with Luc, I just accepted it without protest. My mouth was tingling from his kisses, my clit still throbbing and wanting more stimulation, and I'd completely forgone not just logic, but all else as well. The only thing I could think of was him fucking me in his hotel room, and my hand went down his body, over his abs to brush against his throbbing member.

Our two minds must have been linked, because in perfect unison with my touch, his hand came down to rub over that triangle of black, damp thong. He rubbed at my moist cunny through it until his man came back, the two of us wrapped up in the moment.

"Very good," Luc said as he looked back and found his man holding what must have been a lavishly expensive fur coat. Long and exquisite. He took it in his hands and put it around me. It was long, draped all the way down to my calves and was so warm, too warm for how hot I felt right then.

"Come along," he offered his arm to me as he instructed. "Anything you leave behind can be easily replaced when we get the time," he said.

I grabbed for my purse, but abandoned my leather rhinestone skirt and top, oblivious to everything but him. His touch. I just wanted to be naked, then and there, and the fact that I had to wait was driving me mental.

Though the fact that with every step, I was a little bit closer to finally seeing his cock, did make it a bit better. I couldn't believe how much I wanted it. My hormones were going crazy, and all I could think about was his fucking me.

But something made me think that even when we got back to the hotel, he'd make me wait.

He knew how bad I wanted it, and if he was going to punish me, it wouldn't be by fucking me the second we crossed the threshold.

I'd seen strippers do the walk of shame, slip out of the building with a high paying client for obscene amounts of cash. But there I was, strutting through the heart of the club upon Luc's arm, letting him escort me through shamelessly.

His shiny, black vehicle awaited, and his chauffeur opened the door. Another large, well dressed thug-like man.

Luc let me in first, but the moment we were both on the back seat together, his hands returned to my flesh. They slipped inside the coat to find my sweltering skin, fondly my breasts as he kissed me.

I wanted so badly to be back in his lap, but I knew there was no way he'd stand for that. I was moving out of my territory and into his, and I wasn't sure I knew what that meant. The club was safety for me, it was a secure home.

And I was taking a big risk, making out with a criminal, and wanting more than anything to feel his raw cock enter my pussy.

His fingers served as a temporary replacement after they slid down over my bare stomach, then snaked in beneath my moist panties to tease those puffy, wet folds of mine. He had such a masterful touch, and he teased and excited me so expertly, circling my clit and making it feel oh so good.

Though it wasn't long before we were there, and we had to pull ourselves apart as his guard waited outside the door for us to finish.

"I know you want to be a good girl," he said, plucking his slick fingers from my cunny, glistening with my moisture. "But you just can't help it tonight, can you?" he said, licking his digits to taste my flavour and savour it so lewdly, right before offering what was left to me.

My mouth dropped open as he licked his fingers, only to be presented with them.

I'd never been a particularly kinky girl, stripper or no,

and tasting myself from his fingers was pretty high up there on my list of things I wouldn't think I was into.

But my mouth captured his digits and suckled him free of that sweet honey, even as my heart raced.

"I've never been bad," I said, the taste of my own cunny lingering upon my tongue.

"I believe it. You taste so sweet and delicious after all," he said to me with such fond sincerity. He gave the signal and the door opened, leaving him just enough time to do up the fur coat again.

Luc got out and helped me out next, my heels clicking upon the pavement in front of the ritziest hotel in the city. After that it was all so dizzying, the lights and glamour of that expensive place, the staff eager to be of help to Luc and I, but were kept at bay by the glowering guards.

He claimed an elevator just for us, and his guard shooed off another man before inserting a key to take us to a private level.

The moment that was done though, Luc was upon me again, opening my coat and putting his arm in around my bare waist as he kissed me. That guard of his not daring to look our way as Luc's lips went to my neck, nibbling and suckling.

I know, it's strange that I dance, naked, for a crowded room of strangers and that I'd feel embarrassed with some PDA, but it was more what he was making me feel. On stage, I might feel excited, or powerful, but when Luc's lips pressed against my throat it was like the lewdest and most sensual thoughts in the world were visible to all.

I couldn't hide my moan, the way I was gulping for breath, how flushed my skin was.

That elevator ride was agonizingly long and short all at once, it was titillating and embarrassing having Luc experience me like he did so lewdly. Yet I didn't want it to end, but end it did when we got to his room. A lavish suite that looked like it must've taken up most of the floor all by itself.

Maybe it did!

We abandoned his guard there at the door in an alcove, shutting the door to that entry room. I should've been more impressed by the lavish room, its numerous row of windows overlooking the city. But Luc made it hard to focus on anything but him.

He guided me along, arm about my waist as my fur coat sank down from her shoulders, hanging from my elbows. He took me over towards the large leather sofa and stopped, looking me over, inspecting me again.

"Exquisite," he remarked. "I am taken with your beauty, my ex-dancer. Now tell me. What is your real name?" he asked, like so many other men had before him, though they had so much less going for them than him.

For one, I'd never been so turned on in my life.

My lips dropped open, and for a second I wanted to delay it. To not tell him, to make him want to punish me all the more.

But more than teasing him, I wanted him to take me, and my real name tumbled forth despite any caution or worry I should've felt.

"Alice," I murmured.

He repeated my name, making it sound so much sexier in his gruff, gravelly voice. He let his hard, strong hands slide up beneath the fur coat, pulling it slowly from my arms and leaving me nude but for my panties and heels.

"Bend over the end of the sofa, Alice," he told me, tossing the coat to the floor out of the way, treating such an expensive item with casual dismissal as all his attention was reserved for me.

"Nobody can break one of my rules without consequence," he explained so evenly. "Not even a stunning beauty like you," he said, reaching up to cup my cheek and stroke his thumb along my lower lip.

I suckled it in, looking up at him with wide eyes that betrayed a little of my fear and my fire. My desire to argue and tell him he was wrong, that I needed my job back. That I never would've broken the rules if I hadn't been scared or known he was the boss.

But it would've been a lie.

I wasn't scared.

I just wanted him inside me. And if bending over the sofa might get me his cock faster...

I pulled back slightly, looking to the armrest, then back to him.

"What are you going to do to me?"

"Just do, don't ask," he said to me in that even tempered voice of his that betrayed no unpleasantness. No mistrust. He shrugged his blazer off his shoulders, and slipped it slowly off. It left him in his fine shirt and tie, with that holster dangling from one side, showing the gleaming metal of his handgun.

He carefully draped his jacket over the coffee table and loosened his tie, watching me all the while he removed it.

My eyes dropped to the gun, taking it in silently before I looked back to the end of the sofa. I was already so bare, in only my black Maryjane platform heels and the dripping panties, but I felt even more exposed as I turned, walking the small distance towards the end of the couch, resting my forearms on it, tilted at a 90 degree angle as I watched him intently.

He shed his expensive, European cut tie, removed the holster that held that weapon and set both aside on the opulent chair that waited there. His eyes upon me all the while he undid his sleeves and rolled them up to his elbows, showing those thick, bulging forearms of his, rippling with veins and muscles.

He finished finally, and made his way over to me.

"It's okay," he said, stroking my hair the arch of my spine, being so gentle as his other hand cupped my ass cheeks and gave them a squeeze.

Though I knew something was to come.

The first crack of his palm let me know what exactly. That hard, strong hand smacking across my round cheeks with a loud sound that filled the room. He wasn't gentle, but he wasn't brutal either, it was a focussed, smooth smack of his hand upon my flesh.

But with how excited my nerves were, it felt like my world went white with the jolt.

My posture went hard, and for the briefest seconds, I wanted to walk out. To leave him, to just run home and hide from all the bad decisions I'd already made without going another step further.

As I teetered in my heels, forearms pressing into the fine sofa, my vision returned and I sucked in a breath.

I had to do something. To say that wasn't acceptable.

I stood up, or, well, I tried to. That hand on my spine kept me pinned.

He must have felt the conflict in me, because he stroked my spine comfortingly, spoke to me in a hushed voice that was so fatherly with its paternal concern.

"Shh, it's okay. Just a little bit more," he said before the next smack of his hand landed, and he continued to spank me, lightly at first, bringing that blood to the surface and making my pale flesh go rouge. I looked over my shoulders at him, at my ass, and shuddered as the sting went through me.

Another came, and that powerful mobster just exacted the price for my indiscretions. My out of control lusts that had made me break the rules for the first time in my life.

But he was just warming me up, getting my nerves primed and ready for the true assault.

It made the spanks of earlier seem like childsplay as his hand cracked down upon my supple ass with such force it drove me forwards and I nearly collapsed at the shocking and quick punishment.

"No!" I cried, but there was no one to hear me. We were alone in his penthouse, all but his guard completely blocked out from hearing my cries.

And a swanky hotel, for the penthouse? I was almost positive it had to have some soundproofing for the wealthy clientele. Especially when they included the mob.

My eyes went to the gun on the table, and I felt a shiver go through me of real terror, but then his hand cracked down on me again and I lost my vision for a moment.

"No girl breaks the rules in my club," he chastised, and for a moment I hated him. He'd teased me, turned me on to the point that I couldn't help but cum. He'd tempted me to break the rules, forced me to teeter along that line.

My knees trembled as his hand rubbed my stinging flesh, the soft touch contrasting to the hard spank that followed.

"Shhh," he said to me about my whimpering, taking hold of my cheek and guiding my face towards his again. "It's okay," he said, rubbing some of the moisture from my cheek with his thumb.

"It had to be done, because I don't want to hold anything against you, sweet Alice," he said so calmly and affectionately, leaning in and placing another of his soft, romantic kisses to my lips.

My body was still quivering as I stood, as I reluctantly wrapped my arms around his neck. It was such a contrast, the warmth and softness of his kiss contrasting against the angry heat of my backside.

I didn't even notice until kissing him that I was breathing so hard, my chest heaving as I tried to suck in oxygen through my nose.

Those big strong arms wrapped around me, and he wasn't using them to make me hurt anymore, he was instead holding me, comforting me, rubbing me fondly. Such hard hands upon my soft flesh. As our tongues entwined, he lifted me up off the floor and carried me in his arms on into the bedroom.

The large, lavish bed was room enough for a whole group, but he laid me out gently among the sea of cushioning comforters and pillows.

He rose back then, and I watched as he unbuttoned his shirt, showing off that thick, ripped chest of his. Bulging pecs and abs, biceps that could be used to easily crush a man. Suddenly those spanks of his no longer seemed like the worst he could do; they were controlled and gentle compared to what he was capable of.

And there, along his right arm, he had a large, black tattoo. Something I didn't recognize, a symbol maybe? But it looked scary, ominous even. Another adorned his chest, of a simple rose.

I'd been with my last boyfriend since I was 18, and I'd never been with anyone else. Even when I was dancing, that had always been business, and I never mixed it with pleasure.

Until Luc.

I looked over his body with such curiosity, such interest, and couldn't help but compare him to my ex. He was so much more filled out, so much more masculine, and I found myself staring at the tattoo, trying to figure out what it was. My hands went to it, curiously rubbing over his veins and the dark symbol.

"What's it mean?" I asked, breathlessly.

He watched me, let my soft fingers roam over the hard muscles and jutting veins of his body as he unbuttoned his pants at the side of the bed.

"That one means in matters of life and death, I am judge as the right hand of God," he stated so casually. "It means I am The Boss. The boss of bosses, with no higher authority on earth," he said just half a moment before he dropped his pants and the snug boxer-briefs beneath it, letting a thick slab of meaty cock spring out, so long and hard, suspended over a pair of heavy balls.

I should've been more concerned at his words. He was the right hand of God? In control of life and death?

Those were definite things that should've made me run back to my simple life, beg for my job back, and live the rest of my life with my head low.

But instead, my eyes were on his package, and my hand gripped his arm tighter.

I could feel my entire body ache, and I had to squirm just at the sight of his organ. Even my mouth was watering, and I'd never been much of a fan of giving blow jobs. But Luc... He could reform me.

He shed his clothes entirely and got up onto the bed with me upon his knees, those thick, muscular thighs spread as he got in close, his hand stroking my hair, guiding me towards that massive, rigid cock of his.

"I know you want to taste," he said to me, the masculine musk off that organ clean but heady and strong. "Just like I had to have a taste of you, sweet Alice."

My stomach flipped.

It was so crass, but I couldn't deny my mouth was

watering and I was curious. Just to see what it'd feel like in my mouth, so hard and thick.

I gulped for a breath, trying to hide my excitement, my shyness, as they warred with each other, but I didn't have a choice. His fingers were entwined with my dark hair and he brought my head right before his throbbing member so that I didn't have a choice but to grab it. To hold onto it before it smacked me in the face.

I was scared, but I opened my mouth, and took him in, letting my tongue flick against the head before running along the underside of his cock.

A low groan rumbled from deep within his chest as he watched me work my tongue along his thick, swollen cock. The simple act of my tasting that thick, marvellously stony crown making the large man look so pleased.

He pet my hair with one hand, while the other reached down and stroked the cusp of my breast, reaching in to knead his palm over that mound of supple flesh. All while his cock throbbed obscenely in my mouth, stretching my jaw as he watched.

"Good girl. I knew you were a good girl from the moment we laid eyes on each other," he husked in a gravelly voice.

I would've liked to think I'd have argued, that I would've reminded him that I just lost my job for being naughty, but instead my mouth moved further along his shaft.

He was huge. Like, bigger than my dildo huge.

I was practically quivering with need, and I brought a hand down to my thighs, pressing in beneath the panties and feeling how soaking wet I was. My shaved little pussy was dripping with my juices and my fingers slid into my cunny so easily.

But they didn't bring anything more than another tease,

because what I wanted most was in my mouth, and I didn't want to relinquish it. My tongue went back and forth against his cock, feeling his veins throb against me as I brought him in as deep as I could, until I felt my breath choke off, the flared tip pressing against the back of my throat as his hand remained on the back of my head.

I managed to coax another deep moan from that big, terrifying mobster with that before he rocked back his hips and let his thick cock slip from my mouth. That gloriously large member glistening wetly as he took it from the reach of my mouth.

"I'm glad you enjoyed that," he said to me, so confident and sure of himself. He never needed to ask what I felt. "But I am done with waiting. I will take what I really want now," he stated firmly, moving to my hips, his two hands taking hold of my panties and tugging them away, leaving my wet cunny bare.

He showed no signs of being concerned for a condom or protection either, he just got between my legs, lifted my arms and let his thick, granite shaft prod against my bare slit.

"I'm not on the pill," I said, my legs spread, my hips angled to him.

I mean, I had to tell him, right? I couldn't just let him fuck me raw without us both knowing the consequences.

But at the same time, I dreaded his reaction to those words, and my legs wrapped around him, trying to draw him in to my fertile cunny. My nipples were so hard they could cut glass, and while my one hand still lay against my clit, the other went up, grabbing my breast and tweaking the nipple.

"I could smell you like we were animals in heat," he said, as if that too was something he knew without my ever needing to tell him. "It's all the better. Just as a man and woman should be," he stated before he bent over me, resting all his weight upon one fist beside me, letting me get a full view of that gloriously sculpted chest of his.

Then he thrust in. That thick, bulging shaft disappeared into my cunny, spearing into my depths and thrusting me open wide. He stretched my cunny taut about his girth and gave a low moan for his pleasure.

I didn't hold back my scream of pleasure. I didn't want to. He was so big against me, his masculine form making me feel so small and breakable. As he thrust in, my still stinging ass was pushed into the comforter and reminded me of his earlier sting.

It made a slight sound of wetness as he pierced me, and for a moment, I was embarrassed by just how wet he'd made me, but it didn't last long.

"You might knock me up," I gasped, and despite all I knew of him, it surprised me he'd take that chance and be so reckless with me.

Those words only seemed to goad the giant, muscular man on. And I watched as his broad, muscle-bulging frame swelled with each thrust. The sinew rippling across his whole body as he plunged deep into me, forcing my body to accommodate to a girth of cock I'd never before dreamed of having to take.

With his free hand he reached up, took hold of my face again. Somehow amid the rough fury of his thrusts, pounding me down into the bed, he managed to force me to look into his eyes with the same composure of our more relaxed time in the club. Our heavy breathing peppering the air as he seemed to peer into my soul.

"I want to," he said, his voice a low growl of desire.

My heart was racing as I stared at him, mouth agape.

But my body betrayed my mind once more and I smiled

a dark smile. It was as though, for once, I had him at my will rather than the other way around.

The words tumbled from me before I could stop them.

"You wanna cum in my pussy raw?" I cooed darkly, my eyes fluttering closed as I lifted my hips and grounds against him. But even when I was trying to reclaim some of that control and power, he took it from me by way of a harder thrust that stole my breath and made my body tremble.

"I'm going to," he growled back to me, moving his body so that his powerful thighs supported him as he pumped into me. His two hard, strong hands groping at my flesh. He felt my breasts, kneaded their perky skin, then one hand dipped down to reach his thumb in towards my clit, nudging my own hand away. That thick digit prodding and circling my sensitive bud provoking it.

"You wanted me to breed your tight little pussy since the club," he said to me, never failing to amaze me. "You ground out your greedy little climax like a bitch in heat. And now I'll give you exactly what you wanted and more," he seemed to roar the longer he went on, his body moving with such composed savagery.

His words sent me spinning, and as his hand rubbed my clit, there was no running from it. Not from him, not from my desires and needs, not from the truth.

I couldn't hide it if I wanted to, my body trembling against his as a spark grew in the low of my belly before jolting out. Every nerve in my body came alive once more, my vision fogging and I had to close my eyes as I screamed out, "Yes!"

My pussy squeezed his, begging for just what he threatened me with. But he wouldn't relent, not yet. His actions stilled, instead focusing on rubbing my sensitive clit, making it throb against him until I was so sensitive and raw that I could barely take it any longer.

I thrashed beneath him, my limbs flailing, but still he didn't relent.

Not until my pussy gushed hot liquid around him and I screamed louder, shame and arousal writ on the high notes of my messy orgasm.

Then and only then, did that brute of a mobster blow his load in me.

All that rippling, hard muscle writhing as he grunted and heaved with the intensity of his release. He ploughed deep into me, right to the utmost depths of my fertile cunny and let loose such a torrent of cum like I'd never experienced or heard tale of.

All through our combined climaxes, his hand on my face kept me locked in place, kept my gaze upon his as we both shook with orgasm.

I stared into the eyes of a hard, criminal man as he dumped all his seed into me, his every intent carnal and lewd.

"You're mine," he rumbled out as his dick swelled and thick gouts of semen shot into me, his hips rocking as he milked out every last drop of his spunk into my fertile depths.

Everything in me shook, pleasure and fear wrapping around one another as I stared up at him. My world spun, my body was raw and still quivering with the aftershocks of bliss, and I was so desperately trying to find my breath.

It was the most intense sex of my life, and I hungered for more, grinding against him like... like a bitch in heat. Just as he'd said. I wanted every bit of his cum in me, just primal need.

Even my ex-boyfriend would not have been able to deliver it to me so promptly as that, but that stallion of a man, Luc, was not daunted. He began to pump his hips again, stealing his gaze away from mine to peer at the sight of my puffy, reddened cunny lips clinging to his thick shaft as he began to tug and thrust his magnificent tool.

I wasn't sure what I was getting into, because that big brute of a man seemed to know no limits. He was revving up to fuck me into oblivion, the thick, virile cum that filled me being pounded into my womb as he thrust into my tight cunny.

He reached under me, grabbing my thighs as he pulled himself up, and me to him, letting him angle me just the right way so that I screamed again.

"Too soon!" I pleaded, but there was no reprieve as he held me there, pinned between him and my shoulders, held in place as he thrust in, the thick cock rubbing against my g-spot. I didn't even know it really existed, but he found it so promptly, and riding so high from my last orgasms, I was rendered into a twitching mess, trying to squirm free of the pleasure.

However, Luc was in full control. That massive, terrifying mobster who should've sent me running, but instead held me ensnared. He'd fucked me raw, blew his load in me and tried to knock me up, and there I was, pinned between his muscular body and the bed as he worked himself up towards another climax.

Watching him fuck me was like nothing I could've imagined. He had the physique of a bodybuilder, but the hard, rugged look of a man who knew the rough side of life. Yet he treated me with care even as he pounded me senseless and sought to knock me up in my lust-filled stupor.

I looked along the flat of my body and could see his cock thrusting into my puffy slit, soaking wet and pink with arousal, and oh... I wanted it. More.

I wasn't thinking straight. I knew I wasn't.

If I was, I wouldn't have growled, "Please... Luc... Cum in me again."

He was in charge, he held the reins, but he knew what I wanted even before I did. And he was barreling towards that next climax, making my body sing as he worked towards hammering me into bliss.

I could see his handsome, stoic face contort with pleasure. Such a savage brute brought to bear by the soft, tightness of my feminine form. His shoulders hunched forward, his balls tightened, and he rammed into me, growing closer and closer to his next release.

"I am going to make you my personal little fuck slut," he growled, at long last his body giving in and his dick throbbing thickly as he blasted another virile load into my depths.

I couldn't help it. I screamed again, the sound reverberating through the luxurious room as he hilted within me so deeply that my mind went blank. It was beautiful, silent bliss, my mind shut off for a few seconds, leaving me to luxuriate in the bliss he bestowed upon me.

We were a tangle of flesh, hard on soft, but both sweaty and glistening. He'd fucked me like I'd never dreamed I could be fucked, and he pressed down upon me. Kissing at my pouty lips as he embraced me fully, his dick still embedded as we made out atop that sprawling first-class bed.

Come to think of it, that was how we spent not only the night, but the morning too.

The next day even, as he sat at breakfast, shirt on, but undone. I had sat in his lap as he fed me, and I him. Just as he'd promised.

A warm smile lit up his broad face as I sat atop him, his cock lodged inside my well-fucked pussy, lodged there after yet another load he'd blown inside me. It was a strange thing to describe, the thrill I got from the feel of his cold pistol against my bare flesh. By rights I was too sore to go again after his long, morning pounding. But as I sat on his lap and felt that metal against me, I was compelled to grind his dick and provoke him to yet another climax.

"What are your plans for today?" I asked that massive man, another foolish question I probably shouldn't have asked such a deadly man. Yet he humoured me as he always had.

"I am heading back home now, to my place up north in Montreal," he stated simply, feeding me a grape from the mini-breakfast buffet that was brought for us. Though my heart sank at the idea of him leaving... especially after all we had done. The risks we'd taken.

"You will come with me, yes?" he added so casually, head tilted just so, brow raised in question.

How could I do anything but nod? A thrill ran down my spine, and I wanted nothing more than to be in Luc's arms forever.

DESPERATE FOR IT

*B*ook Themes:
Interracial Sex and Risky Sex.
Word Count:
6,844

~

AN EXPEDITION of aspiring scholars carried out its study in the overgrown subterranean ruins. The curious fungal growths bloomed ever larger through the previously vibrant and beautiful tunnel system that lay beneath the sands of the jungle above.

The five of them stood upon dusty stone floors, each hoping to make a name for themselves on this trip, to put themselves one more notch above the other graduate students. Well, all but the lone guide. Asher was his name, though none of the budding geniuses had bothered to ask it, much less acknowledge that he was, in practice, their guard.

The group was disproportionately male. In fact, all but

one fell under that category. An all too common occurrence, even in modern times. Three budding young men pushed forward shoulder to shoulder as the group combed over the tight tunnels and caves.

Asher, the towering muscular 'meathead', as one of the other students dubbed him, wore a neat cream vest and a dark shirt rolled up at the sleeves, letting his biceps bulge out. "It's time for us to head back," he intoned in his deep, masculine voice.

Groans of complaint answered him, but he was already turning back.

That left Alexandra with little time. The specimen she'd sighted was delicate, like nothing she'd seen before. If she left it be until they returned the next day, one of the men might find it and beat her to the punch. So quickly, she wrapped her sample bag around the bizarre mushroom and took it.

"Hurry," came the echoing voice of their guide, his thick brown travel boots thudding on the stones as he made his way back. "It's supposed to rain tonight," he added, his words accentuated by a thick accent, "and these caverns might flood when it does."

She had it. Without further delay, Alex turned and followed the others.

BACK AT THE CAMP ABOVE, the large tents looked dim in the fading light of the day. The towering Asher took the fore as he checked the tents for any possible wildlife that might've crept in. There were dangers everywhere in the jungle, and he brandished a machete towards the ground just in case.

When the all-clear cry came, the scholars went first to

their study tent, where they had microscopes and cata-loguing equipment.

Alexandra walked towards her own station. Where the other scholars were busy just locking up unremarkable samples, she was dying to get a better look at her own unique find. So much so, it must've shown through. One of the other men, Dave, took notice.

"What'cha got there?" he inquired petulantly, crowding in on her.

"If it were any of your business, you'd know it," she retorted a bit harsher than was necessary. Still, she always had a hard time getting her point across when she played polite, and even with an acidic tongue she knew he was more likely to pry than not. "Besides, we just got back. I have to examine it before it gets dark, gimme some space."

She had her hair pulled back tight in a ponytail and it prickled her scalp with the heat of walking all day, and she knew her expedition outfit probably smelled of mustiness. Moving her shoulder to try to block her small, delicate find from Dave, she pushed her black rimmed glasses back up to the bridge of her nose.

"Is she holdin' out?" came the voice of prissy Pete, the pretentious blonde walking around the table between them and heading over towards her.

Dave was already looming over her, "She is, I think!" he chimed, trying to grasp at the sample. "Just let us see it," he protested as James, the third male in their party, came wandering over.

"I never heard her say a word about finding anything down there," he pouted, the three pushing in at such an angle it was impossible for her to get anything done. Their three male bodies crowding around her so that her dainty elbow bumped into one by accident. When she went to glare at the offender, another took the opportunity to grab the sample bag.

"Shit, what kind of mushroom is this?" Dave said, holding up the bag and studying it before the light that dangled from the steepled tent ceiling.

"I've never seen anything like that before," mused Pete, trying to take it from the other man. Two of the tall men held the sample out of her reach.

She was too short to put up a fight, clearing in at only five feet on a good day, and she wouldn't debase herself by playing monkey-in-the-middle with them. Instead, she folded her arms tightly beneath her chest and glowered.

"It is mine, now give it back so that I might answer your incessant questions. Remember, that's what we do?" Alexandra narrowed her hazel eyes at them, hoping it'd be enough to get them to back off.

"Yeah yeah," came Dave's voice, "just let us get a look." He was opening the bag up, trying to get a closer look at the thing when Peter made a grab for it.

"What's that strange colour underneath?" he whined like an irritating toddler as he knocked the bag, and a cloud of pollen filled the clear-plastic.

"Careful!" came James' voice strangely, though rather than doing anything to promote carefulness he banged into Dave's shoulder and the contents spilled out. Alexandra watched in horror as her mushroom dropped, a cloud of spores filled the air around them.

"Assholes!" she gasped out, her face instantly falling as she went to try to recover her precious, mysterious find. "You three are such amateurs!"

The three of them coughed and one sneezed as she returned the mushroom to a sample bag. The cloud of spores were slow to settle form their lofty height. "Fuck," said more than one of the clods as they batted their hands in the air and stepped away from what they'd just inhaled.

"Is it ruined?" came James voice, the only one showing even a bit of worry at the possibility of such a unique find being destroyed. The others, she reflected, were probably only concerned with themselves and so if a new type of fungus was lost, so be it. Wasn't their find anyhow.

She sneered at the three of them, her face contorted in annoyance. "Good work. You three might have destroyed the only thing to come out of this expedition, and wasted all of your time. Heaven knows none of you are liable to find anything worthwhile!" Her rage boiled over as she sealed the baggy again.

The towering dark guard pulled back the tarp, his shaved pate poking through followed by his thick upper body. "Is everything okay in here?" he asked in that rich accent of his. South African, Alexandra thought.

She met the guard's eyes and took a deep breath, trying not to cough as she felt the weird dust tickle her throat. "If there were four less people in here, it'd be just swell."

Asher didn't seem to take the dig personally as he looked over the other three men. "You should know not to make so much noise. It can attract predators from the jungle," he warned crisply, like a patient father to the young men who considered themselves his superior in every manner.

Though the three men didn't seem to be absorbing his words at all. They didn't seem to be caring for much of anything but Alexandra in fact. Their pupils dilated as they stared at her with such obvious lewd desire as she went about storing away her damaged sample.

"Shit, I never noticed how hot you are," came Dave's chilling voice as he stepped in behind her to an uncomfortably close degree.

Pete was fast in next, as if heeding some call to circle the prey. "Yeah, how about we forget the whole sample nonsense for now," he proposed, reaching out and placing a very unwanted hand upon her hip as he grinned.

"What the fuck, Pete?" She'd thought he was gay... For all their faults, she'd never felt as if they lusted for her in such an unprofessional way. She didn't even have time to digest how quickly, how strangely it was all happening as she backed away. "And I did *no*T say you could touch me," she reprimanded as she slapped his hand away.

When she backed into James, however, his arms went around her. The sudden change in the men – piggish egomaniacs that they were – was jarring. The grinding of James' bulge was alarming, in fact.

"Fuck, we've been out here for so long," murmured Dave, starting to undo his pants, while Pete was opening his shirt, showing his own pale chest.

"Yeah," followed Pete, "I'm gonna bust if we don't do somethin' about it."

Alexandra bucked, her head knocking back towards James and only managing to knock her ponytail into his chest. Her legs flailed out, kicking in front of her, but she was panicking and not taking the time to aim, to think things through. She just needed to get the fuck away, and she screamed out, "Asher, do something!"

Pete went down in a flash, his scrawny form crumpling into a spindly heap. It was clear by how fast the towering Asher took him out that her cry for help hadn't been needed. Though the strange thing was, Dave was so fixated on her he didn't even turn to address the towering man deliberately moving to stop him.

With a grab of Dave's arm, Asher twisted it around making him cry out in agony as he pinned him down to the ground. The guard had pinned his arm in such a way that any struggle against the thick boot in his back would only bring more pain.

Still, James didn't stop groping at her, his hands moving up to her chest. Yet even with one arm and leg busy tying down Dave, Asher reached out, grabbed the brown haired scholar about the neck, and threw him down to the ground with the rest.

She didn't care to think of how the physics of the defense worked, but she was grateful for the freedom and stumbled forward, towards the exit. Her heart was pounding and her palms were sweaty as she made her way to the freedom of the jungle air, breathing in the moist oxygen in quick gulps.

She could hear Asher's voice calling to her as she ran out, "The hell is wrong with them?"

Though it was a few moments more before he emerged. And, she noted, the lack of the thick, yellow rope at his side. He must've taken the time to bind them up properly, so they wouldn't come after. The muffled cries and grunts from inside made it clear he did more than tie them up, they must've been gagged too.

"Have they done anything like this before?" asked the towering man as he emerged behind her, eyes wide with confusion as he looked to her. Clearly the situation utterly mystified him as he stood there, rubbing his one set of knuckles from putting his fist to Pete's head.

"Never," she admitted breathily, her gaze moving over his hands, then up to his face, as if seeing him for the first time. She blinked something from her eyes then made a show of looking behind him. "I'm not going to feel safe around them again. Especially not at night."

His hands were so large, more than enough to match the impressively sized man. His fingers thick with muscle, veins bulging up across the backs of his knuckles and on down across his trunk-like forearms to his mountainous biceps and shoulders.

"They are tied up," he affirmed simply, reassuringly. "I was not expecting to have to use my cord for such a thing, but they are secured safe and firm. They won't be troubling you until we let them out," he said with absolute certainty, his dark eyes roaming over her, though not in the same way the other men had. It was clear it was innocent. He was searching for any signs of injury.

"I can have the call put in to have them arrested immediately," he added in his smooth, husky voice, which was beginning to sound more and more delectable all the time. The giant in khakis suddenly so gentle, alone with her.

They'd pretty much ignored him the entire trip, so far. Too arrogant to admit they needed some brawn, some local knowledge, to get anything done. But now that she was really taking the time to look at him, she found she appreciated the large man before her in ways she'd never known.

"I just need somewhere to process this. Somewhere safe," she said, her arms folding beneath her breasts once more. "Take me to your tent."

His broad, well-sculpted jaw was set as he nodded. It was smoothly shaven, just as his head was, clearly showing the cleft in his chin.

Leading the way she got some time to appreciate the way his rather impressive bottom showed through the thick khakis he wore. Two large and impossibly firm cheeks locked away beneath. It was inappropriate timing for such thoughts, of course, but it was oddly difficult to keep her mind from going there.

He pulled open his tent for her, showing a neat setup. Tidy and simple. Only the bare necessities, all kept in an orderly fashion, but for an ereader that was left upon the cot in its leather sleeve.

"Anything you need," he invited in a smooth, sincere voice. No intent there but for her safety and security. His dark chest showing through the parted-v of his shirt and vest, his rock hard pecs holding a light sheen from the jungle's heat and humidity.

She went to the ereader, making herself at home already. She found herself feeling less frightened, more secure, already. Just being in his presence was enough to quell any worry that the three beasts back there might come for her.

"What are you reading, hmm?" she asked as she touched the screen lightly, trying to tease it on from its sleeping state.

He didn't look like he intended to follow her in, but when she asked the question he gently stepped inside. As high as the expedition tents were made, he could barely fit in, having to duck his head a little. "Just something for fun," he said with a light, friendly smile.

True enough, the novel that opened to her prying eyes wasn't the sort of fair she'd expect of such a serious, professional, bodybuilder-lookin' man. It was some tale of romance set in a science fiction background. Love in space. So trite she could normally gag.

But instead it made her lips to curl into a smirk as she twirled towards him. One hand still clutched the book, scanning over it quickly, as the other tugged her light hair free from the ponytail. "Is this the trash you read to learn English, too?" she teased.

Her abrupt change in tone made him raise a brow at her. "I learned English in a university," he stated simply. He didn't show much annoyance at her condescension, but he did cross his thick arms over his broad chest, the muscles bulging, those full veins so much more prominent upon his brown flesh. "What do you read?" he asked in an innocent attempt to spur more conversation.

Though the longer she stood there with him, the more heightened her awareness seemed to become. Not only did she realize she was noticing every little detail of his chiseled male form, but she swore she could smell his musk on the air. Her nostrils flared and tingled at that alluring masculine aroma.

More importantly, the tingle travelled lower. And much lower again.

God, how long had it been since she felt something so carnal? She licked her lips and placed the ereader down on a table as she walked closer to him. She wanted to smell him, to know him so intimately. Her body felt flushed, and she unbuttoned the top button on her expedition outfit. "Lots of things, Asher. But that's not really important, is it." It was more of a statement than a question. "You don't really care what I read."

The giant of a man looked at her with a calm, steady expression, as if trying to puzzle her out at his own pace. She could smell the virility off him, could feel it feeding into her own desires so that her loins no longer tingled: they burned with need.

With a shrug of his broad shoulders, Asher said, "Why wouldn't I? Talking books is a hobby of mine." Yet she swore she felt desire on his voice, even if he tried to hide it. Or maybe it was just her own state clouding her judgment. Her body on such high alert, her nipples even felt like they might cut through her bra and top.

A thought crept unbidden into her mind: *imagine how big his dick must be.*

A moan escaped her mouth, unbidden. She couldn't control it any more than she could hide it, and she moved so that she was only a few inches from him. She hadn't fucked someone in... what, months? Longer, maybe. She'd been so dedicated and passionate about her career that it'd sort of just fallen to the wayside.

But now, that was all she could think about, and her fingertips brazenly went towards his stomach. "It's just not interesting to me."

The fabric of his vest and shirt were thin, practical for the climate. So through it she could intimately feel the bulges of his hard abs, so pronounced and rigid.

Asher unfurled his thick arms, his dark brown eyes widening as he looked to her. "Are you feeling alright?" he asked with concern as her own mind began to be clouded with such a dizzying array of carnal thoughts. Her body burning with such need so that it felt like if she didn't get a cock inside her – a cock, it had to be a cock, nothing but a man's dick would suffice, she felt–no, *knew* – she'd collapse into a convulsing pile of agony.

Or worse.

Her fingertips trailed lower, more aggressively, as her breathing quickened. "Shut up," she ordered him, tired of his deep voice, of his mild mannered concern. She didn't need that right now. All she needed was him.

When her hand touched upon the bulge of his manhood, she was delighted to find such a thick, meaty shaft already aroused. She was right! She grasped at it, fondled it through his pants. His own powerful hand reached down, those strong fingers wrapped about her delicate little wrist.

Yet he never pulled her hand away, nor even stopped her.

He stared down at her, that pale arm in his grasp as he licked his full lips. "Are you sure you want to do this?" he asked in his deep tone of voice, and then she felt it... his cock throbbed. And grew. He wasn't hard at all. That girth she held was him at not even half-mast.

Oh God, yes. How could she have ever wanted something more in her life?

She didn't respond, at least not verbally, but her hand rubbed against him with the eagerness of a virgin, so desperate for him to get fully hard. To see how big it would get, to feel him tear her asunder. Her other hand went to his package as well, both working in tandem as she felt the oppressive heat of the jungle weigh down upon her, his breathing growing harder as he watched her.

His chest swelled beneath his clothes, the light outside growing dimmer as sunset approached. Yet as it waned, his manhood waxed against her excited touches.

Asher slid his hand up her arm to her petite shoulder, the other joining it at the opposing one. His dick was swelling so fast that it began to strain the confines of his pants.

"You don't owe me anything," he reminded in a gentle, reassuring voice. Yet it was the most irrelevant thing imaginable as far as her mind was concerned. "It was only what any decent man would do," his voice growing deeper, huskier. His eyes soaking in her dainty, pale form in a different light.

"You talk a lot," she sighed, but it didn't matter. He could be reciting poetry for all she cared. Whatever he needed to do to just let her do whatever she wanted. She needed him, and she rubbed him faster to get what she wanted.

One hand finally moved away from his groin, resisting the delightful pull of his cock and instead setting about unbuttoning his shirt. Already a sheen of perspiration had developed on her skin, but it didn't feel like the sweat of being in the jungle all day. Instead, it was like the clean, sweet wetness of arousal, of desire. Her entire body was responding to him, and her pussy throbbed with need.

She didn't know how much longer she could manage.

His vest and shirt came undone easily, showing that beautiful, dark flesh, so hard and so beautifully sculpted it belonged in a magazine. While his dick strained the fabric of his khakis to such an extent she could hear its fabric groan. He was a beast of a man in size, his dick bigger than any she'd ever felt by far. Bigger than she'd ever seen, certainly

His thumbs rubbed at her shoulders and he licked his lips again, a low little groan escaping his lips. "I don't even have a condom out here," he blurted quickly, as if the large man's mind couldn't even be deflected from trying to talk her out of sex as she rubbed his dick.

"Shut up." She felt his flesh not with the delicate, tender love of a paramour, but like a needy coed that was in a hurry. Trying to incite him, quickly, so that her parents wouldn't catch them. Nothing could stop her from getting what she needed, though.

Not even him.

Maybe she'd fondled him to the point he could no longer handle it, but he finally shrugged his clothes back off his shoulders, standing before her topless in his glorious dark physique. His hands returned to her smooth, those thick fingers moving with surprising nimbleness as they began to undo the buttons of her shirt.

"What has gotten into you girl?" It was a rhetorical question as he gave into her crude advances, his dick swollen so thick she could feel that one hand of hers wouldn't be enough to do it. That is, if she planned to use her hands on it any longer. Which she didn't, not with that fiery need in her loins making her knees wobble.

"Listen, I just need you to shut up and fuck me, alright?"

Her voice was hard, laced with lust and arousal like she'd never known.

There weren't words to describe how badly, how immediately she needed him, and she wasn't willing to wait. Condom or no, there was only one way he could cure her of this tremendous craving, and she practically shivered with anticipation. She didn't know how he'd fit, but with how soaking wet her panties were already, she knew it would be a lot easier than usual.

He finally shut his mouth then, peeling back her shirt to show her petite breasts in their tiny cups. If he read romance, it wasn't because he was inexperienced, because his large hands brushed against her back as he deftly undid the bra and let those perky tits free, the pinkened nipples so stiff they ached.

Her own fingers, working with such feverish need, shaking uncontrollably from her condition, took longer to work open his pants, but when she got it and his belt undone, the weight in his pockets dragged it down. Showing his cock covered only by grey boxer-briefs.

Or at least, partially covered. That behemoth couldn't be contained by them it seemed, his thick, cum-laden balls bulging beneath, while his dick prodded up over the waist band with its thick need. A patch of neatly trimmed pubic hair showing he was well-groomed all around.

Asher leaned in, kissing at her beneath her ear with his full lips, a low groan of desire escaping his mouth.

His touch, his caress, they didn't quell her passions at all. Didn't for a moment calm that throbbing between her thighs, and her knees nearly giving out with weakness. She never needed anyone, anything, so bad as she needed him at this instant.

His lips felt so full against her tender flesh, those places left untouched for so long. Her nipples were so hard, begging to be touched and rubbed, to be pinched and bit. The mere thought made her moan again, louder, throatier.

Her hand went beneath his boxers, touching that molten flesh and grasping him in her hand so tightly. "Fuck, you're huge," she groaned, unashamed.

In reward for her unrestrained praise, she got a thick throb of his meaty dick, jutting veins prodding into her palm.

With a low groan of desire, he slid his hands down from her shoulders, cupped her tiny little tits and squeezed them to his palm. She could feel that he wanted to dally there, to savour the little morsels – and part of her wanted that too – but even he picked up on the greater need at hand. He reached down, undid her pants to let them slip away, pressing a palm to her lower stomach as he curled a finger in and stroked her slit through her panties.

They were soaked. Her pussy burned with need, and she went dizzy for a moment at his touch, her body responding with such intense sensation that she never could have expressed in words. Never could have thought herself possible, with her bookish good looks and prissy attitude. Most guys didn't like her – they called her a bitch when they thought she couldn't hear – but she never cared. She wasn't interested in that stuff.

But her drive to cram Asher's immense cock inside her forced out a scream when his hand finally cupped her womanhood, and her eyes met his.

"Hard, fast, don't take my shit," she ordered with that same haughty tone she usually carried, but there was an intensity there that was usually absent.

He stared into her gaze for a moment, before suddenly he grasped her by her shoulder and the waist of her panties. He twisted her around, her body as easy to manipulate for him as a doll's.

He bent her over his cot, and yanked her panties to the side, exposing that slick puffy pink cunt of hers. She'd never felt it in such a state before, that incessant need straining her labial folds with their dire need to be filled.

He took a moment to rub them bare, the man surprised by just how wet she was, his fingers coated in her glistening honey immediately. "Jesus," she heard him curse in surprise before he got down on his knees behind her. Dropping his boxers, that slab of dark cock slapped to her backside before he grasped it in hand, rolled back the foreskin from his purple tip, then teased her quim.

Stars exploded behind her eyes as she kept herself posed for him, her legs spreading wantonly. Her delicate sex parted for him, eagerly kissing his head and savouring the electric waves of unimpeded pleasure as she pushed back against him, gasping once she really felt how big he was. It was too much, so much larger than anyone else she'd fucked, and her momentary worry was replaced with hedonistic need.

"Come on!" she ordered, sick of his teasing, of the way he was working her body into an unbelievable frenzy.

Maybe he was heeding her earlier words, or maybe he did just have enough of her shit. He grabbed hold of her shoulder roughly, clutching onto her as he pushed that big, fat crown of his cock into her cunt. The puffy labia flowering around his girth as he sank in, the tightness of her embrace making him give a deep, low groan.

Tears welled in her eyes as ecstasy washed up her sex. It was such a tight fit, she'd never have normally been able to even conceive of taking him inside her, not without long foreplay and preparation. Yet her pussy was so honey slick he managed to force himself in raw, moaning as he sank deeper, pushing himself faster than he likely should've.

"Fuck you're tight, girl," he grunted out just moments before he jarringly but the head of his cock to her cervix.

Her eyes stung with tears, but never could she remember feeling more whole, so complete, and she trembled at the sensation.

Sure, she knew in the unwanted back of her mind that it was wrong to let some near stranger fuck her raw, but she didn't care. She wanted to feel him pump into her until she couldn't take any more. That repression was wholly tossed aside now. She wanted, needed a jet of cum so deep within her. Risk it all, throw it all away, it didn't matter.

All that mattered was him taking her, and fast.

He didn't hesitate in delivering, pulling back his strong hips he began to pump into her. His raw strength and her slickness letting him to slide his cock back as her cunny-walls clung to him, only to slam back in with calculated power. His heavy balls would swing up on each thrust, smacking against her messy-wet clit as he smacked her pert little pale ass cheek with his free palm and let loose a loud moan of his own.

Those strong fingers rubbed at her burning flesh as he rutted into her, mimicking the exquisite mixture of pain and pleasure she felt in her sundered, over-stretched cunt.

Her hair formed a curtain around her face, sticking to her wet skin as she gasped and gulped, little murmurs for more escaping her plush lips. She was so much smaller than he, her slender body being rocked with each thrust, and it made her feel utterly powerless despite her words.

And, for once, she didn't care. She didn't care about anything, just so long as he fucked her.

Thankfully, he seemed of just the mind to do so. His gorgeously masculine body, so honed and refined from long hikes in these jungles, completely committed to pounding that thick meaty dick into her, the slap of his balls between her thighs growing louder as he grunted. The tip of his dick jarring her whole body as he took her roughly, some of his precum escaping into her over-wet canal.

His own brown flesh glistened with a light sheen in the dim light of the tent, the generator-powered lamp letting off only a dull glow as the two fucked so recklessly. Asher's grunts and groans grew louder, more regular as he pumped into her. And then he delighted her before she even realized what he was doing. He curled his fingers into her hair and pulled back upon it like a leash.

"Ah!" she cried out, her throat stretched as her head was yanked back, her spine arching and thrusting her breasts forward. It hurt, but it was in that perfect, wonderful way. The way she'd never usually let a stranger make her feel, and her pussy contracted around him in reward for a job well done, even as she spit out, "Asshole!"

With a growl he smacked her ass again, his palm bringing forth a bright red glow in her pale cheek as it stung beneath his hand. Though not being content at that, he plowed into her harder, keeping her body in his grasp so she didn't lunge away from him at the force of his thrusts.

A lesser man would've been slowed by that tight clench of her little pussy canal, but his powerful thighs, abs and hips kept him pistoning at such an impressive rate as he rammed his manhood into her at an increasing pace.

And he never stopped, or relented, even at her anger. The risk of it all, the chance she was taking with him, all that only excited her to new heights, and as he used her body for his own ends, she used his for hers.

Her lower muscles tightened around him, massaging his cock as his heavy sac struck again and again at her clit. They were so moist from her own juices, and he was thrusting with such power that she felt her body begin to tense, moving her closer and closer to her own inevitable release.

Asher showed no sign of slowing, rushing onward like a waterfall, steady and unstoppable. He smacked her pert little rear again and grabbed her waist as he kept thrusting, plowing into her tight little twat with a furious tenacity no other man she'd ever met could even hope to match. Never mind his sheer size.

He took her to that release, and his own hard body tensed. His shoulders pushed forward and out, his muscles bulging as he rut into her with a fierceness that belied his intent to bring her to pleasure.

But it was just what she needed, just what she ordered, and she screamed out as his rushing body threw her over that precipice. It was another few moments before that hot, sticky juice coated his cock, running down his length to coat his balls before dripping in a pool onto the floor. Yet still she could feel her body's need for more, and she pressed back into him with a furious speed.

The hulking giant of a man was far from exhausted or weary, but with her screaming finish, he slowed, preparing to pull from her. Yet when she began to hump back upon his dick, needfully wanting more, he stared at her in disbelief.

The sweet young woman a mystery to the man. He exhaled and began to pump his hips into her faster once more. Her tenacity took him by surprise, but the mighty man was determined to satisfy her, grunting behind her as his hard hips struck her tender ass, his heavy, cum-laden balls slapping against her flesh in a wet, messy smack each time as he began to pant amid his moans.

She could barely stand. Hell, she probably would have been huddled in a twitching pile on the floor if not for his powerful grasp, the way he was manipulating her body to stay erect. She rode in against him, meeting his thrusts with her own little motions that didn't have the strength or ability of him, but had more than enough enthusiasm.

Asher pounded into her without any apparent end in sight, his glorious male physique highlighted by a thin sheen of perspiration. After pounding into her for so long, he finally paused. Though not out of exhaustion as she feared. Instead, he lifted her up and laid her onto her back on the cot.

Climbing up over her, he bent back her legs to his shoulders and clutched onto her petite, pale form. From there she was able to appreciate every twitch and spasm of his muscular body, the bulges of his forearms as he held her down, the poetic beauty of how he pistoned his gloriously thick cock down into her pussy, stretching her poor cunt nearly to the point of breaking.

She couldn't deny to herself that it hurt, even in the haziest depths of her mind that still had reasoning and thought beyond rutting with this man. But the hurt was what made it so good, so powerful, and even as she squealed and squirmed and tried to escape his powerful body, it didn't matter. He was so much stronger and larger than she, and the helplessness filled her with desire.

Together the two of them rutted for what seemed to be the better part of the night, her body racked with such pleasures as he wore her down, testing the limits of her once delicate body that she'd never thought she could stand.

Yet through the mess he'd made of her cunt, through climax after climax, she finally saw him begin to wane. The hulking brute tensing up, his balls no longer smacking against her in a noisy mess as they were pulled tautly up against his body.

She could feel it, see it in every part of him that he was perched so close to his own release, after holding it back for so very, very long in his efforts to please her. His eyes were shut, his broad jaw clenching then unclenching, his mouth opening as he gasped.

All it would take is one more little squeeze to topple him over as he slowed inside her. If it was devilishness or something else she didn't know, but it pushed her to give him just the release he begged for with his hips.

With a noisy cry he bucked into her wildly in the final throes of his ecstasy. That massive, obsidian shaft pumping into her wildly as he spurted his rich, thick seed right into her depths, plastering her insides with his cum, lathering the walls of her cunt with its rich mix before it ran out of room and spurted out around his dick to splatter her thighs and dribble down her crack.

She whimpered, but it was for some deep, strange reason she couldn't name. A mourning that it was over, and a triumph at the same time. She squeezed him tighter, milking him of every last drop as she panted beneath him, a broken down mess of a woman. Her long forgotten glasses were askew, but it didn't matter. Her vision was already blurred from the lack of sleep, and her hair felt knotted, but something inside her told her that this was right. This was how it should be, from now on.

DISCIPLINE THE DANCER

*B*ook Themes:
Stripper, Rough Sex, Anal Sex, Spanking, Whipping with a Belt, Unsafe Sex, Dominance, Submission, and Punishment

Word Count:
7,000

⁓

THE BASS and drums boomed throughout the packed club, cigarette smoke mixing with various herbs in a heavy cloud hovering a few inches above the crowd. A few people sat around on the navy and silver plush benches, though most stood, either surrounding the bar or pressing against one of the small circular stages with the silver poles sticking out of the ground, a lithe woman straddling each.

There were four of the small stages, spread around the room to allow proper space to stare, to tip, to hope for a fleeting glance or a brush of skin against skin. The strip club was packed. It hadn't been this busy in many weeks, and the people at the front of the stages were all being crushed into it. Most didn't seem to mind, their eyes inevitably working their way up and staring between the thin legs of the dancers.

The main stage, however, was larger, with plenty of room for movement and play. While the girls on the mini stages twirled and shimmied, the main stage was alive with more elegant, graceful movements. Large motions of legs and arms, the nudity of the woman aglow in the vibrant lights, not a hint of modesty or insecurity in her buxom form.

Her legs were shapely, with a prominent curve to her calf, and thicker thigh, rounded hips and a sumptuous rear. Her waist was petite, the soft outline of her abdominal muscles apparent, and her large breasts topping her ribs. Her shoulders were narrow, her neck thin and graceful, her ebony hair pulled into two, long pigtails.

The outfit that she had so recently worn was strewn carelessly to the side, over top of her purse, covering it from the greedy eyes. A few stray bills were pushed politely into the bucket as she used the pole to slide to the ground, parting her legs and lifting one up straight, revealing her most guarded area. It was a quick and teasing gesture before she curled onto her knees, her back arching as she presented her rear towards the crowd and then crawled away, her motions serpentine in nature.

The music paused at the end of the song and she sat on her rear, her legs folded in hiding, her arms cupping her chest, teasing the onlookers.

When the music began once more, she stood with absolute grace and beauty, her long hair flicking off her tanned shoulder blades as she curved her neck and back. Again she was on her feet, adorned in nothing more than the heels she skilfully moved, the silver jewellery clasped above her hips, and the tight collar she wore on her neck.

She spun around the pole, one leg bent at the knee, the other stretched straight, her toes pointed towards the crowd as she masterfully commanded her body to grip and stretch and display, her large breasts on prominent show. As she slid down from the pole, her shoulder and butt pressed into it, her lower back slender and arched, she gave the crowd a knowing smile, assured that not a man alive could resist her curves and her grace.

A drunk in the crowd, however, disagreed. He taunted her, his bulbous head flushed from the drink, his meaty hands motioning to her. Though she couldn't hear him over the music, she already had plenty of drugs coursing through her system and pressing her on. Immediately her sex kitten façade was broken and she looked with rage at those standing at the stage, their clammy fists clamped on their meagre bills, her tip bucket only half as full as usual when the club was three times as packed.

She stared at the meathead, and took a few steps back, her azure eyes narrowed in her rage. With a few long strides, she was in the air, soaring over the crowd before landing clumsily on the drunk's head, collapsing him to the ground, her own body striking it soon after. The drugs numbed the pain in her elbows and knees, her hands scratched from a broken bottle on the ground as she quickly moved to take advantage of the stunned oaf.

The tiny stripper began pummelling the much larger man, her fists flying and full of malice for the crappy tippers and those who want way more than they can afford, her face red with anger as the crowd moved from the stage to try to get a better look at the little firecracker.

It felt like eternity, but it was only a few seconds before the bouncer pulled her off, his strong hands and arms easily moving her, even in her frantic fury, lifting her into the air. Two other bouncers moved in right after, lifting the heavyweight drunk off his bewildered arse, promptly bringing him to the door and shoving him into the cool evening.

Scarlett stropped her struggling, though she turned at yelled angrily at the bouncer, "I need my money!" and she squirmed away, running back to the stage and collecting her purse and clothes, storming back into the mirrored changing room, the bouncer hot on her step the entire way.

"What was that?!" he growled, grabbing her arm and spinning her to face him. Bangs clung to her wet forehead, though all her anger had faded away to light amusement. She reached into her purse and withdrew a joint, bringing it to her lips and waiting, expectantly, for him to light it. Instead he grabbed it from her lips and pointed at her with it, "This stuff is making you crazy!"

His voice was loud and commanding, matching the rest of his look. His hair was short, clipped close to his head, his neck broad, and his jaw strong. His body was muscled, tanned, and his hands were rough and large. He once got stabbed by a guy he started pummelling the face of after nicking a drink. Two days later he asked if he could come back to work, after losing two pints of blood.

They said he was crazy, but Scarlett liked that he was strong. She smiled up at him with her typical, smarmy grin, shimmying her narrow arm from his hand and turning to look in the mirror, idly fixing her hair and any minor imperfections in her makeup.

"He was rubbing me the wrong way. Besides, what's with all the cheapos tonight?" she groaned, folding her arms under her chest, perking them for his benefit. His pale green eyes didn't move from her mirrored gaze.

"You're our feature, you can't behave like this," he said gruffly, and she responded by a simple shrug of her shoulders, going back to rubbing her finger along her lips, then reaching to grab her red lipstick.

"But I do," she responded simply, an impish smile raising her cheeks.

He glowered at her, pocketing the joint and moving in, his large body towering over hers. He was easily a foot taller than her, even in her heels. His head moved downwards, resting it on her shoulder as he spoke darkly in her ear, "The manager is going to try to get you kicked out again, you keep this up," he stared at her mirrored reflection, "if I tell him, you'll be gone before you could bitch."

She narrowed her eyes at the threat, "Then you won't tell him." Her voice was laced with promise, even as she moved to press a large sum of money into his expectant palm. The light flickered above the mirror, casting a long shadow along the length of her nude form.

The wad of bills was clasped in his hand, then pressed into his black pants, his fingers resting atop the tip of her rear, "I'll need something more."

Scarlett sighed and turned to face him, hopping her bottom up on the makeup table, her legs wrapped around him, the heels digging into his calves and beckoning him closer. He easily turned from her and barked over his shoulder, "Just go finish your set properly. We'll work out payment later."

Her face flushed hot with another rush of rage and embarrassment at the coarse man's refusal, and she threw her clothes down on her bag, snatching her purse and returning out to the club, nude.

They stared, and it wasn't hard to see why. She was a beauty, with firm, generous curves, and a tight waist. Her long, black hair flowed easily around her shoulders and always seemed to find its place. She stuck out, but that wasn't any good to her if she wasn't rolling in bills. Her favoured vices were not cheap, after all.

Legrasse had come with her when she needed to get away from the drugs last time, and she kept him along because she trusted him to protect her assets. Still, he took his job seriously, and on nights like this she hated him for it.

Her body undulated in the movements of her hard and confident walk, her legs one in front of the other, graceful, even under the influence. She took the stairs, stepped onto the stage and once more the sex kitten took over, spinning and shimmying and rolling on the ground, flexing and posing for the crowd. The tipping had picked up in her absence and she rewarded the generous even more graciously.

A small, mousy man in the front stared up at her with pure awe and she crawled close to him, leaning in to whisper into his stunted ear, "Would you like to see more after I'm done up here?"

She pulled back, coyly, sitting on her calves, her torso upright. Her finger darted in between her lips and she sucked it teasingly, biting the tip and enjoyed as his hazel eyes traveled up her body, pausing on all the important bits. His eyes didn't rise above her collarbone before he nodded. Scarlett grinned and turned over, exposing her rear to him, leaning her ass close to his face, then pulling away, crawling and standing, grabbing the money and ducking offstage.

Walking straight over to her target, she whispered low, "Did you want me to start out dressed?" A soft purr was followed by his nod. She quickly turned to dash back to the dressing room and grab her clothes. A true expert in her field, the thong and the triangle top was laced around her body easily, the material a fine and innocent white, contrasting against her bronzed skin.

By the time she got back out to her mark, however, there was a black woman laughing in his lap, fawning all over his ugly maw. Scarlett's brow narrowed and she immediately stomped over, her lips finding his ear once more, "I'm ready for you, baby," she pulled away and smiled, inviting him. He glanced from her, to the other woman, his mind obviously reeling with the choice. Scarlett licked her lips, the other stroked his balding head; Scarlett's fingers found the edge of her bikini top and traced along it, her competition stroked his chest.

The other woman was narrow up top, not much to gloat about, though her hips and thighs were large and pleasing, a full pear shape. She wore a pink bikini top with a full back boy shorts, ribbons laced around her midsection and calves, her skin a smooth toffee colour. Her eyes were almonds, a rich hazelnut brown, and her lashes were long and dark. Her hair was a brilliant auburn with hints of gold flecks that caught in the light as she moved.

His voice came out high and unpleasant, choked with cotton balls, "Can I have you both?"

The two women looked at each other, the competitiveness in both of them evident, even as they agreed, "Double the price," they said at the same time. The woman's voice, whom Scarlett barely recalled went by Cassandra, was high and girly, belied by her womanly body, those child rearing hips, and her ample thighs. Scarlett's was lower, laced with lust and the edge of one fine cigarette too many, coming out rich and thick, like honey. They both took the tiny man in either arm, both of them towering over his diminutive and stout form. He was just barely over five feet, and the women took the time to look over one another.

Legrasse's eyes followed Scarlett as she walked up the steps, the muscles in her legs pulling taut as they took her up another stair, relaxing once the pressure was off. She drank in Cassandra's stride, the woman standing a few inches above her, and she enjoyed the look of her small chest and the shake of the zaftig rear.

By the time they reached the private booth and slid in, Scarlett had planned on taking advantage of the situation. The booth was lavish and contained a small bed, navy and silver sheets and pillows, a lighter blue booth fashioned at the end of it. The girls pressed him into his seat and sat atop both of his thick thighs, their hands immediately finding one another's hips, "The money," Scarlett cooed, "we need the money first, and then we can get started." Her emerald eyes rose to the cocoa eyes of her companion, "and I want to play with her real bad." There was a twinge of truth that caused Cassandra to flinch for a moment, though her own façade quickly wiped it away and she licked her full, chestnut coloured lips.

The bills were quickly produced and set atop the corner of the bed. The two women looked at it hungrily, and Scarlett counted it quickly. She smiled at him warmly, ignoring the wrinkles and the bad teeth and the balding head and seeing nothing but a rich and fabulous suitor. "My, you must have been away for some time," she smiled, crawling off his lap and onto the bed, "we shouldn't keep you waiting." She patted the mattress and invited Cassandra to crawl up with her.

Cassandra was obedient, if nothing else. Her hair draped over her shoulders, grazing over the flesh, then hanging in the air, hiding her body as she crawled towards Scarlett. She turned and sat, facing the man, allowing her to take over.

Scarlett moved slowly and in a feline manner, her

shoulders poked off more than necessary as she displayed her prowess and awareness of the situation. Her hands moved down over the other woman and she shifted to allow the customer a better visual as she turned to straddle the woman in reverse, her wet pussy mere inches from Cassandra's face as she moved downward, trailing her tongue over the silken flesh of her co-worker.

The mirror beside the bed reflected it all, showing a twin vision of two beautiful women as their bodies pressed together, the bronze skin on smooth, light brown. The customer flicked his eyes between both the real and the mirrored version of their show, growing stiff beneath his pants.

The one way mirrors were installed as a way to watch the strippers and make sure they weren't breaking any of the rules. Hidden viewing panels were squirreled away beside each booth, and the bouncers had enjoyed the more pleasing purposes. When the manager had found out, he locked the viewing rooms up, but this one had a trick side that was easily pushed away. Legrasse figured he was the only one that knew about it, since he never ran into another guy in there.

He had, however, told Scarlett and advised her to always use the adjacent booth whenever possible if she knew what was in her best interest. She had that much common sense, and knew that, in the mood he was in, she best treat him to a real show.

Though she was grateful to the girls for following the rules and making her job easier, Scarlett was never so good at following them herself. She was a staunch supporter of them, but would make little side deals with her clients for after work specials. The other women had their suspicions, of course, but nothing was done on club property and there was little they could do about it.

She was, however, known for her unabashed treatment of the other women.

Legrasse sat behind the booth, squirreled into a corner, the mirror inside the booth allowing him a proper view at his most valuable asset. Indeed, she paid him well, in both cash and in small tokens of appreciation, but she was going to have to give much more in order to cover up for her high flying act.

He sat and watched the women's slow and careful movements as they eagerly drained the customer's pockets dry, Legrasse's large hands rested on his own thighs. He brought the joint from his tight pants to his lips, lighting it. The small tendril of smoke warped around and then hit off the ceiling of the box, the tiny area quickly filling with the rich scent of acrid drugs. He leaned back, casually, watching as Scarlett took over and was consumed by the ecstasy of her tongue trailing down Cassandra's breasts, over the cusps of her top, then down to encircle the belly button. She teased it with her adept tongue, jade eyes not leaving the man at her mercy.

The other woman was pressed back to the bed, her hair fanned out around her pretty face, her thick eyelashes closed and showing the smoky cocoa eye shadow she had applied earlier in the night. There was a slight crease to it at the tops, which Scarlett both held against the girl and found endearing.

Legrasse shifted in his seat, the smoky air hindering his sight, his eyes squinting faintly as he leaned forward to get closer to the glass. She looked right at him, or, at least, where she assumed him to be, her thong clad ass facing the customer as she wantonly pulled her breasts free of their meagre confines. Letting the bikini strings sit to the side of either of her large tits and underneath, the material pressed them together and allowed them to hang before leaving them to the affects of gravity.

His breath caught in his throat as he watched, holding the smoke deep in his chest. His face was handsome, in a rugged manner, broad and stern. His eyebrows were thick and drew attention to his bright eyes, his skin deeply tanned, obviously spending much time in the sun, despite his night job. His lips were a pale pink, nearly a straight line, his teeth a faded white, pleasant and non-obtrusive. He smiled and gave a slight grunt as he moved back in his seat, his calloused hand teasingly moving overtop of himself.

Scarlett pulled Cassandra's thong to the side, treating both of the voyeurs to a long and slow tease as she bobbed in closer and closer, her kittenish tongue at the ready as it first found the tip of her thigh, then delved lower and lower until finally that sweet, smooth taste hit her. Her tongue ran along the other woman's outer lips before parting deeper, the back of her tongue tracing up against her inner petals.

Cassandra had let out a gasp but she was easily silenced by another skilful lash of the pink tongue, turning the woman's sound of surprise to one of bliss. Her tongue slowly wound around the woman's clit, lavishing attention on it, Scarlett's eyes still locked on that mirror, enjoying the sight of her eating the other woman's cunt and knowing exactly what Legrasse was seeing on the other side.

By the time the money was spent, both of the female bodies were glistening with the dew of sweat and the high lights had come up in the club. With sunrise, the club closed, and the disgruntled sounds of drunks who weren't drunk enough, or didn't get enough of what they wanted, wafted up the balcony to the private booths.

The money was split cleanly between Scarlett and Cassandra, except for a slight favourable accounting error on Scarlett's part, and they left ways, as if nothing odd in the slightest had happened between them. As though nothing special had been exchanged. It was just a job.

SCARLETT DIDN'T HAVE to turn to know that Legrasse was stalking behind her, his eyes clouded with the drug. She walked down the steps quickly, clutching the discarded clothes to her chest along with her purse. The club was always so strange at this hour, as if reality were intruding upon a place that it had no right to visit. Everyone blinked to adjust to the brightness and stared in confusion at the flawed women who were, under the illusion of gentle lights and ample darkness, goddesses. The light never bothered Scarlett at all, and she dared them to stare as she made her way to the dressing room, tucking her skimpy clothing into her bag and drew out a black corset and skirt.

Legrasse waited at the door, watching as she tugged up the skirt and carefully laced the corset, making him wait and stare, knowing full well what he had just witnessed. She tugged the pig tails out and shook the long raven hair, the tips of it brushing over the top of her backside. With a slow application of fresh, ruby lipgloss, she turned, grabbing her things and now ready for her escort back to her room. She never bothered changing from her impossibly high heels.

He allowed her out in front, his hand pressed firmly against the slope of her back, urging on her lazy saunter as she waved goodbye to this gent or another. The top of the corset dug into the skin of her shoulder blade, and his eyes focussed on it, that little measure of tender exposure, something unplanned and unintended, for his eyes to devour.

Onto the cold streets, the sun just was peaking over the lowest of the buildings, her heels clicking on the cement ground. The loud thump of his heavy leather, steel toed boots followed after her, though they otherwise walked in silence until they finally reached her condo.

It was several stories up and had a beautiful view of a small park below, even though the staircase was so narrow that they had to walk up one at a time and it looked as though it could use a new layer of paint. She stopped in front of her door and searched for her key, idly, pressing the cash and makeup aside.

Legrasse noticed her procrastination, however, and the thick web of his hand found the nape of her neck, pressing into it and slamming her face into the door, her cheek pressed against the cool wood roughly. She yelped in surprise, and immediately her hand was on her key and the key was in the door. He snatched it from her before she could return it to the purse and, with a snarl, reminded "I'm not paying. I don't need to wait."

Her eyes fluttered in a measure of shock and arousal, her heart thumping loudly in her chest, blood rushing from her head at the forceful reminder. He pushed her in through the door, slamming it shut behind him.

The condo was pleasant and wide open, more akin to an artist's loft than a true home, though it did have some of the necessities. It lacked a kitchen and there were boxes of discarded and finished food tossed in a bag at the side of the door. A cat pranced up and tried to wrap around her feet but she kicked at it as he guided her, his hand still gripping her neck painfully tight, the blood red hue apparent beneath his grasp. He guided her past the open living room and the opulent couches and tables and up a steel staircase. Her heel slipped through the gated stairs, but his pressure didn't subside and so she trotted up the rest of the way with a limp.

Upstairs there was no door, no room, just an open balcony that looked down on her living room and served as her bedroom. A large vanity was pressed against the wall, and beside it was a larger wardrobe. A dresser that was messily overflowing flanked the other side of the vanity; several looked at and discarded outfits thrown above it and on top of the bed.

The bed itself was large and plush, round and covered with a custom tailored comforter. The pillows were propped up around the side. She was pushed headlong towards it and, with her already tender ankle, sent sprawling onto it. At the first chance she got, she turned onto her back, staring up at the man with anger and annoyance, even as he reached for his belt.

"You don't have to be so rough!" she protested, her ruby lips pouted in annoyance. His eyes didn't soften and he took the belt from his pants, clasping it in a loop between his hands.

"You don't learn otherwise," he retorted, his voice edged with the drugs, "I could get fired for covering for you again." A sneer parted his lips and he moved to tower over the woman, "You just. Don't. Learn."

Scarlett's eyes went to the belt and widened with fear, "Hey!" she cried out, struggling backwards on the bed, "Calm down! I didn't..."

Her words were interrupted by the feeling of hard leather being slapped across her shin, the momentary sting causing her to recoil, the corset and leather collar digging into her flesh with the sudden movements. Her eyes were angry and glistened with fresh tears, her flesh ablaze with fury "Fuck you!"

He laughed at her, cruelly, moving a step forward and snapping the leather, "See what I mean, bitch?" His voice was hard, no measure of sympathy apparent in it as he reached down and grabbed a clump of shiny, dark hair, tugging on it. She squealed as she was lifted from the bed, her high-heeled feet struggling for balance and a relief of the pain, her ankles warbling on the cushioned mattress.

In a quick and steady movement he brought her body back to the bed, crashing face down into the mattress and holding her there against her struggles. He easily moved to the back of her head, holding her into the mattress as she flailed, her nose dug painfully into the material, breathing becoming more difficult. He moved behind her and crawled onto the bed, a knee finding the low of her back and pinning her there roughly.

The frills of the black skirt were lifted and his eyes ran over her smooth backside, hungrily and wanting, his cock pulsing roughly against his pants as he raised the belt and brought it down with a loud crack to her ass, an inch wide welt rising almost immediately. Scarlett's head struggled to push up, but he forbid it with the pressure of his hand, her screams coming out as muffled and desperate attempts at breath.

Again the belt found her bottom, and again she struggled to breath, only to be denied the air she needed.

His cock throbbed angrily as his belt found that round ass again and again, leaving it nothing but a welted red mess before he finally tossed it away, trading it for the palm of his hand. His finger delved between her crevice and sought downwards, towards the heat of her swollen pussy, red with desire and angry at his denial. His finger found the part of her inner lips, pushing inwards and, though she struggled, he could feel her throb lightly around his digit.

"You never learn, Scarlett," he lifted the hand from her head and she gasped for air. Messily she tried to wipe the tears free from her face, the blanket beneath her moist with the salty residue.

Deftly he unbuttoned his pants and pushed them downwards, releasing his hard cock from its confines. Pulling her up onto his lap, her bosom pressed roughly into the mattress. He grabbed the base of his cock and pointed it towards her dripping entrance, rubbing it along her outer folds. She shivered with the anticipation, pulsing as his head strummed over her clit, then back again, teasing the slit.

She shimmied, begging him with her body for release, a tiny mewl coming from her lips in pleasurable want, but his cock slid further up her crevice, instead finding her darkened hole. Both of his hands angrily pried her tender ass cheeks apart, ignorant of the pain it caused her, before bringing a singular hand back to guide his throbbing piece into her.

With a grunt and a snarl he impaled her, first with his head, then further, inch by inch fighting inward as she clawed at the bed, desperately begging him to go slow; to stop hurting her; to stop delving deeper and deeper into her forbidden caverns. A swift hand to her battered backside paused the protests for a moment as he finally was able to hilt himself fully within her, the hot hole pressed tightly against his impressive cock.

It wasn't her first time, yet still she squealed with the pain, her tiny feet kicking against the mattress on either side of him as he looked down at the scene of her blood red ass cheeks splayed against his hips, his prick invading her body. The sight of her corseted back, the ribbon so neatly tied, of her black hair, knotted from his hard hand, her frilled skirt tipped up to her waist. He began thrusting into her dryly, and she cried out noisily, even as her pussy burned hot for him.

He knew she wanted him, craved him mind, body and soul. Yet he denied her, his hands grabbing onto her perfect hips and pulling her to him every time she tried to squirm away. Her round ass pushed up against his hard pelvis, the softer flesh giving way and indenting, and each tug caused her to moan in anguish.

Her ass was so red from the belt, and the sight only made him throb harder, and the fact that each pulse brought with it a whimper of pain from his dearest friend only made things sweeter. He had her right where he wanted her, pinned down and vulnerable, begging for him to fuck her right. Every time she reached for her clit he smacked her hand away, denying her that sweet release of endorphins that would lessen the pain of what he was doing to her.

He wanted her to feel it, every pulse of his cock, every swell, every twitch of bliss as he pressed into her again and again, despite her body's resistance of the invading organ. It looked so hot, his cock so tightly siphoned by that dark hole, watching as his pole disappeared first between her large, round cheeks and then into the torturously tight canal.

He wanted to make it last, but wasn't long before his ramming became more wanton, less predictable as the familiar fire travelled through his body. Legrasse's desire for the woman rarely ebbed, regardless of her moods and behaviours, and seeing her so helpless beneath him brought him to the point of no return. He pulled out before the final push, bringing his powerful hand to his cock and giving it that last tug, the creamy liquid eagerly releasing over the battered woman below him, strands collapsing into her hair, onto her corset, her skirt, marking her as his.

He smiled down affectionately at the mess he caused, at her sobbing face, wiping the remains of his cum laden cock off on her battered ass. He stared at her as he caught his breath, his leather clad chest heavy with the excitement and exertion, "What did you learn?" he growled lowly.

All Scarlett could manage, however, was tears. He grabbed the bottom of her corset and dragged her limp body from the bed, dropping her to the floor. Legrasse looked down at her, his voice stony, "I want to sleep in today, so best you not wake me." He watched her as she nodded her head, making sure she understood before he pulled the comforter over his body, his muscles relaxing as a deep and restful sleep found him.

FERTILE BIMBO

*B*ook Themes:
Bimbofication and Sex in the Office
Word Count:
4,198

THERE WERE ALWAYS rumours about how Roxy had gotten her position as senior manager of the warehouse facilities. For good reason too. She was still fairly new to the business herself, only working there for two years, and that included the last year, which she had spent in some level of management.

Truth be told, the rumours were well founded. The owner had a thing for her—busty and beautiful as she was, of course he did. Despite her best efforts at remaining professional, she had given in and spent a few nights with the man. It wasn't even unpleasant. Truthfully, the only thing that kept her from giving in more was her desire to be taken seriously. It's something that would make her mother proud.

Since her duties in the summer months revolved mainly around instructing the new hires, young men in for summer jobs, she was able to avoid the knowing stares from the older workers. Though, by no means did that mean she got to avoid the leers.

Tending to a group of virile young men fresh out of high school on their summer break meant quite the opposite.

One of them in particular always seemed to catch her eye with a grin. A handsome young man, tall and broad shouldered, well built. So well built... which was on prominent display as he usually shed his shirt early on each morning. His well-toned physique catching the glint of the sun as he toted the heavy cargo to and from the warehouse.

Somehow, despite all his time bare and exposed, that skin of his remained a nice peachy colour. His short cut hair a brilliant blonde.

He had chest hair, but it matched his head and so was almost invisible upon his skin unless the light glinted off it the right way or she was really close... like now, where she could see the soft trail it made down across his abs towards his groin, that was just barely out of view by his low-hanging jeans.

"Roxy?" he asked, trying to gain her attention as he stood in front of her desk, just a few feet away. Clearly aware of her staring.

Her eyes jumped back to his face, as if her hand was caught in a very delicious cookie jar. "Yes, Chris?" Roxy's dark skin hid her flush, and she was thankful for it, but it still glistened under the heat of her sheer blouse and tight skirt. She'd forgone her tights for the summer and her inner thighs were sticky from the humidity and she squirmed a little, hoping for relief but finding none.

Chris tugged off his work gloves, the one piece of clothing he wore above the belt. "Wanted to have a little chat with you," he said, a smile upon his handsome face as he ran a hand through his short, spiky blonde hair. Without another word he helped himself to leaning over her desk, resting one palm upon it as he looked her straight in the eyes. "You and me, tonight after work. We're gonna go out. Sound good, Roxy?" The youthful cockiness and supreme confidence just oozing from his every word.

So much so that she wanted to leap at the chance, to smile and feel excited, like she would have when she was younger. Instead, her dark eyes met his, and her lips went tight. "Well, Chris, I'm flattered, but I don't think it would be a good idea."

He tilted his head and gave her a disappointed look. "Well alright then. How about I shut that door and you bend over this desk right now? Last offer, Roxy," he said with a smug smile that irritatingly only enhanced his handsome features, those bright blue eyes of his.

Her lips dropped open in shock, but something about the fullness of her mouth, the glint in her eyes, it all made it more seductive than intended, even as she shook her head and that full head of curly hair bounced against her high cheekbones. "That is not appropriate language, Chris."

With a shrug of those bare, glistening shoulders he reached into his back pocket and pulled out his phone. "Was it appropriate language last month when I saw you in this office with the owner?" he said, and with a press of the screen he started a video playing that was all too familiar.

In it she could see herself on her knees, sucking on the owner's cock as the moaning man knotted his fingers in her curls and spoke so filthily. "That's it, baby, suck daddy's cock. Suck it good," he said in that deep voice she was so familiar with.

"Seems to me you don't mind that kinda language, Roxy," Chris remarked to her, the office door wide open, and even though it lay high above the floor of the warehouse, secluded from everything else, she felt particularly vulnerable there to being overheard.

She stood up from her desk, snatching for the phone only for him to yank it away. "Give me that!"

Smiling still, he tucked the phone into his back pocket again. "Don't worry, I got it saved at home too," he explained, rolling his shoulders and seeming to relax himself more as he sat upon the corner of her desk. "Now, are you gonna bend over this desk as I shut the door and blinds, or am I gonna have to let that video slip? What's it gonna be, Roxy? I mean... I tried to play this nice, offered to take you out for a date." He gave her a look-over, those bright blue eyes of his so obviously eating up her curvaceous form.

Her dark eyes were wide as she stared at him with disbelief. "Listen, you don't understand," she pleaded, walking around his desk and towards him, her knees shaking so hard that she was having trouble walking in her high heels that were probably two inches too tall for a workplace. "It's not what it looks like."

Chris never stopped looking her over, appreciating the way her calves were shaped as she walked over to him, or how her short skirt clung to her shapely rear. "Well, it's not so much what I would think, right? I mean, I saw it, and I still wanted to date you, right, Roxy?" he said with such a sweet-looking smile, those peached lips stretched wide. "But what about the folks in the office? Or hey, the owner's wife! I mean... once she finds out he'll have no choice but to let you go..."

"You wouldn't!" It felt like all of the air had been sucked from her lungs, and her hand fluttered to the open collar of her translucent, white blouse. She fidgeted, looking to the open door and quickly moving to close it.

"Listen, Chris," she started in, but what could she say? She needed this job. She'd gotten too accustomed to living off a manager's salary, and she liked working here. It was good, honest work that managed to pay for a few designer pieces along with her small but gorgeous apartment.

"Maybe we could go out, talk this over, okay?" she pleaded. She had the better part of a decade on him, but she felt like she was so much younger with how strange her voice sounded.

"Yeah," he said to that, and so casually reached out to grab her ass. That strong worker's hand of his sinking into her soft, yet supple, flesh, making it swell between his long, slender fingers. "We'll do that date, right? But first," he said as he stood up, towering back over her again, but standing so close she could smell his musk and the sweat of his labour. "First, you're gonna bend over this desk, because you owe me an apology for your rude refusal."

How was he so tall? With her heels she almost always was equal height to most men, taller than some. But she felt overshadowed by the young man, and had to wonder if it was her mind playing tricks on her. Making him seem so much bigger than life.

"I wasn't rude, Chris," she rebuffed, taking a step away as she tried to slap his wrist. "But I can't sleep with my employees. What I did... that was... wrong of me."

So why are you breathing so fast? And why is your body tingling with anticipation? she asked herself, but she didn't have an answer.

The insistent young man didn't let her remove his hand, and instead he wrapped his other arm about her too.

He pulled her in against his hard chest, let her hefty bosoms smush against his firm muscles as he looked into her eyes. "C'mon," he said to her in a low, lust-laden voice, "I know you want me. Now you be a good lil' bimbo slut, I'm bein' real nice to you because I like you, Roxy. But I ain't the most patient man."

"Stop this, Chris," she commanded, but that tone lacked oomph. Her heart raced and it was like he was surrounding her, smothering her body with his, and it felt so good. It'd been too long for her, but then, a week was too long. Still, she was trying to control herself, her urges.

Sex had become an addiction to her, and she'd gone from man to man, never finding one that could satisfy her for long. She was a serial monogamist for a while before she just turned to dating ads. Then, after a horrifying encounter, she'd quit.

Cold turkey.

Well, almost.

"C'mon, Roxy," he said insistently, and he switched their positions, pushing her round ass up against the top of the desk as he pressed her knees apart with his own. Those strong hands of his slid down to her hips, then over the short length of her skirt to her bare thighs before sliding up in under the fabric. "I don't wanna get you fired. I love every opportunity I get to check out that ass. These big beautiful tits of yours, nearly popping out of your blouse," he said with such supreme relish, even as his fingers curled into her panties and began to tug them downwards.

"Holy fuck, Chris," she hissed, but it didn't sound all mad. In fact, the more he took control, the crueler and nastier he got, the more she noticed the way her body responded to it. Her head felt clouded by lust, but still she tried to fight his hands off, her ass grinding against the desk. "Someone could walk in at any second!"

Why didn't she lock the damn door? Why did she think she could handle this?

Instead of addressing her worries, he silenced them with his peachy lips pressed to her painted ones, that moist tongue of his so hot as it penetrated her mouth, swirling about and tasting her as he slipped her panties down to her ankles and left them there. He didn't ease up on her, didn't heed her words.he simply grabbed hold of her thigh and reached up, beginning to pluck open her buttons on her top as he went for her breasts next.

Things felt like they were moving in slow motion and yet so very, very fast. She could barely respond to one motion before he was on to another, his hands and hips and mouth all devouring her in tandem.

She tried to push his chest away, but when she felt the bare skin, the bristly hairs beneath her palms, she got distracted.

"Chris, please," she murmured.

Her blouse was open, and immediately she felt his hands working the clasp of her bra. With a smack of their lips he tugged the garment open and let her ample bust spill out to slap heavily against her chest. "I'm done headin' to the washroom to rub one out because your slutty ass saunters on by, Roxy," he said in a gravelly voice as he pushed her back and grabbed a breast.

How had he unbuttoned her and unclasped her so easily? So quickly?

It was if she was standing still as time sped by her, leaving her confused and in its wake.

Her body, though, seemed to know precisely what was happening and her dark areola and nipple hardened into his hand. She was so eager for touch, yet her dark eyes were filled with pleading. "Not here."

"Too late," was all she heard from him as he kissed, bit,

and suckled his way down her neck, that strong hand of his squeezing and kneading her breast. She could feel each digit sink into those thick mounds, the peachy skin enveloped in her chocolatey tit flesh.

He was ravenous for her, so strong and moving so fast. She could hear his belt buckle, then feel his jeans lower as a thick, veiny cock popped free of its confines. He was a tall man, and with a big cock that smeared its precum against her inner thigh as he throbbed between her knees.

She wanted to scream "no," to shove him away and hit him. To punish him for being so cruel to her.

But there was a stronger part of her that didn't want to lose this moment, in all its fucked-up glory. The way his body felt, the need she had between her legs, it was all so damn... good. She needed this. She needed him.

"Chris," she gasped, his cock throbbing against her damp skin, and she shifted towards it, rather than away from it. "We can't do this. You're my subordinate!"

"Not anymore," he bit back, and she felt his fingers grip her thick curls and tug her head back roughly. "You're my little fuckslit, Roxy," he growled to her, feeling him lift one of her thighs as he pushed in between them, his hips rubbing against her smooth flesh. "You're gonna be my little cum Dumpster from now on. Each and every day we got work."

With a twist of his fingers in her hair, he reiterated sharply as she felt that throbbing manhood brush against her labia, "A man needs to keep his mind clear to focus. And you're just the cock sleeve to make it happen, aren't ya, Roxy?"

Oh god. He was being such a douchebag, but she couldn't help how horny his words made her. The promise of an available, beautiful stud waiting for her every morning, ready and willing and eager for her body was what she wanted. It was like her cocaine, and her heart was pounding just thinking of it, even as she pushed his chest again. It made his fingers tug her curly, natural hair harder and sharp little stabbing sensations went through her, but she didn't care.

She couldn't succumb to this. To him!

"Stop this right now!"

The words were barely finished when he bit into her neck and thrust his cock up into her all at once. That throbbing peachy shaft shoved into her slick quim, letting her honeyed canal grip about him so tight as he buried his length to the hilt within her.

A low, growling groan rumbled out of his chest as he lodged himself there, and she could feel him twitch and spasm with his desire. "You're mine now, Roxy," he said just a moment before he tugged back his hard ass and then thrust into her again.

"I'm not on the pill!" she nearly screeched. It was, after all, why she was giving her boss head.

She'd decided to get off it to give her extra incentive to stay professional. To give sex a break while she got her lusts under control.

It didn't seem it was working well, considering how tightly she was gripping him, her dark flesh so welcoming of his toned body. He was gorgeous and cruel, and she knew this was blackmail, but somewhere along the lines her body had decided it didn't care.

The next thrust came harder, more brutal than the last, and it jarred her body as the wet smack of his loins hitting hers filled the office, his heavy balls slapping against her ass. That strong hand of his gripped one of her large tits tighter and he grunted as his thrusts became a hammering pace. "Too bad you fuckin' turned down my date," he said in a husky voice as he began to pant over her. "I mighta given a shit then, slut."

She cursed herself, her skin, her body, her everything, for the way it prickled with sensation and made her feel such intensity. Hatred and fear and lust and passion all combined into something ugly and horrifying as she tried to squirm away from him. Yet the only thing she accomplished was shrinking more beneath him, her back nearly pressed to her ledger and phone.

He was fucking her.

It had almost not dawned on her, or not sunk in fully, but she knew it all the same. The way he spread her delicate, sensitive lips. How full that helm was against her cervix. The rhythmic slap of his body against her moist form.

He was really fucking her, and she was barely struggling.

It was almost as if she wanted this.

Looking up at that gorgeous male body of his, he certainly wanted it. Even through his crassness and cruelty, the look of pleasure on his face was unmistakable. He pumped his cock into her with increasing vigor, every muscle upon his hard, toned physique twitching and bulging as he split her up the middle from between her legs, pounding his dick into her cunt.

"F–Fuck," he cursed, and she could feel his dick twitch inside her, perched so close to the precipice as he leaned over her and lunged for her free breast, biting it, then licking over her areola and suckling the stiff nipple into his mouth hungrily.

Oh god. Her cunny was on fire, her breasts just large bundles of excited, angry nerves that wanted for more. Greedily, she hungered for him, even as she tried to push him away.

Yet if she really didn't want it, why was she letting her strength falter? Why was she secretly hoping he'd fight her off?

"Chris, please," she pleaded one more time, and she wasn't sure she knew what she wanted the answer to be. It was so wrong, so very wrong, but it wasn't her fault. She couldn't be held responsible for the actions of another.

Her cunt had grown so wet that his thrusts each produced such a noisy smack, his hard, thickly throbbing shaft pounding into her wet honey-slick cunt again and again. He started to grow erratic, she noticed, the timing of his hips off just slightly. Then abruptly the rough suckling he was giving her stiff teat ended and he arched his neck.

The noisy moan he gave echoed out hoarsely through the office as she felt his arms squeeze her thigh and breast, and he gave two final thrusts into her. The thick streams of his seed spurting deep within, splattering and smearing over the entrance to her womb as he so heedlessly shot his load deep inside her warm quim.

Her eyes stung as her back arched and her throat caught. It was the single most intense moment she'd ever felt, the combination of pleasure and anguish something so pure it silenced all other thoughts.

The final throes of his climax came with hammering stabs of his hefty manhood, spurting the very last of his seed into her as he grunted and groaned so roughly. He was like a wild beast atop her in that moment, growling, snarling, and full of raw drive to rut and fuck her voluptuous figure.

As the moment slowly came to a halt, she looked up and saw his glistening physique, his sculpted pecs so perfectly outlined, the light blonde hair there damp with perspiration.

He pushed himself back up and rubbed his hand over

his spiky hair. "You better take care of that pill issue, if you know what's good for you," he said so casually, yanking his still thick, meaty cock from her cunt as he began to tug up his jeans and boxer briefs. "I'll be takin' you home after work, so wait up for me," he said with a wry grin, "boss."

FERTILE CELEBRITY: AIDA

$\mathcal{B}$ook Themes:
Cuckolding, Breeding, Impregnating Creampies, Cheating, and Oral Sex
Word Count:
5,285

I'D WORKED backstage as a stagehand for so long, for many of these lingerie fashion shows, that they were all starting to bleed together. That all of the women just sort of started to look the same, with their fake tans and their long, perfect hair, and the sneer they always had for me as I hammered the set, or fixed up one of the stage props.

I knew most of my buddies thought I had the best job in the world, but being surrounded by supermodels wasn't all it was cracked up to be.

Not until I saw her, crying in the dressing room as everyone else pretended she wasn't there. But I couldn't help that it tugged my heartstrings to see the pretty young woman looking so broken up.

When I went over and knelt before her, asking what's wrong, though, I couldn't believe my ears.

"My husband's sterile!" she whimpered, her hand unfolding and revealing the phone she must have just hung up on. My face fell. I already had two beautiful kids, but they lived with my ex-wife. I'd be devastated, though, if I couldn't have had them, so I understood her pain.

I don't even really remember how the conversation went after that. Not until she asked me if I might help her out.

WE MET AT MY PLACE, my bachelor pad. The apartment I took out after my ex-wife and I split up. It was a decent place. After all, I made a good living and needed somewhere decent to take my kids for those weekends I had them.

It was in a brick building downtown, with ostensibly two floors. The master bedroom up above, the small guest bedrooms below with the living room and kitchen.

I dressed nice for her visit, or at least as nice as I felt comfortable doing. I wasn't a fancy guy, usually denims and plaid shirts. Hey, I was a workin' guy, alright? But this time, I went for a nice turtleneck black sweater… and dark denims. Okay, it wasn't *that* different.

But I did brush my dark hair, groom my beard and splash on a bit of cologne. Just a tiny hint though. I couldn't stand artificial scents, and so it was just the slightest accent to go along with my natural musk.

When the buzzer to my place went off, I let her on up, and waited for her knock. I was a little nervous. The models had a knack for looking rather intimidating and holier-than-thou. I mean, I was a handsome guy, six foot four, well built and muscular. I took care of myself and I certainly didn't look my age. But I wasn't rich, and I was used to a humble lifestyle.

Beer with friends, and working hard. That sums up most of my life now that my kids are off with my ex-wife.

The knock finally came, and I opened the door. I honestly don't know what I was expecting from the whole thing, but I'll tell you this: I wasn't expecting what came of it all.

She was dressed to the nines, her dark hair pulled back from her face, high cheekbones and smoky eyes batting up at me. She still had on her killer stilettos, her black and silver dress hugging the curves I was already familiar with from the dressing room, and the little leather jacket she wore over her shoulders was quickly stripped away and offered to me as she glanced around.

"This is a cute place," she said, not meaning to sound as condescending as she did, I could tell. I'd wipe that smug grin off her face before long, though. After all, she's the one that needed me in all this.

She then lifted her hand, holding out a brown paper bag to me. "I brought champagne."

I hung her coat up by the door and took the bottle from her, pulling it out of the bag to find a decent bottle of booze. Not the sort of thing I'd buy for myself, but then I didn't even like champagne.

"Looks good," I said with a smile, gesturing her over towards my living room. A black sofa, white sofa-chair, and a coffee table next to the TV and the large windows overlooking the town. "I'll just go poor this up for us," I said, and did just that in the kitchen.

Luckily I carried a couple wine glasses for just such

occasions I might have some special lady come over. A bachelor can't be caught off guard after all.

"You find the place alright?" I asked before emerging, glasses in hand.

"I had my driver bring me," she said with a smile that was part way too smug, but mostly just oblivious to the things she was saying as she accepted the drink. Considering how sullen and sad I'd seen her, I knew she was human, with real emotions. She just worked hard to hide it beneath this veil of pride, if you could call it that.

She sat upon my sofa, her long legs crossed daintily as her high heeled foot bobbed in the air, the muscles in her thighs outlined so beautifully.

I sat myself on down next to her, my arm up on the back of the sofa as I took a sip of the champagne. I didn't care for it much honestly, not at all, but whatever, I drank it down and smiled sympathetically to her.

"It must be tough. Even with what happened between my ex-wife and I, my kids are the most important thing in my life," I said, looking at her and trying not to oggle. "You're a beautiful, successful woman too, you have every reason and right to want to have a child of your own while in the prime of your life."

She let out a bitter laugh.

"Tell that to Tony. He couldn't be more pleased with the news. He thinks I should wait until my career's over in my 30s, but I'm not waiting that long. I'm already 22, and who's to say what's going to happen next?" she asked, rhetorically, as she rolled her eyes. She sipped back the champagne, clearly taking more joy in it than I was.

"So, fuck him."

I didn't know what to say to that exactly, not at first, so I drank more of the champagne and looked her over.

"You're thinking of leaving him then?" I asked lowly,

my voice steady. "If your two views on life don't mesh up on such a big issue as having kids, then... that'll be a rough one to make work." Which was true enough, and I didn't want to question her judgment. I knew that wouldn't go over well with her.

"I don't know," she said, her eye twitching for a moment before she tipped back the rest of her drink, settling the empty glass on the table and reaching over to me, gripping my nice sweater in her fist as she looked at me. "But I know you're going to fuck me, bare, and you're going to leave me dripping in your seed, and I'm going to make him clean me up in the morning."

Her sudden shift took me by surprise. I knew many of the models could be downright domineering, but this? I wasn't expecting it at all. I reached over to lay down my drink and looked at her in shock.

However, I'd be a fucking liar if I said I wasn't turned on by it. By her. And the opportunity to knock up a model.

"Are... are you sure?" was all I managed to stammer out then at that point, but my eyes couldn't help but roam down over her svelte form.

"I'm sure," she said, with not as much bite as she had before, but lacking none of her sincerity, that wicked little smile of hers growing wider. "I've never been more certain of anything."

Maybe it was the lack of sex in my own life for so long, or maybe it was the urge to just have such a ravishing beauty. Or maybe yet, it was the fact that her saucy attitude made me want to take her. Have her. Make her scream and bend to me, as payment for how she and all the other models had treated me.

Whatever the reason, I pulled my sweater off over my head, and flung it to the floor, letting my bare, somewhat hairy chest show. I was packed with muscle, hard bodied and manly, not like the pretty boys most of her model friends knew. I wanted to see her reaction to a real man.

But her shock was perfect. It opened her pretty eyes, made her mouth into an 'o' that I just wanted to press my cock into. But it quickly faded to a more hooded and devious smile as she licked her lips with a purr.

"Well, hello," she said as she brought her hand back to my rock hard chest, her fingers lost in the forest of my hair, tugging on it just a little.

I let her have her way for a while, allowing her slender fingers to rake through my thick forest of hair. Scratch over that hard muscle, feel it all so intimately, and know what a real man was like. But then my patience ran out. I reached out and grasped her hips in my two powerful hands, and turned her towards me.

Her mouth parted, about to object, but I reached down, undid my belt, my trousers, and I made the crass look upon her face fade as I peeled down my pants, and unveiled the massive bulge of my cock through those black cotton boxer-briefs.

There certainly wasn't as much buildup as I'd expected of the princess. I thought that she'd required a bit of convincing, maybe even changed her mind, but she wasn't lying. She was absolutely certain that she wanted to fuck me, raw and without holding anything back.

It was an intense stare she gave that throbbing piece of meat in my boxers, and I swore, she was close to drooling over it.

I reached down again, sliding my rough, worker's hands up her outer thighs toward her hips. I rolled her dress up, exposing her panties beneath, looking her over upon my sofa before I spoke. My voice came out gruff and hard, a real commanding tone.

"How's that, huh? Bigger'n your limp dicked, sterile

boyfriend's?" I taunted her. Tested her. Was she serious about doing this? Part of me didn't think so, and wanted to push her to back out once the realization of what she was doing kicked in. Be a responsible man. Taking a shot at someone's lover had a way of reminding them of how they really felt.

And even though she looked borderline disgusted, I saw some glimmer in her eyes, and she wouldn't take her gaze off my package. She didn't even seem to mind the fact that I could see her underthings, though as a woman who made a living walking down a runway in them, having one guy see her like that mustn't have been a big thing.

"Yea," she admitted, breathless as she licked over her lips. "Yea, it is."

"C'mon," I said to her, my voice gravelly and hard. "Take it out. Get a feel for the thick fuckstick that's gonna breed you," and I was being crass. Vulgar. If she wanted this, she was gonna have to put up with some rough shit. I wasn't gonna sugarcoat it for her.

You don't take it on yourself to abandon your significant other with me if you aren't serious. I don't take that sorta thing lightly.

She reached forward, that delicate little hand fluttering like a bird in flight, uncertain for a moment against the wind before she reached out, grabbing me through the fabric and giving a rub, testing me out before her hand moved up. Fingertips breached the top of my boxers, and she delved into the heat, grabbing my tool and unleashing it to the air.

Her eyes widened and she let out a gasp of delight as she dragged her hand down, looking at my cock and all its meaty glory with a lustful look.

I was a big guy in general, tall, built. But my cock? Yeah, that was the pride and joy of my physical self. It was a monster. A big thick shaft, with a bulbous crown, all well shaped though, like it was cut from stone, my ex-wife said. Too big for some women, and with those heavy nuts swinging below, I packed a hefty wallop of seed. I knocked up my ex-wife without even trying once, and the first time we actually tried she was pregnant that week.

"Like that, huh?" I said, licking my lips as she felt those dainty fingers over my beefy shaft, feeling the jutting veins. "If a kid's what you want, I'll knock you the fuck up with this beast in no time, beautiful."

She liked my compliment. That wasn't like a lot of women, especially a model, and especially one so drop dead gorgeous. She was the type of girl that had to be used to hearing she was beautiful on a constant basis, but oh, she was thrilled at me calling her beautiful.

It was almost funny. Thinking of her being the lucky one, when I was living every guy's dream.

"Only stipulation," I said, drawing it out. "Is that there's no chasing me down for child support, no calling me up in ten years begging for money for the kid's shoes. Once I knock you up?" I said, letting the words hang, "And I will knock you up. That's your responsibility."

She nodded, her eyes never leaving my shaft.

"Oh, yea," she purred. "I agree to that."

All the while she had been fondling my dick, feeling the stiff, meaty shaft, the way it throbbed and filled her grasp. It was a big, meaty organ and having it out, I just felt more confident in general. I mean, hard not to feel like a big, in charge man when you're jutting out a massive cock like mine and blowing the mind of a gorgeous super model.

"Give it a kiss then," I told her roughly. "And beg for some virile cum, like your lil' boy toy'll never be able to give you."

She made the sweetest noise I ever heard, the soft little

pleading and whimpering. She shimmied towards me, still haphazardly dressed as her kittenish tongue prodded out.

She went for the head, first. Bringing her lips right to my tip, to the bit of precum that leaked out, that she could clearly taste the sweet tang. Hey, I liked my fruit, I knew I had to taste pretty good. And the way she cooed was absolutely wonderful.

She even said, "Yum," as she licked it again, her eyes upon me as she kissed and licked.

I was putting on a stoic face, looking down at her with a hard gaze as I kept one hand upon the back of the sofa. But I can't deny that I was moved by her display, my dick throbbing lewdly, my tongue running along my lips as I watched that shaft bulge out beneath her fingers and tongue.

"A little beauty like you belongs on your knees before a real man anyhow," I muttered to her, reaching out my free hand to stroke along her hair. "Not these prissy lil' girly men you always end up."

She probably would've protested, if not for the fact that she'd just taken me fully into her mouth the second I spoke, a low hum trailing through my flesh.

It only took her a second though, before she moved again, rearranging herself so that she was there, rested between my knees and her chest resting on the couch. Her head bobbed down, hand working in tandem with it as she sucked me so desperately.

It'd been a while since I'd gotten a woman to suck my dick off. Not because of a lack of dates or girlfriends even, I've had those. But because the ones I did get this far with were too daunted to even take my dick into their mouths. Too big! They'd always say. Not this little model slut though.

I couldn't help but groan, my eyes almost shutting as I

got lost in the pleasure of that mouth working on my cock. She was young, much younger than me, but she knew how to work a man, even one of my size. My dick spurted precum onto her tongue and down her throat, and I knit my rough fingers through her hair, urging her on. Just to show her who's in charge.

"Knew you could be a good girl if there was some dick and cum in it for you," I growled out.

Her back prickled at that comment, I could tell. I was striking into her, getting underneath her skin, but it didn't stop her. No, if anything, it encouraged her.

Maybe she just needed a nobody to treat her like nothing. Who knew? People were complicated.

But her speed picked up, though it wasn't easy to squeeze that girth into her mouth, but she was a real trooper. Licking and sucking like a champ, even making those little noises I could feel vibrate along my skin.

"Yeah, that's it," I crooned again roughly, watching her bob along my dick again and again. Her long, curly dark hair bouncing around her head as she moved. The scent of my musk filling her nostrils as she would push down my thick shaft to the root, my dick making her throat bulge as I groaned.

"You're gonna have to milk this brute right to the edge," I told her gruffly. "I don't stick this bad boy into a stuck up princess like you until you earn it."

God, I thought I was laying it on pretty thick. I was certain she'd have slugged me for less — much less — but she just kept going, choking herself on my cock. Every time she had to move up for air, she coughed up some thick saliva, further lubricating my shaft.

I let loose a deep moan that set my barrel chest to rumbling, I grasped a hold of her hair after a long while and tugged her off my dick, leaving that big shaft to throb before her, glistening with her saliva which only enhanced how big and perfectly shaped it seemed.

"Gettin' me close," I told her, still holding her hair. "Now suck my nuts," I commanded her, pulling her back in against that cum-laden sac, which was already starting to tense up a little with how close she was getting me to orgasm. "Show me you're worth a load of my seed."

She hesitated, and for a moment I thought that I'd gone too far. She looked at me with more confusion than anger, as if she'd never had to debase herself like that.

But then her hand squeezed my cock and her eyes went to my sac, and I wondered if she'd do it. If this little lingerie model would really suck my balls, all in exchange for me to knock her up.

It felt like a long time before she brought her head in, her tongue licking against the textured flesh, feeling out the strange sensation before pulling away. Her face was already red from sucking my cock, her eyes a bit watery, but she was determined, I'll give her that.

She couldn't fit both of those hefty nuts into her mouth at once, but she tried as much as she dared without risking discomfort to me. Instead though, she ultimately satisfied herself with suckling at one at a time. My dick spurting more precum that ran down its length, and over her dainty little fingers.

"Perfect," I said with a big, hefty sigh that made my broad, hard chest heave. "This is how a beautiful vixen like you belongs. Now come here," I told her, pulling her off my balls again. "Get out of those panties and beg for a real man's cum," I commanded.

With how silent and obedient she'd been, I forgot what a sass mouth she could have, and as she stood up in her high heels, she looked like she was going to say something. The look on my face, though, stopped her. There was that implicit threat that she wasn't going to get what she wanted if she said a word, and so she brought her fingers to the back of her dress, unzipping it.

She tossed it aside, revealing her toned, perfect body. She'd just done a show, so she was at her peak, all lean muscle as she then brought her fingers to the back of her black, lacy bra. It was no strip tease, but her eyes were on me all the while as she unclasped it.

She let it fall away from her natural and incredibly full breasts, the darker nipples hard already as she then pushed down her panties.

She was completely hairless below the neck, her skin softer than I could ever believe as I reached out to grab her thigh with my hard hand.

I took that bit of control by grasping onto her, my dick throbbing before me thickly as I pointedly looked her over. I had a hard look, but I nodded appreciatively and then leaned in, wrapping my lips about one of her nipples and suckling at it, tugging at the sensitive bud roughly. I did it for my own benefit, not hers. Enjoying the moment of suckling at her large, supple breast before I plucked my lips off at her gasp.

"I said beg," I reiterated, standing up, looming over her as I shed the rest of my clothes entirely.

Even in her heels, she couldn't come close to my height, let alone match my broad shoulders and thick arms. I was a brute next to a dainty princess.

But her devious smile was back.

"Okay, big boy," she grinned at me, her hand back in my chest hair. "I want you to knock me up with your super sperm. I want you to shoot your load right into me, every last ounce. Please."

"Good enough, gorgeous," I said after a moment's hesitation, and I grasped her shoulder, forcibly guiding her to bend over my sofa, hands upon the back of it. I got in behind her, and set her high heeled feet apart wide to make room for me, splaying her pussy open as I reached down, cupping that cunt and feeling how wet it was.

The answer? Very fucking wet. Soaking in fact.

"Damn, you are in dire need of some real dick," I said to her, clapping a hand to her ass cheek as I took hold, then grasped the base of my cock as I guided the thick crown up to her slit. I didn't toy then, I gave her exactly what she wanted, and I just impaled her on my dick nice and hard, burying the full length in her with a merciless amount of force that forced her narrow little cunt to stretch taut about a size of dick she'd never taken before.

And oh, how she screamed. It rocked my sofa, the sound reverberating through the air. It was feminine and soft and yet intense, her entire body trying to squirm away from me before she realizes she was able to take it, and instead yielding to pleasure.

"Oh fuck," she called out, not holding anything back, neighbours be damned.

I began to pump my hips, grasping her waist tightly as I fucked that prissy supermodel. I watched for a while as my big, meaty shaft splayed her pussy lips wide, sinking in and out. While beneath, she looked back, seeing the sight of her lower stomach bulge out each time I sank in deep. It was incredible, and she was so damn tight.

"Mmm," I moaned aloud as my hard body crashed against her form. "You could squeeze water out of a rock with this tight lil' cunt of yours," I said, my cock throbbing inside her, and so close to cumming already. Of course, all that preparation she did on her knees, helped.

And she was desperate for it. There were no second guesses, no reluctance about going through with it.

"Fucking cum in me," she commanded, pleaded, begged.

It was all so hard to tell, as it swirled together and rolled off her tongue.

Her heels were digging into my calves, her dainty thighs pressed into my hips, and the idea that I was going to be the one to get this super model pregnant, make her have to take a break from work as her body contorted... that was hot.

The fact that she wanted it so badly?

That was what really did me in.

I would've liked to tease her, make her beg some more, but my dick was tingling with pleasure and I was so damn close to cumming. So instead I just let it go, and my eyes shut, head rolled back and I let loose a deep bellowing moan as I came. That fat cock of mine burying itself inside of her as I shot off such thick, creamy gouts of seed deep into her cunt, filling her womb as I twitched and bucked erratically.

I had so much of that spunk saved up in my balls, and I blew it in her fertile little pussy.

"Just like hubby never could," I groaned aloud, sinking my fingers into her ass and hips so tight.

She screamed with me, as my cock pressed against her cervix, emptying so much cum right within her. I'd be shocked if she wasn't pregnant within the hour, especially as I ground my hips into her, mashing my seed into her as deep as possible.

I stilled for a while, letting my cock throb and spurt the last of its essence into her, until finally my heaving chest still and I slapped my hand to her ass.

"Another before you go," I told her, and I reached down, gathered her up in my two powerful arms and laid her out on the floor upon her back.

I just shoved myself on back into her cum-sodden cunt, and began to pump my hips again. This time with a merciless tempo, thrusting hard, fast, filling her up so completely as I grunted and moaned. I was almost forty, but I was in good shape, and I took care of myself. I'd pound her against the floor until I had another load for her fertile little twat.

She tried to take it without protest, without admitting defeat. She was a hard nut to crack, looking so calm and in control even as she drooled my seed. Even as her face was red and cut off from breath by the overwhelming thrusts of my cock. Even as I asked her to beg. All through it she'd acted so in control.

But after I'd been hammering into her for a while, the facade started to slip away, and I got to see the real her. The one that was desperate for a little pain, to feel a little bit less than.

Her legs relaxed at my side, her eyes fluttering open as her mouth parted, nothing but pleasure left in her gaze.

I took hold of her two slender arms, and pinned them up over her head to the floor. I took absolute control of that gorgeous, supermodel body and I rocked it. Rocked her whole world. Looked across her, watched those thick tits jiggle and bounce, saw my raw, hard dick pound into her again and again as my heavy balls slapped her ass.

I didn't show any mercy, I was going to have her leave my place walking funny and aching from the sweet time we'd spent together.

Her hands balled into fists then relaxed as her head rocked back, little gasps and pants filling the air.

"Yes!" she managed, her entire body rocking, her stomach tightening and her pussy squeezing me. She was desperate for more, even through her hazy mind. I'd pummelled that bit of rebellion right out of her.

She gulped in air as she struggled to wrap her legs

171

around me once more, begging me in as she whimpered and moaned.

I easily kept her arms locked to the floor with just one hand, while the other went down over her body, felt her two thick tits, sank my fingers into their supple mounds and indulged in their soft, pliant feel. Then went onto tease my thumb around her clit, provoking that little nub as I continued to hammer into her cunt.

"You're gonna cum for me, princess," I growled out.

"Yes!" she shouted again, this time louder, with more passion, as her pelvis lifted towards me. She knew just what she liked, and she wriggled until I was hitting her just so, and then her body began to tense. She was wound so tight, so slick and wet against my cock, it was a miracle that she'd held off on cumming as long as she had.

But almost as soon as my rough finger touched her, her body began that slow coiling up, getting ready.

And then it instantly came crashing down on her, and she screeched so loud I thought my ears would pop, and her cunny squeezed so tight, I could barely piston back in.

The two of us had been fucking for so long, our bodies were coated in a thin sheen of perspiration, her tits and my hard pecs and abs all glistening. But I wasn't tired, and I continued to pound into her, making her squirming, climaxing form rock beneath my hammering dick.

I kept up that intense pressure, working my way slowly up to a second climax. It was a slow build, but watching her squeal and scream underneath my thrusting tool was helping. Oh, it helped so much.

She knocked her head on my floor as she bucked and writhed, and I could tell she was desperate for me to cum again but too weak to even beg. I'd fucked the model to the point of oblivion, and she was left with nothing more than a stupid grin on her face.

Finally, after pounding her little pussy raw, I worked myself up to my second climax. My balls tightened, and I could feel the fire of release travel up my thick shaft as it swelled within her. Until finally... finally...

I hilted into her once more, arched my back and let loose another thick flood of creamy, virile seed. I flooded that young model's cunt with so much of my man milk it could no longer all fit in there with my dick, and I made a mess of her loins.

Finally, I stopped, my dark-haired chest heaving as I looked down at her, exhausted and weary.

And as I stilled, I could see that her smile had changed from that dopey, post-climatic smile to a more serious grin. She lifted her head from the floor, bringing her lips to mine and swiping her tongue along the seam of our mouths.

"Thanks, stud," she purred, though there was still that exhaustion there. I'd gotten the better of her, she just didn't want to admit it. But I could hear the unspoken promise. She'd be back for more.

FERTILE CELEBRITY: ZOE

*B*ook Themes:
Cuckolding, Breeding, and Impregnating Creampies
Word Count:
5,122

I'D GONE to every one of her movies, even the romantic comedy ones that made me roll my eyes, just so that I could see her again. We'd fallen out of touch over the fifteen years after graduating high school, but she'd always be my first love, my high school sweetheart. Until she moved away to pursue her acting career, and I went off to law school. We'd tried to make it work, but it all fell apart.

Now she was married to a gorgeous hunk, and I'd read on one of those slimy magazine covers that they were going to try for a baby. All the world's eyes were on them, tabloids angling into every bit of their business.

So maybe I shouldn't have been so bowled over when

she called me and asked me to meet her in person. She was flying into New York for a shoot, and we'd still kept in touch on social media, after all.

But when she asked me to do her and her husband a favour?

And that favour involved having unprotected sex with her, to knock her up and let the world figure that it was her husband's baby?

Well, second chances come in weird ways, and I couldn't say no.

I DID my best to not seem desperate, of course. Didn't jump at her request – her plea – for me to knock her up right then and there. I instead said I'd think about it and that we'd meet up again that evening. Fair enough.

Of course, by the time that evening came, I was dying to blow a load in my old crush. I showed up at the hotel in a nice business suit, but ditched the tie in my car. Of course, I wanted to look more casual after leaving the office. Besides, it was her that came to me for help now. Not like the days long ago when I was salivating after her through high school, but could never impress her enough to be only mine, for good.

Since then I'd kept in shape: early morning workouts with some of the partners were not only healthy but a good networking potential. So my shoulders were broad and built, my biceps and torso filled out well. I was a catch, which is why I never settled down into a long term thing with one woman; I figured I'd use my prime years to look around, have fun.

Besides, I didn't want some gold digger coming along and spoiling my future. But Zoe was no gold digger. She had fortunes amassed beyond compare, with mansions around the world.

The hotel she was staying at, though, wasn't the nicest in the city. She was trying to keep a low profile for her clandestine meeting with me, no doubt. The fact that she felt she could trust me, though? Yea, I couldn't help but be a little flattered that I'd mattered that much, even after all these years.

When she answered the door, she was dressed fairly casually in a navy dress that hugged her curves. Her skin was pale and pristine, her ruby lips so full and her eyes still wide and youthful, despite the years between when I'd first fallen for her.

She was just past 30, and yet her skin was radiant and her long, curled hair was clearly styled. She smiled as she saw me, just like she used to, with excitement and affection twinkling behind her eyes as she let me in.

"I'm so glad you decided to come back, Alex," she said with a respectful bow of her head, all cordiality.

Of course I'd come back. Knocking up my high school crush / movie star topped my list of desires. Even if at the end of it she went home to her husband on the other side of the country.

"I can't leave you hangin'," I said as I stepped on into her hotel room, a smile on my face as I took it in. It certainly wasn't the nicest, but it was far from the worst hotel room either. After a quick survey of the black and grey, modern-style furnishings, I smiled back at her.

"Funny to think of us together after all these years," I remarked, looking her over casually. "I'm glad you thought of me when this problem came up," I said, which was honest enough. I was glad.

Just maybe not for all the same reasons she hoped for.

She brought me further into the room, and there was a

bottle of wine, chilled on ice, and she gave a lopsided smile that had always endeared me.

"I don't really know how to go about this, so I figured... Wine's always the best way," Clarissa said. "Would loosen us up a little."

I plucked the bottle of wine out of the ice and looked it over, seemed an expensive label, not that I was an expert. Though when you deal with fancy clients, you learn to fake it. I plucked up the glasses and helped myself to pouring us up some, handing her one and taking my own.

"To old friends," I said in a toast, holding out my glass to her.

She raised her glass to mine, a little too eager to drink it back, but she looked more relaxed even before the alcohol could pollute her system. Just the act alone seemed to calm some of her frayed nerves.

"God, crazy how things have changed," she said, looking me over with, what I thought to be, appreciation. Couldn't help but feel my ego puff up a little bit at that.

I topped her glass off for her again as we took a seat upon the edge of the bed.

"It's a lot of time between now and then," I said, reaching over and patting my hand atop her knee, rubbing over her thigh just a little. "We were just kids then, only starting to come into our own. There's been college, career and movies that have changed us both since then," I said with a smile. "Which you've been great in, I might add," I said to her with a warm smile, enjoying her scent so close as I was.

She let out a soft laugh.

"I didn't figure you'd have seen any of them. Wasn't... I mean, I didn't want to hope they might be your thing. They've all meant a lot to me," she said with such sincerity as her face lifted to mine, her large eyes sparkling.

"You look really good," she finally managed. "I'm not just saying that."

"Thank you," I responded with a smile, tracing my hand down over my shirt, which only served to highlight the hard pecs and abs just beneath. "And I saw every one of your movies," I confessed with a shrug, drinking some of my own wine. "Even the ones that weren't very manly of me to go see," I jested with a half-cocked smirk. "You made them all worth it. As fine an actress as there is, more beautiful than your high school days by far."

The giggle she had was still the same, the modest way she lowered her eyes. I guess beyond the bright lights of Hollywood, she was still a person, just like before. Still a little uncertain, a little shy, she just learned to fake it for the cameras and the media.

But now she was alone with me, asking a favour, and she went back to the girl I'd dated in high school.

Her hand rest atop mine on her knee, looking at me with such affection.

"I hope this won't be weird," she said gently.

"Maybe a little," I said with a wink then downed the rest of my own glass before laying it aside on the night stand. "But hey, it was weird just dating all those years ago. Because we were new to the whole thing. New to our changing selves. That's life, weird new circumstances that you just get used to," I said, so confident and assured. Ten years of law had taught me how to be confident and in control, even when standing among a sea of hostile faces.

Compared to the prosecution and jury, my old crush, come back to beg my help, hardly seemed like a challenge. So I squeezed her knee and rubbed her thigh a little as I leaned into her.

"You were really great in that last movie," I said, the sex

scene foremost in my mind at that point, though I tried to will it away.

Her skin warmed against my hand, her slender legs parting just slightly as she took another sip of her wine. It certainly wasn't enough liquor to alter her actions, but it was enough to relieve some of that tightness between her shoulders, making her look at me with just slightly lidded eyes.

"You watch it in theatres?"

"Yeah," I said, nodding my head slowly as my arm wound around her, rubbed at her shoulder. My grasp was strong, and she was dainty, that Hollywood movie star frame of hers so delicate in my grasp as I worked the tension from her. "Though you make it all feel so personal... so intensely romantic, it feels almost feels scandalous watching you in public like that," I teased with a smile, leaning in and touching my lips to her cheek with a soft kiss.

She giggled again, though it was laced with nerves, anxiousness, affection. She nibbled on her lower lip, glancing up at me from the corner of her eyes. She'd always been a good girl in high school, dating around but never going all the way. I'd only ever got to second base with her before, and I couldn't deny the thought of finally fucking her, raw, was exciting.

My hand travelled up her thigh, and I couldn't help myself, I just leaned in and placed my lips to her neck. I kissed her, suckled at her neck just a little as I squeezed her body to mine. I didn't want to spend all night warming into it, easing into the mood. I wanted her bad, and I wanted that spark to flare up.

I rubbed my hand over her back as I felt her out, her slender body pressed up against my hard muscles. I wanted to feel in her some of the desire she had for me.

She gasped at my kiss, but instead of recoiling, she moved closer.

Sure, kissing her wasn't part of the deal, not that we'd really hashed out a list of things I could and couldn't do. The only stipulation was that I'd fuck her, raw, and hopefully knock her up.

And that I'd, at the very least, spend the night to see her off in the morning as well. Didn't want to miss an opportunity.

So maybe she'd been a bit shocked at my kiss, the way my tongue grazed across the surface of her flesh, tasting her. It certainly sent a shiver down her body, her nipples stiffening beneath her dress.

My hand travelled up from her thigh, on over her body to cup at her breast. I could feel that nipple prod against my palm as I felt her up, let my fingers sink into her supple flesh, feel her out as I kissed my way up her neck to her ear. I suckled at her lobe, tugged upon it as my body pressed to hers, slowly pushing her back towards the bed.

I wanted her bad, and already that fact was plainly clear by the bulge in my groin. My cock was rock solid, and I wanted to be inside her desperately.

She set aside the empty wineglass, her eyes upon me and I could only describe her gaze as smoldering. She was shy, sure. Reserved, a little. But her legs spread softly, as if I wouldn't notice, and her lips dropped open and let out a little whimper as I kissed and nipped her neck and ear.

How long had I dreamed about doing this? Yet never, no matter how wild they got, did I think she'd call me up, asking me to bang her raw, get her pregnant with my seed. That was out of the realm of even my fantasies, yet it was quickly becoming my reality.

For years I'd been so careful with girlfriends, never wanting to be stuck with a kid I didn't want. Always packing condoms despite my urges to trust in the pill and enjoy some raw sex. But now I got to have it, and better yet… I'd get to knock her up and not worry about the consequences.

My hand slid back down from her breast to her leg, I rubbed over her smooth thigh, then on up underneath her dress, my grasp tightened about her hip, thumb rubbing inwards. I was just dying to get in between her legs, and I felt out the source of her feminine heat.

"God," she muttered, her head rolling back into the pillow, her body arching upwards, breasts thrust into to air as her legs spread further for me. She was already so damn wet, her panties soaking, and I rubbed them into her, making her writhe beneath me. That shyness was quickly fading away as she moaned, and it was such a familiar sound from her movies. I wondered how into it she got, all those people watching as she pretended to get fucked.

I guess I'd soon find out how good her acting really was.

I rose up over her, looking down at her beautiful body, face so flush, watching her writhe as I rubbed her cunny. I rolled my shoulders back and slowly slipped off my jacket before I began to work open my shirt. I'd let her appreciate my body, how well I'd taken care of myself in the years since we'd last been together.

My shirt came off and then I reached up beneath her dress, to hook my fingers into her panties and slowly peel them away from her quim and off her legs. I gave them a toss onto the nightstand, letting them hook around my wine glass as I got back over her, my black pants bulging with my desire.

Her hands kept trailing over me, manicured nails teasing my skin as her legs spread, wider and wider until I was able to comfortably fit between them. Her dress pulled up, I could see the perfectly smooth slit, the dainty little labia as her sex parted for me, the petals already so damp.

She smelled clean and fresh, and she even flushed as she saw me looking at her prized pussy, the thing I'd thought about while beating off on more than one occasion, and it was even better than I could have imagined.

I reached down and undid the buckle of my pants, ignoring the look of appreciative awe on her face as she stared at my chest. I tugged open the belt, then undid the pants below before shimmying out of them and my boxers.

When my rock hard dick sprang free, I could see the look of surprise on her face. I was big, my cock so veiny and pulsating. It was a good looking dick. I knew that. I'd had enough girlfriends be impressed to know it was true. And now I was angling my hips down to nudge against her slick petals, to tease her honeyed quick with my thick fuckrod.

Her gaze kept following my cock, though, not tilting back and pretending like I was her husband. She was staring with desire, licking her lips as her inhibitions slowly melted away. I supposed she somewhere along the line decided that if she was going to sleep with someone not her husband, she was going to enjoy it, because she pressed her breasts up from under the dress, squeezing her left tit as she watched me tease her cunny.

I was happy to oblige, because it was a dream come true for me. The girl of my dreams, mine at last. If only for a night.

I brought the bulging, purple tip of my cock on up to the apex of her slit, teased her clit and made her shiver. That was so very satisfying, and I worked my dick on down again, slowly sinking my loins into her pussy. The sight of those puffy labia blossoming around the crown of my cock before swallowing me up as I sank on in was gorgeous. I got carried away with it all, and thrust the rest in, the two of us watching my veiny shaft vanish into her slick, honeyed canal immediately.

"Oh God," she gasped, but never did she tear her eyes away as I impaled her upon my thick shaft, spreading her open so lewdly.

Her hand squeezed her breast harder, shivering in delight as she ground against me, her pussy so tight and wet. It was like a perfect little sleeve, and she was already desperate for me, her breathing becoming quicker, her nails digging half-moons into her firm chest.

I reached up, pulling down the shoulder strap of her dress to expose her other tit to my gaze. Grasping hold of that fleshy, supple mound, I only then began to pump into her. Rocking my strong hips to tug my cock from her tight little cunny, only to then thrust it back in. Though honestly, the tight pull of her depths helped there. I barely felt like I could tug back a few inches without her grip hauling me back in.

I found myself moaning uncontrollably, my cock throbbing inside her as I looked down upon her beautiful form. Damn, she truly was more gorgeous than ever.

Especially with how into it she seemed. Maybe she'd just been nervous, shy at first, about needing my help. Needing to rely on her old high school flame to come and knock her up.

But now that I was deep within her, fucking her just right, her body came alive and she writhed for me.

"Oh God, Alex," she moaned my name. "God, I couldn't stop thinking about this."

If one of us were to confess that, I thought it'd be me. To hear her say it? Surreal. But it only fueled my passions, made me fuck her harder, faster. Pound my hips down into her. We weren't kids anymore, we were grown up and ravenous, and I wasn't going to hold back.

The slap of my balls against her ass resounded, filling the room as I groaned and pounded harder. Harder. My fingers sank into her breast and I clenched its supple curve so tightly as I enjoyed its feel.

"Fuck," I cursed aloud. "I've dreamt of making you my fuck toy for so damn long!" I said in a husky, groaning voice.

Some women might have been put off on that, but not Clarissa. No, her legs just kept crawling higher upon my hips until I was forced to grab both of them, putting them over my shoulders and letting me ram in deeper, harder, battering against her cervix as her tits jiggled.

She was screaming beneath me, warbled cries of pleasure and desire. It was crazy how fast she'd gone from a reserved and closed off woman to this absolutely out of control slut upon my dick, but I was grateful for the fact.

I ran my hand over her body, appreciating every little curve of her form, sliding across her taut tummy, then down. I let my thumb dip, teasing her clit as I bucked harder, harder. I could feel my balls slowly beginning to tighten, my loins on fire as I approached my climax. I wanted so bad to blow my load, but I was committed to making her cum first. Or cum right with me.

"Cum on my dick," I commanded her. "Cum on it just like you should've years ago," I said in a husky voice, so rough and full of lust.

She let loose such a moan at the touch, her entire body bucking against me, and her heat only growing at my words. She could barely keep her eyes opened, but she wanted so badly to watch as I impaled her sweet little pussy again and again.

"Oh God," she hissed once more, grabbing her breast so

hard that flesh dimpled between her fingers, her lips trembling. "God, I want you to knock me up," she groaned, and those words made her quiver even harder. Apparently they'd sent a prominent jolt of excitement through her, since she didn't stop.

"Just breed me like some dumb slut," she gasped, and another jolt went through her, making her hips buck. "Make me yours."

Her enthusiasm – her raw vulgarity – did me in. Oh sure, I had started it, tipped her over the edge with my own dirty talk, but hearing her reciprocate? I lost it. I hammered into her, pounded her body as I let loose such a loud roar of desire. My balls unleashed a fiery pleasant sensation, travelling up my thick, pulsating shaft until I was shooting my thick, creamy load of virile seed deep into her.

"Take it," I told her amid my bucking, my hard body tensing and clenching, muscles twitching. I was shooting my cum deep into her as I worked her clit with my thumb so desperately. I needed her to cum with me, wanted it so bad...

"My little knocked up movie star slut," I called her upon my groaning, satisfied voice.

And those words, more than anything, got her to that explosive tipping point. She didn't hold back, wasn't a meek little mouse squeaking out her pleasure. Nor was she the all seductive moans and groans as she was on the movie screen.

No, instead, she was shrieking and writhing, her hair a mess and her face contorted and red.

She wasn't holding anything back, not at all, as she gushed along my dick.

That warm flood of feminine honey across my dick, and running on down over my balls, was so satisfying.

Nothing between us, nothing separating our pleasure, nothing in the way. Just my dick, blasting her fertile womb with my cum.

Ohh, it was so very sweet. The finest moment in my life, better than making the bar, getting promoted at my firm, or winning a big case. Much better than any time I'd fucked a woman before.

I rocked my hips, milking out every last drop of my cum into her depths as I groaned, reaching a hand up to grasp at her breast and fondle it affectionately.

"Good girl," I husked, then repeated it. My hard body glistening before her gaze with a light sheen of perspiration.

She whimpered and writhed, her mind emptied of all thoughts as she stared in a blissful daze. Her beautiful lips were parted, her hips still grinding against me as little panted breaths escaped her, making her breast jiggle in my hand as her pussy twitched against my sensitive, spent dick.

WE WENT AGAIN, and drank wine until we passed out in a sweaty heap at some point during the night. I awoke the next day, the two of us nude, and laying in bed with the sheets an utter mess. But there she was still… sound asleep and so ravishing.

She wouldn't be staying much longer, but I knew I had to have her more. She was flying out that very day, off to another movie shoot. And I wanted to leave her with that baby in her belly.

I brushed the hair back from her lovely face, and very gingerly – without waking her – I turned her onto her back, and very softly parted her legs. She was damp, I felt it right away as I cupped her sex. And I wasted no time.

I got up, rock hard with my morning wood, and got between her thighs.

I moved so slow, pressed to her so gently, she didn't wake up until I was already pressing down into her and moaning hoarsely.

"Ah," she whimpered, not having expected to wake up to a cock impaling her, taking her already in her groggy state, and though she tensed for a second, she instantly stilled. The room stank of sex, her body laced with my scent, and she pressed her firm loins towards me.

"Alex," she groaned, without even opening her eyes, and already her body was slickening further for me, responding in such a lewd manner.

"I'm going to knock you up before you leave this room," I pledged to her, my voice raw and rough in my early morning state. It added an edge to my words, making them so much harsher, more commanding.

My hands grasped her legs, fingers sinking into her soft thigh flesh as I began to pump. I stuffed her tight cunt full of my cock, again and again, stretching out her narrow little canal as I moved, making the bed creak beneath us with the motions.

"My sweet lil' Clarissa," I husked appreciatively, the smacks of our bodies together rising up higher, higher.

She moaned such a beautiful little song, her voice almost purring from the sleep.

"Yes," she whimpered, her back arching as she lifted her hips towards me, making me hit her so deeply with that stiff wood. "Fuck, yes."

She must have been sore, that pretty little pussy red and swollen, but she didn't act like it. She was too lusty for me, desperate to take my cock.

I didn't take it easy on her, I gave it to her with all I got, pounding her. Wanting to make her remember her time with me for as long as possible, make the sting of our long, repeated rutting linger in her mind as she found out she was pregnant. Make my breeding of her a mark on her flesh as well as her life.

My dick throbbed inside her, stretching her out as I bent back her legs and made her tits jiggle atop her chest.

"Fuck, you're such a gorgeous lil' beauty, Clarissa. I'm gonna breed you such a beautiful lil' baby," I growled.

Even without me touching that sensitive little clit, she whimpered and a thrill went through her, pussy vibrating around me. My words had such an effect on her, and she bit down on her lower lip to silence a loud scream.

But she couldn't stay quiet for long, before she closed her eyes and said such filthy things. "Yea, you better knock me up." Her legs curved around my ass. "Cum in me nice and deep."

The sweet little girl I knew back in high school, now a beautiful movie star, saying such filthy things to me as I tried to knock her up. It was the stuff of boyish dreams.

I grasped hold of her two hips, lifted her body up off the bed as I pounded away. I put my strength to good use, reminding her of my raw power, hammering in nice and deep as I moaned aloud. Again my hard, ripped abs and pecs glistened with a thin sheen of perspiration, and I groaned loudly.

"C'mon," I growled at her. "Milk my dick of every drop of cum… earn my seed, you desperate lil' slut!"

She cried out as her pussy muscles tightened around me, so obediently. She was really working for my cum, desperate for it, and her entire body was writhing and bucking as she sought it out. I was seeing her the way no one ever could on the big screen, her hair dishevelled, her face bare of makeup and lighting, absolute pleasure contorting her features. Never would they allow her to be seen so raw, but I committed it to memory, knowing I could relive it again and again.

She was going to fly out of my life again soon, but not before I shook her world, I determined.

I looked down across her body, over the soft, supple curves of her feminine form, on down to the place where my hard, muscle-ripped body hammered into her. Those puffy folds of hers swallowing up my cock as I thrust on in, again and again. Hammering away as my balls smacked her ass cheeks, so laden with cum that awaited its chance at knocking her up.

I didn't need a picture or video of that to emblazon it in my memory forever. I'd never forget that gorgeous sight. And just seeing it made my dick throb and swell, stretching her out.

"Fuck! I'm gonna cum in this tight lil' pussy of yours again Clarissa," I growled out. "And then I'm gonna see you on all the news, swollen with child... and know it's mine, you desperate lil' slut."

And it was with my words that she screamed, her body spasming against me, pulling towards my own inevitability. Her cries were enough to wake the neighbourhood, as electric fire ripped through her, her body jerking and tightening against mine.

Her body spasmed and squeezed about me, and I found my thrusts hitting their own ragged end. I was pulled into her tight, fertile body and my dick was drained dry once more. I couldn't suppress the deep groans, the satisfied grunts as I twitched and bucked, pumping the full load of creamy jism straight into her.

I was packing a big, thick load of virile seed, and I was dumping it all in as deep as I could, right into her womb.

That high was a feeling I could never forget, but seemed impossible to ever hope to match again.

Especially not as she looked up at me, with a mix of lust, affection, and raw, animal need in her expression. She was spent, but that teasing little smirk, that way she licked her lips...

I knew she wasn't going to disappear from my life now.

I HAD ONLY JUST FINISHED READING an article about her. Seeing a picture of her on the award's show runway, her beautiful black gown swollen by a child in her belly. It was a sight that took me away, reminded me of our time together in that hotel room. Made me pang for her again.

But before the pang could become sadness, a call came through on my phone.

"Hello," I answered simply, not recognizing the number. But then, she never stuck with the same phone for long, not with how paparazzi kept cracking celebrity's personal devices.

"I want to see you again. Soon," she confessed immediately, that voice unmistakable. I couldn't help but grin.

FERTILE FIRST TIME TOURIST

Book Themes:
 Barely Legal, Breeding, and Virgin
 Word Count:
 5,469

~

Parents, what a drag.

I'm done with high school and suddenly I'm expected to pack up and ship out to some Ivy League college, to compete with eggheads and boring blabber mouths. A whole bunch of dull try-hards. Sounds like hell, if you ask me.

But my parents didn't ask me. Okay, well they did. But for once they didn't listen. And so here I am, facing the prospect of flying across the country to do yet more school work in just a couple months.

I couldn't imagine a bigger downer for my summer vacation.

And that was how I managed to get a simple vacation out of them.

Somewhere nice, somewhere hot, somewhere Caribbean.

Mom and dad were both busy with business meetings all summer, so they couldn't take me. That meant that they would only agree to let me go on my own, if it was somewhere safe, and I got a full time tour guide. I agreed — reluctantly! — but when they said they were sending me to Cuba because it was so safe, I didn't know what to make of it. Isn't that where communist terrorists come from or something?

Well, if it was, it sure didn't stop it from being beautiful. Because from the moment I started flying over it, I was impressed. And I don't easily impress, trust me.

Landing down and going through customs was a bore, but then on my way out of the airport... there he was.

You see, my parents insisted on a full time tour guide, but I got to pick him myself. And I looked around online, and found the perfect one.

Romy.

Pictures didn't do the man justice. And neither did the endless reams of gushing — frankly fangirling — reviews left by countless women for him. It was easy to see why such a massive hunk was so popular.

The heat when I arrived was intense, but Romy stood there in a white button down shirt, gently flowing in the breeze, with a pair of khakis on. Simple, right? Except that white shirt was practically see-through, and what was there to see was worth it. Bulging pecs and abs, a hard body to just die for. With dark hair, and handsome good looks like out of a movie, Romy trampled all expectations.

"Miss Julia?" he said, his voice tinged with such delightful accent as he flipped his sunglasses up and revealed his sparkling, dark eyes. "I am Romy, your personal guide."

I'd originally looked for someone who didn't speak English — better to be seen than heard, right? — but with his reviews, well, I figured I could shut him up easily enough.

Though now I didn't want him to stop.

"That's me!" I said with a flirty flip of my hair that I knew drove guys wild. I had a nickname in school, one no one dared call me to my face, but I knew it anyways.

Cocktease.

I actually loved it.

It was what I was.

What I still am.

Romy had a way of making even the most adamant cocktease want to give in though.

"More lovely than mere pixels can convey," he said, reaching out to take my hand in both of his, the smooth hard skin of his fingerpads so delightfully well-kept yet masculine. The smell of some sort of coconut-y aftershave upon him, but oh so light.

"I hope your flight was pleasant. Or at least as pleasant as flights can be," he remarked, his voice husky and deep, but so beautifully lyrical in that Caribbean accent of his.

I couldn't have been more pleased with my choice, especially as he pressed his plush lips to the back of my hand.

He was a few years older than me, but definitely in his prime.

He had no idea what I had in store for him.

For us.

"Come with me, I'll take us to the hotel, you'll love it, I promise," he said, and I believed him. He had a way about him that made a woman want to trust him after all.

I was told that Cuba was all old fashioned cars, and that sounded awful to me. But when we got to his vehicle, it was actually shiny and modern, very comfortable. He put my things into the trunk, and then offered me a seat inside. It was a two-seater, very swanky with a convertible roof. I'd tell you the name of the car, but I don't know dick about them, hun, sorry.

The sun shone down so bright and lovely as he drove us along the coast, the heat would've easily been too much for me but there was always a lovely breeze off the ocean adding to the wind that whipped by.

We chatted on the way, those beautiful lips of his having no shortage of interesting things to say. He told me all about his life on the island, growing up. And while I usually nodded off during such things, I actually wanted to know more about Romy's life.

The hotel itself was pretty nice, in Havana itself, not in one of those touristy resorts everyone else was going to. I'd heard all the resorts were filled with nothing but stuffy old tourists, and who wants a vacation like that? The hotel was an older style, well kept. Though everything was looking so much sunnier with Romy guiding me along.

He took my things up to my room for me and I got a glimpse of the large, spacious area, and the big king sized bed. There was a balcony overlooking the ocean, and the sight was delightful.

"I hope you approve," he remarked, placing my luggage down and showing me about the place. "I picked this all out for you myself," he said, and it's true. I hired him to look after all the details of my trip for me.

My parents spared no expense, not after how much I pleaded and begged and bargained. If they wanted me to do well in College, I argued, I had to be well rested and prepared.

So the hotel was likely one of the best in the city, but I still looked around it like I was used to nicer things and places. I didn't want Romy to get too swollen of a head. Not yet.

"Oh, it'll do fine."

The smile he gave me held a sparkle, and it was like he could read right through me and see I was more than approving of it all.

"If you are hungry," he remarked, opening the balcony doors open wide, "I can have food brought up, or we could go downstairs and eat. Or I could even show you some lovely spots to dine around town. I know all the best, either way," he boasted.

"Oh... I suppose I might as well have a taste of the town," I said. Even though I was practically starving by that point, he made his knowledge of the town sound so intimate, I just wanted to rush out and see what he had to show me.

The streets of Havana were beautiful, old fashioned but lively and well kept. The kind of thing I probably wouldn't have appreciated if not for the handsome man guiding me down the streets to the lovely restaurant overlooking the historic city.

Everything was so tall, but it wasn't like home. The side streets were narrow and filled with people and colour, and the main streets were flooded with noise. Beautiful, shiny cars drove by in outlandish colours that would've been gaudy if it didn't seem to fit in with the city so well.

A bunch of schoolgirls in blue rushed ahead of us, glancing back at Romy and giggling before they took off down a side street. Some people glanced at us as we walked at a leisurely pace that I wasn't quite used to but it seemed that was how everyone walked. Leisurely.

To get to the restaurant itself, we had to climb these

winding, narrow stairs, and I thought for a moment on how strange it seemed. But once we got to the top, it was a beautiful place. Old fashioned but classy, with a live band and some other, well-to-do tourists sitting down with locals, talking, enjoying drinks and good looking food.

"I think you should try the special," Romy said to me, nodding with a smile to the manager or owner before guiding me to a table and pulling out the seat for me. "I hope you eat meat," he asked, "because the pork here is excellent."

I wasn't a very adventurous eater, truly. Though something in me made me not want to admit that. Which was, honestly, a first. Usually everyone knew how I felt just as soon as I did.

I brushed some of my straight, blonde hair behind my ear, looking at him. Just drinking him in.

What my parents didn't know, was that I had a plan. A plan so that I never had to go to school again.

I smiled seductively at Romy. "I'm sure it'll be fine."

He ordered for me and the meal was delightful, the drinks delicious, the music so calming and pleasant. Yet it was the company that truly made the evening special.

"I have a confession to make," Romy said, smiling at me across the table as we savoured our drinks as the sun slowly made its way to setting.

"What's that?" I asked, batting my long, curved lashes at him as I tilted my head back, letting my blond hair slip away from my slender neck a little.

"You are far younger and more beautiful than my usual clientele, Julia. By leaps and bounds unmeasurable," he said before raising his mojito to me in toast.

I couldn't help but feel smug at that, and I let the top of my foot graze against his calf as if by accident.

"Oh really, Romy?" I purred, leaning in and letting my shirt fall away from my chest a little bit.

He held my gaze for a moment, but then very casually let his eyes dip down. The way he took a peek at my breasts made it feel as if he wasn't letting me get away with pretending to be so casual about it. It was like he turned the tables on me with but a few simple facial expressions. Pulling me out of my hiding spot to gaze at me with such casual interest.

"Luscious and ravishing," he stated so calmly in that smooth, charming voice of his.

His accent made it sound even more exotic, and he certainly had a way with words that none of those dumb boys at school could ever dream of. He was way too calm and in control.

And that excited me.

My lip quirked into a smile and I watched him for a moment. "Thank you," I said before taking my straw back into my mouth, finishing off the rest of my drink.

We were walking on out, through the darkening streets of Havana when I had to put my arms about his for support. The drinks had been so strong, stronger than I was used to, but any excuse to cling to his muscular arm for support was welcome.

I could feel the bulge of his muscles, the veins rising up on his flesh. He was so well sculpted, nothing just for show about this hunk of a man.

"We could go enjoy some of Habana's night life," he remarked, looking to me from the corner of his gaze. "But maybe your trip here has been long enough already, and you could use some rest. Tomorrow I am going to take you into the jungle, after all. Show you a beautiful spot in the mountains that you will just adore."

But the salsa music was already spilling out onto the

streets, and I could feel it in my hips, my bones. I wanted an excuse to get close to him.

It wasn't that I needed to seduce him. I knew what guys were like. If I'd asked him to take me back to the hotel and bone me without a condom, he totally would. Probably wouldn't even be bothered that I was still a virgin.

No, wanting to dance with him had nothing to do with him and everything to do with me.

"Naw, let's go dance!"

Romy looked at me with a wry smirk, some mild surprise on his face at my sudden brazenness.

"Dance you say?" he remarked, and I thought for a moment he might try to talk me out of it. But instead, he guided me off our path and took me down a different road. "I know just the club," he said with a smile.

It wasn't hard to tell where he was taking me, the lights and sounds of the club were apparent from far away. The beautiful music and gorgeous people spilling out into the streets even, as we approached. It was such a remarkable place!

Again, Romy seemed to know people, the man at the door let us both pass with barely a word, just some friendly hand gesture between the two of them. We headed on in, the thrum of the music and the sights of so many stunning, scantily clad people grinding, swaying and cutting amazing moves all around us.

It was unlike anything I'd ever seen, and the music was already thrumming in my veins, making me feel so hot in all the right ways. Like I was invincible.

I dragged him towards the small, free spot on the dance floor, my soft hand in his before I tugged him in. My arms wrapped around his neck, and instantly my hips started swaying.

I knew I had a good body. My parents paid for a

personal trainer for me since I was fourteen, and I didn't skimp or cheat.

If you ever met Helga, you wouldn't either. She was an Amazonian woman, and mean as they come, but she whipped my ass into perfect shape.

The perfect shape for Romy's big hands to cup and gently squeeze, which was exactly what he helped himself to as we began to dance. The handsome, smiling man showing no sheepishness in holding me so personally, and for a moment I debated whether it was just the hot Latin nature of the place, or if it was all him and his charming bravado.

Either way, worked for me!

He certainly showed no lack of moves on the dance floor, his ripped body moving with such ease and masculine grace.

"You dance well," he said to me with a smile. "Especially for such a pretty, fair girl from away," he tacked on playfully.

I was letting myself fall for him. Really fall for him. Forcing those barriers down as I enjoyed the music pumping through our veins.

I pressed my breasts into his hard chest, looking up at him with a devilish smirk.

"That's not all I do well," I taunted, though honestly, the furthest I'd gone with a guy was hand stuff.

Romy didn't know that though, and he grasped hold of my hips and spun me about, sliding one hand up to grasp mine before pulling me back in against him. We moved with the music, our bodies twisting and turning, until my rear was pressed up against his groin, and we were grinding so shamelessly in the middle of the club.

So shamelessly that Romy made not an effort to hide

the thick bulge that quickly grew to a full — and startlingly impressive — size against my two cheeks.

I even swear I heard a low groan over the sound of the music.

And I know I said it wasn't for him, and it wasn't. But his reaction, that's what I needed. To know that he wanted me. Not just a little, but that he couldn't think unless he had me.

I got off on the power, on making guys want more and then pulling away.

But instead, I ground against him closer, my mouth parted as I lifted my arms up, wrapping them around him and drawing his head in towards my shoulder so that I could feel his breath on my ear.

There he was, held in thrall to me as one of his big, muscular arms went about my waist. I could feel his bulging, hard forearm press into my tummy as his fingers splayed and slid down over my mons atop my dress. He hovered his mouth so near to my skin I could feel the warm, moistness of his breath.

He felt glorious, hard, tall and broad, like a man should be. And he rocked his hips in tune with me, grinding his manhood into me as we swayed and danced. Until finally those lips of his dared brush against my earlobe, my neck. A soft, light kiss.

My tummy flipped, and I felt a tingle between my thighs. It wasn't anything explosive, but my body certainly didn't seem to care that it was *just* a kiss.

No, my body was responding like he'd just managed to find a hidden part of me, a sensitive and secret place, and open it with such expertise...

I was losing at my own game, but then, that was the plan. To let myself give in to passion, and do what felt right. What felt natural.

For once.

And Romy was the perfect man to let go with. Those big, strong hands rubbing over my flesh, soaking me all in, appreciating every inch of my body. Every little brush of his fingertips was like fire and ice, exciting and calming at once.

Before long I lost all connection with what I was doing, there were only the pleasurable sensations of our two bodies contacting, with no clear idea of where I stood, or that I was even a distinct being, separate from him. It was like we'd both just... evaporated into tingling, excited energy.

Mere moments of clarity got through, and I heard myself moan as Romy's lips tugged my earlobe into his mouth, and he suckled upon it.

It was like a warm chill went through me, my nerves responding with such eager delight.

My panties were already soaking wet, and I wanted him like I'd never wanted anyone before. My lips parted, and I panted out, gently, "Let's go."

His grip upon my hips tightened for a moment, and those strong fingers sank into my flesh right above my womanhood, slowly pulling my dress up fractions of an inch. Then finally he let go, and spun me back around, looking into my eyes with his intense gaze before he began to lead me out.

His hand was around mine as he guided me, taking me into the cool night air, which made my overheated skin tingle. No sooner than we were free and clear in the open, he put his arm around my back and pulled me close, guiding me towards the hotel.

No words passed between us, but once we were in the elevator, he pressed me up against the wall and kissed me on the lips. Hard, passionately.

He still tasted of the minty mojito, and my tongue lashed against his, hungrily. He was a skilled kisser, and his hands roamed over my body, over my clothes, and it felt like such a long ride up to the top.

My arms around his neck, we practically fell out of the elevator when it arrived on my floor, nearly crashing into a couple waiting for it. I giggled as I tugged Romy's hand, leading him into my room.

The door shut behind us, and I was suddenly glad he had the foresight to leave the balcony windows open, because I was still so hot and the cool air was helping keep me from passing out with the heat of desire.

It was mere moments before we were toppling over onto the big, king sized bed. That strong, hard body of his over me, my hands running along his broad shoulders. The swell and throb of his manhood against my cunny and lower belly as he lifted a knee and loomed over me as our lips smacked moistly.

I didn't want to tell him I was still a virgin and give him cause to stop or slow down, but at the same time, I was a little worried. Would it hurt?

But those thoughts were quickly swept away as his hand cupped my breast, squeezing it firmly and not treating it like a radio dial. He was paying attention to the whole mound, and that just brought my arousal to the next level.

"Fuck me," I begged him, my voice low with lust.

His lips moved from mine, making their way on down my neck as I arched it out to the side. He undid his shirt all the while, so that his white cotton top came undone, and his dark tanned flesh was bare for my wandering hands to appreciate. To feel the smooth skin and its light peppering of dark hairs.

He raised my dress up to my hips, then let his thumb

trace along my lace panties, on in towards my mound, where he traced the outline of my labia, all the way down my slit, making me mewl in response.

He was perfect.

Our child would be the cutest little thing, I just knew it.

My legs parted and my entire body flushed with heat as he revealed more and more of my skin to his gaze. The buzz of the mojito had mostly worn off, but was replaced with my lust for him. I hooked my hands in to each side of my panties, beginning to strip them down.

Romy watched my unveiling so intensely, his gaze glued to the sight of my glistening slit, licking his lips as he watched their reveal. He helped me at the end tug those panties away before reaching to his own belt. He unbuckled it, then lowered his pants, showing the large bulge of his manhood.

He knelt upon the edge of the bed on his knees, those thick, muscular thighs showing as he then reached into the waistband of his briefs and slowly peeled them away. The big, pulsating shaft that sprang free was glorious. So much bigger than any of the boys I'd played with and teased over the years.

Though before he bent over me, he reached into his pants pocket and pulled out a condom.

That was not the plan.

My brows furrowed and I placed my hand on his wrist, holding it away.

"We don't need that," I said, pulling my panties off my feet and bringing my other hand between my legs, petting myself lewdly.

He looked at my dainty hand at his wrist, then back to my eyes. He pondered for a moment, perhaps taking measure of me. But then his decision was made.

The condom was tossed aside, and he got over me, his

big, broad body suspended over mine as he leaned in for another passionate kiss. He brought his free hand to my hip, stroked his fingers on down across my thigh, until he was tugging my leg up to his hip and letting that big, beefy cock of his slide along my bare slit.

"As a warning," he said, his voice husky, deep, and ripe with desire, "I can't see me being able to pull out of you."

"Good," I purred, and I swear, I was nearly passing out with need and excitement. It felt like we'd been making out and touching one another for an eternity, and my body was on high alert. I couldn't wait to find out what it felt to have a man inside me, and I reached out, gingerly touching his hardness.

The big shaft twitched against my hand, and I could feel its pulsating hotness so distinctly. He was immense! Put all the boys I teased to shame, and I stroked back along his length gingerly, watched the glistening purple crown as it flared near my wrist.

My gentle, exploratory touches elicited a big, lusty groan from the man, and his eyes nearly shut. Instead though, he splayed my legs open wide as the pleasant air breezed on by us, and I used that big tip of his to tease at my sensitive clit.

"Mmm," he let loose in a big groan. "Your little pussy is going to look so perfect stretched around my cock, chica."

My eyes rolled back in my head and I thought I was going to pass right out. His seductive words, the way he was making me feel, it was all so good.

I moaned out loud, grinding against him wantonly. "I need you to fuck me," I said, trying to sound commanding but instead sounding so breathy and small.

It was only my first night there, and already I was splayed out, putty in Romy's hands. He took hold of my hip in one hand and angled his own torso, pointing that big, hard dick right along my cunny.

"I'll fuck you, baby," he growled out, then began to push himself into me. That thick tool stretching my cunny open wide, breaking my hymen as he let loose such a deep moan. "So goddamn tight!" he declared.

I screamed a little, because it fucking hurt like hell for a moment, even though I was so wet, so turned on. I bit down on my lower lip to try to hide a bit of my pain, but as he rammed inside of me, I couldn't help but emit a few little whimpers.

Once he was deep inside though, and my little cunny was stretched wide about his shaft, there was only the pleasure of being full for the first time in my life. Being completely whole, with a man deep inside me... it was bliss.

Romy reached his hand up to my breast, tugging down my dress to expose the supple mound and squeeze it so masterfully as he began to tug back. My narrow sleeve of a quim clung to his girth, and he groaned, but then he was soon thrusting back into me, pumping his girth inside again and again.

"So tight... so damn tight," he groaned out aloud.

"So... big," I managed to pant out in kind, my head swimming as my eyes rolled back in my head. I arched my back, pushing my breast into his hand as I took all of his cock between my spread legs. My slickness helped, after the pain ebbed, and I knew that after this, I'd be addicted.

Just watching him work at me, his body undulate as he thrust, that eight-pack of abs moving so sensually... seeing thick, corded muscle shift and bulge so gloriously. All as my body experienced every delightful bulge and throb of his organ inside me.

Each new thrust brought a slap of his heavy, cum-laden

balls against my ass, growing louder with each rougher thrust into me.

Once he warmed me up, no longer was he treating me like a delicate doll. No, he was pounding into me, making all of my body feel alive. I screamed, uncaring who might hear, as my fingernails dug into his shoulders, keeping me rooted in place against him.

The panting, moaning and screaming we made together carried out the window into the streets of Havana, but on we went. His big, beautiful form glistening with a thin sheen of perspiration, highlighting his hard musculature as he pounded me into the lush mattress.

This man I'd only met a few hours before, was taking me so passionately all on my parent's dime. It was intense, and I couldn't help but reach out a hand and rub it all over his bulging, muscular chest, adoring the grooves of his sinew.

He felt amazing, and I clung to him, my legs wrapping around his back and clinging to the cusp of his ass, forcing him in deeper. Letting our bodies grow hot and sticky against one another as I lost all rational thought and simply succumbed to the illicit, exquisite pleasure.

"You feel so good," I whimpered.

He growled out his words, "So do you," and brought his hand from my thigh up to my hip. His thumb reached in, and with an expert touch he began to circle and prod at my clit, stoking my fires higher, bringing me closer to true bliss.

His balls tightened, and he pounded me harder, faster, building up to a bigger frenzy.

"I'm going to cum in your little cunt," he seemed to roar. "Cum for me. Cum on my cock," he commanded.

It was... sublime. I'd never felt anything like it, and it only took seconds before that bundle of nerves started to feel strange. Tingling, the sensation growing stronger and stronger until it was like a wave crashed over me and I was lost at sea, just bucking and screaming beneath my Latin lover.

Romy pounded into me all through it, fucking me like a wild animal lost to passion. My moist cunny juices flowed about his girth and our bodies smacked with a loud, wet crash each time he hammered into me. He continued like that, stoking my fires, teasing my clit and drawing out my orgasm until finally, just as the fog of pleasure began to clear enough for me to see clearly…

I got to watch him lose himself to his own satisfaction.

He thrust in roughly, his dick spasming as he stretched my pussy wider. Loud moans bursting from his lips as he abruptly began to spew his load. Thick gouts of virile seed firing deep inside me as he thrust in to the hilt and coated my womb in his cum.

He knew just as well as I did the risks we were taking, the risks we both wanted to take, in part.

My toned legs tightened around his ass as he came, holding him into me so that he couldn't try to pull away.

I bit down on his shoulder, muffling my cries, my sound of pleasure, against his warm, salty flesh.

His spine was arched, and he stayed imbedded in me as my pussy drained his manhood dry of every little drop of seed. He shuddered and groaned, squeezing and kneading my breast as he continued to flick my clit and make me squirm and writhe.

"Ohhh fuck yes," he husked out. "Your pussy is heavenly."

I was panting for breath, almost too sensitive for words as I licked and suckled at his flesh. He was so perfect, so exquisite, and even though my entire body was singing, I couldn't stop grinding against him, taking me to that point of explosive bliss once more.

Even as the last of his seed was milked from him into the narrow canal of my cunt, I shuddered, moaned and spasmed. His magnificent hand working my clit, bringing me to such a boil as he watched, enjoying the jiggle of my breasts, the way my face flushed a bright red at the oncoming of my second orgasm.

"Cum for me," he husked so charmingly. "Cum on my dick."

My entire body was shaking, like a vibrator, and my pussy clenched him so hard I could feel his body pulsing with life.

"Oh God," I cried out as I hit that peak again, and felt the rush go through my body, flooding his dick in my sweet juices.

He moaned and rocked his hips, grinding our bodies together as I rode out my second, intense orgasm. I was a sweaty, messy heap, and as I gazed up at my big, buff hunk of a lover... I realized my vacation had only just begun.

So that was just the start of my trip. But here I am, ready to see my parents again for the first time in a while.

Oh, there's so much more to tell about my trip, but sorry. Right now my mind is on something more dire...

"Sweetie! It's so good to see you again," mom says, and dad comes in for a hug.

"How's college?" dad asks.

"Are you doing well?" mom chimes in, the barrage of questions endless.

"I need to drop out," I say, and their faces look horror-stricken.

"You can't!" mom cries.

"You've barely even started!" dad protests.

But now I'm reaching down, cradling my stomach with one hand, and the tiny swell there as I whip out the test stick in the other hand.

"I can't stay. I'm preggers," I say, and lord help me, I can't help but smirk a little despite the aghast look on their faces.

FERTILE FIRST TIME WITH A BAD BOY BIKER

Book Themes:
Breeding, Barely Legal, Virgin, and Bad Boy
Word Count:
6,576

~

Makeup wasn't somethin' I had a lot of opportunity to practice with back home. Livin' in the middle of farm country meant there weren't a lot of chances to buy any makeup, and certainly not the kind I really wanted to try. Just the corner store sellin' a couple sticks of red lipstick, one sort of eyeliner.

So the moment I got my chance to head on to the big city… well, I went a little wild.

I found myself givin' in to some crazy desires, not just makeup, but clothes too. I bought a whole new outfit right away, and once I'd got myself all dolled up in my new attire, well… I was a little surprised by how well it turned out.

The old me, with the red pigtails and country tan could hardly be seen. Now it was lots of blacks and pale skin from a long winter spent in school and hospital. It was a whole new look for me, for a whole new life.

I knew the term 'goth', but for me it was somethin' only in the abstract. A cool appearance I saw from my brief experiences with watchin' TV at my grandparents. (Our farm didn't get TV, we didn't have the hookups far out where we lived! And only solar power.)

I remember first seein' it in a show, long ago, and lovin' it. Something about it really spoke to me. And when I stumbled upon a real dark store in the big city, that sold all kinds of freaky leather and frilly goth clothes, I knew I'd found *my* style.

I knew my natural red hair looked okay, but it was more faded than I wanted, so I grabbed a bottle of Manic Panic hair dye that was called Vampire's Kiss, and after I did that, well, I looked like a whole other person. With black eyeliner and my eyebrows all thinned out and partially drawn on, and my dark purple lipstick, it was like I was my true self and also kinda hidin'. Like I was totally anonymous, and bein' myself, all at once.

I zipped up the leather corset and the short, frilly skirt, fastening the torn fishnets onto my legs, and I felt ready. Confident. Sexy.

Now all was left was to go out and put my new look to work. I'd asked the shop clerk where I could find a party, and though I still musta sounded like a total hick — judgin' by the way she gave me a sceptical once-over — she told me about a dark club not far from my new apartment. So that's where I was gonna go.

She couldn't shake me. I knew I looked good!

∽

The loud thump of the music carried down the street, and there was a flow of people comin' and going from the club. There was a bit of a lineup, but I guess I must've got the look right, or the bouncer just thought I looked good, 'cause he flagged me down before I even got to the back of the line and invited me on in.

"Go ahead sweet cheeks, no need to wait," the big fella said, even as others looked on in annoyance at my line-skippin' abilities.

Though it wasn't long before that little high was forgotten, as I saw the dark-light club in motion, so many scandalously clad bodies moving.

My knees were quakin', and I felt so out of place. Or, well, I woulda, if not for my costume. My *armour*. That made me feel a lot safer as I looked down the stairs towards the club proper. There were some little areas guarded off with some fabric, and I couldn't help but wonder what was behind them.

But first, I worked my way down the steps, one platformed boot in front of another. I just had to get to the bar, find some safety there. Then I could really drink in the place.

The music was loud, too loud, and it was so hard to hear as that heavy beat rocked through my body, the industrial sounds being remixed into a song I faintly recognized from the radio.

The place was pretty packed, at least by my naive standards, but I was able to elbow my way up to the bar, thanks to the eager shuffling of the many men that watched me approach. Their lips formed into wry little smiles as they nursed their drinks, and right away, before I could even order, one of them offered.

"Can I get you somethin', hun?" He wasn't a pretty guy,

nor a pleasant sounding one, but his charity was forthcoming.

Yet again, before I could act, another man stepped on in. This one, however, was both big and striking. Broad shouldered, clearly well built in his tight short-sleeved top, he butt in between me and the other fella, looked me over slowly then declared:

"I think this lady is a vodka gal." He looked to the barkeep, "Cranberry and vodka for the lady. Straight for me. Make it the Russian stuff, from the top shelf."

And it was as if the world bent to this dark haired man's whims.

I barely knew what to say, or what my new persona'd say, so I muttered out a, "Thank you," before I realized he probably couldn't hear me over the music. I went up on tiptoes, which was pretty hard in my heels, and shouted, "Thanks, Mister!"

And I immediately regretted it. Mister? Why'd I have to call him Mister? Why not dude or something... hipper?

I might've gotten the new costume, but I wasn't exactly equipped with the life experience to act the role, I feared.

For his part, he gave me a crooked grin, looking amused by me at least. But before anything more could be said or done, the other guy — whom he'd cut in on — grabbed his arm and tried to twist him around. But failed.

Instead the tall man grabbed the fellow's hand, twisted his thumb until he came around to face him. Though even that display of violence didn't quite deter the uglier man, who undoubtedly had a few drinks on him already.

"Hey, I was talkin' to that bitch first," the ugly fella said.

I was worried there'd be some kind of fight, and rightfully so. No sooner than the drinks were put before me, than the staredown came to an end, as the taller man head-butted the other fella, causing a spurt of blood to shoot from his nose. A swift punch to the gut then doubled him over and he grabbed the man's hair and slammed him to the bar sendin' him to the floor.

The club was so packed not a whole lot of people were aware of the fight, and fewer still knew how casually it all started, with so little instigation. The instigation being me. But still some people cried out and gasped, even heard over the music, before the tall fella looked back to me.

He rubbed a hand over his blood-spattered forehead, and wiped back his dark hair before taking up his straight vodka and knocking it back.

"Better down this thing quickly babe, you and me need to get out of here real fast," he said, giving a stern stare to the bartender and a tap of his glass, ensuring the man refilled him despite his fear.

I looked at him, then at the other man, and I didn't know what to do. It was like I was frozen in place.

I only just got here and already I was causin' issues!

It wasn't fair, but I took my drink, because I hoped it'd calm my nerves a little. Make whatever was happenin' a bit easier to swallow!

I hadn't had an experience with drinkin' by then, so I just downed the thing. And it was so smooth, I was surprised. Somehow I'd expected something worse. But then... it hit my gut. But before I could object, the bartender refilled my glass and the grinning man before me slipped a bill across the table.

"C'mon, real quick now," he urged me to down the other shot as he did his. And I saw through the crowd at least two big guys coming, and judging by the look on the handsome man's face, I could only assume they were friends of the man who was now bleeding and uncon-scious on the floor.

"Down it now babe, or I'm gonna have to bust a few

more noses on your account," he said, as if it'd all been unavoidably my fault.

I didn't think it was, and maybe I was just a sucker for anyone that talked with authority, because I drank it down just as he said. I blinked as a bit of dizziness hit me, but it tasted just like juice.

"I didn't mean to cause no trouble," I said, but I knew the music was drowning out half my words.

"You're too damn hot babe, you're trouble on a pair of sexy legs," he said, grabbing my arm and guiding me away from the bar just in the nick of time. We avoided the arrival of the other two, though a quick glance back showed me they weren't going to take long before they followed after us through the crowd.

All while I was towed along by some towering beefcake of a guy I didn't even know the name of.

The music was becoming almost suffocating, the press of the bodies around me as my fear mounted.

What was goin' on? Why'd I have to get myself into this mess? I should've just stayed home, safe and bored on the farm!

But it seemed a little late for that, as I tagged along behind that big man, in his tight black jeans and top. Though a glance behind me showed the two big men picking up their friend and then looking at us with daggers in their eyes.

I don't need to tell you they started shovin' folks out of the way as they came for us.

But through the loud music the man who held my arm pushed us on ahead.

"What's your name, babe?" he asked me over the din of noise as he guided me around to the back exit, it seemed.

"E-ember," I managed. Short for Emberlynn, but I

thought just the first part sounded more exotic and so I'd gone with that since I made the big move.

"Glad to meet'cha, Ember," he said back at me with a grin, as those three guys now were closing in on us in their hurry for revenge. "My friends call me Truck. 'Cause I hit like one," he remarked, and it wasn't hard to see that. His fists alone looked like they could crush my skull.

Though carrying on a conversation as I hurried through the crowds and out into the cool night air was difficult.

Truck paused for a moment, looked around and spotted a motorcycle. He went to it and hopped on, riding back in the seat, but tossing the helmet onto the sidewalk as he started it up with a roar.

"Now or never, Ember," he said, gesturing for me to hop on in front of him.

What in the devil was I doing?

But what choice did I have? I was being chased by those... those... thugs! At least Truck had been nice to me, but even then, I knew he was violent. I should've been so much more scared, but instead I walked up to the bike. Though then I hesitated.

"Where're you going to take me? I don't know the city..."

"Now you know me, and that's all you need to know to get by," he said so calmly, that deep, husky voice of his radiating authority as he looked to me unflinchingly.

Though the decision was made for me when the three guys came out the door, looked around and shortly thereafter found us.

"No time," Truck said, grabbing me again and pulling me onto the bike before he sped off. The three men running towards us, away from the crowd of smokers milling about the doorway.

As we started to head on by though, Truck kicked out his leg, knocking over one motorcycle, and then that toppled into another and both fell. The shouts of curses from the three men indicated it was theirs.

I couldn't stop thinking what I'd gotten myself into, and I squirmed a little under the pressure as my arms wrapped around Truck's waist. He was huge, and hard, and scary.

And I was ridin' off to who-knows-where with him.

I was sat side-saddle style, arms about his hard torso as we drove on through the city streets. The thrum of the motorcycle beneath me so very loud. Then something occurred to me...

"Why'd you toss your helmet away? And... why'd they only have two motorcycles if there was three of them?" Though even as I asked the question, the answer became apparent.

Truck laughed and revved the engine, cruising on down the streets faster. The lit up roads a mystery to me, in a city I was only just barely getting acquainted with.

"If he wanted to keep his bike he shouldn't have called you a bitch," he said with a grin, as the rumble of the engine reverberated up through me.

"This is *stolen?*" I said even though I knew the answer and didn't really want to hear it out loud. But it just came out of my lips without permission.

I wanted to leap off, but my legs were totally exposed and we were going really fast. I'd hurt myself somethin' awful if I jumped. I made my choice and had to live with it.

"It was probably stolen before I even took it, Ember, don't fret over it," he remarked so nonchalantly, tearing on down the road, taking these smooth, practiced turns. It might not have been his motorcycle, but he knew how to drive it, that was for certain.

Then I noticed we were heading into a darker neighbourhood, residential, where the street lights were broken as often as not.

"I don't know this place," I said, worry edging into my voice. What if he took me captive and killed me!

My parents warned me that would happen if I left for the big city, and I was shiverin', not just from the cold but also 'cause of the thought of him doin' somethin' horrible.

"Don't worry your pretty lil' head, Ember," he said to me as we approached this one house, with a motorcycle out front, a few people loafing about, drinking and smoking. It looked like a place people in TV shows went to buy drugs.

And it was where he pulled us up to.

"This is my pad," he declared so casually, as if that was supposed to be reassuring. Though with him coming to a stop and lifting his leg up off the bike, he pulled me from my seat and grinned down at me.

I knew I was far from my own apartment, and maybe it was the two drinks, but I gave him a small, cautious smile. I had enough money to get a cab, if I needed it, I reasoned. So maybe it wouldn't be so bad to just have another drink with him...

He reached a hand up and slid it along my neck to my chin, before some guy came rushin' up.

"Hey Truck," he said, clearly younger than the big man.

"Ditch the bike, Tommy. I'm takin' my new girl up into the house," he declared, having put a claim to me as easy as that, it seemed. He took my hand and led me on up the walkway, over the stairs as Tommy rode off as instructed.

The sound of blaring music lifted out of the house, as if another party awaited me. And judging by the bodies that milled about outside, smoking and drinking, I could imagine there were only more inside.

"Hey Truck," said one of the scandalously clad, bomb-shells outside his door. "Who's the goth?"

"Shut up," he said to her so flippantly. "She's my gal," there it was again as he led me into the house, a party defi-nitely going on, though it wasn't as packed as the club was. It more seemed like a group of friends and lovers hanging out... making themselves *quite* at home.

I didn't really like bein' claimed like I'm his pet or somethin' like that, but at the same time... I did. Or, my body did. It made my heart thump and my stomach flip with excitement or somethin'. Maybe it wasn't so bad. I'd never been to a house party before, and I had to avert my eyes from the people makin' out and grindin' on the couch, but it felt like it was bad.

And didn't I want to be a little bad?

The large living room had a bar of its own, and Truck took me over to it, giving a grunt or a nod to some of the people as they greeted him, but staying focussed. He took up a large bottle of vodka, like the stuff he'd ordered me at the club, and poured us both up a glass, this time without the cranberry juice for me.

"To livin' fast, and fun times, huh?" he said in a toast to me, grinning as we clinked glasses before he downed his and poured another up quickly thereafter.

The fresh air must've taken away a lot of the effects of the first drinks, because when I took it straight, I felt it not a minute after. A warm, soothing feeling. It hardly had any taste to it, but I could feel it as I pushed the glass away.

But when he poured me up another, I drank that back too. I didn't want him thinkin' I was a goody-goody or nothin'.

As people came up, payin' their respects to him, he seemed focussed solely on me. Restin' his hand upon my hip as he smiled and shared the vodka with me, it was clear Truck was somethin' of a leader of these hard tickets.

"You handled that situation back at the club well," he said in his deep, gravelly voice, a glint in his eyes as we drank.

I giggled.

"I didn't handle it at all. I didn't do anything. All I wanted was to go to the bar for a drink," I reminded him, and the vodka was makin' my tongue looser.

His big, strong hand rubbed and squeezed at my side, his thumb roamin' in over my belly.

"You kept your cool through it all. That's an important quality in a woman. In anyone really," he said, knocking back another vodka before topping us both up, the alcohol seeming to have no effect on the giant man. "Knew from the moment you walked in, I had to score some time with you."

I laughed, my nervousness beginning to drift away a little. Whether it was the alcohol or the fact that we were no longer running from a bunch of scary bikers, I didn't know, but whatever it was, I liked it.

"There wasn't another choice other than keepin' calm and just goin' with what needed done..."

He grinned at me as I downed my drink, leaned in and kissed at my neck, much to my surprise. His lips workin' their way up towards my ear, but no sooner than the glass was away from my lips, he moved on in and claimed 'em with a moist kiss.

My very first kiss, despite the dark look I was rockin'.

Though judgin' by how pleasant and skillful he was, it wasn't anywhere close to bein' his first.

And he felt... really, really good.

I'd never even fantasized about something feeling so good. It affected me from my lips right down to my toes and back up again, makin' my body feel chilled and hot, all at once.

I hadn't really thought about what I wanted out there at the club, I was just tryin' to find myself, but instead I found a bad boy with a mouth of sin.

Before I knew it, his glass was discarded on the bar and he had both hands upon me. One at my hip and stomach, the other movin' up to cup my breasts. Suddenly I wasn't just in a room full of lewd people, I was part of 'em.

I was engaged in somethin' indecent, before all eyes, as Truck's big hands felt me up, his lips worked at mine, and he gave a deep, husky growl of approval. He sounded like some sort of large, intimidatin' beast.

I pulled away, touchin' my fingertips to my lower lip. It was almost like it was numb but not quite, and I was breathin' so fast, his hands still wanderin' over my body.

"Truck, maybe we should... slow down," I said, though my body hated me for it. And, honestly, part of my mind, too. I was supposed to be someone different than my prudish, virginal self. I wanted to leave that girl behind.

But I was nervous. It was all happenin' so fast. Or I think it was... I was so tipsy by that point. Way too much vodka for my first-timer self to handle.

My words seemed to almost confuse him, but he took a look around at the place, as if that was the problem.

"C'mon," he said, but this time he didn't take my hand and drag me along like I feared he might — having to wobble on those high heeled boots with all that vodka in me felt like it'd be suicide — instead he swept me off my feet, literally, and carried me on over to the stairs, holdin' my whole body up as if I weighed nothin'!

It impressed me, not gonna lie about that. I wrapped my arms around his neck, and even though my feelings were all strange and out of sorts, I admit... I was excited to be held by him. He was the kinda guy who'd never even look my way when I was in school.

The kinda guy I'd giggle over with my girlfriends, knowin' he was way too hunky for me. I'd have facebook stalked him and all that but this was beyond even my fantasies of what'd happen.

"Where're you takin' me?"

"Somewhere private," was all he said as he pushed past another couple making out in the upstairs hallway. "Outta the way," he growled as they hurriedly shifted to make way for him and I; though mostly him of course.

He kicked open a door and took me on in to what must've been his bedroom. It was a mess, but the king sized bed and blankets all looked nice, just unmade. With some of his clothes on the floor. No garbage or anything around, thankfully.

Slamming the door behind us with his foot he gave me a toss onto the bed, and my whole world went wildly spinning, thanks to both the trip and the alcohol. I couldn't help but cry out — mostly in amusement — but he pounced atop me in no time, kissing at my neck as soon as I settled into place.

He felt so amazing. His mouth, the way he knew to touch me, it was surreal. When he found that one spot on my neck, I was putty in his arms, my mind shutting down so that I was left with only pleasure.

I moaned, unintentionally, and took in several quick breaths.

This was definitely not how Emberlynn would react... but Ember? She's been dreaming about this day for a decade.

Don't get me wrong, I was wrapped up in somethin' way over my head. I was dealin' with shady folk and a dark, violent guy I didn't even really know, and if I didn't have a ton of vodka in me I'm sure I'd have screamed in terror and ran for my life.

If I was allowed.

But instead, I was pinned beneath that big muscle head bruiser Truck, his hands roamin' up and down my sides, feelin' the fishnets over my thighs, workin' in under my skirt. He felt me up in such a way it was like he was payin' homage to every inch of me. No rush to get to the act, just feelin' out every bit of my body as he groaned and growled, licked and nibbled.

I wasn't thinkin' straight, that much was for sure, and when he finally took a break from kissin' my neck, and some of my thoughts returned to me, I managed out some words. "I can't do this," I said, hand on his chest.

His big, hard chest. Which felt like smooth, polished stone through his shirt.

"Sure you can," he said, and he rose up, grasping his shirt from the back and tugging it up over his head in one swift motion, leaving his upper body bare. Leaving me to gaze up at the mounds of muscle that were his pecs, abs and biceps. The kind of sculpted body I'd never come close to seein' out in the country. With a peppering of dark hair that travelled on down his stomach to his low hanging jeans, as if the trail led beneath to something greater still.

And with him undoing his pants, I had a feelin' I'd find out soon.

I was panickin' a little, but my heart was racin' 'cause I was excited too. 'Cause a part of me — a big part of me — just wanted to go with it. Virginity be damned.

But maybe I was a prude.

"I've never... with anyone," I murmured.

He paused, his jeans undone and peeled open to show an obscene bulge in his black briefs. He looked at me, half-grin on his face, a look of disbelief on his face.

"You're fucking with me," he said after another once-over look across my body, so darkly clad, making me look like Ember; naughty girl.

With that reassurance he tugged down his jeans and underwear, and I got to see what laid at the end of his dark trail: a big, throbbing heft of cock meat. Thick and veiny, it bounded out from its confines, full of desire and bigger than I thought it'd be. With a pair of heavy balls beneath to complement its hefty girth.

Part of me was gettin' scared, but the bigger part...

I was gawkin'. I knew that. My mouth was parted, my ruby lipstick probably all gone, a little crack in my mask. My grey eyes widened, and I couldn't turn away.

And really... what was I hoping for? Romance and fire-works? An 'I love you'?

I'd gone to the club lookin' for sex whether I wanted to admit it or not. I just didn't think I'd get it.

Once I had that big, strong, nude man up over me, his hands freely roamin' up my legs and beneath my skirt, it was hard to battle instinct. And alcohol.

He touched my bare, pale skin beneath the frills of my skirt, and hooked his fingers into the elastic of my panties. He tugged 'em on down and removed the black, frilly undergarment, liftin' 'em up to his nose for a deep inhale.

"Ahh, damn... now that's the scent of a woman," he growled before letting the panties drop and spreading my legs out wide before him, sliding his fingers up my inner thighs.

I watched him with rapt, though slightly blurred, atten-tion, the corset feeling so constraining against my quick-ened breathing. My breasts held tight to my ribs as he touched me, inhaled me so crassly. It was like nothin' I'd even heard girls gossipin' about.

It was so much more... intimate.

I'd shaved *down there*, and I was suddenly shy by the fact that he could see all of my most private parts, so I tried to close my legs but those hard hands wouldn't let me.

He was in the driver seat, and it was clear he intended to savour every part of me. Every glimpse of me. His eyes glued to the sight of my glistening slit.

"Damn… that is the prettiest pussy I've ever seen," he said in a growl, licking his lips. And I didn't need to wonder if he was lying. Truck wasn't the kind of guy who had to lie to make women swoon. He just had to be his brutish self. No false compliments necessary.

Though almost as powerful as his words, was the touch of his finger to my cunny, feeling the moist folds and teasing my delicate clit.

I nearly screamed. Or maybe I did. I kind've lost all control when he touched me, because it felt so unreal. So amazing. My body tensed a little, embarrassment and modesty interfering with my moment before they, too, disappeared in the flood of pleasurable sensations.

By the time my alcohol-fuzzed mind managed to focus and I looked down, I realized Truck — the big brute of a man he was — had his head between my legs. His tongue was slidin' up over my slit and tastin' my femininity like it was his to do with as he wished.

With a rumbling growl he seemed to think it was.

"Mmmmm, damn girl… your cunt is fuckin' fine," he said before lashing his tongue over my cunny again, teasing my clit so expertly as he indulged in me at his whims.

It felt phenomenal. Unreal. Heavenly, even!

I was over the moon, and clutching onto the bed, just trying to keep myself balanced in the sea of pleasure.

"Truck!" I gasped, my milky thighs pressed so hard against his head I doubt he could hear me.

He ate my pussy with such smooth expertise, expert lashes of his tongues doing things to my lady parts I couldn't have even fantasized before! His two big hands grasping my thighs and ass as he lashed his tongue over my slit again and again, savouring my flavour. He was ravenous! A wild, muscular beast who just saw me, knew he had to have me, and made it happen.

I know we didn't meet on the most conventional of terms, but lordy, he was makin' me sing!

"Truck!" I screamed again, one of my hands going down to the top of his head, holding him there as suddenly it was like my body started to tense up, the good feelings becoming almost too much to tolerate.

Even if I wanted to push him away, he was an immovable object. His body couldn't be dislodged by my shoving, no way! He just sank his fingers into my flesh and continued to eat me out at his (and my) pleasure.

The big, loud grunts that came from him made there be no confusion as to his own satisfaction in the act. He was enjoying it, savouring me like a fine meal as he licked my folds and tasted my honey.

And then something happened that I'd never felt before, not even close. It was like my body started just tensing up, all my muscles going tight and then they all released in a burst of sensation unlike anything I'd dreamed of.

I screamed out loud as the pleasure struck through me like lightening, my hand tangled in Truck's hair, my legs pressing to him so hard I thought I might hurt him.

He clung on though, continuing to trace his tongue along the edge of my clit, provoking my pleasure through the earth shattering climax I was experiencing. He made my skin hum, my blood boil and hiss, and he ravenously devoured the flood of my honey that came forth across his tongue and face.

It was too much, and I was buckin' and moanin', my limbs flailing and then tightening as I just completely and utterly lost myself to his mouth.

I swear I must've blacked out, or very nearly so! It was all so intense!

But by the time I came to my senses, there he was again, loomin' over me.

His dick was hard as ever, and he held one of my legs in one arm, and with the other he wiped around his mouth with the back of his wrist, cleaning up the glistening mess of my honey even as he licked at his lips.

"Damn tasty," he said in his guttural, growling voice.

I was still wearin' almost all my carefully chosen clothes, except for those panties, and my booted calf was wrapped with his hand as he bent it back a little. It was so lewd, but I was spinning in a lust filled haze, and all I wanted was more.

Was him.

I wanted him to fuck me.

Even just the thought of it made me blush, though I'm sure my face was already red from the heavy breathin' I'd been doin'.

Then he did somethin' I'll never forget, because the sight of him reachin' his hand down to his long member, and takin' hold of that shaft was burned into my memory. Watchin' such a big, hunky man stroke his own cock was beyond compare, and he did it as he stared down at my glistening, wet pussy, takin' such pleasure in touchin' himself as he watched me.

"Such a gorgeous fuckin' babe," he growled at me before he leaned on in, using his hand's grasp upon his dick to guide it into my pussy, raw. That big, purple crown of his kissing my cunny lips as he began to sink on in bareback and groan in bliss of his own.

I cried out again. I'd always heard that it hurt the first time, so maybe it was the vodka, or maybe the fact that he'd eaten me out for so long and I felt so good and relaxed, but it didn't really hurt. Not like I expected.

But he grunted like it was takin' him force to feed that dick into me, and I squirmed, wanting more.

Slowly as he sank on in, I could feel the pressure build. He was such a big fella, and my lil' pussy was so tiny by comparison! It stretched to accommodate him though, and it never hurt like I feared, it only felt good to feel so full.

And I watched as he took hold of my hips in one hand, my leg in the other, and just sank his big, meaty shaft all the way into me, until his dark pubic hair was pressed up to my shaved mound. Such a beautiful fit.

"You weren't lying," he growled out, his dark eyes on me.

He grunted and groaned, and I could feel him twitch inside of me excitedly! But it wasn't long before he was tuggin' his hips back and beginnin' to thrust into me, startin' a tempo as we fucked unprotected.

My fingers clasped the sheet, my knuckles white as I held on for dear life.

I moaned louder, my more feminine sounds combining with the raw masculine growls, and my legs wrapped around his calves.

"I'm a virgin," I answered back, my throat tight and sore.

Truck lifted my ass up off the bed as he began to pump his hips faster, harder, his big cock splaying my pussy as he thrust in again and again. He looked on down over my body, and slid his hand from my leg on up to cup and squeeze my breasts through my corset.

"You aren't anymore, babe," he growled between moans, his dick pulsing with a twitch of pleasured excitement.

The way he said it made me almost cum again, my body still vibrating on high, filled with such delightful little aftershocks of pleasure. Every time his hips rammed into me, I jolted again, my breathing getting so hard.

I was getting close again to that point of no return, and he must've been able to tell because one of his hands relinquished my hip and instead went to that throbbing, needy clit.

He was master of the female form it seemed, master of my body. Because he thrust into me so deliciously, and worked his thumb over that sensitive little bud with masterful precision, the two actions working in concert — three if you count his delightful kneading of my breast — as he drove me to the precipice, my pleasure mounting beyond control.

Though one look at his broad-jawed face showed he was reaching his own pleasured peak. His eyes shutting and his dick throbbing inside me wildly.

"Cum on my dick," he commanded me, harsh and simple.

And maybe I was going to anyways, or maybe those words drove me over the edge, but either way, I did just as he said and that rush of bliss went through me like a wave crashing onto shore. I screamed and bucked against him, writhing against his hard cock and diligent hand, gasping for breath.

Though as I was racked with overwhelming pleasure, he too reached his peak as a wave of my honey crested over his cock. The slickness coated our loins, and he hammered into me harder than ever, pounding and pounding as he moaned loudly. His broad, hard chest puffed up and I could feel his dick swell as he lost himself in me.

He arched his spine and with one final thrust, shoved his dick to my very limits, jammed his tip against my womb and let loose a flood of his virile seed, filling my fertile depths with spurt after spurt of that thick, creamy spunk.

I lost track of how much time passed, and how many of those waves washed over me, but when I finally came back to awareness, we were wrapped together, my arms around him. I was breathing in the combined scent of our arousal and pleasure, the tangy salt of our perspiration as I felt his weight atop me.

I'd done it. I'd just lost my virginity!

Truck was glistening with a thin sheen of perspiration, which highlighted the intensity of his sculpted muscles. And he leaned on in, lowering me to the bed as he wrapped his bulging arms about me, held me tight as he kissed my lips.

It felt so oddly... romantic, for such a brute who just took me after only meeting me, but that's how it was!

Right up until his hips began to move again, and I knew he was already hankerin' for another go at my tight pussy.

So that was how we met, and how I lost my virginity.

And how I got this bundle of joy growin' inside me too, the same one I feel beneath my hand as I stroke my belly.

Yeah, I got knocked up on my first time. And yeah, I left the next day, ran on back to my apartment and planned to head home before I got myself into more trouble.

But it didn't last. I came on back. Tracked Truck down to his place...

Whoops! Here he is, his big ol' arms goin' around me from behind.

"C'mon babe. I got a hunger like you wouldn't believe," he says in a growl, kissing my neck and nibblin' at it before he hoists me up from behind in his arms.

EXPOSED

*B*ook Themes:
virgin, breeding, older man younger woman, stripper

Word Count:
5776

THE MUSIC IS PUMPING, my body is saturated with a shimmery combination of sweat and glitter, and there's pure adrenaline running through my veins. I feel good. No, better than good. I feel like a million bucks, and it doesn't take a rocket scientist to figure out why. The club is absolutely jumping tonight. Every direction I turn my head, there's another flash of hundreds in some guy's hand. I wish I could say I was the kind of girl who doesn't get excited by the sight of a wad of cash across the club floor, but I would be lying. These days, it feels like nothing turns me on quite like money does. Maybe there's just something in the air.

And white-hot electricity running up and down the length of my body as I bend and sway to the pulsating beat. The bass is loud and powerful under my six-inch heels, giving a heady dizziness to my dance routine. My fingers curl around the glossy metal pole, the neon lights casting hues of bright turquoise and hot pink across my body. It only adds to my mystique, drawing in the whiskey-soaked gazes of the men scattered around the stage like lost boys. Their eyes are wide, their vacant looks quickly replaced with stares of pure desire. I lick my lips, running my tongue along my full, plump lower lip, the gesture stretching effortlessly into a winning smile. Turns out, it doesn't take much to reel in one of these guys. They are ready to party and ready to part with a lot of cash in exchange for a little taste of something new, something almost forbidden.

Almost. Except that I'm not *completely* untouchable. There's one surefire magic spell to get me alone in one of those VIP rooms in the back of the club. No incantations necessary, just enough cash to get my heart pounding and my pussy slick. Maybe it makes me a little shallow. But I don't care.

I need the money, and I am more than willing to bend over backwards-- and forwards-- to get it. I spin around the pole slowly, arching my back and letting my legs stretch out. I stand out from the crowd, even among the other beautiful women who work here. My long, curly blonde hair spills over my pale, bare shoulders. My honey-brown eyes smolder in the low light, and once they land on my catch of the night, there's no going back.

I set my sights on a guy at the edge of the stage. He's tall and broad-shouldered, his face obscured by shadow. He's well-dressed, especially compared to most of the frat guys

CANDY QUINN'S DIRTY FANTASIES

and lonely older men who come in every night for lack of anywhere cooler to go. He looks like he has money out the wazoo, but it's more than his obvious cash flow that has my attention. Something about this guy draws me down from the stage, my feet barely touching the ground as I swish up to him. All I have to do is bite my lip and bat my long lashes and he's mine. He leads me by the hand, totally silent, all the way back to the VIP room. The door shuts behind us and we're alone. Just how I like it. Just what he wants, too, by the way he slides into his chair and waves me over.

Suddenly, all I can think about is his anatomy and mine, the science of blood reallocating, of hormones and endorphins rushing at breakneck speed to keep up with our money-laced tryst. I straddle him, careful not to actually touch him even though my thighs are burning to make contact. I move my hips and trace my manicured nails down his muscular shoulders. Somehow, even though his face is still shadowed, I can feel his eyes on me. Locked with mine as I gyrate and twist. I wonder if he knows how wet I am between my thighs. I wonder if he knows how desperately I want to slip my lacy black panties aside and tug his tailored pants down to his ankles, climb on top of him, and ride him until we're both sore and spent. Never mind the fact that I'm a virgin. Never mind the fact that he's a perfect stranger-- emphasis on the perfect. I want him. My body wants his. And when he breaks the rules to run his huge, powerful hands down my slender sides, I forget all about the lapdance. He pulls me down into his lap and a burst of bright, searing lust explodes in my chest. I lean in to kiss him. I need to know how he tastes.

But as soon as my lips brush against his, my eyes flutter open and the club melts away, along with my irresistible mystery patron. The adrenaline dies down and I sigh, realizing that I'm now staring up at the vaulted ceiling of my bedroom in between the four posts of my bed. I sigh and roll over in the silky sheets, my eyes narrowing at the number on the clock.

Half past nine. I groan and sit up stretching.

"Just a dream," I murmur. Even I'm surprised at how disappointed I sound.

I slide out of bed, my toes curling as they hit the pink carpet I've had since I was eleven. And the sheer number of horse posters hanging there are indication enough that my bedroom is in desperate need of an update. Not that my parents have noticed that. In fact, it wouldn't surprise me at all if they still think I *am* eleven, even though I'm enrolled in college and I'm almost old enough to order my own whiskey at the club.

But who am I to burst their bubble? I don't need their help anyway. I have a plan.

I trudge into my bathroom, which is just as pink and frilly as my bedroom. I strip off my silky PJs and step into the steamy rain shower. I sigh as the hot water hits my bare skin, beading in thick droplets down my naked body. The remnants of my sensual dream come floating back to me, along with a flush of warmth between my thighs.

I can't help but answer the siren's call, and before long my fingers are slowly working my clit. I bite my lip and close my eyes, giving in to the sensations and letting that mysterious stranger come back into my thoughts. I imagine his big hands running down my thighs, gripping me by the hips, squeezing my ass, my slender waist. I shiver at the thought of his hard cock straining to break free, aching for *me*. I reach up and take the fancy detachable showerhead out of its cradle and switch it to the pulse setting, and with a little sigh of pleasure I point the pounding water at my sensitive clit. Leaning against the shower wall, I rock my hips and whimper with need as the showerhead circles that tight little bud of nerves. I'm not going to last long at this rate, especially when I picture my dream-patron unzipping his pants and pulling me down to rut against the growing bulge in his boxers. He's gripping me tight, whispering filthy, pretty words in my ear as I spin closer and closer to the edge. I imagine a low, growly voice calling me 'princess' and telling me I'm a good girl, and that's all it takes.

"Oh my god," I groan as an orgasm vibrates through my whole body. My knees buckle, and it's all I can do to stay upright and finish my shower with my legs all trembly and my heart racing at breakneck speed.

I hop out and wrap a towel around myself, then step into my walk-in closet to pick out a blouse and jeans. In contrast to this modest outfit, I also grab a pair of fishnets, a matching black lace panty and bra set, and some staggeringly high heels, which I toss into a tote bag alongside my purse and school bag. If there's one thing I've learned about living a double life, it's that you tend to accrue a lot of dirty laundry. But it's a small price to pay for independence. I don't need my parents for money, and I don't need a man to make me cum. And thank god, because I'm still a virgin.

Still, I can only imagine how good an orgasm must feel with someone else.

"Someday," I tell my reflection as I towel-dry my blonde curls.

I skip out on a makeup routine for now, but I pack the essentials for later. Right now, I'm just a good student heading off to class. Nothing risque. But tonight, I'm going to don that black lingerie and a smokey eye and feel like a million dollars. I feel so powerful when I assume the night-time version of myself, like I can conquer the whole world and crush it beneath my platform heels. Today is Friday, which means I can stay out all night and blame it on a study session or hang-out fest with my friends. My parents will have no clue what their little girl is really doing, and that's the way I like it. They'd just try to stop me.

I comb my curls and hoist my bags over my shoulder. I give myself one more quick glance in the mirror before I walk out, and I'm satisfied with the reflection. I look the part of a normal college student... for now.

As I head down the hallway to the stairs, I'm met with several staff members who greet me with a warm but professional, "Good morning, Miss Holloway." I do what I always do, which is smile and respond with politeness. I'm accustomed to this. My father likes to keep a full staff on the property, since he's always jetting off to foreign coun-tries to attend meetings. He's a real estate mogul. My mom is a former supermodel. She attends fashion shows and makes guest appearances all over the globe.

It's always been this way. My parents check in with me all the time and make sure I have everything I need, but they're not here to see the changes in me. They don't see that I'm not their little princess anymore. I used to dream about being a princess, but nowadays... apparently I just dream about big, hard cocks. Talk about character devel-opment, right? Not that my parents have noticed I'm not a kid anymore. They don't know anything about my life.

Hence my former nanny, Maggie, who happens to be in the kitchen chatting with Rodrigo, our personal chef, when I walk in. It may seem strange to still have her on staff when I'm no longer a child who needs a nanny, but at this point Maggie is basically family. She's been with our family since I was a toddler, so there are sentimental reasons for her continued position on the staff. But it goes deeper than that. Maggie also keeps an eye on me and makes sure my parents are in the loop. She's their spy. Which means I need to be extra cautious around her so she doesn't figure out my secret plan and go blabbing about it to my mom and dad.

"Good morning, Prissy! Did you sleep well?" she greets me brightly.

It's Priscilla, I want to insist. Prissy is a childhood nickname I can't seem to escape, and one that no longer fits me. But instead of telling her that, I just smile so she doesn't suspect anything is amiss.

"Morning," I reply, reaching for one of the waffles Rodrigo has stacked on a plate. "I slept fine. How are you two?"

"*Bene*," chirps Rodrigo.

"Good. Heading to class?" Maggie says.

I nod. "Yep."

"Bright and early," she remarks. "Which class is it? Fashion design?"

"I've got three classes today," I answer, dodging the actual question.

I make sure to keep my arm over my school bag to hide the spines of my textbooks so she can't see the titles. That's yet another lie I'm carrying. My parents think I'm going to college for a fashion degree, like my mom always wanted. But it's not my passion, it's hers. And I can't fulfill someone else's dreams. I can only push toward my own.

"Ooh, busy day," Maggie says. Her tone is light and casual, but the way she's looking at me I can tell she's angling for a firmer answer. Time to pull out the big guns.

I take out a pink binder covered with a collage of cutouts from fashion magazines and pretend to flip through it for a second. As soon as her eyes land on the binder, her gaze softens. There we go. Easy peasy. I give her another winning smile.

"Well, I better go or I'll be late. Parking is a nightmare on campus," I remark.

"See you later, kiddo!" she replies.

"Actually, I'm going to a study group at a classmate's house tonight so I'll see you tomorrow," I tell her as I hurry out of the kitchen.

"Oh! Okay! Well, be careful and make sure that homework gets done," she calls after me.

"Will do!" I shout back before stepping out into the glorious sunny morning.

Phew. Glad that's over. I hurry down the steps and climb into my Mercedes, tossing my bags into the passenger seat. I drive down the long, winding driveway to the road and finally out to the highway. I glance at my rearview mirror to check the line of cars merging behind me, then turn on some upbeat music to get my energy flowing. Traffic is crazy, probably mostly students like me rushing to class. There are a few cars going the same way as me, including a heavily-tinted black luxury sedan. I wonder what kind of student drives a car like that. Then again, I'm sure all my classmates think it's odd that a nursing student like me happens to drive a Mercedes. Granted, it's an old model since I got it for my sixteenth birthday, but it's still a Benz. I know what kind of stereotypes I'm working against here. Everyone I know thinks I'm going to college for some frivolous degree, but underneath that fashion-mag binder is a gigantic anatomy textbook. I want to learn to be a nurse and take care of other people instead of relying on other people to take care of me forever like my parents expect. I just need a chance to prove I can stand on my own two feet.

Once I get to campus, it's the usual battle for a parking spot. There's a line behind me of students looking for the same thing, including that black sedan. Although, once I miraculously find two open spots next to each other, the sedan drives right past it and keeps going.

"Weird. Guess they decided to ditch class instead," I murmur to myself as I gather my belongings and get out of the Benz.

I quickly put the black sedan out of my mind, focusing on the day of classes I have in front of me. Anatomy, microbiology, medicinal botany. A far cry from the fashion, yoga, and pottery classes my mom insisted on. I smile proudly to myself as I walk into class and take a seat. It's not that I enjoy lying to my family, but I'd be lying to myself if I said it didn't give me a little bit of a thrill. I can't help it. Besides, I'm not using my parents' money for these classes. I'm not touching the limitless credit cards they gave me anymore either. If I'm going to be a nurse and, more than that, an independent adult, I have to handle things myself.

The day runs smoothly and I enjoy my classes. I'm finished by mid-afternoon so I head off to a cafe for a caffeine pick-me-up and a homework sesh. To my surprise, I happen to notice a black car waiting in the drive-thru line outside the window while I work. I do a double take as I see the car slowly pull out of the line and park. I hold my breath, my heart racing. Is this person following me? I strain my eyes to try and see who's at the wheel. I can vaguely make out a dark, large figure-- definitely a guy, and definitely way bigger than most guys, too. I wait to see if he'll come inside to confront me or something. Maybe Prissy would be afraid right now, but

Priscilla can handle it. In fact, I make the decision that if he does come in and get in line at the counter, I'm going to pull a power move by anonymously paying for his order. Just to make him nervous. But before I can live out my perfect plot, the car promptly pulls back out and drives away.

"Damn," I whisper.

I'm disappointed. The driver's bulky frame reminds me of the mystery man in my sex dream from this morning and I wanted to get a better look. Oh well. I focus on my homework and get it done in time for me to take a moment's rest before I get back in my car and head across town to my next destination. The sun is starting to sink toward the horizon, casting pink and golden light across the sky. My adrenaline is pumping. This is what I've been looking forward to all day: my chance to prove myself and hustle my own money.

The sun's gone down by the time I pull up to the strip club. I grab my tote bag and quickly make my way to the back entrance. Immediately, all of my senses are hit with the sounds and sights and smells of the place. I can feel the bass pumping from the front of the club, and it gently vibrates the glossy floor beneath my feet, seeming to reverberate through the very walls. The lights are down low, with orange, hot pink, and turquoise hues casting the hallway into a dreamy nocturnal vibe. It's like stepping into another world. I forget about who I have to pretend to be during the day, about how many secrets I'm keeping. Here, nobody knows me as Prissy. In fact, nobody even knows my real name. We all go by pseudonyms here anyway.

I walk into the dressing room and am greeted with a cheerful chorus of, "Hey, Scarlet!" from the other women.

Out on the floor, we may look like competitors for the

attention and cash of the clientele, but in the dressing room our true feelings come out. We can be vulnerable here together while we apply makeup, tease our hair into a little sexy volume, and change into our sexy outfits for the stage. We support each other, crack jokes about crappy or ridiculous clients, talk (quiet) smack about management, and help zip or unzip each other's strappy getups.

"How's everybody doing tonight?" I greet them as I open my locker and start peeling off my boring daytime clothes to change into the black lingerie set.

"Katrina got a heavy hitter earlier," remarks Destiny.

"I thought he was going to be a dead end, but turns out there was a bunch of cash in those ugly, stained cargo pants," Katrina laughs.

"Don't judge a book by its cover," I reply with a wink.

"Or a patron by his number of pockets," giggles Juliette.

"Friday night, girls," says Ruby. "We're all gonna rock it."

"Hell yeah," agrees Destiny. "There's a bachelor party out there."

"Easy pickings," I say with a grin.

Once I've amped up my look, I head out onto the club floor, thrumming with excitement. I get onstage after Fiona steps down and I take her place at the pole, wrapping my slender body around the cool metal. I drop my head back and shake out my bouncy curls while I arch my back. The song playing is one of my favorite jams, and I feel sexy and powerful. Every time another dollar lands at my high-heeled feet, I get a little rush. There's a group of guys accumulating at the front of the stage, all of them clearly buzzed and utterly entranced by my undulating body. This must be the bachelor party, and by the looks of it, they came ready to spend. Drunk, attentive, and spendy, just how I like them. Well, except for the bachelor himself, who is definitely drunk but not the friendly kind. I see him shove through the crowd to stand at the side of the stage, watching me with bleary, narrowed eyes. I can hardly tell if he's turned on or angry, but either way I keep dancing and bringing in cash.

When my song is over, I blow a kiss and step down from the stage. My feet have barely touched the floor before I feel a hand grip my arm. I whip around to see that the bachelor himself is in my face, looking me up and down with a hungry gaze. I can smell alcohol on his breath when he leans in close, and it's all I can do to not jerk away from him.

"What's a guy gotta do to get some alone time with you?" he slurs in my ear.

"Let me take you to a VIP room for a lapdance," I reply, always the good hostess.

There are alarm bells ringing at top volume in my head but I can't turn down a paying customer. I gently pull away and gesture for him to follow me as I lead him back. As soon as we step into the tiny room, he shuts the door and lunges for me, his hands gripping my arms as he pins me against the wall. I let out a yelp of fear as I try to fight him off, but he has his hand on my ass and he's so strong.

Suddenly, the door bursts open and a massive figure rushes into the room. It takes me only a few seconds to register that the man ripping the bachelor away from me is none other than the guy in the black sedan! My eyes widen as I watch him grab the handsy bachelor by the collar, throw him against the opposite wall, and I hear a sickening crunch as his fist connects with a jawbone. The bachelor drops to the floor instantly, and I don't get a chance to react before my mystery follower scoops me over his shoulder.

"What are you doing?" I gasp.

"Saving your ass," he growls.

There's no use in fighting-- he's too powerful. He carries me out of the VIP room, across the club, and out into the night. He hurriedly shoves me into the passenger seat of his car and peels off into the night. I stare at him in utter shock.

"Did you just kidnap me?" I splutter.

"Kidnap is a strong word," he replies. "Besides, you're not a kid."

"Who the hell are you? What do you want? You've been tailing me all day!" I retort.

"Good thing, too. You need someone to watch over you."

"Excuse me? I can handle myself, thanks. And my parents will literally have your head on a platter for this!" I snap.

"Unlikely," he says. "Considering they hired me to do this."

My blood runs cold. "What?" I murmur. "Why?"

"You stopped using your credit cards. They want to know where you're getting your money," he explains. "I'm a private investigator."

"My own parents hired a PI to follow me?" I burst out. "And where are you taking me? Wait. Please don't take me home. Look, your knuckles are bleeding from... hitting that guy. Oh god, I'm going to get fired."

"Judging by what I saw tonight, that might be for the best," he says. "Put on that t-shirt in the back seat so you're decent."

I reach back and grab the oversized t-shirt, pulling it on over my head. I get a little thrill when I realize it just be one of his. It's massive on me.

"You're the one bleeding all over the place," I shoot

back. "I'm training to be a nurse. You should let me bandage you up. Maybe... at your place?"

"You're serious," he says.

He sounds surprised and honestly, so am I. But I don't feel afraid of this man, despite the fact that he just stole me right off the club floor. I trust him. He did kind of save me. More than that, though... I want to be near him. I can't help feeling like I've met him before.

Maybe even in my dreams.

"It's got to be better than going home," I tell him.

"I'll figure out what to do with you there," he growls back.

My heart skips a beat. It worked! Far from the fear I was feeling at the club, I find myself simply excited. By the time we pull up to his modern, luxury apartment which seems to double as his PI office, my body is buzzing and my heart pounding like mad. He hustles me into the apartment, which is just as beautiful on the inside as the outside. It's meticulously clean, if a little spartan. He leads me through the office area to the kitchen, where I pull up a chair and make him sit down while I find a bottle of alcohol and a washcloth to start tending his bloody knuckles. Being this close to him is intoxicating, and for the first time I get to see him in better lighting. He's even more handsome than I thought when I saw him in low light. As I hold his injured hand in mine, I feel my body getting hot.

"It's really not fair," I say suddenly. "You seem to know a lot about me but I don't even know your name."

"Vince," he replies. "And you can stay here for the night, but I'm taking you home tomorrow. I'll make you a cot on the couch."

"Aren't you worried I'll try to run away or something?" I tease.

"Not if I keep an eye on you," Vince remarks.

I quirk an eyebrow. "All night?"

"If that's what it takes," he answers.

"You were right earlier," I tell him slyly. "I'm not a child. Let me prove it to you."

He crosses his thick arms over that powerful chest and watches me, waiting. I flash him a devilish smile and take a step back. Slowly, I play with the hem of the oversized t-shirt, teasing him with little tastes of what's underneath. He's watching me ever so closely and I can see the fierce desire burning in his gaze. It's a thrill to want and be wanted in the same degree. I've never craved anything the way I crave him. I don't quite know what to expect, but I know I want whatever he has to offer me. I long to feel every part of him.

I run my hands down my body and hold eye contact with Vince while I gently tug the shirt up over my head. I toss it aside and begin to rock my hips. My fingers course through my blonde curls and I let out a soft sigh. I can feel his eyes burning into my very soul while I seduce him. He doesn't look away for a single second while I step closer and drape my arms over his muscular shoulders. I can't help but feel like my sexy dream is coming true. It feels totally surreal. I'm giving my mystery guy a lap dance, but not in the club. Not for money.

For something I've never had before.

And judging by the thick bulge I see, Vince is after the same thing. I sway and gently brush up against him, then peel off my black lacy panties and bra to let them fall on the floor. My fingers traipse down his back as I slide closer. I lean close to tease his lips with mine, bestowing an impossibly soft kiss. My hands move to cup his face and I revel in the sharp cut of his jaw, the rough stubble shadowing there. Every inch of me is on fire for him. I'm acutely aware of his heat, his quiet strength, his scent—everything about this man is addictive to me.

Vince can't resist anymore. His hands grip my slender waist and rove down my thighs. He flicks a fingertip along my wetness, just for a moment, just enough to make me gasp.

He leans in close to raspily whisper in my ear, sending sparks of desire through my body.

"You want to be a grown-up, I'll gladly treat you like one. But you have a lot to learn, don't you?"

I shiver. "Yes. I-I'm a virgin. But please, I want to learn. I want you to teach me, Vince."

"As you wish. On your knees," he growls.

"Yes, sir," I reply breathlessly.

I drop to my knees and watch enraptured as he unzips his pants and pulls them down with his boxers. My heart is pounding. I can't believe this is really happening. His massive, hard cock bounces free and my mouth waters to taste him. I've never wanted anything the way I want him. I've never done this before, but Vince guides me down with his hands pressing gently at the back of my head and weaving through my hair.

"Open your mouth and relax your jaw for me," Vince orders softly.

I do as I'm told, and I'm rewarded with the satisfying sensation of his cock pushing into my mouth and tickling my throat. I groan and feel another rush of wetness between my thighs. I begin to bob up and down on his shaft, reveling in the way he stretches my cheeks and fills me up. He grumbles with pleasure when I pick up the pace. I was made for this. Made for him. I feel him tensing up, but he lightly pushes me back before I can get him to the edge. His cock slips out of my mouth with a wet pop. There's a fierce hunger in his dark eyes as he grabs me and picks me up, my legs wrapping around his waist. He carries me down the hall to his neat, sleek bedroom and lays me back on the king-sized bed. The breath catches in my throat when he moves down between my legs and runs the stiff tip of his tongue along my wet slit. I cry out and he pushes my thighs further apart with his hands, diving in to nibble and suck at my swollen clit.

"Oh, it feels so good," I whimper.

His tongue traces perfect, delicious circles around the sensitive bundle of nerves there while his finger teases my right little opening. Before long, I'm bucking my hips and rocking against his face. The pleasure becomes overwhelming and I go limp as the most powerful orgasm of my life vibrates through me— and it doesn't stop at one. I come again and again with his tongue and fingers between my legs until I'm no longer even coherent.

"Are you ready for me, Priscilla?" he rasps.

I can only nod vigorously and say, "Please."

Vince positions himself carefully, guiding the head of his stuff cock to my aching hole. I press up against him needfully. I hiss with a combination of pleasure and pain when he pushes inside, millimeter by millimeter until he's fully sheathed down to the hilt. My pussy contracts and pulses around him. The feeling of fullness, of being whole is almost too much.

But Vince leans down to gently kiss me while he withdraws and slides back in, gradually moving faster and harder. I'm so tight that we can both feel every twinge. The head of his cock bumps against a secret spot deep inside of me that makes me see stars. My pussy blooms for him, unfolding to let him in.

I know what a risk it is, taking him inside me, without any protection. I don't care. Hell, maybe I even like it. The thought of him knocking me up, marking me as his for all time...

He caresses my breasts, my stomach, my face, while his rod spears into me over and over again. I can feel him starting to lose control and that sends me over the edge. My legs tremble through another climax, and the way my pussy squeezes his cock is enough to bring him over the line with me. With a few more rapid thrusts, Vince tenses up and growls my name fiercely while he empties his virile seed deep inside of me. We shudder together through the powerful waves, clinging to one another. He rests his forehead against mine for a few sweet moments. My heart surges with affection and I feel so completely connected to him on a soul level.

When we're both spent, he pulls out and collapses beside me, tugging me close. I giggle and drape an arm across his chest while we come down from the enormous high.

"Well, if I wasn't a grown ass woman before, I am definitely one now," I sigh contentedly.

"Yes, you are," he agrees with a smile.

"Listen," I whisper sleepily, "I don't want my parents' money. I also don't want them to worry about me. Please let me keep my secret. Just for now."

"I don't need your parents' money either," he answers after a short pause. "I'm not going to turn you in. But I have conditions."

"Go on," I urge him, snuggling closer.

"I'll give you cover and protection if you promise to be more careful and find a less dangerous job. You also have to promise you'll let me help you," Vince commands.

"I promise," I tell him.

"And Priscilla?" he prompts.

"Mhm?" I mumble.

"I think you should start spending your nights here. With me. You know, for safety's sake," Vince insinuates. He traces a finger across my cheek. The softness underneath his words is reflected in his gentle touch. For the first time in a while, I feel truly safe. And happy.

Like this is where I'm supposed to be.

I smile against his warm skin as I drift off to blissful sleep.

FERTILE MODEL:
LIGHTS_ON_LYDIA

$\mathcal{B}$ook Themes:
      breeding, first time
Word Count:
5600

THE SHEETS WERE SO crisp and white, Lydia felt like she was leaning back into a cloud. A smile of soft elation spread across her face as her powder-blue eyes absently counted the tiles on the ceiling. There was crown moulding in the corners, pillars bridging the archway to the bathroom on the other end of the top-floor suite. The bed had tall-rising posts from which veils of gauzy, sheer curtain hung gently waving in the breeze. Lydia liked to keep a window cracked when she came to the city like this. Even though she was a country girl used to sleeping amid the gentle buzz of insects and wind through tree branches outside her cozy townhouse, there was something so alluring about the city soundtrack. It would keep her awake most of the night, but then again, she wouldn't have been able to sleep through the excitement anyway. This was a much nicer hotel than she was accustomed to. She couldn't help but wonder what kind of man could afford a place like this--and for two nights!

It made her feel tingly between the thighs, picturing a big, strong hand reaching into a fine leather wallet to pull out a thick wad of cash. Then the same hand sliding down the back of her floaty summer dress, sending goosebumps down her spine. A little shiver she could not hold back, and just the hint he was looking for. The go-ahead. The proof in the pudding. That faint indication that she perhaps might be in this business, in this room, in front of this particular camera lens for more than just professional reasons. It was an unspoken, untouched conversation. An exchange that could be tipped to one side with just the soft, nuanced nudge in the filthy direction. Just a slip of the strap down her shoulder or a tilt of her head, the flutter of her lashes, a gaze that lingers longer than necessary to focus the lens.

Lydia gasped, realizing with a little pinch of hot shame that she had been holding her breath, too focused on the fantasy unraveling vividly in her head. She sank back into the pillow and sighed, letting her hands trail down the front of her white lace bodice. She had picked up the frilly top from a thrift store, and the black skirt she paired it with had come from a friend's closet back home. Sure, there were glamorous bits and pieces of her occupation. Hair and makeup on a very good day, designer digs and duds on the best days. Lydia loved being all gussied up with makeup artists flitting around her with various brushes and sweet-smelling, high-end products. She loved having a hair team arrange her luscious tresses into even more stunning looks. And the excitement of being assigned a stylist to pick out her clothes and dress her to the nines was potent. It kept her coming back for more, even through the much-less exciting and much more common experience of lowkey, low-exposure shoots she normally landed. So she lived as though she had a foot in each world: the high-gloss fashion editorial world and the lifestyle-slash-boudoir content of her daily gigs. One foot in a Manolo Blahnik, the other in a consignment shop mary-jane, at least proverbially speaking.

She kicked her feet gently back and forth as she stared straight up, careful not to let the filthy bottoms of her shoes grime up the white sheets. In stark contrast, the silky panties and thigh-high stockings under her thrift-store clothes were high-dollar items. Of course, it was easier to afford nice things on someone else's budget. When a client required a prop or clothing item beyond her reach, she had the option of seeing if the photographer might supply it-- or even better, add a little extra to her bill. If there was anything her scrappy single mom had taught her, it was how to make the most of what she was given.

And what Lydia was given... was a soft, curvaceous body with broad, rounded hips and full, perky breasts. Her stomach was a pale, flat plane, but not so toned as to be hard to the touch. There was only the gentlest impression of the well-worked abdominal core muscles underneath her alabaster skin. In fact, just about everything about Lydia was soft. Like silk stretched ever so tautly over feather pillows. Her friends often sweetly described her as "extremely huggable." Lydia melted into whoever she was close to, like she was even hungrier for touch than they were. Maybe there was even some truth to it.

That was saying something, because she had the kind of body that men really liked to look at. That they could not *help* but to look at. Coupled with a stunned double-take, most of the time. It was impossible for her to go out without the stares and the whispers following close behind. Lydia was kind of used to it, but it gave her a thrill every time.

She could tell by the look in a man's gaze as he looked at her that his fingertips were downright itching to touch her, to lightly trace every rounded edge of her supple body. She often imagined the exact same thing they did, rough, calloused fingers gently tweaking those perfect, pale-pink nipples, sending a branch of electricity through her whole body. Making her back curl into a perfect arch, her thighs parting to let those hands wander wherever they so desired.

Theoretically, of course. It was all just a moving picture in her head, but it was real, too. She could only imagine what these men wanted to do to her, but it wasn't hard to get it right, even as innocent as she was. Lydia was unpracticed, but even she knew the hunger they felt for her, their mouths watering to taste her sweet lips, on her face and between her flawless thighs. But it wasn't just her outer beauty that drew them to her like love drunk flies to sweet, sticky honey. Lydia put out into the world a sort of quiet, magnetic energy that drove men wild. They wanted to figure her out, to chart every curve and memorize every place that made her sigh when touched. She was the most tempting puzzle. The most precious code to crack open. Pretty as a picture, but not just as easily captured.

From the moment they caught sight of her, these guys wanted to get her in frame-- whether it was a picture frame or the frame of a cushy bed. Lydia was not totally naive; she understood that the answer was more often than not 'both.' But she was careful. Maybe more so than she even needed to be. She couldn't help it. She was shy. The world of sex was something she bordered alongside but never crossed into-- not in real life, anyway. Lydia was cautious about setting boundaries, about keeping her professional work... professional. As much as she could, at least. It was half out of self-preservation and half out of shyness. She could use the excuse of her working reputation as a shield against having to give herself over, body and soul, to someone else. In her head, though, it was a different story. Fantasies weaving intricate webs of desire and longing as her fingertips fluttered softly and familiarly between her thighs. Daydreams stealing her focus and catching her in an infinite, starry-eyed loop. Sometimes it even struck her in the middle of a photoshoot. She would cast her soft gaze toward the camera and surprise the photographer with the quiet intensity of her look. Like she could melt glaciers with such heat.

It helped that the camera lovingly hugged every slope and line of her body and her angelic face, making magic on film and digital like a superpower she could wield against the world. She looked good in any kind of fashion, any style, any flavor. Whatever size and brand of muse the photographer needed her to turn into. She was it, and well on her way to becoming an It Girl, too. All she needed was one big flash, one loud, unignorable bright spot that would cast her into the supernova level of stardom. Maybe one day it would come. Lydia would be on a billboard. She would really be something. At last, she could solidify her identity and persona to the public, mold her reputation as she truly desired. But for now, she had to wear many labels, put on many costumes. She could be herself, but only underneath the mask she wore for pictures.

Luckily for Lydia, she was an effective chameleon, happy to shapeshift with the mystical power of makeup and styling to suit whatever the shoot called for. High fashion one day, street style the next. Glam in the streets, barefaced beauty in the sheets. Metaphorically, of course. She had a face that took well to makeup, but she glowed with natural softness, too. All in all, she was an easily marketable product, able to succeed gracefully at every gig.

But for all her talents and charms, there was no beating around the bush. There was a sort of unspoken truth she had to confront: the *real* money, the *real* notoriety, would come falling in the second her clothes came off. Not that she had done that yet, not all the way like so many models she knew. It had crossed her mind so many times, the idea of increasing her fees for decreasing her modesty. She knew it paid to loosen up and lose the clothes, but that was a line she had yet to cross-- not just in front of a camera, but in front of another person, period.

Lydia, for all her coquettish poses and attitudes that were so convincing in a camera frame, was a virgin. Some people didn't believe her. That was to be expected. Some people were all too eager to believe. That was even more expected. But the truth of the matter was that she remained untouched by hands other than her own. And at the quivering age of eighteen, she was all but on fire with untapped lust. It used to be easy for her to put those occasional naughty thoughts aside. But it was like the closer she inched toward true adulthood, the closer those thoughts inched in. The harder it was to ignore her deepest, most blushing desires when they breached the surface of her mind. She was always pushing them down, pushing them away, pretending not to feel herself getting wet every time one of those hot, older men moved in closer to her, one eye squinched and the other hidden behind a viewfinder. She was the view to find, but only ever to be viewed.

Not touched.

Not even when the tension in the room reached uncomfortably hot levels.

Not even when the urge to just peel off the layer of clothes separating stiff cock from slick pussy was almost overwhelming. Oh well, she always thought as she walked away from a particularly almost-steamy shoot. At least she could hold onto those memories in her mind, revisit them when the mood struck. She was a virgin, but she also had an awfully active imagination. It was a frustrating combination to deal with, from her perspective. At least right now she had a little time to herself before the photographer showed up... and the luxe hotel sheets did nothing to discourage her.

Her fingers slipped under the hem of her silky panties and smoothed lightly over the warm mound between her thighs. She bit her lip, inhaling sharply when the tip of her finger ever so delicately grazed the tight bud of nerves at the hood of her flower. She was wet before she even touched herself. These days, it felt like she was constantly teetering on the edge. Every flash of the camera, every twist of her body under harsh lights, every night spent awake tossing and turning while rampant fantasies tore through her head... it was all getting to be too much for Lydia. She needed a release.

"Oh," she squeaked, feeling a rush of endorphins through her body.

Her fingertips circled her clit slowly, catching a gentle, lulling rhythm. The model's beautiful blue eyes rolled back in her head and closed, lashes fluttering. Her cheeks flushed like pale pink roses. Her slender body arched in a perfect semi-circle with her head tilted back. Her fiery red hair spilled out around her like a halo on the soft white sheets. Some of the curls slid down to gather at her shoulders as she bit her full, pouty bottom lip. Lightly at first, then a little harder. She applied the same technique with her fingers between her legs. A tingle of pleasure rolled up through her body at the flutter of her fingers across her aching clit, but she momentarily lost her breath when she rubbed a hard, tight circle around it. Soft or hard, two urges always fighting inside of her. The softness she expected. But her longing to be touched with less caution and more force came along with some insecurities. She felt dirty for wanting it, but feeling dirty kind of just made her want it more. It was a vicious cycle, and it kept her eternally on the edge. Lydia was in a never-ending foreplay and guilt routine in her own mind and, indeed, her own body. Which led her to moments like this: desperately touching herself on the hotel bed while she waited for her professional colleague to show up, which could happen at any second.

The thought both chilled and thrilled Lydia completely. She could get caught. Like this. Fingers circling her clit while her panties became dangerously slick-- what if the photographer could see her arousal in the photos? What if he could see her arousal... there. In person. During the shoot?

"Oh god," she whimpered. Her heart stumbled at the notion. Caught. Exposed.

She had to be oh so careful. A momentary lapse in modesty could undo her. Lydia knew she had to stop. Were those footsteps she heard coming rhythmically up the hall? Was someone-- someone large-- approaching the door? Surely he would have to knock, right? He wouldn't have a key to the room. Or would he? After all, he was the one who paid for the room.

Her stomach dropped at the unmistakable sound of the door handle jostling. She let out a little yelp of surprise and hastily pushed her skirt down, pulling herself up to her feet. He wasn't knocking! In fact, he wasn't using a key either.

The door simply creaked open, pushed by the edge of a large black boot. Lydia's wide blue eyes slowly panned up the statuesque shadow in the doorway. She swallowed hard, her whole body stricken rigid with shock. As he stepped forward into the light of the lamp, Lydia stepped back instinctively, like a trembling fawn shying from a grizzly bear. But when she saw his face, she could hardly believe her eyes. He smirked, one eyebrow raised.

"Not what you expected?" he said in a low, growly voice.

Lydia was totally tongue-tied. "I--I, um. I didn't--"

"Lock the door. You didn't lock the door," the man quipped. He nudged the door shut behind him, never taking those blazing brown eyes off of Lydia.

"I thought I did," she answered meekly.

"Mm, well, next time you make sure," he said, still eyeing her like she was the most delicious dessert he had ever seen. "Good thing I'm the guy who was supposed to show up here today. Not that you know that."

Lydia frowned. "Are you?" she asked.

The guy chuckled, all fear melting out of Lydia's body as the tiny laugh lines deepened around his eyes. Suddenly, he wasn't so scary. He was ruggedly handsome. Tall, broad in the shoulders like an athlete, his plain white shirt barely containing the muscles that rippled underneath. And he was smiling. It was like a beam of sunshine right to the heart. Lydia found herself smiling back.

He held out his huge hand for her to shake, still grinning.

"I'm Noel. Nice to meet you," he said.

Lydia's shoulders relaxed and a smile flickered across her face. "NoelEyeFilm85," she said shyly. She took his hand, trying not to gawk at how his downright dwarfed her own delicate hands.

The photographer nodded. "Yep. That's my dorky social media handle," he said.

"No worse than mine," Lydia giggled.

"Oh, I think LightsOnLydia is a pretty cute handle. It suits you. At least I think it does," Noel mused.

Lydia's heart thumped. She found herself desperately curious as to what this almost-stranger thought about her. She was hungry for his approval. He was already more affable than some of the aloof, self-absorbed photographers she had shot with. He was definitely more handsome. In fact, Lydia caught herself doing double and triple takes at him. The tables were turned for once.

"Oh? You think so?" she asked, strangely a little breathless. There was a glimmer in his brown eyes.

"Well, I can't know for sure if you're a lights on or lights off kind of girl, but I'll take your word for it," he tossed back, just as casually as anything.

It even took Lydia a second to realize what he was implying. Her cheeks flushed pink. Before she could even formulate a response, he walked to the bed. Lydia turned slowly to look at him, still in awe. The bed? Why was he going to the bed?

He shrugged off his bulging black backpack, letting it fall gently on the sheets. Oh. He was just putting his stuff down. Of course. That made sense.

Noel hummed under his breath as he looked through the bag of equipment, taking out the usual suspects. He had a slick, well-kept, but easily portable setup. All good signs, from Lydia's perspective. He looked like he truly knew what he was doing, unlike some of the bumbling, nervous amateurs she had worked with before. What a relief.

He turned and quickly raised an old-fashioned-looking camera to his eye, effortlessly squaring Lydia in frame. She startled, sweeping the hair out of her eyes. She was nervous. Why?

"Don't worry," Noel murmured. "I'm just testing the light for my settings here. You don't have to look pretty yet. Although, I don't think you have a choice with a gorgeous face like that."

Lydia was flustered. It wasn't like she was new to compliments. She got them all the time from photographers, makeup artists, random strangers. But coming so smoothly from Noel's lips, it brought new feelings. The tingly kind.

"Oh. Thank you," she murmured. Her cheeks flushed pink and she fought the reflex to look away.

"And that body? I bet you look good in anything," Noel went on. "I can see why you make an excellent model. Most of the work here is already done; I just have to capture the masterpiece in front of me. But don't worry, I'm pretty good at what I do."

His tone was utterly casual, like he was describing the weather, but it was having all kinds of unseen effects on Lydia. Or at least she hoped they were unseen. Between her thighs, her petals were trembling and dewy with need. There was just something about Noel, the way he spoke so brazenly and unabashedly about her body.

He lowered the camera and smiled, his eyes twinkling bright. Damn, she thought. He even had two perfect dimples. So symmetrical. So handsome.

"You've modeled, too," Lydia blurted out.

Noel raised an eyebrow and took a step closer.

"Good eye. But that was a lifetime ago," he said. "I prefer to stand on this side of the lens."

"Why?" Lydia asked.

He smirked. "I guess I just prefer to feel more in

control. I like to capture beauty in a tiny square. And I'm obsessed with the technical side of things."

"I feel more in control when I'm being watched," she replied, then immediately blanched when she realized the possible double entendre in her words.

Noel laughed and stepped closer. The breath caught in Lydia's throat. He was so close now, only a bulky camera's length between them. She could feel the heat radiating off of him.

"I could watch you all day long," he said softly.

Lydia's eyes widened and her heart began to pound. "Really?" she breathed.

The camera clicked and a little light puffed on for a moment, snapping a photo. Lydia blinked in the bright light.

"Sorry. Your face... I just had to," Noel laughed. "You're stunning. I can't stop noticing that you're different."

"Different?" she pressed.

"In a good way," he assured her. "I mean that you are just as beautiful in person as you are in a photograph. Most people are either-or. But not you."

"Thank you. I think," she replied. "Are you this nice to all your models?"

"I can be nice to anyone. But something tells me you need something more than nice," he insinuated.

"Like what?" Lydia murmured. She felt her nipples twinge and stiffen underneath the fabric of her lingerie.

"Look," he said, setting down the camera. He turned back to look at her with something akin to mischief in his gaze. "I've been waiting for the right model to do this with."

"Do what?"

"A sort of passion project I've been holding onto for a long time. A self-study, full exposure. But I won't do it alone. I need someone to match my energy. Someone who is an expert in her craft."

He quickly closed the space between them and softly cupped her face in both of his giant hands. She felt so small and vulnerable with him this close, towering over her. A little thrill rolled down her spine. As nervous as she was, she didn't want him to stop.

"It's been forever since I stepped in front of the camera, and you are the perfect model to take into this self portrait project with me. Do you accept?" he asked.

She knew how crazy it sounded. How dangerous. If any of her friends described a situation like this, she would've advised them to leave. But there was something so authentic about Noel. And irresistible.

"You feel it too," he murmured. "I can tell."

"I-I do," she admitted. Her body burned for him. He smirked back down at her.

"You're smart. You would run if you were afraid. If you didn't trust me. If you didn't want it just as badly as I do," Noel asserted.

She bit her lip. He was right. It was all moving so fast, but it felt fine. Better than fine. Exhilarating.

"This is insane," she said. "I-I don't normally do this kind of thing."

"I know. I don't either. But I'll take good care of you," he said. "It'll be a fun journey together."

He hooked an arm around her waist and pulled her flush against him. She felt his hard cock, huge and stiff against her soft thigh. He spun her around and walked her backward to the bed. He leaned down to press a button on the camera. A record button. She knew it was. And for some reason, she didn't care.

After all, there was truth to what she'd said: she did very much love the idea of being watched. Recorded.

Forever caught in the act. Every inch of her body was silently crying out for intimacy and danger and risk and so, so much reward. She saw all of that and so much more waiting for her in the enchanting depths of Noel's eyes. He caught her in his arms and leaned in close, his lips hovering not even a full inch apart from hers.

"I ask again," he whispered. "Do you accept?"

Lydia nodded. "Yes. I accept."

"Good girl," he growled.

Noel dove in and kissed her hard, stealing her breath as she folded into his arms. She felt the tall brick wall of her defenses start to crumble and fall to tiny irregular pieces. There was a veritable cacophony of alarm bells ringing in her head, nearly screaming at her to be more careful, to remember her smarter instincts. To think with her head instead of the pulsating warmth between her soft thighs. But there was no use in applying reason or rhyme to what was rapidly kindling between Noel and Lydia in the hotel room that night. For once, there was no violent yanking of the chains that bound her to demure isolation. She was not recoiling from a fiery touch this time. She was not politely rejecting the sloppy advances of some lonely camera guy or insomniac photo editor. She was acquiescing happily to a personal project.

Although, she wondered to herself through the fog of lust crowding her mind, maybe she ought to do her due diligence. While she diligently did whatever Noel wanted to do to her.

"So this project," she gasped between fervent kisses as he pinned her down on the bed. "Tell me more. I-I want to know what I'm performing in."

Noel pulled back slowly and gazed at her, his brown eyes lidded with desire. A devilishly handsome smile spread slowly across his face.

"You really are a good girl, aren't you? A real good girl," he mused.

Lydia swallowed hard. He was eyeing her with equal parts awe and hunger.

"I'm a professional," she replied.

"Oh, I could see that from the moment I saw your photo," he said.

"Really?" she breathed.

He dipped down to kiss her again. "Yes. And then walking into this room and seeing you here, in the flesh, just as magnetic and captivating in person as on celluloid... I knew you were even more than I bargained for. You, LightsOnLydia, are something special. The one I've been hoping to find. I didn't go looking for you, not consciously. But here you are."

"Here I am," she agreed with an exhilarated smile.

He had her totally at his mercy, pinned beneath his massive, powerful frame. She was so delicate and dainty under him, her soft curves a profound contrast to his hard body. He rocked his hips ever so slightly and Lydia gasped. She felt his hard cock straining through the fabric at his crotch, lightly brushing across her mound. When he heard her whimper, he pressed against her with more purpose, eliciting another soft moan. He was pleased... and so very, very turned on. He had found his muse, the one to explore this videography endeavor with.

"I'll explain," Noel offered. He grasped her wrists with both massive hands.

Lydia arched her back to meet him, making his cock twinge.

"This will be the first in a series. Our debut video, the one to kick it off. Every new installment, I will find a new way to please you. A new way to connect your body and mine," he explained. "I know we've only just met, but that's kind of the schtick."

Lydia was on fire. She found herself desperate to get rid of the thin fabric separating the two of them on the bed. She needed to be closer to him. Skin on skin. She wanted to feel it all, one thousand percent. Still, though, she forced herself to be as rational as she could in between totally irrational waves of passionate need.

"We're making... porn?" she hissed. The word felt unwieldy on her tongue. In fact, she wasn't sure if she had ever even said it out loud before. What was it about Noel that made her so brave, so reckless?

"Some people might see it that way," Noel admitted. He bent to nip and whisper in her ear. Lydia shivered and felt another little gush of honey between her legs. "But I see it as art. We are two artists coming together as strangers to make an explosion of creative juices."

"An explosion," Lydia repeated, biting her lip.

"Two bodies converging in the ultimate tableau. Getting to pay around in the sandboxes of one another's minds, free of predetermined hangups," he went on, pausing to graze his teeth lightly across her throat.

"Uh-huh," she squeaked back, utterly frozen in place by the shivers rolling up and down her spine. "Sandboxes."

"I have a tendency to get a little metaphysical when I talk about art sometimes," he admitted. "My bad."

"No, no. I love it," Lydia blurted out. "Please. Don't stop."

"I won't," Noel growled back.

And he didn't.

Even as he went on explaining the technical side and the aesthetic details of his project involving Lydia, he artfully slid his hands back up her arms and down the sides of her quivering body. He lifted the lacy hem of her lingerie and peeled it up He stopped to bend down and kiss her while the garment was up past her head but still binding her arms.

"It's the ultimate performance art. The testing of two bodies in a vacuum, a neutral overlapping location," he said as he slipped off his shirt and jeans.

"Like a hotel room," Lydia supplied.

"Exactly," he said, grinning. "See, you get it. Already. Of course, you do."

"But if we're recording right now, and talking about it out loud…" she trailed off.

Her thought process stopped short when Noel's hand slipped under the elastic waistband of her panties and between her soft lips. She uttered a faint moan and closed her eyes. Noel was lucid, though his voice was rough with lust, as he went on.

"It's all very meta, I know," he said. His fingertips circled the tingling bud of nerves at the hood of her flower. "But when you've been behind the camera and in front of it for as long as I have, you start to question everything. Lose the facade. Get real."

"Are we getting real?" Lydia murmured.

Noel looked her straight in the eye as he tugged down her panties and his own well-fitted underwear in one smooth pull. She could see the fire blazing in his stare. It was clear: there was something more than just professional chemistry between them. Maybe this was what it was all about. Maybe this was the crux of her lackadaisical foray into modeling, that every flash and every pose had been a stepping stone to this moment.

"Yes. We are," Noel growled.

And with that, he sheathed the full length of his swollen cock inside of her, and Lydia's mind went white-hot like a flash. Her body tensed up for a moment as he pushed inside, the walls of her pussy clenching tightly around him, pulling him in deeper. He held her hand with his left and her waist with his right, holding her in place while he picked up the pace.

"We are experiencing each other without plan or prejudice. No bias, no expectations beyond whatever we create together in this room," he grunted.

Lydia was even more turned on to hear the roughness in his voice, how obvious it was that his feelings and sensations were distracting his philosophical endeavors. He bent to kiss her again, their tongues probing as he rocked in and out, harder and faster with every stroke.

"Feels like magic," Lydia gasped, her body starting to shake all over.

"It is magic," he agreed.

Goosebumps prickled sharply down his arms and legs, both of them hurtling violently toward a gripping climax. Lydia felt something rise up inside of her, something she had never experienced before. It was like something had taken over her body and mind, her very soul exposed like a raw nerve.

The thick head of Noel's cock slammed again and again into that deep, dark ache within Lydia's cunny. Every stroke brought branches of white-hot lightning through her body. She hooked her legs around his waist tightly and held him close, her perfectly-manicured nails raking down his back as his cock pounded her toward oblivion.

"Yes. Oh my… oh my god," Lydia whimpered, her head falling back limply.

"That's right. That's my good girl," Noel groaned.

"Oh, right there. Right there!" the model yelped. "I'm… oh my god!"

"Oh fuck," Noel gasped, feeling her clench and convulse around him. Lydia was coming, and she was both totally out of body and yet more in tune with and comfortable with her body at the same time. The waves of throat-clenching pleasure rocked her hard, her mind short-circuiting as she gushed slippery juices all over Noel's cock.

He followed mere seconds after with a low groan, his hips pistoning rapidly back and forth while he speared into her, pumping every last drop of his thick come inside of her aching pussy. He slid in and out of her a few more times, milking himself into her before slipping out and gracefully collapsing next to her.

They both stared at the ceiling for a moment, their hands grasped between them on the come-soaked hotel sheets.

"It was a pleasure making art with you," he said, smirking down at her as she rested her chin on his chest, fingers stroking her hair.

She giggled. "Most definitely a pleasure," Lydia sighed.

"And only just the start," he said.

Lydia beamed. She could hardly wait for the second installment of their project.

HIS FERTILE GROUPIE

Book Themes:
Breeding, creampie, simultaneous orgasms, and a very horny groupie with a dominant jerk.
Word Count:
5,293

ALLY COULDN'T BELIEVE her luck. After months of following *The Buzz* around on tour, dreaming of the sexy-as-sin singer, he'd finally noticed her. But more than that, he'd invited her to a special gig, on a private island in the Caribbean.

Only eighteen, she thought she'd experienced all of the pain in the world, and she'd found purpose in their music. But more than that, she spent her nights lusting about their front man. Flynt Slader.

That gorgeous man with the kohl rimmed eyes and the soul that spoke to her. His piercing blue gaze stared into the deepest parts of her. She swore all of his lyrics were written about her life, and she knew they could heal one another's broken hearts.

She'd just been getting out of a bad relationship when she first heard The Buzz come on the radio, with their hit song, and she listened to it on repeat.

She'd even dropped out of college to follow him around on tour. Every night she styled her bottle-blonde hair into a wild mess of curls and she hoped her dark eyes and full lips and tiny bra tops would entice him. Finally, one night, it did, and she was invited backstage.

That was when he invited her to his private concert, on an island in the tropical Caribbean. He'd told her it was a fundraiser, just a small show for a select few very special fans.

He even shelled out for a private jet for her.

But when she stepped off the luxurious jet, dressed in her nicest and sluttiest black dress with her suitcase in hand, she wasn't expecting what she saw as she was driven towards her hotel.

Everything seemed so rustic and quaint, as if she'd gone back in time a hundred years. Even the fine manor that she pulled up in front of, with its colonial styling and large support beams out front, reminded her more of an old historical museum rather than the lavish hotel of the rich and famous.

Yet there he was, Flynt Slade, sat outside with his guitar in his lap, strumming idly as he rocked back and forth on the porch swing.

She couldn't believe her eyes. He was dressed better than he did for his shows, in a nice pair of jeans and a black vest atop a white linen button down. He looked up as she arrived, sweeping his hand through his black hair, making it spike up a bit more.

"Hey, Ally," he said, and she nearly fainted that he'd

remembered her name. She inconspicuously pushed up her cleavage, though her push up bra did most of the work. She stepped towards him, her long, slender legs moving gracefully in her high heels.

She was almost over joyed, too excited to exist, and she couldn't help that she went to him faster than she should have, acting like a little girl getting a puppy.

"Oh my God," she said, looking up over the old building. "Is this really where I'm staying?"

"Yeah that's right," he said with a smile her way, that uneven expression so charming on his face. He looked like such a bad boy in every way. So handsome and dashing, a devious looking black goatee, and looks that could kill. Even if he wasn't a musician, he could probably get away with murder on that devilish smile alone.

"We both are," he remarked, strumming upon that guitar idly, producing such a hypnotic melody as he lowered his dark-rimmed eyes down to the instrument.

"Oh my *God*," she repeated, this time louder and with more emphasis. Every bit of control she had was quickly slipping away as she closed the distance between them. She smelled of vanilla up close, her cleavage absolutely scandalous as she stared at him.

"I can't even believe it," she added on with a full scale blush, her tanned skin turning pink beneath her cheeks.

He looked back up at her, though not without stopping at her luscious breasts to stare a while.

"I like to come here to relax, get myself back together after a tour," he said simply, in that dark voice of his that produced such beautiful lyrical sounds. "And a man can't be expected to relax with a fine piece of ass around, now can he?" he remarked bluntly, looking back to his instrument and trying a few more chords.

Ally was such a smitten fan girl around him, so excited

that he was checking her out that she barely comprehended his words. When they finally sank in, though, she blushed towards the ground, taking a step backwards and towards the house.

"Oh, yea, totally! I'm so sorry," she said, her luggage resting against her firm leg. "Totally didn't mean to interrupt your music, it's just, I'm your biggest fan and had to, like, thank you for getting me this spot!"

He didn't seem to pay her much mind, just playing some beautiful notes, practicing little pieces of what she no doubt thought would eventually become new masterpieces of his. Until finally he looked back at her in that scandalous outfit.

"Just leave your things out here," he instructed her. "Your place is upstairs, right next to the big one. Mine. You can go up there, freshen up. Left a few treats in there for you, to help get you in the spirits before this evening," he stated bluntly, though an offering of anything from him was something she couldn't possibly refuse.

Immediately she set down her luggage, backing towards the door another foot or so.

"Oh my God," she repeated, breathlessly. Right next to his? There was no restraining the thrill that gave her, blue eyes widening with such excitement!

"Okay! This evening, right, of course!" she said, though she had little idea what was in store for her. What plans he truly had for his willingly little groupie. But she could dream.

"I'll see you tonight, then!" She took another step back inwards, her breathing so quick before she turned and quickly moved towards the stairs.

He didn't say a word more, just peered back over his shoulder and watched her hurry on up the large, curving stairs through the manor. She saw no other people there yet, but she understood a true artist like Flynt needed his peace.

When she arrived upstairs, there was no mistaking the place he meant. There at the center of the upstairs hall was a set of double doors, old and exquisite, leading the way to what must have been his room. Then, right next to it a small, single door. It was unlocked, and she went right in.

Inside, the old colonial style room was small compared to what his must've been, but lavish and beautiful. An adjoining bathroom with a large tub awaited her, and there to her right... a locked door that could only have led directly into his room.

In all her excitement about that, she almost didn't notice the silver tray next to the bathroom. There, a decanter with some fluid awaited her, right next to a fancy gold tin. Opening it up she found inside some pills, and knew immediately they had to be what he meant below.

She looked at them curiously, fingers roaming over them before she went to the bathtub and turned it on, letting the hot steam begin to fill the air.

It had been a long flight and she stripped down, looking at herself in the full length mirror next to the bath. Her breasts were large and capped with tight pink nipples, her stomach flat and her ass firm. She was proud of her body and smiled at it before she pulled her hair up into a bun and stepped into the steaming water.

She let it wash over her, breasts disappearing beneath the surface as she kept her hands dry.

With those, she reached towards the pills and the water. She poured herself a glass, the cool drink contrasting against the hot steam, and she held it in her mouth as she popped a pill between her lips and swallowed.

It was risky not knowing what the pill was, how she'd

react, but it was thrilling at the same time. A way of learning what type of high Flynt liked.

Little did she know, though, that it wasn't that type of pill at all.

As she bathed she swore she heard someone enter into her room, and assumed it was the help with her bags as to be expected. But by the time she was done and got out of the tub, she looked into her bedroom only to see her clothing gone and an outfit laid out for her on the bed.

Her bags were nowhere in sight, and a peek into the drawers showed nothing of her own.

She assumed it was all part of Flynt's plans, and went to the clothes he'd laid out for her.

Outfit was perhaps being a bit generous, as it was a see-through white dress, a pair of matching high heels, and nothing else more but gold chains. A waist sized one, a neck sized one and four others that looked ankle or wrist sized.

She looked them over curiously, uncertain of what to make of it.

She didn't yet feel any high from the drugs, though the bath had relaxed her and she felt fresh and clean. She'd shaved just before she left, and used the lotion provided so that she was soft as anything.

Even though she was accustomed to dressing sluttily the clothes provided for her made her blush, and she drew her lower lip into her mouth.

Yet there weren't any other options, and so she pulled on the dress, amazed that her nipples were so visible from beneath it.

There was no way she could go out looking like that, especially without a bra. It felt so scandalous, the way her breasts swayed as she moved.

As the minutes ticked on and the sun began to set,

though, she knew she didn't have the luxury of time, and went towards that door that led to his room. Perhaps if she could just ask for her things...

She knocked twice, listening to see if she could hear anything from within.

It was locked to her though and she couldn't hear anything from the other side. For that matter the door to the hall was also locked, and though that should've made her panic she merely reasoned it had to have been for her own security. Right?

She kept herself calm, and decided to take it easy, enjoy the tropical air by the balcony. She wasn't sure how long she sat there before the sound of music came wafting by her, sounding like it was coming from Flynt's room next door, out the open balcony door next to hers.

She went back to the door that joined their rooms, and though her first inclination was to knock, she didn't want to interrupt him in the middle of his performing.

So instead, she gently turned the knob to test it, and surprisingly found it unlocked.

When she opened it up, she saw his massive, spacious room, a giant four-poster bed big enough to fit a family, and then him... sat down by the window.

His vest was gone then, just the shirt on, left wide open, showing his hard, well-toned abs and pecs beneath as he played the guitar. And he looked utterly wrapped up in what he was doing, the random pieces of music from before slowly coalescing into something nearer to a song.

She leaned against the door, feeling quite the voyeur as she watched. She lost track of how long he played as she stood there in nothing more than her translucent dress, the rest of her outfit still resting upon her bed.

The music, as always, spoke to her soul. It touched her

in such a deep and meaningful way, and she slumped down a little, closing her eyes as she listened.

At last he stopped and put the guitar aside, casting his gaze her way as he if he knew she'd been watching all that time. His blue eyes ran up and down her figure, able to see her areolas through that white, slinky dress.

"Where's the rest of it?" he asked curtly, his voice rough and impatient.

She started as he spoke, straightening up and glancing behind her to the door she'd just come through.

"Oh, I'm sorry!" she said nervously. "It's just... my clothes? Where are they?" She didn't know why she was so nervous. She'd hoped to be able to fuck him for so long, but dressing in such revealing clothing, clothing that wasn't hers, it made her feel more uncertain.

"I gave you better clothes," he stated bluntly. "Why the fuck would you want the other stuff back?" He sounded impatient with her, and got up from his seat, going over to one of the stands and pouring himself up a drink into a tumbler. He took a sip then looked her over, "You tellin' me you came all the fuckin' way out here just to get hung up about some stupid shit you brought with you?"

He was so crass, so rude, but damn he looked good. His hard body on such display, those tight jeans hugging his firm thighs, his round package, dipping low to show the dark hairs that pointed towards his manhood.

She caught herself staring as she took a step back, towards her room. She felt like such an idiot. A confused little girl, and not the badass sex bomb she pretended to be.

"Oh God, I'm so sorry. I didn't mean to offend you," she said as she went back into her room fully, reaching for one of the gold chains and wrapping the long strand about her waist.

She then repeated it along her limbs, her throat, before

stepping into the heels. Though she couldn't stop blushing, feeling so stupid in front of her crush.

When she came back into the room she found him pouring another drink. He cast a look her way, noting the gold chains back upon her.

"That's better," he stated a bit gruffly, leaning his tight, round ass back against the dresser behind him and sliding a hand down over his rocky abs. "Did you take the pill I left you at least?" he asked, and then very unceremoniously undid the top button of his jeans. She couldn't see anything but for the way he slid his fingers down into the gap so lewdly.

It distracted her from his question for a second and she had to force her mind free of thoughts of him unzipping his pants further. At what he'd look like. Smell like. Taste like.

She licked over her lips and forced her eyes away as she finally nodded.

"Yea, but, like, it hasn't kicked in yet," she said confidently. "I took it before my bath."

"It's not that kinda pill," he said to her downing some more of his rum before he jerked his head in a 'come here' gesture. "Take 'em twice a day while you're here, got it?" He instructed as he looked her up and down, "Unless you want me to bring in some other fan who's willing to have some real fun."

"Real fun?" she asked, tilting her head to the side as she walked towards him. "What's it, like... vitamins?" A teasing grin warped her lips as she bit down on the corner of them seductively.

"Somethin' like that," he said, sizing her up with such casual interest as she got up close to him. "They're good for a woman like you," he said of the younger woman, pulling his hand from his pants and casually reaching out to lightly squeeze her breast through her top, and sink his thumb into that fleshy mound.

She couldn't help how broad her smile was, how thrilled she was at his touch. Sure she'd understood all the signs, of her being put in a room next to his, of being forced to dress in such revealing clothes, of being so controlled by the domineering rock star.

Feeling his hand on her, though, was completely different.

"You're not on the pill are you?" he asked, so bluntly. "IUD? Anythin' like that?"

He'd asked her that stuff before he invited her along, and she'd answered him then, but she figured he was being safe.

She shook her head no. She had problems with those types of birth control and always relied on condoms to keep her safe.

"Good," he said simply, rolling his thumb over her growing nipple, teasing that stiff little nub through the thin, see-through fabric of her white dress. "Can't stand fuckin' broads with that stuff," he said, finishing his drink and laying the tumbler down on the stand beside him.

Then, her rockstar crush did such a lewd thing, and he reached his free hand down, popping open another button, then another, tugging down his pants to free that thick, long cock of his. She could see immediately that it wasn't even fully hard yet, but it was immense. Bigger than any she'd ever seen, and he was exposing it to her right before her eyes. Even the two heavy cum-laden balls beneath.

"On your knees and suck it," he commanded her.

She wasn't expecting it to happen like that. She didn't know what she *did* expect to happen, but not that.

The God she'd worshipped for so long, the man she

thought understood her soul, commanding her so forcefully.

And yet stranger still was how obedient she was about it. She'd lusted for him for so long that she couldn't resist dropping down, staring right at his cock with such a curious hunger. Her friends would never believe her!

Her mouth opened as her hand gripped the base of his thickening shaft, holding him tight in her fingers. Her tongue poked out, tasting his masculine musk with such relish. Her cunny was throbbing so hard as she went down the length of his shaft, suckling him so eagerly.

Flynt reached out and put his hand upon her head, sinking his digits in through her hair as he began to forcibly guide her actions. His dick was so big, and as it rested along her tongue she could feel it swelling up, thicker, thicker. It soon became hard for her to fit it in her mouth! It strained her jaw just to keep going, but that forceful hand in her hair made sure she continued.

"That's it," he said in a low tone of voice, the husky sound of pleasure on his tongue as he spoke to her. "I didn't fly you all this way for nothin' after all," he said, the tip of his cock probing her throat as he urged her on.

One look up showed his eyes struggling to stay open as she worked that thick cock of his, his chiselled abs and pecs tensed as his chest rose and fell.

She'd never been with a man so huge, and as her airways were temporarily blocked, she gripped his thigh tight, her other hand wrapping around his cock more fully. It gave her a bit more leeway so she wasn't taking him down her throat.

And yet the idea of it made her throb excitedly, and she wriggled on the floor.

A soft moan went over his cock, her pleasured sound so

deep that it vibrated his flesh, her tongue working along his veins so intently.

She worked her mouth over his dick so diligently, throwing all her excited enthusiasm into making him moan and twitch with pleasure. He still grasped her head and hair, but finally he groaned and yanked her off his long, hard cock.

"Fuck!" He cursed loudly, "Nearly made me cum, bitch. Careful what you're fuckin' doing." It was confusing to see him so upset at her nearly doing exactly what she thought was her duty, but he looked down at her crossly. "Here," he said, shoving her face in under the shaft to his two large, heavy balls. "Suck these for now."

He was so much crasser than she'd expected and she was delighted by it. As though he had ignited a fire in her loins, and so she went to his sac and suckled it in. His heavy cock rest across her face, and she was once more surprised by its length and heft.

But she turned all that attention she'd paid his cock to his balls, lapping them up so hungrily.

The masculine taste of his loins was so intensely unique; he was all man and as that thick, meaty shaft rested over her face, she swore she felt a trill of excitement course through her. It throbbed, spurted its thick precum that she'd only moments before tasted upon her tongue, but now ran down his length and onto her face.

His girth was so hot, and pulsating with desire as she suckled and licked his two heavy balls, struggling to fit them into her mouth one at a time without grazing them with her teeth.

"That's it," he husked, hand still on her head as he watched her slather his sac with her tongue and saliva. "You're not the brightest girl, but you catch on eventual-ly," he instructed. "I don't want you spillin' any of that seed in those balls until I'm good and ready to give it to you."

His words did a dangerous thing to her, that thinly veiled threat, the questions about birth control, all swirling about in her mind.

And yet she wanted it. So badly did she want it, and she pressed her face more firmly into his sac, her tongue running across his balls so eagerly, dragging her tongue along his flesh.

A low hum went across his flesh as she squirmed, the throbbing in her loins almost too much to ignore.

He shuddered, letting his head arch back as he released a low, lewd moan, all that chiseled, hard flesh of his on display as she slathered over his balls. When his dick pulsed and spurted another jet of precum down its length he pulled her off his balls once more and looked down at her. His gaze was hard.

"Go stand up on the balcony, bend over the railing," he instructed her, tugging her hair to guide her in the direction, though it made her teeter.

Her mind was spinning. She couldn't believe that he was so into her, his hard behaviour only making her want to please him more. She walked as quickly as she could towards the balcony, her arms going to the railing as she leaned over, flushing as the skirt of her dress rolled up over her hips and exposed her fleshy ass.

Her blonde hair feathered over her face, hiding her blush in its golden curtain, and her feet even spread to hip width, inviting him in.

It'd been so long since she had sex, not that she lacked the opportunities.

No, she was saving herself. For him.

He strolled up behind her, staring at that ample, round ass of hers on display, and the sight of her bare cunny bared between her thighs. He swaggered on up behind her, reaching his hand out to stroke along the smooth curve of her two cheeks, then dip down, to touch that warm, wet slit below.

"You are one eager slut," he remarked at the slickness of her cunt, that thick hard dick of his prodding her thigh as he felt her up. "Here's the thing," he said to her firmly, grasping the base of his dick as he walked in behind her. "That pill you took? That was some fertility drugs I had brought in just for you," and he slapped the raw flesh of his dick to her pussy, making a wet smack in the night air. "You know why?" he asked, as if speaking to a child in need of instruction and guidance.

Her mind was reeling, and she tossed her hair over her shoulder as she looked at him, mind swimming with confusion. She may not be a kid, but she certainly couldn't understand why he'd feed her fertility drugs, come to this island and be his little sex toy with so much risk!

Flynt looked at her with that cocky smirk, the same one he wore on stage, except now he was rubbing his raw dick along her puffy, wet slit, teasing her clit with his thick, throbbing cock.

"You're gonna be my lil' breeding bitch," he informed her, and for a moment he very nearly stuck his dick right in her, nudging that broad crown against her plush nether lips.

"I'm gonna dump every load I have this trip right in your lil' pussy. And when I'm done? You're gonna be knocked up with my kid in your belly. You hear me?"

His voice was so firm, so resolute. There was no choice offered to her by the way he spoke, yet her mind reeled with indecision.

And arousal.

To be knocked up by her idol?

Nothing could possibly compare to that, and her eyes widened. She wanted it. Everything in her wanted it. It would be the ultimate thrill, the highest reward a groupie like her could ever want for!

"Yes!" she finally said as her mind stopped tumbling with their thoughts, and her legs spread wider.

"That's more like it," he said, giving a smack across her smooth, round ass to make her squeal, using that moment of opportunity to sink his fat dick into her slick little cunt. The feeling of that thick, veiny girth plowing into her deep and raw making her knees quake.

He was huge, his dick as big as his ego, making her feel every inch of it as he sank right down to her utmost depths to nudge against her womb.

"Fuck yeah, you're gonna like being my personal breeding bitch," he said before he tugged back his hips and gave a lewd groan into the tropical night air.

Perhaps she should have been put off by his rude language, but she sensed the desire running beneath it, and those raunchy words did little more than excite her as much as the sensation of his dick filling her did.

She could barely believe what was happening to her, but she pushed back against him with such eagerness. She truly was his personal little slut, so absolutely soaking wet and wanton for him.

She'd always played it safe before, so careful with sexual intercourse, but there she was, bent over a railing, offering up her raw, fertile pussy to her idol. And he was taking it for all its worth.

His two hands grasped her hips and ass cheeks as he rocked his hips, the warm ocean breeze washing over them both as he pummeled her pussy, sliding that thick, bulging cock into her so deep as he claimed her his.

"This is gonna be your new life, slut," he groaned out

amid his moans. "You're gonna live here on my island...
gonna pop out as many kids as I wanna have," he insisted,
and with each word she felt his dick throb with excitement. He wanted her to be the mother of his children so
damn bad.

His enthusiasm was infectious, and for those moments,
she wanted nothing more than to do just that. To be whatever he needed, whatever he wanted, and she shuddered
violently against his cock.

With every thrust, her pussy clenched him, that thick
head pounding so deep into her against her womb, the
threat implicit.

"Yes," she gasped out, her head tilted back and her back
arching as that white dress pulled up a bit more.

Flynt arched his back, letting loose such a lewd,
depraved moan at that clench of her pussy around his dick.
His skin developed a light sheen of perspiration, and all
that hard muscle gleamed in the Caribbean moonlight.

"Fuck!" He cursed, his hefty balls tightening against him
as that first load began to travel up through his shaft like
an intensely burning pleasure. "Gonna knock you up, slut,"
he bit out mere moments before his dick exploded, and all
that virile cum blasted out, thick rivulets of creamy spunk
filling her up.

As big as his dick was, that rich load of semen matched,
pumping her so full as she bent over that railing. He
moaned so deeply, filling the night air with his pleasured
sounds, pumping her fertile womb full of his seed all the
while.

And instead of horrified, she felt so... relieved. Her
mind went numb and all that was left was her emotions,
that sensation of pleasure that twisted its way through her
core.

As his heavy balls slapped against her clit those few

final times, she could barely hold back any longer, her entire body excited and so very near to that brink. She brought one of her hands from the railing, moving it between her legs and touching her wet clit, rubbing it roughly.

He felt her bring her hand down, and though he pulled back, he didn't take his dick out entirely. He grasped the long shaft, and pumped it with one hand, squeezing out the last of his seed into her depths, milking it for another spurt. Then another.

"That's it," he told her, stroking her lower back with his free hand. "Cum for me, slut... make that pussy purr and lap up my cum." He knew it'd only enhance the chances of her conceiving his child, and he egged her on excitedly.

She rubbed her clit so hard and fast, and she was so close that it only took a few seconds before that spark ignited in her loins, spreading out so instantly as her pussy drew him in, clenching his cock so tightly.

"Oh Flynt!" she cried out, lust apparent in her tone as she slammed her hips back against him.

He shuddered, feeling that tight clench of her pussy as it reached climax, and it milked another thick spurt of his virile cum right out of him. He grabbed a hold of her, keeping her in place tightly as she quaked and screeched into the warm, breezy night until they were both panting and sticky.

"Don't fuckin' spill a drop," he warned her so grimly, pushing down on her back to arch her spine and keep her pussy propped up in the air. He plucked his dick from her, leaving it to drool his thick cream, but he very quickly scooped her shapely body up into his arms and lifted her.

Her legs were wobbly, and the heels didn't help, so she was grateful for his strong arms about her. He smelled so masculine and she nuzzled into his neck, inhaling deeply.

He carried her back into the bedroom and laid her out upon the extravagant, thick bed, his hard cock exposed as he grabbed a pillow and propped it in beneath her ass.

"Let that pussy drink it in," he told her in that smooth, lyrical voice of his.

And she felt like it was the time to protest, to move away and escape his hold on her, but she didn't want to.

She didn't know it before that day, but she wanted absolutely nothing more than to have that tie to him, to know that they'd created something together, their souls forever linked. And so she lay on that pillow, his cum draining into her eager womb.

And he'd promised to breed her every day of the vacation!

HIS FERTILE PRESENT

*B*ook **Themes:**
F/M/F Threesome, Breeding, Polyamory,
Multiple Partners, Menage, and Creampie
Word Count:
6,245

IT WAS something he'd always wanted, but honestly, I'd always been a little worried about trying it. There's something about inviting my best friend to join me in the bedroom with my fiancé that made me feel a little jealous... and a lot turned on. Not that I would tell him that. If he knew that I so often touched myself to the thought of him fucking my best friend, raw?

There's no going back from that.

But after last Valentine's Day, when he proposed to me, I knew I had to top him somehow. I was talking about it with Stacey one day at lunch, and I can't even remember how it came up. I blame the mimosas.

I kept watching her lick her full, pretty lips. I was entranced by the way she brushed some of her hair off her cheeks, and her tight little dress looked really great on her. Maybe I brushed against her naked leg a little too often, or maybe it was just the way I kept moving closer to her.

Stacey was single, and gorgeous. She had blonde hair that always fell perfectly around her face and expressive blue eyes. She was stunning, but she was having a hard time finding someone she connected with.

Still, when I felt her hand atop my knee, I couldn't help but clam up. I'd always been the shyer one of us, even though we'd gone to college together and had more than our fair share of crazy exploits.

But I'd never thought I'd ever have the courage to ask for the thing I really wanted. Not until the words tumbled from my lips...

"Stacey... Have you ever thought of joining Todd and I?"

Her hand was still on my knee, and it didn't shift away. Not even at my words. Still, I held my breath as I waited, so nervous that the answer might be something I didn't want to hear. Oh God, did I just ruin our friendship? Did I just jeopardize everything I had with my best friend, just for a chance that she'd join my fiancé and me in the bedroom?

I was so nervous that I barely noticed the fact that her fingers had worked their way up higher along my knee, playing against my thigh as she stared at me.

"I think about it a lot," she admitted, breathily, and I couldn't believe what I was hearing. I couldn't! It took me a long few heartbeats before my eyes went to her, exploring those baby-blues of hers.

"Really?" I asked, and it was part hopeful, part surprised. I squirmed and found her hand had crawled higher upon my thigh.

"Yes," she murmured, leaning in towards my ear.

I was dumbstruck.

"What about... Do you have anything for Valentine's Day?" I asked gently, and she shook her head from side to side.

"Nothing I wouldn't skip in a heartbeat to join you two."

I had trouble believing it was all happening so easily. My best friend and I were often on the same wavelength, but this was uncanny. Even our deepest, darkest desires were shared? It was a bit much to wrap my head around.

"Then... maybe you'd be up for making it a very special day for Todd," I said sheepishly, but all the same I found my hand reaching out to rest atop hers on my thigh. "He's a great man, the best really—" I said unable to keep from gushing about him, even though I did my best not to make her jealous, usually. "Great enough to share," I added on, fluttering my lashes anxiously.

And Stacey's grin really said it all. I mean, neither of us were going to get drunk on a couple of mimosas, but there was definitely that warmth in my heart and my tongue was a bit loosened.

"We could just do dinner first, see where it leads," I offered, even though she already looked so into it. She was licking her lips, leaning in so close to me that I could smell her sweet perfume.

"It's a date," she agreed, and her fingers teased a bit higher on my bare, inner thighs, exciting the skin. Sure it was February and I was freezing, but what's a little bit of discomfort to look good, right? And now I was so ecstatic that I'd skipped the tights.

I couldn't help but breathe a sigh of relief and smile at her happily. I'd been so anxious about bringing that up with her I realized, and time was an issue too, since I had no real other idea how to make Valentine's special for Todd this year.

"I'm so glad Stacey," I said, and I leaned over, wrapping my arms about her so that our breasts pressed together in our embrace. Able to smell her delightful scent, I felt more intoxicated than I had from the drinks. "You're so special to me, I want to share everything with you."

And I truly meant it. Todd and I were something great, but Stacey and I were special too. Girlfriends of a different caliber, and seeing such a beautiful, smart, clever woman alone killed me. I'd share my man with her in a heartbeat just to make her happy.

It wasn't just the sex, though I had to admit... I wanted her. I'd wanted her for a long time, and now that she'd agreed I was practically having to beg myself not to leap for joy.

Her hand coiled along my back, feeling out the flesh there, and everything about the embrace seemed different. Unusual. New.

Exciting.

She purred in my ear, "Do you want it to be a surprise?"

I nodded, quickly. It would be perfect. Just perfect.

TODD ARRIVED home with an enormous bundle of red roses in his hand, his immaculate business suit crisp and perfectly fitted. He was a professional man when it came to work, always looked the role of boss. The silvery-grey of his sports jacket contrasted the maroon of his tie, and the light blue of his shirt, yet it was the handsome, tall man that filled it out which really drew the eye.

Todd had a well-groomed beard and stylish blonde hair, his eyes were a curious mix of light sky blue and grey,

296

and I often got lost staring into them. Especially when pinned beneath him.

My mind gets away from me so easily when it comes to Todd. He radiates masculinity, sex. Even though he's so calm, cool and in control.

Or maybe because of it.

Regardless, I knew I'd lucked out when I'd ran into him at the grocery store and struck up a conversation about the ripeness of some melons or something equally as trite. I'd never felt so lucky as the day that I met him.

Well, every day since only got better and better.

My hand went to his chest as I accepted the bouquet, kissing his mouth with such affection. I was trying to act calm as well, but I couldn't help it. I was abuzz with energy, and I couldn't wait for him to find out what his present really was.

"Thank you!" I purred against his mouth.

His strong forearm pressed into my lower back and he held me to him tightly as we kissed. My handsome man was never one for short kisses; he wanted to savour my lips each time and was never too shy to let it happen. Never too macho to kiss his woman in public, regardless.

"Well it's just the tip of the iceberg, my sweet," he said to me in that deep, velvety voice of his. His every word so rich and firm. His newly freely hand went to my side, down to my hip where he squeezed my ample flesh tightly.

I couldn't help but grin at just how right he was. If he thought he had something for me that would top my gift, he had another thing coming.

"Well there's no way you could do better than last year," I teased.

"Oh, I don't know about that," he said to me with that self-assured confidence, smiling down with a twinkle in his beautiful eyes.

He lifted a hand up to cup my cheek, the engagement ring cool, such a contrast to the rest of his hard, warm grasp.

"Remember how we talked about having that baby?" he said to me smoothly, holding my gaze.

How could I forget? Months of asking him to ignore his traditional families wishes and just forget the condoms for a little while? To get a start on the family before we exchanged vows?

The conversations has gone as well as I'd assumed, but I was so ready for a baby and I didn't want to have to wait another few months, that much was certain.

But I didn't want to hope that he'd changed his mind...

"Of course," I said, pulling away and tucking some of my dark, wavy hair behind my ear. "Why?"

He took his time answering me, that steely gaze of his travelling down over me, soaking in every inch of my figure as if I was the most ravishing woman in the world.

"I was thinking you'd look at least as beautiful in your wedding dress with a pregnant belly," he said, cracking one of those devilish smiles of his that made him look even more handsome still.

I was floored. Positively and utterly struck dumb for a long few moments as his hands roamed over my tight, red dress. I nearly dropped the roses before I came to, startling my way out of my thoughts.

"Are you kidding me?" I asked, and for a moment I forgot all about Stacey and our plans for later.

He trailed his hand back over my cheek, ran his fingers lightly through my hair in that appreciative manner of his which carefully avoided messing up my hairdo.

"Do I ever kid with you about something so important?" he asked, his voice rich and husky as he pulled be slowly back in against him, let me feel his hard, athletic body pressed against me. "I want you to have my child. And after that, I want you to have another. And another. And we can't very well wait around forever if we're going to make the kind of quota I have in mind," he said with a quirky smile upon his full lips.

"Exactly!" I said, louder than I intended. I was just about to lose it, and I squirmed against him. Hell, I wanted to throw away all our plans then and there just to feel him take me, raw, for the first time. I'd always had problems with other types of birth control, but I couldn't help but really crave his dick, bare and throbbing for me.

My hand went down his chest, over his abs, grabbing at his belt.

"We have forty five minutes before the reservation..." I breathed out, unfastening it and bringing my hand lower to rub at his package. Just the idea of him getting me knocked up had me wet as a hurricane.

That wasn't a lot of time to fuck, get ourselves back together then cross town to the restaurant, but neither of us seemed like we'd be able say no once I started loosening his belt. Todd's package swelled through his tailor-fit pants, and his hands felt out my ample breasts through my top as I went about freeing the beast. That thick cock of his locked behind a final layer of cotton beneath those pant, which I then peeled back to let that throbbing, veiny girth pounce forth.

"You're lucky," he said breathily as he took hold of me, guided me to the wall and bent up over up against it. "I've been saving a big load for you as a special Valentine's Day present," he growled as his dick throbbed behind me, his hands rolling up my dress to expose my cunny.

My hands braced myself as I looked over my shoulder at him. I couldn't see him well as he brought the dress up over my hips, finding me without any panties, shaved smooth, and already soaking wet. I parted my legs, arching my back as I purred at him.

"Fuck me hard," I pleaded, my plans, the flowers, everything forgotten with the promise of feeling his raw cock.

Later I'd share him with Stacey, but for now, my rich and successful man would be all mine, and I felt his bare, unsheathed dick sink into me. A single, slow thrust and he was buried to the hilt inside me, that broad, vein-bulging shaft spearing me open. But this time, there was no layer of nasty rubber between us, no knowledge that he was going to pull out to ruin the whole thing for me.

He let loose a deep, throaty moan as he ploughed in deep and pulsated with excitement. Delaying that brief moment before he began to pump his hips, hard and growing faster with each thrust.

It felt better than I could have ever imagined. He was so big and warm, and my juices let him thrust quickly. My back arched, pussy clenching his dick as I moaned out his name.

"God, you feel so good," I managed breathily, taking in a couple short gasps. "I can't wait to feel your cum in me."

Todd was a man of power and control, and until he decided he was going to knock me up with a cool head, I knew he'd never fumble. He'd never ridden me raw, except on the rare occasion we indulged ourselves and he pulled out. He'd never fail, of course. But this time...

He'd never fail, but the goal was different.

Those heavy, cum-laden balls of his swung up between my parted thighs and smacked against my clit, again and again. Each of his hard thrusts punctuated with the wet smack of our bodies colliding.

"You're gonna be my beautiful lil' breeder," he growled to me, and I could feel the excited pulse through his cock.

Those words made me quiver with desire and I

squeezed his dick with my tight pussy, needing so bad to feel his creamy jism fill me. I was so excited I could barely contain myself, those little vibrations and spasm of pleasure going through me with such urgency.

Todd was buff and athletic, his body a well-tuned machine, and he put it to use pounding his cock into me so magnificently. He thrust hard and fast, building such an intense tempo as I felt his cock throb with urgency, his own release held barely in check. I knew he couldn't last too long, not in the face of that tight, clenching pussy of mine.

I managed to coax a deep, pleasured moan from him and he bent over me, pressed me up against the wall harder as he ploughed into my fertile depths. And, oh, they were fertile.

We'd both been checked out to make sure we'd have no trouble conceiving when the time came, and we were — in the doctor's words — the ripest couple he'd ever met. Todd had sperm to breed the most barren of wombs, and I was ready for his seed to sow.

"Cumming!" he grunted out, moments before his balls tightened and he began to blow that thick, rich stream of seed into me.

It was the sweetest gift he could have given me, and I accepted it all with a scream of my own. I was ravenous for his cum and slammed my ass into his hips, forcing the head of his huge dick to press painfully against my inner most depths. But even that brought me a sense of pleasured joy, more so knowing that with that one act, our choice was likely made.

In that brief tryst before dinner, Todd had undoubtedly planted his seed within me. I just had a sense for it as I felt him empty his loins into me, all that thick rich cum spurting and filling me up, so much my pussy couldn't handle it all. I was left overflowing with his cum as he bucked and twitched a few final times, groaning in pleasure all the while.

"Good girl," he husked approvingly, leaning over me and pressing a kiss to the back of my head. "And happy Valentine's Day," he whispered softly before slowly pulling back out of me, leaving me so sadly empty. But for his cum, that is.

Yet I knew what I had planned for him would blow his mind, just as his gift had done for me.

～

HE AGREED to knock me up!

I hit send on the text as soon as I sat into Todd's luxury car, and couldn't wait to see Stacey's reply as we started our way towards the high scale restaurant Todd had chosen. I had to talk to one of my contacts there to change our table from two to three, but I knew calling in that favour would be worth it.

OMG Really? When?

Stacey texted back.

Just now. We might be running late...

All she sent back to that was a winking smiley face, and I grinned wider.

This was going to be a night to remember...

～

THE LOOK on Todd's face when the waiter took us to an already occupied table was priceless. Not that he betrayed much in that stoic expression of his, but it was the little things that said it all.

"No no, this is our table, sweetie," I said, clinging to her arm as I tugged him to the seats. The waiter managed to beat him to the punch at pulling out my chair.

A first.

Even my man could be shaken with surprise it seemed.

It might have seemed rather strange, to invite my best friend along to our get together, but it didn't take long for me to get the message across to Todd. Flanked by two women, Stacey's hand reaching out to touch his thigh, mine upon his other, I leaned in and murmured to him seductively.

"Happy Valentine's Day, sweetie. Double the women in your life," I said in such a lusty voice, so ripe with lurid intent.

He was shocked into silence, and I grinned across him towards my best friend. Stacey was wearing a sexy black dress that showed off her ample cleavage, and with the dark rimmed eyes and red lips, she looked like a bombshell.

Maybe I should've been worried about feeling jealous, but honestly... that kind of turned me on too. And I couldn't help but find myself attracted to her toned, beautiful body and her sweet yet seductive face.

I squeezed Todd's thigh again, and snaked it higher and higher as the meal progressed and he started relaxing into it.

Todd was not unfamiliar with Stacey, and the three of us got to chatting naturally before long, getting my husband-to-be over the awkwardness of his new present. The dinner was a beautiful, high class affair, and Todd was able to embrace the fact he shared it with two stunning women, one on each arm.

When it came time for dessert and we were finishing our lovely evening out, I snuck my hand up over his thigh and took a feel of his groin. I could feel his stiff cock,

raging hard once more after our earlier tryst, and then...
Stacey's hand joined me. The two of us gently massaging
that beastly sized dick, making it throb and bulge beneath
our fingers until the bill was brought and taken care of.

I bit in upon my lip as my hand skirted hers and then
retreated as Todd went to stand, his motions a bit more
cautious. Then, they'd have to be to hide that huge
package.

I wondered what others thought, and glanced around,
briefly, at the packed restaurant filled with couples and
then... us. It probably seemed like we were prostitutes or
something, and the thought nearly made me laugh out
loud.

Stacey moved towards me, letting Todd lead us out and
back to his car. Unfortunately he'd brought his two seater,
but that wasn't any problem for us.

Taking off down the road with Stacey in my lap, her
smooth thighs pressed against me as she wriggled with
excitement... How could I complain?

She leaned back, whispering to me so that Todd
couldn't hear.

"So he's really aiming to knock you up?"

I nodded, my cheek pressed against hers. "He already
took me bare tonight," I confessed with a lusty growl.

She pulled back for a second, considering that information before she whispered something in my ear I'll never
forget.

"Think he'll do me too?"

My eyes flashed wide at the brazen nature of the question, but I couldn't help but grin. Todd was my man, and
though I was excited to share him with her...

I was already certain he'd knocked me up.

I giggled and gave her rear a pinch as best I could, it

was so firm after all, then the two of us shot a conspirato-rial look over at Todd, who spared just a glance.

"What are you two planning?" he asked, like a loving father talking to his two daughters.

"Nothing," I said, drawing out the word and giving him such a wicked grin. I couldn't help it.

The thought of him knocking up my best friend was making me squirm, and I could already feel my clit throbbing with need.

It was a struggle to make it back to our place, though Stacey and I made the most of it. The two of us like college girls again, pawing, prodding at one another in rather inappropriate ways, catching Todd's gaze time and again as one of us would cop a feel of the other's breast, or up between the thighs.

We took the elevator back up to our place, and Stacey and I were all over him, flanking him on either side. Feeling him up, fawning over my man even as other riders briefly hopped aboard until at last we were at our destination.

The flowers were still abandoned on the side table, but we barely noticed anything about our front foyer as I grabbed onto Todd's tie, dragging him towards our bedroom. We weren't overly kinky people or anything, and this was definitely the most risky thing we'd done together.

I couldn't even believe how turned on I was as I led the two of them into our room. We had a king sized bed with gold and maroon sheets and cherry wood furniture, and I turned the lights on just a bit to illuminate the room in a gentle wash of light.

Stacey was already helping Todd undress, sliding her hands in under his sports jacket, slipping it back off his shoulders. Leaving me to undo his tie, then slowly thread his buttons through the holes, undoing his shirt to reveal his hard, toned physique beneath.

My man was such a looker, and he took great care to stay in shape, as the two of us helped undress him, Stacey got her first, full appreciation for just how studly of a man my Todd was.

And I took such delight in watching her mouth fall open in a bit of surprise, licking over her lips as she eye-fucked him.

"So Todd," I purred. "Why don't you open your present?

I watched as his gorgeous eyes met mine, checking to make sure everything was okay in a silent manner before his hand moved to Stacey's back. He found the zipper at her back arched with excitement, her erect nipples visible beneath the dress.

He watched me at first as that zipper came down, exposing Stacey's beautiful, unblemished back. But when he began to slip it from her figure and leave her bare from the waist up, he looked and appreciated my best friend's figure for how stunningly gorgeous it was.

Stacey helped by taking hold of his hand, guiding it up to cup one of her ample breasts, urging him to sink his fingers into that supple flesh and enjoy its feel. The throb in his bulge said he enjoyed it immensely at that, his gaze flitting from the sight of her tit in his palm, nipple prodding betwixt his fingers, over to me.

I was transfixed. Never had I seen him touch another woman, nor even look at one. He was always a perfect gentleman with me, and this was far beyond what I was used to.

So I wasn't prepared for the way my heart pounded and my pussy throbbed, my breath caught as my fiancé squeezed my best friend's breast. Stacey moaned, and I squirmed with my own arousal. It was going to be hard not jumping him then and there, making him take me again, hard and raw.

No, I had to contain myself, force myself to watch as my man felt up my best friend, enjoyed her smooth skin, slid his free hand down across her hip and helped her shimmy out of that dress entirely. Which revealed that just like me, Stacey wore nothing beneath. Scandalously bare, and oh so wet with arousal.

I broke from my frozen position to come over behind Todd, shedding my own dress before I pressed my bare breasts to his back and snaked my limbs around him. My two hands coming to his belt and unbuckling it, working it through the hoop before I undid his trousers.

"It's okay to enjoy her," I said in a lusty, whispering voice, my hand slipping into his boxer-briefs to wrap about his dick and feel just how intensely aroused he was.

He throbbed in my hand, that cock so stiff and long.

I peaked around his body in order to look at Stacey, to lick my lips as I freed him from his pants and boxers.

"I told you he was huge," I said confidently, giving my man another stroke before unleashing him, letting him bounce before my best friend. God, how did it turn me on so damn much?

I looked at Stacey's fit body, her large breasts, the smooth curve of her ass and thighs, and I wanted to touch her, to take her. But this wasn't about what I wanted. It was a night about Todd.

She certainly wasn't new to seduction herself, and when she bent herself over, leaning atop the edge of the bed, she curved her spine in such a seductive manner, offering up her plush, round ass, and the glistening slit betwixt her thighs.

I could see the thrill of excitement in Todd. What man didn't want to have two gorgeous women, after all? And judging by the intense throbbing in his cock, my virile man was no exception.

"Get me a condom from the nightstand," he told me as he grasped Stacey's hips and fondled her figure, down to her firm ass cheeks.

But I didn't want a condom to ruin any of this, and I kissed his back, stood up on my tip-toes to reach his shoulders as I whispered.

"It would be so much more perfect without a nasty ol' condom though, don't you think?" I said, reaching down to cup his heavy, cum-laden balls and fondle them gently.

Stacey flipped her hair back and peered behind at us both.

"You can cum right in me, it's okay," she said, her voice so seductive, so wanting. "I need it in me so bad," and it sounded so honest and genuine.

I rubbed my thumb along his sac as I groaned. My other hand went to his stiff, wanting cock, trying to guide him to my friend's shaved pussy. I could smell the soft, feminine scent of her arousal in the air, and it was making me so horny I could hardly stand it.

Perhaps the two of us combined finally managed to shake Todd's stoicism. Or maybe with his decision to knock me up, he was willing to go all out with her too. Either way, he let me guide the fat, purple crown of his cock to her bare pussy, and once the two of them touched loins together, he slid in to the hilt and the both of them moaned loudly.

I watched his hands grip at her hips and ass tightly as he began to pump into her, watched my best friend's face contort with such pleasure as my husband-to-be stretched her little cunny open wide with his thick cock.

The sight took my breath away and I couldn't do

anything more than squirm, stepping aside to watch as that throbbing organ pierced her.

Before I knew what I was doing, my hand was between my legs and I was touching myself, prodding my own throbbing clit and trying to find some measure of relief. But that touch only brought me up higher, and I ground into my hand, messing my fingers up with my own juices.

Seeing Todd pound into Stacey from behind, making her firm ass ripple with each impact, was enthralling. I was captivated by those glimpses of his cock pulling back, tugging her labia with him as they were so tightly wrapped about his girth.

Stacey and I were so alike, and I realized that watching Todd fuck her was like a mirror for all the times he'd fucked me. And I got an even greater appreciation for our own love making then, because this was utterly rapturous to behold.

I came back in, pressed my bare tits to Todd's side and kissed his lips as he fucked my best friend. I lingered there a while as my free hand trailed up over her back and into her hair, before I broke away from his lips and came up beside her, to kiss her shoulder. Only she wasn't satisfied by merely a kiss on the shoulder, and our lips met then, and we made out as she was bounced by his thrusts.

Todd got a full view of us kissing, tonguing and enjoying each other's mouths as he fucked Stacey harder and faster.

I was getting really wrapped up in it then. It wasn't the quiet arousal of watching two others fuck, but the full on heat and need of my body meeting another's. One I'd appreciated and laughed and cried with, and had such a crush on for so long in my own way.

My tongue swiped against hers and I moaned as I dipped

one of my hands down to touch her large, bouncing tit. My other hand brushed some of Stacey's blonde hair from her face, cupping her jaw as my mouth moved against hers.

Our beautiful moment together only made Todd pump and thrust all the rougher, the sight of his woman and her best friend making out able to drive him to new heights of virility. The two of us gals savoured it, and I fondled her breast, kissed her deeply.

I could sense Todd getting closer to his climax with the way he panted and moaned, the slight hitch in his otherwise flawlessly rhythmic pace. Something occurred to me then: I remembered reading in the news once that a woman climaxing in time with the man enhanced the chances of conception. And I wanted Stacey to conceive with me that night.

I released her face, and switch hands. One cupped her full, heavy breast, the other slid down to prod at her sensitive clit. My dainty digits circling and provoking that lovely little nub buried amid her puffy pink labia.

Looking back, I watched Todd pound away, could see all his prominent abs and pecs glistening with a thin sheen of perspiration as he battered at her pussy, hammering towards his finale.

"Come on baby," I cooed to him. "Fill her up... we both need your seed so bad," I said.

I watched his face contort, could see the pleasure written upon his face as he buckled forward just a little, edging closer... closer...

He rammed in deep with each thrust, and then I watched it all happen. The convulsion through his broad shoulders, on down across his rippling physique as he blew his load into her. Another thick stream of cum lancing out of his hard, immense cock, but this time it wasn't into me, it was into my best friend's fertile little pussy.

And I couldn't have been happier.

I reminded myself of what I was doing, and worked Stacey's clit harder, faster. Brought her pleasure to such heights so that she came hard upon his dick in return. Just in time to receive Todd's creamy gift, same as I had earlier that night.

I lost control of myself, and while still squeezing Stacey's breast, I dove in to kiss Todd passionately. He'd bred my best friend and I in the same night, I just knew it, but I only wanted him more than ever because of it.

My slick fingers went from Stacey's clit around to grasp the base of Todd's cock, and as he pulled back just a little, I pumped his dick to squeeze out every last drop.

And keep him nice and hard for me.

Todd and I had been together long enough for me to know his limits, and three times in one night was not beyond him. Certainly not with two hot women who wanted his cock and cum.

He plucked his cock from Stacey's pussy at last, leaving a thick, creamy load to dribble from her slit. Though he pushed me from the kiss just long enough to appreciate the sight of that creampie.

"You're next," he said in a deep growl, so primal and needy.

Todd pushed me down onto the bed upon my back, and he mounted atop me. That glistening shaft of his sank in deep, still coated in Stacey's moist fluids as he made me moan. Though my best friend was far from forgotten, as my fiancé began to pound into me, he pulled her into his side as she toyed with her cum-filled pussy.

I watched him bend his head down and kiss at her tits, lick at the edge of her areola before making his way back up to her lips. I was being fucked by my man as he made out with my best friend...

Maybe I should have felt jealous, envious, but instead I felt so incredibly hot, and I clung to the comforter atop the bed as I moaned and wailed, soaking it all in.

Stacey looked to me, first to see if I was okay with their kissing, then to watch my thick tits bounce and sway atop my chest. There was nothing more exhilarating in the world than watching them make out, my fiancé so eager for another woman even as he pounded into me.

The three of us worked so well together, and she slid her hand down behind him, beneath his ass to cradle his balls and fondle them oh so gently. It produced a sweet moan from him, and he returned a similar gesture, cupping her cunt and fingering her as he pounded me. The sound of her pussy so wet thanks to the mess in her folds.

We were all moaning and wailing from the pleasure, and it all went on so long.

We switched positions multiple times, until near the end, I was atop him, having him watch my tits bounce as Stacey licked his shaft the brief moments it came into view from my pussy. Then as I felt him grow close, I tugged her face up, felt her lips latch onto my stiff nipple and savoured them both as Todd blasted another hearty load of cum deep into me, filling me up with all that rich cream.

We were a sweaty, messy lot, but that was the happiest Valentine's Day of our lives. At least, so far.

I HAD no idea my kinky Valentine's gift idea would have such repercussions though. I was letting desire guide me, not my brain.

Though I could hardly complain when Stacey moved in with us. We made a great team, and even as our bellies swelled in perfect unison, we continued to get on as good as ever. Even better in fact!

And Todd?

I'd never seen him so happy as those times he had us two pregnant women upon his arms as he strolled into a fancy restaurant, or merely woke up to us in the mornings, or at the end of the day, to place a kiss on each of our lips. To let his hands roam over the growing life in our bellies.

"We'll make that quota of yours in half the time now," I jested to him one morning, unable to hide the stiffness of my nipples atop those two, engorged breasts. I was horny damn near all the time, and I wasn't sure if it was the pregnancy or the fact I had the two people I lusted for most with me all the time.

"Or maybe..." Todd said with a wry grin or me, holding us both to his sides.

"We should double it," Stacey finished for him with such a mischievous smile, her fingers moving down over his stomach towards his belt.

Too bad for her, mine had already beaten her to it.

HIS FERTILE SWEETHEART

Book Themes:
Bareback, Breeding, School Girl Roleplay, and Military Man
Word Count:
3,896

EVERY STEP BROUGHT another click of those heels, the hallway of the hotel so empty upon the fifteenth floor of the Intercontinental. Gnawing her lower lip, Sylvia slipped the card through the lock, though her hands were shaking so much it didn't register. Tucking back some of her thick blonde curls, she slid the keycard through again, this time the red light turned green with a beep, followed by the unclicking of the lock.

With a deep exhale, she tried to calm herself, to still her petite body before pushing open the door and stepping inside. Of course he wouldn't be in there, but part of her somehow expected he would be somehow.

Instead, the large room was all to herself. A large king sized bed to the right wall opposite the TV, and there before her the windows overlooking Toronto behind a large desk. She'd stayed there before of course, but it was alone, on a work trip half a year ago.

Stepping inside she left the door unlocked as she rolled her suitcase in. A glance in the bathroom showed her it was neat and tidy as to be expected, and she went in.

Within her tiny chest she could feel her heart beating, thudding noisily as she ran some water and then lightly patted some of the cold spray onto her cheeks, careful of her light makeup. Just a bit of lipstick and eyeliner, but she didn't wish to ruin it after all.

Looking herself over in the mirror, however, she knew the business outfit had to go for their first encounter. She undid the blazer, poked each button through the blouse beneath, and shed both. Next came the simple white bra, showing her pinkened areolas and stiff little nipples, fast growing aroused from the cool air of the bathroom and thoughts of the rendezvous to come.

She next wriggled her hips as she pushed her thumbs into the skirt, sliding it on down around her rear and to the floor. She took her time, doing it all smoothly, not in a rush. She was too nervous to rush things, worried she'd botch it all. As if a stray thread would ruin everything.

Out of the suitcase she pulled the outfits she'd brought with her. It was something she'd bought a while back, flushing the entire time she was in the store. The new blouse was tighter, more girlish, and less professional. Its white fabric clinging to her tiny upper body. Then came the plaid, pleated skirt. Too short to wear out, it barely covered her pale round bottom.

She twirled about to look at herself from behind. She

was too short to see herself fully, but she patted over her ass, making sure all the wrinkles in the pleats were gone.

On the dressing went, as if it were a ritual. Tugging up a pair of white stockings over her slender calves before she heard a noise at the door...

CONNOR WASN'T sure how long he'd been standing there. It could have been seconds, no more than a minute, but that moment seemed to drag on for what felt like an eternity. His head was a closet of ensemble emotions seeking to burst forth, and somehow in the middle of it all, he was relatively calm, almost nonchalant.

That was normal, right? He glanced down at himself, afraid he'd not impress with his attire; freshly returned from serving overseas he had only some casual clothing to wear. Brown desert boots tapped the floor, mostly covered by a loose pair of khakis, the back end of which just barely managed to avoid dragging on the ground; he wasn't one for normally wearing military get-up in public, but the boots were probably the most comfortable thing he owned.

The belt he wore wasn't visible, but he felt like it was suffocating his waist at the moment. He wore a brown jacket, the leather worn but well fitted, under which could be seen a faded shirt; off-white for the most part save for the sun blasted stitching around his breast pockets on his chest. He drew a hand to his cheek, rubbing his face to make sure it was clean shaven, and followed it with one last tussle of his hair, which was also well-kept and short in a military style.

He took one last deep breath, closed his eyes, and exhaled, before letting a friendly, if somewhat devious smile line his lips. He knocked on the door of the hotel room, and did the only thing he could at that point: waited.

~

SHE HESITATED, frozen not by reluctance but by a worry that if she let herself, she'd race to the door and throw it open like an over-eager child and embarrass herself.

Instead, she forced calm through a moment of concentration then walked over to the door. Taking a deep breath, she braced herself one last time as she peered through the eye-hole, seeing it was him. Just like his pictures. A little more weather-worn, but it only made him more handsome than he was years ago. When they were both too young to do what was right by each other.

Her mouth went dry, and she began to turn the knob. Only then she realized she hadn't completed the outfit, and hadn't put on the black Mary Jane shoes to go with it, nor the little tie.

It's too late now, she told herself, and pulled open the door.

She meant to greet him with a confident smile, but instead found herself unable to resist tucking her chin down, letting her eyes gaze up at him sheepishly from beneath her long lashes, and those thick blonde curls which fell down into her face.

Without her usual shoes on, though, she seemed even shorter than usual. Her white socked feet twisting upon the wine coloured carpet.

"Hey," she said, her voice soft and airy. "Come on in," she managed, forcing a bit more life into her voice as she found her smile growing despite her anxiousness.

~

HE WAS FROZEN THERE with a look on his face that was somewhere between anxious or friendly, and stupefied. His breath stuck in his throat for a moment before he caught himself staring, hoping to God that his cheeks weren't as red as they felt. Despite the nervousness, he found his voice was still working, and seeing her own reaction to him was about as comforting as he could've hoped.

His smile widened, briefly recalling the stories she'd told him about her school-girl get up. Despite the obvious choice of her attire, somehow he hadn't anticipated it through all his nervous musing. He was laughing on the inside, and it put him at ease. The momentary silence hung between them as she stood waiting, her invitation to enter still looming, and he nodded, taking a step towards her and pulling her into a warm hug.

When he embraced her it did something to her own nervousness. She flung her arms around him, squeezing him tightly in return and feeling that masculine frame against her with warm delight.

"You know, I should've expected the outfit, but you look way sexier in it than I could've imagined." He said it with some joviality, but he was dead serious, his heart racing as he pulled her body against his.

You can prepare yourself for anything, have it all planned out in your head, but nothing ever goes how it's planned, he reminded himself.

A simple giggle escaped her pouty, pink lips as she pulled back enough to look up at him.

"I didn't think anything else would be appropriate after so long," she said in a soft voice, her scent like a mixture of bubble gum and flowers, an intentionally girlish aroma, reminding them both of when they were younger. And they didn't have things to worry about like a career in the military.

She was smaller than he remembered, cuter than he imagined, and he was more of a nervous wreck than he anticipated, but seeing her standing there sheepishly gave him the needed motivation to make sure their encounter lived up to all their hopes and expectations.

First impressions be damned, they had agreed to meet at the hotel for a reason, and his loins were already beginning to stir, washing away all hesitation before the cresting wave of his carnal need.

Him stirring against her only made her grin wider. She bit down upon her lower lip to try and stymy it, but it didn't quite work.

He let her go from the brief embrace, her scent still clinging to him as he stepped into the room, offering a brief inspection of his new surroundings as he pulled his jacket off. The fabric of his shirt beneath was thin, and it did a fair job of outlining his frame, which was on the whole well built, with some hard muscle showing through, particularly around his triceps and shoulders.

"I'm glad to finally see you again." He grinned at her, though his eyes were less than conspicuous as he took her in from head to toe, admiring her dainty body and cosplay attire.

"At long last," she said sweetly. She grasped his thick forearm with one hand, feeling the hard muscle as she raised the other, pushing back some of her blonde curls from her delicate facial features. "I can't believe the moments finally here," she confessed.

He had to try so hard not to stare. He shifted his gaze away, but the goofy grin on his lips didn't fade any. Normally, he'd have been much more reserved, but the situation was entirely different.

Months of contact over the internet and phone, their sexual fantasies confessed, and now they were finally meeting for the first time in a very long while. It was like a strange dream, the good kind where nothing goes wrong, and after it was over, you were left with a moment of consciousness where you couldn't tell if it was real or fake, but it made you smile anyway.

Every little move she made, from the way she bit her lip, the way she looked at him, and the way she touched him, sent shivers up his spine. It was really happening. A man could only resist temptation so much before he caved in.

In this case, he embraced it.

He turned into her, his arms wrapping around her once more, bending slightly as his hands snaked around to her lower back, slipping down the edge of her short skirt as he pulled her up against him, lifting her off the ground entirely, not wasting any time in locking his lips with hers. His senses were assaulted by her essence, her scent, taste, feel... It was overwhelming, and he hadn't felt the touch of a woman in so long.

"We don't want to waste a second of it, either," he said to her in a deep, needy husk.

He breathed between a broken kiss, before his lips sought hers once more, pulling her over to the bed where he set her down gently on the edge, separating them for that brief moment... A moment long enough for him to peel his shirt off.

Easing into it be damned, they'd waited too long for that moment.

"Not a second," she affirmed in a breathy whisper.

The way he lifted her up off the ground made her swoon, the ease with which his strong arms carried her to the bed only to lay her out before him, her bottom bouncing on the mattress just a little.

Clearly the military had been good to him. It certainly filled out his cut figure, his skin a nice tone, his body so strong.

She found herself blatantly staring at him as he peeled away his shirt, one hand reaching out to snake her tiny little fingers up over his rocky abs and across his chest. She had earlier shed her own bra, and the light pink of her nipples showed through her see-through white blouse as her chest heaved with her heavy breathing.

Nodding to him she licked her lips again, leaving them with a glossy sheen.

Bringing her second hand to him, her two dainty sets of fingers began to work open that uncomfortably tight belt to help him.

He busied his hands while she undid his belt, a simple thing to loosen, and when he felt it pop he breathed a sigh of relief. At that angle, she could see the growing bulge against the fabric of his khakis, his member poking out against the leg of his inner thigh, obviously eager to be free.

He slid his hands over hers, feeling her soft skin as he trailed along her arm, and then shifted onto the bed, his knee between her legs as he moved his hands over her thighs, touching her bare skin just above the stockings. Those lightly calloused hands massaging her as he trailed them down over her calves and then back up before he leaned over her completely, staring down into her eyes, drawn in by those long lashes and acutely aware of the blonde curls sprawled out in a halo around her head.

She shuddered beneath him, feeling that rough, masculine touch upon her milky skin the cause of her excitement. To feel how manly and hard he was, compared to her smooth, soft flesh. She laid back, kissed him in turn with moist smacks of their lips as she worked open his pants. Her shaky grasp slow to free his manhood, but finally managing to grasp hold of that girth and pull it free.

He leaned in again, kissing her more fiercely this time, pressing his face against hers. Their lips melded together as he slid his tongue against hers before withdrawing, his teeth nibbling at her lower lip. His nostrils flared with each quickened breath, his own rapid heartbeat just a dull throbbing in his ears.

Those tiny fingers worked over the shaft, feeling it out as she pointed it down towards her, her tongue swirling about his as they entangled for the first time in the flesh. A low little moan thrummed out of her throat and she felt herself squirm beneath him as her unblemished skin developed little goose bumps.

They'd been in love all those years ago, but were too young, foolish and ambitious to give it time and make it work. Now, after so long of talking about what had been, what might have become, they were enacting on what might be...

He throbbed against her hand as she toyed with him. He was already as full as he could get, a stiff pillar in her palm, but he moaned as she stroked him. That lurid connection between them, the heat of his cock melding with the soft warmth of her hand.

She lifted a leg up onto the bed, bending her knee up alongside his waist. The act flipped her skirt up, showing the white thong that covered her slit, just a tiny little triangle of fabric that hugged the shape of her dainty labia.

"Mmm," he moaned against her, his cock throbbing in her dainty hand, swelling at her touch, the tip already moist with pre-cum as he shuddered from her teasing. He snuck a glance down, as if to make sure her hand was actually on him, like he didn't expect it. As if she and the whole scenario would fade away, and he'd be back in some dingy tent on the other side of the planet again. Locked in a fantasy too good to be reality.

To find it was real only served to entice him even more. He peeled his mouth from hers, licking his lips as he slid a hand between her thighs, pressing his finger against her tight slit through the thin fabric of the thong, a fleeting touch before the fabric was pulled aside exposing her to the cool air of the room.

He marvelled at the smoothness of her body, at how swollen and red her slit was. Her fragrance grew in the air and he inhaled that heady, feminine scent. It was the smell that made it real, most of all. Her sweet, girlish perfume mixing with that primal smell of her sex.

He used his knee to spread her other leg further as he brought his hips down between her thighs, arms flexed as he held himself up, pants halfway down his ass, and his thick manhood pressing down against her pussy. Another shudder escaped him as he felt that initial contact, the moist lips inviting him to enter, warm, soft, and welcoming as he teased her with the head of his shaft.

There was no way it could've been a cruel illusion. There was nothing that felt like that but a real woman.

She whimpered at the first touch of his bare member against her little slit, the pinkened folds tingling from that first illicit contact. She arched her spine in an almost feline sort of manner, angling her hips and cunny in a way that let him slip in easier, all by instinct alone.

He hadn't even stuck it in yet, and he was already prepared to explode.

"You'll have to forgive me...it's been awhile." He confessed between breaths, kissing her again as he shifted his hips forward.

Lifting a free hand up, she stroked her smooth little fingertips over his cleanly shaven jawline, back towards his hair, the giddy smile on her face saying all that needed to be said about how little she'd mind. They'd talked about it for ages, and she was anxious to be the woman who broke his long streak of celibacy in 'exile'.

"It's been too long for you. I'll fix that," she said, though she gasped barely a moment later as he pressed down into her, burying himself into that tight little cunny.

The narrow canal took a little bit of extra force to squeeze inside, and it in turn squeezed him back as her long curved lashes fluttered, and her almond-shaped eyes shut tight.

"Yesss," she hissed out as he sank between those pink labia and down into her depths, able to fit the fullness of his manhood snugly inside her. There was so little foreplay or preamble, but she was just as aroused as him, if not more so. All day she'd been fantasizing about that blissful moment, and it lived up to every one of her expectations.

He closed his eyes and tried to relax, though the attempt failed miserably. His body was tense, almost rigid as he sank his thick cock into her wet folds. He eased in slowly, his skin rippling with goose bumps as he felt every inch of his manhood being squeezed by her tight confines, which were simultaneously being stretched by his engorged member.

He grunted, letting a sigh slip between his lips that came out as more of a gasp.

That large, hard body of his began to piston. His round ass pushing up into the air before his hips came down, thrusting that thick, veiny girth into her tight little cunny. It was sheer exquisite pleasure, feeling that narrow little moist quim wrapped about his cock.

The fantasy did not measure up to the reality of their

long lusted for reunion. He never could've conjured up such intense smells, such amazing sensations, all within the confines of his mind as he was out in the desert.

His hard body rocked over her, her soft, feminine moans filling the air of the hotel room as he fucked her. She spread her legs wide to hook them about his hips. He glanced down in sheer delight down between their bodies, over the peaks of her perky little breasts as his thick cock vanished into her body.

It was the sweetest sight he'd ever seen, and a little bulge in her lower belly rose up each time he sank in completely.

Her hands moved over her shoulder, across his neck, feeling the sinuous muscle along his frame, while one dipped down, to stroke her digits over his heavy pecs, appreciating every inch of his hard, well-trained body.

His body trembled as he eased back out of her, pausing just before he was out completely, and thrust back inside of her. Fingers dug into the sheets of the bed, and his arms flexed as he began to pump his hips uncontrollably, his balls contracting as he felt the long-needed tension relieving itself at last.

"God..." He muttered, falling to his elbows, his chest pressed against hers, his face buried against her neck and hair as he fucked her for those fleeting moments. They weren't using protection, and he knew it as well as her. That was also covered in those flirty emails and letters.

They wanted to feel one another, bare, primal. They wanted their first time, the time they'd been waiting so long for, to be real.

"Cum in me," she pleaded, putting words to the things they were both feeling. "Please fill me with your cum."

He gasped as he came, his body convulsing slightly as he shot his thick seed inside of her, coating her canal with his cum, his cock swelling as it released his load. For a moment, he thought he was going to die, and as her tight cunt squeezed around him, the pleasure nearly turned into pain it was so exquisite.

The feel of that raw cock, so long desired and now finally inside her, pumping briefly into her tight little cunt, made her tremble and nearly convulse. She was so primed, and as she grasped onto his bicep and dug her nails slightly into his back, she let loose a slightly shrill little wail as she felt him swell and unload within her.

The sensation of him unleashing his seed into her raw and unhindered, filling her fertile depths up inside made her cling to him tighter, lifting one slender leg to hook around his waist and press against his ass.

She'd never let a man cum inside her when the risk was so high, and it titillated her. All the greater knowing it was him, her crush of old. That they had talked about and teased one another with the prospect for so long.

She moaned and whimpered, her body writhing, her narrow little cunny squeezing around him, seeming to knead his dick and milk out every last drop into her waiting depths.

Kissing his neck, cheek and ear, she panted softly from the excitement more than the brief rutting itself. "Yesss," she hissed softly. "I've waited so long for this..."

It had been so brief, but neither of them begrudged that. She'd teased him, coaxed him. She yearned for that moment when she got to be the one to relieve him of all tension and desire.

He breathed heavily, kissing along her shoulder, over her slender stalk of a neck up to her ear. His voice a low rasp there.

"You were worth the wait," he said, and with how she

trembled beneath him — around him — he knew the feeling was mutual.

That long ago missed chance when they were both young and in love... Curled up together on the bed, it hardly seemed lost at all.

LITTLE BRAT PEEPS ON: FIONA'S FIRST TIME

*B*ook Themes:
Voyeur, Virgin, First Time, Older Man / Younger Woman, Creampie, Peeping, Breeding, and Barely Legal.

Word Count:
6,777

~

THE FARM HAD ALWAYS BEEN RUN by us for as long as I can remember. My ma and pa passed when I was just a baby, and so my oldest sister, Rose, she took over. Then the twins, Mary and Lizzy came of age and they started helping out. Then Fiona, she graduated high school, and you guessed it, she started workin' on the farm too.

But I wanted something more than that. I wanted to go away to the big city, to see the flashing lights and a city that never sleeps. I wanted to lose myself in a new place, and meet new people. But Rose, she didn't want that, and neither did any of the others. They were pleadin' with me not to go away for college.

My grades sure were somethin', and I always was the teacher's favourite. Reading far beyond my own level, but our town's library wasn't at all big, and there was still so much I wanted to learn.

So I guess we came to a compromise. I'd stay until I turned 19 at least, and help out on the farm. In return, they were gonna hire me someone they called a tutor, which I guess was just a teacher who would be able to teach me in private. From home.

I wasn't lookin' forward to it, not at all. It was just somethin' I was agreeing to to get them all off my back for a little while when I finally decided to take off.

But Mr. Roberts, well... he made me have some second thoughts, I'll admit.

THE FIRST DAY Mr. Roberts arrived was a pretty momentous occasion for our sleepy lil' farm. My sisters never saw a whole lot of men folk in their day to day, and neither did I for that matter. The local school house was run by the church, and so boys and girls were taught in separate halves of the buildin'. Which meant even in our school days, we never had much of a run in with fellas.

But when he first got there, I watched from my upstairs window. There he was, a dapper lookin' fellow, wearin' a smart lookin' suit the likes of which I'd never seen. I'll admit here and now, my opinion about having a tutor immediately changed. If only a little.

Rose was the one most eager to greet him, though not for the reasons ya might think. She was the boss of the farm, as the oldest, and she had it in her head that she was our protector. And a fella on the farm meant she had some idea that she had to scope him out and make sure he'd be safe to have around.

Even she was a lil' surprised to see such a fancy lookin' fella at our door though. Tall, dark and handsome would be the cliché way of puttin' it. He wasn't big and burly like the few other local farmers we did encounter, he was lean and fair. With a pair of glasses, though they didn't make him look dorky or nothin', lil' bookish perhaps, but that was okay. I loved my books.

I never heard their first talk, but I could imagine how it went, knowing Rose well enough, and their body language.

She stomped on up, past my three other sisters who were there to greet him first. Rose pushed on up to the front, hair tied back in a ponytail, her old work shirt tied up in front, skin tanned and glistenin' from a hard mornings work as she stood there in her jeans.

She was welcomin' him, but layin' down the rules too. She was big on rules, especially for guests. But while she barked and blustered, I could see Mary and Lizzy talkin' between each other with masked excitement, eyin' him up and gigglin'. Then there was Fiona, lookin' stern as she could manage, though that's how she always was. I knew beneath it all that she was just as excited for the touch of change, almost as much as me she wanted sometin' else. Don't think she ever liked bein' the "middle child". Felt she never got enough due.

Which was why when Mr. Roberts started to greetin' them all, takin' Fiona's hand first of all and kissin' the back of it, I could tell she was smitten. Though the twins weren't fussed at bein' second and third place. While Rose would have none of that fancy do!

~

MY FIRST TIME MEETIN' him came shortly after of course. Well, shorts a relative thing. Rose kept him out there for ages, showin' him around, impressin' upon him the importance of his duties to teach me. She could go on a while, I'll tell you.

I swear, she thought she really was my ma.

But this part of the story ain't about me and Mr. Roberts, not yet.

My sisters didn't tend to notice me so much, 'cause I was quiet and kept to myself. Or so they thought. But truth of the matter was, I was a great listener, and I had a knack for sneakin' about, keepin' tabs on what everyone else was doin'. Usually it weren't nothin' too interestin', but with Mr. Roberts on our farm, things took a turn for the interesting, and I wanted to be in on it.

Fiona had changed her clothes since Mr. Roberts first arrived, even though it was only a couple hours later. That weren't like her at all, but then again, Fiona was a different kinda woman altogether when there was a fella involved I was learnin'.

I knew she had an inklin' to leave the farm. We'd talked about it in times past, but she never wanted to do it by her lonesome. And she never wanted to do it with me much either. Fact of the matter was, though she'd never admit it, I think she just wanted to meet a fella and move off together.

Seein' her dolled up in a nice dress as she went out to the guest house confirmed it. She brought a plate with her, holdin' a lil' mini cake she'd baked herself to bring to the man as a dessert.

When Mr. Roberts answered the door, his tie was gone, and his collar undone, but the man looked only more handsome still.

"Oh hello Fiona, sorry, I wasn't expecting company, I

was just unpacking and trying to settle in," he said, a bright, friendly smile upon his face as he held the door open. "Come on in," he invited immediately.

Fiona goin' into the tutor's room? Well, that was against one of the rules, and I knew it. Could have screamed bloody murder and Rose'd come running, and she'd chase him out of the house then and there just for invitin' Fiona in. We were all pretty close in age, me and my sisters, but Rose acted like she was fifty when she was only half that.

Now, I know Fiona didn't always get lots of attention, but truth be told, it wasn't her looks. She was a pretty girl, and none too stupid. But she just always was overshadowed by Rose. Or the twins. They teased her somethin' awful at times, so Fiona sometimes acted like she was the loneliest girl in the world.

"Sure, I'd love to Mr. Roberts," she said with a cheerful smile on those ruby lips of hers. She even got dolled up with makeup!

Now, here's about where my knowledge of the situation might be expected to die off, but I knew our farm in and out, better than any of my sisters even. And every place had its own little peep holes or quiet nooks to nose in on, and the guest house was no exception.

"What's that you have there?" he said, eying the little cake with fascination as Fiona waltzed on in, swayin' her hips so wide.

It was a little weird, watchin' her like that, I had to admit. Kinda exciting, though. I just knew somethin' funny was goin' on with how she was movin' and biting down on her lower lip like she was real nervous as she offered him her baked good.

"I made this just for you, Mr. Roberts," she said, as she blushed real bright.

It was a pretty lookin' lil' cake too, I had to give her

that. Chocolate, looked like a lil' volcano with some choco-late sauce runnin' down the sides to the base. It set my tummy to rumblin' then and there, but I had more impor-tant things to keep track of.

"Wow, it looks delicious! So fast too," he exclaimed in surprise, smiling as he took the cake from her and laid it down on the small table that was his own personal eating nook, just two chairs and a table next to his mini-kitchen.

I was watchin' from my hidey-hole that I crept into from beneath, and I could see it all.

"Would you like to share it with me?" he asked, fetching two forks from the drawer as I studied his room. He wasn't lying, he was fast settlin' in, putting out his suits, a little ornate globe and an array of books he'd brought with them.

I couldn't wait to get my hands on 'em! But it wasn't the time…

Naw, I was learnin' about something different alto-gether. I was learning about how men and womenfolk talk together. I practiced pressing my lips together like Fiona was doing, but it felt strange.

"I would love that," she said, and even her voice was different. Had a strange little lilt to it. Like it was a bit lower, and she really emphasized the world 'love'.

She went to sit down, but then Mr. Roberts did a surprisin' thing, he took hold of the chair for her and pulled it out, offerin' it up to her like she was some sorta princess or somethin'. Guess he just had some refined manners that the local boys didn't.

"Such a gentleman," Fiona said, and she came over, holding her red dress up at one side between her index finger and thumb as she sat down more dainty than I'd ever seen her behave. It was such a strange shift in her behaviour, but I couldn't help but be entranced by it. I was learnin' something real different. Like for instance, that beneath her red dress, Fiona weren't wearin' a stitch! Nothin'! I could even see her bush!

"Ah well, when a man entertains a lovely lady in his residence after she brings him a delicious looking cake, he has to treat her right," he said, setting the table, pouring them both up some milk before he sat down with her.

He was pretty smooth, my new tutor-to-be. I wondered if he'd treat me like that, but I shook the thought from my head. I was just the baby of the family. No one wanted to treat me like that, and I never could have thought to make him a cake like that. I should've, though. That would have made him like me loads more and wanna teach me even better.

She crossed her legs and I couldn't see between them no more except for along the sides, her tan legs nice and muscular from all her hard work around the farm. Fiona wasn't a slouch.

She might've chafed at Rose always bein' so bossy, but she worked as hard as any, harder! Just to prove she was as good as any of the rest of us.

They dug into the cake, but right away Mr. Roberts was taken. You'd think he'd just bitten into the most delightfully tasty thing he'd ever put in his mouth!

"Mmm mmm! Oh my, Fiona, you must be the baker of the family," he said with such appreciation, and I bought it, didn't think someone could fake such enjoyment of a simple cake!

But oh, Fiona, she was bright red, and I watched as the top of her foot ran up his shin a little. I thought that was weird, her messin' up his nice pants like that. But he didn't look upset at all, and she was grinning like some fool.

"Thank you for sayin' so, Mr. Roberts, but normally I leave the cookin' and bakin' to the twins. It's only when special company comes by that I like to break out my... culinary skills," she said, her voice like I'd never heard it before, so... enticing and erotic.

For his part, Mr. Roberts reached on over, placed his big hand upon her knee, right at the edge of her dress skirts and gave a squeeze as he smiled.

"A shame you don't get to exercise those skills a bit more then, you're clearly well suited to them," he said with a smile.

And I knew for a fact that Fiona never cared for baking and cooking, heck, she downright loathed it normally! Or at least, pretended to. But suddenly with Mr. Roberts there you'd think she was Martha Stewart! Heck, I wouldn't have been surprised if the twins had baked that cake and she was just takin' credit.

Her foot kept rubbin' on him, and she shimmied a little bit closer to him, bringing the fork to her lips and pressing the cake between them. And she made a sound, but it wasn't a normal dinner-time sound. It was more like a moan, and she was lookin' at him the entire time. That was really strange, I figured, but I didn't know nothin' about this sort of thing.

I'd have to practice when I got to my room, makin' that sound.

They continued a while like that, the two of 'em eating and looking at one another across the table like somethin' was strange. If I didn't know better I'd say they wanted to eat each other more than the cake.

There on her knee, Mr. Roberts' hand lingered, and her foot — still in that high heel I'd never seen her wear before! — kept tracin' up and down his calf.

I knew the cake was done because I heard the forks hit their plates, but still they kept touchin' one another a little.

"Mr. Roberts," my sister began, as if somethin' was on

her mind rather serious, "I know you're going to be busy with teaching Lily, but..." she stopped there.

"Go on," he said, urging her as his hand rubbed up from her knee to her thigh, raising her dress a little and letting his palm and those long fingers touch her thigh. "What's on your mind?"

"Well... I was thinkin' you and I could spend some time together now and then. Get to know one another. I'd be ever so interested in hearin' your stories about travel and such. Maybe... tonight. After the other girls have gone to bed," she said, an impish lil' smile on her ruby lips.

"Fiona," he said and it sounded more like a wolf growlin' than a man speaking, and he leaned closer to her.

"I'd enjoy that quite a lot."

I couldn't believe what I was hearing. Fiona was gonna get her behind tanned if Rose ever found out about this!

Yet there she was, Mr. Roberts barely havin' time to get through the door and she was enticin' him off to do things that were strictly not allowed. More than that, her high heeled shoe was left upon the floor and her bare foot trailed up from his calf in between his thighs so brazen like I figured he'd jump up!

But he didn't.

"There's a creek nearby, where the farm gets its water. But there's some trees off to the west, and that's where the old tree house is. You and me can have some private time there, lookin' out over the water... the moon and all above us," she said so sultrily, I had no idea where she got it from!

Mr. Roberts stiffened in his seat a little, and I could see he was breathin' heavier.

"I'll meet you there then," he said.

"After all the lights go out in the farmhouse," she added, smilin' so happily with herself.

I couldn't believe my eyes, nor what I was hearin'. One

thing I knew for certain, though. There was no way I was going to miss what was to happen later that night.

～

I KNEW full well what treehouse Fiona was talkin' about. I'd spent much of my time up there readin' to get out of chores over the years. Never did I think Fiona would be usin' it for somethin' so… naughty, though.

But soon as the lights went out, I waited for it: the sound of Fiona sneakin' off. It was so soft you'd have to be expectin' it to hear. She was a crafty one, craftier than I gave her credit for, that's for sure.

I went after her shortly thereafter, my PJs nice and thick, so I didn't need to worry none about gettin' cold. But her? I could see her ahead in the moonlight dressed in the same outfit as earlier, but holdin' her heels in her hand until she got to the edge of the farm, and slipped 'em back on.

I had to be cautious, because I didn't know when Mr. Roberts would be comin' behind, but as Fiona got into her heels and waited, I took my station.

Y'see, later on, Rose found out about my secret tree house, and she'd come and drag me back to the farm to do chores. So I created a second little hideaway in the trees. Tucked in underneath the treehouse was a lil' box, obscured by the branches and leaves, where I was able to hide out.

I had to get into the treehouse before either of 'em though, slide the secret hatch out of the way and climb down in. None too soon either, 'cause I heard a giggle and a laugh.

I was beneath 'em again, but this time I had a much better vantage point. My little hideaway was made to avoid

Rose, but for that I needed to keep a good eye on her too. It helped that when Mr. Roberts and her climbed up, they turned on a lantern, lightin' them both up so I could see 'em clear as day.

There came Mr. Roberts, a fine back jacket on, but no tie again. He looked slicker than before, and his glasses were gone too. He was downright dashin' without 'em.

"So this is your little fortress of solitude, Fiona, hmm? A nice hideaway," he said with a grin.

It was my hideaway. A little flare of jealousy went up in my heart, but I squished it back down. I didn't have time for none of that. If she wanted to use it, I wished she'd have asked, but I understood why she didn't. I wouldn't tell her if I was sneakin' out after lights-out. That would be a recipe for disaster.

But she was touchin' on his chest, and that made me feel a little jealous too, though I didn't know why. I barely knew the teacher, and I didn't want to be the one touching on his chest. So why did it make me feel weird?

She beckoned him in, biting her lower lip anxiously as he followed after her. From his angle, he could even get a glimpse up her dress skirts, and I wondered if she was still not wearin' any panties like before.

"Just a convenient lil' get away for us, under the circumstances," she said to him, and I noticed her dress was awful low cut. She must've done somethin' to make it even worse than earlier that day, because her breasts were showin', big round mounds swelled up into cleavage from the red dress.

"So why are you so interested in my travel stories, huh? I figured you had to be very happy here on the farm. After all, it was young Lily that's the one trying to get away," he said, already being filled in on that personal tidbit.

I kinda resented being 'young Lily'. I wasn't a baby

anymore, and I felt a bit hot and angry, but Fiona started talkin' again and what she said shocked the anger right out of me.

"I've been thinkin' of running off for a while now. You know, really experiencing what the world has to offer. But with you right here, I figured maybe you could just show me."

I didn't understand it wholly, but I knew that tone wasn't to be used in polite conversations.

I saw as Mr. Roberts gaze dropped low, then looked to Fiona and saw her legs were spread, and spreading wider. Her dress hiked up, and from my angle below I could see, she was bein' downright shameless with how she was showin' her flower to the newly arrived man!

I mean, we all had fantasies and such, but this fella had only just arrived, and there was my older sister showin' him her privates so shamelessly!

"Looks like you've got a lot to show me too, Fiona," he said, his voice deeper and huskier than usual as he stared between her legs, making my sister grin and bite down upon her lower lip. "You're as pretty beneath your dress as you are outside it," he said.

I thought it might not go no further than that, but then Mr. Roberts reached out, his long fingers extending to touch along her inner thighs, stroking the backs of his digits along her smooth skin. He traced along her, enjoying the feel of her skin quite obviously.

It sent a shiver down my spine, truth be told. My breath held, and it wasn't that I was scared they'd find me. They were both too distracted for that.

But I just couldn't find my breathing. It was weird, but I could almost feel it myself, that light tracing of fingers along my sensitive flesh. But that didn't stop how wrong my sister was. I wondered if I should stop her, tell her she better get back into the house to apologize to Rose straight away.

But instead I just waited for what would happen next.

"I'm glad ya think so, sir," Fiona said, just lettin' him touch on her! His fingers tracin' in closer and closer to her cunny. He weren't just lookin' at her most private of privates now, he was touchin' 'em! His fingers grazin' along the edges of her puffy, reddened lips, so swole up.

I've seen my own get like that on rare occasion, only when I awoke from a rather... naughty dream. And it looked like my older sis was havin' a doozy by the looks of how red and glossy it was.

"I've been around the world, visited a lot of countries," Mr. Roberts said, studying Fiona's little flower, brushing his thumb against those folds, makin' her shiver and whimper. "But there's more beauty to be found on this simple farm than I've found in all my journeys."

Again I felt that weird little pang, wishin' that he could've said that to me. But instead I was just young Lily, nothing like my overconfident sister and her way with him. She wasn't embarrassed or shy, not at all. I'd never seen her be so up front to someone, not ever.

"You mean that?" Fiona said, brushin' back some of her hair from her face, and I could see she had a touch of blush to her cheeks. She wasn't as brazen as I'd given her credit for, although... only by a bit.

She had the nerve to show off her lady bits to the man, but she still felt at least a lil' embarrassment over it.

Mr. Roberts didn't answer her right away though, and I thought for a moment he'd confess to not meanin' it. Instead, he brought his free hand up, stroked two fingers along the mound of her bulging breast, then curled them into the cup of her dress. He helped himself to tugging down her dress, exposing her right breast — which was so

341

much bigger than my own! I felt jealous. Then he was stroking about her pinkened areolas, and stiffened nipple.

"It's confirmed," he said with a confident smile, so smooth and undaunted by it all. "Absolutely beautiful."

I was breathing heavier, though I was trying to keep still. It was uncomfortable, cramped like I was, but I barely noticed. My eyes were glued on the two of them, on how they were touchin' each other.

Fiona let out the sound like she did when eating the cake, this low moan, and she pushed her breast into his hand, her legs spreading even wider.

Mr. Roberts leaned in to her closer, his hand workin' at her lil' cunny in such a curiously precise fashion, makin' lil' circles near the top, makin' my older sister moan and whimper some more. While his other hand squeezed at her breast, sank into that fleshy mound and toyed with her sensitive nipple, makin' her flinch now and then.

"Have you ever been with a man before, Fiona?" he asked her, and I almost answered 'no' for her. None of us had!

"Yeah," she said, and my eyes went wide! I had no idea!

But my older sister stared into his eyes, lost in the moment, breathin' heavily as her chest heaved.

"He was older'n me," she continued. "He passes through now and then to sell things to the local shop."

I immediately knew who she meant. Mr. Erics. The travellin' salesman! He worked for some company or another, and he pitched products to Herbert family for their local store. I couldn't believe it! Fiona and Mr. Erics?

"How far did you go?" Mr. Roberts asked, continuing to work at her body.

She couldn't have done what they were doin', not like this. He wasn't ever around long enough for that, I was certain. But then, I'd been certain she'd never done somethin' like this before at all just a moment before.

Didn't she know what Rose would do to her?

It was enough to make me wanna scream, to try to protect her from her bad decisions, but Mr. Roberts was touching her so lovingly, and I stayed put. Part of me didn't want to interrupt.

"We touched some, like this," she said to him slowly, her voice heavy with her lusty breathing. "He took me behind the shop, and we showed each other all we had. We was gonna go all the way... but then he got transferred to a new area," she said with a whimper as Mr. Roberts seemed to find some special way of stroking her.

"So you've never had a man slip his cock into your pussy," Mr. Roberts said, his words so crass I felt my cheeks turn blood red! "Such a shame. We'll have to fix that tonight," he said with such a smile I felt a chill run down my spine.

I wanted to run out, to hide from all this. I was curious, sure, but that language... I couldn't believe my ears. I know there was no way that I'd be innocent, not after seeing what was happening in my treehouse.

But there wasn't a way out. I was trapped, unless I wanted to expose myself, and then I'd be in as much trouble as Fiona for not telling sooner!

"Please," my sister said in a whimper, "please fix that for me, Mr. Roberts."

I couldn't believe my ears! My sister was beggin' for it! For the nasty things that dashing stranger was sayin' to her!

He withdrew his hand from her chest, leaving her breast to fall back to her chest with a jiggle as he began to undo his top. Now, I'd never seen a man naked, not once.

But I'd seen one topless a time or two, but none compared to Mr. Roberts.

He was lean, but he was fit. Beneath his shirt was hard, lined muscle, and just a sprinkling of hair over it. He stripped away his shirt to show his statuesque pecs and abs, and my sister and I were transfixed as he exposed himself.

She was the first to break the spell though, reachin' out, and runnin' her hand along his chest, feeling him up with such relish.

"You're so handsome," she said, soundin' younger than me with her excitement.

I had to put my hand over my mouth to quiet myself then, because I was getting really scared and feeling really hot. Not just my cheeks from being embarrassed, but between my legs too. I pressed them together tighter and took in a deep breath through my nose.

I couldn't make a sound. I had to be as quiet as a mouse, even as her hand went lower and lower along his abs.

Mr. Roberts paused his own hands after he stripped off his shirt and jacket entirely, his broad shoulders rotating.

"I'll leave that to you," he said, as my sister's hand got to his belt at his wait.

She nibbled her lower lip anxiously, but did as he said. Her two hands going to that leather belt and unbuckling it, the excitement in her clear as day as she began to undo the man's pants right before my eyes!

"There you go," he said in a deep husk, right before she peeled his pants open... and reached into his underwear!

Dear lord! How'd she manage to do such a thing?!

I'll never know!

Fiona was grabbing at his maleness, right before my eyes, squeezing him and keeping her eyes on his the entire time. She was being so brazen, I couldn't believe it.

And I really didn't understand why my own breathing was getting shallower. It wasn't happening to me, after all, but I could almost imagine it was. I had to shake those thoughts away though. They weren't proper, not at all, and I couldn't stand to think about them.

Then she pulled him out of his pants, though, and my sex throbbed in response. I couldn't believe it. It looked so strange and foreign, that big, meaty stick that she held in her hands. It wasn't like us girls at all, and I leaned forward to get a better look.

That big tool was ribbed with pulsing veins, jutting off its meaty length. It rose up at a slight upwards curve towards the tip, where her stroking hand revealed a big, glistening purple crown! It was... well, magnificent. I never saw a thing like it in my life and yet I immediately knew I wanted it. Craved it.

It was embarrassing to even think that, but it was the truth, and I could feel it down below. Watching those twin balls swing out of his drawers, so heavy and big, I was breathless!

"God, you're a big man," Fiona said breathily, and though I had no point of comparison I felt he had to be! I was wonderin' how he was gonna squeeze that thing into my sister — or me! — and not sure how it could be possible.

He grinned at my sister's compliment, stroking the hairline along her cheek and pushing some of her hair back as he watched her. She was touching his most private of parts, and he was just looking at her like it was all a big laugh or something. That it wasn't nothing to be ashamed of.

I forced myself to take in some breath, because I was getting a bit dizzy, and I had to close my eyes for a few seconds just to steady myself. When I finally opened them again, he was kissing her right on the mouth as she started to run her hand up and down his shaft.

The two of 'em were poised above me, showin' their naughty parts with not an ounce of shame, makin' out and touchin' one another as if it were no big thing. I couldn't hardly believe it, but there it was, right before me.

He pressed Fiona back, laying her out on the floor of the treehouse as he got down over her, in between her legs. Now, that might've made it hard for me to see, but nope! Fiona's legs spread so gosh darn wide that her dress slipped up to her ass, and I watched from beneath as her hand guided him in to her. That big, bulging tip of his pressed to her puffy, wet folds, and they prepared to lock parts just a few inches from my face!

I could smell the soft scent of them both on the air, and maybe that was what was causing me to be so dizzy. My heart was pounding in my chest and I was worried that they'd find me, but they didn't seem to hear a thing over their own heavy breathing.

I wanted to reach down and touch myself, truth be told, but I was a good girl. I wasn't going to do something like that, or something like what Fiona was doing. It wasn't right, but I was transfixed as he started to push into her.

It was like something was stopping him, at first, and I figured it was just too big to fit into that tiny little twat. She made a face like it hurt, but she kept her legs open wide.

"Just break it," she said, and I was scared for her. Break what? Break her?

I wanted to yell at him not to, but what could I do? I was trapped, and I had to stay still and quiet. And even if I wanted to, I couldn't stop him because he bucked his hips forward in one movement, and she screamed somethin' awful.

He stayed still for a second as she quieted down, her body relaxing a little bit and she smiled.

I didn't understand that! She'd just screamed bloody murder and now there she was, smiling like a maniac.

I looked back to where their bodies met, his thick organ splaying her folds so lewdly, his balls pressed up against her ass. Then as he began to pull slowly back, I could see that little trickle of red that stained his bulging shaft. He'd hurt her!

But the way she was moanin' as he pulled back, then thrust in again, said she wasn't hurtin' no more. Fast as that.

Mr. Roberts was pumpin' that big dick of his into my sister right before my eyes, and the pungent aroma of their sex was fillin' the air as they grew faster, more heated.

"Fuck," he cursed so crassly all the time with her. "You've got such a tight hold on my cock, I feel like you're gonna milk my nuts dry in no time," he said, staring at her tits as they swayed with the motions of their rutting.

I puzzled at those words. I didn't know what milking nuts meant, and it took me a second's pause before I decided to look it up when I got back. Try to find it in one of the books I had, though I knew I didn't have nothing that talked about what they were doing.

My lips parted as Fiona moaned back in response, "Oh yea, big boy?"

She obviously understood what he was talking about!

Fiona clearly had more experience with men than me, and I reckoned that the salesman had shown her quite a few things behind the shop judgin' by her familiarity with it all… but I was so focussed on what they were doin'. The slap of their flesh, his heavy balls smacking against her ass, the wet noise of his dick plunging into her cunny again and again.

I was so close I could smell and see it all, every lil' detail! The way her tight little quim swallowed up his dick each time he thrust forward, only for her folds to cling to him as he tugged back. It was gross and yet beautiful in its own way. I'd never seen a thing like it, and I should've been horrified, but hearin' them moan as they did it, I knew there was nothin' but good feelings to come from it all.

"Fuck you've got such a tight little cunt," he said in a deep, rumbling voice. "I'm gonna fill it with so much cum, you'll be bursting," he growled.

I didn't know what he meant, of course, but I knew from the way Fiona was squirming beneath him, begging him with those whimpered, "Yes, yes," sounds, that it was good. It had to be real, real good, and I wanted it too.

I was jealous, and my hand went between my thighs, just to try to stop my bits from throbbing.

I had no idea how long it'd all gone on for, but it felt like an eternity to me. With how my privates were pulsing with need, aching for some relief, I felt like I was ready to die.

Yet above me, I watched my sister get fucked by that handsome stranger, ploughed into by his thick cock again and again, their pace rising. I watched as a curious thing happened, and those big, heavy balls of his began to tighten up, and no longer slapped my sister's ass anymore.

He gave a big, loud groan, and his rough thrusts became erratic, and Fiona cried out loudly, screamin' for him to fill her. Then I watched it all from beneath as if in slow motion. That big dick of his pulsed, and even though he came to a halt, it swelled up as if it was pumping all on its own.

And I began to understand it all better then. He was filling her full alright, and it wasn't long after I found out with what. Because once he pulled back that thick, creamy white spunk began to drool from her puffy lil' slit, and I could see it begin to run down towards me.

I was going to have to move or else it'd drip down and hit me in the face, but I didn't. I don't know, maybe a part of me was just too curious to wanna hide from it, and I watched as those few little drops went down between the cracks, dropping on my nose.

It smelled so strongly, and my nostrils flared.

And then I did something I'm not too proud of. I brought my finger up to my nose, to those little drops, and I smeared them away before...

Before bringing my finger right to my lips, and tasting their combined juices.

As I tasted my first drop of cum, the two of them above me made out passionately. While I was delighted by the salty tang of that milky seed, and another drop landed upon my lips this time where I licked it away, they fondled and felt each other up.

I got so wrapped up in my own experience, fondlin' myself beneath my PJs and tasting his seed, that I got carried away and made a moan myself. It got the attention of the two of them above me and I froze in my tracks.

"Did you hear that?" Fiona asked Mr. Roberts as he felt up her big tits.

"Probably just some animal," he replied, not wanting to be distracted from her body.

"We should get on back before Rose notices I'm missin'," Fiona said, suddenly worried about getting caught again, now that she had the man's cum dribbling out of her pussy.

"Alright," he said and he pulled back from her with a final smack of their lips.

"Thanks for showin' me somethin' new," Fiona said

with a blushing grin as she pulled her dress back into place.

"Thanks for the warm welcome," he echoed in response as he tucked his big tool back into his underwear and pants with some effort.

And then, before I knew it, it was all over. They were disappeared back out into the darkness, and I was left in the treehouse by myself, the smell of their sex so heavy in the air. I couldn't believe what I'd witnessed that night, and I figured it was goin' to be the only time I'd ever see something like that.

But following around Mr. Roberts, it didn't seem he was all too content with just one of my sisters, and when I noticed him eyeing up the twins one day, I took to spying again...

NYMPHO FOR THE BILLIONAIRES

Book Themes:
Nymphomania, Creampie, Breeding, Multiple Sex Partners, Prostitution

Word Count:

5,150 words

~

HE'S the biggest guy in the building, six and a half feet tall, broad shoulders, lots of muscle. And he has me pinned against wall, hammering me with his thick cock. He's got me crying out, my body reeling each time he pounds into me with that meaty girth of his. My skirt's become little more than a belt, my high heels keeping me up as my knees quiver and my breasts jiggle.

I'm crying out loudly, and I'd be worried about violating the noise rules except everyone knows this is just how it goes. If they don't like my moans and cries as I'm fucked by a hot stud, they can take it up with the guy about to blow his load inside me.

Mr. Torenson is a great lover, and my favourite tenant in the building, even if he is the most demanding. He always leaves me breathless and satisfied. He's got a hot bod and knows how to make me quake with pleasure.

He's getting close too, his own gruff moans filling the air, his cock throbbing inside me, stretching out my poor little pussy, making those pink labia turn reddish from strain. He's not wearing a condom, which is a special little treat for himself that he's entitled to.

Even if it means I'm at risk of being a mom... again.

I'm not complaining though, not really. Not only do I get a thrill from it as he moans loudly, throws back his head and buries his dick inside me, blowing that thick load, but I kinda like the whole idea. Mr. Torenson and the other tenants take good care of me, and I take good care of them in return. So I make sure to clench my pussy around his dick and milk it nice and good, moaning as I press my ass back against him, draining every last spurt from his hefty balls.

But hey, what's a thirty-something woman like me doing being railed against a condo wall, hitting climax for the fourth time today on my work hours? Well, I'm the superintendent for the building. What's that got to do with it you ask? It's complicated...

YEARS AGO, when I was another pretty twenty-something looking for solid work, worrying about where my next month's rent was gonna come from, something happened out of the blue.

The cute guy I was dating had an offer for me.

No, not marriage. He wasn't the type. He was so wrapped up in his startup business and its early success he had no time for being serious. But he did want to tell me about his new condo and the opportunity there.

"It's a swanky condo for successful bachelor's who are busy. Y'know, too busy to settle down and start a family all on their own," Doug told me.

But I didn't get it.

"What makes a condo specific to successful bachelor's?" I asked him, and he smiled crooked at me, a little bashful.

He took his time, slowly warming me up to the idea.

"Like I said, none of us have the time to really take dating, marriage or kids seriously. Not on our own. But what we do have is money," he explained to me, but I was slow to wrap my head around it.

"Wait, so you want to rent a family for the condo? I don't get it," I told him flat out.

"Look, it's a superintendent job, I think you'd be great for it. You've got the looks, you're charming, everyone loves you," he said adoringly, and I always did like that about him. He was always sweet and sincere. "It'll pay a lot, comes with a four bedroom condo all your own that you don't have to pay a dime for, and..."

He stalled. There had to be a catch. It was like a dream come true, but his pause was making me tear up my napkin anxiously.

"And?" I pushed, getting a little annoyed at that point, though I really couldn't afford to be. I was about to be out on my ass in the cold.

"Look, keep an open mind, okay?" He said, wetting his lips. He wore glasses, and was a bit of a dork, but he was sweet, cute and kind. So I was patient as he explained it to me in full. "In addition to the usual tasks of just tidying up the building, you'll have... *other* responsibilities."

That sounded ominous.

"C'mon, just tell me already!" I whined. This sounded too good and I just wanted to hear it all.

"The guys all get to sleep with you," he blurted out at last, looking bashful. My jaw must've dropped, because I was speechless. "You'd be like... wife to the group, kinda. And since none of us have the time to commit to you solely, together we'd be enough to keep you busy with dates and such."

"And sex!" I blurted out, shocked! My sensibilities were shaken to the core.

"Yeah but like... you're more like girlfriend, wife or even mom to us than--" he didn't finish before I said.

"Prostitute?!"

I wouldn't say that now; it's sex work and that's fine. Sex work is work. But I was still naive then.

"Right, I mean... you don't have to make a decision right away. Come over, meet with everyone, interview for it. I think you're a shoe in. If, y'know... You want it I mean," he explained.

And at first I was kinda offended. But after a while of thinking about it, I began to waiver...

THAT WEEKEND I got to meet with a bunch of the guys. Not all at once of course, since they're a busy bunch, and all working long, different schedules. Doug introduced me to them, and we all hit it off. One by one I warmed up to Greg, Bret, Amir, Mr. Torenson and all the others.

And so I gave in, as a "trial". I started work, with my own office and my own massive condo, with more bedrooms than I knew what to do with then. But little did I stop to think about what they'd be for later on.

The men were mostly very nice and charming. They

began slow, treating me to dinner at their swanky places, or out to nice restaurants. It was like I was dating them all, but nobody really got jealous or offended.

The first time I faced the reality of my new job I was in my office, going over a few things when Ken came in. He's a total hunk. I gotta admit. If there was one of these guys to break me into my new life as girlfriend to over a dozen different guys, it was Ken.

He's a bodybuilder when not running his business, and he's absolutely ripped. But I came to know a side effect of working out so often: Ken was horny. Badly horny. After every workout. And so he came into my office, tank top nearly tearing as it stretched over his broad chest, outlining his pecs and abs, those jeans he had on strained by the thick outline of his cock.

"Hey babe, I know you're still settling in and all, but…" he took out the tenant's card. A digital tracker the condo residents used to keep track of when and who was withdrawing supplies from the community lot.

Or, in this case, he was cashing in on screwing me.

He slipped the card through the reader on my desk before I could say anything, and he licked his lips with anticipation.

"I really gotta have you," he said, staring at me like I was the most beautiful woman to ever walk the earth. He leaned atop my desk, bent towards me, and it showed off his bulging, rippling biceps and those thick forearms, criss-crossed by rigid veins. He was eye candy alright.

"Um, Ken…" I stood up, dressed in my work outfit, which was one part professional, one part sexy. It was a lovely blouse and skirt, capped off with heels. But the skirt was just a bit too short for most offices, the blouse just a bit too see-through.

What can I say? I justified it in my head other ways, but

I really liked these guys from the get go and wanted to look good for when they stopped by or saw me working in the building. I just hadn't really anticipated it would all happen so soon.

"What do you say? I got a big meetin' with some investors in a couple hours, and I've had you on my mind ever since I first saw you." He reached down, tugging his belt off, opening his pants so I could see that thick bulge separated between us only by a thin layer of cotton. "No amount of jackin' it has been able to get my libido to calm down with you around, know what I'm sayin'?" He said.

And frankly, I was already weak in the knees. Before I even knew it I was pulling the glasses from my face and neatly tucking them aside on my desk.

I couldn't believe I was doing it. I couldn't believe I *wanted* to do it. I'd been raised the same way as most, to believe in one true love and marriage.

But Ken... he tossed my upbringing to the side and started making me wonder if maybe this couldn't be the new normal. My eyes roamed over his body before I finally came up with enough justification that I didn't feel bad for bobbing my head yes. After all, it was my job. How could I refuse him?

That made all the guilt and internalized slut-shaming that was keeping me so tightly wound slip away.

"Okay," I said. "Where would you like--"

Before I could finish the question, Ken was tugging off his boxers, and letting that thick cock spill out. It thwacked against the desk top with a meaty thud that surprised and excited me.

"This is gonna be so good," he rumbled lowly as I began to sheepishly undo my blouse, letting my own milky white breasts spill out.

But Ken had other ideas, he rounded my desk and took

hold of my shoulders and hip. He guided me forward, bending me over the desk, and then hiked up my skirt. He gave a deep, lewd groan of excitement, rubbing his hands over my ass cheeks, groping and fondling them, letting the flesh swell between his fingers as he sized me up.

That was part of the deal. No panties.

"God damn you look tasty," he groaned, and then prying my cheeks apart, he did the unexpected: he got down on his knees behind me and brought his mouth to my pussy.

I couldn't help but gasp as he lashed his tongue over my slit, tasted my womanhood with such enthusiasm. He gave a low rumble that hummed through my sensitive nethers, making me moan aloud as he parted my folds and licked excitedly.

I could barely believe it. The pleasure he was giving me... it was exquisite. It wasn't at all like what I'd fear it'd be, all about his orgasm and nothing else. Some of my boyfriends in the past didn't even like eating me out.

And none were as good as Ken. I parted my legs, teetering forward in my heels as my thighs pressed into the desk.

Ken had me moaning wildly, grasping onto the edge of the desk as he ravished me, his hunger for me insatiable. He licked and worked at my pussy with such ravenous desire and expert tongue work. My spine was arching before I knew it as pleasure coiled up within me, and I swear the only thing that made him stop at all was that I came so hard I gushed honey over his face and nearly choked the poor man!

"Fuck," he said, pulling back, gasping in air, licking his face and wiping up the thick honey about his mouth.

I felt embarrassed and self-conscious for a moment, worried he was displeased.

"That was amazing!" He said instead, squeezing my two ass cheeks once more, giving me a kiss on them before he rose up. "You taste like heaven, doll," he remarked, standing behind me, grasping that thick shaft and lining up the tip with my pussy.

I was dizzy from his touch, from what he'd just done to my body, but the touch of his crown against my sensitive pussy... It was heaven. Absolutely divine.

My moan said as much as my head tilted back, my flesh simply begging for more. How quickly I'd turned from apprehensive but curious to downright lustful! The thoughts that were running through my mind... The things I wanted him to do to me!

It made all my nerves more sensitive, my entire body jolted with delight.

There he was, this big, successful, muscular adonis behind me, staring down at me like I was the hottest girl in all the world... and then he was pushing that thick cock inside me, stretching my pussy wide, making me moan as he sank on inside. And he was moaning too, grasping my ass cheeks so tightly as he throbbed wildly with each inch he sunk in.

"Ohhh fuck!" he moaned, kneading my ass cheeks as he hilted himself inside me, filling me up and savouring it a moment. "You feel better than I imagined," he said, wasting no time as he tugged back his hips and began to pump his shaft into me, my tight little canal clinging to him, clenching around him and fighting him every step of the way.

But that only made the man love it all the more as he claimed me, first of the men.

And the fact that he was bareback inside me?

Well that was a pleasure I'd never known before. I was always so cautious, so frightened about getting pregnant. But it was in my contract, so it wasn't like I could refuse.

It wasn't like I wanted to, either. Not after feeling how good a raw, hard cock was inside of me. I swear, I was a trembling mess after not even a minute, the sensation of him fucking me turning me on like I couldn't believe.

Ken's pace picked up, faster, harder, making my ass cheeks quake as he pumped into me deeply. I saw in the office mirror a reflection of myself being pounded by him, and it was glorious. The image imprinted on my brain and never left since. That big, broad, muscled brute, pounding his thick cock into me, making my face red as I moaned and cried out, his pecs, abs and biceps all glistening with a thin sheen of perspiration that made him look irresistible.

It was that heavenly image that finally drove me over the edge again, and I was screaming out as I came upon Ken's cock, coating him in my honey as I shivered and shook, losing my mind with pleasure. It was the best fuck of my life, by far.

And maybe part of it was because it felt forbidden. It was illicit, like we were up to no good. I mean, fucking in my office? Fucking someone just because they paid? There was definitely a thrill to that and a part of me loved it. A big part of me, I came to realize.

Ken showed me more things I loved that day, his pounding continuing, faster, harder... until that big sexy brute began to lose his rhythm, and I knew he was getting close. His heavy balls were no longer slapping against my clit. They were tightening up, getting ready to blow.

And when he did, it was with such a loud, uproarious thundering bellow. He jackhammered that cock into me, blowing his load with such intensity. He grunted, shuddered, bent over me a little as he blew so much thick, virile seed into me, until we were both left panting.

"God dammit, babe," he moaned, running his hands up and down my body. "That was just what I needed..." he said so dotingly, kissing along my back to my shoulder.

In some ways, it really did feel like my boyfriend came to my office for a quickie to clear his head. I guess that was part of the reason why I started to feel I might be a natural at it. Because I smiled so broadly, happy to have been able to help him get some release.

It didn't feel normal, but it definitely felt natural to me.

I turned my head slightly, smiling at him, and his lips found mine. It was unexpected, but only made me smile broader.

Ken was a sweetie. After I told him where they were, he grabbed a wet wipe from my desk drawer for me, helped me tidy up. Then he even gave me a kiss on the lips and a warm smile.

"Thanks babe," he said, "that really helped me like you wouldn't believe." He gave my ass a tender squeeze, smiled at me and said his goodbyes. "I'll take you out to a nice show soon. And hey," he said, right before he left, "I'll be back for you tomorrow too."

That charming grin on his face was a nice little goodbye.

"You bet you will," I said, blushing a little, already looking forward to the next day. But that was only the beginning.

I LOVE MY JOB, but it's not always easy. These guys I tend to are rich and successful, handsome men all, but some of them can really take me for a ride, and by the end of the day I can be left feeling so sore sometimes.

Mr. Greenly is a big reason for that. He's a nice, older

gentleman, but oh he lasts so long! No matter how much I tighten up my pussy around him, he keeps pounding away!

I've tried it all to get him to cum quicker, but nothing seems to work. So here I am, glistening in a sheen of perspiration after he's been ramming me on his bed for so long, moaning. My tits bouncing and swaying as he ogles me.

I know he enjoys it, there's no mistaking his moans and the way he stares at me as he fucks me, but damn he wears me out!

He's still gonna be a while too, is the worst of it! But I enjoy it despite my complaints.

But when my phone lights up with an emergency condo management call, I have to answer it despite the moment.

"Sorry hun!" I say, reaching to the side, where my discarded clothes lay, taking up the phone as he pumps away.

"Yeah?" I answer, and take care of the business. But I notice something immediately, Mr. Greenly is trying to be quiet even as he keeps thrusting into me, but he's trembling.

"I see. I'll have that taken care of as soon as possible," I say, and then the miraculous happens... As I'm clutching my phone, taking care of business, he just... loses it. His handsome, hairy chest buckles forward, and he gives a suppressed moan as he unloads in me on the spot.

In all the time I'd been managing the condo, and tending to his cock's needs, I'd never seen such a thing. He just lost it, his dick pulsing immediately as I watched with wide eyes, hearing the voice on the other end of the phone.

"Right away. Thanks," I said, before hitting the end call button, watching him pant as he spurt every last blast of his seed into my tight, wet pussy without any protection.

"Wow, I should take all my business calls when I'm with you from now on," I said with a teasing smile.

He grinned at me a bit bashfully, still lodged deep inside.

"I might like that," he admitted, still panting a bit over me even after he'd lost it so suddenly.

It was adorable. And on the plus side, I'd finally found a kink to get Mr. Greenly off real good: apparently he liked being ignored as he fucked me.

Normally I'd take my time ending things, but he seemed to like my being all business about things, so I shooed him out of me, let his cum drool from my slit as I got up and did a quick tidy. A real clean would have to wait until I got back to my place, as I slipped back into my skirt and blouse.

"See you again soon!" he called out eagerly, like I'd never heard him before. And instead of saying bye I just smirked at him over my shoulders, and sashayed my bubbly round butt on out of there.

He ate it up.

I left his place, and headed on towards my office, but before I could even get there, I saw Mr. Steele. He was tall, fit, and always had an insatiable appetite for me, and there he was, waiting for me to return to my office.

"There you are," he said, a smile blossoming on his face.

"Been waiting long, hun?" I asked as I unlocked the door, flashing him a smile.

He didn't waste any time, coming up behind me, putting his strong hands on my hips, pressing his groin to my ass.

"I need you," he husked into my ear in that low growly voice of desire. His dick already rock hard, I could feel it so completely.

"Okay sweetie, I just need to clean up real quick. Just

362

finished with another resident," I said calmly, but he squeezed me tightly and kissed my neck.

"I can't wait. Let's go now," he growled, and we pushed into my office together.

Most of the tenants were such clean and neat freaks, being in tech and business as they were, and Mr. Steele was normally too. But he had such desire for me, he could barely contain himself usually. He really made a girl feel wanted.

It was exciting, to know that he'd forget all about how dirty I was. Or maybe that was just what he was in the mood for today. Men are complicated beings, far more complicated than most women give them credit for. I had to learn that fast, because being the condo manager for this place? I'd be eaten alive if I didn't appreciate every nuance of these delicious men.

"You want to be a little naughty, don't you?" I pretended to tsk tsk. I looked so prim and proper in my blouse and pencil skirt, with my stiletto heels and black thigh-highs accentuating my legs in a subtly sexy way.

But beneath my skirt, I wore no panties, and my bra was so sheer you could see my stiff nipples through my blouse.

I was anything but prim and proper.

Mr. Steele was ravenous, his mouth lunging for my neck, kissing, licking, nipping at me hungrily as my thighs hit the edge of the desk. I could feel that cock of his throbbing incessantly, his two big hands groping at my waist, my hips, one pawing at my breasts then through my blouse and bra.

"I want you any and every which way," he said, that touch of an English accent still on his voice, as he ground himself in against my bubbly round ass. "You're haunting my dreams, my waking fantasies."

What girl could resist hearing those words and not feel a shiver of joy and pride. I wanted to infest his every thought. I wanted to be *irreplaceable*. And it seemed it was working. I ground up against him, letting my ass get him harder and harder.

"And what way do you want me first?" I purred over my shoulder.

His strong hand fondled my breast while the other dipped low, sliding along my thigh, edging up my skirt to expose the smooth supple flesh of my ass. His lips never stalling as he kissed and suckled at my neck.

"Any way, I just need to be inside you, so bad," he groaned out huskily, reaching his hand to his own shirt, undoing the buttons, sliding open his trousers to let his hard, veiny cock pulse against my bare ass.

"Mmm. What's gotten you in such a mood," I ask as I shimmy up my skirt so that it's little more than a belt, revealing my slick, shaven pussy. I part my legs, bending over the desk as I glance over my shoulder at him.

I got a full view of his sculpted chest, his hard pecs and rippling abs as he took hold of that thick cock. It was such a lovely shaped organ, thick and full with just the right amount of upwards curve to it so he'd hit me perfectly once inside.

"I know it's the right time... for you," he said suggestively, teasing his cock against my slick, cum-stained pussy. "And I really wanna make sure that I have a shot at being the one who plants a baby in that beautiful body of yours," he rumbles with desire.

I bit down on my lip and moaned, my eyes fluttering shut. I couldn't believe how much those words brought a blush to my body, and made me feel so alive. I'd never thought about it in that way before, and I had no idea I'd be so turned on by the idea of getting knocked up.

"Yea?" I mutter dumbly, my head too fuzzy with desire to even be able to form a complete sentence, apparently.

The men all signed on for the same deal: unprotected sex with me, all of them having responsibility to pay out for the kid's future as if it was theirs. And they were fine with that, they got to have a family, but with less responsibility, since it was shared. And I got as much male support as I could handle, and then some.

"Fuck yeah, baby. I want to be in you... now," he husked, shoving his dick inside me suddenly, spreading me open despite the other man's cum still there, and letting loose a deep moan.

It sent such an erotic jolt through me, it felt like I was struck by lightning. I cried out, my limbs quivering, my body shaking with excitement and ecstasy.

"Fuck, you're big," I gasp out, my mouth hanging open, my shoulders slumping for a second as I got used to his huge cock, stretching me out.

I've been with all the guys I look after, of course. It's my job, and my passion. They love me, I adore them. Not all of them are so invested in knocking me up, but the ones like Mr. Steele or Torenson, make life interesting.

Without wasting much time, I feel that throbbing cock pull back, and that eager man begin to pump his hard cock into me. It was a good thing I'd just gotten warmed up by Mr. Greenly, because this was going to be a ride. The hard, incessant pumps of Mr. Steele's cock needfully filling me up, thrusting into the hilt as he so desperately wanted to knock me up.

"You're such a hot babe," he grunted out, his one hand sliding up my side to fondle my breast again.

My nipples were so stiff, they prickled at his touch, sending intense vibrations right into my chest. I flipped my long hair to the side so I could look back at him, see his face as it contorted into pleasure. I loved watching them get off on me. To see them at their most vulnerable.

I guess they helped awaken a lot of my own sexual desires as well. I had no idea I was so into making men weak in the knees for my pussy.

So into watching them eagerly compete to fuck me and fill me with their cum.

I got to watch his hard body rock and tense, as he pumped those hips, filling me up with his needy, anxious cock that was so eager to pump me full of his seed. But then he reached down beneath me with his free hand, his fingers teasing at my clit as he grunted and his dick swelled.

"I wanna feel you cum on my cock... for real, no faking," he said in his deep, lust-laden voice.

Another tremor went through me, his words and his touch exciting such desire in me. I sucked on my lower lips as I let my head fall between my shoulders. I closed my eyes, simply focusing on the sensations. His cock, spearing me open. His fingers, rubbing my throbbing, slick little clit. The way my breasts swayed with each thrust, and how he teased my nipples stiffer and stiffer.

But what really did me in was his breathing. The moans and grunts of him behind me, filled with such lust and need. It all combined to really and truly topple me over the edge.

No faking.

And as I squealed and moaned, he lost all control too. He'd been holding back for some time, I could tell. And as my pussy gushed warm, hot honey over his shaft and balls, squeezing around him, he pulsed, throbbed thickly, and hilted himself inside me.

"Ohhh yess!" he moaned out, his dick exploding in thick, creamy gouts of virile seed, flooding my fertile depths. He wasn't the first this day, not by a long shot, but he was clearly saving up for this moment, to increase his odds at being the one to knock me up and he kept cumming for such a long time as he thrust and moaned.

Knowing why he wanted to cum in me, knowing he wanted to breed me, was such a turn on. It wasn't something I'd thought a lot about in my time working there. It was always just something I knew was part of the deal, not something I was excited for or dreading.

Suddenly, he'd unlocked something in me I didn't even know was there, and I tightened my pussy around him, milking him of every last drop.

He leaned over me as he panted, keeping his cock locked inside me even after the last spurts splattered against my deepest depths, his husky, pleasured voice in my ear as he kissed my neck.

"The female climax increases the odds of insemination. I really want it to be mine this time," he husked, holding me a bit possessively.

My guys were such horny dorks sometimes. But each one made me happy in his own way. And at this rate, there'd be a third kid on the way soon.

Especially when that knock came at my office door, signalling another tenant in need.

It's hard work, but it's rewarding.

PROFESSOR'S PET

Book Themes:
Teacher/Student, May/December Relations, Risky Sex, Breeding, and Barely Legal
Word Count:
6,341

BRITTANY SAT ANXIOUSLY at her desk. It was the last day of school for the year before exams began, her eighteenth birthday behind her. Yet she knew things didn't look good. Whether she passed or failed entirely rested upon her performance on the exams, and she was just awful at them. Awful at the assignments too, for that matter. In fact, about the only thing she was good at was attendance.

Of course... she had reason for that: school was where the boys were. Where the men loomed over them all.

Mr. Hawthorne closed the door to the classroom, shutting out the noise in the hall before he turned and made his way back towards her.

He was her favourite teacher, for obvious reasons. So big and tall, a fit man who worked out on his lunch breaks, he had a great sense of style to boot. Always in nice European-cut pants, with rich shirts undone a couple buttons, and a shiny vest atop that. Sometimes a fetching blazer.

He wore glasses, but he made them look good, with his thick, luxurious golden hair framing his face. He was twice her age, but always reminded her of the father she'd not had since she was but a little girl.

"Brittany," he said, in that smooth, masculine voice of his as he sat down on the edge of his desk and brought his emerald gaze to bear upon her. "You're not about to pass your exams without help, are you?" That authoritative voice challenged her to defy his logic.

And, of course, she couldn't. Her blue eyes glimmered for a moment before she tried to hide them from him under the long, dark lashes. She wore plenty of mascara to make up for just how fair they usually were, with her natural blonde hair and porcelain skin. She'd tried to tan, but all it had done was given her a cute brush of freckles across her nose and cheeks that she hid with concealer and powder and blush.

Still, they were mildly visible under the harsh glare of the school lights.

"I've been studyin' really hard," she replied, batting her eyes at him flirtatiously. "I just have a lot on my mind distracting me."

"Studying?" he said questioningly, sounding surprised with her, his full lips shifting into an amused grin. He reached out, his long fingers sliding over her cheek before his large palm cupped it. "Why are you wasting time at that, hun?" he said, his glittering eyes studying her, admiring her beauty. "We both know you're not the kind of girl made for that sorta work, don't we?"

She bit in her lower lip, tasting the vanilla lip gloss she loved, and held his gaze. She played a bit shy, but only because she knew it got to him.

She drew in a large breath, her silver chain sparkled along her collarbone, the delicate cross hanging lower beneath the cusp of her white blouse.

"What else am I supposed to do at night, when you're home with a family and responsibilities?"

He gave her a crooked smile as his thumb traced along her lips, feeling the thick lower one softly as he admired her beautiful features. Wetting his own mouth with his moist tongue, he said, "Now, Brittany, I'm separated, but that's not the point of this talk..." he remarked, growing increasingly enraptured with her by the moment, she could feel it. One thing she did know, just instinctually, was men. "We could come to an arrangement for me to get you a passing grade, but what good would that do you, huh? You'd only bomb your other courses, right?"

She paused for a moment before reluctantly nodding. "Probably."

He was so near to her, she could smell some soft, woody aroma from him, and she leaned in to inhale him deeper into her. Just as instinctually as she knew men, she lusted for them. Was desperate for them.

Him in particular.

He gave her a gentle, tender sort of smile as he continued to softly stroke her cheek, letting his fingertips graze back over her ear and hair. "I knew your mom way back when," he remarked off-handedly. "You're a lot like her. Bet you're just as man crazy as she was, huh?" he said with a bit of a wry grin forming. "You're much prettier than she ever was though." His voice grew progressively deeper and sexier as he spoke and she licked her lower lip hungrily.

"She and I don't talk much about that stuff," Brittany admitted, but she quickly started remembering the comments her mother had made over the years and it all started falling into place. Her lips curved upwards and her cheeks dimpled in such a complimentary manner, a bit smug with the favourable comparison.

"Take my word for it then," he said in that husky, paternal voice of his laced with that added layer of lust. "Now, Brittany. Knowing who your mom is, and watching you very closely every day in class"—and the look he gave her said it all, truly—"I could offer to give you a passing grade if you agree to get down and suck my cock." He let that hang a moment as he studied her reaction. "Or…"

He trailed off there, his fingers curling in her hair and giving just the slightest hint of a tug on the blonde strands.

Her lip trembled at his… request? Demand? It didn't matter. Her stomach still flipped and she squeezed her thighs together beneath her navy-blue skirt.

She was a fairly thin woman, yet she'd been blessed with an ample bottom and full chest that threatened to make the buttons on her blouse pop open at any moment. Her breath caught again and they rose even higher, so deliciously near to his hand, begging to be touched.

"Or?"

He gave her an approving little smile, and his fingers uncurled from her hair as he leaned forward, his masculine musk so clear and pleasant to her as he neared her. He filled his suit so well, she noted, looking so professional yet stunning as he trailed the backs of his fingers along her collarbone and grazed along her breast flesh. "Or you can forget this silly learning nonsense, and focus on what you were made for, darling. You can come over to my place after class, accept you're gonna be a high school dropout, and I'll teach you what you really need to know to survive in the world. How about that, hm?"

"Oh god."

The words slipped out of her throat, so breathy and raw and instinctual, filled with such longing. As if he'd plucked from thin air just what she needed to hear, and her legs squeezed tight again, her pussy throbbing against her panties.

Her throat felt so raw and her stomach was twisted with her emotions.

She wanted that.

"But my mom will be so upset," Brittany managed in protest, but her smoldering gaze dared him to tell her she was wrong.

WIth a shrug of his shoulders he said, "So what? You're eighteen now. High school's behind you, and you can do what you want. Besides" —he gave her a cocky, knowing grin— "she did it when she was even younger than you. I should know, I advised her to do the same back then."

His thumb trailed along her lower lip, pushing the moist morsel down as he leaned in close to her, those green eyes of his seeming fiery with desire. "If it'll ease your mind, after you come stay with me, I'll go over and calm her down some. How's that sound?"

She swiped her tongue along the salty, textured pad of his thumb, staring at him intensely.

Regardless of what transpired in this classroom, she knew that she would flunk out before the year was through.

And she wanted him so bad.

With his thumb still between her full lips, she murmured, "Promise?"

She watched as his Adam's apple bobbed as he swallowed, seeing and feeling her taste his digit exciting him even further. "Promise," he said, smoothly withdrawing his hand to reach behind him and grab a notepad. He jotted something on it then handed it to her. "Here's instructions to my place. Nice and detailed. Can't be seen giving you a ride home yet, doll, so you come on over after class and I'll start teaching you the only stuff that'll ever matter to you."

He stood up then, dangling that piece of paper before her, a commanding look on his face that said it was no longer an option. The choice was made.

She grabbed for it eagerly.

BRITTANY NEVER WENT HOME, but straight to his place, following the directions on his note.

It led her to a quiet neighbourhood, and then right up to his house, which was a lovely place. It was a bit nicer than a teacher typically had, but then he had a wife before, seperated now, so it must've been bought then.

His car was in the driveway, and she recognized it immediately. It was a nice, silver Lexus that looked only a couple years old.

Heading on up to the door, she rang the bell. She was a bit nervous, she had to admit. She'd never done anything quite like this, though she had thought about it so often. Fantasized about following him home one night or hiding away in his backseat, just waiting to pounce on him in private.

She'd fixed up her lipstick and straightened her skirt, but still she stood in those Mary Janes, the navy skirt that just grazed her white knee high-stockings, and her pressed white blouse. She knew it showed off the red, lacy bra beneath if anyone stared hard enough, and it always made her wet to think about.

To know that the boys and men around her were going to their rooms with the teasing glimpses of her cleavage and thighs on their mind.

It felt like an eternity, but a few moments later he appeared there before her, opening up the door and welcoming her in.

"Come on in, babe," he said to her with such a casual air of confident control, gesturing her up the stairs to his living room. His home was well furnished inside, the living room nice and big with a bar on one end. She noted his sleeves were pulled back, showing his thick, bulging forearms, the veins protruding prominently.

She nearly stumbled as she stared, but forced her way up, slowly.

She knew what he could see if he followed just the right distance behind. Those little flashes of milky flesh, so tender and ripe.

"Thank you, Mr. Hawthorne."

He never corrected her, never told her to call him anything else, but after staring up her skirt at the round swells of her ass cheeks as she climbed those stairs, he then very casually placed his hand upon her hip. "I'll get you a drink," he said, his strong fingers sliding down over the curve of her rear and giving her backside a squeeze.

She didn't bother suppressing her moan.

It was a slow, purposeful gesture, and he then walked over to the bar, taking out some vodka and a few other drinks as he went about mixing something for her. "Make yourself comfortable," he said, gesturing around the room, with its two large, plush sofas around a beautiful fireplace and TV; it was obviously meant for entertaining a large crowd.

"Oh, the parties I could have here," she said apprecia- tively, walking towards one of the couches and taking a seat, crossing her legs at the knee, and staring at him. It was almost like she was seeing him for the first time, her eyes traveling up his body with slow, steady purpose.

She popped open one of the buttons on the top of her blouse, revealing more of that hidden cross as it teased between her cleavage.

As he mixed their drinks he looked across the room at her, a wry smile upon his face. "There'll be plenty of parties here, Brittany, and you'll be here for 'em all from now on." He was so purposeful and matter-of-fact about it, even as his words dripped with heavy sexual meaning. "Your mom used to be a real party girl too. Wasn't how I met her, but it was how I got to know her way back when."

Brittany couldn't help but feel a bit curious, and almost relieved, to hear him say that. It was comforting to know that she wasn't... broken. She'd always looked up to her mom. She always worked hard, even if they didn't always see eye to eye.

Still, she found it a bit odd for her teacher to be talking about her mother in such a... sexual setting.

"Are you still close?"

He finished fixing the drinks, pouring a couple White Russians for them before heading over to the sofa with her. "Not as close as you and I are gonna get, Brittany," he said in a low voice, handing her the drink as he slipped down beside her, putting an arm around her shoulders. He was closer than he'd ever been with her, his hard body pressed up beside her, really accentuating just how much bigger the man was than her.

Leaning in, he inhaled her feminine scent and smiled. "Everything about you is just fuckin' beautiful, doll."

She loved the constant barrage of familiar nicknames, the feel of him... lusting for her. Wanting her.

And yet she knew she wasn't the one in control. She wasn't the one calling the shots.

He was.

She licked her lower lip before sipping the creamy liqueur, her eyelids fluttering pleasurably. "I never thought this is where I'd be tonight. Or any night."

He took a sip of his own drink then laid the glass down on a coaster on the coffee table before reaching over and resting his hand upon her knee. "Never?" he questioned her, as if doubting her. Those strong fingers of his rubbing over her inner thigh as he moved from her knee. "I guess imagination's not your forte, doll. It's okay," he said soothingly, smiling fondly at her.

She smirked back at him, already feeling the effects of the alcohol. Or, more likely, her youthful idea of the effects of the alcohol, combined with her own burning lust.

"I said I never thought this is where I'd be. Not that I didn't want it."

Some music seemed to start playing all of its own accord, or perhaps Brittany didn't notice him start it up. The rhythm of it starting off smooth and getting rather lively before long, though she didn't recognize it at all.

"You know, I've been waiting for this day to come for quite some time, doll," he said in his deep voice, rubbing her shoulder and along her thigh as he edged his fingers beneath her skirt. "Watched you grow up. Saw the telltale signs that you were becoming such a little sex bomb all the time." He gave a big, broad smile. "I don't think you could've turned out any more promising."

She uncrossed her legs and her knees pressed together, that throbbing of her pussy nearly driving her mad as she drank more of the White Russian. It was nerves. She knew it was. Her stomach was flipping and dancing unlike it ever had before, and she was feeling so damned hot.

"Oh?" she practically stammered, and cursed herself for not being better at keeping herself calm and collected. Uncaring of her teacher's desire for her.

He tilted his head, his thick blonde hair spilling to the side as he smiled at her. "Yeah, that's right. I was looking out for you even if you didn't notice it as such," he explained, his hand squeezing her leg as he moved in so daringly close to her feminine heat, forcibly prying her thighs apart enough to graze over her panties. "You're a very special woman, Brittany. A beautiful little airheaded bimbo," he said, as if it were the highest compliment.

"Oh god," she pleaded again, her head tilting back and her long, straight hair spilling over the cushion on the back of the sofa. Her entire body felt like it was on fire, and when he touched her, she barely knew what to do with herself. Her hands shook as she brought the rest of the drink into her mouth, eager for the creamy coolness to ease the scorching heat, but it only inflamed her more.

Mr. Hawthorne leaned over her, his mouth finding her neck and kissing upon her smooth, pale skin as his hand crept up to rub over her panties. His long finger tracing the outline of her slit as he kissed and suckled her neck up towards her ear, where he nibbled her lobe.

She could hear his rising breathing, and his low, lust-laden voice so quiet yet right there against her. "You're a walking, talking dickteaser in the flesh," he husked as he felt her dampness through her panties. "You're pure sex, and you've got no room in that head for anything else, just like you should be."

Brittany made a small noise, but it was incoherent. Halfway between a moan and a protest, her hips writhed against him of their own volition.

Her teacher was touching her.

Mr. Hawthorne was touching her.

Kissing her.

Purring in her ear.

She was putty in his hands as she put the glass on the end table, her body pressed to his eagerly.

He was so different from the way he acted during class, that warm, knowledgeable veneer replaced with bawdy talk and lewd touches. This was the man in his own home, acting with her as he truly wanted to, she realized.

The handsome, dashing man she had a crush on for so long feeling her up, pressing his long, powerful fingers into the cleft of her womanhood. Prying those well-trimmed digits in under her panties and tugging them aside so he could touch her slit bare, with nothing between them. He gave such an expert little swirl of his fingers around her sensitive clit and stoked her excitement so high.

"You were always an obedient girl, weren't ya, Brittany? Just never so good at the follow-through on all that boring schoolwork," he said in a low, lusty voice, eying her so hungrily.

She was squirming against him without even realizing, her body needing him so badly. Wanting for him so badly.

Her lithe thighs parted and she pulled back from him to stare at him with her bedroom eyes, her lips partially parted. "We shouldn't be doing this," she moaned, and begged for him to tell her she was wrong. Her back arched, her chest lifted, and she pushed herself towards him, her arms wrapping around his neck.

"Shhh." He hushed her softly as he continued to tease and excite her, kissing along her jaw towards her pouty lips where he licked and sucked those luscious morsels. "You leave the thinking to me, doll," he said quite firmly.

He pulled from her, despite her attempts to get nearer

to him. Lifting those cunny-slick fingers to his lips he licked and tasted them, his eyes fluttering nearly shut as he seemed to revel in her flavour. "Mm, be a good slut and get down on your hands and knees," he commanded sternly.

Her stomach twisted, but she knew she wouldn't disobey. She couldn't. The way he was looking at her was driving her crazy and she whimpered as she leaned closer to him. But she knew that wouldn't be good enough, that she couldn't beg her way back into his lap and arms.

So she did what every good girl should.

She crawled off the couch and her navy skirt fluttered around her thighs as her knees pressed against the hard floor. Staring up at him beneath those dark lashes, she inhaled deeply and awaited his instructions.

That strong jaw of his squared off in a satisfied grin as he watched her fall to her knees so obediently, and he got up from the couch, straightening his vest as he lowered himself down behind her on one knee. Very casually he reached out, hooked his fingers upon her pleated skirt, and lifted it up, revealing the smooth, round cheeks beneath.

"Such a beautiful ass you've got, Brittany," he remarked just a moment before he casually turned one cheek red with a rough crack of his strong palm.

Her eyes went wide as she jolted forward with shock. "Ow!" She wasn't expecting that, not at all, but then the pain lessened and left a tingly feeling along the swell of her behind and her breath caught.

That was nice.

Letting her skirt rest on her lower back, he stroked his one hand up her spine, like stroking a good pet. The other rubbed over her stinging cheek, prodding those tingling nerves, putting them to the test as he smiled approvingly at both her beautiful body and her acceptance of the spank.

"That's for being such a little cocktease all this time,

doll," he said, his fingers curling into her blonde hair, wrapping the strands about his digits as he struck at her ass once more, making the flesh burn hot.

"Ah!" Her eyes widened and then shut, her body folding to his whims, her scalp prickling, and her ass stinging.

Yet she couldn't remember ever being so turned on, so needy. The amount of control, of buildup that he was creating was something unusual for her. She shivered at the tension in the air, at her desire for him to simply take her.

And at the same time, she wanted him to take her to the limit.

His fingers tightened their grasp and he twisted his fist, punching her hair up and pulling back her head as he gave her stinging cheeks a pat, bringing more of the blood to the surface before he cracked his hand against the still pale and unpunished half of her ass. "You're gonna be a good lil' cock sleeve for me from now on, Brittany. Aren't you?" he said in a husky, commanding voice that so darkened the handsome man's words.

This was her teacher. The man who graded her papers, who knew her mother, who went to parent-teacher meetings and talked about her performance.

And now she was down on her knees, her skin stinging from his abuses, and all she could do was want more. Her ass even stuck out a bit more, begging for his harsh hand, even though it tugged her hair more.

Worst still, it all caused her to moan like a wanton whore.

He cracked his palm against her ass again, harder this time, and the sound of it filled his beautiful entertainment room. "I asked you a question, slut. That's a rare opportunity for you to use your words," he chastised as she heard him work his belt behind her. Was he undoing his pants?

She couldn't tell, not with him holding her head in place so tightly.

She tried to look, but it only gave her more of that painful sensation to her scalp and she moaned louder. But she knew better than to disappoint twice, and she managed out a meek "yes," just to please him. To make him happy.

Then, instead of feeling the hot flesh of his manhood, he moved her body to the side just slightly, and... the crack of his belt across her ass landed along both cheeks, narrowly avoiding the puffy wet slit between. "That's better," he remarked in his hard, authoritative voice, over her cry of anguish.

She'd never felt something so intense in her life, and her cunny throbbed hot with need. Why wouldn't he just take her? Why was he insisting on punishing her so?

"Please," she breathed, but she didn't know what she was begging for. Leniency? Forgiveness?

Or for him to fuck her?

"Please?" he repeated questioningly as he let go of her hair and reached to her arms. He wrapped her wrists in his leather belt, then tied it up tight, locking them together securely. Grasping the back of her hair, he pulled her head up as he leaned in and bit her earlobe. A low growl rumbled from his throat and he husked out to her, "Please what?" Then a crack of his hand across her ruddy, battered cheeks came fast behind.

"Ah!" she screamed, this time a bit louder, and she hoped that no one could hear how hungry she sounded.

No one but her teacher.

She tested her hands, her fingers playing with the tongue of the belt as she squirmed on the hard floor. She didn't know what to say, what he wanted, and so she just whimpered again. "Please..."

He growled into her ear, "That's the best you've got for

me, you bimbo slut? Just a 'please'? Please what?" He was insistent—demanding—and he struck her ass again, though this time after the loud crack of impact he left his palm to rest there upon her cheek, his fingers sliding over her glistening slit, testing her needful cunt. "Even a dumb slut like you has words enough to tell me what you want."

Her mouth hung open and never had she felt dumber. Not when she was failing his class, not when she'd first hit on him and he politely refused.

Never.

It was like all the thoughts simply left her mind, leaving her feeling vacant and a little haze before she licked her lips.

"You," she managed out finally. "I want you."

He gave a harsh little laugh and bit at her ear, tugging the lobe before letting it snap back to her. "You want me to fuck you, is that it? Then say it," he prodded, his fingers stroking over her cunny, swirling about her clit before trailing her warm honey across her stinging ass cheeks. "You're a bimbo slut, use your words like one," he chided, his hand cracking across her cheeks, the moisture of her cunt only making the sting worse.

This was so humiliating, to have him insult her like that. To use such degrading and horrible language.

But she was so fucking turned on by it, she could barely contain herself from turning into a quivering, stammering pile on his floor.

"Please fuck me," Brittany pleaded, her voice so desperate.

"Good girl," he complimented her, and very quickly she heard his fine black pants come undone behind her. A low thud resounded as his heavy cock smacked against her stinging ass cheeks. That hefty shaft bulging with throbbing veins, glistening at the tip with his precum.

He trailed that beast of a dick down along her cunny, teasing her slick womanhood as he grasped her hips with both of his strong, manicured hands. "This has been a long time in the coming, slut," he remarked, letting his digits sink into her flesh before he speared her upon his thickly throbbing manhood, taking her up to the hilt as he nestled his crown against her womb.

Her thighs tightened as she yanked herself forward, trying to balance herself against that sudden thrust and the sharp pain that followed as he went too deep, too soon. It took her breath away, and the feel of his hips against her stinging ass only accentuated her own feeling of pain.

"Holy fuck," she moaned out, her prissy skirt falling back around the top of her ass and his hips as she squirmed.

Those powerful hands of his grabbed her tight and pulled her back into place as he grunted his approval at her tight pussy. "Fuck, you're a good cunt," he growled, and she could feel the instinctual throb of his excited cock inside of her, twitching and filling her so completely. Pushing the walls of her narrow quim outwards so widely as he just enjoyed resting inside her warm, wet confines.

She couldn't believe this was happening. Maybe it was just the alcohol that made her slower to realize it than she should have, but her teacher was inside her. He was oh, so deep inside her, and she swallowed deeply because her stomach was roiling with butterflies and her mind was quickly growing hazy.

"Mr. Hawthorne," she whimpered, wanting him to be gentle, to go slow, and yet... not.

It didn't matter, as he went the pace he wanted.

He tugged back his hips, letting his thick girth slip from her, slick and hot before pounding it back inside with a satisfied grunt. He didn't ease it in her at all, but began to set a slow, hard pace that grew in tempo. The wet slap of her cunt against his groin, the smack of his heavy balls against her clit as he took her in the middle of his living room.

Took her was the right word, as those powerful hands of his grasped her so tight, taking control of her. Making her bound body his to command and use.

Her fingers tightened around the leather belt and her back arched before she gasped.

She couldn't remember him putting on a condom.

She couldn't feel a condom.

Brittany tried to pull away, partially falling off balance but for his strong hands keeping her pressed to him. "Are you... Did you put one on?"

That insistent throb of his cock inside her was so hot and real, so complete, there was no way some rubbery sheath separated him from her. His thrusting shaft pumped into her without a hitch in its rhythm, the loud smacks of his groin and balls striking her uninterrupted as he slapped her ass and reached out to tug her hair once more.

"Don't put your head to thinking, slut," he growled as he fucked her a little rougher in response. "I want the full experience."

Her heart beat angrily against her chest and she knew this was wrong. So very wrong.

He should be smarter than that.

She should have been smarter than that.

So why did her cunny pulse so wantonly, begging his cock into her deeper and deeper despite the stinging of her ass and scalp?

She was gasping for air and couldn't fill her lungs, couldn't clear her head enough to argue with him.

Despite all sense and reason he pounded into her

harder and faster, that handsome, civilized teacher of hers fucking her wildly. The sounds of their rutting filled the room as he pushed her head down onto the floor, bending her body to his will as he kept her ass pushed up in the air only to be beaten so mercilessly with his thrusts.

"C'mon, you want this, don't ya, slut?" he growled at her, his voice ripe with need as she felt him swell and throb inside her. Again and again he pulsed so eagerly, and she could feel him tensing, working himself closer and closer to his climax within her abused body.

She couldn't keep track of the thoughts and sensations that filled her. They came on too hard, too fast, and then left before she could grasp them. Her mouth hung open as she panted like a dog, her body contorting to his whims.

It was a long few heartbeats before she understood his question, and before she could stop herself, the answer fluttered out. "Yes!"

That was just the answer he wanted, and with one hand upon her hips and the other pushing her cheek down onto the floor he rutted into her with a rabid intensity. Again and again he savaged her poor, battered behind, until… she felt him come to to a screeching halt as he pummeled her depths one final time. His body tensed as he came intensely, letting out a loud, wanton moan of satisfaction.

More than that, she could feel the incessant throbs of his manhood as he shot his load right inside her, deeply filling her honey-slick canal. Spurt after spurt of that rich, virile seed flooding and filling her nubile depths.

"Fuck… yes," he grunted, squeezing her hip so tight as he shook intensely.

She thought, for a moment, she might be sick. Sick of herself, of what she'd let this man do to her.

But it quickly passed and she was filled with nothing but relief. Pleasure.

She groaned as he bucked again, weaker this time, and her eyes rolled back partway in her head as she tried to catch her breath.

He was panting over top of her as his cock twitched out its last pangs of release, unloading every last drop into her unprotected cunt. Bending over her, he leaned in and licked her cheek before nibbling her ear and lowly rumbling his pleasure to her.

"Good work," he praised her lowly. "We've got a bit more work for you to do before you're ready to be the star of this weekend's party, but… you're off to a good start, my little bimbo," he said, the name having no bite to it. Just pure praise. Pure approval.

"A party?" she whimpered, and she couldn't make sense of it.

And then, slowly, it began to sink in and she swallowed hard. "What?"

He slid back onto his haunches, but he took her with him, lifting her up off the floor with his hand in her hair and the other arm about her waist. He was still lodged inside her, and she could feel his pearly-white cum slowly dribbling out of her puffy slit as he spoke into her ear. "Going to hold a nice party here, for me and my good friends. And you're going to be the chief entertainment, doll."

She couldn't see his grin, but could feel it, knew it was there somehow as he held her to his lean, fit physique. "Excited?"

She shivered in his arms and didn't know what to say.

But she wouldn't deny the thrill that went down and settled in her core, making her breath quicken and her back push into his more eagerly. Her bound hands pressed against his stomach and she ran her fingers over him as she began to nod.

"Good," he husked into her ear as he nuzzled his cheek to her blonde hair and squeezed her tighter in his arms. "Until then, you've got a lot of practice to put in. You've still got a little too much pretense in you, my burgeoning bimbo," he said with a hint of amusement as he clutched her breast and squeezed it oh, so tight.

PUNISHED BY THE PRINCIPAL

$\mathcal{B}$ook Themes:
      barely legal, virgin, breeding, teacher/student, creampie

Word Count:

5,475

~

I SHOULDN'T BE HERE. I'm not dumb, I know that sneaking around after hours is going to get me in trouble. But I can't help it. There's only three weeks left of class, and if I don't find out now, it's going to bug me for the rest of my life.

See, my Principal is best friends with my dad, and a couple nights ago, I heard my dad cussing his friend out something fierce.

"How can you spy on Haley like that, Rick? She's just turned 18."

"Oh come on, Hank. I didn't mean nothing by it, but you can't tell me you haven't noticed—"

"Rick! I don't like where this is going, and if you don't

stop what you're doing right now, I'm going to have to take action. Those pictures on your hard drive are inappropriate!"

"It's just innocent," Rick protested, but I could see the way his lip curled into a smirk, and I knew it wasn't.

I hoped it wasn't. I'd always had a crush on him ever since he was little, and he used to treat me like a grown up instead of a kid. And now that I'm not a kid, his lips put bad, bad thoughts in my head.

But hearing them fight like that was strange, especially over me. I haven't been able to stop thinking about it, about what Rick might have on his computer. So I decided to stay late after school today and sneak into the Principal's office. How hard can it be?

I know it might not even be on this computer. Maybe it's at Rick's home, but dad hasn't brought me over there since last summer for a BBQ and I know how weird it'd be if I just showed up out of the blue trying to get on his computer.

Nervously, I bite in on my lower lip as I walk through the school halls. It's creepy at night. Even with the lights on, and the janitors here and there, it feels too quiet and abandoned. Like the ceilings are too high and the walls are too wide, and yet it's almost claustrophobic, like everything's closing in on me.

I try to reign in my fear and continue my walk towards the end of the hall. I remind myself of why I'm here.

To find out what pictures Rick has of me.

Earlier that day I'd gone into the secretary's office and when she wasn't looking, I put a little piece of tape over the door hole so it wouldn't lock all the way. When I finally get to the door, I gratefully find out that no one noticed, and I slip into the inner office.

I stare at the nameplate on his door. Principal Rick

Wood. All the others called him Mr. Dick Wood behind his back, but I never did. Mostly because I was afraid that if I did, I'd moan out the word or something like that. I didn't want anyone to know how much I thought about his dick.

I turn the knob and push the door in, but it makes a surprisingly loud noise and I cringe and stop. But I hear nothing, can't see anyone around. So I continue and push on into his office.

The light from his monitor is still on, which means he must've forgot to turn it off when he left work. But all the better for me, because it means that I can get onto his computer more easily.

And it's doubly good, because I see he hasn't logged out of his account! No guessing his password. Which is good, because I have no idea how I'd go about that. I wasn't thinking straight, or planning ahead, clearly!

I sit myself on down, the chair squeaking noisily, but no sooner than I start moving the mouse about to click through folders do I notice the dark silhouette of a tall, broad-shouldered man looking in from the door.

"This kinda thing gets a girl a whole ton of detention… or worse," came that dark, gravelly voice that was so familiar.

Oh crap! He must have heard me come in through the receptionist's door.

"It's not what it looks like!" I protest instantly, the words coming to my tongue no sooner than I'd thought it. I push myself away from the computer as if it's hot lava and I somehow won't get in trouble if I'm not touching it anymore. My blonde bangs brush against my forehead as I shift, and suddenly I'm more aware of everything.

Of the smell of him in the air, the rich cologne filling my senses. It's so dark, but my eyes adjust slowly, and I can see how good he looks in his suit, the way he's undoing the collar of his button down shirt.

He steps towards me slowly, purposefully, placing his two palms upon the desk and leaning forward. I can feel his dark gaze on me, boring through me as he sizes me up, licking his lips slowly.

"Y'know, if you were anyone else... I'd be about to expel you, Andrea," he says to me, each word a deep, husky delight on my ears as he says them.

"No," I whimper, my shoulders slumped, my school outfit crinkling. I'm hot beneath my blouse and vest, and my skirt suddenly feels itchy around my thighs. I can't let my dad find out I was sneaking into his best friend's office at night, that I would have been expelled if he didn't know me so well!

Those perfect, masculine lips of his quirked up into a wry smirk, and as he sizes me up again, I feel downright trapped. So I stand up to leave, but he so casually steps in my way, blocking the only route around his desk with his tall, towering form.

"Andrea," he says, my name rolling off his tongue so smoothly as he reaches out and cups my chin and cheek, stroking his thumb along my smooth skin. "Where do you think you're going? We haven't come to any arrangement here yet," he says.

My nose crinkles, and his eyes twinkle. He's teasing me. I know that look better than any. It's like he caught my hand in the cookie jar and now he's asking what I'll do for him to not tell dad.

"What kind of arrangement?" I ask, and I'm surprised by how lusty my voice is. I feel scared, sure, but he keeps stroking my cheek, and I can feel my body start to flush.

"Well," he begins, taking his time as he looms over me, his natural musk tinged with some light manly aroma of cologne. My eyes are the perfect level to stare at the bare triangle of his hard, masculine pecs. "I can't very well let you off with just a warning in lieu of an expulsion Andrea, now can I? Some kind of punishment or service has to be rendered," he explains slowly, those long, hard fingers of his knitting back into my hair.

When did it get so hot in here? I swallow hard and lick my lips before lightly crossing my arms beneath my heaving breasts.

"I'll wash your car for you every day after class," I promise, knowing very well how much he prizes his car. His dad gave it to him years ago, and he's looked after his Cadillac like it was his child. I guess since he never married, he needed something to care for.

"Wash and polish my car, huh?" he says, brow raised, sounding sceptical of my proposal. "You think that's all it's gonna take to wipe the slate clean, lil' girl?" he taunts me, goads me as those dark eyes of his flash wide a moment and he looks down over me. "I think we'll have to step things up a notch, don't you?"

I'm dying to know what pictures he has of me, but that look in his eyes...

I'm a virgin. I've never been interested in other guys, especially not those my own age. But Mr. Wood is so sexy, and way out of my league. So why does it look like he wants me? Why does he keep looking at my pink-lipglossed lips? Every time I lick them, he looks at them almost enviously.

There's no way.

Is there?

"Like what?" I manage out finally, my voice soft and cautious.

He brushes his fingers back through my blonde hair, stroking it as he tilts his head and admires my face with that warm smile. A warm smile that contains a hint of something else entirely. Something more than warm. But hot.

"You're telling me a beautiful young woman such as yourself doesn't have any ideas, Andrea?" he asks, and I can hear a bit of that suave charm in his gravelly voice, and it's melting my knees.

But he called me beautiful. The word is slow to seep into my mind. Usually he'd call me cute, or pretty. Never beautiful.

I tilt my head and feel his thumb brush against the shell of my earlobe. He strokes it tenderly, and it sends something straight through my core.

"Mr. Wood?" I murmur curiously, "What should I do?"

He doesn't remove that hand from my face, but his other one comes up, grasps my hip and holds me. Keeps me from floating away. Or that's how I feel anyhow, with him looming over me so closely, holding and caressing me.

"Whatever it takes," he says with a certain gravel to his voice, leaning down towards me, until I realize his lips are within a hair's breadth of touching mine.

I can almost taste the cinnamon mint on his breathe, and I don't know what to do. I'm like a startled animal caught in the headlights.

Yet at the same time, excitement thrums through me. For so long I've fantasized about him, wanted him to just... take me. And now he's so close, I could just... lean forward and kiss him.

But when my mouth touches his, I'm shocked by my brazenness! I didn't mean to actually do it!

Whether I meant to or not though, he takes the kiss, and deepens it.

His head tilts, and his tongue lashes along my lips, parts them and probes into my mouth just a little. He's holding my face and guiding the tempo, making me swim in a sea of excitement until…

He pulls away, and looks down at me with that dashing smile of his.

"You can't kiss your way out of this entirely, young lady," he says with such smooth authority, his hand on my hip running around until it's skirting the top of my bottom. "But maybe a few spanks and I can see through to letting you off with this… and we can get back to that kissing," he says, just as his palm slides down around the curve of my ass.

Oh God. I wonder if he can feel how hot I am?

If he just moved his fingers just a little further, no doubt he could sense the heat that's radiating from between my thighs. I want it so bad that I'm distracted from his words.

"Spanks?" I ask with some confusion. I haven't been spanked since I was a little girl, and certainly never by someone not my parents. That was always a childish punishment thing.

So why does the thought of him spanking me turn me on?

That hand of his strokes over the round part of my rear, and it's done so softly, so tenderly, but it feels like such a tingling tease of what he's saying.

"C'mon now, Andrea. Bend over this desk here and we'll sort out your punishment," he says, and his hand leaves my face at last, but only to reach down, take hold of my hand and guide me to his desk. He's placing my hands to the top of that hardwood, doing it all so tenderly, but I can feel the strength in his grasp as he slides his hand back to my waist and hip, and pushes me into a bent-over position.

I'm in a daze, and feel so prone bent over, my skirt

hiking up over the backs of my creamy thighs. My stockings end right above my knees, and my flesh is so vulnerable and bare. But I can't find the will to protest or stop him. I don't know if it's just fear of being caught, or wanting to make amends.

In fact, the only thing I do know, is that the longer his hands are on me, the harder my pussy throbs with need. Why would punishment turn me on like this?

That big, strong hand of his is stroking over the swell of my pert rear again, and I can hear him step around me, switching sides. The pathway to the door is open now, but I can't will myself to move. Not even as he squeezes my cheek.

"Alright sweetie, that's a good girl, it'll all be over soon," he husks, and not long after the first crack of his palm lands, smacking over my skirt against the flesh of my rear. A firm, crack of his palm, so easy and casual for him, but enough to make me gasp out loud.

It's so much different than the spankings I took before. I don't know what it is. Maybe just my feelings for him, my desire, but it's almost like the stern punishment is a reward instead. A juicy treat of humiliation and pain, and his hand on a part of me that he should never touch.

Whatever it was, it only does me better with the second spank he lands on my rear, and I swear my gasp is tinged with a bit of a moan. But he does it again, and there's no denying it then.

"Now now," he says, stroking his hand over that part of my rear he'd just struck three times! "I think this skirt is making things too easy on you," he muses, and I feel his long digits curl in around the edge of my skirt and slowly hitch it up higher. Higher. Until my pale butt is exposed.

"This is more like it, don't you think?" he asks, leaning

over my, his gravelly voice so close to my ear as I feel his hand taunting my cheeks.

Oh my God. I've wanted and dreamed about this for so long. His hands touching my bare, sensitive skin that now buzzes with sensation.

It makes me buck towards him like some mindless animal, wanting to feel his touch so damned bad. Even if it stings, it's still his hand touching me. My dad would kill us if he knew. Oh, and if he could read my thoughts, I'd be killed twice!

"This is so bad," I say, but it comes out like a delicious groan of desire.

"Perfectly suited for a bad girl," he says right back to me without missing a beat, and his strong hand strokes along the curve of my ass, skirting the crack of my cheeks only barely... but he pauses low, and I know he can feel my feminine heat there. It's so strong, my desire too strong.

"Fitting punishment for snooping around like such a bad, bad girl," he says with such devious delight, right before his hand smacks my rear again, but this time it's harder. Or maybe it's just the lack of clothing separating us, but his bare hand hit my cheek and makes me cry out in time with the sharp crack.

I gasp, but he's right. I am a bad girl, and I deserve to be punished. This is just more than I ever could have dreamed of or anticipated. It's more of a forbidden treat than anything, and then I feel like the dirtiest girl alive for thinking that.

But I can't help envisioning his fingers going between my thighs, pressing into my white panties...

Instead I get another, harder, slap across my rear and I cry out louder than ever! He follows it up with another, and my butt is stinging, but then... then he's caressing the red hot flesh so tenderly. Gingerly exploring that smooth skin.

"There there. You're a bad, naughty girl Andrea," he says in that deliciously dark rasp of his, "but you're in good hands. I'm going to take care of you. But not before I mark you and lay claim to this pretty lil' body of yours, starting with this sweet ass," he growls out the last of his words, before smacking me again, then again and then the spanks blur together until...

Until he's cradling me, stroking my stinging flesh again and...

He's doing it.

I can feel him sliding his fingers between my cheeks, over the fabric of my panties. Feeling the fiery warmth and dampness over my pussy.

I almost feel drunk or like this is all a dream, the haziness of the pain dripping away and instead replaced by the purest pleasure I've ever know. Sure, I've touched myself once or twice, but I've never been touched by a man. Especially not a man twice my age and best friends with my dad!

I can hear his breathing in my ear, deep and husky, tinged with such lust as he rubs me through my panties. He's ravenous for me, I can tell even before he bites my neck then kisses it, making me tilt my head to the side to make room for his hungry mouth. That thin stalk so sensitive to his ravishing mouth, but the feeling of him petting my pussy down below is so distracting.

"Mmm, you're an even badder girl than I thought," he growls, and then I feel his finger hook into my panties, grazing over the raw flesh of my femininity as he peels them away from the source of my wetness. "Damn, your little cunt's so wet from this spanking, Andrea," he says, tugging down my panties, dragging them down my thighs to my knees, then letting them slip further down.

"Does any of this even count on punishment if you were getting off on it like this?" he asks me, bringing his hands back up to cup my slick, naked mound.

I don't have answers for him. The first time a man's ever done anything like this to me, and I'm helpless against my lusts. I never anticipated I would let it go this far, but now I don't want to stop. I need to feel him inside of me, even if it's just his fingers, and I spread my legs slightly.

"I'll do anything you want, Mr. Wood," I moan out truthfully.

"That's right, you will," he growls into my ear, and his hands slip away from me and I feel him pull back. But when I peer over my shoulder, I see him undoing his belt, hear it jangle as he pulls it free, then the buttons of his pants come undone.

"You know all about safe sex, don't you Andrea? Come on, tell me," he says as he pulls his pants down, and hooks his thumbs into the waistband of his boxer-briefs. The tight, black cotton hugging that thick bulge which snaked left.

"Always use a condom, and abstinence is the only safe sex," I recite from my lackluster sex ed classes. But when I'm watching him undress, I know abstinence is not an option.

"That's right," he says just before pulling down his briefs, and letting that thick, long shaft topple out so rigid and huge. That veiny length pulsating with such desire as the purple tip glistened with precum. And then those balls, heavy and big, dangled beneath as he nudges my feet wider, causing me to spread my legs.

"And have you been a good, clean, safe sex girl, hmm?"

he asks me, taking hold of my two butt cheeks and prying them apart.

I feel anything but clean, but I understand what he's asking.

So do I lie? Or do I tell him that I'm a virgin?

I lick my lips, not sure of what to do, and then I feel another crack on my bare ass. My skirt is up around my waist, my panties dropped to my maryjane shoes, and I feel so vulnerable and yet... it's good. Really good. I arch my back, digging my palms into the hard wood of his desk.

"Answer the question," he demands sternly, and I know I shouldn't be caught in a lie. Not now.

"I've... abstained."

He goes silent for a moment, and I can tell he's shocked, not sure if he should believe me.

"You're lying," he says, but I can feel his finger exploring along the seam of my slit, and then... probing on in. Parting my labia, he dips his middle finger into my cunny and I can feel myself wrapped about that digit. And I moan.

"Damn, you weren't lying... you're tighter than a stubborn knot," he says with such growling approval before plucking his finger out of me and sizing up the glistening digit. He pops it in his mouth and tastes my honey, giving a deep, throaty 'Mmm'.

"Well then sweetheart, you learned all that safe sex stuff for nothin'," he says, and I feel him hefting his thick cock to guide the tip along my moist slit.

"What?" I murmur, looking over my shoulder at him, watching as he suckles on it. I want him so bad, but I don't want to get pregnant!

He unbuttons his shirt all the way, and as I peer back I get an eyeful of his broad, bare chest. The toned muscles, the hard pecs and ripped abs, and then... his manhood. So big and hard as it presses against my most private of places.

"That's the price for being a bad girl tonight," he says, and slowly he begins to pierce my virginity. That thickness of his sinking in, stretching me wider than I've ever been before, and him groaning with such pleasure as he does it. "Or are you sayin' you don't want me in you?" he growls, taking hold of my hips so tightly.

"I do!" I protest instinctually, and even though I was going to follow it up with a big 'but!' he pushes in and my words die on my tongue. He's so big, and even though I'm wetter than I've ever been, it stings as he takes my virginity, making me into the bad girl he thought me to be.

He moans so lewdly as he pushes on into the hilt, filling me up completely as our debauched sounds of pleasure fill the air. And I can feel him inside me, pulsating, stretching me with each new throb of desire.

"Ohhh fuck yeah," he growls, his fingers sinking into my flesh so tight it almost hurts, but it keeps me anchored and in place to have him grasping my hips and waist like that. "You've got the tightest, sweetest little pussy I've ever been in, sweetheart," he rumbles to me.

He stays there for a few moments, letting me get used to his size, to the fact that there's a man inside me! And then the throbbing pain dulls, and is replaced by something much nicer. He grinds against me, not moving in or out, but with each rotation of his hips his body collides with mine, his hips pressing into my tender ass.

My breasts flatten into the wood as he holds my ass up in the air so that I have to go on tip toes, even in my shoes, and then he begins to pull out.

But he doesn't pull out all the way, and I can feel his thick crown snugly inside me still before he pushes back in, and starts to build up a slow budding tempo. His deep, husky moans filling the air.

"Mmm," he gives a long, deep moan. "I can feel your lil' pussy lips clingin' to me as I slide back... like they don't want me to go," he says, smacking into my ass a little as his pace grows. "This tight lil' pussy of yours needed a nice hard cock so bad, huh? Makes you willin' to be such a naughty girl," he husks, his breathing growing heavier.

I know the risks, I know that what we're doing is so wrong, but he feels so right. Like I'm meant to be here, pinned between him and his desk, with nothing between us. It's even better than I fantasized, and I push my ass into him, wanting him deeper.

"You feel so good," I gasp, shuddering when he fills me completely.

"You feel like heaven, you devilish girl," he growls back at me through his own heady lust, but everything is getting lost in the slap of flesh. The way his cock plunges in deep, fills me up, stretches me wide and makes my toes curl with bliss.

My stinging cheeks are taking a beating from his thrusts, but I can barely feel it as he pumps into me. His heavy balls swing up, smacking my clit before he reaches in under, and those long fingers of his find that sensitive bud themselves.

"Ohhh, you feel so good sweetheart... but now it's time for you to cum on my cock," he says with such an insistence. Like I have no choice in the matter.

But it's not like I could hold back, even if I wanted to. His fingers... Oh God his fingers. It's like every nerve in my body is being caressed all at once, and when he strokes along my soaking pussy, I begin to tremor. I've never felt anything like this, and he rubs a bit harder, more insistent.

I buck forwards, the sensation almost too much! He has

me pinned to the desk, though, and there's no real escaping him. Ohh, not that I want to!

"Ah!" I gasp out, and his rough fingertip swirls around my clit. "Ohh!"

And then there's fireworks going off behind my eyelids, and my pussy clenches his dick so hard that he can barely pull out.

But as pleasure explodes within me, I don't think he's trying too hard to pull out. He pumps into me, the gush of my honey flooding around his shaft, then coating his balls as they smack wetly against my body.

His deep, growling moans fill the air with my squeals and cries, and he's pumping me into the desk so hard.

As I lose all control and become a spasming, twitching mess, he takes over. He bends down, ceasing his thrusts long enough to take my leg and twist me around. He lifts me up, puts me down onto my back atop his desk and places my calves against his shoulders.

"That's it," he says, licking his lips as he starts to pump again, reaching his two thick forearms out as he undoes my blouse, one button at a time.

I can't help but knock his pencil holder to the ground, folders under my ass as he holds me in position. I can see his face in the dim light as he opens my blouse to find my red, lacy bra that I had to hide from my dad whenever I needed to wash it.

My breasts heave as he fucks me deeper, so deep that I almost feel like I'm going to black out!

But then he reaches out, grasps my breasts with his two powerful hands, sinks his fingers into the twin mounds. His greedy grasp pulls the bra away, to get at the stiff nipples, to maul and manipulate them as he continues to pump his hips and pound his dick into me.

"You'll be doin' more than just wash my car from here

on out, lil' girl," he growls so possessively as I watch his ripped chest ripple with his motions, his abs and pecs glistening with a thin sheen of perspiration.

We're wrapped in each other like a game of twister, but so much better. Though at his promise — or threat? — I shudder again. My stiff nipples are clasped between his fingers and thumbs, and he pinches them hard enough to send a jolt of pain and pleasure through my entire body. My pussy tightens around his cock, and he feels so good, I've long forgotten about my worries of getting knocked up. All I know is that I don't want him to stop yet!

I watch him pound into me, more and more powerfully, all that hard muscle and sinew rippling as he makes me body quiver and quake. He's a beast as he takes me, thrusting so hard and fast now as my pussy is stretched out around him. And all the while he's fondly my breasts, squeezing and manhandling them, teasing my stiff nipples.

"Oh fuck... I'm gonna cum in this tight little cunt of yours," he growls, and reluctantly relinquishes one of my breasts to reach down and tweak my clit again. "Cum with me," he demands.

And his finger on my clit is all it takes for my mind to go numb and forget all about how he definitely should not cum inside me.

Instead... I like the thought. Of making my dad's best friend, my principal, cum in me. It'd be the ultimate rebellion, and I start grinding into him, but I'm already so sensitive. It only takes a second before I gasp for air, and the waves of pleasure come crashing down on me.

I can hear him moan out loudly, and he's grasping my body so tight as he fucks me through my orgasm.

"I am gonna pump you so full of my cum," he growls amid his huffs and moans of pleasure, "I'll take you away and make you my lil' breeding bitch if that's what it takes!" And no sooner than those filthy words were out of his mouth, he was ploughing into me one last time and exploding.

Thick gouts of his virile seed shooting into me as he lets loose such a gravelly, long moan. His hips bucking as he spurts more and more of that creamy load, filling me up to capacity and then some.

"Take it!" he growls, twitching as he blows his load into my raw, unprotected pussy.

My pussy is vibrating against him as jolts of pleasure go through me, and I hear something heavy crash to the ground as I flail desperately against the sexy older man.

When I finally come down from my erotic high, I'm gasping for air, covered in a thin layer of perspiration.

When the last of his cum flows into me, he falls over on top of me, his hard chest crushing atop my breasts as his lips find mine. We're making out, our chests heaving as his tongue invades my mouth and we lay there atop his desk, sweaty and entangled.

Somehow, kissing him like that is even more intimate than having sex, and my arms wrap around him. I'm scared he's going to leave. That after this moment, he'll realize what we've done, and how wrong it all is, and he'll run. For just a few moments longer, I want to savour him in all his masculine glory.

∾

A FEW WEEKS HAVE PASSED, and here I am. Staring down at this pregnancy test, letting it tell me what I already know: I'm pregnant.

I rub a hand over my belly and head on out. Mr. Wood is waiting for me in his car, and I can see him there, smiling my way. I head on over to his Cadillac, and slip into the passenger seat.

Immediately his hand is on my bare thigh, and he's leaning in to kiss me on the neck. But I'm a bit tense.

"What's the matter?" he asks, concerned.

"Mr. Wood... I'm pregnant," I say, hanging my head a little.

He pauses, but then laughs and squeezes me thigh.

"Of course you are babe," he says and nips my earlobe. "That was my intention all along," he says with such devious delight.

"But what'll I do?! I'm too young!" I protest.

"You'll move on in with me baby," he says, rubbing my thigh, letting his hand drift on up between my legs close to my pussy. "And when that belly grows big I'll make it bounce, and keep you forever," he declares possessively.

I glance up at him, biting in on my lower lip. He always knows just what to say to make me feel better, and dad... he'll come to accept it in time. After all, Mr. Wood is his best friend, so who wouldn't want the best for their daughter?

TEASE

Book Themes:
Bareback, breeding, boss/employee, stripper
Word Count:
5,264

~

HIGH HEELS AND A CORSET, that's about all I have on as I stroll through the club, swaying my hips. I just finished another dance set on stage, the clothes came off, I showed off my tits, and then collected the tips. It was good work, as far as I'm concerned. Lots of money, flexible hours.

Plus I always get a thrill from stripping.

It was terrifying at first, taking off my clothes before a crowd of horny men. But now it just feels... powerful.

I've got a drink in hand, a nice cocktail, courtesy of a customer, of course. And I let it burn its way down my throat as a reward. I can handle my drink.

Of course, from out of the crowd I couldn't help but notice the club's owner was watching me as I swayed and twisted around the pole. His eyes caressing me no less than my own hands fondled my supple breasts, and squeezed my two ass cheeks for the crowd to see.

Most club owners are dicks, but this guy...

Tall, broad shouldered, handsome. Always dressed in a nice suit, fit for a club like ours. And on top of that, he never stiffs us girls on pay, doesn't bilk us for every dime like other clubs do. In fact, he appointed one of us as manager, replacing the former guy who was constantly messing with us.

So I was happening to watch him as he got down from his booth, and headed back to his office. I saw him murmur something to the manager. And her eyes turn to me.

"The boss wants to speak with you in his office," she came over to me and said, hand on my shoulder.

"Ohh, I hope I'm not in trouble," I teased her, my dark lipstick contrasting my ivory teeth as I grinned. "Thanks for letting me know. If anyone asks for me, tell them I'm the most popular girl here and they should be quicker to offer me their wallets next time," I giggle, the sound uncharacteristic against the bad girl persona I've developed here.

She rolled her eyes at me, but couldn't hide the amused grin as I sauntered on by, down the back hallway towards the bosses office. It was a big space, with a nice desk, all the usual stuff a boss fills their office with. And he was stood there, over his desk, phone in hand.

"Yeah, get it done," he said, holding up a finger to me then indicating for me to shut the door. "I know. I'll cover it."

He hung up and looked to me.

"Great job up there, as usual," he told me in that deep,

smokey voice of his. "You're a favourite with the clients, as always."

I smiled back at him, not feeling at all uncomfortable, despite the fact that all I wore was a tight corset, a collar, panties, and 7" high heels. I was a natural shorty, so that barely brought me up to his shoulders. It would be almost comical if I were barefoot.

"What can I say, money is a wonderful motivator to do a great job," I said as I sipped my cocktail. "But I doubt that's why you asked me back here."

"You're right," he said to me as he took out a bottle of whiskey from his own desk, and poured up some in a tumbler. He downed it and looked at me. "I hear tell you're doing extras," he said to me blatantly, his voice not sounding angry or incriminating, but... my heart did skip a beat, because... well, guilty. "Taking guys home after work, for extra pay. Fucking them. Maybe even on the club premises."

I rolled my eyes at the last part.

"I don't shit where I eat boss, come on," I scoffed. Besides, I could charge a whole lot more for after hours work outside of the club. Doing it *in* the club was just a way to make quick cash and then lose the steady revenue.

"That's good," he said, moving around the desk and sitting on the corner of it. He was still taller than me, even sitting like that. "Don't want you to get the club or the other girls in trouble," he remarked, sipping his whiskey as his eyes scanned over me. "How much you charge?" he asked me point black after that moment's delay of his eyes devouring my skin.

I stared back at him, wondering if this wasn't the worst idea I've had. At least the worst idea of the night. But I own my baggage, and I own my choices. I might be a lot of things, but a liar isn't top of that list.

"As much as I think I can get away with," I finally said, unable to stop my smirk from twisting my lips. "Isn't that what they teach you business manager types?"

He cracked a smile at that, and ran a hand along his chiselled jaw, over his light sprinkling of stubble that had cropped up by that evening.

"Good girl," he said approvingly, perhaps just amused by my antics. "But how would you feel about making an exception? Just the once. About some side business... here. In the club," he posed to me, his smouldering dark eyes locked on mine.

"Sounds like entrapment. Are you trying to entrap me?" I asked, my dark eyes narrowed at him suspiciously, even though my amusement dripped in my voice.

He laughed at that, then put his tumbler down, and reached into his pocket. He pulled out his wallet and peeled off a few bills. Four fifties. Then held them out to me.

"Here. For your time. And patience. Take it and go back to work if you like, no hard feelings. But..." he shrugged his broad shoulders a little, looking so casual about it all. "If you want to earn more, name your price."

I took the offered money, tucking it into my little hand purse as I stared at him. He was so... respectful. I mean, sure, he was my boss offering me money to fuck me in the strip club, but it wasn't the weirdest thing to happen at my job, and definitely not an unpleasant thing.

Maybe it was just because he was hot and I was feeling a bit curious.

After all, I was wearing a choker that said 'slut' on it. Not like my tastes were chaste.

"That's a dangerous offer, boss. I know how much money this place rakes in from drinks."

"I never promised I'd say yes," he replied after a brief

chuckle. "But go on, name a price. And any stipulations. This is a negotiation after all," he said as he pulled a second glass next to his, and poured some whiskey into both.

Of course, I still had a bit of my mixed drink left, but that was easy enough to handle.

"You're the top girl here. So I want to keep you happy. I can only promise not to negotiate too hard," he joked with a grin.

"I thought negotiating hard was precisely what we were doing, huh?" I quipped before I tossed down the rest of my drink. I leaned forward towards him, placing my empty glass next to his hip. "But I like my job and keeping you happy *does* seem advantageous. So how about you give me half the profits from the club this week? I'll even help you sell some extra drinks this weekend."

His eyes never left mine as I stalked closer to him, but his brow raised at my offer, surprised by it.

"Half the profits? You always manage to surprise," he said with a slight laugh. He let his gaze trail down over me again, making no effort to hide his stare at my cleavage pushing out the top of my corset.

"I could agree to that... but what's it get me? Oral? Vaginal? Anal? Whatever I want?" he asked, sipping some more whiskey as our eyes locked once more.

Being hit on by my boss should've felt awkward. Would've in any other situation. But he'd been respectful with the offer, and I believe he was sincere when he said I could walk off, take the cash and he'd not hold it against me. But of course... I knew he'd be happier if I said yes. And having people with money happy with you is always a good business strategy.

Not to mention, he was a tall, broad, gorgeous man and I was curious to see what he was packing.

"Would you give that all up for a sloppy blow job?" I

teased, leaning in to him so close, but not quite touching him. He could smell my subtle perfume, feel my body heat against him, but I remained just out of touch.

"Bit hefty just for a blow job..." he rumbled in his dark, lusty voice. I could feel the desire rising in him, hear it in his words. "Though I'm sure having you suck me off would be worth every penny," he remarked, not breaking that thin gap between us as his arousal rose, straining against his pants.

"We can start there," he added. "But it has to end inside your pussy. Just to be clear what I'm about," he grinned confidently at me, his nostrils flaring at my sexed up scent.

I tilted my head, scanning his face.

"I doubt you bring condoms to work, huh?"

"And you don't? Not even for an off-chance at a little extra side-hustle?" he asked me, raising a hand as if about to caress my cheek, but instead his big grasp just very carefully tucked a stray strand of dark hair behind my ear. "Or do you normally offer it up bareback for the right amount?"

"There's a corner store just down the street that's open all hours," I purr in his ear. "I wouldn't want to get fired if my boss found a condom on me."

He spoke back to me in my ear, his dusky voice sending a shiver down my spine.

"Half the profits. And we do it bareback. What do you say? I'll even throw in a paid day off, whenever you want it," he responded, so close I swear I could feel his light stubble graze me.

My heart thudded so loud in my chest I thought I might be going deaf, and not just because of the heavy thump of the music outside his office door. I put my hand on his thigh, my thumb nail just grazing along the bulge in his pants.

"In your office?"

With that touch I gave him, it was like suddenly the floodgates were opened. His big, strong hand came up, fingers sliding along my outer thigh until he was grasping my hip.

"Right here," he confirmed as his dick swelled so thickly my thumb felt it bulge out. "You like the sound of that?" he asked me, his lips wrapping around my earlobe, tugging it gently, suckling at it as we teased and negotiated.

It was so wrong, but that just meant my panties were already soaked, and I was quickly losing my composure. I didn't even need the whiskey he offered me to feel that burning lust growing hotter and hotter by the moment.

"The club will be half mine for the week... I think I can afford to go raw this once."

"That's it. Knew we could see eye to eye," he practically growled into my ear, sounding feral with desire. For me.

And then his own drink was discarded, his other hand coming to my body, sliding up over my waist, and squeezing my breast through the corseted top I wore. He pulled me against him, releasing my earlobe and kissing down my neck with a ravenous desire as I felt his hard cock straining through his pants against me.

My skin was so pale against his tanned flesh, goose-bumps pricking up with excitement.

I couldn't believe what I'd just agreed to. The door to his office wasn't even locked, but that didn't stop my hand from cupping his bulge. Or, at least, as much as I was able to. It was far longer than my hand could fit, and that just made my pussy slicken even more.

"You want your office to smell like me, huh?"

"I want it to smell like your cunt, specifically," he rumbled in response, not balking at my taunt as he fondled and groped me, his lips kissing and suckling, tongue taking little laps of my flesh as he made his way to my shoulder, then back up to my face.

All the while his hands growing increasingly greedy for me, causing one of my breasts to spill from my corset, his thumb grazing against my nipple as his dick pulsed wildly with desire.

Luckily, I was a pragmatic stripper, so I was quickly able to unhook my corset with one hand, letting the tight fabric fall between us. I never stopped groping his cock all the while, my motions only getting more firm and intentional as I tried to get it to grow as big as it could, making him strain against his pants.

His eyes went right to my tits, same as any other man's would. They were a good pair. Big for a girl of my size, perky and firm still, yet soft and supple. And he enjoyed the feel of that flesh swelling between his fingers as he fondled them.

But the real show for me was in his pants, that massive dick so thick I could feel the outline of its veins through his underwear and pants distinctly. It strained the confines of his clothes, and he grunted as he reached a hand down to unbuckle his belt.

"I was promised a sloppy blow job to start with," he remarked in his gravelly husk.

I had *not* forgotten that. Though I wondered how on earth I was supposed to manage putting *that* in my mouth. I supposed I'd have to find a way, and I took a step back, watching him intently as he began to reveal his masculinity.

He watched me as I watched him, those two big hands going to his trousers as he peeled back his belt, opened up the button with a burst. I was amazed that button hadn't popped off frankly, as the silhouette of his dick bulged out through his underwear.

"You're the hottest stripper I've ever seen in action," he remarked of me, eyes devouring me as he unbuttoned his shirt, showing off rippling abs, peppered with dark hair, trying to make me wait for that final unveiling.

I scowled at him before I caught myself, frustrated by being teased. Still, it wasn't a bad sight. Definitely something I'd be remembering for a long, long time.

I was just thirsty for his cock, and I didn't want to be made to wait. I crawled up on his desk, pushing a few things out of the way so that I could get on hands and knees at his side.

He even gave me a hand, disregard for his own items getting in the way of our debauchery.

With one hand he reached up, caressing my shoulder, my neck. His fingers going into my dark hair as the other hooked a thumb into his boxer-briefs. He peeled them down at last, and that thick shaft burst out.

It was glorious.

Not only was he big and girthy, but his dick had a magnificent shape to it. With a broad, perfectly shaped tip that glistened with precum. All perched over top of the two largest balls I'd ever seen.

I wrapped my hands around the root of his cock, my mouth watering as I stared at it. He looked even better in my tiny, manicured hands. Both of them stacked on top of each other still couldn't hide his tip and I moaned in appreciation.

I lowered my head, letting my tongue gather up that precum, swallowing it down as if it were a Michelin star meal.

I was rewarded with a husky moan, rumbling up from deep within his broad, bare chest. And that strong hand held tightly onto the back of my head and hair, not forcing me, but keeping me locked there as I tasted his strongly flavoured masculinity.

"Mmph, yeah," he grunted as another dollop of precum surged out to replace the last.

I licked that one up faster before letting one of my hands fall away from his shaft, holding myself up on his thigh as I forced my mouth down as deep as I could. My dark lips barely even kissed my remaining hand before I was forced to retreat, leaving behind thick, viscous saliva along his cock. I inhaled sharply through my nose as I pushed myself down again, intent on feeling his crown against the back of my throat.

But as much as I craved that thick, meaty cock of his, it was the toughest dick I'd ever sucked. My jaw strained to take him, and I had to force myself down to get him back there. But as he moaned and his cock throbbed excitedly, he pushed down on my head to help me out. And before long I felt that bulbous crown of his manhood jabbing against the back of my throat.

"Fuuuck," he groaned out, the muscles of his torso rippling as he tensed and relaxed, and more precum spurt down my throat.

My knees pressed down on the desk, my thighs clamped tight together as I struggled to hold myself there. It ached in the best possible way, and my clit was throbbing against the fabric of my panties. I dug my manicured nails into his thigh as my tongue desperately shifted from side to side, barely able to even do that.

Finally after savouring the oral squeeze for a while, he released that hold and let me move freely again. All while he breathed heavier, his moans tumbling from his lips.

"God damn, you got it in there deep," he rumbled with admiration, as his hand slid down my back, feeling my pale skin on his way to cup and grope my ass cheek.

My back arched into his hand like a cat being stroked, and his encouragement made me want to take him even deeper, but even as I moved my hand down his shaft, there wasn't much more my mouth could handle. I began stroking his root, even as I struggled and failed to take him deeper in against my throat. I decided the best option was, then, to simply make it as sloppy as possible, and began pulling myself off him before pushing back down, finding a simple rhythm, since that was all his massive member would permit.

If I was afraid of disappointing, it was silly. Because he moaned with a deep satisfaction, sounding like a man who had never been so pleased, despite the fact that a gorgeous, well off man like him had to be drowning in pussy and blow jobs if he wanted it.

"Uhn… you suck like no other," he growled in appreciation, his hand groping my ass, those long fingers stretching in between the crack, teasing down from my anal pucker to my pussy.

I was so incredibly wet, and a more chaste woman might be embarrassed by that, but I wanted him to know. I wanted him to feel just what he was doing to me, and my legs parted, my body shifting to give him better access to my dripping wet cunt, still trapped beneath my thong.

If I bobbed up closer to his crown I was more able to use my tongue to swirl around his tip, feel out those thick, gorgeous veins. But it wasn't long before I couldn't resist being choked by his cock again.

He shuddered. That giant, sculpted man shivering with pleasure as I blew his cock, giving it the finest suck job it'd ever had. And he in return moaned and hooked his fingers into my thong, tugging it aside to expose my pussy.

"I fantasized you were as good of a fuck as you were a dancer… never thought it'd be true," he rumbled to me as his bare fingers touched my slit, a luxury I didn't afford other men. Even the ones who paid. "But you're as daring, slutty and fun as you look."

I was at a disadvantage, unable to respond with words. But the way my hips angled to let him feel me out, and how my head dived back down on his cock told him all he needed to know. I was addicted to his cock, and he was going to have to force me away from his dick or I would be intent on tasting his cum.

He was tempting fate letting me suck him so long. That is, if he was hoping to dump that load in my pussy as he promised.

But he took some time to toy with my slit, those large fingers teasing my labia, stretching my little cunny around them just a hint, as he began to tease and encircle my clit. Those expert fingers stoking my pussy to tingling highs as I tasted more and more of his salty pre with each excited bob of my head milking it from him.

The thump of the music from the club was so rhythmic, it created almost a cocoon, the rest of the world falling away and just leaving the two of us. I was losing myself to the moment, my poise and calm disintegrating as I sought out our mutual destruction. My head and hand moved faster and more purposefully along his dick as my hips ground against his hand.

The ache of my jaw straining to fit his dick was forgotten in the moment, and I just savoured his raw masculinity as he stoked my own fires higher. I could feel his dick tensing up, his balls tightening, and I knew I was getting him close.

But it was then that his other hand grasped my hair again, and wrenched me off his cock by force.

"Aw now… I have other plans," he panted out, breathing heavily, his tanned body glistening as his chest heaved.

A thick strand of saliva clung between us like a spider web and I quickly pressed out my tongue to gather it up into my mouth like the greedy slut I was. I didn't make him wait, though. I moved with all the grace that being a stripper afforded me so that I was straddling his lap, his cock pressed between us. I made the mistake of looking down and seeing that thick, wet shaft as it rose up above my pierced belly button.

He was going to absolutely wreck me.

And judging by the way his cock pulsed with excitement, he realized that too. And relished the thought.

Those strong hands of his grasped me, holding onto my hip and arm. He took control of my body, and ground his dick to my pussy as I straddled over him. But he was ravenous still, and his mouth kissed and bit at my shoulder, my neck.

"Fuck, you are the perfect slut... the perfect whore," he rumbled, nothing but appreciation in those words. They weren't insults, they were affectionate praise on his deep, husky voice.

I had lost the ability to be sarcastic, to have those little quips I so loved to make. All I could do was moan like a bitch in heat, and I ground against him so needfully. I wanted to be wrecked by him. I wanted to feel his cock stretch me to my limits. I was losing my patience and he could feel that, but still he had control, and still he forced my desires higher and higher as he made me wait.

He was a man of control. He ran the club, he was in charge of everything in his daily life. But even his resolve to draw out the moment waned as his dick throbbed incessantly against my cunt, and he finally took hold of me, lifting me up. He positioned my hips over his dick, let that thick, bulbous tip prod at my slit.

"You on the pill?" he asked me in his breathy voice, that

consideration having not come up until his raw, hard cock was nudging against my unprotected pussy.

I shook my head, but there was no turning back. I'd already made my bed, and now it was just up to luck and chance what would happen after tonight.

The worst part is, that made my pussy throb excitedly at the very thought of the risk we were taking.

I'd always been clean and cautious when I fucked guys on the side for some money. Always used condoms, never even let them touch my pussy bare. But here I was, atop my boss, his raw hard cock stretching my slit open, straining to my limits as he edged himself into me, no sign of wanting to stop at my confession, and--

I screamed out as his dick was suddenly slammed into me. The strength of his hips meeting that of his hands, as he drew me down atop him roughly. His own low voice erupting with a grunt as I felt that behemoth of a cock pulse, throb, strain against my slick canal.

My head was thrown back, my body arching as he slammed so deep into me I thought I might pass out. It was *perfection* like I'd never felt before, and my thighs tightened around his hips as I clung to him for support.

I had straddled atop him, to take control of things, but with his bulging biceps and strong hands, he had full power. He lifted me up, then slammed me back down, my poor, pink pussy stretched until it was nearly red from that thick girth. And we were both moaning like virgins for our first time.

I couldn't help but let a squeal out as he pounded into me, and then... he slid off the desk, hoisting me up in his hands as he turned around and laid me out atop the desk. His control so complete his dick never slipped from me for a moment as he got atop me. His mouth hungrily diving down to devour my breast.

My nipple was pierced and that made it even more sensitive as his tongue and teeth toyed with it. My legs wrapped around his hips, holding myself in place as best I could against the powerful thrusts of his body. I was losing my mind in the absolute best of ways. I'd never been fucked like this, and a large part of me felt like I should be paying him for this intense session.

The view itself was sublime. His shirt slipping back from his broad shoulders, showing more and more of his sculpted body. Showing that he really was in the gym every morning, as he said. Not just pissing off to some golf club like most bosses.

No, from my position below him I got the intense view of his thick cock pistoning into my tiny pussy. His body full of hard, toned muscle just rippling, undulating with each hard thrust into me that shook my body and made my free breast ripple. The view only improved when he pulled off my breast and let roar a deep moan of desire.

I've never been more turned on by a man than in that moment, with his thick cock spreading me open, my legs wrapped around him, my nails digging into his back as our bodies met in exquisite, raw lust. I didn't care about who might see us there, who might be talking about what we were doing in his office for so long. That didn't matter.

It didn't even matter that he might breed me like the slut I was.

All that mattered was the way his veins pulsed, and my clit throbbed, both of us on the way to oblivion together.

He looked over my body, having to force his eyes open as he fondled my breasts, slid down over my nipped waist. He appreciated every inch of me it seemed, before finally grasping my hips, to help him fuck me harder, faster. His balls slapping to my ass as he hammered me more intensely than I'd ever been before.

But I knew it couldn't last forever. As gorgeous and muscled and in control as he was, my body, my blow job, had taken their toll. And his dick was like an iron pole inside me, strained to its absolute thickest as he grunted and shuddered. Though as his orgasm approached, he reached his thumb for my clit, working it perfectly.

I was already on the brink, and that was all it took. His skillful machinations didn't just topple me over the edge, they catapulted me into the abyss. I screamed so loud that even over the music, I'm sure someone could have heard me, and my pussy started milking my boss's dick with such a primal urge to be bred.

And he didn't let me down. Not at all. His dick exploded in near perfect timing. His roar filling the room as he blew his load. Thick jets of his virile seed flooding my raw, unprotected depths. The head of his cock jammed against the entrance to my womb as it disgorged more cum than most men could produce in a week.

It was… exquisite. And I got to admire the way this adonis' body tensed, trembled, glistened with a thin sheen of perspiration, as he bust his nut inside me, paying for the privilege of risking knocking me up.

He panted, moaned, shuddered, all as I squealed and cried out, tightening around him, milking every last spurt from his glorious shaft. Until he was bent over me, panting, the two of us in a sex stupor.

My brain was hazy, my entire body aching and exhausted, tingling with the aftershocks of my orgasm. Every time one passed through me, he reaped the benefits as well, my walls massaging his cock, forcing his cum deeper inside me.

He was in no rush to pull out of me though. His dick locking that seed in my pussy, as his lips kissed over my neck, my shoulder, face. His free strong hand caressing my breast, my body.

"Mmm... that was worth every penny," he rumbled between smacks of his lips.

"Yuhhuh," I agreed dumbly, still working on catching my breath as his mouth worked over my tingling skin. I moaned softly, arching into him as my legs began to go lax around his hips.

WE DIDN'T RUSH an end to things. Instead he took his time, and when he finally pulled out, he had a kerchief ready to cup my loins and help me clean up. A handsome, dashing gentleman to the last.

And after I'd finished cleaning up, I sauntered back out into the club with some extra wiggle to my step. A happy smile on my face as--unknowingly--my bosses seed was sewing itself inside me, the beginning's of my first child planted, as I remembered his last words to me.

"Offer stands for next week too," he'd said, buttoning his shirt back up, hiding away those glorious abs and pecs. Just for now.

Until next week.

THE BET

*B*ook Themes:
  Bareback, breeding, billionaires, strippers
Word Count:
6,959

WORKING at a high profile strip club, you see a lot of celebrities and high rollers come through. Like just the other night, I happened to walk into a private dance booth that was occupied. Whoops! But the sight that greeted me was worth the momentary embarrassment, because I got to glimpse one of my friends doing more than the regular show.

There she was, that pretty angel of a girl, riding in the lap of one of the hottest rock stars around. And I don't mean a lap dance. Yeah, she was breaking the rules, and the law, but she was riding that dick like a woman possessed. The fat shaft spreading her open as she bounced, a giddy look on her face as she had her arms around him.

I mean, plenty of girls fuck rock stars just for the hell of it. My friend did it and got paid. What's not to love about that?!

So I didn't tell the manager or the bouncers. I mean, girls selling extras is bad for all of us. But in a case like that, how can I judge? I'd have gone home with that hunk whether he paid me or charged me.

I've never been so lucky. I rock a good look, and clients love me, but I've never cashed in big off a rock star. And y'know, I've never been too down about it. Some of the girls tell me that the big celebs are often stingy, they expect extras for free just because of how popular they are. And if that's the case, sure, I'll suck it up and rub one out on my own time to thoughts of my friend banging on that big, veiny dick. (Except it'll be me in my fantasy, trust me.)

A steady flow of high paying clients for me to dance for, works just fine.

But then *he* walked into my club.

Oh, he's not a rockstar. In fact, I didn't even recognize him at first. All I could see was that he was a tall, well-shaped man in a very expensive suit. But that doesn't necessarily mean anything. Plenty of guys come into strip clubs after big business meetings, weddings, you name it. And they wear the most expensive thing they own.

But this guy had *style*. Real style. Like, it was no polyester suit he wore. It was tailored, custom fit to his impressive frame. Fancy cufflinks and a french-cut shirt that I adored. And the tie was a thick european cut, that alone probably cost $500 at least, and I wouldn't be surprised if it was more.

Beyond his clothes though, he was downright dreamy. A broad jawline and dark, long hair that was slicked back in a perfect style. He was a man that knew how to show off his rugged good looks. And he did look rugged and manly, trust me. The expensive suit was just a bit of flair to show that in addition to being a hard as rock macho man, he knew how to impress.

So when two other girls got to him first, I was a bit heartbroken, you can imagine. But I didn't let it get me down -- too much -- I had a stage show to put on anyhow.

So instead, I popped my lips to finish off my gloss, flicked back my long, blonde hair, and strut towards the stage. In my gold bikini, and with my hard-fought-for curves, I always drew more than a few heads.

But I just wanted his.

The other girl was just finishing up her stage show, lamenting the lack of tips, and giving me a commiserate stare. "I hate it when it's dead like this," she said, pulling on her white bikini. "Too many girls here, and way too few guys."

I had to admit she was right, it's a bit slow, but she's the type that'd complain if the room was full, so I just smiled her off. Nothing's going to kill my buzz before my show. And the second my song comes on, I was instantly in the groove. I walked up to the stage with a killer stare, commanding everyone's attention.

I was in the zone, but I'd be lying if I didn't see that gorgeous hunk sit himself down near the stage in a booth, the other two dancers still clinging to his side. Even though his eyes were slowly pulled from the two hot girls on his arms to me.

That meant one of two things.

Either he was a broke ass fool who'd say he *didn't get dances in a place like this*.

Or, the alternative, which I much preferred: he was so into me that no girl could break the spell I was weaving around him.

I licked my lips in that exaggerated way, and sauntered

towards the pole in the middle of the dance floor. Usually on a night like tonight, I wouldn't bother giving a good show. But this guy has lust in his eyes, and I want to make sure that's all for me.

I grabbed the pole in my hand, letting my fingers rub up and down it in a teasing manner, all while staring right at the stud in the booth. I gave an exaggerated wink before I swung myself up, my thighs wrapping around the pole, my high heels way above my head as I spun. I gave him a good look over my ass, my strong legs, my slender tummy, and when I finally descended, I pressed the pole between my huge breasts, all while looking right at him.

His gaze was mine. I owned it. Even as the two beautiful women at his sides pawed at his chest, pressing in on his tailored shirt so that I could see the outlines of his pecs and abs, he watched me perform. Even as one of them tugged upon his expensive tie, I had his attention.

He was smitten with me. I could tell, even if his gaze was steely, betraying no emotion. He was a rugged man, but his unblinking gaze didn't lie.

As my first song drew to a close, I leaned in against the pole and reached behind my back. It was a perfected move. I pulled on the string of my bikini, and in a snap, it wraps around the pole, exposing my nipples to the chilly air.

I moaned, my eyes fluttering shut as I removed the top entirely, spinning it around my finger before mock-flinging it at him. I winked again before tossing it towards my purse at the end of the stage.

His stony expression broke, and even though the two women were desperate for his attention, he grinned wryly at me. They were about ready to give up on him, I so owned his gaze, that one of them looked to me and gave an exasperated roll of her eyes before peering off. But then he did something, he pulled a roll of bills from his jacket and handed a thick stack to each of them. And they weren't ones, I could tell you that much.

The two girls were torn between excitement and disappointment. If that was how much he'd pay for them to sit with him a spell, he was certainly going to give it *all* up to me after my show.

I turned, spanking my ass and letting the flesh ripple as the second song got into it, and before it'd barely gotten started, I was climbing up that pole once more. I spun, I stretched, I teased and touched and smiled and shon up there on the stage, and when my song finally ended and I was gathering my bikini, I know I'm going to make bank tonight.

True to form, the two women got up and leave his side, albeit a bit morosely. With the impressive sum in hand, one of them struts up to meet me as I get off stage.

"He wants you," she said, doing a good job of hiding her jealousy with a smile and a pat of my arm. "Goodluck," she said before heading off to search for another client.

Leaving me and the handsome man, who had ordered two drinks in the meantime. So that when I come to his table, he was holding a cranberry vodka and there was my favourite waiting for me.

"Never seen a show like that before. Or maybe it's just the girl performing it that has me wowed," he remarked in a deep, husky voice that's tantalizingly rough.

I giggled, patting his arm teasingly. "Oh, maybe it was both," I said as I joined him, dressed once more in my skimpy micro-bikini. "But someone inspired me to do extra good tonight."

"I hope that someone's me, or I might have to get rough with some other guy," he jested with an uneven smile. "Private dances, for you and me. How much? I bet you go for at least five times what the other girls charge here," he said in a brazen display, plunking down half a grand in front of me, "or am I wrong?" he asked, playing his own little game with me.

"That might get you a song or two," I said with a teasing grin, reaching out for that cold, hard cash. "Let's see what we can do."

I grabbed my drink and his hand, leading him towards the champagne room. It's the higher class place to go, and I'm not even going to bother asking if that's what he wants. His money has said as much, and I tip out the room attendant before taking him to the nicest one we have.

He helped himself into the booth, unbuttoning his jacket as he reclines back in the center of the seat, drink in one hand as he eyes me.

"Not much of a strip club man," he said to me over the music, "but I had a special feeling tonight. Guess I was wise to listen to that little voice in my head. Oh, and don't worry about if I want more. Just hold out your hand when you're gettin' antsy about owed dances, and I'll fork it over."

"My kind of man," I grinned as I down my wine. It was the priciest thing they have in there, but really, I just loved the taste of it. Besides, it tells me if the guys are worth my time or not.

"So what were you doing tonight? Business?" I asked, as my hand goes to his chest. The next song hasn't started, and paid or not, I don't start 'til the music does. It's bad luck to start in the middle of a song.

"Business is done for the day," he said, locking eyes with me after a sweep of my body. "And when I conclude the business deal of my life, I want to celebrate with the most beautiful woman I can find," he declared with a charming smile that could easily steal most women's time for free.

It was a wonder he didn't just head to a bar. But it worked out well for me, to say the least.

"And what business are you in, baby?"

He looked a little surprised at first, his brows furrowing, then relaxing as he seemed to find some peace in my not recognizing him.

"Guess you aren't much for business news, huh?" he remarked, pulling out his phone, and in a second popped up a story from CNN to show to me. And there it was, his distinguished face beneath the headline, 'Aron Wolfe Concludes Military Contract for $4billion'.

"Now that is a very, very sexy name," I said, though suddenly I'm finding myself very hungry. Holy fuck that's a lot of money. A guy that looks this good definitely should not have that much money too. It's not fair to the rest of the world.

My fingers go to his tie, playing with it, "So why not a regular bar, huh?"

"Because you weren't in it," he said boldly, his two big hands coming around me to cup my ass cheeks, his steely eyes locked on mine. "I said I was after the most beautiful girl I could find. And this is where she is," he declared.

My fingers teased along his jawline as the song switches over and I stand up.

"Ohh, knowing the future would definitely be handy for the military," I agreed with another light giggle. It's not often I meet a guy who is both gorgeous, rich, and can make me blush. But he definitely held that power.

His eyes only left mine once again as I started to dance, enjoying the movement of my body like only the best clients can.

"Tell me about it," he responded after a bit of time enjoying my movements. "That's what got me where I am, intuition. But this is the first time it's really paid off in leading me to a gorgeous girl," he said with approval. "You move like a pro, but you look like a fresh faced angel," he remarked of me, the big guy sounding a bit smitten.

Teasing and pleasing a normal guy was always a thrill, but being able to turn a guy so out of my leagues into a puppy was always a rare treat.

And he looked, and smelled, and felt like a rare treat. Not like those bad boy rockers who are perfectly content to pump and dump into anything with a pussy, not like those old money snobs who think they're better than everyone.

Aron was young, hot, and clearly brilliant. No dumb man makes four billion off the military, and my fingers went to the back of his neck, sharing a breath with him for a moment.

"I feel like a very lucky girl, then. To have caught your eye."

"Then we're both lucky this evening," he said with that handsome, wry smile of his, his two big hands -- a bit hard, not soft like every other wealthy man I'd dealt with -- touching me. "Say, would you be all that offended if I asked you to just sit in my lap, wrap your arms around me and enjoy a bit of your company more personally?" he asked. But there was no risk of offense in how he said it, trust me.

My legs were wrapped around his waist before he even finished speaking, my arms around his neck as my fingers went to his hair. I pressed my breasts into his face, making them jiggle against his flesh. "If you're a breast man, that's all you had to say, baby."

"When it comes to you, I'm finding out I'm an every-thing-man," he retorted without delay, those big, strong hands stroking over my smooth skin, feeling me out with great relish. And though he was big, strong, obscenely wealthy and in control, he had a way of making me feel in control. Or at least calm. "But damn if these aren't the most glorious tits," he declared, letting his eyes rest upon them as his hands wandered up to cup the pair of breasts in his palms.

"I thought you'd never touch me," I teased, pulling away just enough so that we could both watch his fingers dig into the pillowy flesh.

"I've learned how to savour a moment," he said with that disarming grin, his big, strong hands not relenting, enjoying the feel of my tits, the way the flesh rippling with his fondling fingers. "I was offered ten million for my company just a year ago," he confessed to me. "Everyone called me a fool for passing it up. Now I'm a billionaire, and I've still got my company," he said with no undeserved amount of self-satisfaction.

"And the hottest girl in the city in your lap," I reminded him as I started rolling my hips, grinding in his lap in a slow, teasing manner. My fingers went to his jawline, stroking him tenderly. "What did you want to do to celebrate?"

He was big, broad-shouldered and apparently made of steel-concrete judging by the way his hard muscles felt through his clothes, but when I ground on his lap I made him tremble a little in excitement.

"Hottest girl in the city?" He said, a dubious look on his face. "Try hemisphere, at least," he said with confidence and appreciation, not holding back the low groan of plea-sure that rose from his throat. "As for celebration…" he tongued his lower lip slowly, "all I can think about is a way I can get you out of here and back to my place. Even if the attempt risks me becoming another quaint client, overly smitten with you. I bet you get a dozen of those a night," he said with wry amusement.

"On a slow night," I teased back, my fingers going to his

hair, nails massaging his scalp. "But they weren't brought here by destiny, were they."

That brought delight to his chiselled features, and he gave me a good squeeze in return.

"Ten grand to come back to my place and celebrate with me," he said boldly, without hesitation. "Not to fuck," he clarified, "just for your time and company." But his lips grew into a wry smile, "The fucking would be for fun. If it happens," he said with the confidence of a man who wasn't used to losing bets.

I roll my eyes with a matched confidence that I didn't earn in the same way as him. Oh no, I'd earned that by coming into the strip club five nights a week and working my ass off.

"You can't tell a girl you're a billionaire and offer her low five figures," I giggled, though my lips found his ears, and a conspiratorial whisper crossed them, "You'd at least need to offer me dinner."

He tilted his powerful neck as I teased his ear with those wispy words, and his hands grasped me all the tighter.

"Dinner, breakfast, you name it," he rumbled to me so deliciously. "I imagine a gorgeous, talented girl like you will have no trouble wringing more from me over the course of an evening." He reached down and gave me ass a bit of a smack, a light strike for a man so strong as him. "Twenty thousand, but you'll have to stick around until morning to let me withdraw the cash. And to take you to breakfast."

"You'd also have to pay my fees for leaving early," I chided him, but I couldn't help but grin.

I'd have easily gone back with him for free, and I have never, ever, *ever* done that with a client.

"Hardball negotiator," he said as his eyes nearly shut

from the roll of my hips upon his groin. "Mm, but I'm in no position to say no, am I?" he remarked. "Done. It's a deal," he declared as his hands slid down to my hips and ass, his fingers sinking into my cheeks.

Honestly, getting out early was only a couple hundred bucks, absolutely nothing compared to what he'd already dropped on me. Mostly, it was just the embarrassment of going home with a client. I'm not the type of girl that did that, so no doubt lips would be flappin'.

But let them talk.

I stood up, reaching for his hand and guiding him back to my manager where they quickly handled the transaction for me getting off early.

I darted back into the dressing room, quickly pulling on my skirt and sweater before saying goodbye to Juliane, my stripper bestie. I promised I'd text her all the details the next morning.

She told me to be careful, and I was back on Aron's arm within a couple of minutes.

Immediately he made me feel like I was his lady, rather than the woman he paid to accompany him back. The familiar way his arm snaked around me and rested upon my hip, how he guided me out to his shiny, brand-new BMW. And by brand-new, I meant brand-spanking-new.

"Just driven off the lot earlier today," he told me, before opening the door for me, a gentleman to the core it seemed. "Another little celebration," he remarked with a kiss to the back of my hand before he shut the door and went around, getting into the driver seat and heading us off back to his place.

I couldn't blame the man. I'd make sure to get more than a couple of fun new toys if I suddenly found myself with that many extra bills burning up my pocket.

But soon I found my hand resting on his lap, my fingers

rubbing his thigh. Something had definitely come over me, and though it was the money that got me out the door, it wasn't money that kept me there, touching him.

Aron flashed me a look from the corner of his view, and though he had every reason to be cocky, he wasn't. He just looked strikingly handsome and fond of me. And that had a special meaning in and of itself. I'd got the attention of this capable and fabulously wealthy man.

We didn't quite drive to the ritziest part of town, to my surprise. But to a section reserved mainly for business offices.

"You'll excuse the place," he remarked before getting out, and opening the door for me in the underground parking garage. "I'll be moving on out soon," he said, offering me his hand and helping me out of his vehicle. "But can't do everything in one day," he said with a cheeky grin, pulling me into a close embrace for a moment before taking me to the elevators.

I couldn't help but laugh. Despite my job, and my hustle, I wasn't a snob. Not on my off hours.

But was that truly what this was? My off hours?

I couldn't really be sure. But I'd never gone home with anyone before, and it certainly wasn't desperation for the cash. I could've milked him dry back in the club. Well, not dry, not in one night.

But it was something else that made me decide to come back with him. Something far more valuable than cash.

He took us up to the top floor, where frosted glass office-style doors greeted us. He had to unlock them before leading us in. There, the whole floor spanned out, divided by partition walls, with a very trendy but eclectic taste in furniture. He had a large living room area, dining area, the whole works.

"Used to be my company's first office," he said, helping

me out of my coat after flipping on the lights, the view a gorgeous view of the city all lit up. "When we had to move to bigger premises, well... I turned this into a spacious little home pad for myself. Don't tell anyone though," he said with a playful shushing gesture, "they'll kick me out if you do."

"Naughty, naughty," I chided him, even as I took a look around. But then my eyes found his again. He was gorgeous. He was the whole package. Everything I'd been looking for and couldn't find in a man, and then some.

And he'd chosen me.

I licked my lips before taking off my high heels, setting them at the door and approaching him. I was a foot and a half shorter than him without them, and it made me feel both self conscious and something else... something I wasn't sure I had words for.

But once he put his arms around me, and those big hands came to rest upon my ass again, I felt certain it was a good feeling.

"Four billion dollars," he began in a low, husky voice, "and you're the most exciting part of my day." It was hard to accept it as mere flattery, not with the conviction in his voice. He leaned in to kiss me, first on my cheek at the corner of my lips, then plush upon my mouth.

I melted into him. There wasn't any other way to describe it. His kiss was amazing, and twenty grand or not, he and I were definitely on the same wavelength. It was the highlight of my day, too.

My arms went up around his neck, my sweater lifting to reveal my stomach as I pushed against him.

Those powerful hands helped lift me up and close the immense distance between the towering giant of business and me, my weight nothing in his palms it seemed as his tongue penetrated my lips and lashed at my mouth. He might've been a business genius, but he was a master kisser, and I got so lost in the feel of our connection I didn't notice that he'd moved us, and my back touched a wall. A wall nowhere near where we began, but I was too enraptured to notice.

Little details like that were beyond us as he pressed into me with his throbbing manhood, a thick bulge that put to shame any other man I had danced upon the lap of.

I had to admit, it was something out of this world. Just the power of his kiss was enough to make my heart leap, and my body tighten. How could he be so amazing? How could I be doing this with a stranger I just met?

But honestly, the question that plagued me the most, was how could I leave after a one night stand with him? There would be no comparing to the night, I could already tell, and that made me even more heated. I had to make the moment between us last.

I had to have it to hold onto, forever.

He was as reluctant to tear his lips away from mine as I was from his, but eventually with a moist smack of our mouths, he did. And those steely eyes stared into mine.

"I need you," he rumbled from deep within his chest. With my back pressed to the wall, it freed him up to reach up, tug his tie loose and undoing his shirt. "I need to fuck you," he declared, the word sounding more crass on his lips than any lewd customer ever could make it, yet at the same time, far more seductive than even those egotistical sorts imagined it was.

The fact he sealed his declaration with another passionate kiss and carried me through the door into his spacious bedroom, only to fall atop me on his king sized bed, certainly helped.

I wasn't going to resist. Hell no!

I wanted him just as badly as he wanted me, even

though I'd been trying to play it cool. But with him, that was impossible. My legs were around his waist, my skirt around my stomach just as quickly as he laid me down, and I ground against him with an urgency I didn't know I could feel.

We made out with a desperate passion for one another, he was everything an ideal man could be. And to him I was everything an ideal woman should be. His desire matched mine, and he shed his blazer, shirt and tie as we kissed, unveiling that gorgeously sculpted torso of his, those bulging muscles a delight to explore with my manicured fingers, to slip between the ridges of and appreciate what must've been at least a few hours of gym work a day for him.

His pants came next, belt jangling as he pushed down his boxer-briefs to let his startlingly large cock pounce out, thick and throbbing with need.

For me.

I was starved for him at that point. I'd never been so wet in all my life, and I reached for his cock, greedily. My breathing was so quick, my chest heaving as I went to the side of my bikini, beneath my skirt, and undid it. I repeated the action, a little more awkwardly, with the other side. I didn't want to let go of his heated dick for even a moment.

He watched my display before lunging in to devour my mouth again, hungry for my kisses, my tongue. He pushed his hips towards me, and with a glancing touch of his cock against my naked pussy he groaned in a low, gravelly voice then said.

"No condom," the words terse and gruff. "If I get you off first... I get to cum inside."

A bet. Just like that. But what was in it for me? Other than receiving this gorgeous man's seed in my unprotected pussy.

My nails ran through his hair, more roughly, with more abandon, all as I stroked his cock.

"And if I get you off first?"

He stared into my eyes with an intensity that startled me, his dick pulsating in my hand so thickly it made my fingers stretch out, unable to encompass his full girth.

"Name it. Anything," he said, as if challenging me. So confident in his own abilities.

Problem was, of course, that I wanted his dick in me right then and there. I didn't want to have to dream up other things I wanted, because all I wanted was looming over me, threatening to make me cum, then fill me with his seed.

So I just said the first thing I could think of that wasn't: 'you'.

"I don't know. A million bucks," I said, laughing a little. I just wanted him to stop playing with me. I wanted him inside me.

"Done," he said without hesitation, either in full confidence of his abilities to get me off with his dick, or because he thought pumping me full of his virile seed was worth every penny of that million dollars.

It didn't matter.

Because he took my hand away and then speared me upon that massive dick. The thickest cock I'd not only felt but seen stretched my cunt wide open as he sank into the hilt and let loose a mighty roar of a moan. The thick, jutting veins of his dick pulsating out, stretching me wider as my labia strained to wrap around his full girth.

It was divine. There was no other way of describing it. He was phenomenal, and I quivered right then and there. But there was no way I was going to lose the bet. Not only was I definitely not ready for kids, but damn, there was a million dollars on the line.

Instead, my pussy squeezed his cock as tight as I could manage, even as my mouth found his once more.

I made him moan with that clench of my cunt, but when he began to pump his dick into me, I started to have some second guesses. His gorgeously sculpted body pumped into me with such powerful thrusts, his balls slapping my ass as he claimed me atop his bed.

He was an adonis, a greek man-god etched in marble by the feel of it, and his dick was no less exquisite. Filling me up to my very limits as he pounded into me, his chiselled face looking tormented by pleasure as he angled his hips and hit me at the exact, intensely satisfying angle that made me cry out.

I tried to squirm away, but there was no where to go. He had me pinned, and he knew he was hitting my g-spot just from the way I cried out, and he wasn't going to relent. I reached down, trying to grab his cock, to squeeze him, to make him feel so fucking good he couldn't hold back but he gathered my wrists in his hand and pinned me to the bed.

In retaliation, those big, beautifully strong hands grasped my breast and my hip. His thumb worked around my clit, teasing in just the right manner as his other other hand pinched and twisted my nipple lightly, torturing me with pleasure as he continued that perfect thrusting without missing a beat, without marring that flawless tempo.

But he moaned aloud, his dick swelling, the pleasure I was giving him taking a toll despite his own masterful efforts.

I tried to use my newly freed hands to bat him off, but it wasn't enough. Even as I childishly fought at him, I could feel myself grow closer to that brink, and I wasn't sure what I could do to stave that off.

Worse, my thoughts were growing fuzzy and I started to forget even why I wanted to fight him off.

What was at stake.

Instead I was awash in the rising tempo of his pounding, thrusting into me harder, making me and the whole massive bed quake and cry out. It was like being caught in a tidal wave, being crashed and beaten upon the shore mercilessly as he claimed me there atop his bed. This was the best day of his life, the pinnacle of his achievement, and making me cum upon his dick was his new, final victory for the day. A celebration of his triumph as he claimed the most beautiful woman he'd laid eyes on, making me squirm and moan and scream out in pleasure from the motions of his gloriously muscled body.

He'd won the bet.

And I didn't even care.

I was too swept up in the most intense orgasm I've ever had, and my screams were echoing all around us as he held me there. It wasn't until my warm juices flooded his cock that I was able to think at all, and even then, it was only about how much I wanted more.

More of him. More of his cock.

The slaps of his body striking mine grew wetter as my slick honey coated his groin and balls, and his victory was celebrated in the way he desired most. With a loud moan and an unleashing of all that pent up desire.

He must've been mere moments from caving himself, and with that flood of my climax coating him he just let go. His cock pulsated, throbbed thickly as he hammered into me erratically, letting loose his rich, creamy seed, flooding my fertile depths with his virility.

I'd lost the bet, and there he was, this gorgeous, powerful, rich man pumping me full of his seed, unprotected and heedless, hammering each spurt deep inside me until he hilted himself in, his dick twitching on its own as he emptied his balls to the last drop inside me.

It took us long moments to come down off our highs, panting for breath and trying to regain some control of our minds, but all the while my hands roamed over his back. We were sticky, and spent, but I wanted to remember the moment, and how he felt against me.

His broad chest swelled with each breath, and slowly his eyes opened again to gaze down at me. He'd won, spectacularly. But he held me in his arms, never gloated, but kissed me deeply, lovingly.

He eventually pulled from me after a long time in his arms, much to my sadness, but gathered a warm, damp cloth and cupped my cum-dripping cunt. He lifted his covers and carried me inside them, to hold me and caress me longer.

"Double or nothing," he dared me to bet again, his smile a wry, devious thing as I felt his cock throb back to full mast against my body.

I lost that one too.

And it was the last I saw him.

It was a glorious night with him. One I'll never forget. Especially since that night a couple months ago, I've learned he left me with more than the twenty grand he promised me for my time.

I was due up for a stage show again soon, but I was drawn to the sight of my tummy in the change room mirror. Nobody had yet noticed it, except me that was. But my tummy was a bit swollen. And the pregnancy tests all said the same. I was knocked up.

I went to his place to tell him, but he had moved, true to

his word. Off to some gorgeous, billionaire's penthouse I guess.

I had to get to work again, as I heard my song begin to play. I had to prepare to care for a new person someday, after all.

But as I strut out there, trying to well up all my confidence, I see him. Back in his same spot, he paid the stripper at his side and she left him. His eyes are on me, that confident smile back on his face.

I lick my lips, a surge of emotions combatting within me. Anger that he felt he could just walk back into my life, months later, without having said a word. Annoyance, that his leaving me had hurt so bad.

And relief. Relief to see his gorgeous face once more, in person. I'd been trying to find out more about him since he left, but he'd gone quiet after making that deal, and I'm ashamed to admit how often I found myself staring at his picture from the day he met me, wondering what'd gone wrong.

But I suck that feeling down, and just focus it all into anger as I strut over to him. My black one-piece suit shows off my cleavage and hides my stomach, and I know I looked hot as hell, and I'm not about to let him walk all over me.

"Celebrating another big win?"

"Remains to be seen," he says with that confident smile on his face. I don't know what he's getting at, but I'm determined to not be trampled on, even if he's been the stuff of my late night fantasies ever since. "Been away, setting up operations for the military," he explains, "but now I'm back and looking to resolve something that's been on my mind ever since."

He looks me over slowly, sizing me up, and paying a bit of undue attention to my tummy. Does he suspect?

"I'm not pregnant," I lie, shrugging my shoulders and flicking my hair over my shoulder. "If that's what you're curious about. So don't worry, I'm not going to be hounding you for child support."

He looks disappointed, which I guess means I at least win one round with him.

Kinda.

"Well," he reaches into his stylish, even more expensive blazer, pulling out a small, velvet box. "Up for a bet?" he asks me, looking so serious. "Double or nothing," he says before slowly opening up the jewelry box, showing off the most ridiculously lavish diamond engagement ring I've ever seen. "And this time, if I knock you up, you get the ring to keep too."

I don't know what to make of it, I really don't. It's like I just hit my head and went into a coma and am now having the best dream of my life.

This can't be reality.

Reality like this doesn't happen in a strip club.

My knees start to shake, and the towering stripper heels aren't helping me keep my balance, so I hold onto the table.

"What?" I ask, stupidly.

He wets his luscious lips slowly, pushing the ring towards me.

"Come stay with me a while. Join me on my business trips from now on. And..." he shrugs his shoulders, "take our chances together. Maybe we hit it off. And, if you get pregnant along the way... well, then we've definitely hit it off." He smiles at me so charmingly all over again. "If you're not interested in commitment though... I'll make it worth your time," and then his calm, cool front melts before my eyes. "I just want you with me. One way or another."

445

My heart pounds hard in my chest, and I can feel the tears threaten my mascara. I can tell there's more than a few eyes on us, and this is definitely not my most badass moment.

But it's a moment I know I'll remember 'til I die.

"But you left..."

"Military contract," he says with a deep sigh, "hush hush. Had to sign a million waivers, go out of communication for a while." His strong hand reaches beneath the table to grasp my thigh, "But the whole time I was thinking of you. Wished I would've asked you to come along, instead of trying to play it cool. A man needs a good woman to make it through life. Something I learned after just one night with you."

The tears start falling and I desperately try to swipe them away, but I can't play it cool anymore either. My arms are around his neck, and my head is in his chest as I hold onto him for dear life.

He wraps those thick, bulging biceps about me in turn and squeezes me.

"That a yes?" he asks me after a while of holding me quietly, stroking my back in the most reassuring manner possible.

I nod my head. I take in a deep breath, though, and reach for his hand, bringing it to my stomach. I can't find the words to speak, but I want him to know.

I need him to know I'm carrying his baby.

He's a smart man, I've read all about him online and in the papers. But it takes even him a moment to catch on before his eyes widen and his confident smile returns.

"I knew it," he declares in triumph. "I fuckin' knew it. You're mine, babe. Never gonna let you go now," he says, pushing the most passionate kiss to my lips I've ever experienced.

446

THE BILLIONAIRE'S FERTILE SUBMISSIVE

*B*ook Themes:
   BDSM, Barely Legal, and Breeding
Word Count:
6,880

~

As MY PRIVATE jet landed on the small airstrip, I looked at all the warmth, the green of the land. This time of year, New York seemed ashen and grey, and compared to this tropical paradise, it might as well have been in black and white. Everything was vibrant and lush, the blue of the sky so bright, the water along the horizon a beautiful sea foam teal.

I'd changed for the flight into a more comfortable outfit, discarding my usual suit and ties and instead opting for plain cotton pants and a half unbuttoned linen shirt. Sunglasses hid my eyes, my brown hair left a bit shaggier and wilder than its usual style.

I was ready to relax for the first time in months. No

meetings. No calls. No visits with Presidents and Prime Ministers from around the world, no expectations placed upon me at all.

Stepping from the plane, I looked around with a sense of excitement and vigor I hadn't had since my much younger days, and there was an extra pep in my step as I made my way towards the classic car that awaited me.

Gleaming and a brilliant blue to match the sky, I took a second to appreciate it before I saw her.

My prized package, all wrapped up in a gauzy dress, looking at me expectantly. She wasn't a local — it didn't make me feel powerful to have a poor woman with few options serve me. No, she'd been shipped in as well, an import from home. I'd ordered her as others ordered movies.

Blonde hair cascaded down her shoulders, her fit and firm body porcelain coloured.

I couldn't help but smile. The agency had delivered me the perfect woman, and as she made her way over to me, she seemed so small and delicate. Her head tilted and those full lips parted as she waited my first order.

Well, that wasn't true. My first order had been that she wasn't to speak unless spoken to, and she was fulfilling that wonderfully.

Pretty and demure, that lovely young woman walked up to sheepishly press against my side, as if she were longing to be my latest adornment. Such perfect white teeth in that smile, such a bright excited glimmer in her eyes. She was mine for the trip, but she didn't look unhappy to be. Perhaps she was pleased to find out her keeper for the trip was handsome and fit, rather than the stereotype of what guy requires her services.

Who could blame her for that bit of relief?

I patted her on the head and motioned towards the car.

"Get into the backseat," I instructed slowly, as if talking to a child. She was legal, of course. I only dealt with reputable companies, after all, and ensured that there'd be no public fallout should they get wind of my excursion. But who can blame me for wanting to treat the little beauty like that?

I turned my back on her, trusting her to do as I'd instructed as I looked to my guard and right hand man. Elliot had been with me almost since the start, and I trusted him with everything. He was already getting my suitcases, ready to load them into the trunk, but I still watched him as my pet lifted her near see-through dress and climbed into the back seat.

Those long, shapely legs of hers were ivory coloured and so beautiful. The kind that just made you want to kiss them, rub your hands along them, all before feeling them wrap about your waist and cling to you.

She slipped in deep to the center of the back seat, adjusting her blonde hair as she waited for me, leaving that slender stalk of a neck exposed facing me.

Elliot finished packing the trunk as I stood quietly watching, just letting her stew in anticipation, to see what she'd do and how she responded to pressure.

But she had the patience of an angel, and I couldn't help but smile as I saw her sparkling blue eyes look at me.

I moved to the back seat with her, the hard seat against my back and ass as I looked to her.

"What's your name?" I asked.

"Angela," she said without pause, but what was most remarkable was just how beautiful that voice was. 'Voice of an angel' didn't do her justice, and it made me regret having silenced her for as long as I did.

She was the whole package, a body that belonged on the cover of magazines and billboards, a voice that should be singing before a crowd. The grace of a lady far her senior in years and social standing. Her every little move so dainty and meticulous as she crossed her legs and let her hands rest over her knee.

"Well, Angel," I said, taking ownership of that name and rebranding her. "I think you're going to have a wonderful vacation." My hand went to her thin, toned thigh, resting atop it and squeezing as Elliot went into the front seat and started us on our journey.

With the windows down, it blew her blond hair away from her perfect cheekbones, the little button nose that made her look so youthful.

She leaned in against me, slender arms coiling about my own as she pressed her surprisingly ample bust to my bicep. She was the full package, and as she gazed up at me with such sparkling eyes, I could see down that dress to the sight of such ample, pale breasts on display.

"I know we will, Sir," she said with such reverence and respect in each word.

I was only a man, and I couldn't control the way I began to swell at those sweet words, at the press of her body to mine. I leaned back, trying to look more relaxed, when all I could think about was getting to the hotel and ravishing her.

She wasn't just any companion, after all. She was chosen for my tastes, and I throbbed again just thinking about it.

Thinking about making her mine.

IT WAS an old colonial style building, settled amongst the trees and overlooking the ocean. Beautiful sand and water spread out before us, the cities and towns hidden by the lush foliage. The sea air blew in, and it was as if all my worries simply melted away. Especially with beautiful Angel still shimmying into me, needy for approval that I never truly gave.

Elliot opened my door, and I held out my hand to help Angel out as I looked upon the great hotel. It could easily house a couple dozen families, but it was far more exclusive than that, and only a few cars were parked nearby.

I strode towards the building with the same slow, measured gait of the locals, taking my time to enjoy the warm sun on my skin and the breeze in my hair.

I felt so relaxed, and yet, I also felt this excitement beneath the surface of my skin. I didn't want to rush, though. I wanted to soak in every moment of my vacation.

"What do you think, Angel?"

She looked like a kid in a candy store, eyes wide and shimmering, excitement radiating from her as she bit her lower lip and soaked it all in.

"It's beautiful, simply beautiful," she said soft and breathlessly. The ravishing young vixen nearly bouncing along my side with her excitement, rubbing against me with her supple, yielding breasts. She was the perfect, soft woman, who looked like she'd ever be in need of a hard, guiding father figure.

"Where are we staying, Sir?" she asked delightedly.

I smiled, taking a moment to stop and point to the east wing. "That's us," I said, "so that we can enjoy sunrise together."

The way her eyes sparkled at that said she was delighted with the response, but then looking at her stare at our place for the vacation, I wouldn't have been surprised if she'd reacted that way to whatever I said. She looked absolutely delighted just to be at my side.

Either she was a really good actress, or she was actually

the real deal. An innocent little thing who wanted nothing more than to be taken care of.

A rare and true pet.

I'd find out soon enough, and I draped my arm around her delicate shoulders as I guided her inside.

Beautiful artwork surrounded us in the lobby. It wasn't just the hung paintings, but the marble carvings, the way the ceiling as shaped as if to tell a story, it was beyond lavish. And it wasn't like the high class places in New York, stripped of emotion and personality. It was true artisan work, and I couldn't help but appreciate it.

I was a lover of the arts, and my own condo was filled with colour and passion. It was one of the few things that motivated me to earn as much as I did.

The second thing was the pristine young woman on my arm.

I led her up the marble staircase, listening to her heel click against the smooth stone, the two of us left alone as I showed her to our suite.

We had the entire wing to ourselves. I didn't scrimp on things like this. I worked hard, and I deserved the best, and while the hotel technically housed other guests, I ensured they'd be nowhere near me and my Angel.

The room was adorned in red and gold, the king sized bed nestled next to the large window that looked out over the ocean.

But lavish rooms and high class living weren't the only things the hotel was known for, and I greedily took in the little instruments I'd requested, laid out with care on the bed. A blindfold, five strips of leather with their metal Os, a paddle.

All I needed.

Angel reacted with sheer awe, gazing about as if she'd never seen so magnificent a place before in all her life, and of course she hadn't. Though when her gaze came to rest upon the sight of those kinky implements, her eyes dipped and I could see the blush fill her pale cheeks.

Though sweetest of all was how she clung to my arm a little tighter as she forced her gaze away.

"It's spectacular," she said breathlessly.

I stroked over her shoulder, warm from the heat of the sun, and yet even still, my touch made her skin bump.

I shut the door, locking it.

I didn't want to waste even a single moment with her, and I pulled away from her.

"I didn't give you permission to talk, Angel," I said with a tut-tut to my voice, my eyes flicking to the bed. The sun was higher in the sky now and the room was a bit darker than outside, a warm orange flooding the bed.

"You're going to have to be taught what happens when you speak out of turn."

The poor girl looked mortified. Her round, exotic looking eyes wide and glossy, her face appearing simply aghast. Those pouty lips of hers trembled, about to speak before she realized better and hung her head. Those little hands clasped before her as she awaited her punishment.

What a sweet young thing.

I had to hide my smile, though. My excitement.

That was the hardest part, for me. It wasn't doling out the punishment, it wasn't listening to the girls scream in pain and pleasure, or feeling them wriggle and writhe.

It was trying to pretend it didn't affect me until it was time.

I motioned towards the bed.

"Keep your dress on, but go to the bed," I said sternly, though I'd like to think I wasn't cold about it.

She obeyed perfectly, that beautiful young woman moving with such angelic steps, her dress streaming behind her as she went and tucked the skirts beneath her thighs and took a seat. She glanced over at me with those big blue eyes of hers before hiding back beneath her blonde hair.

I stepped towards her as she settled in, and I hoped her heart was racing like mine.

I had a specific set of instructions for the company that sent her, and so far as I could tell, they obeyed my every word.

My index finger went to her jawline, touching along it and making her look up at me again.

"I want you to be as quiet as a mouse," I instructed as I reached towards the leather collar at her side. My thumb ran along it, the cold metal pressed to my palm. Rubies adorned it all around in an intricate pattern and I smiled at the craftsmanship as I brought it to her throat.

She tilted her head back, chin up as she let me put that collar about her neck, tying it tight about her slender little stalk.

Up close like that I got to appreciate just how long and curved her lashes were, they fluttered before me beautifully as she let me take control. Her anxious swallow straining the confines of that collar, yet she restrained her squirm.

I looked down on her with such appreciation as I went for the next piece of leather, this one suited for her wrist. I lifted her hand from her lap and she kept it in place as I fastened it, the rubies glittering alongside that metal O ring.

I took a moment to feel her slender, smooth arm and smile.

I was so damned excited. The thought of having her, fully, excited me like nothing else. No meeting with the most powerful people in the world, no amount of money, could compare to the way I felt before taking a beautiful young woman for the first time, claiming her for myself.

To feel that milky white skin, with its smooth, flawless complexion. She was a work of art, like a statue carved by the finest of artisans, I wasn't sure such a girl as her could exist before then. But there she was, sitting so demurely, obediently. Offered up to me as I strapped her into the leather, claiming her as mine.

She of course never uttered a word, just cast furtive glances at me as I went about my work, took liberties with feeling her skin.

As I fastened the last one around her ankle, stroking up along her calf with such a calm sense of entitlement, my heart thudded faster and I could barely contain myself. I let her bare feet rest against my thighs, both of them held by my hands, as I looked up at her.

I reached for the blindfold, and beckoned her head towards me so that I could rob her of her sight.

She did just as I wished without a word said, leaning forward and letting me wrap that blindfold about her head, tucking her beautiful blonde hair out of the way. She was so still and quiet, but there through her gauzy dress, I could see the outlines of her stiffened nipples, betraying the excitement she felt as I took my time with her.

Those full, pink lips parted as she breathed heavier, her bosom rising and falling with each breath.

Without her being able to see, I was able to finally smile. To let my eyes trace along her beautiful body and finally let myself seem weak to her utter beauty.

I throbbed in my pants, and I wanted so badly for her to touch it, for her to know what she was doing to me, but that wasn't part of the game. The fun part was seeing how long I could resist. How far I could take her before I simply had to have her.

My hand cupped her jaw and forced her blinded face to me, so that my forehead rest against hers.

"Are you ready, Angel?"

That beautiful swan of a woman gave a light nod, her magnificent voice so soft and light.

"Yes, Sir," she said, ready to offer herself up to me fully, completely. She was the full package, no hesitation, no reservation. She wasn't just mine, she wanted to be mine. Such a rare treat in a submissive.

I smiled and stroked her cheek as I stood. I didn't want to bind her, not yet. I wanted to see what she'd do, how she'd react. I wanted to give her some freedom, just to see her limits and what she'd do with it.

"Alright, Angel. I want you on all fours on the bed."

She obeyed, but blinded as she was she had to feel her way up onto the bed, her dainty fingers feeling out the rich blankets as she climbed in. That dress of hers didn't cover even half of her thighs like that though, her pert little rear wagging in my face as she bent away from me, bare feet dangling over the edge of the bed.

I liked disorienting them just a little. Making them enter my world, rely on me more.

What could I say other than that it got me hard?

I stood behind her, watching her ass sway with uncertainty, little tremors running down her spine, and I licked my lips as I undid my belt slowly so as not to give myself away.

"How do you feel, Angel?"

She was hesitant to answer me, I could tell, but she obeyed. That soft little voice so sweet and light.

"I'm not sure, Sir... a little nervous," and that much was obvious, with the way her slender limbs shivered now and again. Her much tinier form so frail compared to mine, her skin looking porcelain and untouched in the Caribbean light that streamed through the open windows along with the ocean breeze.

"First times will do that," I said, though I wasn't sure if I intended it to be comforting so much as a statement of fact.

"What do you want me to do?" I asked, and that time I knew I was just curious. Interested.

That question obviously threw her, the poor little dove flinching and faced me with confusion written on her beautiful pale face around the blindfold.

She took her time, wet her lips, leaving them glossy and moist.

"I… I'm not sure, Sir," she said faintly. Though she'd sold her virginity off to a rich man she'd not yet met, and I could see the stiffness of her nipples prodding down through her see-through dress.

Maybe it was just the money, but I didn't believe so. Not with how selective I'd been, not with how many boxes on the checklist she had to say yes to.

I brought my hand to the back of her thigh, rubbing the backs of my fingers along that smooth, sensitive flesh."Did you shave like I asked?"

Her blush deepened at that question, and I felt her thighs quiver a little. Those beautiful milky stems in my hand so soft and pure. She nodded her head and said to me softly, "Yes, Sir. Of course."

She'd never miss so big of an instruction as that, but I just wanted to see her reaction.

Especially as my hand trailed up her inner thigh with such a slow, teasing motion, closer and closer to that prize of hers. That little bit of herself that she sold to me.

Though I knew I got more than that. I didn't just want a girl's virginity.

I wanted them to be mine, willingly, happily.

I could feel the gentle heat of her femininity as my hand grew near along her thigh. That soft inner thigh flesh led me up towards it, where her bare little cunny — so smooth from her shaving and slick with excitement — greeted the light brush of my hand.

That momentary contact made her gasp audibly and her whole body stiffen in surprise. She bit down upon her puffy pink lower lip and suckled it into her mouth as she tried her best to remain quiet.

"Did you shave like I asked?"

Her blush deepened at that question, and I felt her thighs quiver a little. Those beautiful milky stems in my hand so soft and pure. She nodded her head and said to me softly, "Yes, Sir. Of course."

She'd never miss so big of an instruction as that, but I just wanted to see her reaction.

Especially as my hand trailed up her inner thigh with such a slow, teasing motion, closer and closer to that prize of hers. That little bit of herself that she sold to me.

Though I knew I got more than that. I didn't just want a girl's virginity.

I wanted them to be mine, willingly, happily.

I could feel the gentle heat of her femininity as my hand grew near along her thigh. That soft inner thigh flesh led me up towards it, where her bare little cunny — so smooth from her shaving and slick with excitement — greeted the light brush of my hand.

That momentary contact made her gasp audibly and her whole body stiffen in surprise. She bit down upon her puffy pink lower lip and suckled it into her mouth as she tried her best to remain quiet.

It was so sweetly endearing, and I couldn't help but throb once again, so eager to feel that tight little pussy around me. But more that even that, I wanted to taste her.

First, however, I had to do what I promised.

I brought my finger, laced with her juices, away from her smooth and untouched sex, hands instead pushing up the flirty dress she'd chosen so that I could look over her pristine ass cheeks. They were so pale, so delightfully gorgeous, and I stroked along her left cheek, feeling her out.

I rubbed it, first. Greedily, letting the soft flesh caress my hand and get the blood flowing to the surface.

She was like a mewling little kitten, half in heat, half awkwardly shy. She didn't know what to do with herself, trembling with the anticipation so innocently, a soft little sigh escaping those pouty pink lips of hers.

"This is for your own good," I said before bringing my hand down.

Crack!

The sound filled the air, and I stayed still for a while as she got that wail out. Her slender throat put to work producing a surprised squeal as my hard hand met her soft, delicate skin.

I felt almost heady with the sensation, greedily taking in her response and letting it ease my troubles away.

Back in the big city, I have a few trysts, when I care to. But overall, my tastes are so selective that regular sex just didn't thrill me. Not in the way that training new subs did. Those with a curiosity and a high price tag.

I brought my hand down again and watched as my handprint marred her beautiful, pale flesh for just a moment.

It wasn't just about the sex. It was never just about the sex, or even the power.

I wouldn't call myself benevolent, but I couldn't deny that a part of me wanted to imprint upon the women I've been with. That I wanted to have an impact that I couldn't have as just a suitor, just another john.

And so I brought my hand down again, shhing her in a gentle and warm manner as my hand stilled on her ass, rubbing the heated flesh.

Her pristine, pale flesh tanned red beneath my hand so quickly, her sensitive body prickling with pain as she cried out again and again, each crack of my palm making that gorgeous girl teeter forward on her slender limbs and reel back in.

It was easy to see that the intensity of my punishment was a bit hard for her to take, but she never relented, never showed a sign of failing me. She was a beautiful work of art, and I was making my mark upon her as she cried out.

I didn't want to take it too far. This was a ballet, and one that I knew needed time before it reached the final, beautiful, marvelous act. I enjoyed every moment of it as I brought my hand down once more, softer this time though it still met her skin with a loud crack.

"Because it's your first time, sweet Angel, I'll let you off if you say sorry."

She was whimpering, quivering before me upon all fours as she did her best to topple face first into the blankets.

"I'm sorry!" she said with little hesitation, her voice wavering a little with the pain she felt rising through her throat into her words. "Please, I'm sorry!" she bleated like a white little lamb.

She couldn't see my smile, or what those words did to me.

I had to watch my breathing so that it didn't get away from me, and I stroked her thigh tenderly.

"It wasn't all that bad, was it?"

"N-no, Sir," she said to me through trembling lips, the

pretty little thing clearly enjoying it despite her delicate nature. Her flushed cheeks betrayed the depths of that sweet woman's reluctant interest.

She bit down upon her pouty lower lip, suckled upon it so sweetly as she knelt there before me. Looking utterly desperate for me to claim her, make her my own.

I couldn't help myself. I wanted to see her, and I wanted her to see me.

My hand went to her cheek, guiding her with such a tender, yet commanding, touch before my fingers wrapped around the back of her head, unveiling her to me like a delicate present.

I could see the moisture in her eyes beaded between her long, curves lashes as they fluttered and her gaze shut.

I then guided her towards my mouth.

I wanted to taste her, to feel the warmth of her worried lips against mine as she trembled. My other hand went to her shoulder, holding her aloft.

Those soft lips were pressed to mine, so perfectly smooth and damp. It was such a delight, the loveliest pair of lips I did ever kiss, and I could've savoured them for hours.

That sweet girl made kissing feel new and interesting again, like it weren't the prelude to something but the whole show. Intensely satisfying and exciting.

Especially with how her little tongue probed mine, testing it out, tasting me as well. I couldn't hide the fact that I throbbed beneath my pants at her enthusiasm, at the way she was eager for me despite the pink hue of her perfect ass.

The warm, tropical wind blew the curtains inwards, filling the air with the scent of sand and the ocean, the sound of foreign birds calling in the distance. It was the perfect vacation atmosphere with her kissing me so delicately.

I pulled back, coiling my hand around her ear, thumb rubbing along her cheek.

"How did you envision losing your virginity, Angel?"

Her eyes fluttered open once more and she looked at me, anxiously gnawing her lower lip a moment before she mustered up the courage to answer me.

"A strong, handsome older man... who guides me, takes me from behind," she swallowed anxiously. "I've resisted temptation..." she said, and I could feel the need in her words. She'd been a good girl for so long; too long.

My hand roamed over her face, tenderly, just getting a sense of that softness of her cheek, down over her jaw and further towards her throat as I smiled.

That's another reason I love these arrangements. They're mutually beneficial. There's no drama for them in giving away their virginity, no boy that's going to play games or judge her for not knowing what to do.

It was simple, and pure, and again I throbbed in my pants as I motioned towards the head of the bed.

"Crawl back into place, honey. What have you done with others, mmm?"

She obediently got back into place, her alabaster skin so perfect and smooth, such sweet glimpses up her dress skirt as she faced away from me, towards the headboard.

"Just... some touching and making out," she said, sounding oh so embarrassed. Her naivety worn like a mark of shame rather than pride, because she was a little too old to be carrying around that innocence still.

My hand traced over her still stinging ass and she flinched, but stayed right where I wanted her. I trailed my finger along the handprint, teasing it as I spoke.

"I'm going to lift my rule for just a little while, Angel. I want to hear every little thought, every little word, said aloud, alright?"

She bit her lip and nodded adamantly, choosing to agree with me silently in such an odd manner. As if not sure what to do with the newfound freedom I'd given her at first.

"Yes Sir," she said, and I could sense her pushing back against my palm just a little bit. Feel the heat not only from her reddened cheek, but from her cunny so close by.

"I... I—" she stammered, struggling with confessing dirty feelings aloud. "I can't help but imagine what you'll feel like. Inside me," she added on, those last words such a faint whisper.

I leaned back on the bed, my heart beating faster at her shy confession. Was there anything in this world sweeter than an innocent woman speaking dirty?

I licked my lips as I brought my hand along the cusp of her ass, touching her tenderly, teasing towards her slit.

"What else, Angel?"

As my hand neared that cunny of hers, I felt her shudder and heard her give a sweet whimper.

"I— I want you to touch me," she said, her voice a little strained with desire. "I don't want to be ignorant of it all! I don't want to be a virgin anymore," she confessed in such sweet tones, some of her warm slickness touching my fingers as I neared her quim.

I granted her a brush of my fingers against her smooth, shaven slit. She was absolutely soaking wet, and I couldn't help but feel a little bit of pride.

"You're going to have to do better than that, sweetness," I said lowly, just to tease her. To test how far she was willing to go, to see which desperation was worse for her.

She gave a suffering groan, so girlish and soft. It was filled with want and frustration.

"Please," she said, eyes shut, neck arched back as her spine curved in a feline sort of manner. "I want to feel you! Your... your cock," she said, her pale cheeks turning such a deep red as she begged for what she'd never known.

I brushed the back of my fingers against her pussy once more, just enjoying the slippery, smooth feel of her sex. I wanted her to reach her brink, and I knew she was already growing close. She didn't have the words to voice what she really wanted.

"Raw though, right Angel? You want the real thing?"

She was flustered, but she nodded, her vibrant hair bouncing with the motion.

"Y-yes! I don't want my first time spoiled," she said, arching her spine deeper and daring to press her needful cunny back against my fingers just the slightest bit. "I want you to make my first time perfect. Just like I always dreamed! Nothing in between us..." those last words uttered with such a lusty tone.

I intended to laugh, but it came out as more of a growl as I rubbed her pussy, up along her labia and towards her clit, circling there.

"And you want me to cum in you, don't you, Angel? To always have that link to me?"

It was easy to see she'd never been touched directly there before, because as my fingers teased her clit she moaned, shuddered and struggled to resist a flail from the intensity of her nerves being prodded.

"Y-yes! Cum in me! I want it to be real! Complete!" she begged me, that tone of desire unmistakable, unfakeable.

And I wanted to reward her for her good behaviour, but not before I rubbed that bundle of nerves once more, dragging my hand down along her slit and prying her inner labia open. I just wanted to see that perfect, pristine cunny before I filled her up.

She mewled for me as I inspected that perfect, pink slit. The hymen narrow, too taut for her to have been penetrated before. The proof of her virginity right there before me, promising such a tight squeeze when I finally sank into that cunny.

"Please," she begged again. "I don't know if I can wait any longer!"

What a sweetheart. I normally didn't like being rushed, but I was only a man, and her dulcet voice was driving me just as wild. Not to mention the sweet scent of her arousal.

I pulled back and brought my clean hand to my trousers, unbuttoning my pants before standing. I then went to my shirt, watching her as I undid it, letting her see as I throbbed beneath my cotton trousers before I finally stripped.

Watching her squirm, I could see her struggle with resisting moving, her blue eyes flicking to the side even as she tried her best to avoid doing so. She wanted to see my cock. Gaze upon it, know what was about to fill her. And she caught a good glimpse of its thick, vein-lined shaft, pulsating with desire for her. And it made her whimper with need all over again.

I stroked it, once more trying to tease her, to make me need to punish her. But she was so obedient. I don't think I'd ever met a girl like her, and I couldn't help but grin.

I went back on the bed, behind her, bringing my cock to her slit, rubbing my heated member against her labia. The warmth of the air had covered me in a bit of a sheen already, the tropical breeze relaxing me.

She moaned, a genuine, honest, beautiful moan from the very touch of my bare cock against her cunny. My thick, purple crown stretched her hymen gently, working it wider as she quivered and writhed.

"Oh god…" she said, and I wasn't sure for a moment

whether she was speaking to me or not, with how she said it. "Please don't stop... I need your cock inside me," she said breathily.

No one could resist her plea, least of all me.

I placed a hand on her ass, parting her cheeks a little as I began to guide myself into her. There was that wonderful, blissful pressure as I eased in and then that final give as I thrust my hips forward, claiming her for myself forever.

I made her cry out, a loud squeal followed by a throaty moan as I sank my thick, pulsating member deep into that tight, once-virginal cunt of hers. And I felt the fullness of just how tight and untouched she was. The narrow clench of her womanhood upon my raw cock, knowing for certain she was the cleanest, most pure little woman a man could ever hope to sink his dick into.

She cried out for me as I watched those puffy pink cunny lips cling to the base of my shaft.

"Oh god... yes!" she said in a quivering voice.

My other hand shifted away from my cock, going instead to her hips on either side as I brought her back against me. I hilted within her sweet, tight pussy and just held her there, luxuriating in her wetness and the almost-too-tight clench as I growled.

Of course, it was all part of what was arranged. Such a sweet, willing virginal woman, who was tested to meet my needs. Yet what made it so good was how genuine it was, her moans, the way her tight little pussy squeezed my cock as I lingered in her, savouring her depths. She was the real deal, not a phony simply in it for the money.

"Please please please!" she wailed wantonly. "You're so big... I need you to take me," she said breathlessly.

I didn't delay or linger any longer. Not with those words tumbling from her lips.

Both of my hands dug into her ass cheeks, pulling them

apart as I tugged out before slamming my hips back against her, watching my cock disappear within her again. There was a slight taint of red to my cock, mingling with her sweet, feminine juices, and I began rutting into her full force.

As the hammering blows of my cock reigned upon her, battering her ass cheeks with my groin, thrusting deep to her utmost limits with my throbbing cock, she buckled and fell face first into the pillows. She moaned and wailed, squealing and writhing as my dick plumbed her depths again and again.

"Oh yes, yesss…!" she gave an unintelligible wail and I could feel her body heating up, almost as if her pussy was coiling about me tighter as she wound up towards her climax. "I- I think I'm cumming!" she said, and the way she did so made it sound like she'd never had an orgasm before to judge by.

And I slammed into her harder, the head of my cock hitting against the depths of her body as I brought my hand around front. If she thought she was cumming, well… I'd make certain of that.

My index finger found her clit, that little heated bud almost buzzing with energy, and I pressed against it, circling it with firm motions as I kept hammering my cock into her.

That did her in, the sweet little angel's eyes were shut and she was flailing about, writhing beneath me as she screamed and hit her peak. A flood of warm juices coated my cock and she was like an out of control creature, limbs reaching out, nails digging into the bed sheets as she lost herself to not only her first fuck, but her first climax.

'Ohhhhh!" her voice warbled, "Yes! Yes Sir! God!"

"Yea, Angel," I growled. "Cum all over my cock."

It was hard to resist the way her cunny was tightening

around me, squeezing me with such need. As if it weren't just her that needed my seed, but her body as well. It felt so primitive, so lewd, and I knew I couldn't last much longer.

Not against that tight cling of her pussy. The slick grasp of its folds!

She clenched about me, just as her clawing at the sheets tore them down towards her, and she twisted about, moaning and squealing.

"Cum in me! Cum deep inside me, please Sir!" she begged of me, desperate for it. Insane with need for our breeding.

I didn't resist the urge then. It took me not more than a second to find my own end, holding her still upon my dick as I unleashed those torrents of cum deep within her, splattering her insides with my creamy jism.

I growled out something unintelligible, grinding up against her as I brought my free hand down upon her stinging ass.

She seemed almost as ecstatic to have me cum inside her as I was to do it. She cried out with excitement as I flooded her fertile womb with my seed, spurt after thick, virile spurt filling her up as I hammered out every last drop into her.

She shut her eyes, relished it all as she moaned continuously, filled with such deep satisfaction as she let herself be lost to the full experience of her first time. A long, warbling moan passed out of her throat as she quivered and called out for me.

It was sweet, warm bliss and I stayed nestled within her folds for some time, just enjoying the little cries and whimpers and moans of pleasure that kept coming from her. She was such a beauty, and I ground my hips before finally pulling away and freeing my dick with a pop.

But I didn't let her relax. No, instead my hand went

once more to her pussy, prying apart those sweet, flushed lips and saw my cream pooling within, threatening to spatter to the bed.

The sweet girl mewled and flinched just a little. Her puffy folds were reddened from being stretched, and oh so sensitive, but she craned her neck and watched with me as that pearly white seed drooled from her slit so beautifully.

"That was magnificent," she said breathlessly, her ample chest rising and falling with her heavy breathing.

My lips curled into a grin as I saw the change I'd brought about in her body, drawing out a little of the cum and rubbing it along her clit just to tease.

She shivered and my grin broadened.

"It only gets better for you from here, Angel. We're going to be spending a lot of time together." My fingers delved into her messy cunny, making her moan once more. "You're my girl now."

THE FERTILE ACTRESS

*B*ook Themes:
      Cuckolding, Breeding, and Impregnating Creampies
Word Count:
5,122

I'D GONE to every one of her movies, even the romantic comedy ones that made me roll my eyes, just so that I could see her again. We'd fallen out of touch over the fifteen years after graduating high school, but she'd always be my first love, my high school sweetheart. Until she moved away to pursue her acting career, and I went off to law school. We'd tried to make it work, but it all fell apart.

Now she was married to a gorgeous hunk, and I'd read on one of those slimy magazine covers that they were going to try for a baby. All the world's eyes were on them, tabloids angling into every bit of their business.

So maybe I shouldn't have been so bowled over when

she called me and asked me to meet her in person. She was flying into New York for a shoot, and we'd still kept in touch on social media, after all.

But when she asked me to do her and her husband a favour?

And that favour involved having unprotected sex with her, to knock her up and let the world figure that it was her husband's baby?

Well, second chances come in weird ways, and I couldn't say no.

I DID my best to not seem desperate, of course. Didn't jump at her request – her plea – for me to knock her up right then and there. I instead said I'd think about it and that we'd meet up again that evening. Fair enough.

Of course, by the time that evening came, I was dying to blow a load in my old crush. I showed up at the hotel in a nice business suit, but ditched the tie in my car. Of course, I wanted to look more casual after leaving the office. Besides, it was her that came to me for help now. Not like the days long ago when I was salivating after her through high school, but could never impress her enough to be only mine, for good.

Since then I'd kept in shape: early morning workouts with some of the partners were not only healthy but a good networking potential. So my shoulders were broad and built, my biceps and torso filled out well. I was a catch, which is why I never settled down into a long term thing with one woman; I figured I'd use my prime years to look around, have fun.

Besides, I didn't want some gold digger coming along and spoiling my future. But Zoe was no gold digger. She had fortunes amassed beyond compare, with mansions around the world.

The hotel she was staying at, though, wasn't the nicest in the city. She was trying to keep a low profile for her clandestine meeting with me, no doubt. The fact that she felt she could trust me, though? Yea, I couldn't help but be a little flattered that I'd mattered that much, even after all these years.

When she answered the door, she was dressed fairly casually in a navy dress that hugged her curves. Her skin was pale and pristine, her ruby lips so full and her eyes still wide and youthful, despite the years between when I'd first fallen for her.

She was just past 30, and yet her skin was radiant and her long, curled hair was clearly styled. She smiled as she saw me, just like she used to, with excitement and affection twinkling behind her eyes as she let me in.

"I'm so glad you decided to come back, Alex," she said with a respectful bow of her head, all cordiality.

Of course I'd come back. Knocking up my high school crush / movie star topped my list of desires. Even if at the end of it she went home to her husband on the other side of the country.

"I can't leave you hangin'," I said as I stepped on into her hotel room, a smile on my face as I took it in. It certainly wasn't the nicest, but it was far from the worst hotel room either. After a quick survey of the black and grey, modern-style furnishings, I smiled back at her.

"Funny to think of us together after all these years," I remarked, looking her over casually. "I'm glad you thought of me when this problem came up," I said, which was honest enough. I was glad.

Just maybe not for all the same reasons she hoped for.

She brought me further into the room, and there was a

bottle of wine, chilled on ice, and she gave a lopsided smile that had always endeared me.

"I don't really know how to go about this, so I figured... Wine's always the best way," Clarissa said. "Would loosen us up a little."

I plucked the bottle of wine out of the ice and looked it over, seemed an expensive label, not that I was an expert. Though when you deal with fancy clients, you learn to fake it. I plucked up the glasses and helped myself to pouring us up some, handing her one and taking my own.

"To old friends," I said in a toast, holding out my glass to her.

She raised her glass to mine, a little too eager to drink it back, but she looked more relaxed even before the alcohol could pollute her system. Just the act alone seemed to calm some of her frayed nerves.

"God, crazy how things have changed," she said, looking me over with, what I thought to be, appreciation. Couldn't help but feel my ego puff up a little bit at that.

I topped her glass off for her again as we took a seat upon the edge of the bed.

"It's a lot of time between now and then," I said, reaching over and patting my hand atop her knee, rubbing over her thigh just a little. "We were just kids then, only starting to come into our own. There's been college, career and movies that have changed us both since then," I said with a smile. "Which you've been great in, I might add," I said to her with a warm smile, enjoying her scent so close as I was.

She let out a soft laugh.

"I didn't figure you'd have seen any of them. Wasn't... I mean, I didn't want to hope they might be your thing. They've all meant a lot to me," she said with such sincerity as her face lifted to mine, her large eyes sparkling.

"You look really good," she finally managed. "I'm not just saying that."

"Thank you," I responded with a smile, tracing my hand down over my shirt, which only served to highlight the hard pecs and abs just beneath. "And I saw every one of your movies," I confessed with a shrug, drinking some of my own wine. "Even the ones that weren't very manly of me to go see," I jested with a half-cocked smirk. "You made them all worth it. As fine an actress as there is, more beautiful than your high school days by far."

The giggle she had was still the same, the modest way she lowered her eyes. I guess beyond the bright lights of Hollywood, she was still a person, just like before. Still a little uncertain, a little shy, she just learned to fake it for the cameras and the media.

But now she was alone with me, asking a favour, and she went back to the girl I'd dated in high school.

Her hand rest atop mine on her knee, looking at me with such affection.

"I hope this won't be weird," she said gently.

"Maybe a little," I said with a wink then downed the rest of my own glass before laying it aside on the night stand. "But hey, it was weird just dating all those years ago. Because we were new to the whole thing. New to our changing selves. That's life, weird new circumstances that you just get used to," I said, so confident and assured. Ten years of law had taught me how to be confident and in control, even when standing among a sea of hostile faces.

Compared to the prosecution and jury, my old crush, come back to beg my help, hardly seemed like a challenge. So I squeezed her knee and rubbed her thigh a little as I leaned into her.

"You were really great in that last movie," I said, the sex

scene foremost in my mind at that point, though I tried to will it away.

Her skin warmed against my hand, her slender legs parting just slightly as she took another sip of her wine. It certainly wasn't enough liquor to alter her actions, but it was enough to relieve some of that tightness between her shoulders, making her look at me with just slightly lidded eyes.

"You watch it in theatres?"

"Yeah," I said, nodding my head slowly as my arm wound around her, rubbed at her shoulder. My grasp was strong, and she was dainty, that Hollywood movie star frame of hers so delicate in my grasp as I worked the tension from her. "Though you make it all feel so personal... so intensely romantic, it feels almost feels scandalous watching you in public like that," I teased with a smile, leaning in and touching my lips to her cheek with a soft kiss.

She giggled again, though it was laced with nerves, anxiousness, affection. She nibbled on her lower lip, glancing up at me from the corner of her eyes. She'd always been a good girl in high school, dating around but never going all the way. I'd only ever got to second base with her before, and I couldn't deny the thought of finally fucking her, raw, was exciting.

My hand travelled up her thigh, and I couldn't help myself, I just leaned in and placed my lips to her neck. I kissed her, suckled at her neck just a little as I squeezed her body to mine. I didn't want to spend all night warming into it, easing into the mood. I wanted her bad, and I wanted that spark to flare up.

I rubbed my hand over her back as I felt her out, her slender body pressed up against my hard muscles. I wanted to feel in her some of the desire she had for me.

476

She gasped at my kiss, but instead of recoiling, she moved closer.

Sure, kissing her wasn't part of the deal, not that we'd really hashed out a list of things I could and couldn't do. The only stipulation was that I'd fuck her, raw, and hopefully knock her up.

And that I'd, at the very least, spend the night to see her off in the morning as well. Didn't want to miss an opportunity.

So maybe she'd been a bit shocked at my kiss, the way my tongue grazed across the surface of her flesh, tasting her. It certainly sent a shiver down her body, her nipples stiffening beneath her dress.

My hand travelled up from her thigh, on over her body to cup at her breast. I could feel that nipple prod against my palm as I felt her up, let my fingers sink into her supple flesh, feel her out as I kissed my way up her neck to her ear. I suckled at her lobe, tugged upon it as my body pressed to hers, slowly pushing her back towards the bed.

I wanted her bad, and already that fact was plainly clear by the bulge in my groin. My cock was rock solid, and I wanted to be inside her desperately.

She set aside the empty wineglass, her eyes upon me and I could only describe her gaze as smoldering. She was shy, sure. Reserved, a little. But her legs spread softly, as if I wouldn't notice, and her lips dropped open and let out a little whimper as I kissed and nipped her neck and ear.

How long had I dreamed about doing this? Yet never, no matter how wild they got, did I think she'd call me up, asking me to bang her raw, get her pregnant with my seed. That was out of the realm of even my fantasies, yet it was quickly becoming my reality.

For years I'd been so careful with girlfriends, never wanting to be stuck with a kid I didn't want. Always packing condoms despite my urges to trust in the pill and enjoy some raw sex. But now I got to have it, and better yet... I'd get to knock her up and not worry about the consequences.

My hand slid back down from her breast to her leg, I rubbed over her smooth thigh, then on up underneath her dress, my grasp tightened about her hip, thumb rubbing inwards. I was just dying to get in between her legs, and I felt out the source of her feminine heat.

"God," she muttered, her head rolling back into the pillow, her body arching upwards, breasts thrust into to air as her legs spread further for me. She was already so damn wet, her panties soaking, and I rubbed them into her, making her writhe beneath me. That shyness was quickly fading away as she moaned, and it was such a familiar sound from her movies. I wondered how into it she got, all those people watching as she pretended to get fucked.

I guess I'd soon find out how good her acting really was.

I rose up over her, looking down at her beautiful body, face so flush, watching her writhe as I rubbed her cunny. I rolled my shoulders back and slowly slipped off my jacket before I began to work open my shirt. I'd let her appreciate my body, how well I'd taken care of myself in the years since we'd last been together.

My shirt came off and then I reached up beneath her dress, to hook my fingers into her panties and slowly peel them away from her quim and off her legs. I gave them a toss onto the nightstand, letting them hook around my wine glass as I got back over her, my black pants bulging with my desire.

Her hands kept trailing over me, manicured nails teasing my skin as her legs spread, wider and wider until I was able to comfortably fit between them. Her dress pulled up, I could see the perfectly smooth slit, the dainty little labia as her sex parted for me, the petals already so damp.

She smelled clean and fresh, and she even flushed as she saw me looking at her prized pussy, the thing I'd thought about while beating off on more than one occasion, and it was even better than I could have imagined.

I reached down and undid the buckle of my pants, ignoring the look of appreciative awe on her face as she stared at my chest. I tugged open the belt, then undid the pants below before shimmying out of them and my boxers.

When my rock hard dick sprang free, I could see the look of surprise on her face. I was big, my cock so veiny and pulsating. It was a good looking dick. I knew that. I'd had enough girlfriends be impressed to know it was true. And now I was angling my hips down to nudge against her slick petals, to tease her honeyed quick with my thick fuckrod.

Her gaze kept following my cock, though, not tilting back and pretending like I was her husband. She was staring with desire, licking her lips as her inhibitions slowly melted away. I supposed she somewhere along the line decided that if she was going to sleep with someone not her husband, she was going to enjoy it, because she pressed her breasts up from under the dress, squeezing her left tit as she watched me tease her cunny.

I was happy to oblige, because it was a dream come true for me. The girl of my dreams, mine at last. If only for a night.

I brought the bulging, purple tip of my cock on up to the apex of her slit, teased her clit and made her shiver. That was so very satisfying, and I worked my dick on down again, slowly sinking my loins into her pussy. The sight of those puffy labia blossoming around the crown of my cock before swallowing me up as I sank on in was gorgeous. I got carried away with it all, and thrust the rest in, the two of us watching my veiny shaft vanish into her slick, honeyed canal immediately.

"Oh God," she gasped, but never did she tear her eyes away as I impaled her upon my thick shaft, spreading her open so lewdly.

Her hand squeezed her breast harder, shivering in delight as she ground against me, her pussy so tight and wet. It was like a perfect little sleeve, and she was already desperate for me, her breathing becoming quicker, her nails digging half-moons into her firm chest.

I reached up, pulling down the shoulder strap of her dress to expose her other tit to my gaze. Grasping hold of that fleshy, supple mound, I only then began to pump into her. Rocking my strong hips to tug my cock from her tight little cunny, only to then thrust it back in. Though honestly, the tight pull of her depths helped there. I barely felt like I could tug back a few inches without her grip hauling me back in.

I found myself moaning uncontrollably, my cock throbbing inside her as I looked down upon her beautiful form. Damn, she truly was more gorgeous than ever.

Especially with how into it she seemed. Maybe she'd just been nervous, shy at first, about needing my help. Needing to rely on her old high school flame to come and knock her up.

But now that I was deep within her, fucking her just right, her body came alive and she writhed for me.

"Oh God, Alex," she moaned my name. "God, I couldn't stop thinking about this."

If one of us were to confess that, I thought it'd be me. To hear her say it? Surreal. But it only fueled my passions, made me fuck her harder, faster. Pound my hips down into her. We weren't kids anymore, we were grown up and ravenous, and I wasn't going to hold back.

The slap of my balls against her ass resounded, filling the room as I groaned and pounded harder. Harder. My fingers sank into her breast and I clenched its supple curve so tightly as I enjoyed its feel.

"Fuck," I cursed aloud. "I've dreamt of making you my fuck toy for so damn long!" I said in a husky, groaning voice.

Some women might have been put off on that, but not Clarissa. No, her legs just kept crawling higher upon my hips until I was forced to grab both of them, putting them over my shoulders and letting me ram in deeper, harder, battering against her cervix as her tits jiggled.

She was screaming beneath me, warbled cries of pleasure and desire. It was crazy how fast she'd gone from a reserved and closed off woman to this absolutely out of control slut upon my dick, but I was grateful for the fact.

I ran my hand over her body, appreciating every little curve of her form, sliding across her taut tummy, then down. I let my thumb dip, teasing her clit as I bucked harder, harder. I could feel my balls slowly beginning to tighten, my loins on fire as I approached my climax. I wanted so bad to blow my load, but I was committed to making her cum first. Or cum right with me.

"Cum on my dick," I commanded her. "Cum on it just like you should've years ago," I said in a husky voice, so rough and full of lust.

She let loose such a moan at the touch, her entire body bucking against me, and her heat only growing at my words. She could barely keep her eyes opened, but she wanted so badly to watch as I impaled her sweet little pussy again and again.

"Oh God," she hissed once more, grabbing her breast so

hard that flesh dimpled between her fingers, her lips trembling. "God, I want you to knock me up," she groaned, and those words made her quiver even harder. Apparently they'd sent a prominent jolt of excitement through her, since she didn't stop.

"Just breed me like some dumb slut," she gasped, and another jolt went through her, making her hips buck. "Make me yours."

Her enthusiasm – her raw vulgarity – did me in. Oh sure, I had started it, tipped her over the edge with my own dirty talk, but hearing her reciprocate? I lost it. I hammered into her, pounded her body as I let loose such a loud roar of desire. My balls unleashed a fiery pleasant sensation, travelling up my thick, pulsating shaft until I was shooting my thick, creamy load of virile seed deep into her.

"Take it," I told her amid my bucking, my hard body tensing and clenching, muscles twitching. I was shooting my cum deep into her as I worked her clit with my thumb so desperately. I needed her to cum with me, wanted it so bad...

"My little knocked up movie star slut," I called her upon my groaning, satisfied voice.

And those words, more than anything, got her to that explosive tipping point. She didn't hold back, wasn't a meek little mouse squeaking out her pleasure. Nor was she the all seductive moans and groans as she was on the movie screen.

No, instead, she was shrieking and writhing, her hair a mess and her face contorted and red.

She wasn't holding anything back, not at all, as she gushed along my dick.

That warm flood of feminine honey across my dick, and running on down over my balls, was so satisfying.

Nothing between us, nothing separating our pleasure, nothing in the way. Just my dick, blasting her fertile womb with my cum.

Ohh, it was so very sweet. The finest moment in my life, better than making the bar, getting promoted at my firm, or winning a big case. Much better than any time I'd fucked a woman before.

I rocked my hips, milking out every last drop of my cum into her depths as I groaned, reaching a hand up to grasp at her breast and fondle it affectionately.

"Good girl," I husked, then repeated it. My hard body glistening before her gaze with a light sheen of perspiration.

She whimpered and writhed, her mind emptied of all thoughts as she stared in a blissful daze. Her beautiful lips were parted, her hips still grinding against me as little panted breaths escaped her, making her breast jiggle in my hand as her pussy twitched against my sensitive, spent dick.

WE WENT AGAIN, and drank wine until we passed out in a sweaty heap at some point during the night. I awoke the next day, the two of us nude, and laying in bed with the sheets an utter mess. But there she was still... sound asleep and so ravishing.

She wouldn't be staying much longer, but I knew I had to have her more. She was flying out that very day, off to another movie shoot. And I wanted to leave her with that baby in her belly.

I brushed the hair back from her lovely face, and very gingerly – without waking her – I turned her onto her back, and very softly parted her legs. She was damp, I felt it right away as I cupped her sex. And I wasted no time.

I got up, rock hard with my morning wood, and got between her thighs.

I moved so slow, pressed to her so gently, she didn't wake up until I was already pressing down into her and moaning hoarsely.

"Ah," she whimpered, not having expected to wake up to a cock impaling her, taking her already in her groggy state, and though she tensed for a second, she instantly stilled. The room stank of sex, her body laced with my scent, and she pressed her firm loins towards me.

"Alex," she groaned, without even opening her eyes, and already her body was slickening further for me, responding in such a lewd manner.

"I'm going to knock you up before you leave this room," I pledged to her, my voice raw and rough in my early morning state. It added an edge to my words, making them so much harsher, more commanding.

My hands grasped her legs, fingers sinking into her soft thigh flesh as I began to pump. I stuffed her tight cunt full of my cock, again and again, stretching out her narrow little canal as I moved, making the bed creak beneath us with the motions.

"My sweet lil' Clarissa," I husked appreciatively, the smacks of our bodies together rising up higher, higher.

She moaned such a beautiful little song, her voice almost purring from the sleep.

"Yes," she whimpered, her back arching as she lifted her hips towards me, making me hit her so deeply with that stiff wood. "Fuck, yes."

She must have been sore, that pretty little pussy red and swollen, but she didn't act like it. She was too lusty for me, desperate to take my cock.

I didn't take it easy on her, I gave it to her with all I got, pounding her. Wanting to make her remember her time with me for as long as possible, make the sting of our long, repeated rutting linger in her mind as she found out she was pregnant. Make my breeding of her a mark on her flesh as well as her life.

My dick throbbed inside her, stretching her out as I bent back her legs and made her tits jiggle atop her chest.

"Fuck, you're such a gorgeous lil' beauty, Clarissa. I'm gonna breed you such a beautiful lil' baby," I growled.

Even without me touching that sensitive little clit, she whimpered and a thrill went through her, pussy vibrating around me. My words had such an effect on her, and she bit down on her lower lip to silence a loud scream.

But she couldn't stay quiet for long, before she closed her eyes and said such filthy things. "Yea, you better knock me up." Her legs curved around my ass. "Cum in me nice and deep."

The sweet little girl I knew back in high school, now a beautiful movie star, saying such filthy things to me as I tried to knock her up. It was the stuff of boyish dreams.

I grasped hold of her two hips, lifted her body up off the bed as I pounded away. I put my strength to good use, reminding her of my raw power, hammering in nice and deep as I moaned aloud. Again my hard, ripped abs and pecs glistened with a thin sheen of perspiration, and I groaned loudly.

"C'mon," I growled at her. "Milk my dick of every drop of cum... earn my seed, you desperate lil' slut!"

She cried out as her pussy muscles tightened around me, so obediently. She was really working for my cum, desperate for it, and her entire body was writhing and bucking as she sought it out. I was seeing her the way no one ever could on the big screen, her hair dishevelled, her face bare of makeup and lighting, absolute pleasure contorting her features. Never would they allow her to be seen so raw, but I committed it to memory, knowing I could relive it again and again.

She was going to fly out of my life again soon, but not before I shook her world, I determined.

I looked down across her body, over the soft, supple curves of her feminine form, on down to the place where my hard, muscle-ripped body hammered into her. Those puffy folds of hers swallowing up my cock as I thrust on in, again and again. Hammering away as my balls smacked her ass cheeks, so laden with cum that awaited its chance at knocking her up.

I didn't need a picture or video of that to emblazon it in my memory forever. I'd never forget that gorgeous sight. And just seeing it made my dick throb and swell, stretching her out.

"Fuck! I'm gonna cum in this tight lil' pussy of yours again Clarissa," I growled out. "And then I'm gonna see you on all the news, swollen with child… and know it's mine, you desperate lil' slut."

And it was with my words that she screamed, her body spasming against me, pulling towards my own inevitability. Her cries were enough to wake the neighbourhood, as electric fire ripped through her, her body jerking and tightening against mine.

Her body spasmed and squeezed about me, and I found my thrusts hitting their own ragged end. I was pulled into her tight, fertile body and my dick was drained dry once more. I couldn't suppress the deep groans, the satisfied grunts as I twitched and bucked, pumping the full load of creamy jism straight into her.

I was packing a big, thick load of virile seed, and I was dumping it all in as deep as I could, right into her womb.

That high was a feeling I could never forget, but seemed impossible to ever hope to match again.

Especially not as she looked up at me, with a mix of lust, affection, and raw, animal need in her expression. She was spent, but that teasing little smirk, that way she licked her lips...

I knew she wasn't going to disappear from my life now.

I HAD ONLY JUST FINISHED READING an article about her. Seeing a picture of her on the award's show runway, her beautiful black gown swollen by a child in her belly. It was a sight that took me away, reminded me of our time together in that hotel room. Made me pang for her again.

But before the pang could become sadness, a call came through on my phone.

"Hello," I answered simply, not recognizing the number. But then, she never stuck with the same phone for long, not with how paparazzi kept cracking celebrity's personal devices.

"I want to see you again. Soon," she confessed immediately, that voice unmistakable. I couldn't help but grin.

THE FERTILE BEAUTY QUEEN

*B*ook Themes: Cuckolding, Breeding, Impregnating Creampies, and Public Sex
Word Count:
5,122

~

My ears were still ringing, but clearly talk still went on around me. Oliver and Sue, my wife, mostly. Sue was very animated, a little red faced and upset at the whole proposition. Which I couldn't blame her for. Oliver was desperately trying to make his case, but neither of their words were getting through to me.

Out of us all, it was strangely the two most affected that were quiet. Me and Marisa.

The neighbour's wife was a beauty queen. And I don't mean that glibly, she was literally a beauty queen. Slender but shapely, she was well cut and clearly worked out, with beautiful long, auburn hair and a rack to die for.

I'd be lying if I said I hadn't thought of her a few times over the years, mid-coitus, or paused to look out the second story window at her sunbathing in her backyard. But what they'd just proposed?

It was clear it was her husband's idea; he was the one defending it to my wife, and Marisa sat, knees together, looking down at her lap with embarrassment.

At that moment I thought it was absurd, never gonna happen.

Funny how things can turn out.

IT TOOK some convincing to get my wife on board. She was, after all, the mother of my two children. We'd been together for over ten years, and had no real hitches in our love life. But those qualities were what the neighbours were after.

I was a fit man, successful in my business, and clearly virile with my two kids. Hell, it took too much of our energy just trying to prevent more from happening. Now I was expected to turn back the clock.

The offer of money helped convince my wife, but more so was that powerful desire she had to let me call the shots. And getting paid five grand to knock up the beauty queen next door was not the kind of deal any normal man turns down. Once she'd calmed down, she gave her consent.

Fantasy is one thing though. Actually going through with it though? That was another.

The day came when I was to start, Oliver was gone on some excuse to be away from the house no doubt, and my own wife was away with the kids to a football game. That left me to waltz on over on that warm, sunny day to seal the deal.

It was all planned of course, hell, down to the details: I'd come fuck her three times a day. This was just the first planned, on a nice sunny morning.

I dressed nice, but not too nice. A white polo that hugged my own well-toned chest, and a pair of black jeans.

Her though?

Seems her task for the morning was more sunbathing in the backyard, so when she came to the door, she was glistening and oh so ravishing.

Her tight, white bikini clung to her tanned body, her sculpted abs and large breasts. I was certain they had to be implants on size alone, but it was so hard to tell with the talent of surgeons nowadays.

Her blonde hair was bleached, and her lips were bright pink as she smiled at me.

"Hey, Perry," she said as she stepped aside, letting me into her home. It was almost exactly like mine except for the furniture and art that adorned the walls, erotic black and white images that were more sensual than anything else.

"How're ya doing, Marisa?" I asked, trying to play it all as casual as I could, not make it any more awkward than need be. Though truth be told my dick was already swelling in my pants, not just at the prospect of fucking such a gorgeous woman as Marisa, but at being able to plant my seed in her.

Sure, I had kids and didn't want to raise anymore myself, but this was different. I'd knock Marisa up, and then what came after would be none of my responsibility.

Just $5,000, sitting in my bank, ready for me to blow it on whatever I wanted.

After I blew my load in her, of course.

She lowered her eyes to the ground to hide that smile, and she was so endearing when she blushed. She'd always traipsed around the neighbourhood, high and mighty, but here I was, rendering her to school girl status.

It felt good.

"Did you want anything?" she asked, and maybe she had the same thought as me. That it'd have been less awkward for our first time if it were later, if there were champagne and darkness to hide in.

Yet something in me relished this early morning tryst, and starting my day off by relieving what had already began as a rather stiff bit of early morning wood.

"Nah I'm good," I said simply and reached out, placing my hand on her arm to rub it smoothly. It was the most casual way I could find to first touch her, initiate that bit of contact, and I left my hand on her, feeling that incredibly soft, smooth skin. I don't know what she used, but whatever it was, it beat the hell out of my wife's moisturizers, because she felt like heaven.

She shut the door behind them, clicking the lock shut. She clearly didn't want to be disturbed.

Taking a step in, her head bobbed towards the stairs. "Our—" she stopped herself. "My bedroom is just up here."

Of course I knew that. The master bedrooms in this subdivision were all in more or less the same place.

Her bare feet lightly compressed in the carpet as she turned away from me, beginning to lead up the stairs and giving me a fantastic view of the curves of her firm ass as she walked upwards.

I had no idea how it was going to go, but I hoped I'd eventually get a chance to grab hold of those cheeks from behind as I plowed into her. As I stared at those two perfectly round mounds, there was nothing I wanted more.

When we got upstairs, I discovered their bedroom was set up like a young girl's version of a beautiful marital bedroom. With a large canopy bed, with white drapes about it, and delightfully antique adornments around the room. She clearly was even more of a sweetheart inside than she appeared, living out an adorable fantasy of married life in her bedroom.

There was no point in wasting time, not if we were gonna be screwing three times a day for a while. And so I started things off by pulling my polo up over my head, revealing my toned, hairy chest and abs. As she turned and saw me, that look she gave seemed to indicate she thought I was a little more impressive than her usual. Her husband.

The way she took in the corner of her lip, nibbling down on it so seductively as her head tilted to the side. Those bleached blonde waves curled down over her tanned skin, a full length mirror off to the side reflecting that perfect ass back at me.

She took in a deep breath, letting go of her lower lip with a pop as she looked me up and down.

"Do you... have a preference?" she asked, as if she, the beauty queen with the rocking body, was actually nervous about pleasing me!

"We'll start with it from behind," I suggested so help-fully, though really my mind was on that ass of hers, and it seemed the perfect opportunity to grab a hold of those two cheeks and make 'em rock before my eyes. "Y'know, ease into things," I said with a smile as I undid my pants and slowly let my gaze trail over her, up and down.

She was one stunning woman, there was no denying it. Thank god for sterile next door neighbours.

She nodded so obediently. It was going to be the easiest five grand I ever made. It was especially obvious as she tilted her head forward, both hands going up to bring her curls to either side of her shoulders, freeing her back and neck from the stray hairs as she tugged her swimsuit top's string. It fell forward, but she stopped it before it fully revealed her breasts.

Not that she really had to show me the goods. That wasn't part of the deal. I just had to knock her up, but I'd accept this.

Her left hand held up her bikini top, that sparkling diamond ring still prominently on her finger as her right hand went behind her, tugging upon the lower bow. Then there was no stopping it. The white bikini top shrank in upon itself, and her large breasts were revealed.

I knew, instantly, they couldn't have been fake. They were firm, sure, but they still had that trademark teardrop of natural breasts as they rested atop her ribs. All the while as she looked at me nervously.

I would've loved to fake the need for some help, maybe even got her to suck my cock a little to get things going, but once I dropped my jeans and my boxer-briefs with them, there was no hiding the thick, raging erection I was sporting. And judging by the wide-eyed look of surprise on her face, she was impressed to boot.

"Come on," I said to her softly, stepping in close and putting one arm around her to her opposing hip, the other on her arm, letting my fingers brush against the side of her breast just momentarily. Yeah, that supple feel was not fake. "It'll be alright," I said in a husky, reassuring voice.

"Let's... just get this over with," she breathed out, but I could hear the excitement there that she was desperately trying to hide. Maybe she'd told herself one too many times that she wouldn't enjoy it, being fucked and bred by me. To be knocked up by another man, to have someone else in her marital bed.

If she truly was a little princess in this lavish, perfect bedroom, certainly she'd never had such impure thoughts like spreading her legs for her neighbour.

She shimmied away from my grasp as she went to the bed, her fingers working in tandem to undo both sides of her bikini bottoms and letting them fall away.

She had a little trail of hair just above her slit, as if beckoning me downwards, towards that sacred v.

It was a pretty little slit, and I would never undersell it. While her breasts her big and supple, her ass round and firm, her pussy was a sweet little thing with nice, puffy little labia that I just craved to sink my dick in between.

I climbed up onto the bed behind her, reached out, placing one hand casually on her ass to sink my fingers into that cheek under the pretense of getting a grasp. When really all I wanted to do was fondle that award-winning rear.

With my other hand, I took hold of my veiny, throbbing dick and pressed the bulbous, purple crown up against her cunny, slowly pressing myself in against her, moving it in just the slightest little tease up by her clit.

I was surprised by how wet she was. Sure, the idea of fucking a beauty queen was guaranteed to turn me on, but the idea of a beauty queen being turned on by the thought of being fucked by me?

That was the stuff that my teen dreams had been made of.

Her legs spread wider as she looked at the headboard, her spine arched as she pressed in against me. It was hard to control myself when that heated snatch was rubbing up against me, her wetness adding to the precum of my crown.

Her toes brushed against the outside of my calf before she shifted them away, clearly afraid of this becoming something more than just a transaction.

"Just... stick it in," she pleaded with me.

And I obliged.

Sinking into that tight cunt was sheer bliss. The outsides matched the insides when it came to perfect. That slick little canal gripping my hard dick so tight I could've lost my load then and there. I wasn't about to let that happen though. Business it may be, but that'd just be downright embarrassing. And a waste of a good opportunity.

I gave a low, husky moan as I sank in balls deep, and I couldn't even help it. My dick pulsated and throbbed against her, and I had to pause a moment.

"Sorry," I said breathily, "you're just so damn tight."

"It's fine," she gasped, and she even squeezed me, those pussy muscles trying to bring me over the edge as her hips rolled.

God, she wanted me to breed her so bad. Desperate for it, even.

But I wanted to enjoy my first time in her hot body, even knowing that right after work, I'd be back in her again.

Wrapping my hands about her waist and letting my thumbs sink back into her ass cheeks I held her in place as I began to pump my dick into her. The slow, building motions rising as I worked myself up into a powerful thrusting pace.

My heavy balls swung up and smacked against her pubic mound as I began to rock her body, each thrust making those firm cheeks of hers ripple with the impact just a bit. She was utterly stunning, and I couldn't help but marvel at every aspect of her as I prepared to lay claim to her womb with my seed.

It was a connection that wouldn't be easily matched, not even by her husband. Part of me wondered if he got off on it, knowing that I was going to mark her as forever mine, but in the end I didn't care.

Especially not when I had her on my dick, milking it with her tight little pussy and the sweet cunny-lips kissing my hard cock.

I didn't want to drag out the first time too long, get her worried, and it was already a struggle to hold back then. She was the tightest woman I'd ever stuck my dick in, and the rest of her beautiful body didn't help either.

"I'm gonna cum soon," I muttered amid the moans, my cock throbbing inside her as she milked my dick, I just couldn't handle what a slice of perfection she was. I gave her some harder thrusts there as I approached my limit, pounding her forward upon the end of my dick.

"Yes!" she said, flipping her hair as she turned to glance back at me. That one single word was filled with such raw emotion, though. She wasn't viewing it as a simple transaction, I could tell, and instantly knew that next time she'd be much more ready to really have some fun with this.

That realization made it all the sweeter when my dick swelled up and I shot my load right into her fertile womb. She was damn ready, the tests had been done, and she was ovulating. There was no more ripe and fertile woman on the planet and I was dumping my load into her. Thick, heavy spurts of my seed pumping into her, filling her up deep inside as I kept my cock lodged in her pussy.

My hands slid down from her waist to squeeze at her ass tightly, savouring the feel of that firm flesh as my balls emptied all they had right into her.

She made such a soft, sweet coo as the tip of my dick struck against her cervix, pressing that stream into her as far as I could. Her shoulders slumped, her breasts dropped towards the bed as she still writhed against me, clinging to me and letting her hips rise up.

I could tell she was trying to keep her ass in the air, let that cum pour into her.

I gave my dick a few slow pumps to milk the last of my seed out into her depths, just a few final spurts before I had no more to empty into her. I couldn't suppress the deep moan that rolled off my tongue then.

"I'll see you at my office for lunch then," was about all I could manage to say as he slid my dick from her achingly tight little cunt.

She stayed posed upright, though, her ass still in the air, her pussy so red and wanting. Her face contorted and I could tell she wanted more. I'd left her pent up, but that didn't stop me from standing and walking towards my pants, even as her ass swayed back and forth.

If she wanted me to get her off, well, she was going to have to beg for it like a good girl.

Instead she nodded, her face pressed into the pillow.

"Noon?"

"That's right," I said with a smile as I pulled up my jeans and got dressed. "Make sure you get there on time, I've got a meeting right after, and I don't wanna short change you," I said so casually, flashing her a wink and looking more cocky than I felt. Because right then all I wanted to do was go balls deep in her again for another go.

She nodded again, still splayed so lewdly, and I took the time to step back behind her, to look at those spread asscheeks and the rose bud between them, her delicate sex so red with arousal.

I reached down between them, brushing my fingers over her clit. Two digits, sliding up over her wetness and then pressing inwards with such bravado and confidence that it made her wriggle and moan.

"Sorry, you were going to drip," I explained as I pulled my fingers from her once more and wiped them on the bed. "See you then, Marisa."

~

IF I SAID that by ty the time our lunch date arrived, it'd slipped my mind, I'd be lying. As busy as that day got at the office, I couldn't get my mind off the next opportunity to pump a load into that beautiful Marisa.

I'd shed my blazer earlier as I talked on the phone with one of our suppliers, and then the call came in.

"A woman is here to see you sir, says her name is Marisa," came my secretary's voice over the intercom.

"Let her in, she's my business appointment," I instructed. "And hold my calls."

"Yes, sir," she replied and not a moment later Marisa was in my office, shutting the door behind her.

She'd changed into a simple blue dress with a blazer overtop it, black thigh-highs and pumps making her look far more put together than she had that morning. She set aside her purse as she looked back to the door, tucking her sunglasses away.

"Is it safe here?" she asked in that soft, sweet voice. "Maybe we should just go to a motel."

I pressed a button on my desk and she could hear the electronic lock click it shut as I stood up.

"Nah, I don't wanna waste any of our time. Maybe if this doesn't work out, we'll do the motel next time, huh?" I said with a casual smile as I loosened my tie and began to work open my shirt.

"You look good," I added on nice and casual, my gaze sliding up and down her form, appreciating her look as I tugged open my shirt to show my broad chest.

She smiled as her fingers went to the hem of her dress, tugging it upwards over her fine ass and revealing nothing but the thigh-highs beneath it. Her pussy was still so red, as if she'd been rubbing at it furiously all morning, and she smelled so strongly of sex and my seed.

It was intoxicating, and she looked at me nervously once more.

"How should we do this?" she asked. Clearly, she wanted me to be the one calling the shots.

I reached out and patted my hand on my desk, which I'd cleared off in expectation of her.

"Park your pretty ass up here, and face me this time," I said with a smile, stripping my shirt off entirely before I freed myself of my pants and let my dick burst out, thick and hard. Still wasn't gonna be faking a need for some oral stimulation yet, I lamented, but dumping another load in that tight little pussy would be real nice.

She pulled her dress up higher until it rest around her waist and pushed her ass onto my desk. She was going to leave her mark, no doubt about that, as her pretty, wet pussy met the cold wood of my desk.

She shrugged off the blazer and threw it behind her, leaving her shoulders bare, a gemstone resting between her two, large tits.

Her heels hooked into the armrests of the two chairs facing my desk and her hands went behind her, thrusting out her chest as she exposed herself for me.

I moved in towards her, taking hold of my thick, throbbing cock and bringing it to her waiting, wet slit, teasing those puffy red folds a moment. Then I just couldn't help myself.

I reached up, and very casually hooked my finger into her blue dress strap and tugged it down from her shoulder around her arm, then repeated it on the other side, exposing her two thick tits before me.

"Seeing these'll help me give you what you want faster," I explained so calmly, a simple smile on my face as I looked to meet her gaze, then back down to those two glorious tits. Yeah, I wasn't gonna miss my opportunity to stare at those perfect fuckjugs.

Her nipples stiffened as she drew in a breath, her eyes going up towards the ceiling as I looked over her, the way those perfect, tanned breasts rose and fell with her nervous breaths as the scent of her sex swirled in the air.

"I'm ready," she said softly.

And the way she rolled her hips...

Oh yea, she was ready to be my little broodmare.

I grasped her hips and angled my own, sliding my dick into her with a low, rumbling groan of pleasure. She was still so damn tight, even after my first time stretching her open that morning, and I knew this was a woman I'd never have trouble dumping my load in.

I gave a sharp little thrust to bury myself in first off, and it made her tits jiggle before my eyes deliciously. Maybe I should've been more professional about it, but as I began to roll my own hips and rock my cock into her, I reached up and cupped one of her breasts, squeezed that supple mound as I began to fuck her atop my desk.

She didn't seem to mind, though. Her nipple tightened, begging for me to pinch it between my fingers, and she arched her back as I did just that. Those pretty, pink areolas and their hardened peaks responded so eagerly to my touch.

As did her pussy as those muscles tightened around me, still so wet and juicy from earlier. But now, her hips were rolling, and panted breaths peppered the air between us as still she kept her eyes closed, her head slightly upwards.

Maybe she was trying to assuage her guilt by not looking at me, but I knew there was no way her husband could fill her like I was. No way he could do her like I was doing. So I thrust harder, made her feel that thick, pulsating dick of mine as it stabbed in deep and stretched her tight little canal.

"How's a man to resist breeding you?" I muttered aloud, and wasn't even sure what I was saying at that point. It just felt so damn good inside her, and I wanted to draw her mind towards me, and what I was doing to her.

I kneaded her breasts a little more firmly, working that supple flesh so deliciously in my strong grasp. A woman like her was wasted on my neighbour. Though I guessed he'd serve his purpose when I was done knocking her up.

My other hand went from her thigh to the back of her head, making her look at me. Meet my eyes.

Her dark lashes slowly fluttered open, glittering gaze meeting mine as she moaned out lowly. Oh, that sweet, lyrical sound that she couldn't bite back in time.

"He wants this," I reminded her, trying to assuage that guilt. To get my beauty queen to come out of her shell and scream my name.

She gave a brief nod, her eyes fluttering between closed and opened as she swallowed back another moan.

She was too fucking gorgeous for words, and I wanted to make her squeal atop my dick. I thrust harder, pumping my hips as my cock throbbed, that warm, wet little hole so delightful I could cry out. And I did in a way, I let loose such a noisy groan even I started to worry about being overheard.

Though it was just a momentary flicker of a concern, I wanted to bang that beauty queen straight into submissive bliss. And I kept her face locked on mine with one hand, the other groping at her ass cheek with the other.

"You've got a tight lil' pussy like a vice grip," I told her in the most flattering of manners possible for dirty talk.

But she seemed to like it dirty. There were those little tells, like in poker, except obviously a lot more fun to figure out. Like how her chest brushed against mine, or the fact that her breathing held for just that second, emitting a throaty moan into the air.

Or the fact that her gaze held mine completely.

Normally I'd go to the gym and get a quick workout on my lunch breaks, but instead I was gettin' all my exercise knocking up the hottest woman I knew. And I decided to make a show of it. I lifted her up off the desk in my powerful grasp, made her whole body bounce off my dick as I watched her. It did delightful things to those two heavy breasts of hers as well, and I took a moment to look down at them, lick my lips and let her know I was appreciating every little bit of her.

She wrapped those slender arms around my neck, tugging herself towards me, and yet... she didn't squeeze her breasts into my chest. Almost as if she realized I was enjoying staring at them and didn't want to stop me.

There was certainly nothing modest about her actions, and her breathing was picking up. Oh, my neighbour's wife was quickly warming up to having my dick in her.

"You like havin' my dick in you, don't ya?" I asked her brazenly, and I knew I was letting it all get to my head. Fucking the beauty queen next door with the intent of planting a baby in her belly was inflating my ego, but I was eating up every moment of it. The deep, throaty moan I gave testified that I was getting close though and I lowered her back down to my desk, resting her back there as I pounded atop her.

Wouldn't do any good to let some of my spunk go to waste, even if part of me wanted that. To keep this up as long as possible, to keep having an excuse to bang her.

She squeaked a bit, trying to bite down on her lower lip and silence it, but it only half succeeded. Her back arched, revealing that glorious, huge chest to me again, the tits jiggling with each hard thrust.

I reached up and grabbed one of those jiggling mounds, sank my fingers into its supple flesh and enjoyed the delightful feel of it. I wanted to do more, wanted to kiss her, and partly leaned in to do so. But I stopped myself as I felt my dick swell, throbbing excitedly inside her as I barreled towards my finish.

"You want this cum, huh? Want me to knock you up? Beg for it," I told her, even though I knew it was all but guaranteed at that point, just a few moments more…

But she wasted absolutely not even a second, those words tumbling from her lips instantly.

"Cum in me, Perry. Knock me up," she pleaded, her voice so sweet and soft.

I obliged with a deep, chest rumbling groan of pleasure. I plowed my dick deep into her and blew my load so hard, I thought I'd suffer an aneurism. My body shook, my balls tightened, and I dumped such an incredibly thick load of cum into her, even I was amazed. It was my second time that day, after all, and it flooded her cunny, filled her womb where I did my best to deposit it directly.

I shuddered and squeezed her tit nice and tight as I rocked myself into her, milking out that last bit of seed.

"There you go, babe," I said in a deep, gravelly voice.

Her head tilted back, and I swore my secretary had to have heard that. At least discretion wasn't of the utmost, and it gave me kind of a rush.

A lot of a rush.

Especially when she breathed out my name and squeezed my cock so tight, milking me of every last drop.

I gave her a wry smile and slowly rose up. I pulled my dick from her pussy just a little, reaching down beneath my hard abs to grip that shaft and make a show of squeezing out every last drop. Though really it was just another excuse to stare at her gorgeous body, the way it meshed with mine, and how obscenely large my cock looked with that cunt of hers wrapped around it.

I let my fingers lightly tease her clit in a momentary brush as well, just for good measure.

She leaned into me more, chasing that finger, though not forcing the issue as she settled back, reaching for my box of tissues, readying herself to keep every ounce of my cum within her.

"I'll see you tonight next," I said to her with that confident smile. "We'll make the final load of the day nice and special," I added on pointedly.

And that lusty look she gave me...

It's going to be a fun couple of months.

THE FERTILE BEAUTY QUEEN &
MY WIFE

*B*ook Themes:
  Cuckolding, Breeding, Impregnating
Creampies, Oral Sex, and Simultaneous Orgasm
Word Count:
5,680

~

WHEN THE END of the workday came, my mind was still buzzing with the events of the day. Not the deals that'd make me more money at my business, not the talk I had to have with my secretary.

But of how I'd fucked my neighbor's wife twice already that day, dumped two thick loads of cum into her cunt with the intent of knocking her up.

Oh, and that I was due for one more visit with her that night.

First there was the matter of dinner with my wife and kids however, but as I pulled into the driveway I noticed a certain lack of something. The noise of children.

I got out of my car and headed to the front door with just a momentary look in the direction of Marisa and Oliver's place. I have to admit, I wasn't too surprised to see Marisa looking down at me from her window expectantly before disappearing inside.

It brought a grin to my face as I headed on into my own home.

"I'm home honey," I called out. "Where's the kids?" I was already loosening my tie and getting ready to unwind and get changed.

"They've gone to my mom's place," she said from the kitchen. I couldn't see her, but the food she was cooking smelled divine. Honestly, she was always a good cook, but hadn't been putting as much effort into it lately. With the kids being a handful, I didn't hold that against her, but it was a nice surprise regardless.

An even nicer surprise when she came out of the kitchen in nothing more than a white apron. Her dark hair was pulled back and she was wearing flattering makeup, her pale curves mostly hidden but still seductive.

She smiled at me with all the vigor in the world, like she hadn't looked at me in so long.

My wife was no officially declared beauty queen like the one next door, but she was in my books. That's not just love speaking, she was quite the looker, and had I not nabbed her up I'm sure she would've had her pick of rich and successful men.

I let loose a whistle at her appearance as he tugged my tie free and undid the collar of my shirt.

"Damn, I knew I was gonna like what you had for me, but I didn't expect it this much," I said with a cheeky grin, walking up to her slowly as he stripped off my blazer.

She kissed me with such warmth, and I couldn't help but feel that maybe this hook-up with the woman next door hadn't done something to re-ignite my wife's desires as well. Certainly she hadn't touched my cheek in just that way since the honeymoon period wore off.

Sure, we were still in love, and still quite affectionate, even after the kids.

I hadn't even noticed that spark of desire had been missing in her gaze until I caught a glimpse of it then and there.

"I'm making your favourite," she cooed, "but it won't be for another hour or so."

I reached a hand up and cupped one of her breasts through that apron, and it might not have been as firm as the beauty queen Marisa's next door, but it was bigger, and oh so delightfully soft to squeeze and touch.

"Another hour, huh?" I remarked, brow raised as I looked around coyly. "What'll we do for a whole hour, hun? Kids aren't even around," I adopted a smug little grin as I looked her over, and without even realizing it I was licking my lips. As great as it was fucking the woman next door, having my wife know about and getting so turned on by it only made it sweeter.

"Mhm," she purred, thrusting her breast into my hand, her nipple stiffening so enticingly.

"Well," she cooed, fingers working my buttons through the holes casually as her wide eyes went up to mine, her long, dark hair trailing down her back.

"I know we agreed you'd fuck her three times a day. But I thought, maybe..."

For a second I was worried she'd ask me to skip the third trip, and leave Marisa wanting. Instead, what she said absolutely shocked me.

"Maybe I could get you ready."

I couldn't help but grin at her. My wife. The little minx. My dick was already getting stiff between us.

"Well your resume checks out," I remarked, letting her work open my clothes so familiarly. "You've had no trouble gettin' me nice and hard before. Even got two kids to testify to that fact," I remarked, slowly pulling her apron away from her breast so I could fondle that pale, soft flesh of her breast more fully.

She was still so into me, even after ten years of marriage, and she quickly wrenched the apron from my hands, lifting it over her head and leaving herself absolutely bare. She was full figured, with a nice nip in her waist and a full ass. She was a sexy woman that knew just what I liked, and her hands were already working my belt open as soon as the apron was tossed aside.

"I've been thinking about you all day."

I reached down and cupped her breast, lifting that heavy mound up to fondle and squeeze as my other arm reached down over her pubic mound to test her slit. I wanted to see just how damn wet she was for me. And the answer: very fucking wet.

"Oh yeah?" I said, and I would've liked to say the same to her, but who're we kidding here? My wife would see through that in an instant. I'd fucked a beauty queen twice that day and was set to do her a third time. I'm not a saint of monogamous love, we both know that.

Besides, that look in her eyes? She didn't want me to lie to her. It was the truth that had gotten her this worked up. Those dirty thoughts worming their way through her skull, the knowledge that her husband was fucking another woman.

And hell, maybe the money was enough to assuage her guilt over enjoying it as much as she was. But her fingers worked down my zipper and removed my cock from my boxers, and we both knew she could still feel the other woman's stickiness there. Smell it so thick in the air.

Yet still, my wife lowered herself to her knees and brought her mouth to the bottom of my shaft and licked.

I watched her get down before me with such excitement, I couldn't help it. Every time she sucked my cock it was special, this time especially so. It was a special act of submission, not like it was all the times before, where she merely put herself towards my pleasure selflessly, but did so while paying homage to the fact I got to fuck another woman on the side too. It was a more complete submission out of my wife, and I relished it.

"My good girl," I cooed to her, reaching down and stroking her hair with one hand, cupping her cheek with the other.

She moved into that touch with such appreciation, but never did she forget her real reason for being down there. Her lips worked along my excited, throbbing veins and hummed into them, before going full on animalistic against me.

That taste of the other woman must have sent her on a ravenous spell, because she utterly impaled herself on my cock, repressing a gag as her tongue swiped along the underside of my dick and then pulled her way up again to swallow that taste into her stomach.

I couldn't help but groan from that deep treatment, and I rocked my hips, helping nudge my thick cock down her throat a little further. I petted her fondly, adoring that sweet attention she was giving me.

"Oh fuck baby," I moaned out the words, letting my eyes shut after taking an eyeful of her sucking off my dick. "Even after today, you know exactly how to get your man nice and hard for you," I said appreciatively, rocking my cock into her mouth as it throbbed.

The way her head bobbed with such skill. It'd been a while since she last gave me a nice blow job, but she certainly hadn't lost any of her skills. Her form was perfection, and the way her perky ass stuck out behind her was just another treat.

Once again I couldn't restrain those moans, the way she worked my dick, the patter of flesh as my balls struck her chin. It was delightful, and I shuddered all over before reaching down and grasped up a bundle of her long hair and helped use it to guide her mouth quicker.

"I've not had this much fun since I first set to blowing my loads in your cunt and knocking you up," I said in a low, rumbly voice.

It was a risky thing to say to someone's wife, but not mine. She was practically purring against my dick, her legs spreading wider as her arousal grew and her fingers went to play with my sac. Twice I'd cum today, and I was feeling the effects of it, but she was so gentle and loving in her touch.

I knew I should've saved myself for Marisa, but with my wife suckling at my prick so expertly, and seeing her give herself up to me so beautifully submissively, I just didn't wanna hold back.

"Wish I could plant another one in you too," I blurted out as my cock throbbed in her mouth. I don't know what I was thinking, probably not thinking at all. Just acting on pure instinct. And my instinct had me in the mood to breed. The beauty queen next door. My wife. Any lovely woman I could get my dick into, I wanted to breed her.

She rolled my sac between her thumb and index finger, gripping me with just the right amount of firmness as her spit began to run down my length and drip onto my balls. Her tongue reached out further, but she wasn't able to take me in all the way, not without gagging.

My head rolled on back and I let loose such a deep moan. Nobody worked my dick like my wife. Nobody. She was a fucking pro at working those balls with fingers and tongue, and my knees shook from the satisfaction of it.

"C'mere," I said, tugging her mouth off my dick to let its glistening length rest against her face, up over her cheek and nose. "Fuck Marisa, this next load belongs in your pussy," I said down to her.

She pulled herself off me with such reluctance. She loved that taste of my spent cock, her lips fuller from sucking me, but she stood obediently. Always so obedient.

Well, until she spoke again.

"Ever since Marisa and Oliver were over... It made me start thinking and," she leaned upwards, pressing her naked body to my half clothed one. "I haven't taken my pill since."

That news should've bothered me, because I didn't want another kid. Not rationally. But then and there, amid all the heat of breeding my neighbour's wife? I wanted to bust my nut in my wife's womb and make her carry my third child more than anything.

I grasped her tightly, wrapping my one arm around her tightly, then reaching up and squeezing her breast with the other.

"Good," I said nice and hard. "I haven't bred you enough all these years," and I absolutely fucking meant it.

I pulled her along over towards the sofa before I fell back onto its plush surface.

"You gotta earn this load though babe, all the way. Ride me 'til I pop," I commanded her, my dick standing up so damn hard.

And my wifey was so willing as she spread her legs around my waist. She pushed her breasts into my face before she lowered herself, hand pointing my cock right at her dripping pussy. Fuck, she hadn't been this wet for me in months.

Though honestly, I hadn't been this turned on in months either, and I still spread her wide, made her gasp for air after the crown popped through those engorged lips.

The feel of those thick, soft mounds around my face, I could just die happy suffocating in those tits of hers. And the thoughts of how they'd swell with milk again soon just made me rock hard, and want to suckle them all the more. I clamped my lips about one teat and went at it a little more excitedly than I intended, suckling at her nipple as one hand went to her hip and wrapped around to her ass, helping guide her up and down my dick.

She'd already worked me into a frenzy with her blowjob, so the sensation was just divine. I felt electric, each touch creating a shock of pleasure through my body.

She moaned loudly at my sucking, not holding back. She had no reason to, now that the kids were gone, and she was always such a little screamer in the sack. Now it was amped up to the max as her pelvis ground against mine, hips rolling as she tugged my face into her soft tits.

My hands sank into her voluptuous ass cheeks as I devoured her tits, loving the way they jiggled with her motions, her whole body rocking atop mine with such beautifully smooth action. I'd find a fourth load for Marisa, I knew I would. Hell I could probably find a fifth for that beauty queen. But I knew my wife was getting the third. I could already feel my dick throbbing, percolating towards that next hot explosion.

Besides, getting off just before going over to my neighbour's house was a perfect excuse to prolong things with her. Make her really work for that next load of baby makin' seed.

My wife let out such a throaty growl, her cunny quivering about mine as if it somehow knew what was coming, could sense that tensing in my loins.

This was my wife though, not Oliver's, and I slid my one hand around to rub my thumb over her clit. I'd give my wife her orgasm because I wanted her to have one. Marisa would have to beg for hers.

"Cum on my dick baby," I commanded her in a husky tone of voice, strained by my impending climax. "Cum right as I shoot this next load into you and knock your pretty ass up," I told her, swirling my digit about her sensitive clit again and again in perfectly practiced precision.

I knew her body almost as well as I knew my own and responded with just the perfect tempo and pressure to topple her over the edge with a scream that threatened to pop my eardrums. Her cunt clasped around my over sensitive dick, begging that load from me as she slammed her hips down hard.

Our loins were clamped together and I bucked into her, giving a hard groan as I shot my third load of creamy spunk right up into my wife's cunt. Her tense, climaxing body siphoned up that rich seed so perfectly as I grasped hold of her, emptying all I had into her body, kissing and suckling at her thick tits all the while.

I'd knocked her up twice before, yet the notion of doing so again was no less thrilling, and I savoured the moment, every pulse of my dick another extra shot at planting that baby in her belly.

And oh how she screamed for it. My name, her desires, all come out in a spill of words that were barely comprehensible, all the while clinging her tits to my mouth.

She was sopping wet but still squeezed me free of those last few drops, still grinding her hips and begging for punishment.

I couldn't help but shiver with the overwhelming sensations of her clinging pussy about my hard dick, and I slapped her ass nice and hard for it.

"Bad lil' girl," I husked, a grin stretching across my face as I gave her tits another few kisses.

She wrapped her arms around me and there was such affection and desire in her actions, her lips pressed to the crown of my head.

"I love you," she said softly, those words holding such emotion and tenderness.

I smiled at that declaration, couldn't help it. I always did when she said that. Even after ten years.

I gave her body a tight squeeze, a warm embrace, and kissed her back and said it in return.

"I love you," but I knew I still had one more woman to teach a bit of submission to yet that night.

OUR FINAL MEETING of the day was right before bed, nice and late, so I had time to let supper settle. Marisa's husband was long gone again, giving us time to meet up, and I made my way over.

I dressed up a little nicer this time than I had in the morning, a nice button up shirt, with the collar done down nice and low to compensate. A fine pair of pants to go with it. The other two times were warmups, but this time? I knew I'd have Marisa eating out of my hand, and I went up to her door ready to make the evening special.

She was waiting for me. Oh, that little hop-skip of my heart in joy as she opened the door almost as soon as my knuckles had hit it.

She, too, had gone all out for our last tryst of the day. Her blonde hair was tugged back off her shoulders into a low ponytail, her makeup gone, but I barely noticed any of that.

Not with that sexy black negligee that showed off her tits through the transparent lace. It barely even covered her ass, and her long legs were so deliciously bare. Her tanned skin was still warm from the day as I brought my large hand to her bicep, and she smiled at the contact.

"Come in," she said softly as she stepped out of the way of the door, closing it behind me.

I didn't let that contact break for more than a moment, I came on in like she was mine, and slipped my arm around her waist, pulling her in closer to me as I stroked her side, along that narrow waist and down over her hip and skirting her rear.

"Been lookin' forward to this?" I asked her, a confident smile on my lips as I reached a hand up and lightly brushed the backs of my knuckles over her breast atop her negligee.

She'd been shy the first time, as I took her in her marital bed.

She was louder the second time, in my office.

By this third time, I had her figured out and already eating out of my hand as she nodded enthusiastically, pressing her large tit into my palm so needily.

"Upstairs?" she asked softly. She was never big on talking, more relying on the drop dead looks to get through life. She hadn't been made a beauty queen for nothing, after all.

I smiled unevenly and took one step back to look her over from head to toe, giving a slow nod of approval

"Yeah, let's mark that bed nice and good with the scent of our fucking, huh?" I said and reached my hand to her ass, giving it a pat and a squeeze before guiding her to her own stairs and only then nudging her forward by her rear.

She outwardly bristled at the comment, at my brazenness, but that certainly didn't cause her to stop or reconsider. I could see that flush to her perfect, tanned skin, and knew she wanted it. By the time I was done with her, she'd not be able to sleep, waiting for tomorrow.

As we climbed the stairs together I had my hand upon her ass, my fingers curling in beneath her nightgown to touch her bare cheeks, and then slide on in between her thighs, lightly teasing her puffy cunny lips. I was getting out of control, I realized, feeling like a damn king with two women at my beck and call, eager for me to knock them up.

"Tell you what," I said as we got to her bedroom. "Third time today, how about you get on your knees and help me out a lil' to get us started, huh?" I said so confidently, inwardly grateful that my wife had managed to tame my instant hardon.

Marisa tilted her head at me, blonde waves cascading down over her tanned shoulder. I knew how wet she was, though. My fingers were already heated with her juices, and she looked down over my body.

I could see the wheels turning behind her eyes, considering... what, exactly? What I was asking her to do?

Or if she should do it?

She licked her lips, though, moving and guiding me to the bench at the foot of her bed, probably some hope chest beneath the pure, white fabric.

"I haven't done this in a while," she admitted as she settled between my knees, her wide eyes up at me.

Hubby didn't get the full treatment, but no matter; she'd learn to get real good on me.

"Don't worry about it," I told her, reaching out and stroking her hair, caressing her smooth, perfect cheek. "I'll give you all the practice you could need," I said as I let her open my fly, reach in and wrap her hand about my cock.

Truth was, I was already well on the way to getting stiff again, had to fight it a little even.

With a beauty queen in a slutty negligee between my legs, begging me to breed her, it was hard not to be a little hard, even if I was working on setting a new record for myself.

Her nose crinkled and it was no doubt she could smell that lingering scent of sex on my cock, and her tongue poked out at it, curiously. Her motions were soft. Kitten-ish. As if she were afraid of it, her eyes darting up at me nervously as she began licking my member.

My gently stroking hand guided her mouth in, encouraging her to taste the flavour of my wife's cunt upon my dick, still so fresh.

"A little more," I said in a low husk. "I know you wanna be a good girl for me," I said encouragingly, my dick throbbing against her tongue just a little.

That jolt or my words, I couldn't tell which, but it egged her on and she took the flared crown between her full, flush lips and tasted the precum at the tip before moving her head downwards. Maybe it was just her own desires getting the better of her, or the fact that sucking dick was like a bicycle and you never forget once you learn, but it was like once she had my cock fully in her lips, she knew just what to do.

Her head moved down over the shaft, licking all the while as she let out a low little whimper of... distaste? Enjoyment? It was hard to tell.

But I helped push her onwards, my fingers in her hair helping urge her down to suckle at my prick, letting it swell within her mouth, bigger, bigger. The veiny underside filling her up, stretching her jaw wider as my dick reached out for the back of her throat and beyond.

"Good girl," I husked. "Even if you aren't a pro, you're a

natural lil' cock sucker," I said to her approvingly through my deep moans.

She gasped around me, her eyes still holding mine as she retreated from the base of my cock. Her eyes were watering a little, just that nice little sparkle that made her look so excited, her nipples poking out from the lace of her negligee.

Seeing those tell-tale signs of her excitement made it all the sweeter, and I helped myself to reaching down, letting my long fingers slide over the mound of her breast atop her negligee. I felt that stiff nipple, teased it a little as she suckled at the tip of my cock.

"If only I could spare a load for your pretty mouth," I said with a deep moan. "Maybe after your belly's swellin' up with my child, huh?" I said with a cocky wink down to her.

She paused for a second before pulling free of my cock, a spiderweb trail of spittle linking us for a moment before she sucked that between her full lips. She stayed there, so obediently, her face risen towards me as she let me fondle her large, firm breast.

She was waiting for my orders, with that ravenous look upon her face.

My cock throbbed before me, glistening with her saliva, and I stood back up over her, peeling my shirt away, then my pants.

"Stand up," I commanded her, and she did just that so obediently. My hand went up her negligee as I stood there naked, and I fondled her breast beneath it, let my fingers sink into that fleshy mound and knead it. "You want it, don't you?" I asked darkly.

Her flesh was so warm from the sunbathing, her arousal, and that nipple stiffened harder between my fingers as I pinched it briefly before going back to groping the full mound.

She stood for a moment, just letting me help myself to her body before she slowly nodded, inhaling sharply. The smell of her arousal was so thick in the air.

I toyed with her breast, tweaked her nipple just so to make her gasp and whimper.

"Get on the bed, spread your legs," I instructed her in such crisp, commanding tones. "Splay them open wide for me, let me see that pussy," taking command of her was so delicious. I'd not had so much fun since I'd first broken my wife in.

She followed my instructions to the very letter, and for a second I was disappointed. After all, correcting disobedience was its own reward, but something about a hot beauty queen who was submitting to my every command as she cuckolds her husband? To get bred by me?

Well, that was just layers upon layers, and with her pretty pink pussy spread for me, my prize for the evening, I couldn't complain.

I got up onto the bed upon my knees, coming in to loom over her, cock in hand as I slowly pumped its length in front of her, watching her eyes linger upon that rigid shaft. She wanted it so damn bad, I could tell. But that wasn't enough.

"You want it?" I asked her in that tone of voice that suggested I was gonna make her do more than give me some sheepish nod for this one.

And she was so much smarter than she looked.

"Yes," she said, her voice still soft but laced with lust-filled intent, her legs spreading wider as the negligee rose up over her firm thighs.

I moved in closer, pressing one palm to her side as I bent over her, cock still in hand as I brought it down to tease along her slit. Her slick, glossy honey coating my dick as I swirled the crown around her clit.

"Say it like a big girl," I chastised softly, unable to fight my grin as I had my cock at the entrance to her sweet little twat, ready to pierce her depths.

"Yes, sir?" she amended, and I could tell she was fighting off a grin. The way her lips quirked and eyes widened for just a moment as she watched me. Her ass lifted from the bed for only a moment, as she took in a deep breath, holding it high in her chest.

I didn't give it to her though, not yet. I slipped the crown of my head just inside her labia, stretching her that little bit before he pulled back out to tease her clit.

"Beg for my cock," I said, licking my lips, watching her tits rise and fall with her breathing. "If you want my cum, you've gotta beg me, babe," I growled to her.

She chewed in upon the corner of her mouth, gnawing at it for a few moments as she watched me with such frustration and arousal. Her hips pushed closer to mine in that silent pleading, but I was more interested in what came after it.

"I need your cum." She started slow. Giving us what we both wanted and knew she needed. The next words, though...

"I need you to fuck me. Hard."

After already ploughing into her twice today, I knew she must be sore, but nothing about her actions gave that away.

Only the puffy red lips of her little pussy betrayed the very real circumstances.

I rewarded her anyhow; if she was sore, so be it. She wanted to be sore, and I'd make it all the worse.

I slammed my hips down, impaling her upon my cock as it throbbed so thickly. I began to pump my hips nice and hard without hesitation, fucking her as she wanted, making the bed creak as I rut the bimbo in heat.

My newly freed hand slipped back up inside her negligee, where I squeezed her breast, fondled it nice and rough to my heart's content.

Marisa gasped as my pelvis struck her delicate, tender folds, but her legs curled up around my waist, begging me in as her tits rocked with each thrust. There was that moment she regretted it, her face contorted in a silent cry, but then it warped into a moan, her wet pussy still clinging to me so tightly, even after taking such a pounding.

Making her whole body rock with the thrusts of my cock was pure heaven to see. I hammered her so hard, her supple tits jiggled and I delighted in every moment of it. It was so sweet I just couldn't help myself after that, and I lunged in, pressing my mouth to hers, kissing her nice and hard and deep.

Knocking her up as part of our deal was one thing, but something as intimate as a kiss was another. And I went to it with such aggressive enthusiasm, my tongue lashing against hers.

Her mouth welcomed mine rather than resisted, and it was such a sweet mingling of tastes.

She purred softly, her breath hitching upon my tongue as such suckled it. Her body jolted against me with each thrust, her blonde hair fanned around her like a halo.

I became insatiable for her then, that kiss helping bring me over the edge so I hammered her all the harder. Thrust after thrust pounding down into her as I made the bed shake, the house full of the sounds of our fucking.

I felt like I owned her then, and I rose back, our lips popping free as I squeezed her breast and felt out her firm tummy on down to her pubic mound. I wanted to tease her to orgasm, but not without her begging.

"Say you're mine," I commanded her darkly, my hard body rocking as I pumped into her. "Say you're mine and maybe I'll let you cum on my cock."

She was clearly torn and for a second I wondered if I'd pushed her too far, found that limit — and so soon! It was only our first day, after all.

Her lower lip quivered as her eyes darted away, but very quickly did that desperation win out. Her mouth parted, drawing in breath before she met my eyes as she spoke.

"I'm. Yours."

Those two words, so clear and unmistakable, filled with such conviction.

I couldn't help but spread my lips into a big ol' grin, and gave her a nice hard fucking to reward her.

My thumb dipped down to the apex of her slit, finding her clit and beginning to work around it, using all the years of my expertise to stoke that little nub up to a high fire. Despite it being my fourth time that day, and me no longer being a spring chicken, I was getting close, and I wanted to make that lil' beauty queen scream before the night was out.

Our earlier trysts had been burning her body to a white heat, and it took so little for her to start trembling. Those warning signs kept building as her body writhed and whimpered, hips arching towards my hand and taking me in so damn deep as that building pleasure started to silence her mind of any doubts.

It couldn't have been more than a minute before she was violently quaking beneath me, her body arched and filled with electricity as she came, her pussy milking my dick.

That tight little cunny drained me dry as it went over that precipice, it's vice grip milking my cock and making my knees buckle. I fell over her, my dick spasming as it shot its thick load out, filling her depths as I quaked and quivered.

Even though it was my fourth time, I gave her a nice, healthy load of creamy seed, pumped right to the very depths of her cunt, splattered against her womb.

I shuddered and groaned as the last of my essence was pulled out of me and into her.

It was almost a shame to think it'd all be over soon. After all, fucking her raw three times a day? She was probably already knocked up.

But as I squeezed her breast and heard the way it made her moan, I wasn't so certain that her being pregnant would stop either of us.

THE FERTILE BRIDE

$\mathcal{B}$ook Themes: Cheating, Bareback, Creampie, Breeding, and Infidelity
Word Count:
4,231

SHE LOOKED at me with such pleading in her eyes, but I still couldn't understand what I was hearing. I was supposed to be the best man at her wedding, stand next to my two friends as they walked down the aisle.

Yet here was Juliet, pleading with me to knock her up before the ceremony. They'd rented out an entire hotel with her daddy's money, and she'd given me a room in a tucked away corner.

"Please, Blake," she said softly, her warm eyes filled with such love and affection. "I wouldn't ask if it wasn't important to me. You don't even have to like it," she said, but that was a load of bullshit. She'd known I'd been into her for years, ever since we first met, but she'd always chosen other guys over me.

My shock was slowly wearing off, leaving in its place a dirty smirk.

"Will you be wearing your dress?" I asked, and even though she blushed and lowered her eyes, I saw her smile too.

IT WAS a strange set of circumstances, I won't deny that. The hotel was rather busy, all the guests for the wedding bustling about, preparing for the big event itself. I never cared for such things, and if I didn't have special plans I would've just been waiting downstairs in the bar.

However, I had a special, albeit secret, role to play that evening. Juliet wanted a baby, and she wanted it to be mine. Was her husband-to-be sterile? Or did she simply want to make sure her kid had an advantage in me as its father?

I told myself it didn't matter anymore.

I made my way along the corridor, headed back to my cozy little room to await her arrival. I had on my suit for the wedding, since the event was set to start before long.

It was risky, I'll give her that. Guests were everywhere, and though it wouldn't be completely outlandish for her to be visiting her best man on the wedding, it'd be a little strange.

I was only best man because Juliet forced the issue, I knew that. Ken never cared much for me, or my relationship with Juliet, but she and I went way back, so it never mattered to either of us.

I walked into my room, looking over at the rather lavish bed, the flowers that adorned the bench before it. I couldn't be certain, but that felt like a special little touch, just for me. The champagne next to the vanity, the mirror that took up most of the anterior wall, the Jacuzzi in the corner, all made the room seem a little romantic and tawdry at the same time.

I knew we wouldn't be using the Jacuzzi yet, though, and that made me frown a little bit. It would be nice to just relax with her, make her wait...

But more than anything, I wanted to fuck her in her wedding dress and send her down the aisle with my seed on her panties.

The thought made me smile, but not so much as the rapped knuckles upon my door.

I looked over the red comforter, into the large mirror and fixed some of the dark hair that had gotten out of place, and made her wait just a moment longer before I opened the door.

Juliet was radiant. She had brown hair and almond eyes, porcelain skin and a killer smile. She was a beauty, svelte and wealthy beyond reason. But that smile she gave me, the way her perfect, white dress clung to her, pressed her small breasts up and making them look full and lush, she was beyond compare.

"Come in," I urged her, opening the door wide so she could push on pass in that wedding gown of hers. The tresses of which dragged out into the corridor a nice ways. She had to come inside and walk deep into the room before I could shut the door behind her.

"The blushing bride," I said with a gravelly taunt, looking her over as I stepped on up. My own tuxedo rather nice, but simple. That was the luxury of being a guy I suppose, got to keep it simple.

The gown had rhinestones embedded in it, along the corset and down into the tulle, her back bare but for the ribbon lacing, showing off her toned shoulders and arms. She turned to look at me, her lips a pretty red, her eyes looking smoky and fluttering lightly.

"God, you wouldn't believe how hard it is going down the stairwell in this," she said, and I knew she'd avoided the elevator to reduce the risk of being caught. Though in her high heels, I could only imagine. Ken was a tall guy, and Juliet was petite, so she was clearly compensating.

But then, as I approached her, looming over her so tall, I was reminded that Ken wasn't the only one.

"Seems like you must've been pretty hard up for somethin' to make such a trek in that dress… and those heels," I taunted, reaching out, touching my fingertips to her arms, lightly grazing up over the dress and sizing her up appreciatively.

I know time was limited, but I wanted to savour what I had. To play with her. Enjoy the moment.

She went to gnaw on her lip, but instantly stopped herself, remembering the lipstick and flushing a bit more naturally.

"I'm… just sorry I didn't ask you when I first wanted to. Or the second time, or third, or any of the other times after that. But you're the only one I really trust, Blake. You're… the only one I want to mark me like that."

It sounded so primal, the way she said that, especially with the way her eyes smoldered at me, contrasting to the glittering of her necklace and earrings. Her hair was pulled back from her face so I could see those high cheekbones of hers.

She looked like a perfect doll some princess out of a movie or some such. It was rather captivating, I had to confess. I could see the appeal of the big, flamboyant wedding after all. At least as I gazed on Juliet, looking so ravishing and pretty.

"Why did you ask me at all anyhow if you're about to get married?" I said, and not even entirely because I wanted to know the answer, or so I told myself, I just wanted to extend the torture as my hands trailed along her. The backs of my fingertips brushing over her cheek, feeling that porcelain skin.

Her nose crinkled, her eyes up at me and no longer downcast in shame or doubt.

"Isn't it obvious, Blake?" she asked me, and no, it wasn't. Not to me, at the least.

She must have saw my confusion, because she took in a deep breath and ran her finger down over the lapel of my tuxedo.

"No man has stood by me like you have," she said, her voice lowering. "And I want us to be linked forever."

I wasn't sure how to take that. Her words struck a certain chord with me. I'd long been into her, but never thought the feelings were returned. So I found myself looking at her rather wide-eyed and confused for just a moment.

"You're a unique woman," was all I could say, shaking my head in disbelief for a moment. "On your wedding day, you want to link us together... forever? One man not enough?" I said, taunting her just a little, but really, I got it. I did.

"We like different people for different reasons, right?" she said with a little half smirk. "And I couldn't get knocked up before my wedding. What would people say? But... I want you first." She licked over her lips, tasting the sweet strawberry gloss before she pushed her mouth to mine and shared it.

Our tongues intertwined, the two moist muscles entangling, lashing at one another as my arms went around her. I wasn't as careful of her intricate dress as I should have been, I know that. But it was hard to care when finally I was able to unleash my desires for her.

My strong hands roamed over her back, felt her bare skin as my palms went down, down, to cup her pert rear and squeeze. Feeling her supple flesh as I enjoyed the moment, savouring the taste of her lips, the flavour of her kiss.

My cock was already stiffening excitedly, throbbing through my fine black pants as I pulled her into me, crushing the white frills with my eagerness for her.

She didn't protest at me crinkling her elaborate gown, or the way I was touching her so brazenly. This was, after all, her idea. It had just been my suggestion she wear the dress as an added little... what? A fuck you to Ken?

Or just an additional thrill for myself?

It didn't matter. Whatever the reason, it worked and made my dick thick with desire as she made out with me, pressing her sweet little tongue in against mine as if she were starving.

We kissed for so long, and I was just ravenous for her. My hands slowly began to bunch up the dress, gathering up its frilly mass as I so desperately wanted to feel the bare flesh beneath.

My long held dream of fucking Juliet was about to come true, I knew that, I felt no hesitation in her. I just wanted to make good on it, to feel her around me in that carnal manner I'd fantasized about so much.

Our lips broke, moist and glistening.

"I've wanted to fuck you since we were little," I confessed, my voice a little gruff in my excitement.

She made a soft whimper as I spoke, her voice going lusty and filled with honey.

"I didn't know how bad I wanted you until I got engaged."

And the words might have stung, if they didn't sound like they were filled with such primal need. Marrying her wasn't something I wanted so much as just... something more. This. Touching her, feeling her, hands travelling over her body as our mouths intertwined once more.

I gathered up her dress skirts enough to reach in under, to place my hands on her ass cheeks, feel the pert and supple ivory flesh, the edge of her lacy panties, the rim of her stockings beneath. I fondled at her flesh, let my fingers knead and luxuriate in that long lusted-for rear of hers.

"Well... I can give you a special wedding gift for the occasion," I said to her, licking my lips with such excitement as my dick throbbed, pulsating with blood that flooded the thick shaft.

She felt even better than she looked, her skin so soft, her ass so firm.

"I need you too," she breathed out, her voice so low and tinged with lust. "I need you to fill me up with your cum."

She licked over her lips, then pressed them back to mine, deeper and harder this time as she ground into me.

We kissed again for so long, our mouths and tongues enmeshed, my two greedy palms groping and squeezing at her ass cheeks until finally, at long last, I could take no more.

I broke away, breathing heavily as our chests rose and fell rapidly.

"Turn around, bend over the dresser," I commanded her, holding up her dress skirts behind her as I eagerly awaited what was to come. My eyes widening as I got to see her ass once more, so perfectly round and delightful.

We didn't have a lot of time, but I still wanted to make it last, to make it count. She went to the dresser, the mirror reflecting her beautiful face and smudged lipstick as she watched me. She pulled the heavy skirt from my hand, lifting it up and up until it was slung across the low of her back, her pussy hidden behind the white lace, her garter clinging to her thigh.

She was so petite, her body toned and gorgeous, and she wiggled her ass at me a little.

I couldn't help myself, I really couldn't, and maybe I should've felt bad about it, but I smacked her ass cheek, nice and hard. A slap across her pale little rear, leaving an imprint of my hand on her pert cheek as I made it tremble before me.

She squeaked her shock, but honestly, she didn't sound pissed. At least not as pissed as she should have, with the way I was marking her up right before her wedding.

"Damn you're gorgeous, Juliet," I said to her in a low growl, and I reached on down, curling my finger into her panties to tug the lace garment aside. I brushed my digit against her soft little labia before I saw them, that perfect little flower of hers, so delightful and wet. There was nothing I wanted more than to fuck that cunt.

"Blake," she whispered so delicately. "I've wanted you for so long," she confessed, trembling against my hand. "I want you now. I can't wait."

Her words were filled with as much sincerity as lust, and I watched her lick her lips in the mirror.

I wanted nothing more than to slide on in and feel her tight little pussy, but I reached down and rubbed two of my fingers over her slit instead. I savoured the feel of that velvety little snatch, the slick moisture so sticky against my fingers. I revelled in the feel of her dampness, teased her stiff little clit and prodded my fingers into that tight little hole, feeling my dick jump at just how tight she was.

All the while she wriggled and writhed against me, and I was watching her face contort in the mirror. Eyes closed, lips dropped open, a slight flush coming to her cheeks... It was amazing to be able to see that as well as her sweet, swollen pussy as it kissed my fingers.

"Alright," I said at last, sliding my fingers out and suckling the tips, tasting her honey before I began to undo my belt and open my pants, letting that thick, throbbing slab of cock meat spring out and slap against her cheeks.

"Oh God," she whimpered, pressing her hips towards me. She wanted me so bad she could hardly contain in. There was no lying, not with how I could see every expression on her face.

Not to brag, but my dick was big. I mean, real big. And seeing it pressed up against her two pale, pert ass cheeks only made it look all the larger. I ground myself against her, rocking my hips and feeling her two cheeks squeeze about the veiny girth of my shaft, until I couldn't take anymore.

"I need to be inside you," I growled out, sliding down the thick tip between her ass cheeks, until it was nestled far enough down against her puffy little pussy. I didn't wait, though. My patience had run out, and so I merely pushed forward, thrusting my dick down deep into her slick little canal, feeling that narrow cunt stretch wide to accommodate my girth. I pulled that slit of hers taut about my meat as I let loose such a deep, gruff moan.

"Blake!" she cried out loud, her head tilting back as she arched her spine, and I watched her expression change from shock, to lust, to that little tiny wince of pain as I hit too deep. It was sweet perfection, and her slender body took me all in, even though it looked so obscene.

Her tits heaved beneath her wedding gown, her lips parted as she let out little gasps of pleasure.

I savoured every little thing about her for as long as I could, and then I began to tug back. Those tight little cunny lips of hers pulling at me in return, clenching my dick and seeming to haul me back inside her. It made it so hard to resist filling the air with my moans as I bucked my hips and pumped sweet Juliet full of my cock. Again and again I thrust forward, smacking into her pert ass cheeks as I sent her reeling against the dresser.

All the while, watching her face as she moaned my name, filled with such appreciation for my thick dick. It was sweet to be able to watch her like this, and her hips pressed back against mine aggressively.

"I used to," she whimpered, "think of you, when I touched myself in the bath," she confessed.

I rewarded her with such a hard, passionate thrust. I made that lavish wedding gown flounce with each push of my hips. I hammered myself into her nice and deep, marking her mine right there on her wedding day, the two of us making so much noise in that tucked-away room.

"I'd beat it to thoughts of your prissy lil' ass and tits," I growled out to her in return, breathing heavier as I began to build up a tempo, making those cheeks ripple before me with the motions of our fucking.

Her body thrummed at my words, a deep chill of pleasure going through her.

"Oh God..." Her eyes fluttered up, and I could tell she was trying to picture it, to imagine him jerking off to thoughts of her.

"I wanted to tell you," she managed out, her breathing so much harder and her voice lustier. "I wanted you so bad, but I didn't want to fuck up the friendship."

Call it a reward for her confession, or a punishment for her wrong decision, but I hammered into her so hard then. Pounded her up against the dresser, my cock throbbing, swelling up with desire as my head filled with thoughts of her and I, pining for each other. Dick hard, pussy wet, but only now meeting up as they should've so long ago.

"Should've come to me so much sooner," I growled out, looking down, to see the sight of my ruddy cock, bulging with thick veins, pumping in and out, glistening with her slick honey. I couldn't contain my excitement, and the loud slap of my balls to her clit resounded through the room.

She wanted me to knock her up, but I wanted to enjoy this. To take my time, to make her really want to come back for more. My hips rocked, my hand trailing down between her bare shoulder blades. I felt her warm skin out, her body slamming back into mine as she let out a long moan.

God, she sounded so sweet, just like the girl I'd first fallen for.

"Blake!" she cried out, body arching against my touch, her hands barely holding her aloft.

She was groaning and her body pulsing with such heat as her heart raced, and I could see such unleashed pleasure on her expression.

The long years of pining for her — and she for me! — were broiling up at long last, and my hands grasped her hips, fingers and thumbs sinking into her pert flesh before I started to let my hands wander. I reached up, sunk my digits into Juliet's breasts, felt the supple flesh of those pale, milky mounds and luxuriated in them. She was absolutely exquisite.

There was no finer girl out there for me than her, and I had her at last, if only for a moment. I could feel my dick swelling, harder than it'd ever been because I was fucking her, and not some runner-up.

I grunted, moaned out her name as we fucked against the dresser, seeing every heavenly expression upon her face. The way my greedy hands ravenously groped at her tits over her dress.

I thought back to prom, when she and the jock she was

dating at the time had won, the way she'd looked at me with a soft little smile. A smile that had more meaning, now. A smile that hid those feelings so well, made me believe that it would never be me on her arm, never be me in her bed.

And now, here I am, fucking her on her wedding day, raw, so recklessly. She wanted a baby, my baby, and I promised I'd breed her. That I'd pump her full of enough cum that there'd be no question who the daddy is.

She pushed back into me, her mouth opened as she cried out against my touch, everything about her looking less refined and yet somehow more perfect as she rammed her ass into my hips.

I couldn't contain myself, the physical joy of being inside her, of feeling those tight walls cling to my manhood. The emotional joy of knowing that she'd wanted me… of knowing that when I came I'd be planting her first child in her womb.

I moaned aloud, hard and noisily. The room shook with our motions, and I took a final look at her gorgeous face, her stunning tits, then closed my eyes. I could feel all the sensations of that slick canal over my shaft, the thick veins rubbing against her inner walls…

My balls began to tighten and I was barreling towards my climax as I hammered into her, squeezing her hip and breast as I raced towards that precipice.

She could obviously feel I was getting close. I could tell by the way her breathing changed, her moans becoming more prolonged as she ground against me.

My balls slapped against her throbbing clit, and each time it sent a spark through her until the fire finally took, and she screamed. There was no way it couldn't have been heard down the hall with how loudly she cried out, her entire body shivering and trembling.

Her hands wrapped around the edge of the desk harder, trying to hold her up as she rocked and jerked.

Then as her cunny spasmed, clenching me so tight, I let loose a roar of my own, my body following after hers. I pounded my dick into her erratically until at last, I hilted inside her warm, wet depths and I loosed all the creamy seed I'd built up in waiting for that moment. It was the most intense sensation of my life, blowing my virile load into my best friend's fertile pussy. Right on her wedding day.

I gasped and bucked as strand after strand of the thick seed lanced into her depths, filling her womb and making her mine. I'd waited for that moment for so very long, fantasized all about it, but nothing approached the reality of knocking up my best friend on her wedding day.

That sigh of pleasure, there couldn't have been music sweeter than that. She was filled with my seed, and it was bliss for her. Never had I seen her face look more serene and filled with love, affection.

She blinked her eyes back open, a bit surprised to find her reflection staring back at her, before she smiled up at me.

Then she caught sight of the digital clock in the background, looking over her shoulder at it with a gasp.

"The wedding's in fifteen minutes!"

We were in a rush then, and I plucked my still hard cock from her cunt, leaving her to drool my creamy spunk before she tugged her panties back over the moist gash of her pussy, locking it within her. I helped her lower her gown down around her, getting it back into place as she tried to tidy herself up, our fucking leaving her a little disheveled and far from the elaborately put-together princess bride that had entered my room.

"You gotta go," I told her as I did up my pants.

"My parents are going to kill me," she said, but there wasn't an ounce of regret there. She pushed her lips to mind as she pushed some of her brown hair back into her bun, standing up straight. She had a healthy glow to her cheeks, and though her lipstick had completely disappeared, she looked so happy.

Because of me.

~

SEEING her walk up the aisle, drooling my seed down her inner thighs was quite the experience, and I'll never forget it. Though even sweeter than seeing her get married with a cum-filled pussy, was what came later.

A few months after, when her honeymoon was over and she was back to town, we got together. And seeing the swell of her pregnant belly and breasts brought such a smile to my face, even if it shouldn't have surprised me.

And even better was how affectionate she was, how dotingly she touched my legs, how much of a glow she had to her cheeks. She was radiant, and when she tugged my hand towards the bed of the unseemly hotel, wriggling out of her jeans, I knew that I'd be seeing much, much more of Juliet over the months.

Though the sweetest moment of all was when she guided my hand to her swollen belly, let me feel the life within and leaned in to softly whisper in my ear.

"It's yours, for sure," then pulled back, gnawing upon her pink lower lip as her eyes glittered with delight.

THE FERTILE FOREIGN EXCHANGE

*B*ook Themes:
Barely Legal, Breeding, Creampie, and Foreign Exchange Student

Word Count:
4,391

SENDING my son off onto a foreign exchange program had to be the best decision of my life. Though I had no idea when I signed up for it, it'd lead me to the most intensely erotic moments of my life.

Nope, when I said goodbye to my son, I thought it was to have to put up with another terror of a young man, looking to cut loose in his college years in a whole new country. Instead, when the time came to pick up Aren from the airport, I was greeted with the most breathtaking of sights.

It wasn't some scruffy Scandinavian punk coming up to

me, but the most delicate looking of beauties I'd laid eyes upon.

Then there was me, standing there with that sign, speechless as she approached and removed all doubts.

Her smile could melt an iceberg with those rosy lips, and the fairest skin I've ever seen. There wasn't a freckle anywhere to be seen, those blue eyes crystal clear and blonde hair so bright.

I found myself fantasizing about touching it, reaching out and grabbing one of those braided pig tails, but I resisted the urge.

Instead I returned her smile as she pulled her pink suit-case up next to her.

She wore a summer dress even though it was only May, and still admittedly chilly. Her shoulders were bare, the yellow fabric accenting her long legs and nipped waist.

"Are you Mr. Chandler?" she asked in that accented voice of hers.

"That I am," I said a little delayed, dumbstruck by her beauty. "Aren?" I asked, even as I reached out to alleviate the young woman's burden. Hell, she could've been the wrong person entirely and I'd still have helped her heft that suitcase out of the airport, just as an excuse to prolong our encounter.

She nodded, her beautiful face dipped from me for a moment, giving me a chance to look over the large swell of her chest.

When she caught my eye again with her baby blues, I swear she'd caught me, her skin pinkening just a little before she relinquished her suitcase to me, her index finger brushing over my coarser digit.

"I'm looking forward to staying with you," she said finally.

I was doubly unsure of how to respond to that, my

mind so wrapped up in that gorgeous young lady, her pristine skin and seeming sweetness. I lifted her bag and gave her a nod and a bright smile.

"It'll be just the two of us, so you shouldn't have to worry about time for study or getting to know the country," I said, but the only thing my mind was on was how I'd get to spend the next few months with this beauty.

And how I might even be able to accomplish something more than merely spending our time together.

After all, it was the expectation that I'd be spending a lot of time with her, showing her around, teaching her all about America. Driving her wherever she needed to go...

I couldn't help my growing bulge, or my widening grin, as I led her to my car.

THE DRIVE back was a struggle to keep myself in check and to summon up all those skills of casual flirtation, which had atrophied in my time with my ex-wife. But when we got back to my spacious home, I took her on up to the spare bedroom, which had been prepared for her arrival.

"Here you go," I said, pushing open the door, showing her the queen sized bed, the simple yet elegant furniture and drapes. "Had I known I was getting a beautiful young lady to stay with me, I would have made sure it prettier itself to compliment you," I remarked, laying down her suitcase at the foot of the bed.

Her giggle was like music as she padded into the room. She was barefoot, now, her legs not hidden beneath stockings or tights. It was just nude, honest flesh, as she felt the cold, hardwood, beneath her feet.

"It's beautiful!" she said earnestly, her arms going out as she did a spin, revelling in the space.

Yet it gave me a chance to revel in how her skirt flew up, unveiling more of that pristine, milky flesh.

I couldn't help but grin like a fool at that sight, she was stunning, happy, like a cheerful nymph that frolicked about my home, making it feel alive again.

"My room's right across the hall," I said pointing to the other door. "So if ever you need anything during the night, you know where to find me," I explained with a smile, wanting her so badly to disturb me with a very particular kind of nightly need.

"So with that," I said, rubbing my hands together, "you hungry?"

◦

THAT WAS how we started out, and luckily the skies were bright and sunny, so she spent little time studying in the face of asking me to take her out and show her around. Chauffeuring a beautiful young minx like her about was a sweet pleasure.

She was always so meek, so willing to go along with my suggestions. I always wanted to take it a step further, but the sense of wrongness held me back. Sure, she was a beautiful young woman, but she was under my care. A surrogate daughter for a few months that I was supposed to look after and protect.

And with her kindness, it seemed she needed protection. She was always asking for coin to hand to the beggars, for an extra sandwich for our picnics so that she could share with anyone who looked to be in need. They stuck out to her, she said, and didn't find it fair that we could have so much while others had so little.

It all changed, though, when we caught a burglar in the house.

Arriving home to the dark and finding a huge, intimidating man in my house wasn't the sort of thing either of us were expecting after a day at the museum.

By rights that should've been terrifying for me. I didn't own a gun and I wasn't a violent man. But something came over me then, and my instincts as a man to protect sweet Aren took the fore, keeping any fear for myself at bay.

I leapt at the man before his surprise was up, and I managed to grab a hold of him and force him to the floor. Like I said, I'm not a violent man, but I keep fit and in shape, and so I was able to get him down and keep him there despite his struggles. There was little of an altercation, and the burglar managed to only get a few smacks at me before it was done and over with, and I got him pinned securely to wait for the police.

That was the exhausting part, because then the adrenaline wore off, and it was just tedium. But the moment they left, I went to Aren, concern for the sweet young girl ripe in my eyes.

"You alright?" I asked, reaching a hand out to rest upon her bare, milky shoulder.

She had been screaming during the fight, I remembered that much, and she was looking like a wounded little bird, startled and scared as she trembled against me. She'd been so strong in front of the police, but now her eyes watered and she went into my chest with a sob.

I wrapped my arms about her, pulled her delicate frame in against me, holding her soft form to my hard chest. My hands roamed over her back and shoulders, rubbing and trying to comfort her as her smaller body heaved with her upset.

"It's okay," I said to her reassuringly, and in that fatherly kind of manner I kissed the top of her head, felt the brush of that perfect blonde hair against my lips and face. "You're safe with me," I assured her, and she was. I'd kept her safe throughout it all.

She stayed there for some time, allowing me to breathe in her scent, to feel strong and as though I were a pillar of security.

Though I don't think I'd ever forget what happened when she pulled away, her watery eyes up at mine.

"I don't want to sleep alone tonight."

Those words. Whatever they did to me, they summoned forth from me more of that male part of me that strove to be a protector. Someone who looks out for the weaker, and Aren, with those puffy blue eyes, watery from tears, was weak and in need of help then.

I scooped her up in my arms as if she were but a feather-stuffed pillow case, and carried her on upstairs.

Sex wasn't on my mind then when I did that, but when I got to my bedroom, and brought her in to my king sized bed, in that well-appointed room, I laid her out and was struck once more by her beauty. How perfect that pale little delight was.

"You'll sleep with me," I said in a firm, hard voice, a protective — even possessive — edge to my words.

She was still in another of her summer dresses — that seemed to be all she brought for the trip! — her feet bare. It looked almost like a nightgown, and she made no protest or move to change first. Instead, she looked up at me, one leg pulled up at the knee, the other rested against the bed.

Her braids caressed her throat as she nodded.

"Yes, Mr. Chandler," she said in deference to my order.

Maybe what I did next was way out of line, but something in me said that she needed more than that. More than merely being next to me for safety through the night. More than my protection. She needed a man to not only protect, but soothe. To defend her and comfort her.

So I leaned in, and I brushed my hand along her cheek, pushing back one of her braids before I pressed my lips to hers and gave her a tender, loving kiss.

Just as I'd thought, her body didn't startle. Instead it softened, a sigh passing from her lips against mine. Her hand went to my arm, touching me so gently, as if just to have a connection and remind herself of my strength and presence. The way her thumb rubbed along my bicep, how she melted into my kiss...

I couldn't have asked for better.

But as much as I desired her in the nubile flesh, she was in need of me, the comfort a strong, older man could provide. So I did what we both yearned for, and I got down atop her, lowering my broad, masculine frame slowly as we kissed, our lips smacking.

She tasted like honey and heaven, such pristine perfection in every way. Her tongue moist and almost cool compared to my own, I just couldn't help but give a deep, husky groan. My arms swelled with the effort of hefting my weight over top of hers, and she felt the bulge of my bicep.

She was still the meek little darling I'd picked up at the airport, in need of my care, and her fingers squeezed around my arm. She let out a moan into my mouth as her legs spread, making room for me between them.

She was shy, I could tell that much by how she kept trying to hide her eyes, to not let me see the flush of her cheeks, or the way her body was softening to mine.

But where she was soft, I was hard. My muscles were firm, my dick a solid pillar then. All that exhilaration of earlier, of getting to protect this fair young maiden, it had filled me with more desire and virility than I'd felt in my entire life. Even the stiff ones I'd popped as a teen paled by comparison.

I rubbed one hand along her thigh, felt her smooth, creamy flesh as I pushed her sun dress up to her hips. I felt like a god among men then, and she was my Aphrodite. The sounds of our lips softly smacking filled the air, and I couldn't help myself but press my bulge in against her, and roll my hips, grinding my groin against her.

Aren looked up at me with uncertainty for a moment before her eyes fluttered shut and her rosy lips parted. I loved how she felt against me, that sweet, foreign exchange student so nubile and youthful. Her skin was like cream, so soft and delightful as my hands went further and further up her hips.

She was breathing nearly as hard as I was, our heartbeats racing against one another's.

My hands pressed up beneath her dress, felt the waistband of her panties before moving on past to delve up, over her broad hips to her slender waist. She felt like heaven to touch, that was the gods honest truth. I could've gotten lost in just exploring her body for eternity, if I wasn't in such an insatiable mindset thanks to the events of that night.

I'd conquered the enemy in my efforts to protect a woman, and now she was mine. That was the stuff of pure masculinity, like a man always yearns for, but so rarely comes.

"I've never done this," she said in her accented voice, and it gave me a moment of surprise. Though it was quickly countered by how her arms wrapped around my neck, as if she were afraid that'd make me want to leave.

As if I could.

Her legs were already spread for me, my cock hard and throbbing against her clothed pussy, and she felt too sweet to pass up. My testosterone was flooding me, and I ground into her as her lips once more found mine, her tongue lashing against me.

I curled my fingers along her hips, into the waistband of her panties and found myself peeling that garment away from her cunny. The slick dampness of her moistened folds making a wet sound as I tugged the cloth away and slid it on down her legs.

I took one look at that pink little slit and felt my dick throb so hard it risked popping free of my pants on its own. Instead though, I focussed myself, and peeled off my own shirt, tugging it up over my head and shoulders, revealing my broad torso, bulging with muscles across my abs and pecs.

I began to work my belt as I gazed down at her tenderly.

"I'll take care of you," I promised her in a deep husk.

Her pussy was swollen with blood, puffy and bare of hair but for a sweet blonde tuft above the slit. It was so wet, and she didn't shy away from my gaze. She may have been a virgin, but there wasn't shame as I stared at her. I let my eyes trace down her face, over her full lips, her large breasts and down to that heated little slit.

She was gorgeous, and I wanted to see so much more of her. All of her. So as I took off my belt, I looked up at her eyes.

"Take off your dress," I ordered, not unkindly. I smiled to take any bite out of my words, and her hands tentatively reached for the sides of her dress. She shifted into a sitting position, pulling the material up over her flat stomach.

Her skin was perfect, and as she took the dress over her head, unveiling her large breasts, held in place by her white and pink flowered bra, they were even bigger than I'd imagined.

She shifted, the breasts bouncing a little as she looked at me.

I undid my pants and shed myself of them, letting my thick, muscular thighs loose, but then more importantly, I tugged down my boxer-briefs. That thick bulge that drew her eyes soon became the full on sight of my bare cock, the broad shaft tumbling out, ribbed by the ridges of my thick veins.

I reached out as she gaped at my manhood, my powerful hands undoing her bra and peeling it away. I wanted to free those tits of hers, and the moment they fell free, so perky and large, I sank my fingers into them, squeezed and kneaded them, enjoying the supple feel of those perfect mounds of flesh.

Her body was so responsive, nipples prodding into my palm as she moaned.

One of her hands went down, resting between her thighs, teasing over the soft flesh as if she wanted to play with herself. But I was paying far more attention to the one that was reaching out for me, for my cock, curious fingers reaching out to touch it as she shimmied closer to me.

I watched as her slender little digits coiled about my cock, feeling out that thick, veiny instrument as I gave a low, gravelly moan. The heat of my shaft pulsed against her palm, the girth stretching her fingers open wider as I leaned down over her.

I kissed at her breasts, again, then again. I took my time, teased around the edges of her pink areolas before giving a light suckle to her stiff nipple. Only stopped once I'd tugged it back and let it snap into position once more.

She gasped, but her nipple stiffened further, and her hand along her thigh couldn't resist anymore.

I didn't think anything could match the sight of her in

her nude glory, but the fact that her fingers went between her thighs and began stroking at her pussy was sublime. Her hand wrapped around me more firmly, though she didn't quite stroke me. No, she was just feeling me throb against her.

My mouth left her nipple as I pulled back and watched as those fingers played with her wet folds, teasing herself. She struggled to find that little clit of hers, and I brought one of my hands to her wrist. Holding it tightly, I changed where her finger lay, forcing the middle digit right over the throbbing nub.

I watched her face as her mouth dropped open in delight, her moan so much lustier as she ground against her finger. I dove down and collected her nipple in my mouth, tugging on that heavy tit with my teeth, her supple form yielding to me as she let out a loud cry.

She was so close, so very close, but I had all I could take, and I grasped hold of her dainty, feminine body and pulled her down the bed a few inches, to get her before me just perfectly. I lowered myself down, letting the thick, purple crown of my cock glide against that virginal little pussy. I couldn't suppress the deep, throaty moan, my desire too intense even for me then as I rolled my hips forward.

I stretched that sweet girl's hymen around my cock, and I pressed on into her, sinking deeper and deeper into her nubile depths. My gruff, thunderous moan filling the air as I sank my dick into her raw and unprotected. No girl's first time should be spoiled with a condom, and what we were doing was raw, animalistic. It was nature at its core. A strong, older man, looking out for a nubile young woman. We had to play it out like it was meant to.

And her sweet little pained moan was all I needed to know I made the right decision. Her fingers retreated a little as I pierced her, but she was so wet and turned on that the pain faded quickly. Just a pinch before I forced myself in further, taking away her innocence, as her legs wrapped around my hips.

"Ah!" she said with a gentle tremor to her figure, her arms going above her head as my darker body sunk into her pristine, pale form.

She was an unreal beauty, like a goddess carved from white stone. And I fucked her, slowly pumping my hips, stretching her tight little cunny with each pass of my thick, veiny cock. I moaned, revelling in the sensation of her moist, warm pussy stretched taut about my dick, my heavy balls slapping against her ass as I built momentum.

It was her first time, but for me, it was my finest time. I made love to that sweet girl with all the devotion a man could muster. She felt exquisite, and I leaned down to kiss her pouty, ruby lips repeatedly as my hard ass rose and fell with each thrust into her fertile depths.

I was her safety, her security, and she clung to me, understanding that all so well. Her soft, buxom form pressed into my large bed...

I'd never felt better, that sweet little pussy wrapped around my dick, her slickness pulling me in. Her long legs wrapped about my hips, cautiously, uncertainly, but as my large hand went to the side of her thigh and held her there comfortingly, she calmed.

Her wide eyes were still upon me as her mouth met mine, again and again, tongue swirling against mine as she let out the sweetest little groans of delight.

"My sweet little Aren," I said in a deep, gravelly voice, filled with such desire and caring. We'd not known each other long yet by that point, but after just that brief moment downstairs, where we were man and woman at our most primal, I felt a bond with her that boiled deep in my blood.

I groaned loudly, filling the air with my deep, basso voice as I fucked her. Her moist cunny smacking to my groin as I plunged deep, filling her up with each new thrust. All the while, my manhood strained the limits of her taut little pussy with each throb, my pleasure mounting just as I mounted her faster and faster.

She felt heavenly, especially when her hand went between us, touching once more to that hidden bundle of pleasure. She touched against it where I'd shown her and I saw her entire body light up. Her cunny clenched me, begging me in deeper.

I wanted so badly to cum in her. I hadn't had a woman raw in a long time, and I'd forgotten how good that bare sensation was, and as she twitched around me, I thought I might blow, right in her fertile depths, but I held back. For now.

I wanted to see her cum first, right on my cock. To make her feel so good, so that she'd always come back for more. So that the next few months, I could expect to have the prissy woman riding my cock like a pro. I'd teach her to be perfect for me, to take that virgin woman, to fill her with my seed, to breed her and make her mine for all time.

I made her body rock with my thrusts, those thick tits jiggling and swaying atop her chest as I ploughed into her utmost depths, filling her up again and again. It was hypnotic, watching her body move with mine, responding to my motions, my desire.

With a deep, husky moan I felt my dick spurt a little precum into her, and knew I wasn't long for the finale. But I did my best to savour every moment inside her tight little virginal pussy. I grasped a hold of her thigh breast and continued to pump my dick, angling it just right to give her the most stimulation.

"Cum for me Aren," I beckoned to her in a deep husk.

God, just the thought of how she'd feel, cumming on my bare dick, was enough to make me spurt a little bit more. A warning that soon, she'd be bred by me, owned, just as it should be.

She shivered at my words, her fingers rubbing herself more urgently as she began to quake and then there was no holding her back.

Her head tilted towards the pillow as she cried out, her body trembling as her pussy tightened around me. It was milking my cock, and there was no way I could hold back, and so we dove into the forbidden bliss together.

I arched my neck back and let loose a deep, bellowing cry as I felt the fire of sensation travel up my shaft and explode outwards. My thick, virile seed flooded her depths, filling up her nubile womb. I pressed into her deep and hard, jamming the tip of my cock up against her cervix and unleashing all the rich cream I had.

There was nowhere else I could have willed myself to blow my load them. We were man and woman, raw and natural, rutting wild with the need of nature broiling in our veins. I had to fuck her, breed her, and she needed that comfort from it.

I shuddered all over, giving a thrust, then another, quaking from pleasure and desire as I finally lowered my lips to kiss at hers through the final throes of our moment together.

She took all of my seed, her pussy still vibrating against my cock, coaxing more and more fluid from me like the ravenous young woman she was. Her body wanted this more than anything, and she let out a low moan of pure desire.

Her fingers stilled at her clit, the other arm going around me and pulling me in closer.

We embraced, her slender arms about me, my thick,

muscular ones about her. We held each other, cradling one another's form in the afterglow of our love making. I kissed her passionately, all over her, from her lips to her cheeks, down her neck to her shoulders, then back up.

We laid there like that for some time, lost in each other's bodies.

She was sore after her first time however, and she went to sleep eventually, her in my arms, her beautiful blonde head rested upon my chest.

But as I lay there, drifting off into sleep, I couldn't stop my smile, feeling her nude body pressed against mine, and knowing her pretty little cunny was filled with my cream.

THE FERTILE LINGERIE MODEL

*B*ook Themes:
Cuckolding, Breeding, Impregnating Creampies, Cheating, and Oral Sex
Word Count:
5,285

~

I'D WORKED backstage as a stagehand for so long, for many of these lingerie fashion shows, that they were all starting to bleed together. That all of the women just sort of started to look the same, with their fake tans and their long, perfect hair, and the sneer they always had for me as I hammered the set, or fixed up one of the stage props.

I knew most of my buddies thought I had the best job in the world, but being surrounded by supermodels wasn't all it was cracked up to be.

Not until I saw her, crying in the dressing room as everyone else pretended she wasn't there. But I couldn't help that it tugged my heartstrings to see the pretty young woman looking so broken up.

When I went over and knelt before her, asking what's wrong, though, I couldn't believe my ears.

"My husband's sterile!" she whimpered, her hand unfolding and revealing the phone she must have just hung up on. My face fell. I already had two beautiful kids, but they lived with my ex-wife. I'd be devastated, though, if I couldn't have had them, so I understood her pain.

I don't even really remember how the conversation went after that. Not until she asked me if I might help her out.

~

WE MET AT MY PLACE, my bachelor pad. The apartment I took out after my ex-wife and I split up. It was a decent place. After all, I made a good living and needed some-where decent to take my kids for those weekends I had them.

It was in a brick building downtown, with ostensibly two floors. The master bedroom up above, the small guest bedrooms below with the living room and kitchen.

I dressed nice for her visit, or at least as nice as I felt comfortable doing. I wasn't a fancy guy, usually denims and plaid shirts. Hey, I was a workin' guy, alright? But this time, I went for a nice turtleneck black sweater... and dark denims. Okay, it wasn't *that* different.

But I did brush my dark hair, groom my beard and splash on a bit of cologne. Just a tiny hint though. I couldn't stand artificial scents, and so it was just the slightest accent to go along with my natural musk.

When the buzzer to my place went off, I let her on up, and waited for her knock. I was a little nervous. The models had a knack for looking rather intimidating and holier-than-thou. I mean, I was a handsome guy, six foot four, well built and muscular. I took care of myself and I certainly didn't look my age. But I wasn't rich, and I was used to a humble lifestyle.

Beer with friends, and working hard. That sums up most of my life now that my kids are off with my ex-wife.

The knock finally came, and I opened the door. I honestly don't know what I was expecting from the whole thing, but I'll tell you this: I wasn't expecting what came of it all.

She was dressed to the nines, her dark hair pulled back from her face, high cheekbones and smoky eyes batting up at me. She still had on her killer stilettos, her black and silver dress hugging the curves I was already familiar with from the dressing room, and the little leather jacket she wore over her shoulders was quickly stripped away and offered to me as she glanced around.

"This is a cute place," she said, not meaning to sound as condescending as she did, I could tell. I'd wipe that smug grin off her face before long, though. After all, she's the one that needed me in all this.

She then lifted her hand, holding out a brown paper bag to me. "I brought champagne."

I hung her coat up by the door and took the bottle from her, pulling it out of the bag to find a decent bottle of booze. Not the sort of thing I'd buy for myself, but then I didn't even like champagne.

"Looks good," I said with a smile, gesturing her over towards my living room. A black sofa, white sofa-chair, and a coffee table next to the TV and the large windows overlooking the town. "I'll just go poor this up for us," I said, and did just that in the kitchen.

Luckily I carried a couple wine glasses for just such

occasions I might have some special lady come over. A bachelor can't be caught off guard after all.

"You find the place alright?" I asked before emerging, glasses in hand.

"I had my driver bring me," she said with a smile that was part way too smug, but mostly just oblivious to the things she was saying as she accepted the drink. Considering how sullen and sad I'd seen her, I knew she was human, with real emotions. She just worked hard to hide it beneath this veil of pride, if you could call it that.

She sat upon my sofa, her long legs crossed daintily as her high heeled foot bobbed in the air, the muscles in her thighs outlined so beautifully.

I sat myself on down next to her, my arm up on the back of the sofa as I took a sip of the champagne. I didn't care for it much honestly, not at all, but whatever, I drank it down and smiled sympathetically to her.

"It must be tough. Even with what happened between my ex-wife and I, my kids are the most important thing in my life," I said, looking at her and trying not to oggle. "You're a beautiful, successful woman too, you have every reason and right to want to have a child of your own while in the prime of your life."

She let out a bitter laugh.

"Tell that to Tony. He couldn't be more pleased with the news. He thinks I should wait until my career's over in my 30s, but I'm not waiting that long. I'm already 22, and who's to say what's going to happen next?" she asked, rhetorically, as she rolled her eyes. She sipped back the champagne, clearly taking more joy in it than I was.

"So, fuck him."

I didn't know what to say to that exactly, not at first, so I drank more of the champagne and looked her over.

"You're thinking of leaving him then?" I asked lowly,

my voice steady. "If your two views on life don't mesh up on such a big issue as having kids, then... that'll be a rough one to make work." Which was true enough, and I didn't want to question her judgment. I knew that wouldn't go over well with her.

"I don't know," she said, her eye twitching for a moment before she tipped back the rest of her drink, settling the empty glass on the table and reaching over to me, gripping my nice sweater in her fist as she looked at me. "But I know you're going to fuck me, bare, and you're going to leave me dripping in your seed, and I'm going to make him clean me up in the morning."

Her sudden shift took me by surprise. I knew many of the models could be downright domineering, but this? I wasn't expecting it at all. I reached over to lay down my drink and looked at her in shock.

However, I'd be a fucking liar if I said I wasn't turned on by it. By her. And the opportunity to knock up a model.

"Are... are you sure?" was all I managed to stammer out then at that point, but my eyes couldn't help but roam down over her svelte form.

"I'm sure," she said, with not as much bite as she had before, but lacking none of her sincerity, that wicked little smile of hers growing wider. "I've never been more certain of anything."

Maybe it was the lack of sex in my own life for so long, or maybe it was the urge to just have such a ravishing beauty. Or maybe yet, it was the fact that her saucy attitude made me want to take her. Have her. Make her scream and bend to me, as payment for how she and all the other models had treated me.

Whatever the reason, I pulled my sweater off over my head, and flung it to the floor, letting my bare, somewhat hairy chest show. I was packed with muscle, hard bodied and manly, not like the pretty boys most of her model friends knew. I wanted to see her reaction to a real man.

But her shock was perfect. It opened her pretty eyes, made her mouth into an 'o' that I just wanted to press my cock into. But it quickly faded to a more hooded and devious smile as she licked her lips with a purr.

"Well, hello," she said as she brought her hand back to my rock hard chest, her fingers lost in the forest of my hair, tugging on it just a little.

I let her have her way for a while, allowing her slender fingers to rake through my thick forest of hair. Scratch over that hard muscle, feel it all so intimately, and know what a real man was like. But then my patience ran out. I reached out and grasped her hips in my two powerful hands, and turned her towards me.

Her mouth parted, about to object, but I reached down, undid my belt, my trousers, and I made the crass look upon her face fade as I peeled down my pants, and unveiled the massive bulge of my cock through those black cotton boxer-briefs.

There certainly wasn't as much buildup as I'd expected of the princess. I thought that she'd required a bit of convincing, maybe even changed her mind, but she wasn't lying. She was absolutely certain that she wanted to fuck me, raw and without holding anything back.

It was an intense stare she gave that throbbing piece of meat in my boxers, and I swore, she was close to drooling over it.

I reached down again, sliding my rough, worker's hands up her outer thighs toward her hips. I rolled her dress up, exposing her panties beneath, looking her over upon my sofa before I spoke. My voice came out gruff and hard, a real commanding tone.

"How's that, huh? Bigger'n your limp dicked, sterile

boyfriend's?" I taunted her. Tested her. Was she serious about doing this? Part of me didn't think so, and wanted to push her to back out once the realization of what she was doing kicked in. Be a responsible man. Taking a shot at someone's lover had a way of reminding them of how they really felt.

And even though she looked borderline disgusted, I saw some glimmer in her eyes, and she wouldn't take her gaze off my package. She didn't even seem to mind the fact that I could see her underthings, though as a woman who made a living walking down a runway in them, having one guy see her like that mustn't have been a big thing.

"Yea," she admitted, breathless as she licked over her lips. "Yea, it is."

"C'mon," I said to her, my voice gravelly and hard. "Take it out. Get a feel for the thick fuckstick that's gonna breed you," and I was being crass. Vulgar. If she wanted this, she was gonna have to put up with some rough shit. I wasn't gonna sugarcoat it for her.

You don't take it on yourself to abandon your significant other with me if you aren't serious. I don't take that sorta thing lightly.

She reached forward, that delicate little hand fluttering like a bird in flight, uncertain for a moment against the wind before she reached out, grabbing me through the fabric and giving a rub, testing me out before her hand moved up. Fingertips breached the top of my boxers, and she delved into the heat, grabbing my tool and unleashing it to the air.

Her eyes widened and she let out a gasp of delight as she dragged her hand down, looking at my cock and all its meaty glory with a lustful look.

I was a big guy in general, tall, built. But my cock? Yeah, that was the pride and joy of my physical self. It was a monster. A big thick shaft, with a bulbous crown, all well shaped though, like it was cut from stone, my ex-wife said. Too big for some women, and with those heavy nuts swinging below, I packed a hefty wallop of seed. I knocked up my ex-wife without even trying once, and the first time we actually tried she was pregnant that week.

"Like that, huh?" I said, licking my lips as she felt those dainty fingers over my beefy shaft, feeling the jutting veins. "If a kid's what you want, I'll knock you the fuck up with this beast in no time, beautiful."

She liked my compliment. That wasn't like a lot of women, especially a model, and especially one so drop dead gorgeous. She was the type of girl that had to be used to hearing she was beautiful on a constant basis, but oh, she was thrilled at me calling her beautiful.

It was almost funny. Thinking of her being the lucky one, when I was living every guy's dream.

"Only stipulation," I said, drawing it out. "Is that there's no chasing me down for child support, no calling me up in ten years begging for money for the kid's shoes. Once I knock you up?" I said, letting the words hang, "And I will knock you up. That's your responsibility."

She nodded, her eyes never leaving my shaft.

"Oh, yea," she purred. "I agree to that."

All the while she had been fondling my dick, feeling the stiff, meaty shaft, the way it throbbed and filled her grasp. It was a big, meaty organ and having it out, I just felt more confident in general. I mean, hard not to feel like a big, in charge man when you're jutting out a massive cock like mine and blowing the mind of a gorgeous super model.

"Give it a kiss then," I told her roughly. "And beg for some virile cum, like your lil' boy toy'll never be able to give you."

She made the sweetest noise I ever heard, the soft little

pleading and whimpering. She shimmied towards me, still haphazardly dressed as her kittenish tongue prodded out.

She went for the head, first. Bringing her lips right to my tip, to the bit of precum that leaked out, that she could clearly taste the sweet tang. Hey, I liked my fruit, I knew I had to taste pretty good. And the way she cooed was absolutely wonderful.

She even said, "Yum," as she licked it again, her eyes upon me as she kissed and licked.

I was putting on a stoic face, looking down at her with a hard gaze as I kept one hand upon the back of the sofa. But I can't deny that I was moved by her display, my dick throbbing lewdly, my tongue running along my lips as I watched that shaft bulge out beneath her fingers and tongue.

"A little beauty like you belongs on your knees before a real man anyhow," I muttered to her, reaching out my free hand to stroke along her hair. "Not these prissy lil' girly men you always end up."

She probably would've protested, if not for the fact that she'd just taken me fully into her mouth the second I spoke, a low hum trailing through my flesh.

It only took her a second though, before she moved again, rearranging herself so that she was there, rested between my knees and her chest resting on the couch. Her head bobbed down, hand working in tandem with it as she sucked me so desperately.

It'd been a while since I'd gotten a woman to suck my dick off. Not because of a lack of dates or girlfriends even, I've had those. But because the ones I did get this far with were too daunted to even take my dick into their mouths. Too big! They'd always say. Not this little model slut though.

I couldn't help but groan, my eyes almost shutting as I

got lost in the pleasure of that mouth working on my cock. She was young, much younger than me, but she knew how to work a man, even one of my size. My dick spurted precum onto her tongue and down her throat, and I knit my rough fingers through her hair, urging her on. Just to show her who's in charge.

"Knew you could be a good girl if there was some dick and cum in it for you," I growled out.

Her back prickled at that comment, I could tell. I was striking into her, getting underneath her skin, but it didn't stop her. No, if anything, it encouraged her.

Maybe she just needed a nobody to treat her like nothing. Who knew? People were complicated.

But her speed picked up, though it wasn't easy to squeeze that girth into her mouth, but she was a real trooper. Licking and sucking like a champ, even making those little noises I could feel vibrate along my skin.

"Yeah, that's it," I crooned again roughly, watching her bob along my dick again and again. Her long, curly dark hair bouncing around her head as she moved. The scent of my musk filling her nostrils as she would push down my thick shaft to the root, my dick making her throat bulge as I groaned.

"You're gonna have to milk this brute right to the edge," I told her gruffly. "I don't stick this bad boy into a stuck up princess like you until you earn it."

God, I thought I was laying it on pretty thick. I was certain she'd have slugged me for less — much less — but she just kept going, choking herself on my cock. Every time she had to move up for air, she coughed up some thick saliva, further lubricating my shaft.

I let loose a deep moan that set my barrel chest to rumbling, I grasped a hold of her hair after a long while and tugged her off my dick, leaving that big shaft to throb before her, glistening with her saliva which only enhanced how big and perfectly shaped it seemed.

"Gettin' me close," I told her, still holding her hair. "Now suck my nuts," I commanded her, pulling her back in against that cum-laden sac, which was already starting to tense up a little with how close she was getting me to orgasm. "Show me you're worth a load of my seed."

She hesitated, and for a moment I thought that I'd gone too far. She looked at me with more confusion than anger, as if she'd never had to debase herself like that.

But then her hand squeezed my cock and her eyes went to my sac, and I wondered if she'd do it. If this little lingerie model would really suck my balls, all in exchange for me to knock her up.

It felt like a long time before she brought her head in, her tongue licking against the textured flesh, feeling out the strange sensation before pulling away. Her face was already red from sucking my cock, her eyes a bit watery, but she was determined, I'll give her that.

She couldn't fit both of those hefty nuts into her mouth at once, but she tried as much as she dared without risking discomfort to me. Instead though, she ultimately satisfied herself with suckling at one at a time. My dick spurting more precum that ran down its length, and over her dainty little fingers.

"Perfect," I said with a big, hefty sigh that made my broad, hard chest heave. "This is how a beautiful vixen like you belongs. Now come here," I told her, pulling her off my balls again. "Get out of those panties and beg for a real man's cum," I commanded.

With how silent and obedient she'd been, I forgot what a sass mouth she could have, and as she stood up in her high heels, she looked like she was going to say something. The look on my face, though, stopped her. There was that implicit threat that she wasn't going to get what she wanted if she said a word, and so she brought her fingers to the back of her dress, unzipping it.

She tossed it aside, revealing her toned, perfect body. She'd just done a show, so she was at her peak, all lean muscle as she then brought her fingers to the back of her black, lacy bra. It was no strip tease, but her eyes were on me all the while as she unclasped it.

She let it fall away from her natural and incredibly full breasts, the darker nipples hard already as she then pushed down her panties.

She was completely hairless below the neck, her skin softer than I could ever believe as I reached out to grab her thigh with my hard hand.

I took that bit of control by grasping onto her, my dick throbbing before me thickly as I pointedly looked her over. I had a hard look, but I nodded appreciatively and then leaned in, wrapping my lips about one of her nipples and suckling at it, tugging at the sensitive bud roughly. I did it for my own benefit, not hers. Enjoying the moment of suckling at her large, supple breast before I plucked my lips off at her gasp.

"I said beg," I reiterated, standing up, looming over her as I shed the rest of my clothes entirely.

Even in her heels, she couldn't come close to my height, let alone match my broad shoulders and thick arms. I was a brute next to a dainty princess.

But her devious smile was back.

"Okay, big boy," she grinned at me, her hand back in my chest hair. "I want you to knock me up with your super sperm. I want you to shoot your load right into me, every last ounce. Please."

"Good enough, gorgeous," I said after a moment's hesitation, and I grasped her shoulder, forcibly guiding her to bend over my sofa, hands upon the back of it. I got in behind her, and set her high heeled feet apart wide to make room for me, splaying her pussy open as I reached down, cupping that cunt and feeling how wet it was.

The answer? Very fucking wet. Soaking in fact.

"Damn, you are in dire need of some real dick," I said to her, clapping a hand to her ass cheek as I took hold, then grasped the base of my cock as I guided the thick crown up to her slit. I didn't toy then, I gave her exactly what she wanted, and I just impaled her on my dick nice and hard, burying the full length in her with a merciless amount of force that forced her narrow little cunt to stretch taut about a size of dick she'd never taken before.

And oh, how she screamed. It rocked my sofa, the sound reverberating through the air. It was feminine and soft and yet intense, her entire body trying to squirm away from me before she realizes she was able to take it, and instead yielding to pleasure.

"Oh fuck," she called out, not holding anything back, neighbours be damned.

I began to pump my hips, grasping her waist tightly as I fucked that prissy supermodel. I watched for a while as my big, meaty shaft splayed her pussy lips wide, sinking in and out. While beneath, she looked back, seeing the sight of her lower stomach bulge out each time I sank in deep. It was incredible, and she was so damn tight.

"Mmm," I moaned aloud as my hard body crashed against her form. "You could squeeze water out of a rock with this tight lil' cunt of yours," I said, my cock throbbing inside her, and so close to cumming already. Of course, all that preparation she did on her knees, helped.

And she was desperate for it. There were no second guesses, no reluctance about going through with it.

"Fucking cum in me," she commanded, pleaded, begged.

It was all so hard to tell, as it swirled together and rolled off her tongue.

Her heels were digging into my calves, her dainty thighs pressed into my hips, and the idea that I was going to be the one to get this super model pregnant, make her have to take a break from work as her body contorted... that was hot.

The fact that she wanted it so badly?

That was what really did me in.

I would've liked to tease her, make her beg some more, but my dick was tingling with pleasure and I was so damn close to cumming. So instead I just let it go, and my eyes shut, head rolled back and I let loose a deep bellowing moan as I came. That fat cock of mine burying itself inside of her as I shot off such thick, creamy gouts of seed deep into her cunt, filling her womb as I twitched and bucked erratically.

I had so much of that spunk saved up in my balls, and I blew it in her fertile little pussy.

"Just like hubby never could," I groaned aloud, sinking my fingers into her ass and hips so tight.

She screamed with me, as my cock pressed against her cervix, emptying so much cum right within her. I'd be shocked if she wasn't pregnant within the hour, especially as I ground my hips into her, mashing my seed into her as deep as possible.

I stilled for a while, letting my cock throb and spurt the last of its essence into her, until finally my heaving chest still and I slapped my hand to her ass.

"Another before you go," I told her, and I reached down, gathered her up in my two powerful arms and laid her out on the floor upon her back.

I just shoved myself on back into her cum-sodden cunt, and began to pump my hips again. This time with a merciless tempo, thrusting hard, fast, filling her up so completely as I grunted and moaned. I was almost forty, but I was in good shape, and I took care of myself. I'd pound her against the floor until I had another load for her fertile little twat.

She tried to take it without protest, without admitting defeat. She was a hard nut to crack, looking so calm and in control even as she drooled my seed. Even as her face was red and cut off from breath by the overwhelming thrusts of my cock. Even as I asked her to beg. All through it she'd acted so in control.

But after I'd been hammering into her for a while, the facade started to slip away, and I got to see the real her. The one that was desperate for a little pain, to feel a little bit less than.

Her legs relaxed at my side, her eyes fluttering open as her mouth parted, nothing but pleasure left in her gaze.

I took hold of her two slender arms, and pinned them up over her head to the floor. I took absolute control of that gorgeous, supermodel body and I rocked it. Rocked her whole world. Looked across her, watched those thick tits jiggle and bounce, saw my raw, hard dick pound into her again and again as my heavy balls slapped her ass.

I didn't show any mercy, I was going to have her leave my place walking funny and aching from the sweet time we'd spent together.

Her hands balled into fists then relaxed as her head rocked back, little gasps and pants filling the air.

"Yes!" she managed, her entire body rocking, her stomach tightening and her pussy squeezing me. She was desperate for more, even through her hazy mind. I'd pummelled that bit of rebellion right out of her.

She gulped in air as she struggled to wrap her legs

around me once more, begging me in as she whimpered and moaned.

I easily kept her arms locked to the floor with just one hand, while the other went down over her body, felt her two thick tits, sank my fingers into their supple mounds and indulged in their soft, pliant feel. Then went onto tease my thumb around her clit, provoking that little nub as I continued to hammer into her cunt.

"You're gonna cum for me, princess," I growled out.

"Yes!" she shouted again, this time louder, with more passion, as her pelvis lifted towards me. She knew just what she liked, and she wriggled until I was hitting her just so, and then her body began to tense. She was wound so tight, so slick and wet against my cock, it was a miracle that she'd held off on cumming as long as she had.

But almost as soon as my rough finger touched her, her body began that slow coiling up, getting ready.

And then it instantly came crashing down on her, and she screeched so loud I thought my ears would pop, and her cunny squeezed so tight, I could barely piston back in.

The two of us had been fucking for so long, our bodies were coated in a thin sheen of perspiration, her tits and my hard pecs and abs all glistening. But I wasn't tired, and I continued to pound into her, making her squirming, climaxing form rock beneath my hammering dick.

I kept up that intense pressure, working my way slowly up to a second climax. It was a slow build, but watching her squeal and scream underneath my thrusting tool was helping. Oh, it helped so much.

She knocked her head on my floor as she bucked and writhed, and I could tell she was desperate for me to cum again but too weak to even beg. I'd fucked the model to the point of oblivion, and she was left with nothing more than a stupid grin on her face.

Finally, after pounding her little pussy raw, I worked myself up to my second climax. My balls tightened, and I could feel the fire of release travel up my thick shaft as it swelled within her. Until finally... finally...

I hilted into her once more, arched my back and let loose another thick flood of creamy, virile seed. I flooded that young model's cunt with so much of my man milk it could no longer all fit in there with my dick, and I made a mess of her loins.

Finally, I stopped, my dark-haired chest heaving as I looked down at her, exhausted and weary.

And as I stilled, I could see that her smile had changed from that dopey, post-climatic smile to a more serious grin. She lifted her head from the floor, bringing her lips to mine and swiping her tongue along the seam of our mouths.

"Thanks, stud," she purred, though there was still that exhaustion there. I'd gotten the better of her, she just didn't want to admit it. But I could hear the unspoken promise. She'd be back for more.

THE FERTILE PET MAID

Book Themes:

Dominance and Submission, Pet Play, Barely Legal, Virgin, and Breeding

Word Count:

9,102

~

If you told me I'd be working for the very man that put my father out of work, and my whole family into poverty, I'd have called you crazy. But it's funny what a few years and the burden of debt can do to you. I already had to drop out of college to look after my ailing father, and I needed work to keep the lights on.

That was how I ended up working at his office. I mean, one of his offices. He was a big capitalist, owned more companies than I had digits to count 'em on I'm sure! And I was just another 'human resource' in the data entry pool. That is… up until the day he came striding in, looked us all over and let his dark gaze rest upon me.

"You," he said, hooking a finger at me, beckoning me into my manager's office, which he commandeered on the spot for our impromptu meeting.

Oh, how I loathed the man... though his gorgeous, dark good looks made it so hard to keep my anger up as he stood there behind the desk in his black suit and maroon tie, a light neatly trimmed layer of beard hair that was oh so fashionable.

Though really, when was getting called into the boss' office, being singled out, ever a good sign? I mentally went over everything I'd done that day, and I knew I was a good worker. Hell, it wasn't that revenge didn't come to mind once in a while, but I liked to think of myself as above that.

More respectable.

"Yes, sir?" I asked as he shut the door behind me, my hands awkwardly at my sides, brushing the edge of the black dress he insisted we all wear.

It was so rare that I actually saw the man himself, always jet setting around the world on business trips I'm sure. Probably shutting down more factories like my father's, and shipping them off to the third world.

"Interested in a substantial raise?" he asked me, sliding his hands into his pockets as he looked me over. His well-tailored suit did wonders at showing off his cut physique, and so without giving away anything at all I could still imagine the ripped muscles beneath his suit.

That just made me hate him more, though, but in that weird way that wasn't comfortable. How could someone be rich and gorgeous and still be so damned cruel?

It wasn't fair.

It especially wasn't fair how my body responded to the thought of a raise, my blue eyes going to his. I'm sure they were sparkling, and my spine was a lot straighter.

"Yes," I answered. Best keep it simple with a guy like him, right?

He wet his lips, taking his time as he inspected me like another of his possessions.

"My previous maid has retired, I need someone to keep up the maintenance of my condo. It's a full time gig, especially since I'm gone for such long stretches. It'll require moving into the maid suite and being on call 24/7, but your pay will be doubled," he said with such curt efficiency.

My head reeled from the prospect, but before I had a moment to even ponder it, he asked.

"Interested?"

I just stared for a second. He was gone, like, all the time, so why did he even need a maid? And what did he mean being on call 24/7? In case there was an emergency dusting?

Then the second part of his statement finally sunk into my thick skull and I was nodding.

Double pay?

I'd give up my life for that, easily enough.

"Very good," he said and reached into his coat to pull out a small card and slide it across the table to me. "This is my address, and on the back is the time and location of a fitting appointment, for your new uniform. Be there on time. I don't wish to drag this process out any more than necessary," he said in that firm, authoritative voice of his.

New uniform?

Who's even going to see me in his condo?

I ran my fingers through my bleached hair as I reached out for the card, looking it over. "When do I have to move in by?"

Not like the moving part would be that hard. I had to

move around a lot the last three years and pruned almost everything down to the necessities.

"Immediately," he said as he began to walk around the table, studying me. "But you won't start work until your uniform arrives."

He pulled open the door and stood aside, waiting for me to leave.

"What are you waiting for? That fitting appointment is…" he checked his watch, "in just twenty minutes."

Panic sank in then, but I nodded and rushed off.

Ready to start my new life as a domestic servant…

The fitting was not what I was expecting. It wasn't some dreary sort of office-oriented uniform dispensary or something, but rather a swanky, upper scale clothing store. Where the shirts cost more than I made in a year!

It almost made me turn on my heel and run right out until I remembered I wasn't the one paying.

The older gentleman who fitted me was professional, albeit thorough and then… off I went.

I went home, bagged up my things, told my family about the promotion — in as little detail as possible, sticking to the point about 'double pay' — then headed over to his penthouse condo overlooking the city. I wondered if rent was included. It better be, because I wasn't prepared for just how swanky it was.

I was so bowled over by it the vista before me, and the expensive furniture, that I missed the first few things his personal assistant said to me.

"Are you getting all this?" he asked, looking at me, brow raised.

"Sorry, what was that?" I said anxiously, brushing back my hair behind an ear.

"Just follow me," he said impatiently, and led me off to the right and down a round stairwell. He took me down to another level — there were apparently at least three! — and led me to a secluded section. My residence, it seemed.

"Here's your room," he said, pushing open the door giving me a brief glimpse of the lovely but sparse area before he moved onto the next door. "Bathroom," he indicated, then last, "kitchen and living area. There's room for guests, but you can't have any. Got that?" he said, but didn't wait for the answer. "Good."

No guests? That was odd.

I arched my brow, but he didn't look like the kind of guy that wanted to deal with any of my questions. He was probably too busy handling all of my boss' bullshit.

I looked over the room again, though, and felt a strange sense of emptiness. It wasn't what I'd expected, after seeing such a luxurious place, but I supposed servant's quarters were never as nice as the Master's.

"How does he like things done? Can I speak to the last maid?"

"No," he said firmly, staring at me through his round glasses, the stick-thin man so severe looking he seemed to rival my boss, but without any of the good looks. "She's moved back with her family and is not to be disturbed. If there are no more questions, you can relax in your new suite for the time being. Once your uniforms arrive, you'll be expected to start cleaning up. Fetching groceries will also be your duty, you'll find the list on the tablet in your closet. Make sure you do regular inventory checks on what's in the kitchen. Understood?"

It was really, really hard not to roll my eyes.

Instead I smiled as I grit my teeth, trying to look pleasant.

"I never got your name," I said brightly.

"Martin," he said in a clipped tone of voice turning back around and leaving me there. "Good luck," was all he said as he climbed those stairs briskly and vanished. Leaving me all alone in the spacious penthouse.

I unpacked my things, which didn't take as long as I expected, and then settled in for a long wait. Luckily, my living area came with just about every form of entertainment I could hope for, the smart TV had access to every streaming service imaginable, with a private computer desk, my own tablet and an expensive phone to boot! All with pre-made accounts intended just for me, with a sticky note that detailed my password and security details.

Though I didn't get long to relax, before a jarring buzz filled the air around me, and my new devices alerted me that it was someone at the front door. By the looks of the security feed that came through my tablet, it was a parcel delivery.

I rushed on up to the door, since it was apparently my responsibility, and answered.

"Hello!" I said a little breathless, having climbed the stairs more enthusiastically than I intended.

"Here's the clothing items Mr. Romy ordered," he said, then held out a digital signing device. "Just jot your name here, ma'am," the young fellow said before the transaction was quickly done.

And I was left alone again.

I took the package to my room and opened it. What lay

inside shocked me! Oh, it was a uniform alright, several of them in fact. But…

I stared, and I knew my jaw was dropped, but I couldn't help it. I felt embarrassed just looking at the package and I quickly shut the top of the box again.

There had to be a mistake. The black dresses that ended just below my ass was one thing. I mean, he had a kink, obviously, but with a guy that rich how couldn't he fetishize the power he had over people? Making them dress and act and talk like he wanted, as if we were all little puppets.

But these outfits wouldn't even give me that much coverage!

I walked away from them, fuming! My brain working wildly as I tried to come to terms with what I'd signed on for. Maybe it wasn't too late to go back to the office… though the more I thought of him, the less I figured he'd put up with one of his peons changing her mind.

I wasn't sure how much time passed with me on the couch, glancing back to my room where the outfits waited, but eventually my phone and tablet both warned me: the boss was due back in an hour, and it was expected I'd be there to greet him. For inspection.

A shiver ran through me, of disgust and… secretly, a little titillation.

Though the idea of getting dressed up in some skimpy maid outfit for the guy who fired my dad and put us all in the hole overwhelmed all else. I was thinking what I'd say to the man, about his nerve! When a call came in, it was Martin.

"Has the package arrived yet?" he asked crisply, no pleasantries.

"Uh, yes, but—"

"Good. I'd suggest you get dressed and get ready.

581

There's several versions there, for different occasions. One for wearing in your leisure time, in case you get called to duty abruptly. It's similar to the usual uniform, but more comfortable, relaxed," he said with such calm, casual certainty.

"Wait... I don't think I can wear *any of this*," I said, cutting him off.

Silence took over for a while.

"You'd best get over that quickly, miss," he said to me. "If you wish to keep your job, I suggest you stuff your qualms in a sack. Otherwise, get out immediately and I'll let him know he needs a replacement."

I went over to the box again, looking at them and feeling my hands tremble.

Not only would I be out my new job, but I wouldn't even have another job to go back to. And let me tell you, if anyone in town was hiring except the guy who fired my dad? I'd already be working there.

"I'll do it," I said softly, a sigh upon my voice. Though Martin had hung up almost immediately upon my acceptance. It was clear I wouldn't get a lot of sympathy from him. He was probably too busy busting his ass for Mr. Romy to care about anyone else.

I squeezed myself into that outfit, just as I was ordered to. Though the stockings, heels and ridiculously-short miniskirt were a challenge, it was the top that snugly hugged my bosoms and made my cleavage bulge out that really was the toughest part. But I suffered it, because I had to, and made my way up to wait by the door for Mr. Romy's arrival.

He came home himself that evening, looking as handsome and hard-nosed as ever. His gaze went to me immediately, and he shut the door behind him as he let his briefcase thunk to the floor.

"Very nice," he said in a gravelly voice, and for once I actually heard what approval sounded like from my boss.

But I just felt like running and hiding. I looked at the briefcase and wondered if I was supposed to bring that in. The job didn't really come with a list of duties other than the few that I'd been told, but more than that, rich guys always wanted their staff to be mind readers.

I shifted in my heels, my hands clasped behind my back. I thought it'd make me look professional but instead it just made my chest stick out more.

"Thank you, Sir."

He took his time sizing me up, but he kept such a calm, cool aura about him all the while, somehow avoiding the disposition of a letch like I was more used to dealing with.

"I approve. You'll get your raise, Miss Tish," he said to me, pushing his shoulders back and looking at me expectantly. "Well?" he asked.

I blanked.

"Excuse me, sir?" I said, and that made him furrow his brow in irritation.

"Didn't you study your new duties?" he asked. "On your tablet?" and I suddenly turned blood red, realizing I must've missed some other things. "Surely Martin told you," he said.

He didn't, I didn't think, but I stared up at him blankly.

"Grocery shopping. Taking an inventory. No guests..." I trailed off, trying to think of what else Martin had told me.

His brows furrowed and he looked irritated.

"Take my briefcase to my office, set the table for supper and await further instructions," he commanded me firmly. "After tonight, I'll expect you to go over the details in the tablet, understood?"

It was less a question like when Martin said that word, and more of a command itself.

My cheeks went hot and I grabbed for the briefcase, my knees trembling a little as I went up the few stairs into the main area, going towards where I figured his office was. I regretted not looking around more earlier, but it felt strange, being in someone else's house all by myself.

It took me longer than I'd hoped just to find the office, what with how big his place was! But at last, the spacious room was in my sights and I laid his case upon his hard-wood desk, taking but a moment to admire the very old-fashioned style of the decor as compared to the more modern look of the rest of his place.

I came out then, rushing to the table, when I found him doing something I'd never thought I'd see: cooking.

There he was, tie and jacket gone, sleeves rolled up to his elbows, working at the stove with such intense focus.

I'd just assumed he had someone to do that as well.

And secretly I was grateful that wasn't another one of my tasks.

I stood for a moment, my head cocked to the side as I drank the sight in. He looked good, and it was nice to see him, without being seen. To study him and let my eyes roam over his hair, his trim figure, the way his forearms bulged from out beneath his dress shirt.

I had to keep my head clear, though. But honestly, it was hard. I was dressed up like some tramp, and you'd have to be someone way more moral than me not to feel exposed and a little turned on. You can't dress up like you would in the bedroom and not feel a bit of that bedroom allure.

I licked my lips and was so aware of the sensation before I pushed it aside. I hated this man. I hated that he dressed me up like a doll.

I just had to keep reminding myself of that.

I walked into the kitchen, looking at the cabinets.

"Place setting for one, Sir?"

"Yes," he said, absent-mindedly, paying me only a tiny morsel of his attention as he focussed himself upon his cooking. The frying pan sizzling as he set to work on whatever culinary creation he had in mind.

Finding the things I needed to set the table was the most troublesome part, but once I was done... I wasn't quite sure what came next. I stood there, a little awkward and confused until his voice came out of the kitchen.

"Grab a bottle of wine from the rack, the one on top," he instructed, not burdening me with the fancy names and boring dates of his wine collection.

When at last it was all done though, he came to the table with his food as I stood there. Not sure what to do with myself as I imitated a living statue.

Though as he began to eat, his eyes would drift to me again now and then.

"Do you have experience in those kind of heels?" he asked me out of the blue, in between bites of his stir fry.

Was I trembling that much? I thought I had it under control.

Honestly, it wasn't the heels that were bothering me so much, though they were way higher than I anticipated. But it was everything else. Nerves.

I brushed my hand over my stomach, smoothing out the fabric though just for an excuse to hide my eyes from him.

"I'll get used to them, Sir. I promise," I raised my eyes, hoping I looked resolute.

He laid down his fork, and wiped his mouth, gesturing to me.

"Stand closer to me," he instructed firmly.

I did as he told me, but it put me within an awkwardly

close distance of him, right up against my towering boss almost.

"This isn't an easy job," he said to me, looking up over my body before resting his gaze upon my face once more. "But the rewards will scale with your effort. Doubling your pay will just be the start, as long as you're willing to put in the commitment," he said smoothly, his voice losing some of that edge. But only a little.

"How does that sound to you?" he asked.

"I've always worked hard," I managed, though I had to wonder why my voice sounded so weak. I swallowed, licking my plush lips and tried to be more confident. "I'm sure I won't let you down."

Though honestly, I had no idea what I was agreeing to. But I needed the money, and if I needed to dress in a skimpy costume to earn it, I'd do it.

He raised his one arm up, and placed his hand upon my lower back, rubbing there... and brushing against the round swell of my rear.

"I knew I had a good feeling about you," he said, touching me so brazenly, feeling my flesh through the thin silk and lace fabric of my uniform. "You'll adapt in no time, I'm sure. Now," he said, continuing to talk before I could object, "are you hungry?"

There he speared his fork through a piece of chicken and broccoli, looking at me with a brow raised in anticipation of my answer.

My stomach being up with my chest, both of them tight with nervousness, made me want to say no.

But Mr. Romy wasn't the type of guy that wanted me to say no.

I instead nodded, my head spinning as I looked at that bit of offered food. It really did smell and look divine, but I was too worried about the precariousness of my situation.

And of what he really wanted.

I wish I'd looked through that list of duties to see if 'let me grab your ass' was on it somewhere.

"On your knees then," he said so firmly, so matter-of-factly. I was a little dazed, but his strong hand upon me guided me down, and I knelt beside his seat as I was ordered. His cruel disposition had vanished, or rather shifted, he was commanding still, but it had a different air to it then...

"Part those luscious lips," he instructed, and I felt like a fool as I obeyed, and he very slowly offered me the food, placing it upon my tongue for me, leaving me to pull it from the fork.

"Good girl," he husked in approval.

What the fuck was happening in my life?

My mind was spinning, and I had to close my eyes as I chewed. I knew this wasn't right. I mean, I knew he wanted to play puppet master, but this was a whole other level.

Part of me wanted to just get off the floor and run home, find something else. Anything else had to be better and less degrading than being fed off my boss' fork, kneeling on the floor at his side.

So why did I stay put? And why wouldn't my body do what I wanted it to?

That cruel man who held my fate — and that of my families — in his hand, speared another forkful of food and fed it to me in turn. His hand stroking over my back, as if I were some dear pet and not a grown woman and employee.

"There you go. It's nice to have some pleasant company for dinner for a change," he said, smiling wryly as he continued the bizarre, demeaning ritual.

I shifted, my knees digging into the marble tile of his condo, my body trembling in barely suppressed rage, laced with desire. I was making myself sick, honestly. What type of person could even think of how great his thighs looked beneath his pants, or how strong his hand felt as it tenderly caressed my body?

I definitely should not be thinking that.

I should be thinking about getting the fuck out of here. No wonder his last maid quit.

So why wasn't I moving? Why was I just staying?

Because this isn't bad.

Shut up, subconscious.

I looked up at him, a furrow in my brows as I swallowed the latest bit of food.

His steady hand continued the ritualized feeding, while I watched his handsome, stern face contort to one of pleasure and amusement.

"You're a very good girl," he said in a breathy murmur. "I have a feeling you shall exceed in this new position of yours." With that, he laid down the fork, the meal at an end as he smiled at me. "Now, clean up," he said, in an almost patronly tone of voice.

Part of me was relieved, mainly the knees, because the floor was so hard! But I got up, took his dirty dishes and brought them away from the dining table in front of that massive window into the kitchen.

When I returned, he was gone, however. And I saw nor heard no sign of him the rest of that night.

My first night with my boss was so bizarre, but after that I had the time to read over the instructions in full. Martin had neglected to tell me about it, but the tablet contained an extensively detailed list of everything required of me, from taking his briefcase and placing it on his desk, to how I should arise early to set out some eggs on Sunday and Thursday mornings, to prepare for him to cook with.

Why they had to be set out early on those days, I couldn't fathom that night.

But the coming morning, a Thursday, I got to see what he did with it at least.

There was no mention of him feeding me, or him touching me upon the list at all, but when he served up his home made waffles for breakfast, it became clear that little event was to happen on repeat.

"Come here," he said as he sat there with the morning light shining upon him and his dark hair. And by his tone of voice, I could tell... he wanted more than for me to merely come closer. "I bet you're hungry," he said, as I looked down on the thick waffles, sprinkled with colourful fruit.

I had to admit, they smelled and looked divine.

I'd spent all night thinking about what I was going to do. Half of me just wanted to tell him to stick his job up his ass.

Then I thought: hey, if I wanted some revenge, knowing these weird little things could only help, right? A weird, sexual scandal could really hurt him, I reasoned with myself.

Funny how elated and relieved I felt when I decided that. Revenge was a dish best served cold, not with a strange tingle between my thighs.

But I knelt at his side without needing to be told, biting in on the corner of my plump lower lip.

"I am, Sir," I said like the obedient lap dog I apparently was.

"Good," he said, and he served me up a neatly pre-cut square of waffle with fruit and syrup, feeding me once more as he pet my hair this time. Luxuriating in the long, blonde strands.

"You can claim the satin cushion from my office for this from now on. No need to risk bruising your precious little knees," he said, half-amused, but half pleasant, as if some part of him wanted to be nice to me despite how cruel his nature was.

This was weird. I knew it was weird.

My mind must have been fucked up, because he was doing messed up things to my body and brain. I swallowed, and it tasted so good.

But his hand felt better.

As the meal went on, a tiny bit of syrup spilled from a bite of waffle onto my chin, and he took up his fancy napkin and gently dabbed it away.

"Hold still," he cautioned as he cleaned me up, removing all trace of that sweet syrup. "Very good girl," he remarked with a smile, a certain glint in his eyes that made me both worried and pleased.

That was how our days went for a while, me setting up his things, cleaning up his home — though little actual cleaning was necessary since he lived alone! — and then kneeling upon a satin cushion at his feet as he fed me for each meal he was home. He bizarrely never made any move to push things further, just his strong hand stroking my hair and my back, on down to my rear.

I just chalked it up to some weird power play. He just liked feeling in control.

I had no idea how to deal with it all, I was lost. My feelings were in turmoil and I nearly stormed off several times, until the end of the week... when I saw my pay deposit.

Not only did he pay me double as he'd said, but he'd tripled it. And I was paid not only for the typical work hours, but every hour I spent at his place. If I put up with his strange behaviour for just a while, I could quit and leave a wealthy woman, I told myself!

Though as time went on, it became clear, he had no guests, not even his assistant would come by. It was just him and I. I grew so used to the quiet and loneliness, that I was cleaning his room one day and became completely startled by his presence!

There he was, sat down on the balcony, bottle of wine beside him as he stared off out over the city scape.

I gasped — and maybe even squealed a little — and he calmly spoke to me.

"Bring me a bowl of fruit, Miss Tish," he said.

"Sorry S-Sir! Right away Sir," I said, and I hustled off, the ruffled plaits of my skirt bobbing as I went downstairs to get him that.

When I returned, he was just as I left him, and I placed the fruit before him.

"Sorry Sir, I had no idea you were home," I explained about my earlier fright, and he looked at me, studying me quietly.

"Getting used to the quiet, are you?" he asked in his gravelly voice.

"I suppose," I said, though honestly, I never quite got used to it. Just expected it. Even when he was home, he wasn't a big talker.

It was hard to hate a man that looked as good as he did and played things so close to his vest.

I stood just a few feet from him, the warm summer

breeze loosening my hair from its barrette. Blonde tresses tickled my cheek and I swept them behind my ear.

"Are you feeling well?" I asked.

He looked out over the city and only glanced back at me, not answering my question, at least not right away. The pause lingered a while, and I wet my lips anxiously.

"What's on your mind?" he asked me.

I reached across my stomach, suddenly feeling uncertain. What was on my mind? I felt like I'd disconnected, become so invested in just work and money and...

And desiring those soft strokes of affection, and his kind words.

I looked out at the city and shrugged my shoulders before looking back at him.

"Just concerned by the... break in routine, I guess."

I'd had no contact with anyone but him all week, and it was starting to take its toll, truth be told. But I didn't want to let him know that.

"Is that all?" he asked, brow raised in that questioning way that made me want to spill every secret I ever held to him.

It got me to confess to something I never meant to.

"Do you... do you intend me to do... y'know," I said.

"What?" he asked pointedly, plucking a grape from the bowl and feeding it to me, touching his thumb to my plush lower lip in the process. I chewed and took my time before answering.

"Sexual... things," I said, my cheeks burning blood red.

"Is that what's on your mind?" he asked, looking not amused nor even upset, just... unfazed by it all. "Would you like that then, hmm?" he asked, and he let his free hand trail low, grasping my round rear through my skirt rather pointedly.

I swear, I was on fire. My skin felt so hot, and my heart was racing.

What'd I just say?

I couldn't look at him, because I did. Because I fucking did, and that was a horrible thing for me to want. It wasn't even about revenge.

It wasn't even the fact that I hadn't had a boyfriend in ages.

It was about all the things I was afraid to admit in myself. That I liked it.

"I..."

I couldn't speak, or eek out more than that one word, that one letter.

"It's okay if it is," he said with that handsome smile of his plastered across his chiselled face, his hand giving my rear a firm squeeze. "But no, I wasn't intending to take such liberties with you... beyond the pleasure of viewing your shapely form," he said, his smile evolving into a wry smirk.

Come on, Tish. This couldn't be your idea.

The things he was making you do!

So why did I believe him? And why was I the one that brought it up?

I fluttered my eyes, and was so aware of his hand on me. I hated this man, I told myself over and over again. He'd cost me so much.

He was arrogant and strange.

But I was drawn to him.

His strong hand wandered low, and I felt vulnerable... like I'd give into him and his cruel charms at any second. But then something popped out of my mouth, some way to deflect that I both instantly regretted and felt grateful for.

"Is this how things were with your former maid?" I asked, and my face burned red.

It only got worse when he laughed at me.

"Bertha?" he said and laughed again, shaking his head. "Oh no. Oh my no," he took such amusement in my question as he took another sip of his wine.

"Why not?" I asked, confused, embarrassed.

"She was more than twice my age, and took care of me since I was a boy. It wasn't like that... like this," he said, looking me over again, with that hint of lasciviousness.

"Why is it like this with me then?" I continued blurting out things I didn't quite want to say, but did all the same.

"Because I saw you around the office. And my mind... burned with questions. Possibilities," he said, his eyes going wide as he looked at me.

"Like what?" I asked.

"Like what you'd look like in a skimpy skirt and high heels," he responded immediately.

Something in me was unravelling. I'd just assumed he'd been a playboy. That he had burned through more maids than I could count, that they couldn't handle his strange demands and behaviours that my body seemed to enjoy and my mind hated that I responded to them so eagerly.

My breathing was high in my chest, my breasts rising and falling quickly.

"But you acted like this was all, like, second nature to you!"

"It is, in a way," he said with that wry little grin on his face that made me want to slap and kiss him all at once. "I'm just acting on impulse. My desires," he said, continuing to stroke the curve of my ass, feeling out the sumptuous flesh.

And it made sense. It wasn't like these little sexual nitpicks were included in the itinerary left for me, after all.

I'd just assumed he hadn't wanted a record of all his plans for me.

I shifted in my heels, my ass growing a little rounder as I put the weight on my leg, looking at him with such mixed feelings.

But mostly, they were all quickly becoming clouded by lust. Desire.

He was the man I hated and wanted most in the world. Maybe working for him so long and realizing he wasn't a complete monster had softened me. Whatever it was, I was throbbing between my legs, and I just wanted to run and hide.

"You never saw me?" he asked, brow raised again in that way that sent shivers down my spine to where his hand rested on my ass. "I could watch you shake your rear about that office all day. The loveliest woman in all my offices. Such fire, such determination," he said, and his appreciation for me dripped from his words so sincere. "You had a passion for life, to get through and make something of yourself."

His appreciation for me came as such a shock, and not just because I was unaware of his attention all that time!

I drew in my lip and knit my brows, but my mind was moving at a snail's pace. I couldn't believe the things he was telling me. That this wasn't just a thing he did.

That I wasn't latest in a line of many desperate women, eating off the floor as he fed them.

As he fed me.

How could I be the only one in all of his little capitalist empire?

Without even realizing he was doing it, he had taken up another grape and offered it to me, like his adored little pet. His intense gaze upon me as I chewed, studying every little thing about me.

"I want you," he said at last, firm and forward. "I want to bend you over this table and claim your body, as well as

595

your soul," his voice taking on a gravelly edge. But his words were making me dizzy, literally dizzy!

"I— but…" I struggled to get out my words, but he had no hesitation slipping his hand in under my little maid's skirt, touching the bare cheek of my rear.

"I don't want to hear a no," he said, eyes half-lidded.

I wanted to give in, quickly, completely. But part of me was still obstinate, stubbornly resistant.

"I can't," I said, my throat dry as I watched his reaction to my refusal.

"Why not?" he said, dark and ominous.

"I don't want to just be your… your play thing. Not knowing how casually you toss off your employees," I said, all those years of angst over what happened to my family bubbling out. My throat had went dry from it, and I desperately tried to swallow and wetten my throat.

I didn't have enough money saved up, not yet, not for all I needed to do. Fear gripped me, but it was more than the loss of the job, and I knew it. How could I lie to myself about what was really scaring me?

The idea that he'd let me walk away.

He stared at me, his brows furrowing at first, but then softening as he reached out a hand and slid his long fingers along my cheek, caressing my smooth skin with his hard pads.

"I've offended you," he said, as if realizing his actions had done me some harm without his intending.

"What? No," I managed, but my knees were trembling and my voice sounded weak and distant. Where was all that fire he saw in me? That determination?

Wilted by his stupid charms. His sexy body. His irresistible smirk.

"No, I have," he said, as if able to read my mind, understand the old hurt there. It made him ponder, think a while, licking his lips before he spoke up again.

"I'll undo whatever I've done. All of what I've done," he said, rectifying his statement as he looked me back over. "As long as you'll be mine," he said, his gaze so intense, his desire palpable.

There wasn't any undoing it though, was there?

I stared at him, and I knew he had to have figured out that he'd been right. I was being pretty obvious about it as I worried my lip, feeling that tremor of anxiety run through me.

"My dad..." I finally managed, taking in a deep breath. He liked my fire? He'd get my fire. "You put him out of a job, even though I'm a slacker compared to him!"

That revelation must've shocked him. He didn't seem to realize it was all so personal to me.

"I'm so sorry," he said, eyes wide. But then... his hard form filled with a certain determination, and he puffed up his chest and knit his fingers back through my blonde hair and leaned in, placing a hard kiss upon my lips. His tongue probed between the two moist morsels, and he held me locked into that embrace for some time, until...

"I'll fix that, regardless of what you say. But I want you," his voice turned to a growl with those last four words. "I want you so bad, Tish. And I need you to be mine. Don't say it... show me... show me and bend over this table like the good girl I know you can be."

My heart was racing, and though it had started out in anger, that bruising kiss turned it into something else entirely. I could barely breathe, and my world suddenly felt so narrow. Like all there was was he and I, and the patio didn't open up to the wideness of the world.

It was amazing. I'd kissed a couple boys growing up, but not like that. Never like that.

His kiss was hard and determined, but had such passion behind it. Not the sloppy over eagerness, but the purest need.

My lips fell open as I tried get catch my breath, my blue eyes slowly working their way to the table.

Could I actually do something like that? What type of person was I if I said yes?

If I agreed to be spanked by my boss? By the same arrogant man that fired my father and put our family into turmoil?

So why did I believe his words that he'd make it right?

And why was all my reasoning being thrown out the window, even if I knew it was wrong?

He rose up from his chair, those strong arms about me, lifting me up and tipping me back over the table as he kissed me so deeply. He had such strength in those arms, and I knew it came from his long sessions in the private gym I so often cleaned up for him. Even bent over like that, he held my ample figure in his grasp as if I were nothing.

"You're too perfect to let go," he murmured in the brief gap that our lips broke their seal, in which I was too dazed to even realize it.

He could have anything, anyone he wanted. So why me?

It made sense, if I was just next up in line for his little experiment in humiliation. I could understand that. Respect it, even, in some weird, twisted way.

But the idea that I was somehow special or different to him? That was throwing me through a loop.

And the fact that all my blood seemed to be rushing throughout the rest of my body and avoiding my brain wasn't helping my situation. I was quickly getting caught up in his charms, letting my guard down. I was weakened by his strength, and I wished I could just let everything else go away so I could enjoy this.

Enjoy him.

But I didn't want to betray my family.

So why did I move my face towards him, my lips pressed against his with such a slow, insistent tenderness?

I was entangled in his powerful grasp, lost against his hard body and passionate embrace. Those long, strong fingers sinking into my flesh, holding me by my hips and shoulder, until at last he laid me down on the table, hovering over me as he plucked a few more kisses from my pouty lips, and moved on down towards the frilled collar of my uniform at my neck.

"I want you to be mine, in every way," he growled, like some beast in heat, drawn to me.

I was losing my mind, losing my everything, but I couldn't fight it forever. I was going mad with desire, and my body needed what he was offering. That touch, those weird rituals, the strange behaviour...

It all spoke to me in some way I could never under-stand, and I'd fantasized about this moment since I first knelt at his table like some pet.

"Oh God," I murmured, my voice sounding so strained.

He rose up, looked down upon me with such a fiery intensity in his eyes. Such a hard man, with such a passionate desire, and he made me want to give into him. That was his trick. That was what made me submit so readily to him, he kindled a desire in me to do what he wanted, as he wanted it.

With his strong hands upon my form, he twisted me about, pressed my ample chest into the table and looked me over, with my short skirt flared upwards.

"Be a good girl and lower your panties," he growled in command.

I'd never done anything like this, not ever. Not even thought about doing it.

Even in my wildest fantasies, I couldn't have conjured up what those words could do to me and how readily I wanted to obey.

My fingers found their way to the waistband of my panties, and I knew that I should stop it all and just walk away, pretend none of this ever happened.

But it did happen. It was happening. I wanted it more than anything, and I was lowering my panties down over my thighs with a youthful glee, and a womanly excitement.

It was so wrong, and I felt the fabric slip down over my calves, gathering around my high heels and leaving me so exposed to the man who made me want to obey, even when I knew it was wrong.

I could feel the cool air graze my nethers, and I shivered with excitement, nervousness. I could hear him working his own belt, the sound of metal and leather, and then the cloth of his pants parting.

I only dared look behind in the glass reflection of the doors, see that towering man there, ready to take me as he pulled down his trousers and revealed his thick, sizable manhood, so rock hard with desire.

"I'm gonna fuck you raw, my pet Tish," he growled hoarsely. "Gonna pump you so full of my cum you'll be knocked up twice over," he pledged as he trailed his thick, purple crown along the seam of my cunny.

I was always a good girl. Always knew to avoid the very thing he was promising to do to me.

But he made me weak. Drew out my secret desires, the ones I wouldn't admit to myself let alone anyone else, and then display them in front of me so blatantly. With such expectation.

He was the type of guy that you never said 'no' to, and all of my good sense was gone and in its place was a girl I didn't recognize. A girl that pushed back against his cock, begging him with her body as a foreign, "Yes..." escaped my lips.

It didn't take much to make him oblige, that gentle little nuzzle of my quim to his manhood, and he was spearing his way into me. A single, rough thrust and he imbed his pulsating pillar deep into my warm, waiting canal.

"Yes!" he roared out, throbbing thickly, stretching my narrow, virginal canal wider with his entry. "You're so damn perfect! The way you feel with your pussy wrapped around my dick," he growled, reaching up, taking hold of my ponytail as he tugged back his hips, pulling the clinging walls of my cunny with him before he thrust back in.

I wondered if he even knew he was my first, if he knew what he was taking from me. What I was giving him. There was a sharp sting, and my body tensed and tightened as he stole my virginity.

I'd never heard him curse like that before, and the idea that I had unhinged a man that was always in control, always so put together... it was a rush. A high unlike any I'd experienced, and I was crying out in unison with him. Pain and pleasure mingled.

I hadn't realized how badly I wanted and needed him inside me until I had it, and suddenly I felt whole. All of my worries and fears slipped away and in their place was just warm, welcoming love and passion and desire.

I slammed my backside against his hips, and his cock hit against a sensitive part of me, sending a jolt of sensation through my entire body. My fingers grasped onto the heavy table, holding myself up as he took me so hard and with such need. The pain ebbed and gave way to a dull ache, and then to nothing more than sweet bliss.

"I've never felt so good as I do now that I'm fucking you," he growled to me, winding my hair about his fingers as he thrust, burying his shaft deep inside me with each thrust. He smacked my ass cheek with his free hand before grabbing hold of my hip to aid in his motions. "You feel so damn good around my cock, pet," he husked into my ear.

I shouldn't want him to think of me as a pet, as a thing he kept and took care of, but that was what I was.

And that was what I wanted to be.

I moaned again, my large breasts flattened into the table as my legs spread. I tilted my hips a bit more as he impaled me on his thick shaft, and he delved into deeper.

The table squeaked as I held onto it tighter, my words peppered with cursing as he fucked me raw. It wasn't what good girls did. It wasn't what I did.

But I didn't want anything to separate us. Not now.

His two hands were holding me, guiding me, and he was thrusting with such rigor. I was captivated by the reflection of our bodies moving together in the glass. The way he pumped his organ into me, filling me up and making my ass cheeks ripple with each impact.

"Take it, take my cock... take me!" he said with such force, but I could feel the yearning in his words. How much he wanted me to accept him, not just physically.

His fingers sank into my fleshy ass cheek, and he swelled inside my raw cunny.

The man who had the entire world, and all he wanted was to take me in such a primal way. My body was trembling, responding to his so acutely. He hit the right tempo, his sac slapping against my clit and threatening to send me over the brink.

But when his fingers wrapped tighter into my hair, tugging on those blond tresses as he went in harder, that was what did it. Maybe I get off on degradation. Whatever it was, I couldn't stop it as every nerve in my body went on fire. My knees were trembling and quaking, and I'd likely have fallen if I weren't pinned between his body and the table.

"Sir!" I screamed, because I couldn't think of his first name at the moment, but I wanted to let him know. Needed to tell him. "I'm cumming!"

But he had to have noticed the way my pussy tensed along his cock, the muscles drawing him in and beckoning him to do the thing he shouldn't. The thing I shouldn't want him to do.

I did, though. Oh, how I wanted him to fill me with his cum, to claim me as his. To bind him to me for eternity.

"Cum on my cock, Tish," he growled, demanding what was already the inevitable. The flood of warm honey coating his length, running down to his sac and adding a wetness to the loud slaps of against me. Though it slowly changed.

As I screamed out my ecstasy, he barreled towards his own. His organ twitched and grew harder inside me, his moans and groans deeper, heavier.

"I'm gonna make you mine, pet," he growled again, and I knew it was coming. He was cumming. And I didn't pull away, didn't fear it. I accepted it as that handsome, powerful man took hold of me and hammered away to his own release, the two of us exploding into a jumble of exploding nerves, the two of us lost to bliss as his virile seed flooded my fertile womb.

The thought, the awareness of what was happening, gave me the sweetest orgasm I could've ever dreamed up. I was soaring, my entire body seeming so disconnected and yet connected at the same time.

My throat was soon coarse, my begging and pleading for him to cum in me mixed with cursing and panting and praying for more. For this to never end.

I didn't want to come down from the high, but as he

pumped those last few streams into me, and slowly stilled, I desperately tried to catch my breath.

Mr. Romy stilled atop me, breathing heavily as his tool twitched and spurt its last inside me, and I laid beneath him. So satisfied… flushed and deflowered. But happily so.

He leaned in, kissed my neck beneath my ear, licked up to my earlobe and suckled it softly. He put one of his arms about me and squeezed me tightly as we lay there atop his balcony table.

"Stay with me… in my room," he husked into my ear lowly. "I'll keep my promises. I'll make everything right. Just be mine," and his plea was so genuine, so needful. He wanted me still, even after having spent his essence inside me.

I trembled, pushing in against him, needing his warmth. The feel of his body against mine, encompassing me.

I brought my hands to his, feeling them as they still gripped my hips, and I shivered gently, because I wanted it. Oh, I wanted it bad.

Before I could stop myself or think rationally, I was nodding.

The story of Mr. Romy and me didn't end there, though. Even if part of me felt no matter what he said, it would. I was always told men say hasty things in the passion of the moment, but despite how bold his promises to me were… he kept them.

Perhaps it helped that the maid uniform he had made for me needed some altering in just a few short months, to accommodate for the growing bulge in my belly. Or how once I was sleeping with him each night, I could coo such

sweet words into his head, and fill him with an appreciation for my feminine gentleness.

Whatever the reasons, when he cradled my pregnant
form, with our child fast on its way, I got to do so guilt
free. Not only did my father get his job back, but all the old
workers did when he opened up a new facility in town,
with better wages and safer conditions than ever before.

The irony of the fact that I was into degradation and
used it to get others the respect they deserved didn't go
unnoticed. And every mealtime, when I kneel at his side,
patiently waiting for the food he lovingly prepared, I
appreciate that — and him — a little bit more.

THE FERTILE STEWARDESS

Book Themes:
      Bareback, Breeding, and Mile High Club
Word Count:
6,245

~

FLYING as attendant for a private jet company got me in with a lot of exclusive people, so that should tell you I'm no stranger to men getting carried away and acting rowdy on a plane. If there's one group of people more prone to flaunting the rules and misbehaving than the rich and powerful, I haven't heard of it.

I could tell you about the time I walked on into the cabin to find a rockstar standin' in the aisle, a beautiful, busty bimbo on her knees sucking him off as half a dozen groupies and band members sat around, watching as they sucked and fucked each other.

Or I could tell you about the time I walked on in to find a movie cast all drunk out of their minds, trashing the plane and fucking each other up, both literally and figuratively. Took the cleanup crew a week to get the cum out of the upholstery, I swear.

But no, that's not the time that sticks out most in my mind. Nor the dozens of other flights where the rich and powerful went wild, like unchained pubescent boys with nobody to tell them they were being bad.

The time that sticks out to me was when a handsome but unsuspecting man stepped on board the jet. Tall, dark and handsome is the cliché, but that's what he was. Sleek, glossy black hair, an outdoorsy tan combined with his casual attire made me think he was nobody special, some guest of an important person maybe. A brother of a CEO, maybe.

But I was so wrong.

Unlike the other usual guests, of powerful out of control men, this guy came on, sat quietly and bided his time. When I first came to him he was polite, which was a refreshing change. I know that commercial flights have their own set of annoyances, but I'm convinced you don't know true annoyance until you realize how callously these people treated their servants. Anyone who was able to hold their tongue and not slap my ass was someone noteworthy to me, but usually meant they were just as poor as I was.

But as I was talking to the captain, he let me in a little something I couldn't quite believe.

"Oh yeah, you didn't hear?" he said, peering back at the closed cockpit door. "That's James Dartmouth, director, author and songwriter. Guy's been responsible for half the big hits across all three mediums. You never heard of him?"

My mouth nearly dropped to the floor, because though I'd heard of him, I'd never seen him before in all my life. He was a middle aged guy, but clearly took care of himself.

And though he was rich, he'd kept his fame low on purpose. He never did interviews or courted his fans.

Down to earth was the term for a guy like him.

Which didn't make sense to me, since he could likely buy and sell anything or anyone he wanted. Could've had groupies and prostitutes all over the plane, making my job a little less fun and a lot more annoying.

Instead, he simply sat, like a normal human being.

"He certainly hasn't seemed to let it go to his head," I murmured to the Captain. I suddenly found myself wanting to look a bit nicer, and so I fixed my black belt along my navy dress, cinching in the couple extra pounds that had creeped on me since the Holidays.

I pat my brown hair, making sure it was neat and tidy beneath the little stewardess hat we still wore on this private airline. The men that flew with us wanted to go back to a time when they were still able to get away with cheating and boozing and treating women like disposable playthings, and the airline paid me well enough to put up with it.

Sauntering on back to check on my one and only passenger, he was gazing off out the window, hand to his chin as he looked deep in thought. I'd come back there full of intention to be all inquisitive and sultry, but seeing him so brooding and thoughtful, I felt like I'd be disturbing a precious moment.

Instead, I found myself standing there like a fool for a while. Appreciating the hard line of his jaw, the way his broad shouldered body filled his button-down shirt and pants so well. He was obviously a man who took care of himself, who looked to the basics of life even as the decadence and frivolousness of wealth and power tempted him elsewhere.

I must've been staring overlong though, because he

turned to look at me, catching my gaze as I stood in the aisle watching him.

"You seem lost in thought too," he remarked to me, his voice deep and creamy, like listening to him was the same as enjoying a fine Belgian chocolate.

I'd always been pretty good at hiding my flush, and I was grateful for it then because I hated to be caught staring. But he had me transfixed.

"I was just coming to check on you, see if you needed anything. Hot towel, massage, champagne," I offered. Massage was definitely not on the standard list of requirements for my job, though.

Can't blame a girl for trying, can you?

His stony facade was cracked with a smile.

"That's quite the list of services," he said, and I worried for a moment that I'd overdone it. "You're quite the all-service flight attendant, aren't you?" he remarked, shifting in his seat and looking to me, not as an employee, as so many others did, but as if I was just another passenger. "Tell me," he said, licking his lips and looking anxious, "what does the crew do up there behind the privacy wall to pass the time?"

Oh lord, on the spot!

If he was really a down to earth guy, maybe he'd appreciate the truth.

"Gossip about how horrid all the passengers are," I said, forcing a grin to my face so that he might be uncertain if I were joking or not. But then my stomach was in knots and I was wondering if that was really the smartest thing to say.

There was a moment of uncertainty, his chiselled good looks frozen in place. But then suddenly he broke into laughter and was grinning at me widely.

"I figured," he said, looking at me with such a genuine

expression across his face. "Say," he said, leaning forward towards me. "How about you and I break into some of that champagne the airline is always trying to push on me, huh?" His words said in such a conspiratorial tone, as if we were good friends about to break the rules.

And rules would have to be broken of course, because I was strictly not allowed to drink on the job. Or do drugs, as so many rich guys offered me.

My company sometimes had no idea the things they were asking me to pass up, and the things that were offered to me in exchange for breaking them.

So why did I want to this time? I'd said no to every man I'd met, over and over again. No, I didn't want to do coke off that stripper's stomach. No, I didn't want to see what his cock looked like. No, I definitely didn't want to join the mile high club.

I licked my lips. Just one more no.

"I'm not really allowed," I said, and my no sounded more like a schoolgirl telling her boyfriend she's not supposed to see him anymore. Like it was an inevitability, and I just needed a push.

He frowned a little, and I worried he was too good of a guy to push at all.

He shifted in his seat, looked out the window then back at me again.

"Well I certainly can't drink by myself. That'd just be depressing," he remarked so casually. "But I really wouldn't want to get you in trouble... I mean, not if there's some way they could find out," he said, brow arched up at me, in silent query.

"For flights like this it's just the pilot, the co-pilot and I..." I trailed off, looking back towards the divide.

Why was I being so silly? I could lose my job, just

because this gorgeous honey seemed so sweet and aloof compared to my usual fare?

But I couldn't deny that the things he was doing to my body with only his eyes and his lips were surreal.

All he had to do was sit there, looking so immaculate and gorgeous, such a fine specimen of what a man should be: strong, thoughtful, confident, modest but accomplished. He was the full package.

Yeah, in retrospect it's no surprise all he had to do was just sit there.

"Well the two of them aren't likely to come back here any time soon, are they?" he asked, brow raised in question. "And tell you what..." he looked around, a playfully dramatic expression as if we might get caught by some hall monitor at any moment before he leaned in and murmured quietly to me. "If you get in trouble, I'll speak up for you. And make sure you get at least a few years pay in recompense."

Now that... didn't sound so bad.

Not like I hadn't been offered money before, but not usually for something I truly wanted to do.

I moved towards the back room, and grabbed the finest bottle we had out of the selection of three. Unless there was a special request, we kept the old favourites on board and nothing else.

Another four hours 'til we crossed the Atlantic Ocean, and already I was losing my mind with wanting to please him. I brought the bottle over to him, uncorking it in an expert manner before pouring up his little plastic champagne glass.

Then he did a surprising thing and took the bottle from me, to pour up a second glass then hand it to me with a bright smile on his face.

"Now, have a seat," he said, patting the spot beside him

so invitingly. "Tell me all about yourself. Because I don't even know your name yet, miss, but I'm dying to find out," he remarked, smiling at me in such a way I felt like I might melt into a puddle before him.

My tummy was flipping about with excitement. I hadn't been so into a guy since high school, and I joined him on the spacious couch, accepting my 'glass' with a furtive glance towards the cockpit and back at him.

"It's Sarah," I said before taking a quick sip of the champagne. I needed it to soothe my nerves.

"Well Sarah, I'm James. It's a pleasure to meet you," he remarked with a smile, drinking down some of his champagne as we sat together there on the comfortable sofa. Better than the one I had at home even. "Where are you from? Is it our destination? New York?" he asked, looking me over, not as some rich brat that I was used to on the plane, but as any interested guy did. As if he was just another studly man in a bar who caught sight of me and found what he saw... intriguing.

I shook my head, the champagne already warming my body, making my tongue looser.

"I'm actually from Maine, but I moved to New York a couple years ago for work," I said with a smile. "It's a big change. I figured you'd be out in L.A. with the other bigwigs, though."

The second the words left me, my stomach flipped. Why'd I admit I knew who he was, like just another crazy fan? Stupid, Sarah!

He smiled at me though, like it was no big deal.

"I can't stand L.A.," he said so casually before sipping more of his champagne. "Too much sun, too easy of a life. Too fake of people," he remarked with a half-smile. "Life should be a little trying, you know? Out there, it's nothing but fake smiles on fake people, all hoping to get a slice of your fame or money. It's tiresome, and unproductive. I'd be just as well off courting a room full of cardboard cut-outs," he said with a playful smirk.

"If you ask me," he added on quickly, leaning in close. "I like real people. Real women, with real lives. Real bodies. Not a persona sculpted to sell themselves."

I couldn't help but giggle. He talked almost like he wrote.

Yea, I'd read most of his books as well. I had a feeling once I got back home I'd be reading a lot more.

"You like the fast paced and cutthroat life of New York better?" I asked with a twitch of my lips.

He gave a slight shrug of those broad, heavyset shoulders and looked at me with a wry smile.

"I might have a nice penthouse apartment there, but I still walk the streets with everyone else. Take the subway and eat with the rest of them. It at least keeps me a *little* grounded," he remarked with some self-deprecating humour. "And it's easier to get people to work for you there who aren't all just looking to lick your boots and tell you whatever they think you want to hear."

I laughed, more genuinely and less uptight as I looked at him with a sparkle in my eyes. I was smitten with the man. He was unlike anything I figured he'd have been, and made me feel so much more comfortable with him even if my heart kept pounding like mad.

"What's your favourite part?"

"Of New York?" he asked, looking away as he thought over my question, giving it serious consideration. He took his time before leaning back in towards me, resting his hand upon my knee and smiling ever so slightly.

"Looking out over the city from my apartment. Seeing the hustle and bustle in the day. The lights at night. I feel like I'm a part of something so much bigger than I am.

Really feel it, you know? Not just a casual knowing it. But I can look out and see the evidence of human accomplishment, of how far we've come and what we can do when we come together," he remarked with a handsome smile on his face, looking straight into my soul it seemed. That strong hand of his resting on my bare knee.

I laughed. Maybe that was rude, but if he liked New York, he must be used to that already.

"Yea, I feel the same looking out my basement studio and seeing the crack addicts fallen down on the sidewalk in the middle of winter." It was dark, but true. With my student loans and a useless degree I couldn't afford the luxury he so casually spoke of.

"That's a shame," he said to me so smoothly, his smile never vanishing, even if it did temper itself to a warmer, modest one. "A lovely, friendly woman such as yourself shouldn't have to live like that," he remarked, looking me over as his strong hand squeezed at my knee. "You should come for a trip with me out to my cabin. Now, don't go getting ideas. I might live in a New York apartment, but when I say cabin... I meant cabin."

He grinned at me, like he was in on some devious secret I wasn't.

Like he wasn't just talking about a McMansion in the woods, I guessed.

Though maybe with his rich way of thinking, what he really meant was that he had one of those huge log monstrosities, bigger than any house I'd ever lived in.

It was hard to say when I was talking to someone so outside of my pay grade.

"What do you mean by cabin, then?" I decided to ask. It was the safest course of action.

He sipped his champagne.

"Single room spot, out in the middle of the woods," he

began, his voice takin' on a deeper, huskier tone. "No road to it. You gotta park your car, then take a canoe, then hike on up to it. Then there it is, in the middle of nowhere. A cabin I built myself. No electricity. No running water. But damn," he shook his head, grinning joyfully at the thought, "it's pleasant. And homey. It's something built with love and care."

He looked to me from the corner of his eyes, as he reflected on that special place to him.

And it sounded nice. Not like I pictured it at all. It sounded more like the place my pop had built when I was a girl. We only got to go a few times before he passed, and then it was too painful for us to go back, but I still thought back on it with fondness.

My eyes softened and went to my lap, the skirt covering the upper parts of my thigh, and he must've noticed because he brought his index finger to my chin, lifting my gaze to his.

"So how about it?" he asked, his deep voice so casual and calm. "Come spend a weekend with me there. Or a week. A month even," he remarked, a grin slowly forming on his face as his eyes locked with mine. "I can arrange it all with your employers, no worries there," he assured.

All through it, he leaned ever so close to me, our lips growing nearer and nearer as our eyes locked.

I was lost to his charms, to that calm, cool demeanor. To the way he held me captive, and made me feel like a real person. I was quickly growing addicted to that sensation, and I nodded my head gently.

"I'd like that," I murmured gently.

He finished the last of his glass and flashed me a handsome grin as he laid his hand atop mine. That tough skin of his not rough, but hard, and clearly the result of manual labour. He rubbed his thumb over my slender fingers, all the while looking into my eyes.

"You know, I've flown a lot on these private planes the studios and publishers arrange for me," he remarked, looking into my soul I felt, with his artist's gaze. "And I've never encountered a flight attendant with such natural feminine beauty that shines forth so radiantly."

He had the words of a poet, and suddenly I understood so perfectly why he was as wealthy as he was. Hearing him speak like that, I'd give up so much to hear more, to lose myself to it. To him.

And it was then the words truly dawned on me, what he was really saying... about me.

I'd never heard someone speak about my looks like that before. Sure, I tried to take care of myself, but I was curvy, with a big chest and a soft stomach. My skin was pale, my brown hair contrasting against it, but I'd always thought myself a bit plain, truthfully.

I was at a loss for words, and I stared at him, agape.

His hand rested atop mine as our gazes were locked, and it was impossible to measure the length of that time period for me. We could have been locked in a trance together for years, for all I know. He held me captivated, captive even. Not with chains and binds, but merely his words and his intense gaze, his handsome face and manly demeanor.

"I really wish to kiss you," he said in his low, husky voice. "If I'm in the wrong for doing so, please just slap me and call me out for the lout I am," he remarked before leaning in, head tilted as he gave me a kiss, plush on the lips.

I was too shocked to slap him, even if I had wanted to, which I didn't.

I couldn't believe how good he tasted, how good he felt,

against me. I hadn't been expecting it, to say the least, and I knew I was trembling. My hands shaking, my body weakened as I melted into his mouth, a little moan silenced on his lips.

He lingered there, kissing me for a while as his tongue ever so gently worked its way into my mouth. He went about it so expertly I didn't even know it was happening until his tongue was caressing mine, and by then I was lost in the moment with him. The two of us making out deeply as we cruised along.

I know people love to talk about the 'Mile High Club', but in reality nothing even remotely romantic seemed to happen with myself or any of the flight attendants I knew. Bathrooms were too cramped, and the job had a habit of being too high pressure to ever allow for the relaxation required to get freaky. But with James?

I couldn't remember ever feeling so at ease, so calm and yet excited at the same time. It was like a really good Christmas as a kid where you're so excited but also just really caught up in the moment, enjoying the pleasures of the day.

I wanted to pull away and be responsible, but I didn't know how I possibly could. Every time I tried, my body put a stop to it. I was putty in his hand.

His free arm went around me, so strong and assertive, he pulled me to the edge of my seat as we made out. He had such a powerful grasp, and I instantly felt an instinctive appreciation for it. His raw masculinity so overpowering.

He brought one hand up, sliding along my side, coming so close to my breast as he skirted the edge of it. The low smack of our lips filling the quiet air about us.

I didn't have a great idea how much longer it'd be until

we landed, honestly. And knowing that I didn't know should've lead me to be more cautious.

Hell, everything about the situation should've made me want to be more cautious. But I was lost to excitement and pleasure like I couldn't believe, and I pushed myself into him, begging him with my body.

Like a predator drawn to its prey, he came after me, accepted my enthusiasm with his own as he leaned over, pressed into our embrace tighter. That hard, muscular form of his against my soft, feminine body, my breasts mashed against his hard chest.

He leaned me back down upon the comfortable sofa-like seating for the VIPs, his body looming over mine as my skirt slid up, inch by inch.

It was, no doubt, the dumbest thing I've ever done and at the same time, even then, I knew I wouldn't regret it. Even if everything went to hell, I was willing to throw it away, because I trusted him.

Funny, since my last breakup hadn't really been... amiable and I'd taken a break from all men since, especially with all the stuff I see at my job.

But, and I know it's a cliché... He was different.

His broad shouldered body got atop me, and I was left with little choice but to part my legs and let him lodge himself between my knees. My skirt rode up so high it was barely more than a belt, and his hand dared to move in, squeezing my breast gently over my top as he worked us both into a higher and higher frenzy.

A low, guttural growl escaped him and I felt the beast inside him, kept in such precarious check as his desires for me bubbled slowly over.

My entire body felt hot, too hot, and I ground against him wantonly. I couldn't hold back with him, like I was under his spell. My arms wrapped around his neck, holding myself against him as I laid back on the couch, my mouth still meeting his in more of a frenzy.

Our passions were rising at a frightening rate, and I could feel the swell of his growing manhood against me as he pressed down upon my softer body. He explored and squeezed my body, relishing the feel of my thick, plump tits, the swell of my hips. He seemed to adore and lust for every part of me, slowly grinding his hips against me between my parted thighs.

Some part of me knew where this would lead, what would happen. I'd stopped taking the pill when I was dumped to give myself an excuse, a reason, not to get into this scenario with a man. But I was being careless, reckless, and I even loved it.

Wanted it.

Prayed he wouldn't suggest stopping.

Luckily my prayers were answered, because instead of stopping or slowing down, James only grew more ravenous with time. His hard, strong hands groping at my flesh, squeezing my breasts, my sides, luxuriating in every part of me. He was easily the most insatiable man I'd ever been with, without all the gross, grubby hands and overzealous pushiness of so many other men.

It was just desire, primal and yet filled without any of that sense of entitlement. I moaned into his mouth, my lips sore and tender from kissing, and I wondered how long we'd been making out, but it had to be for a while to make them feel so numb.

I sucked in a breath as he pulled away for a moment before we were upon one another once more.

His hands roamed up and down my sides, until I felt that my skirt was up to my waist and my panties were sliding down my thighs. He reached in, his thumb rubbing at the lacy fabric of my panties atop my cunny, teasing my loins as he skirted the edge of my nipple above with his other hand.

A dull, low groan escaped his throat as he sought to please and coax me into higher desire along with him.

But already, I was more excited than I'd ever been, my nipple hardening beneath his fingertip, my pussy glowing with heat so near to his hand. I wanted his touch, raw and without all of the hindrances of clothing.

I pulled away for a moment, opening my eyes as I gazed at his face, looking for a sense of questioning or concern.

Instead all I saw was raw desire, and as if he could read my mind he began to undo the buttons of my blouse, freeing my ample chest from its confines as he worked those nimble fingers on down. He was ravenous, like a beast without its feeding in weeks. He tore open my shirt and deftly undid my bra, as his other hand dipped on down to hook into my panties and tug them aside. He traced along the bare lips of my cunny, felt their warm, wet folds and gave a growling husky groan of desire.

My pink nipples stiffened to the cool cabin air, my hot pussy so wet that it sent a shiver up my spine.

He was gorgeous. Far more gorgeous than any man I'd ever been with, and he had a soul — and a bank account — to match. He was everything I'd been looking for and didn't know.

I kept wondering if it was a dream, if it was something I'd be cruelly woken from without a chance to see it through, and so I rushed him on, begging him to touch me as my hands roamed over his shoulders and to the front of his shirt, undressing him as he did me.

I was surprised to find that he looked as good under his clothes as he did over them, his broad shoulders and chest revealed to be brawny and muscular, with a dark peppering of hair. He was every bit the manly man he appeared to be, and he shed his top at my urging so that we were both exposed.

His pants came next, showing the bulge in his boxer-briefs. It looked too big to be true, but my eager, anxious fingers probed along it, felt the thick, veiny shaft beneath and just had to free it. The big, bulging shaft sprang out freely, bulging with veins and a purple crown that glistened with precum. He was hefty and long, the biggest man I'd ever seen in that department.

My mouth hung open, and part of me wanted to taste it. To taste him.

I licked my lips, hungering for it. For him.

I knew I was staring, but I couldn't help it. He was absolutely glorious.

"James," I whimpered, and it was the first word either of us had spoken in so long.

He muttered aloud my name in return, "Sarah" rolling off his tongue as a gravelly utterance as he kissed his way down from my lips, across my neck. Licking and suckling as he went, kneading my breast flesh as he lowered himself down so that the tip of his cock teased at my moist little cunny, prodding and expertly exciting it as he went from my clit on down.

His mouth felt so good on my body, but even that bit of bliss was overshadowed by the exquisiteness of the sensation of his cock rubbing against me. I wanted him to sink it in so badly I didn't know how I could manage another moment longer without it.

"Please!" I begged of him.

"Yes," he growled in response, and he clenched my breast in his hard, powerful hand and then pushed his hips forward. His thick, bulging cock, unsheathed and oh so huge, simply shoved itself betwixt my dainty labia. That bulging monstrosity pierced my womanhood, sinking in deep, deep towards my fertile womb as he let loose a lewd, husky groan of satisfaction.

I was lost to sin, to sinfulness, and I'd never felt so good and alive. I moaned, trying not to scream lest the pilots hear me, my entire body trembling with need and lust.

He felt so good, my wet pussy begging for more.

"Fuck me!" I cried out, so unlike myself.

James obliged, his powerful body coiling back like a snake ready to strike. And his snake did indeed strike; that thick, pulsating cock of his pounding down into me again as he began to thrust. Pumping his girth into me he let loose such throaty groans as he nipped and sucked at my neck, pawing at my tits with his big, strong grasp.

I'd never been prey to such intense, skillful desires before. Such an attentive, masculine man, who catered to myself and him with his every lustful move.

I bit down hard on my lower lip, trying to silence another scream that threatened me as I lifted my hips, begging for him to go deeper.

I was a wanton woman for him, for the pleasure he was giving me, and there was no going back.

With one hand he reached down, cupping the underside of my thick thigh and lifting it up to his side. He continued to thrust and pummel my wanting, pink pussy, his thumb sliding in around my outer thigh to circle and tease my clit.

The lewd, low groans he gave produced a delightful bass to my own moans and cries, his other hand kneading at my breast flesh as we screwed so far up in the air.

"Oh fuck, Sarah," he groaned out so crassly. "You feel so damn good!"

I cried out, sucking in a breath to try to compensate it as he thrust into me. Though just then there was a ding, and the pilot's voice sounded over the system.

"We're heading into a bit of turbulence, though after that it should be smooth flying and we'll be landing at JFK in about forty-five minutes."

Just as he finished, though, the turbulence began, the vibration rocking through the cabin.

There we both lay upon the plush sofa, our bodies rocking, thrusting and grinding as the whole plane shook around us. James' powerful body pummeling my slick, needy cunny as he thrust down betwixt my wet folds, plunging to the very depths of my fertile quim.

He moaned out deeply, his dick throbbing and stretching my narrow canal around his girth.

"You're the most beautiful woman I've ever fucked, Sarah," he said so crassly. But all I could think of was the honour of being this rich and famous man's finest moment.

I could barely believe my ears, but he sounded so genuine, so heartfelt, that I couldn't imagine it being a lie.

And even if it was, I didn't regret it.

The turbulence got heavier, until I was clinging to him, my body grinding against his so desperately.

"I need you!" I cried out.

"Take me, Sarah!" he cried out, thrusting harder, faster, so very, very deeper. "Take all of me!" he bellowed, his cock swelling inside me as our bodies slapped together hard and fast, the moist smack of our loins meeting filling the air as he took me like a savage animal. The whole plane shaking about us as if we made the very sky quake with our bare-back rutting.

I was getting disoriented, dizzy, my mind hazy with lust as I clung to him like my life depended on it. Like he was my everything.

My nails clung to his back, putting little half-moons

into his skin as he slammed into me so hard I worried we might break the expensive sofa.

James had no such worry, he was focussed utterly upon me. On ravaging my body as he thrust and mauled me, rubbed my clit with his hard thumb and groaned so lewdly. He thrust so hard my body bucked, and his harsh voice filled the air.

"I'm going to cum," he grunted out. "I need to cum in you, Sarah," he said, incessantly provoking my delicate clit all the while, attempting to bring me to climax.

The rational, logical part of me was so far gone, she wasn't even on the same continent as me any longer.

Instead, I was the woman shouting, "Yes! Yes!" daring the pilots to hear me, to put a stop to us.

My legs crushed around his hips, holding him against me deep and then there was only bliss as I toppled over the edge of pleasure. My body tensed, squeezing his cock within me as I screamed out his name, my muscles and nerves filled with such amazing sensations that I hadn't felt in so long!

As the waves of slick honey coated his cock and ran down to his balls, he let loose such a loud, boisterous moan of his own. His body tensed, his dick stiffened and swelled inside me, and he thrust in for one big, final push.

I could see his neck tense, the veins bulge out on it as he cried out, and then his virile shaft spewed its rich seed. The thick gouts of creamy spunk filled me up, his whole body tensing and locking with mine as he seeded my womb with his potent cum.

"Ohhh fuck Sarah! You're so gorgeous," he cried out amid his own tidal wave of pleasure.

He held me there, lost to the blur of pleasure, for so long. I lost count of the orgasms as they ripped through me, one crashing into the next.

I didn't even have the power of speech any longer, it was just primal moans and growls of pleasure that barely sounded human. My nails raked his skin, and I knew he'd be red from them for days, but it was beyond me to care.

The two of us were drawn down to our primal states, like two animals in heat and we rode it out to the end, until we were a united, sweaty, panting mess. And the plane was slowly descending towards the ground.

The Captain's voice resounded about us.

"We are descending now, and we'll be arriving in just a few short minutes. Thank you for putting your trust in me."

But there was another man I'd put my trust in that flight.

I'd be lying if I said I wasn't worried. But once we landed, James did the unthinkable: he contacted my employers, arranged for me to have paid time off to come visit his cabin with him. I couldn't believe it, it was like out of a fairy tale, but I was overjoyed.

It was hard, rustic living there, but oh so satisfying. There was something wholesome about getting your hands dirty, making and building things yourself. I understood immediately why he enjoyed it so much.

But all good things had to come to an end, and eventually I had to return to my normal life. It was funny, the obnoxious men on my flights no longer bothered me like they used to. They weren't able to get under my skin any longer.

And it wouldn't be the last time I was swept away to James' private cabin.

Half a year later, there I was again, standing side by side

with him, overlooking the lake. His big, brawny arm about me as I cradled my swollen pregnant belly. And watched the glimmer of the fattest diamond ring I'd ever seen upon my finger.

Sometimes dreams really do come true.

THE FERTILE TOUR GUIDE

*B*ook Themes:
Bareback, Breeding, Creampie, and Sex With Strangers

Word Count:
5,288

AFTER THE MOST BRUTAL and heart wrenching autumn I'd ever experienced, I couldn't help but dream of going south. Of traveling to some place exotic and warm, filled with happiness and salsa music, where I could forget everything about where I'd come from, or the loss I'd just suffered.

I knew I needed to recover from the death of my wife and our child, and I couldn't do that at home, surrounded by their memories.

So, with my work's blessing, I booked myself for a month long vacation in beautiful Havana, where I could immerse myself in a culture so different from my own and find my footing again. I wasn't expecting anything to happen, but the moment I set my eyes on Isabel, my entire world was flipped upside down.

It wasn't just that she was gorgeous — though she was, no sense in lying about that — it was that she had this strange little coy smile, her full lips turning up just at the corner as if everything was an inside joke.

I was the last one onto the tour bus and so she had me sit next to her, and there was a faint scent of mangoes or papaya or some delicious fruit that seemed to emanate from her. Just from that first moment, I was hooked.

The trip we were taking was across the island a ways, and I would be spending hours sitting next to her.

I was quiet at first. Shy, I guess. I'd been married for twelve years, so I wasn't used to speaking to women I didn't know. Especially not women as beautiful as Isabel.

But when we were driving down one of the roads, her hand went to my thigh as she pointed out the window.

"That is the highest bridge on the island," she said in her accented voice, and I could hear the pride there. She was eager to share that bit of knowledge with me.

I might not be the most suave man out there, with my lack of dating experience in the past decade, but I was thankful my tolerance for the heat meant I got away with a nice light pair of linen pants and a short sleeved, button up shirt. I didn't look like the horrible dorky tourists that filled the rest of the bus.

It also helped give me a bit more courage when talking with her.

"Impressive," I said, peering at the bridge and the beautiful valleys beyond it, the lush green jungle all about. "Shame we're not driving over it then," I remarked with a smile.

"There's nothing much out that way other than Varadero," she said, mentioning the closest tourist resort.

I'd wanted a more authentic experience, and so opted for a hotel closer to the capital of Cuba.

I once read that if you wanted to hang out with other Canadians to go to Varadero, but to spend time with Cubans, go to Havana. I was pleased that the advice seemed mostly true.

"Have you ever worked there?" I asked.

"Not usually. I prefer to be closer to the city," she said, her coy smile turning up the corner of her lips once more.

For the next three days I was going to be with her, at her side, as we explored the no-doubt still touristy locations, though I hoped to get a glimpse of what it was really like. To live in Cuba, a place so different from home.

"Me too," I replied, running a hand back over my long, blonde hair. It would undoubtedly be a bit uncomfortably thick in the heat, but I wasn't worried. "The idea of being stuck back there with all the boring tourists doesn't entice me too much," I said with dry humour, hoping it came across alright.

It was almost as if she were laughing at me with that smile, if not for the fact that her hand was still on my thigh.

"Well I'm glad. If you'd stayed out there, I'd have been all by my lonesome up here."

"You? I find it hard to imagine you would ever be left to your lonesome, as beautiful as you are," I said, finding some reservoir of casual flirtatious chit chat to siphon from. Perhaps it was just that smooth, dark hand upon my thigh that was filling me with such vigor.

I always did perform best under duress.

She giggled like a schoolgirl, her face tilting forward and some of her long hair curtaining her face for a moment. She tucked it back — still not removing her other hand from my leg — and looked up at me from beneath her lashes.

"Are you always like this?"

I didn't know how to respond to that right away. After all, I certainly wasn't. I'd not had many ups between my downs since the passing of my loved ones, but finally I was letting go. Moving on. This woman was helping a lot in that department, because the more I looked at her, the less I wanted to think of anyone or anything else.

"Must be all this tropical air, and the beautiful sights," I said to her, my gaze too intense to leave any confusion as to what beautiful sights I was focused upon.

She laughed again, her eyes sparkling as we pulled into what looked to be a farm. She seemed a bit surprised by that, but quickly recovered, standing up just in front of me and stretching enough that I could see her belly button beneath her red blouse.

"This is our first stop for the day, to meet a local tobacco farmer," she announced to the bus, then gave me a personal smile.

My head was abuzz but she was already bounding off the bus, ready to give the tour.

The entire way to the hotel, in between the stops, she always found her way back to me, her hand resting atop my leg. I certainly wasn't complaining.

But night was falling, and the rest of the crowd were tired by the time we pulled up to the hotel, nestled in the jungle. The trip up the hill had been... rocky, and before I knew it, Isabel had been gripping my bicep for dear life and she was hesitant to let go even though we were parked.

"We're here," she breathed out, forcing herself to stand, and look at the others.

"There's a buffet meal you're all welcome to, and a disco

just down at the left for evening entertainment," she announced, the last part directed to me.

I waited until she got off, leaving me the last person off the bus.

I followed behind her, speaking to her quietly as the others rushed to the buffet.

"You look like a dancer," I said, full of warmth. "You have the look of a woman who can really cut-a-rug with the best of them," and I immediately felt dumb about that remark. Not only was it dated, but I wasn't sure she'd get the reference either.

The language barrier was a finicky thing, after all, but though her brows furrowed, it seemed she grasped the warm intention rather than the literal confusion.

"I teach," she said with a pause, "Salsa. On the weekends, as exercise."

She slowly began guiding me towards the restaurant. "Do you dance?"

I followed along with her, having to pace myself, my long stride so easily overtaking hers even at a casual pace.

"I've been known to in my day," I smiled and tried not to let on that my day was now years behind me. It'd been ages since I last danced. "Could use a nice refresher," I said casually, getting the door for her.

"I am told that I am a very good teacher," she said as she walked through, her flirty dress caressing against my pant legs as she went towards the buffet. "I will see you tonight for your first lesson."

I couldn't help but stare a while, until finally some tourist with a vastly over-filled plate needed me to shove out of the way.

∽

WHEN NIGHT CAME, I was surprised by its beauty. The stars above lit the jungle sky, while all around I could see the towering trees, vines and flowers lit by the moon. The little lizards of the day replaced by crickets the size of mice!

I left my room, a pair of shiny black shoes on, polished up nicely for the evening, and a freshly pressed pair of pants, a shirt and jacket from my luggage. I wasn't about to go in looking like a schlep after all.

Good thing I had packed a wide variety of outfits.

It wasn't immediately evident where the disco was, because it was kept tucked away from the resort rooms, so as to not let the noise bother the guests. But once I rounded the right corner, the music called me to it.

It built such anticipation in the air, the sound beckoning me closer, drawing me in with its sweet, warm sound. Wanting me in its embrace.

It was beautiful, and when I finally opened the door and let the sounds flood out into me, there was a sense of peace I hadn't felt in a long time. The dancing bodies, the glowing lights, all flashed about me as laughter rose into the air.

And there was Isabel, dancing with some local, it looked like. She was gorgeous, spinning about and smiling that crooked smile.

It was enchanting, and I was content to just watch for the moment until she caught my eye, and her finger beckoned me closer.

Truth be told, I was a pretty good dancer in my college years, but that was well behind me. By this point all I had going for me were the nice shoes and clothing.

"Impossible to miss you on the dance floor," I remarked to her as I made my way to her, trying to loosen myself up and move with the music, mimic the Latin moves of the local dancers. I was surprised my body was limber enough to even begin to impersonate them!

But I guess part of it came easy. Once the rhythm is in the air and touches your body, you get wrapped up in it.

Though what was better than that, was the fact that her hands went to my hips.

"Not like that, here," she said, making my hips swivel in a certain way, but it seemed awful close to what I was already doing. I wondered if it was just an excuse.

"Who am I to argue with the finer points of dancing from such a talented instructor?" I said with an uneven smile of my own. Then I did a brazen thing and reached out, putting my own hands upon her ample hips and began to move with her.

The two of our bodies moving in the black light, leaving her dark curves so beautifully accentuated.

Everything was a bit hotter in Cuba. The weather, the girls, the music, and especially the dancing. There was something so sensual about the way she moved into me, her lithe legs shown off beneath her fluid skirt.

"You're pretty good," she said with a laugh, still somewhat guiding me.

"Oh, I'm just following you and the others," I responded, the two of us moving so rhythmically together. "I'll need some intensive, one-on-one training to get really good with this and lead," I said with a cheeky smile that did little to hide my true intentions.

I was on vacation, I'll be damned if I was going to pussy foot around this!

After all, I was never going to see her again. Maybe that was part of the appeal. My wife had been my high school sweetheart, and I'd never dated around much. This was the perfect chance.

Her hand went to mine, tickling my skin with an electric buzz as she ran up my ring finger on my left hand, as if checking for a ring.

She found nothing there any longer, and I could see the smile that brought to her lips. In reward, I brought us in closer to one another, stepping in and placing my arm about her lower back to tug her tighter towards me.

"After this I must be allowed to buy you a drink. Or all the drinks," I said with a cocky smile, feeling more sure of myself than I had in a very long time. Something about the island, the jungle, the club and her, most importantly. It brought out some of my brazen spirit.

The part of me I'd thought was locked away for ever.

"I'd like that," she said in response, her hips circling and her legs rubbing along mine seductively. It was all so sensual, the way she danced, the way her body felt against mine. It was terrific and freeing, all the stress dripping from my body as I enjoyed her form.

Those soft, sensual curves of hers, pressed up against my hard, lean form, it was such a delightful mix. That masculine on feminine feel, and my confidence grew. I spun her about and then we locked at the hips again, only now I pressed into her sumptuous ass cheeks, felt their supple flesh as we danced, my hands upon her hips.

I hadn't fully thought things through, I'll confess, because I felt a jump in my cock below, unable to help how excited I got feeling her hot flesh to mine.

"Good," I said, as if none of the intervening actions had interrupted our conversation. "I would've been so sad if I didn't get the chance to treat a beautiful woman such as yourself at least once while I'm here."

She had to have noticed. Not to brag, but I was a big enough guy that a girl would notice if I was getting half a hard-on.

When she ground back into it, I knew for a fact that she

did. She was egging me on, daring me to take it another step further.

"You say that to all the locals?" she laughed.

I bit my lower lip for a second, feeling even more blood run away from my head to my groin, my manhood swelling even further as we ground our bodies together.

"What other locals?" I said, and it was in jest, but truth be told I hadn't so much as done more than glance at the other locals, I was so smitten with her. She'd had my attention from that first touch, and it'd never wavered.

She let out the nicest little giggle, grinding her full ass onto my quickly stiffening cock before she pulled away slightly. I'd lost track of how long we'd been dancing, but she had a slight flush to her, and it was hard to tell if it was the dance or the throbbing in my pants that had really done her in.

I hoped it was the latter.

"I must rest, we have an early morning tomorrow," she said, and I couldn't help but be disappointed. I was certain—

She leaned in towards me once more, whispering, "Tomorrow night, we will be in a nicer place. I will teach you more then."

I didn't bother hiding the feral grin upon my face, but as I pulled away I gave a brush of my lips along her cheek and squeezed her ample hips.

"I can hardly wait," I said, looking into her impishly twinkling eyes with my own steady gaze. "It'll be a dance to remember, I'm sure."

THE NEXT DAY WAS AGONY. I was trying to relax and enjoy my vacation, but I couldn't help but keep looking at her. I was distracted from the beauty of the forests, of the wonderful hike through the jungle.

Though she did stick close to me through most of it, and even though we didn't speak a lot, her presence and the soft brushes of her skin against mine was enough to make me wish I could just take her, then and there. It was a hard thing to resist.

By the time we finally arrived at the hotel, I didn't know if I'd be able to stand another 'dance' lesson. I was already so pent up, and I just wanted to have her.

But she disappeared soon after dinner and I knew there'd only be one place to find her.

All of the hotels seemed to have some disco or night time entertainment, and this one was no different. A much higher end resort, the disco was bigger, the music louder. I could hear it from much further away and the Cuban beat resounded in my heart and loins, drawing me to her.

The Havana night was warm with an edge of crispness to it, but as I rose up to the stairs to the dance floor, the warmth of all those bodies radiated out.

It was covered by a stone roof, held up by pillars all around, right next to a pool where some people watched and drank, a live band played to the other side, and then the beach and the ocean waters laid out ahead.

There was no way to beat such a beautiful view. It was all so perfect, and there amid the gyrating, dancing bodies, was her.

I was hypnotized by her, drawn towards her, step by step, across the dance floor. I weaved through the others, my steps becoming smooth dance moves, as I swayed and made my way towards her like a real suave player.

She smiled when she saw me. A wide, happy grin, before she dialed it back. Maybe she was worried I'd get the wrong idea or something. So instead she just looked a bit cocky as her hand went to my chest, her hips swaying in rhythm to the fast beat.

"You like this music?" she purred.

To be honest, I hadn't given the music a moment's notice. I was drawn to her, not a single other thing occupied my mind.

"Better than anything back home," I retorted, the two of us falling into step together so naturally. It was uncanny how the two of us did that with such ease. Her hand in mine, my other palm grasping her hip, the two of us moving across the floor, dipping and swaying and... it was all so exquisite.

Things were easy with her. Conversation, dancing, just being around her seemed so natural and normal. Which was strange to me, but so welcome.

She smiled at my response, her hand flirty along my chest and shoulder, just feeling me out. I was glad I'd kept in shape all these years. Some guys let themselves go, but I had to keep trim. Wasn't an option.

Isabel leaned up on tippy toes, pressing her large breasts into me.

"Does it make you hot?" she asked.

"Only two things on this island make me hot," I replied, looking her over pointedly, ogling her in that stunning dress. "You and the Cuban sun," I said, giving her no time after that before I took her hand and spun her around, letting her dress skirts spin out with a wide flair before she spun away, then I tugged her back in for another dizzying twirl.

I couldn't help but grin at her then as she was back, pressed into my chest once more. And more than that, able to feel the proof of how hot she made me below.

She giggled again, seeming so thrilled with my flirtation.

I still had it.

She leaned in, and I could tell she was breathless as she panted against me, her pretty lips parted. And then they were pressed against my throat, hot and wanting.

It was lewd and public; right there in the center of the dance floor! But I returned her affection, let my two strong hands feel up her sides, kissed at her shoulder and neck, nibbled at her ear in return, felt her beautiful, black hair against my cheek.

"You're ravishing," I said, my voice an unintentional growl with how high my desire had been provoked.

I didn't know if anyone was staring at us, but I could feel all eyes upon us. Whether that was just my ego or reality speaking, I didn't care to find out. Not when she tasted so sweet.

Her fingers went down along my hips, teasing lower and lower as she ground in against me. We were getting carried away, but never for a second did I think about stopping.

Only the cool ocean breeze was there to stymie the rising heat around us and between us, but it wasn't nearly enough.

I ran one hand up her spine, through her thick, black hair and savoured its rich feel. All the while my lips moved to hers, finding our mouths interlocked and we kissed deeply there, shameless among the whole crowd of vacationers and locals.

She pushed into me, arms wrapping around my neck, as wild passion overtook her. Her body gyrated against mine, and I knew now was the time to take her. She was desperate for me, and the way she moaned into my mouth told me more than anything she could have said.

When she broke away, I took her hand, and we wound our way through the crowd back towards the exit. Though even then she couldn't resist reaching out, touching my ass as I led the way.

I certainly didn't mind, and just led her on towards my room undaunted.

The climb up the stairs was taken over the elevator, because I knew I'd get us there faster that way. Turning to look at her every few moments, appreciating her beauty as we climbed the open-air stairs until we at last reached my floor.

I pressed her up against the door, kissed her plush, pouty lips hard as I fumbled with the keys and door in the other hand. I wanted her so bad, and I couldn't restrain myself now that we'd stopped at last. I slowly worked the door open, until we both swung inwards.

She laughed, my arm jammed behind her, but it just made it easier to embrace her and draw her further into the room. It was pretty nice, all told, with towel swans on the bed that I quickly knocked onto the floor without consideration of them. I had bigger things on my mind.

By bigger I immediately thought of those ample breasts of hers, that threatened to burst free of her dress at any moment. They strained the confines of that gorgeous number, and I reached up to greedily grasp at one of those mounds. To squeeze and fondle that plump tit like it was the first I ever felt.

It wasn't, but it was the finest. Supple and full, firm yet soft.

I gave a low, lewd groan of approval as we fell to the large, king sized bed before the massive glass doors over-looking the balcony and beach beyond.

I felt like a king in the lavish room, but with her pinned beneath me, even more so. She felt like a delicious treat, a delicacy I'd never had, and I kissed down her throat as she offered it up to me, encouraging my downward descent towards her breasts.

I was ravenous by then though, and I lifted my hand up over the full mass of her breast and curled my digits into the fleshy mound. I yanked down her dress, exposing the fullness of her tit just before my kisses made their way to it. I worked on down, supping at the perky teat, made my way around the light areola of her dark breast.

Her skin was so smooth and soft, I was rapturous with delight!

She tasted like the sun, like the warm breeze off the ocean. Her skin was so warm from the heat of the day, and her moan was like sweet music. She arched her back, her hands going to the back of my head and encouraging my supping at her.

Her nipple stiffened quickly against my thumb, and my free hand wrapped around her thigh, pulling it apart before feeling inwards. Seeking my prize between her thighs.

To my surprise and delight, she wore not a stitch of clothing beneath her dress. And my bare hand found her warm, wet cunny without delay, my long digits stroking over her glossy little quim and making her mewl for me.

"You're stunning," I growled out as my cock strained against the fabric of my pants and I worked my fingers up to the apex of her cunny, then back to wriggle through her labia and tease her clit directly, circling and nudging it.

She was grinding against my hand so wantonly, and I could tell how much she wanted it.

No, she needed it.

Me.

It turned me on like I couldn't believe. This hot, exotic woman who was so desperate for me. I didn't know how long I could contain myself, and I sucked her nipple harder, making her purr.

My middle finger pushed between her velvety folds, feeling her clench around it so tightly.

Part of me wished I had just taken her to the beach, fucked her in the sand, but instead I brushed that aside, enjoyed the cool ocean breeze as it brushed in past me through the window, though it couldn't temper our heat. Not even a little.

I fingered and teased her, suckled her teat, but eventually I had to pull back, and before I had a chance to do it myself, her hands went to my shirt. Those nimble little fingers of hers undid my top, exposed my bare, hard chest beneath, my thick pecs and bulging abs. Then on down they went, working open my pants and reaching inside my boxer-briefs, tugging out that thick, meaty shaft.

Her almond-shaped eyes lit up at the sight of it, that hefty beast of a cock resting upon her palm, throbbing with desire from stem to crown. Veins all along its length, pulsating as I stared down at her with desire.

She'd felt it so intimately earlier, while we were dancing and she was grinding in against me, but to see it pleased her. She couldn't wait to have me stick it in, and she gave me a few strokes, warming me up.

Her thumb went to the tip of my cock, teasing out some precum and dragging it down, making my cock shine as her legs spread.

Those smooth, soft inner thighs beckoned me in between them, and I obliged happily. I sank in between, letting her hand guide my throbbing shaft to her cunny, where molten steel met her warm flower.

A kiss of her petals to my cock was followed by the overwhelmingly satisfying feeling of her tight little cunny walls embracing my shaft. I sank down into her, raw and reckless. I wanted her too bad to think, and she never uttered a complaint as I sank down balls deep into her, letting loose a noisy groan of satisfaction as I did.

We were taking such a risk, me fucking her without a bit of protection, but maybe I wanted to walk on the wild side. To just let my worries and fears go and do what felt right.

And her warm, wet pussy around my cock? That felt so right. She was perfect, spreading her legs and then beckoning me in closer. She was ravenous for me, the way she bucked her hips closer so that I could hilt myself in her completely.

It was obscene, the way I was splitting her tight little cunny open, but it looked so right.

Seeing those beautiful, puffy wet petals stretched around my bulging, veiny shaft just got me so damn excited; even on top of my already bursting enthusiasm!

I sank my fingers into her thick tit, squeezing that all-natural breast as I pulled back my hips, watching my cock tug back those folds. It was such a sweet feeling, the tight clench of her narrow cunny as I began to pump back into her, my heavy, cum-laden balls slapping to her dark ass as I fucked her against the bed.

I couldn't remember the last time I'd felt so good. If ever.

It'd been so long since I had sex, but I wasn't a young man anymore. All the same, I pumped into her with all the vigor of a high schooler, but with the stamina of a man much older. Knowing I wasn't going to cum too soon gave me the chance to really enjoy how she felt — how she looked — as I fucked her.

Like how with each thrust, her breasts bounced, and how when I hit her too deep, her thick eyelashes would flutter.

The lack of a condom was dangerous, but oh so satisfying. I could feel every inch of her as it dragged along my cock, as I sank in and she squeezed around me. I could feel it all! And she was exquisitely perfect.

My pace built, and I made those thick, ripe tits jiggle and sway with the impact of my thrusts, again and again I hammered her, made her yelp and squeal and moan as I fucked her raw, manhandled those gorgeous tits of hers.

She squeezed my cock, and I knew she wanted it. Wanted my cum, my seed, deep inside her exotic little twat.

That was beyond my wildest dreams, but everything in my body screamed for that release. To implant myself deep within her and give her what she craved. My fingers squeezed her breast harder, the flesh dimpling beneath my hand as I looked down at her.

She wasn't giving that coy grin any longer. Her eyes were closed, her mouth open as she moaned so loud.

She was lost to the carnal rapture, and I pounded her harder, made those pouty lips moan all the louder for me as I hammered her towards bliss. I felt more alive than I had in so many years, and I let one of my strong hands slide down her soft body, my hard thumb rub at her clit, encircling it as I thrust into her.

My balls were tightening, and I knew my ability to hold back was giving out, and my desire to was long gone. I needed to cum inside that beautiful Cuban woman more than I needed to breathe then, and as the fire of my release traced up my loins, I jackhammered into her so hard and fast, wanting to make that gorgeous dancer cum with me.

And that sweet song, that lilting scream as she quivered was my reward. Her pussy vibrated around my bare cock, milking me of my virile seed. Her hand clutched my bicep, her nails forming half-moons in my arm as she lost herself to pleasure.

Then I went with her, and I blew such a thick, heavy load of cum into her like I'd never had before! Years of pent up desire unleashed into that fertile cunt of hers, and I savoured every mind-blowing moment of it, just as she did. The two of us felt our heads swirl, and I bucked, twitched and moaned aloud as I disgorged every last spurt of rich cum into her utmost depths.

I knocked her up then and there, I felt it even then, but the two of us only thrilled at it, enjoyed the feel of all my seed flooding her depths.

She rocked her hips, taking in all of my offering like a prized gift, her body rolling with all the seduction of the dance floor.

And when finally she laid back, exhausted and spent from her orgasm, she smiled up at me with such warmth. No more coyness. Just affection.

I leaned in, kissing her lips hungrily as I growled, "You're mine now."

She giggled like a schoolgirl but kissed me back with just as much passion.

IT WOULD'VE BEEN easy to move on from that experience. After all, even though we spent the rest of the vacation together, fucking each other's brains out, when it was done, I flew back home and she stayed in Cuba.

Yet the attachment we felt burned hot and fast, but also long. We kept in touch weeks after that, talking on the phone and emailing, and I arranged to return half a year later.

She'd never explicitly said, but I wasn't surprised to see it when I walked off the plane and found her waiting. That beautiful, curvaceous body of hers a little rounder in the belly, fuller in the breasts, looking exactly to be in her final trimester, right on schedule from our first fuck.

I grabbed her up there, spun her around, kissed her and hugged her, without hesitation. It was the finest surprise I could've expected for my second vacation, but I knew that wasn't to be all. There'd be so much more ahead for us, I could see that in her sparkling, dark eyes.

WORLD'S FINEST

Book Themes:
   Escorting, unprotected sex
   Word Count:
   5,049

~

He'd seen her helped out of a limousine but an hour earlier, entering into the swankiest hotel in the whole city. She was dressed to kill in high heels, a slinky burgundy dress, with mink fur wrapped around her neck. Everything about her spoke of two worlds: expensive, but daring. High class, but sleazy.

   She had an air about her of cool collectedness, not that she looked cocky or in control, but as if she watched the world swim by before her and passively soaked it all in as she navigated her course with an eye to a destination far off down river, out of sight of anyone else. She was meticulously put together, with long, flowing black hair, and he couldn't help but notice the large rack she sported, nor those pouty lips as she pulled out a cigarette.

There were only two differences between when she arrived and now. One, the ritzy man she had walked in on the arm of — some senator or businessman that had his face in the news — was gone. And for the keen observer, a ruddy hue tinged her smooth, ivory cheeks that was too natural to be makeup. An hour was gone, and that bomb-shell beauty had only a rosy glow to show for it as she calmly took in the cool night air.

She had his interest from the moment he'd laid eyes on her, when in those first moments she was just a chance encounter. A beautiful face lost in the crowd, never to be seen again. She'd lingered there in the back of his mind as he waited outside the hotel, all notions of duty or responsibility gone as she remained, like an itch he couldn't scratch. But more accurately described like a presence that still hung behind his shoulder, an apparition whose cherry breath tickled the hairs on the back of his neck.

So to see her walk on out of the building again felt too good to be true. And that's why he dismissed her return: too good to be true. A woman like her wasn't meant for him. Nor any man, but certainly not *him*.

She could have anything, claim anyone, break any heart. Yet looked contented to have it all and none at once. She was simply the finest woman he'd ever seen, and he'd not even heard her speak a syllable.

Despite his vow of silence, she caught him dead to rights: staring. But instead of the usual scorn a woman such as her was entitled to pass upon him, she flashed him a smile on her way out the door, and that one single look seemed to hold so much within it.

Her emerald eyes locked on his, and it was like a

magnetic force beyond the power of gravity that tried to pull him into that exotic gaze. A single bat of her long, curved lashes and she was holding out her cigarette in an unassuming manner, perched between two black-gloved slender digits.

"Mind sharing your spark?" she asks, her voice rich and velvety, so smooth it had to have poured from her pouty pink lips. And that's something that became clear as she stood so near: she seemed to wear no makeup, those thick lashes and kohl-lined eyes all natural, those puffy lips a gift of god or devil.

Like a rat to the pied-piper, he followed after her. One leg setting foot in front of the other by no force of will that was his own. And all the while she stood there, her aroma of lavender gently wafting from her feminine form.

He'd forgotten he had a cigarette himself, for it'd hung drooping from between his lips the whole while he'd stood staring.

It was impossible to say her age. For she was flawless in every fine detail, not a line nor crease, her skin blemishless and smooth, like the ivory of some mystical unicorn not a crass earthly beast. Yet she possessed too much casual calm and assuredness to be very young. No mere girl could walk and pose herself with such eye-catching precision, speak with such calm, and maneuver the world of men with such knowing control.

"Sure thing," he said, fishing into his pockets and rooting out a stained brass lighter. He hoped to God the thing wouldn't fail him, because though he'd smoothly pulled that thing out of his pocket to light his smoke a thousand times with practiced precision, he felt almost dumb in her presence.

Heaven must've been on his side though, because with a

most graceful motion he fired up that light and she leaned in, lighting her cigarette upon its flame.

"Thank you, Mister...?" she raised one brow in silent query as the soft aroma of her femininity graced his nostrils and only worked to drive him wild, even in the face of acrid smoke.

"Wells, Bryan Wells," he said with a smile, retracting the lighter as he smiled in her presence, his long charcoal grey coat nice, but nowhere near nice enough to justify talking to her.

"Bryan," she says, and suddenly his own name sounds downright titillating. It was like her moist tongue managed to form that word by sliding around an invisible bundle of nerves he never knew he had. "Thank you, Bryan," she repeats, and that time it sends a shiver down his spine.

Though it wasn't all that impacted him so deep. Everything about her was tickling him to his core. The way her pinkened lips stretched into such a beautiful smile. Not a fake one either; it's the kind of smile that reaches to the corners of one's eyes, all sweetness and sincerity. And more than that, it had a way of making it seem like she was blessed by his attentions and not vice versa.

She held out her hand in dainty offering, and he took it, feeling compelled to bend forward and give the back of her silk-gloved hand a kiss. It was an old-fashioned sort of gentlemanly, but it seemed to fit her.

"I am Natalia," she says with a roll of her tongue, and a tiny hint of something to her voice... was it an accent? A hint of humour? He couldn't tell. But her thumb rubs over the backs of his knuckles.

He felt weak in the knees.

Every little thing about her - the way her eyes glittered as she soaked him in, how she touched upon his hand, or said his name - had a way of making him feel like the most masculine and desirable man in the world.

"Natalia," he repeats and he swore he could taste her name upon his own tongue. "You make it sound as beautiful as befits you. Which is impressive," he says, able to feel his heart thudding so loud he swore she could hear it.

"Thank you, Bryan," she says sweetly, squeezing his hand before letting it slip from his grasp like water.

Part of him wanted to talk about how cigarettes were going to be the end of them, make a joke about it. But part of him felt it'd be too foolish and simple of a remark. The other part didn't believe a woman like her could ever be touched by age or deterioration.

"Tell me, Natalia," he begins, hesitating as his eyes soak her in. That keen inquisitive sense of his noted how she clutched her purse much differently after leaving the hotel than when entering, as if it had now grown far more precious.

"Anything," she says, a hint of something at the corner of her lips and eyes, almost mischievous, but not quite.

"How's a man get to earn some of your time?" he asks, his heart jumping into his throat. He'd noticed she wore no wedding ring, in fact it was the only finger which didn't seem to wear some jewelry.

She laughs softly at his question, covering her mouth with her hand to hide the gesture, but not from his angle. At his angle he got to see her pristine white teeth, so flawlessly formed beyond her glossy pink lips.

"What's so funny?" he asks, smiling and attempting not to look phased.

"You know," she says, ever so simply. Her gaze having only left his for just a moment, but when it returns... it seems to pierce his soul and leave him entwined in her will.

He hesitates, clears his throat then takes a long drag upon his cigarette.

"I do," he says, leaning one shoulder in against the wall near to her, speaking quieter. More confidential. "But what makes you so certain I know? Not like I have good reason to suspect."

"You're a clever man, Mister Wells," she says, her words both fawning and sincere, no mockery. "We could play the game all the same, if that is what you wish though. I just do not think it is," she says.

Bryan couldn't help but arch a brow at her, staring in awe at the beautiful and perceptive woman. He was used to studying people, to learning more info about them in a glance than most would discern from a weekend together. But her? She had a disarming way about her. Made him feel naked yet empowered all at once.

"I couldn't so much as afford the room that last guy took you to," he confessed, a burning in his own cheeks as he spoke so frankly about the matter with her. He'd never so much as seen an exotic dancer in the club, let alone solicited a prostitute. He felt unworthy despite how she built him up in all her subtle ways.

"The room does not matter," she says, reaching over and placing her hand upon his, a reassuring touch. One that made him more confident, even as he felt he was dealing with a femme fatale that could suck his life dry in a matter of moments.

"I've only got three hundred bucks left to my name, and it'd be an insult to offer," he said, feeling his words. They weren't a ploy. A woman like her clearly earned far more for an hour of her time. If he had more, he would offer it. For ten minutes of her time, if that's all he could get. "Especially after what you must've just earned," he adds.

She purses her lips, looks away for just a brief moment before smiling back at him.

"Three hundred, and you forego your duties to spend time with me. That is no small thing," she says with a sweet, understanding smile. Able to understand, through her own inquisitive gaze, intuition or some combination of both, that the man was in the midst of a job, and walking off with her would carry a cost.

"More than I can afford, but all the same... more than I could ever turn down," he says with a growing grin, her own smile almost unchanged, but widening by just enough to show she appreciated the sentiment.

"Spoken like a real man," she says, and with a nimble flick of her wrist casts off the cigarette into it an ashtray on the exterior of the building. She wound her left arm in around his, that slender limb coiling until she was pressed up tightly against him, her ample bosom noticeably supple upon his flesh.

She begins to walk with him after the cash is exchanged, and like that he cast off the job he was hired to do. Forgotten. All that filled his thoughts were her, her figure, her scent. He looked down, and from his vantage point he can see those pillowy mounds of breast flesh pushing up from her dress, silhouetted by soft, black fur.

He was lost in her, losing himself each moment in her beauty and charm. Her laughter ringing down the streets as he guided her towards his place. He could feel her in his bones and not merely the one she was bred to tempt. Her smile so wide and genuine, her eyes a fluttery trap.

As he guided her up the well-worn stairs to his familiar place, it was as if he ascended to heaven. The old was now foreign, but it didn't frighten him.

"After you," he says, opening the door, and for that tiny nicety she made him feel like a knight.

"Merci," she said with fluent grace, his eyes glued upon her, drinking her in even though he was already full to the brim. Full to the point of explosion.

Her long, shapely legs such a treat, calves stretching up to her full thighs. He watched her enter, soak in his place in all its well-worn, unremarkable nature, though the gleam in her eyes made it all seem as if it were Xanadu, and she a humble explorer.

And as he moved in to take her fur from her, smiled as she smiled, appreciated the moment... his soul lamented that the click of her heels would never grace his simple home again. It was too much to hope they ever would. He glanced down, and hoped to see some small scuff of those dauntingly high stilettos upon his floor. Some permanent mark that might be left to remind him of this night on future events.

But there are none. She walks gracefully, and though her heels click with each step, it's as if she does not touch a thing. The only remnants she leave but fleeting impressions of senses that could only ever pale in comparison to the real woman.

Though he knew he would ask himself every night hereafter: was she even real?

"Would you like a drink?" she asks, turning to face him, plucking her gloves from her fingers and draping them over the back of a chair.

"Certainly," he says, moving over to his bar. The one extravagance of his home, with all the accoutrements. "Martini?" he asks, an economy of words taking hold as his heart does dance to the rhythm of her soul.

"That sounds lovely," she says, folding her slender arms beneath her bust, pushing that impressive chest upwards just a bit more as she approaches. "I like your place. So very…" her eyes dance about the room, like a schoolgirl in a candy shop, "You."

"So very me?" he asks, filling the shaker and smiling at her all the while. "You know me well enough to say?"

She shakes her head, those thick black waves bouncing, some dangling above those ivory mounds.

"No. But there is no pretense here. No attempt to hide the person who resides here. Yet it does not stand as a temple of slovenliness," she states. "You are a man of focus. Determination. Single-mindedness. Like a figure out of the past," she explains, looking upon him with that fascinated gaze that both pierced him to his soul and simply let him be.

"So single-minded I blew off the biggest job I've had in years, perhaps ever… just for a moment with a gorgeous lady," he says, shaking the drinks, then serving them up.

"That is what makes this moment so special," she says, accepting her drink even as she steps around the bar, standing right beside him. Against him. Her soft yet supple form pressing against him, her feminine heat so strong and rising as she drank from the martini glass, but never lost eye-contact with him. Never broke that tether of their inner-beings.

"Whatever it is that's brought you here, I'm glad it has," he said before downing his own in one motion.

"I wanted a special night, one I would not soon forget," she says, reaching up with her free hand, trailing her fingers down the front of his suit. Those nimble little digits leaving a trail of undone buttons in their wake, though he never felt more than her tickling nails.

"That's a lot of pressure to put upon a man," he says in jest, but the joke is to hide his anxiousness, his desire. He reaches out, placing his hand on her hip, and in that first contact, that first time he placed his hand upon her flesh, firm and proper?

He felt weak in the knees.

Words were not crafted to describe such a feeling. And though her thin dress separated them, he could feel that soft yet supple flesh so fully. She was unreal. Too real for reality. Like he had never touched another human being in all his life until this moment. That before then it had all been shadowboxing, play at pretend human contact.

"There is no pressure," she says reassuringly, opening his shirt, down over his stomach, somehow taking moments to tease her nails through his chest hair without breaking the flow of her steady motion downwards. "This isn't about impressing me, though you already have," she says, her index finger giving a final little trail down over his stomach, around his belly button before she opens his belt.

"Then what do you want?" he asks a little breathless.

She drinks from her martini glass again, and then it's gone. Her gaze stealing away all his fears, pulling him into her to cleanse him of all his worries.

"I want you to be pleased," she says softly, so sweetly. The words the most honest confession he has ever heard, no doubts about them being a ploy. They weren't the impatient bidding of a working girl who wanted the job done. "I want you to think back on this night and only remember how wonderfully pleased you were in my company."

And he has no doubt about that. Nothing but confidence in that the night would mean more to him than all the nights before it.

When his pants opened, and her soft, lithe fingers descended within, to enwrap themselves about his stiffened manhood, he gasped. And shuddered.

"So big and hard," she says, her voice so achingly soft.

"All for me," and that edge of possessiveness as he watched through narrowed eyes her bosom heave. Her breathing having grown in tune with his own excitement. A ripple passed through those milky mounds as she first began to stroke him, as if every pleasing jolt she caused in him was felt equally in her own flesh.

"God damn," he curses, letting his eyes shut a moment and the feeling of her touch take over. "I've never felt so good just from the touch of a woman's hand... or any other part either, if I'm being honest," he confesses.

Opening his eyes he can see her flushed cheeks and bright smile.

"You sweet talker," she coos at him, reaching her free hand up and back, undoing her straps even as her hand gently pumped his manhood, felt the thick, throbbing veins that criss-crossed its girth. "But it won't end with just my hand... not unless you want it to," she says, and he catches a glimpse of her dress dropping half an inch or so, more of those thick pillowy mounds of breast flesh exposing themselves.

"Oh God," he moans, feeling his cock swell and spill some of its essence. He wanted to give in so desperately. Three hundred bucks and the job of a lifetime for a hand job? Worth it. From her? There was no doubt. But he licked his lips, and persevered, helping her lower her expensive dress, exposing more of her body.

He pulls the fabric down as she lets him, and her large tits slip free, and he stares. For they look too perfect. Too stunningly fantastic, and he'd swear it was all an illusion. But without realizing it, she takes hold of his wrist, guides his hand to those tits, and invites him — no, instructs him — to squeeze. To feel their soft, fleshy texture, the way they meld to his grasp. Or how her soft pink nipple — so stiff! — presses into his palm.

"Or maybe you'd like to finish between these," she says, and through his mind ran the million and one ways he'd like to first experience those milky mounds. How he could satisfy himself with licking and kissing them for hours on end, or hell, just staring at them. She wouldn't even need to move for the first week or so, the bare image of those glorious breasts would be enough.

He didn't know what to say, with her hands upon him, guiding the action he was more than pleased. It was like it was all happening too fast, a race car tearing down a twisting highway, and if he tried to take over he feared he'd spoil the moment.

"Your milky white seed all over these tits," she said, and no matter how dirty her words got, they sounded so perfectly sweet but intense. Her hand moving in such an exquisite motion, twisting as she strokes the full length of his manhood as she guides him to lift one of her breasts, to feel its weighty heft in his palm as she it down upon her puffy pink lower lip.

His fingers sank into her thick breast flesh, watched its perfectly smooth skin dimple and then swell between his digits. He is entranced by every part of her, as if under a spell, though that is a woefully inadequate way of describing how his whole soul seemed to vanish into her.

It was only when she began to guide his hand on down, along the curve of her waist and hips, pulling her slinky dress ever downwards, that he snaps back into enough awareness to notice the chances.

"No," she says, smiling. "I think if that is how you finish, you'll regret. And I don't want you to feel a single regret from this moment."

"I would never regret a moment with you, whatever the price," he says, sincerely.

"Thank you," she says, smiling, her cheeks dimpling as

she steps out of her dress upon the floor, dressed only in her heels and a tiny pair of pink lacy panties. Her long, toned legs lead up to her pert rear where she rests one of his hands. "You're so very nice, Bryan," she says, guiding him towards his room even as she walks backwards on those precarious heels. "There are too few like you."

His room isn't unclean, but it has that familiar smell to it. Not dirty, just...

"It smells like you in here," she says, still holding his cock in her hand as she reclines back onto his bed, twisting at the waist just a little as he watches her, those exposed breasts, those gorgeous legs bent at the knees... all of her. Upon *his* bed.

She only finally lets go of his shaft when she reaches to his other hand, and guides both to her hips, where the band of her pink panties snugly adhere to her skin. She guides him into hooking his fingers into the band, curling into that lacy garment, and then she casts him free, and nature takes over as he peels them away. His eyes glued to the sight of her puffy pink vulva, glistening with honeyed dampness as a train of slick moistness clings them to her undergarments until he gets those panties nearly down to her knees.

Once they're gone, she smiles gleefully and revels in her newfound nudity. Twisting upon his bed she lavishes in the scent of him, the old blankets touching upon her skin, as if she was marking his bed with her aroma for all time.

Only when she's done and a soft giggle of excitement rises from her does he move again, lowering himself down over her as her legs part, exposing that glistening, slick slit of hers once more. Her feminine scent of arousal mingling with her other soft aromas for the most intoxicating incense of his life.

"Can I kiss you?" he asks, his dick throbbing hard down towards her bared slit.

Her answer came fast, her soft fingers sliding over his stubbled jawline, back towards his ear and hair, where she grasps him and guides him in for a kiss. Her pouty lips so soft, so sweet. It is a kiss like no other, and he shuts his eyes, losing all control as her tongue probes his mouth and coyly dances with his own moist muscle.

Mr. Wells would stay like that forever, as he would have done with any one act or sight with her, if left to it. And as is, she kisses him long and deep, her free hand roaming over his masculine torso, feeling out his hard body, guiding him down, down...

Until he feels the wetness of her femininity touch upon his engorged flesh, and like a lightning strike he shivers and moans, breaking their kiss.

"I want to feel you inside me," she says with heated need, her chest heaving with her rapid breaths, her knees bent up on either side of him as his raw glans touch upon hers. "I don't want us to part until you've been inside me, and I've felt you lose yourself there," she says, biting upon her plump lower lip as he holds himself as steady he can with the tremors of desire coursing through him.

It was as if her heart thumped inside his head as he felt their raw flesh touch, hard on moist, but he let desire guide him. Take him towards what he had never dared hope for before now, even when she agreed to his fee.

He pushes his hips forward, guiding his pulsating manhood into her, able to feel each motion as her puffy little labia flower about his girth. A low moan rumbles from him as her own lips part in high pitched ecstasy as he stretches her tight ring about him.

One inch would've been enough to satisfy any man. Just one inch of her carnal embrace could bring tears to the eye of a king, but he sank further into her warm, wet delight, further and further still even when he tried to pause, because her arms and legs wrap about him and pull him in. There is no stopping until he has hilted himself, finds himself fully inside of her and crooning his pleasure as her musical bliss tickles his ears.

It's a sensation like no other, and though he has had sex with many women upon many different occasions in the past, he would not sully her or this moment by comparing that to… this. For while he has gotten into her, he can feel her in his marrow. Her moans resonate onto a level of matter beyond reckoning as she guides him into taking her, his cock pumping as she rakes her nails along his back.

"Ohh Bryan," she calls out amid the many other sounds of pleasure and desire. Her spine arches, and forces himself up enough to watch as he pumps his hips. To see her heavy breasts shake, to see the glorious point of meeting where his loins vanish into hers. The beautiful 'v' of her womanhood seem to pass his glistening cock and then him back into new being.

Tears would well up if he wasn't overwhelmed by pleasure, for as he watches her he feels in love. A kind of love that transcends worldly — earthly — emotions, because this woman is too real. And he feels her flesh tightly plying from him all his feelings, all his pleasure. All he has.

"I'm going to come, Bryan," she says in a wavering voice, so lovely as it quails and shivers. Her body, so smooth and soft beneath him, tensing as pleasure mounts.

"Me too," he pants, realizing that moment of release was fast approaching for some time. His shaft a molten hot rod of fiery pleasure, so much sensation it nearly hurt but it was just overwhelming satisfaction.

She cries out, and he grunts, moans and follows suit. His hips thrust down one final time, his manhood embedded, and he shudders, his whole body quaking as he unleashes the torrent of his passions. The creamy essence of his lusts flowing in thick gouts as she cries out in return, her wails filling the air so beautifully, intoxicating upon the ear as a gush of slick honey coats his shaft and runs down along his milked balls.

He only finished when his seed was spilt, and his body was left shaking and sweaty atop her. Bryan felt more drained than he had ever been, weary and near the point of blacking out. And while he dove into her core, she pulled from him all his insecurities and worries. All she left in its place was the memory of her.

The rest for Bryan was a blur. But she nurses him a long while, tends to him kindly, sweetly. He was a hard man, hard to love, hard to give it, but by the time she has gently rolled him onto his back, kissed and stroked his face, he's content.

When she pulls from him, and his manhood spills out softly, he has only the energy to watch as she walks ever so casually to his bathroom. That stunning woman captivating him to the last as she cleans up, as she wipes away the material of his essence from betwixt her creamy thighs.

But when she comes back, dressed once more as he still lies there exhausted, she kisses him tenderly.

"Thank you," she says, smiling fondly. "I know it cost you dearly, and for that and much more, I'll never forget you or this night," and he can see in her sparkling eyes, beyond those long lashes, the truth of her words. For what he'd given up — a chance at a wanted fugitive, reward of five-hundred grand — paled in comparison to her.

Even three nights later as his friend at the hotel told

him he'd missed the man, he couldn't feel down. It wasn't the night he let half a mil' go, it was the night of *her*. And she'd taken the frustration in him and used it to paint a mural of that night upon his heart.

Besides, he could still smell her in his sheets. Still see her footprints. Long after any worldly remain lingered, leaving him drunk on a love that wouldn't die.

BONUS

Sign up now to get even more sexy books in your email!

If you sign up for my mailing list, you'll get updates on my new books, bundles, giveaways **and**, for a limited time, a **Free, exclusive** book: Twin Passions. This story isn't available anywhere else except to my newsletter, and contains sexy, taboo content.

Here's a snippet:

～

Zach couldn't help but throb against her; that was nature and instinct acting of its own accord. Otherwise he was sweet and tender, stroking a hand over her back and along her shoulder. "I tried not to think about it back then," he confessed, "but yeah, I think so."

His lips kissed softly beneath her ear, "I just wanted more time with you... always. From the moment I first desired women, it was you I wanted to be around, sis." They swayed and stepped back and forth upon the sand with their nuzzling and touches, "This time together was just a blessing... space to let me come to terms with how I felt for you."

"I always noticed. I mean since getting here," she whispered. "I just figured that couldn't be helped. That it was just 'cause you were a boy and I didn't want to embarrass you," she paused and swallowed, and her voice was so quiet it was barely audible over the birds and the waves that sang and crashed around them, "I didn't want to hope."

Zach stilled then, for her words confirmed something more precious and meaningful to him than he would've dared hope. He needed a moment to calm his blood, to let that sink in as he slowly moved along her cheek until their lips aligned.

He kissed her there for the first time, plush and full, no more skirting her mouth sheepishly. His tongue snaked out to lap at her gingerly as he squeezed her body in against his, those full breasts mashed against his hard pecs.

It was so much, their youthful bodies so warm and wanting as her arms encircled him. She tugged him nearer and her mouth worked against his so much more frantically. It wasn't the thoughtful, careful motions of him.

Instead it was passion unleashed, her hand working up along his neck and into his hair, feeling him out so eagerly.

It felt wrong to be doing this, Zach realized, but the rightness of it outweighed that. It was so much better to give in, to let his hands slide over her body, feel out her flesh and move down to palm a cheek and squeeze than it was to resist and be a good brother.

As her excitement grew, so did his, and he gave a low groan as he kissed her back passionately. He was barely even aware of it as his free hand stroked along her spine to find the clasp of her bra, undoing it in his lusty haze as his manhood swelled and pulsed so rapidly.

All you have to do to read the rest of this full length novella is visit here **today** to get your instant, **free** access to this exclusive & sexy story! For fans of BDSM, Siblings & Breeding.

ABOUT THE AUTHOR

Candy Quinn loves writing naughty, dirty stories - both short and sexy, and long and scandalous. Lots of taboo pregnancy, discipline, and first time virgins fill her filthy mind, which she loves to share with you. If you need something to scratch that secret itch, turn to Candy!

Connect with Candy!
candyquinn.com
candy.quinn.erotica@gmail.com

ALSO BY CANDY QUINN

Romance Novellas

Stranded Beauty

Dirty Country Love

The Fugitive: A Romance Novella

Innocent Farm Girl: An E-Romance Novella

Precious Pet: A Billionaire BDSM E-Romance

Sharing Her Series (MFM Breeding)

Buying Her

Catering to Her

Exhibitionist For Her

Teaching Her

Rocking Her

Trading for Her

Stealing Her

Awakening Her

Punishing Her

Blindfolding Her

Nympho - Amber

The Nympho

The Nympho Halloween

Nympho off the Pill

Nympho for the Gang

Nympho Angel

Nympho Valentine

Sugar Daddies Series

Katie's Fertile First Time

Becca's Fertile First Time

First Time College Gangbang (Virgin MFMMM)

Fertile Cheerleader

Fertile Sorority

Fertile Birthday

Fertile Freshman for the Team

The Innocent Tease Series (Breeding)

The Student: Punished by the Priest: #1

The Student: Pleasured by Her Older Friend: #2

The Student: Seducing The Mayor: #3

The Student: Pleasing Her Professor: #4

Biker's Sugar Babe Series (Multiple Partners)

Taken by the Bar: Biker's Sugar Babe (Part 1)

Claimed by the Biker: Biker's Sugar Babe (Part 2)

Taken by the Biker's Gang: Biker's Sugar Babe (Part 3)

Arrested by the Sexy Cop: Biker's Sugar Babe (Part 4)

Sugar Baby (Breeding)

Paige

Claimed by the Bad Boy Biker Series (Breeding)

Book 1

Book 2

Book 3

Laura's Innocence Series (Breeding)

Book 1

Book 2

Breeding Erotica - On The Farm

Nympho Farm Girl

The Farmgirl & The Fugitive: A Fertile First Time

Dixie: Fertile First Time on the Farm

Bought by the Billionaire

The Farmgirl & The Bandit

The Military Man and the Farmgirl

Breeding Erotica - Bad Boys

Bought by the Bad Boy

Fertile First Time with a Bad Boy Biker: The Farmgirl & The Outlaw

Dancing for the Mob Boss

Shipwrecked Beauty: Lost in Lust

Breeding Erotica - Virgins

Summer Heat

Rich Brat

Fertile Model: lights_on_lydia

Shipwrecked Brat

Spoiled Brat

His Brat's Fertile First Time: Deliliah

His Brat's Fertile First Time: Cassidy

Seducing the Man of the House

Honey Trapping the Man of the House

Bratty Chrissy: A Taboo Fertile First Time

Defiling Innocence

Punished by the Principal

The Fertile Pet Maid: BDSM Bareback with a Billionaire

Fertile First Time Tourist: Vacation to Cuba

Professor's Pet: First Time Bareback BDSM

The Billionaire's Obsession

The Billionaire's Fertile Submissive

Teaching the Brat

Forbidden Angel: Taboo M/F/M Erotica

His Brat's Fertile First Time: Blaire: A Taboo Bareback

His Brat's Fertile First Time - Avril: Taboo

The Billionaire & His Brat: A Taboo First Time

Other Erotica

Bombshell

World's Finest

Discipline the Dancer

Anthologies

Forbidden Fertile Brats 1

Too Taboo! 3: A Forbidden Fun Taboo Bundle

Forbidden Fantasies (A Naughty List Taboo Collection)

All for One and One for All 3 (The Naughty List Menage Boxed Set)

50 Forbidden Fantasies

Sting of Lust: 20 Book BDSM Domination Romance Mega Bundle (Excite Spice Boxed Sets)

No Shame in Submission (Shameless Book Bundles 7)

I Love It: 10 Intense Stories to Keep the Passion Alive (Shameless Book Bundles 6)

Hopelessly Outnumbered: 10 Stories. 53 Men. 13 Women. You Do The Math (Shameless Book Bundles)

Take the Heat: A Criminal Romance Anthology

Club Alpha: BDSM Romance Boxed Set

Shades of Surrender: Fifty by Fifty #4: A Billionaire Romance Boxed Set

So Wrong 8: The Ultimate Taboo Box Set

Anything for the Man of the House: Ten Brats who Learn how to Behave (Shameless Book Bundles 5)

GET MORE ROMANCE & EROTICA HERE

Hot Stuff Romance
   Shameless Book Deals.
   Excite Spice.